GORDON POPE THRILLERS

BOOKS 1-3

B. B. GRIFFITH

Griffith Publishing
Denver

Publication Information

Gordon Pope Thrillers: Books 1-3

Copyright © 2021 by Griffith Publishing LLC

Ebook ISBN: 978-1-7353058-4-4

Paperback ISBN: 978-1-7353058-5-1

Written by B. B. Griffith

Cover design by James T. Egan of Bookfly Design

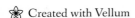 Created with Vellum

THE SLEEPWALKERS

A
PSYCHOLOGICAL
THRILLER

B. B. GRIFFITH

CONTENTS

To Kit, who has cheered me on since day one.

"Dreams are real while they last. Can we say more of life?"

-Havelock Ellis

CHAPTER ONE

At nine in the morning and not a moment earlier, Gordon Pope walked through the doors of the Baltimore City Circuit Courthouse and slowly shuffled through security. He nodded at Harold, the security guard, who watched benignly from behind a scuffed wall of bulletproof plastic as Gordon removed his watch and walked through the metal detector. He beeped, as always. The attendant wanded him, as always, and homed in on the tarnished brass belt buckle holding up his pair of ill-fitting khakis before waving him through. He'd taken his belt off every visit for months before realizing it saved him no time and just made for an awkward re-dressing. He'd lost weight since the divorce, and his pants were hanging on to his hips for dear life.

Harold pointed at the pass-through basin.

Gordon slid in his ID. "'Morning, Harold."

Harold grunted and checked his ID without seeming to see it. He noted the time and nodded him through.

One day, Gordon was going to get Harold to say something. After that, maybe he could get him to smile. That was a small microgoal of the type that Gordon often counseled his patients suffering from depression or signs of depression to set and strive toward in their daily lives. And recently he'd set it for himself.

No smile that day. Maybe next time.

Gordon weaved his way down the tracked marble floors and around harried government workers, following a path he knew by heart toward a bench by the vending machine on the second floor, where the criminal division was located. He sat heavily next to a large woman parked in a scooter, evidently asleep. He eyed the Moon Pies behind the glass for a solid minute before deciding against one. He pulled out his prep papers from a scuffed leather carryall, shuffled through them again, checked his watch. The woman beside him snored loudly once, startling him.

His session was starting in ten minutes. Where the hell was Brighton? He needed that three hundred bucks—knocked down from three fifty because Brighton was generally an asshole and knew Gordon was hard up.

Five minutes from his appearance time, Gordon heard a rapid clacking sound and stood as Brighton slid around the corner on his leather soles.

He held up his phone toward Gordon. "No service around here. I thought I told you. We're on the third floor today. Time to run." He smoothed his hair back then took off toward the stairway without looking back.

Gordon followed along at an awkward lope, holding up his pants with one hand in the pocket. "Third floor? We've never been to the third floor."

"You haven't. I have. Many times." Brighton fastened his double-breasted jacket and slowed to a power walk. He steadied his breathing as they climbed the stairs.

"What's on the third floor?"

"Don't worry about it. You just answer the questions exactly as the prep says. Nothing has changed."

Brighton didn't believe in going into detail with his expert witnesses about the cases in which they were to testify. He thought it muddied the waters. Expert witnesses were there to establish an objective point about which they knew an extensive amount and which had a bearing on the case. They didn't need to know what that bearing was. Quick, easy, clean. That was how Brighton & Associates had become the premier law firm for psychiatric defense. He paid three hundred a testimony. Three fifty if Gordon had stuck to his guns.

Brighton stopped outside of a door labeled Courtroom 7. He held out a hand to still Gordon, who was panting like a dog.

"We're at recess for another"—he looked at his gold watch—"three minutes. Sit in the back. Wait until you're called. You know the drill."

Gordon nodded, an unasked question on his lips, but Brighton patted him encouragingly on the shoulder and threw open the doors. Gordon followed and sat in the back as Brighton walked with a confidence just short of swagger to his place beside the defendant, who was a child. A boy, perhaps twelve years old. Gordon blinked.

"That son of a bitch," Gordon muttered. Brighton knew that Gordon had stopped practicing child psychiatry after the divorce. Gordon had explicitly told him he would not testify in cases involving children. That part of his life was behind him. Thomas Brighton apparently had not listened or, more likely, didn't care.

Gordon started sweating. Too late to back out now. He shuffled through his prep notes again. He skimmed the leading questions and reread his answers. Everything still rang true, from a professional standpoint, regardless of whether the defendant was an adult or a kid. But already his throat was dry. His mind jumped from memory to memory of how his life had been back then, with Karen, before this. His stomach rumbled with the vague nausea of loss. That was what kids did to him nowadays. He plucked his eyeglasses from his face and gave them a wipe down with the sleeve of his jacket. He could do this. He'd diagnosed a thousand kids before the divorce. The only thing that had changed since then was... well, everything.

"The defense calls Dr. Gordon James Pope."

Gordon stood and made his way to the stand, which was little more than a plastic chair behind a low wooden shelf. A glass of water gleamed there next to a microphone, turned off and pushed aside. Gordon counted only nine other people in the courtroom, and all but three sat on the side of the prosecution.

Gordon made himself look forward, and only after he'd been sworn in and turned to sit down did he chance an extended glance at the defendant. The boy was lanky, swimming in what was most likely a borrowed suit, hunched over and staring down at the table in front of him. He had dark-auburn hair that fell unkempt and moppish about his face. He didn't look up when Gordon was announced, didn't even move. He was flanked on either side by who Gordon assumed were his parents, a lean, red-haired man who was practically straining with the effort to appear composed and a fidgety blond woman with spooked eyes who looked about ready to bolt.

The boy seemed the calmest of any of them, on the surface, but Gordon knew better. That was a look of shock. Gordon doubted the boy would even be able to place himself on that day if asked a year or so down the line.

Thomas Brighton leisurely stood and smiled at Gordon as if he'd known him for years, then he approached the bench. He stopped and rested one hand lightly upon the worn wooden balustrade.

"Dr. Pope, would you please state your name and profession for the court."

Gordon cleared his throat and leaned forward as if the microphone were on. "Gordon James Pope, Doctor of Psychiatry from Johns Hopkins University, licensed and practicing psychiatrist with Jefferson and Pope, LP," Gordon said without skipping a beat.

"And how long have you been practicing psychiatry on behalf of Jefferson and Pope?"

"Seven years."

"Currently, you specialize in adult psychiatry, but when your firm first made a name for itself, what type of psychiatry were you practicing?"

That was off the script. Gordon clenched his teeth for the briefest moment before answering.

"Child psychiatry," Gordon said.

"So you have practiced both adult and child psychiatry extensively, for the record?"

"Yes."

Brighton nodded. "Dr. Pope, would you please describe, for the court, what parasomnia is?"

Back on script.

"Well, medically speaking, it's a category of sleep disorder arising from disruptions to the sleep stages," Gordon said, still wary. The script had been odd enough when he read it back at his office in preparation. It seemed even more so when taking into account the boy in front of him, who still hadn't looked up since Gordon's arrival.

"Layman's terms, please, Doctor." Brighton smiled warmly at the judge.

"It's when you do weird things when you're asleep." Gordon resisted the urge to bite the nail of his index finger.

"Things like what?"

"Well, anything from muttering all the way to walking, talking, eating... even driving."

"People drive while asleep?" Brighton asked with a perfect mixture of *are you kidding me?* and *of course they do.*

"Yes, it's been documented. Parasomniacs come in all shapes and sizes. There's a common belief that a sleepwalker has their eyes closed, bumping into walls, mumbling incoherent things, but that's not necessarily true. Many parasomniacs would look perfectly awake to you and me when in fact they are deeply asleep."

It was true, of course, all of it true. Gordon wouldn't sell himself out. He'd go into the poorhouse before he compromised the integrity of his profession. The medical facts stood true, no matter what age you were. But seeing the kid in front of him sent Gordon's mind suddenly racing toward the rest of the prep, extrapolating what it might mean. And it wasn't good.

"How is that possible?" Brighton peered into Gordon's eyes.

"It's simply a matter of missing chemicals in the sleeping brain. When you fall asleep, your brain eventually will become as active as it is when you're awake—this is called REM sleep—it's just that your sleeping brain has secreted a chemical to keep you paralyzed so you don't physically act on the random synapse firings in your head. Extreme parasomniacs don't get the release of this chemical at the right time, so they... aren't paralyzed in sleep." Gordon grasped the glass of water on the stand and took a quick sip. He'd have liked to have downed the whole thing. He could feel his bald head start to glisten with sweat, but he knew wiping at it would look worse.

"*Extreme* parasomniacs? How extreme can we get here?" Brighton asked, unfazed.

"Quite extreme. There is a subset of sleep disorder called violent parasomnia, an estimated four to five percent of the parasomniac population. These individuals can sometimes throw things, like their bedside lamp, or punch walls. People have been known to attack their partners or hurt themselves. People have even killed others in their sleep."

Brighton let that last statement linger. Gordon looked from Brighton to the kid. *You've got to be kidding me.*

"And all of these examples are medically documented?" Brighton asked.

"Extensively. One particularly well-known case, the one we're taught early on in medical school, is the case of Richard Chee. The man in question drove for fourteen miles in his sleep and violently assaulted his in-laws. He actually killed his mother-in-law before turning himself in to the police with blood on his hands and no recollection of what had happened. It was pretty clear he'd been asleep the entire time."

The prosecutor, a woman dressed in a demure black knee-length skirt and jacket, scoffed loudly. "Objection, speculation."

"Sustained," said the judge.

Brighton bowed in allowance. "In the case of Richard Chee, was it the opinion of his medical staff that he'd been asleep the whole time?"

"Yes. It was their opinion," Gordon said.

"And Chee was acquitted?" Brighton added, looking briefly but meaningfully at the boy.

"Yes, he was."

"Objection," said the prosecutor. "Irrelevance."

"Mr. Brighton, let's keep Dr. Pope within the confines of his profession, please. And of this case," said the judge, eyeing them both over a heavy pair of plastic-framed glasses.

"Forgive me," Brighton said, as if he and Gordon hadn't rehearsed this exact back and forth. "One last question, Dr. Pope. When are sleep patterns most irregular in a person's life?"

"During times of stress: changes in environment or routine or changes to one's own person. Mental or physical trauma has been known to trigger parasomnias as well."

"And in your medical opinion, having treated both adults and children, would you say that adolescence is a time of stress?"

Off script again but undeniable. "Yes," Gordon said.

"A time in which one's environment and routine is particularly susceptible to change? Not to mention one's body, which is quite literally changing?"

"Yes."

"Thank you, Dr. Pope. That is all."

Gordon took another slug of water while the prosecuting attorney stood. She walked over to him and gazed directly into his eyes. Gordon wanted nothing more than to look away, but Brighton had counseled him never to look away. No matter what.

"Just a few questions, Dr. Pope," she said. "Have you ever personally treated a violent parasomniac?"

"No, not personally, but—"

"But you've read about them a great deal, yes, I'm sure. Might that be because they are so rare that they're the stuff of collegiate case studies and not much more?"

"Like I said," Gordon stammered, "four to five percent—"

"An *estimated* four to five percent," she interjected.

"That's still a great number of people," Gordon said. "On the whole."

"And what about violent parasomnia in children, Dr. Pope? Do you have any statistics on that?"

Gordon didn't, of course. He hadn't planned on testifying on behalf of a child. He didn't plan on treating any child ever again.

"I don't," Gordon said.

Brighton furrowed his brow slightly, which on him, while in court, was as good as throwing in the towel.

"Neither do I, Dr. Pope. Do you know why? Because it is so rare that they don't keep them."

Brighton stood. "Objection!" he shouted. "Speculation, argumentative"—he ticked off each with his finger—"let's see here, assumption... I could go on."

"Sustained," said the judge, and Gordon thought he caught an eye roll.

The prosecutor backed away then turned. "No further questions."

Gordon nodded, gathered his things, and navigated his way down from the dais. As Gordon walked back down the aisle, he heard Thomas Brighton speaking. "I'd just like to make sure that the record shows that Ethan is twelve years old, just now entering adolescence..."

Gordon registered the boy's name, but he wasn't listening to Brighton any longer. He was a fairly good judge of age and wasn't surprised that his guess was spot on. What nearly stopped Gordon in the aisle was the brief flicker of a glance Ethan gave him as he passed the defendant's table. He'd seen thousands of kids back in the day, but none that looked like Ethan did just then. In fact, of all the kids Gordon had seen, only one reminded him even remotely of the way Ethan looked just then. Lost. Trapped. Cornered. But completely unaware of why.

The boy reminded Gordon of himself at that age.

CHAPTER TWO

G ordon stood outside the closed doors of the courtroom for several minutes, pulling himself together, Ethan's face swimming in his mind. Even in that small glance, he had seen the marbled red of the boy's bloodshot eyes, puffy around the rims. Scratches ran down his face, small but noticeable, like a downward swipe from a cat's paw. Gordon had seen scratches like that before. They could've been from a lot of things. Or from one very particular thing.

He clomped down the stairs in a daze until he found himself back where he'd waited earlier. The electric whine and clunk of the vending machine brought him back to the humming hallway of the courthouse. The scooter lady grabbed the Moon Pie he'd been eyeing, sniffed at him with her nose held high, then whined off.

Why did he even care about the kid? He'd closed the door on that part of his life when Karen left him. Done. Over. He patted the breast pocket of his limp jacket. It crinkled with his measly paycheck, postdated because Brighton was an asshole like that, but still three hundred bucks. And three hundred bucks was three hundred bucks. That was his personal allowance, and he could do with it what he wanted. That was the rule he'd set himself. And usually, that meant booze. He checked his watch—eleven a.m. Too early. His mother would happily call it "brunch" and go hog wild—not at all out of the ordinary for Deborah Pope. He understood all too well the realities of children turning into their parents eventually, but he wasn't yet ready to turn into his mother in that respect.

So coffee it was, then. Good coffee, served by the judgmental baristas at Arnaud's down the block from his office. It was the closest he could come to a good scotch without the scotch. Gordon found himself looking forward to it. He pattered down the stairway, his mind on a perfectly foamed *cortado* and not where he was walking, when he nearly ran headlong into Dana Frisco. Dana sidestepped at the last moment and held out her hand to keep Gordon from taking them both down the stairs and into a wall. Gordon blubbered an apology until he recognized her, then he smiled.

"You always close your eyes when you go down stairs?" she asked.

"Sorry, Officer," he offered, bowing slightly. "Got a lot on my mind."

Dana straightened her gun belt over her sharp hips and moved both herself and Gordon out of the flow of traffic. "Yeah? Like what?"

"Well, money for one. Always money. Or lack thereof. Also booze. So sue me. And coffee." Gordon looked at the ceiling, counting on his fingers as he spoke. "Then there's my failing practice, there's my crazy mother, I'm sort of hungry, so there's that, too. And then the small matter of being an expert witness in a case that came out of the blue and settled right in the pit of my stomach."

Dana held out her hands in surrender. "Is this the sleepwalker?" she asked lightly. The com on her shoulder chattered, and she shut it off with a click.

"I don't know." Gordon looked briefly back up the stairs at the closed doors of the courtroom. "But he sure looked tired as hell."

Dana glanced back up the stairs and stepped in closer to Gordon. Gordon wasn't tall by any means, but Dana was shorter, built like a gymnast. He could smell the shampoo in her fine black hair.

"Brighton's case? The kid?" Dana asked, lowering her voice.

"That's the one," he said, finding himself whispering too. Dana nodded slowly, sadly.

"I processed that case," she said. "It happened on the edge of the city circuit, out in East Baltimore. The parents of the victim fought for jail time, but Brighton worked some magic, entered a temporary insanity plea because the kid had no priors, no history, nothing."

Gordon felt the heat that had flushed his throat while he was on the stand make a reappearance. He tried to swallow it away but struggled, and Dana noticed.

She looked sideways at him for a moment before moving on. "Not that it matters much. Odds are the kid ends up in Ditchfield anyway."

Ditchfield. The name brought back memories for Gordon, none of them good. "That's the juvie psychiatric hospital," he said. "For high-risk kids."

Dana nodded gravely. "You know about it, then."

"Back before... a while ago, I was the psychiatrist of record for a few kids mired in the Ditchfield system. They were..." Gordon sought the right words. He wanted to say, "ruined by the place." But while Dana was a friend, she was still a cop. He settled on "institutionalized."

"Institutionalized my ass," Dana said under her breath. "Cops are institutionalized. Lawyers, bankers, any nine-to-fiver working paycheck to paycheck—that's institutionalized. Those kids come out of Ditchfield like shells if they come out at all."

Gordon wasn't going to argue with that. "Brighton didn't prep me with the case specifics. He never does. I was going to keep talking like I knew what was going on with that kid, but if I don't ask you, I'll probably never know."

Dana looked at Gordon for a long moment. He and Dana had known each other for over a year. She did part-time work managing the holding cells in the basement, so she was often around the courthouse. The reason he'd met her the first time was that she'd struck up a conversation about how gross the water fountains were in the place, and from then on, they just kept running into each other. She knew about the divorce. He'd mentioned it in passing, trying to downplay it as though it was nothing more than a rainy vacation. She knew his practice was struggling, too. Come to think of it, she knew almost everything. Almost. She didn't know the whole of why he'd stopped treating kids, just part. But sometimes, the way she looked at him, he could have sworn she knew everything in his head.

"The kid almost murdered his friend at a sleepover," Dana said, keeping her voice low. "Strangled him in the middle of the night. Put him in a coma before the other kids could scream loud enough to wake up the poor guy's parents. He's at Hopkins Hospital right now. Still hasn't woken up."

Gordon nodded. He knew it must have been something like that. He sensed it as soon as he saw the kid. But the truth still settled upon his shoulders like a slow stream of sand, heavier with each moment.

"Ethan, the defendant, he claims he did it in his sleep." Dana cocked an eyebrow. "Claims he has no memory of it." She paused. Her brow furrowed in concern, as if she could see Gordon slouching before her eyes under the weight. "Hey," she said. "Sorry if I..."

Suddenly, Gordon needed that drink, time of day be damned. Coffee wouldn't cut it.

"No, thank you for telling me. You're the only one around here who would. I'll see you around, Dana."

She only nodded and watched as Gordon made his way past her and down the stairs. Gordon didn't look back. He knew Dana had a thing for reading faces, and he didn't want to be read right then.

Very few people knew that Gordon's office was also his home. His lack of finances called for the double duty. When Karen left him, she basically took their entire child-psychiatry practice with her. Gordon had since come to understand that while she was half of Jefferson & Pope LP in name, she was a good deal more than that in substance.

He'd lost half of his clients outright, and another twenty-five percent shuffled out the door in the years afterward.

No clients meant no referrals from clients, and so the stagnation built upon itself, his wheels spinning in the mud, until his career was basically swallowed up altogether. Almost as if it had never been. When he treated children in the aftermath, he stopped seeing their conditions as challenges with solutions to be unearthed and started seeing in their faces reminders of his loss. The divorce hobbled him, and nobody could sniff out uncertainty like kids, so he stopped treating them. Instead, he started treating their parents. His was a wonky, one-sided family practice. It had no heart, and so he doubted it would ever find legs.

The rare clients he saw these days were always window-shoppers who hadn't yet realized that the Karen Jefferson of *Baltimore's Top of the Town: Doctor Edition* and, more recently, of the *New England Journal of Medicine*, no longer physically practiced in Baltimore. They wandered into his Mount Vernon office building like tourists reading restaurant reviews years out of date—expecting to find a steakhouse but instead coming upon the dollar-a-scoop buffet that had taken over when the steakhouse moved to San Diego and married a powerhouse real-estate agent it had met through a pricey, high-caliber Internet-dating website.

Perhaps one in five of those tourists stayed for a session or two. That let him keep the lights on and the water running but either at his office or at his loft, not both. The loft reminded him too much of Karen, so the office it was. He still needed a place to live, though, so he'd turned the space into a half office, half apartment. The first-floor waiting room was where he worked, and the second floor he'd turned into a de facto studio apartment. He'd plugged in a two-burner stove and had an old college buddy jury-rig the guest bathroom to include a casket of a shower. It was a ramshackle affair, and very probably illegal from a zoning and fire-safety perspective, but it wasn't all bad. One block over and one block down from Gordon's home office stood a classic Baltimore pub. It was clean and dark and had all sorts of cold things on draft and more scotch and bourbon on the shelves than even he could name—the type of place the respectable pirates of old Baltimore would have gone, back a couple of hundred years before when the city was nothing but a smuggler's den. A lot of people, his mother included, would say not much had changed since then, but Gordon disagreed. The city held pockets of brilliance still, and Darrow's Barrel was one of them—especially with their crab-cake sandwich.

Gordon had four hours to kill before his appointment that afternoon, one of three he had scheduled for the entire week. He hadn't eaten out at a legitimate pub since his last expert testimony over a month before. He took his bites slowly, savoring. He'd earned them. He'd come into Darrow's thinking he'd earned an ice-cold mug of beer too. As it turned out, he'd actually earned three. And counting.

He watched the clock, an ancient thing shoved high up on a shelf, where the staff hoped patrons wouldn't see it and would keep drinking. But Gordon saw, and as his appointment approached, he grew increasingly grim. At the last possible minute, he stood up and paid his tab in cash and walked his way back to his office, his hands thrust into his pockets.

Once inside, he popped in a stick of gum, rolled his shoulders, and forced himself to smile as he straightened his office. He dusted off his client's chair and fluffed the pillows on an increasingly worn-looking loveseat. He dimmed the lights and cocked the shades, and by the time his front bell rang, he had halfway convinced himself he was excited to be working.

GORDON FOUND himself tuning in partway through what was no doubt a cathartic story on the part of that afternoon's client, an over-confident, bull-necked executive named Mark Bowman. Mark's company paid for counseling for their C-suite executives, and Mark took everything he could from his company. In their second session together, Gordon had learned Mark was contemplating an affair with his kid's kindergarten teacher ever since they'd hit it off during a parent-teacher conference his wife couldn't attend because she worked nights at the hospital and slept during the days. He hadn't made a move yet, but he also hadn't shut up about it since.

Gordon was fully aware that Mark's plight, if you could call it that, would be the professional envy of many of his colleagues. Once or twice, he'd even thought about referring him to one of them, but then his bank account poked him in the chest again. Better to let the man vent while his company shelled out Gordon's hourly rate. With adult therapy, essentially what he had to do was let the clients run their mouths long enough to find their own solutions to their own problems.

He thought about how Karen would have rolled her eyes at him and told him he tended to wildly oversimplify things he didn't want to deal with, most likely as a coping mechanism. She would tell him to stop feeling vaguely threatened by the mere fact that a man had family enough to *have* marital problems, and she would tell him to do his job. And of course, she would've been right. But she was also in San Diego. Far from there. Far from him. And he was in Baltimore and a bit fuzzy from three beers over lunch. When Gordon blinked back to reality, Mark was in midsentence.

"She thinks it's unnatural to have only one. Says it warps the kid you've got."

Gordon made a noncommittal humming sound and gave a half nod. *What the hell is he talking about?*

"I mean, I'm an only child, and I think by any standard you could call me successful. Frankly, it was a little insulting. Am I wrong?" Mark asked, leaning back in the client's chair with his knees spread wide.

"You're trying to have another child," Gordon said, setting himself back into the conversation.

"She wants three. I've bartered her down to two and a condo. She's not budging on the two, though. And she's got a ticking womb, you know. That's what I like about the teacher, Arielle. There's none of this..." Mark swiped his hand back and forth between his knees, looking for a word.

"Talk of children?" Gordon offered, trying to keep the remnants of that benign smile on his face. "That usually doesn't happen with mistresses, Mark. Not at first, at least. It's the offer they provide of freedom from the classic family model that is the initial allure."

Mark nodded as if he understood completely. "I wouldn't call her my mistress yet. We just text. A lot. But my wife's full of shit, right? About the single-child thing?"

"No, she's not full of shit. Studies have shown that children that grow up with a sibling are better adjusted socially." Gordon was done pandering to the man. So what if he walked away? Gordon was living like a broke college student already. He could stand to be a little bit more broke if it meant he never had to see Mark Bowman again. But Mark didn't counter him. In fact, he seemed not to even have heard him.

"Christ, the one kid is enough. Don't get me wrong, I love Jamie, but he's a train wreck. He's into all these magic card games, spends every waking second talking about them. Won't even consider a sport," Mark said, shaking his head to nobody in particular. "You got kids, doc?"

"No, I don't," Gordon replied evenly.

"Well, think twice. Jamie oughta be seeing a shrink. You know anything about kids' brains?" Mark asked, looking out the window, grabbing blindly at the bowl of nuts on the table.

"Actually, Karen's and my first practice was exclusively child psychiatry," Gordon replied. "Years ago," he added.

"So you know what I'm talking about. You probably saw the real crazies. And now she wants another one?"

Back on the wife again. Gordon muffled his sigh into a yawn.

"Where is Karen? She's pretty famous, right?" Mark asked.

"She's quite talented, yes. And she's on sabbatical, pursuing a post-doctoral fellowship in San Diego for a time. But we both review each other's cases, so she is here in spirit." Gordon smiled blandly.

How many times had he told that little white lie over the past five years? At some point, it wasn't going to hold water. Gordon wondered idly how long a fellowship could reasonably be said to continue. Most were for just the year, and Karen's was long done, so he was already pushing it.

Gordon felt particularly morose after Mark left, vaguely hungover and sluggish, his mind still stuffed with thoughts of the morning's testimony. Had he helped Ethan? Had he hurt Ethan's case? He'd answered everything by the book, aside from the few questions Brighton sprung on him, but those he felt he answered professionally. Dana Frisco's words echoed in his mind: *"Strangled him in the middle of the night... said he did it in his sleep."* And not just the words but the way she'd said them. Like she wanted to rib him with her elbow and add, *"Can you believe that shit?"*

Could he?

For the first time in six months, Gordon walked to the storage closet behind his buzzing computer. After Karen had left, he'd packed up everything even remotely related to their joint practice and shoved it into the closet, in the back, along with a bunch of junk he didn't know what to do with. He walked past his most recent castaways—a broken standing lamp, an old laptop he didn't know how to get rid of, and his ugly metal filing cabinets—and stopped, facing the far wall. Playsets and boxes of toys sat there: Matchbox cars and marbles, action figures by the bucketful, plastic dolls and plush dolls, and stuffed animals of every sort. They were covered in a light coating of dust, but otherwise, they stared at him as if not a day had passed.

Toys had been Gordon's tools back when he worked with Karen. Observing how kids played—or better yet, playing along with them—helped Gordon and Karen begin diagnosing their conditions the way a physician might examine a patient with a stethoscope or a blood-pressure cuff. That was the best part about working with kids. They didn't come out swinging like Mark Bowman, expecting you to validate their neuroses. In fact, a lot of the time, kids wouldn't even give you the time of day if you ask directly. But they will play. And if you're game, they'll let you join in. As to what was really bothering them? The root cause? That was up to the psychiatrist to figure out. Odds are the kid couldn't even tell you if they wanted to. Kids couldn't self-diagnose. They didn't read a bunch of articles on the Internet and proclaim a psychiatry expertise. They never walked in the door ready to tell you what was wrong with them, one hand out and waiting for the antidepressant script.

But coming back to the storage closet was bad. Gordon didn't have to be a shrink to know that. Closing this door in his mind had taken him a long time, and now he'd just opened it without thinking. That was called a regression. Worse was the fact that he also had his phone in his hand and Karen on speed dial, and that he pressed Call before he could talk himself out of it.

He held the phone to his ear. Karen Jefferson picked up after four rings. He counted that as a victory. She hadn't yet shuffled him off to voicemail.

"Gordon, if this isn't some sort of emergency, I'm going to be very disappointed in you," she said. A judgment without sounding like a reprimand. Textbook therapist and not entirely unwarranted.

Right after the divorce, he'd called her a lot—too much. He cringed to think of it. He'd just broken a two-month streak—a personal best for Gordon and one he knew the struggles of which would be completely lost upon Karen.

"It is an emergency. Of sorts. Although not for me," Gordon said, his voice hollow and close in the closet. He was struck by an irrational fear that Karen would know he was staring at his toys, so he covered the receiver and scampered out into his office proper before flopping down on his patient chair.

Karen sighed. "Okay then, let's start at the beginning."

Gordon put his hand to his forehead and slumped deeper. "Is this really necessary? I'm not some pining teenager."

"If you want to talk, it is. You know the drill." Karen cleared her throat and paused. "Gordon, I'm not coming back to you or to Balti-more. You know that, right?" she asked as if reading off a script.

"Sort of," Gordon said, going off of his own script.

"Not *sort of*. Do you want to talk or not?" Karen asked, a note of annoyance in her voice, which was a rare thing and told Gordon more than anything that she took this stupid ritual seriously.

"Yes, I know. Okay? I know. You are not coming back." He paused for a moment. "But I'm keeping your name on the plate out front," he said quickly.

"I know, Gordon. I still get a few calls a month." Her voice was tired.

"You do? What do you tell them?"

"Exactly what we decided on the split, that we review each other's cases. Although I hadn't expected to be saying that still, almost *five years later.*"

"Yeah, well, this time I actually do want to run something by you." He tried not to take her obvious pause of surprise personally. "Karen?" he asked after almost ten seconds.

"Yes. Well, yes, by all means. I'm happy to hear you've got work. What's the case?" she asked.

Gordon told her about his testimony and what Dana Frisco had told him about Ethan's crime. He even told her about how awful his afternoon session had been and how he'd had three beers just to get his mind right enough to even muster that smile for Mark Bowman and his bullshit. Then he took a deep breath and waited.

After a long moment of silence, Karen spoke. "You're telling me you're selling yourself as an expert witness for drinking money?"

Gordon coughed. It sounded bad when she said it out loud. "No. Well... yes. I suppose. In the strictest sense. But can we keep on topic here? Have you ever heard of violent parasomnia manifesting itself so young? Twelve years old?"

Karen made that soft ticking sound with her tongue that instantly took Gordon back to when their two desks shared one office and they would chart patients in the late afternoon, the lazy, heavy sunlight pouring through the big bay window between them, cutting through a ruby decanter of wine and settling upon them both as they worked to the tune of soft piano music in the background. He blinked, and the memory retreated.

"Off the top of my head? No. That type of extreme violence would most likely be the result of REM behavioral disorder, which has a median age of sixty-five, I believe. Children at that age exhibit your more garden-variety parasomnias, though."

"We treated hundreds of them," Gordon said, nodding, "but they were all of the slow-wave sleep variety. Sleep-talking, chronic bed-wetting, sleepwalking..."

"All very benign," Karen said. "I mean, I suppose it wouldn't be completely unheard of for an REM behavioral disorder to manifest at that age. Do you know anything about the child's emotional state? His health history? Violent parasomnia often runs in the family."

"No, I don't know anything about him," Gordon said softly. *Except how lost he looked. How defeated. How confused.* But looks could be deceiving. Gordon agreed with Karen. The science was against him.

"Do you feel some sort of residual guilt here? Is that why you're asking me this? You think you might have helped a killer kid go free?" Karen asked. "You testified that violent parasomnias exists. They do. Twelve is a tricky age. Studies show that children start dreaming as adults do as early as age nine. By twelve, he would be completely capable of exhibiting violent parasomnias. Likely? No. Capable? Yes."

Gordon rubbed his face. "I don't think he's going free. I think he's gonna end up in Ditchfield."

"Ah, I see," Karen said in that infuriating, two-steps-ahead-of-you way she had. "You think you let the child down somehow. Despite knowing nothing about him the second before you walked in the courtroom."

"That's not it," Gordon said weakly. Because he knew that was it —or at least part of it.

"You can't save every child that finds themselves stuck between a rock and a hard place. Not unless you have a time machine. Let me guess. You saw something in this kid that reminded you of someone. Maybe he reminded you of yourself. Maybe of the life you had when you used to treat kids like him. Like if he'd only come to you five years ago, maybe he wouldn't be sitting there on trial?"

Gordon felt depantsed. He couldn't say anything. She'd sniffed him out, and he knew his silence would only serve to confirm it.

"You're projecting, Gordon. And you're unsettled by the very nature of the case. When you get unsettled, you get neurotic. Obsessive." Despite her words, her tone was not impatient. If anything, she sounded a little sad. Still, she paused as if she knew she'd perhaps gone too far. They'd always used to throw diagnoses at each other across the office, half in jest, but Gordon knew that one had heart behind it.

"Well," he said. "This has been a fun chat, Karen. Thanks for talking."

"That was too much," Karen said. "I'm sorry."

"No, I think you're pretty much spot-on. Always were."

"Some part of you has loved every troubled kid you've ever come across. It's a noble thing. Insane, but noble. And part of the reason why I married you."

"Then divorced me," Gordon added. Karen took a deep breath, but he cut in before she could speak. "Divorced me when I couldn't love the one you cared about most." He was baiting her, he knew, lashing out a bit, doing what he could to turn the tables before all the food slid into his lap.

She didn't bite. "Get some sleep. Lay off the booze. Focus on your next patient," she said, not unkindly. "Good-bye, Gordon."

Gordon didn't respond.

"Good-bye, Gordon," she repeated more forcefully. She never used to let them end a phone conversation without a proper good-bye. He wasn't going to win that, either.

"Good-bye, Karen," he said.

That night Gordon had a dream he hadn't had in almost thirty years. He recognized what was happening instantly, and a wave of childlike terror washed over him. The nightmare always started the same way: he found himself standing at the edge of his parents' sprawling Bethesda estate. When he used to have the dream regularly, the place was his home, but he hadn't set foot there in decades. His parents moved after they divorced when he was in his early twenties. But in the dream, the estate was untouched from the days he would run its sprawling lawn as a child. He was facing back toward the house, a stout, four-story structure with two outspread wings, whitewashed and shining in the distance. But he knew he wouldn't be looking at it for long. Very shortly, he would be pulled around, helpless to resist as he was dragged by some unseen force past the manicured edge of the lawn and into the rough outer growth before the forest. He would only be able to watch, paralyzed, as his toes dragged a line through the pine needles and brush into the darkness of the forest beyond. Where the cave was.

The nightmare had happened like that countless times in his youth. It was the single most recurring dream he could remember having, and it was always the same. So Gordon faced his shining house, eyes closed, whimpering, waiting for the pull.

Except the pull never came.

He opened his eyes and looked down at himself and was surprised to find that he was not ten years old. He was a man, with a man's work clothing on and a man's soft paunch and a man's weathered hands. He touched his face and found stubble there. Yet the dream of his childhood remained. As his fear subsided, he turned himself around, prepared to confront the faceless kidnapper of his youth, but he saw nothing, only the forest waving at him like a heat mirage. He felt a strange compulsion to walk toward the woods he used to be pulled toward. And so he did. His feet hit the ground, but they made no sound. Silence stretched tightly between the trees. Had it always been like that? He didn't think so. Another difference.

He walked the route he knew well. He'd been there countless

times in his dreams and also in real life. And so he found himself staring at the mouth of the cave head-on, the mouth that used to swallow him up until he cried out in terror, often awaking. If he was lucky. What was inside was worse. The Red. As a child, he could start to see it there at the mouth—tendrils of red mist snaking their way out of the black. But no red mist met him just then. And the weight of dread he used to feel was instead replaced by the weight of silence. A silence as heavy and unsettling as the terror he used to feel, but different. Manageable.

Gordon walked forward into the cave. Where once red mist had washed over everything like an incoming tide, now he saw only the inside of a cave. Half lit. Hot and damp. Empty. Gordon felt as though he was taking one last look at an apartment he'd moved out of before closing the door. An empty mark stained the rock underfoot where something should have been, a discoloration that meant something, but he no longer knew what. Gordon felt it very important that he remember what was there, that it was vital, even, and somehow connected to something. To... the boy. Ethan.

But as soon as Gordon recalled Ethan and the trial and testimony, the illusion of the dream started to break. He'd become too self-aware.

"No!" he screamed, but no sound came out. "Wait! What is it? What was it?" All his words died as soon as they left his mouth. He grabbed at the walls of the cave, but they came apart in his hands. The dream world crumbled around him. He ran. Not away—not this time—but deeper, deeper into the cave, as fast as he could, but his legs were putty and the cave disintegrating. He pleaded with himself to keep the projection alive for a moment longer until he could figure out what it meant, but his unconscious mind was uncaring.

Gordon shot awake and found himself standing again in his storage room. His heart raced. He felt alien to himself. He forced himself to take breaths. At first, he thought he'd fallen into another dream, but then he looked at the clock on the wall in his office. It ticked steadily. Four fifteen in the morning. So he'd sleepwalked.

That was unsettling in and of itself, but it wasn't new to him. He used to do it all the time as a kid. After several minutes, he was able to pull himself together and pushed off the wall he'd been leaning upon. Karen was right—all this talk of the past was unhealthy for him. He was opening old wounds. He decided to go make himself some chamomile tea, absolutely not have a dram of scotch, and read his book in his office until he felt sleepy again. It was *Finnegan's Wake*, so it shouldn't take long.

He turned to close the closet door, and it caught on something—a Matchbox car, well used, more die-cast metal in color now than the cherry red it used to be. What was it doing out there? Had he picked up any of the old toys when he had been down there last? He couldn't quite remember, but he didn't think so. He'd grabbed it when he was asleep, then. He toed the car inside the closet and shut the door softly.

He was definitely not going to have a dram of scotch. But a sip never killed anyone.

CHAPTER THREE

Gordon drank enough chamomile tea to drug a bear, but he still had a hard time sleeping after revisiting the cave in his dreams. He often counseled patients suffering from insomnia to give sleeping a shot for thirty minutes. If they weren't asleep in thirty minutes, they should leave the bedroom to do a simple task in low light—reading, doing the dishes, putting together a puzzle, things of that nature—until they felt sleepy again. Then they gave it another shot for another thirty minutes. Rinse and repeat. Each of these waking intervals he called a "sit session." Gordon went through four sit sessions before giving up on his own advice and simply lying awake in bed. He'd done all the dishes, read a full twenty pages of *Finnegan's Wake*—which was a minor miracle in and of itself—and didn't own any puzzles. He'd had the one slug of scotch, and the rest of the bottle beckoned to him, a solid, sturdy thing on the shelf in the shifting lights of the night, but he wasn't about to let himself fall down that rabbit hole just yet. So he lay in his bed, damp around the neck from the close heat, counting the number of times his feeble air-conditioning unit kicked on and shut off until he drifted for an hour or two around eight in the morning.

Then, of course, he was sleepy. But he had an appointment, not a professional appointment, but one that sometimes took at least as much out of him those days: lunch with his mother.

Deborah Pope came into the city of Baltimore twice a month, every other Thursday, for lunch with her son at Waterstones, an upscale bistro and grille in the swanky Harbor East neighborhood. Even that she considered risky, convinced as she was that the entirety of the city of Baltimore was one mean look away from erupting into anarchy at any moment. Gordon told her time and again that she didn't have to come if she didn't want to. She told him her love for her only son far outweighed her distaste for the city. But she never let him forget the sacrifice she was making, as if a twenty-five-dollar Cobb salad was the equivalent of a prison visit.

His mother was fond of Caesar, however. Her regular waiter at Waterstones greeted her as if she were royalty every time she came in and had so far resisted all her attempts to smuggle him out of Baltimore and into one of the many white-tablecloth dining establishments in Bethesda, where she still had a condo. When she was being especially pretentious, Gordon tried to slip him an extra ten bucks for putting up with her. Caesar always slipped it back while she was in the restroom. He said he found her hilarious, and besides, she tipped him as if she thought he was living hand-to-mouth in a war zone instead of across from the Walgreens ten blocks away.

"There he is. There's my son," she said, waving Gordon over to her regular table in the center of the garden patio. His mother enjoyed being outdoors but not out *of* doors. She wore large-frame sunglasses with gold accents and had on a cigar-colored straw sunhat wrapped with a coral ribbon. She stood and smoothed her striped sundress before holding out her arms and pulling Gordon into a hug. She was a slight woman, not thin but with refined features that bordered on delicate. Her grip was rock solid though, and she planted a firm kiss on his cheek before pushing herself away and sitting. She settled her necklace and rings before grasping her martini glass, only to find it empty.

Caesar floated in. "Another, Mrs. Pope?"

"Oh, why the hell not. Thank you, Caesar."

Caesar nodded and looked at Gordon.

"Another? How long have you been here, Mother?" Gordon asked.

"Fifteen or so minutes. I get here early. I always assume some sort of breakdown will occur and I'll be reduced to one of those godawful taxi cabs. You might as well shoot me."

Gordon looked blankly at her. So they were having *that* kind of lunch today. He turned to Caesar. "I'll take a scotch on the rocks."

Caesar nodded and swept away. His mother gave him a disapproving eye.

"What, Mom?"

"Scotch? At noon?"

"You're on your second gin martini," Gordon said.

"I'm retired. It's different."

"I'm doing okay, Mom. Thanks for asking. I mean, I'm bleeding patients, and I called Karen last night for the first time in two months, and I'm not really sleeping well, but I'll live."

"Karen? You called her? Oh, Gordon."

"I had a legitimate medical question. She answered. She was actually quite helpful." Gordon grabbed for his scotch as soon as Caesar set it down.

"The usual meal?" Caesar asked.

"Thank you, dear," his mother said. As he spun away, she picked up her own drink, elbow on the table. "Well, she's an outstanding doctor. Brilliant, you might say. As good as I was in my prime. Very talented."

"Mother, she ripped out my heart," Gordon said flatly.

"You didn't let me finish. I was going to say, 'Very talented, that bitch.'" She made no effort to lower her voice. A nearby table of young women turned to look at her, and she looked right back until they turned away.

Gordon stifled a smile. "Well, the fact is she brought in the business. And my current patients are catching on that she might not be coming back."

"*Might* not? She bought a two-and-a-half-million-dollar house in Laguna Beach. She had a kid with that new man of hers... What's his name? The big-shot agent?"

"Chad." Gordon rolled his eyes. As if she didn't know exactly who he was.

"Yes, *Chad*," she said with equal distaste. "The point is, there's no 'might.' She's never coming back."

"I know that. You think I don't know that?" He swirled his ice, the glass already sweating.

"Sometimes I wonder," his mother said over a sip.

"Her name has weight. That's why it's still on the plaque and the website and the phone listing. I can't do this without her."

"Nonsense. You're every bit as talented as she is."

Gordon looked up at his mother to find the sarcasm, but he found none.

"I mean it, Gordon," she said.

Gordon sighed. "Maybe once, but not anymore. She kept doing what she loved, kept researching, kept publishing. That's why she's relevant, and I'm..." He held out his hands, encompassing himself.

His mother watched him through hooded eyes. She wasn't having it. "Oh, *that's* why you're stuck in that housing project with a smattering of clients you don't care about? *That's* why you're still single. Drinking scotch at noon?" She took a sip of gin. "Because you never got published?"

"Well, I was thinking the 'kept doing what she loved' part was more integral. But yes, that too. It goes a long way in our community to get published like she has."

"I am aware of that, Gordon. I was published many times in my day. And as for doing what you love, that's your fault. You made the decision to stop treating children. She didn't make it for you."

Caesar brought their food, and his mother smiled warmly at him in silence as it was presented. As soon as he left, she turned back to

Gordon with a sniff. He crossed his arms and eyed the salad, no longer hungry.

"What I'm saying is it's in your head," she said.

"It's definitely not my head that's the problem," Gordon said.

His mother held up her hand, stopping him.

Caesar stepped up. "Is something wrong with the salad, Mrs. Pope?"

"Oh, I wasn't waving for you, sweetheart. My son was getting vulgar. I'll have one more martini since you're here."

Caesar nodded and breezed away.

His mother ate in silence, ignoring Gordon's stare. She looked up after a bite. "What, you never heard of a three-martini lunch? We used to do it all the time back when I practiced. Then the country got into yoga. The damage was irreparable."

Gordon laughed and took up his fork. "I don't blame you. You did couples therapy for three decades. I'm going on three years, and I feel like it's already driving me to the bottle." He savored the crunch of the chopped peppers and the tang of the mustard vinaigrette. He wouldn't go begging his mother for cash, but he sure as hell would take the Waterstones' Cobb, every time.

"No, dear. See, I actually liked couples therapy—despite being married to your father all those years. Or perhaps because of it. Living in a disaster of a relationship helped me see the signs in others. That was the secret to my success."

Gordon recalled the scattered toys in his closet, the Matchbox car that had seemed to roll itself free. It put Gordon in mind of reliving his own childhood.

"Mom, you remember that night when you found me wandering on the north end of the Bethesda property in that... that cave?" Gordon tried to keep his voice light, picking at his salad as he spoke.

His mother stopped midsip and watched him carefully. "Of course I remember. What brought that up? Is this because I mentioned your father? Did he do something to you? Because if he did and you're coming out with it now, I'll dig that bastard up and kill him again, myself."

"No, Mom. Christ. How many times... He was an asshole, not a criminal," Gordon said. "Forget it."

But his mother wouldn't forget it. "Then why are you bringing up my single most terrifying moment as a parent at an otherwise pleasant lunch?"

"I was an expert witness yesterday in a case where a sleepwalking boy allegedly strangled another child, nearly killed him," Gordon said, lowering his voice. "It really messed with me. It's like it opened up a window in my brain to all this stuff I thought I'd put away."

"Strangled another child? My God. All we ever worried about with you was if you'd sleepwalk into something and kill yourself. And that was plenty to worry about, believe me." When Caesar came around again, she handed him her credit card without looking at it. "For the bill, dear. And would you mind getting me a chilled glass for what's left of my drink? I'd love you forever." Caesar produced one from behind his back, and she hooted. The gin was swapped, and Caesar moved on.

"I do remember you fretting over me. And you rarely fret. So I know I must have been a pretty serious sleepwalker," Gordon said.

His mother snorted. "*Pretty* serious? A sprained ankle is pretty serious, Gordon. We had to lock you in your bedroom at night for years."

"But that night was different. At the cave. That night was worse, right?"

His mother took a deep breath and then a dainty sip of gin. "Yes. Usually, you bumped around your room for a bit. Maybe walked into ours to bump around there. Once, we found you in the garden, bumping around the tomatoes—startling but not frightening. Then, that night. Bam, out of nowhere, you walk nearly a quarter of a mile to that washed-out culvert and end up in this little cave." She shivered at the memory.

"And then what?" Gordon asked. He'd heard it before, many times, but he felt that hearing it again was important.

"You know. You were growling, holding on to a big rock there and swaying a little. I was so horrified and relieved at the same time that I didn't do anything at first. Just watched you. Until you stopped."

"I stopped?"

"Yes, you stopped, and then you sat down, then lay down. Fast asleep. The paramedics took you to the hospital because they thought something was wrong. Turns out you were just deeply asleep. You woke up twelve hours later, smiling. We took you home. Then I went and had several stiff drinks with your father and ended up in some sort of horrible row with him that I can't recall the details of. I think we each accused each other of putting too much pressure on you." She waved the rest of the story off with one hand.

"What happened after that?" Gordon asked.

"Well, we ended up tying your little leg to your superhero bed. Remember that?" His mother smiled out of the corner of her mouth.

Gordon nodded. *That alone would be grounds for therapy.* But that wasn't what he'd meant. "No, I mean, what happened after that night with the sleepwalking? Any more episodes that you can remember?"

"No. Nothing. Eventually, we forgot to strap you in, and then when nothing happened, we even stopped locking the door."

"Just like that. Sleepwalking from the day I could walk, then... bam. Nothing. Over." Gordon was speaking to himself as much as to his mother.

"You outgrew that stage. Thank God. Although you moved from that to picking your nose. You remember that? You still haven't quite outgrown that one completely."

"I don't see how you outgrow something like that in one night," Gordon said. He wasn't about to tell his mother that he'd revisited that cave, that the dream he'd had throughout all those sleepwalking years had come back. The dream was different from before, but the cave was still there. Things weren't quite as buttoned up as his mother thought.

"You're thinking too much about the past, Gordon. Whatever you were working through in that brain of yours as a little boy, you did it. It broke like a fever." His mother signed the bill and tucked her credit card into her clutch. "Now, I have another lunch to get to, with my bridge club, all the way over in Travilah. I need to run. Those witches wait for nobody." She stood and kissed her son on the forehead. "See you in two weeks, sweetheart." Gordon nodded, his mind elsewhere.

As his mother left the table, he turned to her. "Mom, how old was I then? Ten? Eleven?"

She thought for a moment. "You were twelve years old," she said, nodding definitively. "I remember because it was the week before your thirteenth birthday, and I was dreading the questions from the neighbors." She waved again and turned away.

Gordon had thought to finish his food, but he was slowly losing his appetite again. The fact that Gordon's own parasomnia had come to a head at the same age as Ethan might be nothing more than a strange coincidence. Or not.

He could hear Karen's voice in his head. *"You're projecting, Gordon. Leave it alone. Focus your energy elsewhere."* But to Gordon, Ethan was looking less and less like a projection and more like a reflection—a reflection of the boy Gordon had been when he wound up in that cave.

CHAPTER FOUR

When Gordon returned home, he made himself two promises. The first was that he would not call Karen again, not even to discuss her thoughts on how his own parasomnia symptoms could have stopped seemingly overnight. That was a legitimate medical question, but he already knew what she'd say—that the lessening of parasomniac symptoms was well documented at that age although nobody knew why. *"But you already knew that, didn't you, Gordon? So why are you calling me again?"*

Because he missed Karen? Not exactly.

Because he missed working with Karen? Missed the doctor he had been when he was with her? That was more like it.

Bottom line, the call would seem exactly as desperate as it was.

The second promise was that he would not go through the boxes of past case files he had stored right next to his toys in an effort to find anything that resembled Ethan's violent parasomnia, no matter how badly he wanted to. That would be textbook regression. He'd double-taped those boxes shut for a reason. How quickly he'd managed to forget the toll that seeing each kid had taken on him, like a sliver of stone chipped from a statue with each visit. Over the years, he'd been worn down and blunted. That he was good at treating kids almost made it worse. He considered it a special kind of curse to be drawn to a profession that forced him daily to confront his greatest failure.

He turned from the closet door and trekked upstairs to his apartment, but each step seemed to slow him. He might have turned himself around and gone back down and into the closet on the way toward breaking his second promise were it not for his phone ringing in his pocket. He fished it out to silence it and saw who it was: Dana Frisco. He was surprised he had her info in his phone. Had they exchanged numbers? Perhaps, now that he thought about it, many months ago. Something about her offering to keep an eye out for more courthouse work for him. He felt a lurch in his stomach, the kind he got whenever he knew a phone call wasn't going to be good news. He picked up.

"Dana?" he asked. "Are you all right?"

Dana spoke softly. "Hi, Gordon," she began and then paused. "Yeah, I'm fine. I wanted to see if I could... run something by you." She almost sounded embarrassed.

It occurred to him that she might be asking him out. Could that possibly be it? *She gave you her phone number*, he told himself. Stranger things had happened. Of course, he'd taken her number and then sat on it for four months like a hibernating bear. Still, he found himself smiling. Dana would like Darrow's Barrel. He'd buy her the crab-cake sandwich. She'd be impressed. *"Best-kept secret in Baltimore,"* he'd say, leaning in and winking. Maybe not winking. Nobody winks in real life. But the scene was all there. He could picture it: cold beer, the smell of oil on old wood underneath the subtle scent of her shampoo, the sizzle of the fry line in the back—

"Listen, this isn't standard," she said. "Far from it, and they might have my badge if they knew I was calling you like this."

Gordon smirked. He hadn't known he had such a bad-boy reputation down at the precinct.

"We're about to hit that twenty-four-hour window, and I gotta pull out all the stops," she said.

Gordon paused. "What?" he asked.

"It's another kid. A little girl, twelve years old. She's been missing for almost fifteen hours now," Dana said, her voice tight.

"What?" Gordon asked again, partly to cover himself and partly to let his mind catch back up with the reality of the situation. "What can *I* do?"

"I saw the way the Ethan Barret case hit you, and I know you used to work with kids a lot, and I thought maybe you could—"

"Dana, I'm a psychiatrist, not a private eye. I'd rather just disappoint you now," Gordon said.

"I know, I know, but hear me out." Dana took a deep breath. "The girl disappeared from her bed. Okay? A neighbor kid, a young boy, reported seeing a girl in a white nightie walk past his window sometime in the early morning hours."

Gordon went cold. "Sleepwalking?"

"That's the running theory."

"Nobody tried to stop her?"

"The kid thought she was a ghost. He hid under his covers then fell asleep. You know how kids are," Dana said, trying to calm herself. She sounded as though some small part of her wanted to wring that kid's neck. "I know you don't do this stuff anymore. I know. And the last thing I want to do is overstep here, but I don't think I have to tell you the statistics on kids that go missing for over twenty-four hours."

Gordon knew.

"There's something else, too," Dana said. "The missing girl is Ethan Barret's best friend."

The nervous sweat on Gordon's brow sprouted anew.

"Apparently they are, or were, very close," Dana continued. "Sort of like a first boyfriend, girlfriend thing. It was too weird of a coincidence not to call you. See if you could just take a look at the scene here."

Gordon's unfocused gaze fell upon the closet door.

"Tell me where you are," he said.

· · ·

DANA FRISCO TUCKED her phone away and pointedly ignored the lingering stare of her partner, Marty. She focused instead out the windshield, on the buzzing orange streetlight above their squad car. The big bugs of the Baltimore summer slammed into it with the sound of wet hail.

Marty Cicero had been working with her for seven months, which was four months longer than her last partner. He wasn't the type of guy to be the first to look away, even when she was pointedly ignoring him. At a glance, you would lump him in the Jersey Shore brigade. He was dark and built, his chest half again as wide as Dana's. He wore a gold chain, shaved his legs, and had a tribal armband tattoo. Dana had wanted to write him off as nothing more than an East Coast gym rat at first. The problem was he was too damn perceptive, his gaze too keen. And he was too much of a straight cop. He shuffled his mass to face her more fully.

"Did you seriously just call in a psychiatrist?"

Dana nodded slowly.

Marty sat back in his seat, and the fake leather creaked. "Does Lieutenant Duke know about this?"

He already knew the answer was no. Dana knew he wanted her to say it out loud.

"No, Marty. But if Duke ran everything the way he wanted, we'd all be dead of paper cuts long before we found Erica Denbrook."

Dana knew she wasn't quite herself when it came to missing kids. She got a certain look, glassy and dangerous. Marty had been on missing-children calls with Dana before. He was watching her as if she was drunk on moonshine and might snap at any moment. She knew he'd heard the talk around the station about her reputation. She'd had four partners in the past five years. Three of them had gone on to make detective, which in the BPD meant they were on their way. Not her. Never her. In the men's locker room at the station, they called her the bull. That wasn't a flattering thing. The idea was that if you rode with her long enough, if you put in your eight seconds, you'd get promoted. As for why she still sat in a squad car? Dana knew Marty was trying to figure that out. If he asked her directly, which he hadn't yet, she would say it had an awful lot to do with Warren Duke.

"We either find this girl in the next six hours, or odds are she's gone," Dana said. She struggled to keep her voice even and cold, but she could see in Marty's eyes that he knew better. Dana had a daughter of her own, seven years old, named Chloe. She pictured Chloe in every one of these situations. Every call like this she got. She couldn't help it.

Dana watched a fat cicada slam again and again into the street-light until it hit a broken panel and started to fry in the heat.

"Gordon Pope knows how kids think. He can help us," Dana said.

"More cops is what we need. More cops will find this kid, not some psychiatrist," Marty said.

"More cops? We've already got six of them running down the neighborhood from top to bottom. There are three in that spillway alone. They'll just start running into each other."

Dana sat back and waited, turning the car's weak air vents onto her face. Their cruiser sat down the street from a blockaded intersection outside a halfway-constructed tenement neighborhood. A low-lying brick façade to her right read Tivoli Estates, or was supposed to. The *Ti* was missing from Tivoli, and the *E* was missing from Estates. Someone had had great plans for Tivoli Estates. Then the recession hit. The money pulled out and left the handful of families that had moved into the duplexes and single-story ranch houses to fend for themselves. Since then, it had been the *Voli States*. The neighborhood, if you could call it that, was built on an incline leading up to the old Tivoli theatre at the top, so it was easy for Dana to see that, at best, one-third of the buildings were occupied. The rest were abandoned or unfinished.

To her left, three flashlight beams swung like nooses in the wind as they made their way into the neighborhood up a graffiti-pocked spillway clogged with trash and construction debris. To her far right, a flashing cruiser slowed what sparse traffic there was to a stop until two policemen waved each car clear. The cicadas sounded like chain-saws, and Dana could see the mosquitoes already swarming over the heat of the cruiser's engine block. Piles of bricks and rotten wood and pools of standing water lined the sides of the two-lane street leading into the neighborhood, where God willing, a little girl was still just lost somewhere. But more likely than not, in that neighborhood and in that city, if they found anything, it would be a body.

GORDON TOOK the back route Dana had told him about, pulling off Highway 40 a little before the Tivoli Estates exit and meandering down some ugly-looking side streets. The sky was near full dark now, and he could see the blue and red lights flashing in the night haze well before he came upon them, which was the idea. Dana had made no bones about smuggling him in. He realized he was most likely a dead ringer for the profile of somebody that might have taken the girl: a single white male in his midforties. Rumpled and unshaven, smelling vaguely of booze. Driving a shitty car through the scene. Knowing his luck, he'd get arrested while trying to get into the neighborhood to help the girl. But Dana knew what she was doing. She and her partner were waiting back of the blockade, parked along a residential street. She waved him behind her and took the lead, her lights flashing in silence. She spoke a few words at the cordon, and both cars passed by. The policeman stared him down as he crept through, but Gordon looked straight ahead.

Four blocks into the neighborhood, they stopped. Dana threw her car into park, and Gordon did the same. The sound of their car doors slamming echoed against the dark houses. A curtain rustled in a window then stilled. Gordon couldn't help thinking they were walking the neighborhood Ethan lived in as well—the basement of one of these houses was almost a murder scene. The halted development here lent the place a broken air, not so much quiet as empty. He saw signs everywhere of what it might have been—a vibrant neighborhood where kids splashed around the spillway, biked along the sidewalks that zigzagged up the hill, or hiked to the Tivoli to catch a rainy afternoon movie—but all of its potential was clipped, not unlike the future of Ethan himself.

Dana walked right up to him and wasted no time. "The focus is on a spillway that rings the south side of the neighborhood. There's a small sluice of runoff there that they're combing. It's not very deep, but if she hurt herself or fell into it somehow, it's enough to drown in."

Dana's flat, unflinching tone chilled Gordon. She didn't sound like herself. He wanted a better look at her, at her face, but the streetlights above were burned out, so all he saw was the muted shine of her black hair and the silver of her badge reflecting in the ambient light of the cruiser. Her partner was no warmer. He was a squat, powerful-looking man, his arms crossed over a shelf of a chest. Gordon had met him before at the courthouse—Marty Cicero. The man didn't have to say a word for Gordon to know he wasn't exactly happy with Gordon being there. He wondered if the officer might warm to him if he knew Gordon shared the sentiment.

"The roadblocks and sweeps haven't caught anything," she said. "The few neighbors there are said they saw nothing, heard nothing. No cars, no sounds of struggle. It's the type of neighborhood where a sound like that would carry."

"So you think she's still here somewhere?" Gordon asked.

Dana nodded. "The neighbor kid saw her walking south from her house, there, towards the spillway." She pointed at a flat ranch house down the street that was lit up like a stadium, swarming with people, several of them police. "I thought you may have some insight as to how long these things last, you know, or maybe how kids act when they're sleepwalking."

"If she was sleepwalking," he said.

"We don't have a lot to work with here. I think it's as good a theory as any at this point."

"Children shamble when they sleepwalk. They're like cows. It would be unusual for her... What's her name?" he asked, realizing he still didn't know.

"Erica Denbrook," she said softly.

"And she's twelve?" he asked, clearing his throat. That age kept coming back to haunt him.

She nodded.

"It would be unusual for Erica, at her age, to sleepwalk with purpose, with direction. And kids who sleepwalk don't just disappear. If anything, they make themselves conspicuous, like drunkards. If she's been gone for over ten hours, I guarantee you she's woken up by now. Probably some time ago. But she's still not back. That's what should be worrying you," he said.

Cicero snuffled and shifted his stance. Dana scanned the street up and down as if it might offer something new, but Gordon was willing to bet she'd been up and down the street for hours already, to no avail. Her gaze moved in tiny jerks, like a nervous bird, and she swallowed several times as though her fear would come bubbling up out of her if she let it. Gordon felt that anything that might stem that panic, even pretending he could be useful, was better than letting her fear take hold of her, so he spoke again.

"That's the window? The one where the neighbor kid saw her?"

Dana nodded eagerly. "You want to take a look?"

"What about her bedroom?"

"We dusted the bedroom. No forced entry. No foreign prints."

"Can I see the bedroom?"

Dana was quiet. Apprehensively, she eyed the house, still buzzing with activity and the low hum of conversations heard over the still night.

"If I can do anything for you, it's gonna start in there."

Dana nodded. "I'll... I'll make it work. Follow me. Don't say anything."

Gordon heard a soft popping sound when Cicero stepped in behind him. He turned briefly to see the officer tapping his teeth together, eyes set grimly forward.

A policeman in plainclothes was speaking with a distraught man and woman just inside the front door. Erica's parents were young, in their thirties. Dana said their names were Marcus and McKayla. Neither looked to have showered, eaten, or slept in twenty-four hours.

A fat policeman standing on the front lawn stepped up and then paused when he saw Dana. He looked at Gordon, then at Cicero, then back at Gordon.

"He's with me," Dana said, more of a command than an explanation.

The officer shrugged and stepped aside. The plainclothes officer just inside the door wasn't as accommodating. He was a tall man with clean-cut salt-and-pepper hair. He wore dark jeans and a light-pink dress shirt under a gold-buttoned navy jacket. His badge flashed from his hip.

"No press," the man said. "No outside visitors of any sort."

"He's with me, Lieutenant," Dana said again, less forcefully this time.

"Of course he is, Frisco. But he's not with me. And unless you cleared it back at the station, he's not getting in. I'm not having another Rockhurst on my watch."

Dana paused. "I cleared it with the station. And Rockhurst was a simple misunderstanding that—"

The lieutenant held up his hand, stopping Dana cold. He turned to Gordon. "You, what's your name?"

"Gordon Pope."

"Marty, hold him here while I run this guy down." He turned away from them without another word and stepped out of the porch-light. Dana clenched her jaw and watched him go.

"Well, looks like you got about three minutes, Gordon," she said.

Cicero turned broadside to her. "What? Lieutenant Duke said to stay put, Dana."

She looked at him. "You're not Lieutenant Duke's partner. So either you tackle us both, which I have no doubt you could do, by the way, or you be *my* partner."

Cicero's breathing quickened. He flicked his eyes back and forth between Dana and Gordon.

"Don't worry, Marty. You'll have plenty of time to become best buds with Warren Duke when they promote you." She turned to Gordon. "It's down the hall, the room on the right. Three minutes."

Gordon looked at Cicero and took a step toward the hallway, and when Cicero did nothing more than stare bullets at him, he set off. He was in Erica's room in seconds, smiling and feeling as though he'd done something important until he realized he had no idea what he was looking for.

Gordon panned the room. He saw a twin bed in the corner with a brightly striped bedspread, rumpled and pushed to the floor. Posters of bands he didn't recognize. An open pink retainer case on a thin blue side table next to the bed, empty. That was evidence for the sleepwalking theory—Gordon had worn retainers as a kid, and while he wasn't the most social boy, even he wouldn't have been caught dead wearing them outside while under his own power. A whirring laptop, slim and silver, sat on a small corner desk, casting a faint blue pall. The screen constantly refreshed some sort of live chat feed. He moved in for a closer look when Dana's voice suddenly carried down the hall, and he knew he had to go. Gordon had just turned the corner when Warren Duke came back.

The lieutenant stepped inside the foyer and paused, staring at Gordon as if his presence was personally insulting. Then he turned to Dana and said, "He isn't cleared, Dana," his voice terse and low, a school principal's voice. One vein flickered purple at the edge of his tanned temple.

"Must be some mistake, Lieutenant," Dana said. Gordon wanted to shrink back down the hall, but Dana stood her ground. If anything, she stood taller. "I'll take him out, check it out with dispatch myself."

"You do that," Duke said, his voice flat as slate, eyes unblinking.

"This way, Dr. Pope," she said, as if she'd never met him before in her life. Gordon slid sideways around Duke, trying to smile. They left the house along with Cicero and paused in the street outside, beyond the light of the porch.

"Dana, that is exactly the type of shit that I'm talking about," Cicero whispered. "That's the reason you—"

A look from Dana stilled him. Out there, in the darkness, Gordon thought he saw a chink in the armor she'd shown inside. It was in her eyes. They were hurt, but her face was a grim mask. He wondered how many small barbs and jabs that mask had taken over the years from men like Warren Duke.

"Warren Duke, huh?" Gordon said, breaking the silence. "You know, I read a paper once that hypothesized a link between single-syllable last names and social entitlement. It was in the *Saskatchewan Journal of Anthropology*. Hand to God."

Cicero turned to Gordon with narrowed eyes, but Dana laughed. It was a deep laugh, not a high-pitched, nervous laugh. And it snapped the tension between them like a brittle stick. "What about 'Pope'?" she asked. "That's one syllable."

Gordon scratched at his collar for a second. "Eh, it was a garbage paper anyway."

"Did you get anything? From the bedroom?" Dana asked.

"Well, I think you're right about the sleepwalking," Gordon said, "but that's about all I could get. I'm sorry." And try as he might, he couldn't keep the bitter disappointment from his own voice. Nobody had asked for his professional help in something that mattered for a long time. That it was Dana made it all the more biting, especially since she seemed to be taking the weight of this case on her own shoulders.

"It's my fault," Dana said. "I'm not sure what I thought you'd find. And you had no time anyway." She watched Duke still interviewing Erica's parents through the dining room window.

"You could have tried to clear him first," Cicero said, as if telling her the night was black.

"Oh, please. This is the Warren Duke show. I doubt he'd approve of Gordon even if I'd submitted it the second the call came through. I just wanted to act quickly, do what I could to find her in the first twenty-four hours."

Gordon followed her gaze. He watched McKayla Denbrook take a sip of coffee, and her hand shook, but Gordon doubted that was from the caffeine. He looked back at Dana, recalling that she had a child, a girl. He guessed she was placing herself inside, by that window, with that coffee. The remnants of a board game were spread out on the dining room table just past where Duke stood. It looked paused midgame, probably from the evening before, when the family had still been whole. He squinted, stepping forward. The game looked like Chutes and Ladders. He walked forward again, on the porch now. Gordon and his mother had done their fair share of board gaming back in the day. He recognized the old-school yellow checkerboard, the classic design. It was indeed a very well-worn game of Chutes and Ladders, fading around the edges. Buttons stood in for some of the missing pieces. He took another step and nearly walked right into Warren Duke's chest.

"I'm sorry, maybe you didn't understand me," Duke said, holding up a hand that flashed with a gold signet ring. "Interfering with a police investigation is a—"

"That's Chutes and Ladders," Gordon said, ignoring him and speaking to Erica's parents just inside.

Whatever prepared response Duke had died on his lips. McKayla turned toward him, cup in hand. Gordon could see she was so tired and overrun that she was willing to assume any stranger in her house might be a detective or official of some sort.

"Yes," she said. "We've had game night every Wednesday since Erica was five."

"And she likes Chutes and Ladders?"

"She used to like them all, anything we put out there to play," said Marcus. His hair was unsettled, as if he'd been running his hands through it repeatedly. "But nowadays, this is the only one that can get her to the table. If it was up to her, I think she'd be on her phone or in her room on her computer."

"But you still played last night?" Gordon asked, resisting the urge to roll his fingers as if he could speed the man up. Warren Duke already had his hand on Gordon's shoulder and was squeezing sharply.

Marcus nodded. "It's all that's left of family time. She can play online whenever she wants other days, and she does. But Wednesday night is always our night." He spoke as if he was lecturing her. Then his eyes softened again.

His wife began to cry and pressed herself to his chest.

Duke led Gordon away, outside again, past the lights. He was breathing hard through his nose, and once out of earshot of the house, he shoved Gordon forward, off the lawn and into the street next to Dana and Cicero, who didn't look pleased with him either.

"Frisco, I'm writing this up," Duke said. "And if you don't keep this guy under control, I'll make sure everyone knows about it."

With one last shove, he turned away, and that time he closed the front door behind him.

Dana shook her head, her hands on her hips. "As if I didn't fuck this up enough already." Cicero made a move toward him that Gordon knew would end up with him being escorted to his car with a sore shoulder.

"Wait." Gordon held up his hands. He looked around the lawn in a slow spin, his eyes darting everywhere. He settled his gaze on the sidewalk, the one that went past the neighbor's window. "I think I have an idea."

CHAPTER FIVE

Dana watched Gordon walk down the sidewalk and past the neighbor's window, left to right, the direction the boy had seen Erica walk. The streetlights buzzed above him, the dust of a score of moths sifting down to be blown away in the weak breeze of the night. His eyes were wide as his head did a slow pan. Marty watched him with open skepticism, his hands half-clawed, as if they itched to collar Gordon and toss him from the scene. Dana shot a glance back at Erica's house. Warren Duke was the type of guy to have a strict three-strikes-and-you're-out policy. If he caught her dragging her feet again, she was most likely out of a job.

"I'm guessing Erica went to bed around ten? When do kids go to bed these days?" Gordon asked, still scanning the street.

"Her parents said she went to her room around ten. Most likely fell asleep shortly thereafter. The parents went to bed at ten thirty and said the light in her room was off."

"Your timeline puts the neighbor kid's sighting at what... eleven thirty?" Gordon asked.

Dana straightened. "Yes. Approximately eleven thirty. The

neighbor said he looked at his bedside clock. But I don't remember telling you that."

"You didn't. But it makes sense. It takes anywhere from fifty to seventy minutes to go from awake to late-stage and REM sleep, where the strongest dreams occur. Let's call it an even sixty." Gordon pulled up his khaki slacks at the pockets and crouched as he peered down the sidewalk where Erica had last been seen. He leaned slightly against the brick of the low retaining wall to his right, sighting along it with one eye squinted.

"So that puts us at eleven thirty," Marty said flatly. "And Erica dreaming in her bed. Which isn't what happened."

Gordon popped up and turned toward them, his expression intense, as if he'd been staring at the numbers for hours and they were finally starting to come together. "Exactly," he said, pointing at Marty. "It isn't what happened, because she never got to dream."

"With all due respect," Marty said, his tone making it clear he had little to none, "unless you have something concrete to give us that can help, I need to get you out of here before it costs me and my partner our jobs." He looked sidelong at Dana.

Gordon nodded. "There are five stages of sleep," he said. "Stages one and two are light. Hypnagogic. Fleeting images from the day, no real cohesion"—he ticked off the stages on his fingers—"but stages three and four are what's called slow wave. This is where most sleepwalking occurs. Extreme parasomniacs rarely get to stage five, which is REM, deep sleep. They get up before then. Instead of being able to work out whatever their brain needs to work out in their sleep, they act on it. One of the most common reports coming from these cases is that the individual went to sleep dreaming of something on their to-do list and then acted that thing out while unconscious."

"No shit," Dana said, her mind already catching up with Gordon. "The unfinished board game. Chutes and Ladders."

Gordon nodded, a small smile at the corner of his mouth. "And what does this look like to you?" Gordon asked, pointing at the concrete at their feet and the small retaining walls on either side.

"A sidewalk?" Marty offered, holding his hands out.

"See, to me, this looks like a chute."

Gordon stood and massaged his lower back. Above him, the streetlight fizzled brightly for a moment before blinking off, joining most of its kind in the neighborhood as a dark sentry. Gordon looked up at it then swatted at a dive-bombing bug. Dana almost smiled. Even when Gordon got his moment, he couldn't quite get his moment.

"Are you serious?" Marty asked. "You think she's, what, acting out the game?"

"Yes. That is exactly what I think. At least she was when she walked past this window almost twenty-four hours ago."

Hearing the time passed put Dana back in the trenches. The heavy air seemed weighted with the loss of the girl. When you have a little girl of your own and another child goes missing, some part of you goes with that child. Some part of you is that child's mother, clinging to her tea cup as if it held leaves she could divine.

"Well, let's play the game, then," Dana said.

Gordon nodded then spun around again, facing forward. He started walking at an even pace, his head on a swivel. "We're looking for anything that might resemble a chute or a ladder to a child. Think out of the box. The dreaming mind makes wild leaps of connectivity and association, particularly the sleeping mind of a child, but they'll often share a common theme or kernel of similarity—"

"How about that actual ladder?" Marty asked, pointing to the right. Behind the retaining wall and through a break in the overgrown hedge running parallel to the sidewalk was a small access ladder, no more than five feet high.

"Where does that go?" Gordon asked.

"The next block. The neighborhood was supposed to be built at a soft tier, with the Tivoli up top and a greenbelt and runoff plain at the bottom," Dana said. She'd spent nearly an hour staring at the city-planning specs for Tivoli Estates and could picture the layout in her mind. The more she thought about it, the more it seemed set up as a series of steps with runoff chutes and access ladders. She gripped the first rung and climbed up. The men followed.

"What's the Tivoli?" Gordon asked, straining his eyes in the dim streetlights. The next block consisted of a handful of dimly lit houses and the stark skeletons of half again as many abandoned ones, but at the very top was a single structure with a turreted outline.

"The old Tivoli theatre. It has historic status with the city and county. It was supposed to be the centerpiece of the neighborhood, but the restoration money never came through, so it's just as dilapidated as it ever was. We already looked there. Ran the whole place down first thing. There was no sign of her."

The three of them turned to look at the scene below. Spread across the neighborhood were fifteen or so bobbing flashlights—more lights than cops. Good to see that some neighbors cared, at least.

"They were that close? Ethan and Erica?" Gordon asked.

"Marcus Denbrook said they were always together. And when they weren't, they chatted online. Up until the assault. They refused to let her to contact him after that. Apparently, Erica didn't take it well. They got into a fight about it last night, over the board game," Dana said.

"Why didn't you tell me this?" Gordon asked.

"Does it matter? If anything, it gives more credence to the runaway theory, not the sleepwalking theory."

Gordon shook his head. "Trauma and stress before slow-wave sleep is a trigger mechanism for parasomnia."

"What the hell is a trigger mechanism?" Marty asked, tucking the back of his shirt in flush with the rest of his uniform. Gordon turned to him and started to answer but paused. From somewhere above, they heard the faint sound of the neighborhood search party calling Erica's name.

"C'mon," Dana said. "Stay on target. Chutes and Ladders." Dana crouched lower, to the level of what she guessed would be Chloe's line of sight. She pictured Chloe here, walking on a sidewalk that was not a sidewalk. She'd be in her sleep shirt, an XXL freebie her dad had caught out of an air cannon at an Orioles game years before, back before he left them both to go build his beloved bar in Florida. It was still Chloe's favorite shirt. She wouldn't have shoes on, of course, or even socks. *God, the poor girl is barefoot.* The realization quickened her heart—tiny feet walking obliviously through the wreckage of this place.

To their left, the sidewalk continued in a more-or-less straight layout, but to the right it curved upward in a wide arch. "That way," Dana said. "Chute." Dana handed Gordon a spare flashlight and clicked her own on as they walked. "Marty, check the addresses against the all-clear list." Marty nodded and clicked on a Maglite the size of a ladle.

"So you're telling me a person can climb a friggin' ladder in their sleep?" Marty asked, panning toward the sudden barking of a dog behind darkened blinds in the house to his left. He checked the address against a sheet of paper he fished out of his pocket, then moved on.

"Yep," Gordon said.

"And if she cut her feet all up, she wouldn't wake up?" Dana asked.

"Not necessarily. There have been cases where parasomniacs set off in the snow in their sleep and walked to the point of frostbite without waking up. Amputating frostbite."

"That's freaky as hell," Marty said, flashing from his list to the houses and alleys they passed.

"That's the mind at night," Gordon replied. "Anybody see anything? The game jumps around. If she took this road, she won't have stayed on it for long."

"It just drops off over here." Marty ran his flashlight over the open space to his right. "Dana, you got anything?"

Dana was eyeing a drain pipe set into the left side of the road about twenty feet down, a metal hole in the slope of earth, perhaps three feet across. It gaped at her like a darkened basement from the top of the stairs.

"That'll do," Gordon said, following her eye. He walked quickly up to it and ducked underneath the corrugated metal lip. "It goes somewhere, that's for sure, and it's not clogged," he said, his voice echoing. He scurried inside on his elbows. Dana turned around, fully expecting to have to drag Marty behind her, but found him adjusting his belt and unbuttoning the top button on his uniform.

"Time's ticking," he said. "But if there's a flash flood and I'm spit out into the harbor somewhere, I'm gonna be very disappointed in both of you."

Dana smirked, turned around, and ducked in ahead of him.

The three of them crawled on hands and knees through the storm drain in silence. The air was hot and still, but the metal was cold to the touch. A thin layer of scattered debris coated the center bottom, and leaves crunched underneath them. Dana put her hand on something wet and spongy and cringed.

"You all right?" Marty asked.

"Just fabulous," she said.

Sweat was dripping down her face by the time Gordon popped up and out just ahead of her. Moments later, Dana was able to stand. She climbed out of the pipe and found Gordon pondering an offset grate in the dirt.

He took off his steaming glasses and wiped his face of sweat, smearing a fine line of dust into the creases on his forehead. Then he picked up the grate. "Doesn't weigh much. Clearly not bolted in."

"Something a young girl could have lifted?" Dana moved aside as Marty popped out behind her.

He dusted his lapels. "I never liked this game." Marty blew his nose clear. "Not even as a kid. I was more of a Battleship guy." He panned the ground beneath them and paused over a brief trail of crushed leaves.

"It was Risk for me," Gordon said absently. "Hours and hours of Risk. I think she came this way. I think we're on the right track."

"This is the third block," Dana said. "One before the Tivoli. None of these houses were finished."

"This fella barely made it past the skeleton stage," Gordon said. His flashlight traveled from bottom to top of what was supposed to be a split duplex, two stories, with a nice offset porch and a small balcony for each unit. As it stood, it was an off-kilter rectangle of browning particle board, half-covered in tattered plastic that waved at them in the night wind.

Dana walked around the base of the structure, but it was boarded up tight. She stopped in front of a forgotten trellis, two stories tall. *A ladder?* She shook it lightly. It groaned. Dust and yellow paint flaked down through the beam of her light. She looked back at Gordon.

"Looks climbable," Gordon said begrudgingly.

His simple tone—the way he made it entirely plausible that a twelve-year-old girl could have treated this neighborhood like her own personal board game when every other person walking these streets right now probably thought she was already trussed up in the back seat of some shitty van with electrical tape around her tiny ankles—made her question whether she wasn't losing her own mind. It was insane to hope like that. She felt a disparaging comment on her lips but knew that if she let it out, the search would be over and Erica would be gone, so she turned it into a loud, almost angry call of the girl's name. The two men were startled into silence then listened for any reply. There was none. Only the search groups below, who swung their flashlights toward them. One group nearby started moving their way.

"There's an open window well up there," Gordon said, one hand on his hip as he lit up a break in the wall, perhaps ten feet up. It gaped at them, dusty and dark. Dana knew what she had to do. She unbuttoned her collar, slid her flashlight into her belt, and flicked on the smaller light on her shoulder. She took a firm grip of the trellis and started climbing. Marty looked as though he wanted to argue, but Dana shook her head. Before he could say anything, she'd expertly maneuvered up the old trellis, switching her grip and threading inside the bars when she needed to. The trellis shook, and the metal squeaked, but it held. Then she was up and in, her flashlight flickering in the darkness like a jack-o-lantern flame. Below, Gordon told her to be careful in an awkward, motherly whisper that might have made her smile under other circumstances, but he was right about being cautious. The walls were framed with swollen wood that sagged drunkenly inward, and here and there, the floorboards sported the telltale bruise coloring of rot. One wrong step and she would be right back where she started, only with a broken leg.

Then Dana saw something that almost made her cheer out loud. Little footprints, barefoot, about the size of her hand, but clear enough. She followed them with her flashlight, wincing when she saw they'd passed right over a rotten spot on the floor and continued on. They marked the old wood with little dimples of mud and headed toward the back of the second floor.

"Erica? Sweetheart?" Dana asked, trying to keep her voice conversational, trying to keep a reflux of panic from rising in her throat and ultimately failing because what she saw next made her go cold.

Another chute, and this one was real. A trash chute cut into the wall, a long tube of ridged plastic the workers used to toss junk from the upper stories to the ground below. It was basically just a drop.

"Erica?" she called again, louder this time. She picked her way across the room. No answer.

"What's going on up there?" Gordon asked, his voice distant in the rushing of blood to her head.

Erica's path was unmistakable. The tracks led to the chute and nowhere but the chute.

"She went down a garbage chute! Go around back!" She took a step forward, and the floor crunched heavily beneath her. She froze. The ground steadied. She was perhaps ten feet from the chute. She heard Gordon running around the outside of the building. She heard, more distantly, Marty's voice in concert with other, deeper voices— cop voices.

"I see it!" Gordon said. "There's a dumpster here! Erica! Erica, are you there?"

Dana listened, frozen in place, wide-eyed as Gordon hammered at the top of the dumpster and swore. "The stupid thing's locked!" More metallic slamming. Then stillness. "Dana! I hear her! I hear something! She's crying!" More hammering. Or was that her own heart? "Stupid-ass thing, there's a huge metal bar across it. Dana, I think she's hurt."

Dana's mind was already made up. It had been made up as soon as she saw those footprints end. She could hear the crying too, a soft mewling, like a kitten fallen between the slots of a grate.

"Erica, honey, I want you to get away from the opening of the chute if you can, okay? I'm coming in," she said. She secured her utility belt and tied back her hair. The top lip of the chute was already pulling away from the building. Old nails hung from the ribbed plastic like teeth. She flexed her fingers. She didn't weigh much, but she knew the chute wouldn't hold her, not for long. But neither would the trellis if she tried to climb back down that, and the longer she stood there gaping, the less the floor seemed to want to hold her either. She thought light thoughts—feathers, bubbles, dandelion seeds—took a deep breath, and soft-stepped the ten feet to the chute. She heard a big *crack* behind her but didn't stop. The chute was like those slides she hated at the water parks as a kid—the big, steep ones the boys all loved, so she made herself ride them too—the key was just doing the damn thing. She picked up her feet and went in shoes first.

The chute smelled like rotten banana peels and hot street tar. It was rough and tattered, broken from both use and neglect, so she was able to skid to only a half-fall by the time she hit the opening into the dumpster. Still, she slammed her shoulder on the metal lip, which sent a lightning bolt of pain up her neck, and the floor came up to meet her with the force of a slamming door. She sat hard on her tailbone, and all the air left her in a *whuff*. Her chin bounced into her shoulder light and sent the lamp careening into a pile of trash, where it rested, shining directly back into her eyes for a moment before it popped out. The dumpster went black as ink. She'd bitten her tongue too. She spat blood, cursing to herself.

Gordon was slapping on the dumpster from the outside, making the air ring inside. "Dana! Are you all right? Talk to me!" His voice was muffled, but she could hear the panic.

"I'm all right," Dana said. "Stop that banging, I've already got one hell of a headache." She fished her penlight from her breast pocket, clicked it on, and froze. There, illuminated between sharp-angled shadows, huddled against a pile of bricks, and surrounded by the sparkle of shattered glass, lay Erica. Dana scrambled over to her and hovered her hands over the girl for only a brief moment before brushing at her sweat-streaked brow. Her eyes were closed, and she wasn't crying anymore. Her hair was pinned here and there with butterfly clips, but her trip had shaken much of it loose so that it haloed around her head. *Please, please, please...* Dana wasn't even sure who she was pleading with—Erica, sure, but also whatever god had thrown this poor girl down here, broken among the trash. She checked for bleeding but found none. She felt for a pulse, but if it was there, it was weak, and her hands were shaking too much to sense it. She went back to brushing the girl's hair, gently feeling for cuts and wiping her brow. *Please, please, please.*

And then an answer. A flutter. That soft mewling sound.

And then a ripping sound. A puncturing *thunk* followed by more ripping, and a whoosh of cooler night air and yellow moonlight. A grating pop, and then the whole chute was torn away from the opening. Gordon's head shoved through. Marty's voice just behind him, directing. The tinny whine of an approaching ambulance.

"Is she alive?" Gordon asked.

Dana could only gather the little girl slowly to her chest and hold her and smile grimly through her tears because the two of them were crying in the dumpster—both she and Erica—and Dana knew damn well from personal experience that if someone was crying, it meant she was very much alive.

CHAPTER SIX

That night, Gordon took a forty-minute shower, poured himself three fingers of scotch from his dwindling stock, and sat down to watch the news. When he saw Warren Duke take all the credit for finding Erica Denbrook in a snippet from a press conference, he poured himself a fourth finger.

Duke relayed to the press that Erica was dehydrated and had suffered a badly dislocated shoulder but was expected to make a full recovery within the week. He looked exhausted, as if he'd carried her to the hospital himself. Dana was the one who'd risked her job, Dana had climbed into that hellhouse and thrown herself down a trash chute, Dana had literally waded through jagged garbage to find the girl, Dana's was the touch that had brought her back.

And not to be a dick, but some small mention of an intrepid psychiatrist might be nice, Warren. A certain Maryland native, perhaps? Office conveniently located in Baltimore's historic Mount Vernon neighborhood. Currently taking clients. Offering extremely competitive rates.

Gordon snorted into his scotch. He'd known Lieutenant Duke for all of one day, and he already knew the man would do no such thing.

The way Duke framed things when he'd joined the brigade at the dumpster, Dana was lucky she wasn't fired on sight. And Gordon was lucky not to be in jail. Charming fellow. But not surprising. Gordon knew his type. He'd seen them all over Johns Hopkins when he was getting his doctorate there. They were the boat-shoe-clad, pastel-short-wearing, popped-collared undergraduates, the newest generation of East Coast privilege just hitting the upper-management circle. Gordon was willing to bet Duke hadn't so much *made* lieutenant as been *born into* lieutenant. And was on his way up. Gordon knew his type because he'd run in many of the very same circles not too long before Duke came along—bright, privileged, good pedigree—only Gordon had never felt much of a connection with his contemporaries, even back then. Did the generations that came before Gordon find him as foreign as Gordon found Duke?

Probably, but that doesn't make Duke any less of a jackass.

Gordon's glass was empty. He looked at the handle of fire-sale scotch to the left of his television—also empty. He'd hit his dollar limit for the week, as well, and since moonlighting with Brighton wasn't on the horizon anymore, he was going to have to go dry for the next several days.

Or he could call his mother.

He was a phone call away from an allowance, a phone call away from slipping back twenty years and getting a folded check from his mother every month, her holding it out to him with that shine in her eye that said, *"Take it, Gordon. Really. You can't possibly be expected to fend for yourself in a world gone this crazy."*

Gordon shook his head. That was as much as admitting the past twenty years had never happened, and they'd sure as shit happened. Sobriety was nothing compared to a two-decade brain wipe. He could go without his plastic bottle of scotch for a week. He was almost one hundred percent sure of that. Ninety-five percent sure. Okay, at least ninety percent sure.

Gordon wasn't sure when it happened, but one second he was watching the news, sinking into his old chair with the soft weight of a hot shower and a scotch kicker lulling him to sleep, and the next he was back in his cave. He felt a half-second stab of panic, just as in the old days, and a tendril of red mist snaked along the floor, but he slapped it with his loafer to dissipate it, and just like that, he placed himself. His shoes did it. Loafers were adult shoes. He was an adult. The cave couldn't hurt him anymore.

But it *had* once—or very nearly had. He remembered. The mist was an echo of an imprint, but it had held something once. He turned toward the entrance of the cave. It was open, just as it had been when he'd revisited a few nights before. But the cave hadn't always been open. At one point, it had been closed, and he'd been trapped inside of it. With that realization, the dream wavered. He shouted in frustration, but the color of the place was already fading. The damp smell too. Those were the first things to go when someone woke up. He spun around, drinking in the scene with the eyes of his subconscious, trying to see what it was that his brain thought he should see there, and that's when he noticed the rock.

A big, round stone sat just to one side of the entrance—a big, round stone *he* had pushed aside, once. Gordon knew it. But that had taken him years. Years and years to push that stone aside. And before he could do it, he'd been trapped. He'd ripped at it with his fingernails. He ran to it, his feet already sloughing away and back to the waking world. He reached the stone, standing on the stumps of his knees. There, in the large rock, were several gouges, like a pen dragged through wet paper. And bits of fingernail too.

Gordon opened his eyes. He didn't shoot awake. No startled yelp, no bolt of understanding from the sky. He was in his chair again, in front of his droning television, and his hand was out, reaching for something. As the fog of sleep left him, his fingers grasped at something unseen, forgetting they were holding his empty scotch glass. It dropped to the floor and shattered. He stared at it, reminded of the fragmented light in the dumpster, the thousands of pieces of shattered glass that surrounded Dana and Erica in the darkness of their own cave.

After a moment, he realized he wasn't reaching for something he'd seen in the dream but rather reaching for his dream journal, which he'd stopped keeping many years before. His mother had foisted the journal upon him when he was a child in order to deal with his sleepwalking. It was classic Deborah Pope parenting: suggesting a therapeutic dream journal might help calm her son's roiling subconscious and then not so subtly suggesting he was only hurting himself if he didn't produce it every morning for her professional eye. He was nearly a teenager by the end of it, for God's sake. For every dream that ended up in the cave, he'd had two that ended up with morning wood. He wasn't about to write that down for his mother to read.

But he had written almost every dream down. His journaling got so routine that he'd reach for his nightstand first thing in the morning, grasping for his little black Moleskine notebook while still half asleep, determined to capture what he could before it fled him. He'd gone through probably fifty notebooks. Notebooks that his mother had kept and then given him when he said he was going to start a child-psychiatry practice with his now ex-wife. Notebooks that he'd boxed and taped and stashed in a dusty, forgotten corner when he closed the practice.

Notebooks that were in the closet downstairs. Behind the toys. Behind the case files.

The realization made him slowly sit up, then stand. He almost put his left foot down on a jagged edge of glass, his broken tumbler momentarily forgotten. He managed to avoid it with a skipping stumble and then walked right past his dustpan and broom and took the stairs down two at a time. The bare bulb in the closet clicked on and then popped out with a bright flash and a hiss that made Gordon yelp like a child then curse like a sailor. *Where are the damn light bulbs? Do I even have any more light bulbs?* Karen had kept everything in labeled drawers. Gordon tended to leave the lightbulbs on the floor wherever he last changed them. *Forget it.* He knew where the flashlight was.

The boxes holding his old dream journals were in the very back and looked to have been tossed out of a moving van into the rain and then kicked into the closet. Which made sense because they'd been in there so long that Gordon couldn't remember unpacking them for the first move to set up the joint practice, much less the second move that broke apart said practice in all but name. He stripped the tape easily and sat down on another, sturdier box with his flashlight in hand to start rifling.

He found stacks and stacks of black notebooks, smelling like ancient newspaper and looking far more scandalous than they actually were. The first one Gordon picked up detailed a long stretch of nights in his eleventh year, when he'd ended up wetting the bed twice in the span of three months. Same dream—nothing Freudian or Jungian about it. He'd just dreamed he was peeing in a huge toilet. He remembered his father near hysterics, talking about how he wouldn't abide a bed-wetting son, and his mother rolling her eyes in silence when she could have stepped in on his behalf. She knew as well as any psychiatrist that the last thing you do to a bed-wetter is shame him. But she'd held her tongue. *A skill she seems recently to have pointedly forgotten.* He tossed the book away—picked up the whole stack, in fact, and set it aside. That wasn't what he was looking for.

Not until he searched the second box did he find something promising: a series of journals near the bottom, dated to when he was twelve years old, around the Fourth of July. He remembered the wet heat of the cave then, the real cave on the north of the property, and how when he'd come back to himself after sleepwalking, he was shivering and sweating at the same time because of how stifling July was. He flipped through each page, scanning it for any reference to the cave, wiping his damp forehead and leaving fingerprints on the paper. Then he found one entry dated June thirtieth.

I dreamed I went to a red cave. I felt that I had to meet someone there. But when I got there, I was terrified. I wasn't ready. I tried to run, but the cave was blocked. I scraped at the walls of the cave until I woke up. My nails had cut my face. It stings in the shower.

He flipped forward, certain he'd find more entries, at least a mention about the night he woke up in the cave itself. But the next entry was dated July twentieth and detailed some nonsense about finding himself at a math exam he'd never studied for. He flipped back to the cave dream. Forward to the math dream. That was a huge gap. He nearly threw the journal in frustration. The cave dream was the single most traumatizing dream of his childhood. He'd spoken of it countless times with his mother at their lunches.

As an adult, he added to himself. As an adult Gordon.

As a child, he'd apparently written about it once then never again. Could he be remembering things wrong? Had he not dreamt of it as much as he thought he had?

Or had those dreams frightened him so much that he didn't want to remember them?

The journals from there on out had the feel of censored letters from a war front—general platitudes, basic ideas, many things blacked out or left unsaid.

With nothing more to say for himself and the cave dream, he found himself reading again and again the passage he had written. *Red cave?* The cave he'd visited minutes before had a mere dusting of red, no more. *Had to meet someone?* Gordon remembered whatever was in that cave as being something to run from, not to meet. *But I wasn't ready.* Ready for what?

Gordon had a nagging feeling that everything was connected, from Ethan's trial to his own sleepwalking and even to Erica's near-death experience in the dumpster. But the common thread was eluding him. He was missing something. He felt it was there, in his dreams, but he couldn't stay within them long enough to figure it out. The half-formed picture was frustrating enough to drive a man to drink, and the last drink in the house was dried into the carpet upstairs.

He had a sudden, almost desperate urge to call Karen. Either that or to go out to Darrow's Barrel and see how much Riggs the bartender could extend him on credit. Gordon had his spreadsheets, and his spreadsheets said there was no more cash for booze, but a bar tab was different. Gordon looked at his cell phone. He had reasonable cause to call Karen. He could run down his thoughts on the dreams and sound almost as though he wasn't calling just to hear her voice. Or he could just go get a beer.

As it turned out, Riggs said Gordon was good for several beers. Four pints was the final number. Gordon vaguely remembered the kind offer of a fifth, which he politely declined, reasoning that leaving some water in the well was how one continued to get credit, and one never knew when that pint might come in handy. When he went back home, he had no urge to call anyone, which was a victory. His only urge was to hit his pillow.

Gordon woke up in the damp heat of his bedroom the next morning. Baltimore sometimes did a trick where it rained, but the rain made things hotter. He stumbled up, turned on the air-conditioning window-unit he'd neglected, stripped off his damp T-shirt, and fell back into bed again. He fumbled for his cell phone on the nightstand and checked his call history.

No calls to Karen. He did a little fist pump.

He clomped out of his bedroom and toward the sink, eyeing the shattered glass still on the floor with reproach, as if someone else had done it. In fact, all of the day before felt to Gordon as if it had been lived by another man, from running up and down the Tivoli Estates neighborhood to find Erica all the way to washing away the sour taste of his journals with whatever beer Riggs was willing to front him. His time hunched over a flashlight in the storage closet seemed like a strange mania to him in the light of a new day.

Karen would tell him his dreams might say a bit about where his mind dwelled but nothing more. He could hear her in his head, her patient voice saying, *"Dreams are just dreams, Gordon. Don't go all Freudian on me."* And she was right. He wouldn't. The time had come to turn the corner. He needed to confirm his handful of appointments for the remainder of the month and hammer out a concrete plan for getting new clients. Did psychiatrists have social-media accounts nowadays? Could he maybe do some sort of blog? He wasn't much of a writer, but he could at least get his name out there more, figure out how to use a tablet, or something.

Gordon sat at his computer, his browser open, ready to research how to market a small, struggling psychiatry practice. He had a hot cup of fresh French-press coffee steaming next to a dripping glass of ice water. Ambient electronica was playing on his handheld speaker. A steady rain was falling outside, tapping his windows. For once, he was happy he didn't have an appointment all day. He felt so good, in fact, that he pulled out his Brain Journal, a mishmash of medical ideas that he thought stood a chance of growing into publishable journal articles. He felt inspiration fluttering about the eaves of his brain. Something not quite defined was coming, the beginnings of an idea that could bring him professional recognition as Gordon Pope. Not Karen Jefferson and Gordon Pope. Gordon Pope. He tapped the tattered journal in time with the music, sipped his coffee, and watched the rain.

And then his doorbell buzzed. He blinked rapidly. It couldn't be a package. He hadn't ordered a book in months. He wasn't expecting any visitors—hadn't had one of those in months, either. *Probably just a solicitor or someone mistaken about the address.* He decided not to answer and leaned back in his chair and lifted his coffee mug to his lips.

The doorbell buzzed again, longer that time. Too long for a solicitor, too long for a mistaken address. He stood, tucked his robe over himself, and moved to his intercom.

"Yes?" he asked, not quite managing to keep the annoyance from his voice.

"Dr. Pope?" came the reply, a man's voice, small in the background wash of rain.

"Yes?" Gordon replied hesitantly.

"My name is Andrew Barret. You... I believe you testified at my son's hearing? Ethan?"

All of the cozy warmth of the morning slowly seeped from the room. Gordon found himself leaning against the com as if it was the only thing keeping him up.

He pressed the receiver with a trembling hand. "Can I help you?"

"May I speak with you?"

"I'm really not... I have a pretty hectic schedule at the moment—"

"Please. We're sort of at the end of our rope, here."

His voice held an air of desperation, as well as a touch of shame, as if he was hesitant to speak up, even into the com. That made Gordon feel a little ashamed too, of his fumbling and his excuses. Years before, he would have had the man upstairs already, one hand out to take his coat, the other holding out a mug of coffee. Where had that Gordon gone?

He hesitated another moment then pressed the com again. "All right. I'll buzz you in. Take a seat in the study on the main floor. I'll be down in a moment."

Before he could talk himself out of it, he pressed the button that snapped the lock open. He heard the door open and lingered a moment more before dashing back to change, narrowly avoiding the shattered glass a second time. As he threw his robe onto his unmade bed and rifled around his closet for the most professional-looking outfit he had that was also still moderately clean, he recalled Andrew Barret's face. He'd been the strained-looking man sitting at the defense table next to his son, his back straight, gripping his hands in his lap as if he thought he might lose them otherwise. His wife, Jane, was the skittish blond woman on the opposite side of Ethan, looking as though she'd walked into a bad dream, not a courtroom. And in a lot of ways, she had.

They'd probably want coffee or tea, caffeine of some sort. Gordon doubted they'd been sleeping all that well. Gordon wouldn't be sleeping well either if his son was known to assault people in their sleep. In fact, he might never sleep again. He tucked his shirt in, slipped his bare feet into some loafers, checked that his fly was zipped, popped the kettle on, and refilled the press. Then he took a deep breath, grabbed a pair of cups in one hand and the coffee in the other, and took the stairs slowly.

At the bottom, he turned to his guest, only to find not Andrew and Jane, but Andrew and Ethan. Gordon almost made it three shattered cups in twenty-four hours, but he caught himself at the last second and awkwardly set the service down before the whole thing slipped from his hands. Ethan looked thin as a waif, even thinner than he had in the courtroom. His auburn hair was long and a bit stringy and pushed back behind his ears. He had a long chin but a small nose and pensive green eyes. His skin was pale and wet from the rain. His arms were tucked around himself, and he was eyeing the photo of Karen and Gordon that still hung prominently in the foyer, the one where Karen sat on a low-backed leather chair and Gordon rested his arm gently on her shoulder, both of them cheesing for the camera. He turned to Gordon at the sound of the clanking mugs. He looked as though he did not want to be there. In fact, he looked like he did not want to be anywhere but his bed. His father stepped forward between them, hand outstretched.

"Dr. Pope, I'm Andrew Barret," he said a little too eagerly. "Thank you for seeing us."

Gordon shook his clammy hand. "Yes... What is this about?"

"Ethan is out on temporary release," Barret said, his voice low, as if the boy might be spared what had no doubt been emphasized with a gavel in the courtroom.

"What was his sentence?" Gordon asked although he already knew. Ethan watched them both, and he could see it on the boy's face.

"He's to be sent to Ditchfield Medical Facility," Barret said, his voice thin and reedy. He cleared his throat as if the name had stuck there. In the silence that followed, the rain sanded the windows in a flaring gust.

Gordon closed his eyes. He'd expected it, but to hear it spoken as truth hit him surprisingly hard.

"But we have thirty days to appeal," Barret added, craning his neck toward Gordon, his brow furrowed. "Thomas Brighton—you remember Thomas, our attorney?"

"Yeah, I know Thomas."

"Thomas told us that it would be damn near impossible to win an appeal unless Ethan's... condition... was clinically proven and some sort of treatment plan could be outlined."

Gordon said nothing. He turned to look at Ethan, who watched him flatly. So Gordon's testimony alone hadn't been enough to sway the court. He wasn't surprised. Violent parasomnia was tough for people to understand. It was hard enough for clinical psychiatrists to understand, much less a judge or a jury.

"Thomas said that, huh?" Gordon said. "And let me guess, Thomas also gave you my contact information." Thomas didn't like to lose. If he thought there was a chance he could improve his win percentage or up his profile, he'd take it.

"Sort of," Barret said. "He told us the name of your practice and told us to look you up." He clasped his hands together nervously and spun his wedding ring on his finger.

"Did Thomas also tell you I... that Karen and I don't see kids anymore?" Gordon asked. "That it's a policy of mine? Has been for years now?"

"He said you might take some convincing. That's why I've waited until now to come see you. We've approached several practicing child psychiatrists already." Barret looked at his son, who slowly shifted his gaze in return before pulling his phone from the baggy front pocket of his raincoat and tapping idly on it. "They were either booked or out of town or... The fact is, none were willing to take up Ethan's cause. I think that some of them..." He struggled to find the words to finish, so Ethan did it for him.

"They were afraid of me," Ethan said, still focused on his phone, still tapping. His voice was high, and his childish tone made his words all the more surreal.

Gordon had no response. He was still coming to terms with the fact that the boy and his father were standing in his office to begin with.

"Thomas said that with a diagnosis and plan of care, he might stand a chance of appeal," Barret said. "But the deadline to file is in three weeks."

"Look, Mr. Barret, I don't know what Thomas thinks I can do for you, but even if I wanted to, I can't just rubber-stamp a diagnosis and plan of care here. I gave that testimony because I was a compensated expert witness. I had no idea that it would be Ethan's case. I've been meaning to have some words with Thomas about that. He knows my policy on treating children."

"Do you believe he was sleepwalking?" Barret asked point-blank.

Ethan looked up from his phone, his face a blue glow.

Gordon remembered the look of the boy in the courtroom, hunched and frightened, but not just because of what he'd been accused of, not just because he'd nearly killed his friend. But because he didn't understand how he'd ended up there. Gordon knew that because he'd felt the same thing once.

"Yes," Gordon said. He felt what he felt. But that didn't change anything about treating the kid.

Ethan eyed Gordon a moment longer then nodded slightly before looking down at his phone again.

"I knew it," Barret said. "That's what the cop said, but I could see it on the stand. You believe us."

"What cop?" Gordon asked.

"Brighton's office is right next to the courthouse, and there's this police officer that we've bumped into a few times there. She said she helped find Erica Denbrook. Actually, she said without you, the girl wouldn't have been found."

"Dana said that?" Gordon asked.

He nodded. "Which is strange because they never said anything like that on the news."

"Tell me about it."

Gordon doubted that Dana "happened" to run into Andrew Barret. She was in and out of the courthouse in an official capacity often enough, yes, but Gordon was beginning to think that very little Dana Frisco did was by chance.

"Erica and Ethan are friends," Barret said.

"*Were* friends," Ethan said suddenly, his head snapping up from his phone.

"Right," Barret said sadly. "Were friends. But the point is Dana and I struck up a conversation over it, and she suggested I look you up as well. She said you could help. That was twice your name was mentioned. So here we are."

The Chutes and Ladders gamble was one thing, a lucky break he'd pulled out of a snapshot of Erica's life. Diagnosing and crafting a plan of care for a convicted criminal was another. Because that's what Ethan was. Whether or not he was asleep at the time didn't change the fact that he'd come very close to killing another child. Those were the facts. The question was why... and whether he was culpable at the time.

And Dana Frisco thought Gordon could figure it out.

Gordon suddenly felt a little bit warm, and he doubted it was from all the coffee.

"Can you help us?" Barret asked.

"I can't promise anything," Gordon found himself saying, as if his mouth had skipped permission from his brain. "But the least I can do is chat with him."

Barret sagged a little. "Thank God. And thank you. When can you start? Like I said, we have a time frame here—"

"How about right now?"

CHAPTER SEVEN

For the first time in nearly five years, a child sat in the patient chair opposite Gordon Pope. When he'd worked with kids, he had a kid's chair, an identical version of his own leather chair at one-third the size. The kids had loved it, but in his self-cleanse after the divorce, he'd sold it online for a quarter of what he'd paid for it. He was regretting that decision, seeing Ethan's feet dangle from the floor as he sat back and watched Gordon quietly.

Ethan's phone was tucked beside him, and in the silence, he stole occasional glances at the screen. His green eyes were hollowed, the color of dry grass, and lidded with exhaustion. He had the weary, wary air of a child who had been passed from examination room to examination room.

His father tried to join them at first, but Gordon insisted that he meet with Ethan alone. Gordon had forgotten how personally parents often took the one-on-one sessions between psychiatrist and patient. The fact was very few breakthroughs occur with parents in the room. Gordon wanted to know the boy himself, not the son that came out when his dad was around. Barret acquiesced quickly. He seemed to know not to push his luck.

Gordon doubted he would get any sort of immediate opening up, and he wasn't surprised. He was reminded of a well-used quote from Dr. Mort Gladwell, the psychiatry chair at Hopkins in Gordon's day, and an unabashed eccentric. He'd said that the difference between child therapy and adult therapy can be broken down to one statement: With adults, you had to help them find the words, but with children, you had to help them make the words. That was where Gordon came in.

Sitting across from Ethan, he had hoped to find familiarity, a clicking-into-place, a welcome-back feeling. Instead, he was reminded of why his practice with Karen had fallen apart. His heart twinged like an old war wound, which was what he was afraid of. The question for Gordon wasn't so much if he could treat the boy—it was whether he could set aside the broken feeling it gave him long enough to try.

Ground zero, Gordon told himself. *We are at ground zero here.* The basis of every connection made between therapist and patient was built upon trust, and Gordon knew that didn't exist with Ethan. Yet. Still, Gordon had seen worse first visits. He'd had children yell until they were taken out of the room. He'd had children stare at the walls. Scream at him. Run circles around his chair. Throw things at the windows. Honk, grunt, and spit. Anything to avoid the silence that Ethan seemed to have cloaked himself in already. He sat awkwardly on the wide lounger, like a novel teetering between bookends.

"You want to sit on the rug?" Gordon asked, pointing to the round sheepskin rug on the floor beneath them. Ethan said nothing, but nothing wasn't a no.

"C'mon, that chair is way too big. I got it because I was told I needed to be sensitive to the fat people I saw. Turns out I don't even have any fat clients." Gordon slid to the floor himself first. He managed to disguise a grimace as his knees popped. He settled himself with his knees up and his back against the chair.

Ethan slid to the floor much more naturally, the way only kids can do, like a settling Slinky. He reached up for his phone without looking and set it down next to him and started tapping at it, although without any real aim.

I suppose we should start at the beginning. "Hi, Ethan. My name is Gordon."

Ethan nodded, turned from his phone, and picked at the thick carpet for a moment.

"Your dad is right outside, but for now it's just you and me. Do you remember me? From the trial?"

Ethan looked up at Gordon briefly and nodded. "You tried to help me," he said.

Gordon nodded. *Technically, I got paid to say that it was theoretically possible that you could be a violent parasomniac at twelve years old.* But he would take what he could get. "I did what I could."

"It didn't work. Now I've gotta go to jail," Ethan said. His voice held no malice, but his words seemed carefully chosen, as if he was gauging Gordon's response.

"You're not going to jail. Ditchfield is a hospital," Gordon said. Then he paused and decided he wouldn't lie to the boy. "But it's not really any better."

Ethan nodded, seeming to appreciate the blunt answer. "Mom called it a nuthouse for kids." He made eye contact with Gordon in intervals, switching between him, the rug, and the phone with the ease of a driver checking his mirrors. Gordon felt he didn't have the boy's full attention, but he wondered if anything actually did.

"Have you had any more dreams? Any more sleepwalking since the incident at the sleepover?"

"I don't have dreams," Ethan said.

"Everybody has dreams every night. It's just a matter of if you remember them or not."

"Not me. Not anymore. And no, I haven't tried to kill anyone else yet, if that's what you're asking," Ethan snapped his words with a flash of aggression that seemed out of place, as if his brain had flared for a moment. Gordon noted it while appearing to ignore it.

"Forget killing. I'm talking about anything. Any thoughts when you wake up in the middle of the night? Any twitches before you fall asleep? Do you find yourself sitting up or maybe at the door to your bedroom before you know what's going on?"

Ethan stopped scrolling on his phone, and he stopped picking at the rug, and he stopped looking at Gordon. His head inched down, and he stared at his shoes.

"I'm tied to my bed," he whispered.

"Does your dad tie you to the bed?" Gordon asked, keeping his voice neutral. He almost looked past the door to his office, where Andrew Barret sat. It occurred to him that he knew nothing about the man and had assumed good faith on his part. How quickly he had forgotten that the majority of neuroses that manifested themselves in children were directly attributable to their parents in some way. But Ethan cut his thoughts short with a quick shake of his head.

"I tie myself," he said. "With a rope. I took it from the garage without Dad seeing."

"Why do you tie yourself to your own bed?"

"In case."

"In case what?"

Ethan was silent again.

"Do you think you would try to hurt your parents, Ethan?"

Ethan shrugged. "No. But I didn't think I'd hurt Jimmy Tanner either." He left it at that for a moment, but Gordon knew when not to speak. "And sometimes I wake up... twisted. Like I've been fighting in my sleep."

Gordon made another mental note. He'd found that kids didn't like it when he took physical notes, scratching away on a pad while they spoke. To adults, the scratching meant they were getting their money's worth. To kids, it was like he was writing secrets that they couldn't read. It unnerved them. Ethan picked his phone up with both hands and kept refreshing the screen.

"What are you doing on that thing?" Gordon asked.

"Nothing," Ethan said.

"Are you talking to somebody?"

Ethan took a big breath and blew it out. "Not anymore." He tossed the phone gently onto the rug. "What's the point anyway, of all this? It doesn't matter. I've told everyone a billion times everything I thought. Everything I felt. Everything I dreamed. Everything I don't dream. Nobody believes that I don't remember. Erica used to believe me"—he nodded at the phone—"but she won't talk to me anymore either. So now it's nobody."

"I do," Gordon said simply.

Ethan paused, clearly weighing whether he believed Gordon or not. Then he shrugged. "Doesn't matter anyway. Jimmy is in the hospital. He might die. Everyone knows that I did it. Even I know I did it." Despite his attempt at nonchalance, his voice cracked at the end like a blown reed. "It doesn't matter that I don't know why."

"It does matter. It means everything, Ethan. That you were asleep means everything."

"Yeah? What if Jimmy was your kid? You wouldn't be saying that. How would you feel then?"

Another Gladwell-ism came to Gordon's mind: Nobody on earth can smell out a dodged question better than a kid.

"I don't know what I'd do," Gordon said.

"Yeah, you do. You probably have a kid my age." He leaned forward, and the hollow green of his eyes wetted to a sparkle. "Think if I killed him. Like this." He held out his bony fingers and squeezed the air, concentrating to the point where a vein popped up on his temple.

"I can't say how I'd feel," Gordon said, trying to rein in the situation, "because I don't have kids."

Ethan stopped speaking and looked at Gordon as though he'd just dropped a plate of food. "That's weird. Why not?"

Gordon rested his arms on his knees and then his chin on his forearms. A thought occurred to him. He could take a gamble. Everything about the past five years told him not to, but everything about the past five years seemed to be slowly sifting away that afternoon.

Gordon took in a small, barely perceptible breath and peered intently at Ethan.

"I'll tell you a secret if you tell me a secret," Gordon said, his voice low.

Ethan's finger paused above his phone. Secrets were powerful things for children. They often burdened adults, but in Gordon's experience, kids held secrets in almost mystical esteem. Ethan looked as though he was weighing Gordon's words carefully. Gordon was banking on it.

"Okay," Ethan said.

Gordon nodded. "I don't have kids because I can't have kids."

"You mean you don't have a girl," Ethan said, half asking, half stating the obvious.

Gordon snorted. "Well, yes. There's that too. But even when I did have a girl... I couldn't. I can't."

Ethan cocked an eye at Gordon but nodded slowly. He seemed to get it. At least, Gordon thought that whatever Ethan assumed was probably close enough. Gordon was firmly in his forties now, and every day he still had to wrap his head around what it meant to be sterile, around the reason he existed on the earth, if not to continue his little sliver of the human race. He'd been yoked by a solid, steady weight of existential depression since he'd been diagnosed years ago. It grew heavier when Karen had left him because of it, heaviest when he'd had to close up shop because every child reminded him of one that would never spring forth from him.

There, sitting with Ethan, he'd expected the yoke to be heaviest of all, to pin him to the floor next to the boy, but it didn't happen. After he spoke his secret aloud, he sat a little straighter, and was reminded of another reason he'd loved working with kids: they took those things in stride. It was what it was. Children were dealt new cards every day. They shuffled everything into the deck regardless, and to them every card weighed the same. *These things only crush middle-aged men.*

"You're only the third person in the world besides me that knows that," Gordon said, amazing himself with the statement. Other than him, only his mother and Karen knew. That was it.

Ethan sat still, letting the secret settle.

"My turn," Ethan whispered.

Gordon watched him patiently.

"I'm trying to chat with Erica on the phone. She won't talk with me anymore. Not after what happened."

Gordon covered his disappointment. That was hardly quid pro quo. He already knew Erica and Ethan had been tied at the hip once, but it was hardly surprising that she'd keep her distance now, given what she knew he'd done to his other friend. Still, it was a disclosure, and as Karen used to say, every disclosure was a victory. Gordon opened his mouth to speak, but Ethan kept talking.

"We used to sleepwalk together," Ethan said.

Gordon froze and settled again. Ethan seemed not to notice.

"Together?" Gordon asked.

"We'd end up in the same place together, wake up there next to each other. At the Tivoli. It's this old abandoned movie theater at the top of the neighborhood."

"I know of it," Gordon said softly, as if speaking loudly would scare the boy from his train of thought. "You both would wake up there? Not walk there together, but wake up there?"

Ethan nodded but already was moving on. "But that's not my secret. Mom and Dad know about that although they think it only happened once. Here's my secret." Ethan leaned over, close to the ground, his hands buried in the rug. "Whenever we ended up there, we both dreamed the same dream."

Gordon kept a still face. It wasn't unheard of for close friends to dream along similar lines, but for some reason he didn't think that was what Ethan was referring to. When he said same dream, he meant the *same dream*.

"What was the dream?" Gordon asked. Ethan seemed prepared for it.

"Every time we ended up there, it was because we were being chased by Red."

"Red?"

"It's our name for him, except it's not a *him*, really. Not even a thing I can describe, just... Red."

"Like a red mist?" Gordon asked, suddenly sweating, suddenly brought back to his own cave, to the tendrils of red mist that remained there, the last vestiges of a thing he'd clawed his fingernails out to run from.

Ethan nodded. "It's a mist that's not a mist. It makes me feel... like I should kill Jimmy." The last words were barely a whisper, and after Ethan said them, he sat back and watched Gordon wrestle with his own thoughts.

"I know Red," Gordon said. "Do you believe me when I say I know Red?"

"How?"

"I don't know, but I know him. Or I knew him, once."

Ethan nodded. He believed. "But he's gone now. Which is good, right? I wasn't lying when I said I don't dream. I don't see Red anymore. I don't dream at all."

Gordon thought about how the boy who claimed he no longer dreamed still had to tie himself to the bed.

"Everybody dreams, Ethan," Gordon said.

"But if I can't see Red anymore, he must be gone, right? That's good, right?"

Gordon shook his head sadly, deciding not to coddle the boy. "I don't think it is good. And I don't think Red is gone just because you don't see him."

Gordon tucked his knees up and hid his chin behind them. "Where'd he go?"

"I don't know. But you and me are gonna figure it out."

CHAPTER EIGHT

After Ethan and Andrew Barret left his office, and with Ethan's words still ringing in his head, Gordon's willpower finally cracked. He found himself sitting on the floor in his closet with his box of dream journals in front of him, rifling through book after book with the phone cradled in his neck, pressed to his ear and ringing.

"Gordon—" Karen said after picking up.

He heard the barest hint of reprimand on the tip of her tongue, so he cut her off. "I know you're not coming back to me or to Baltimore," Gordon said quickly, getting Karen's ground rules out of the way. "I have a question about dreams. A professional question."

Karen was quiet on the other end. Gordon heard the high wail of a young child somewhere in the background, along with the bark of a dog. And was that a lawn mower? The domestic bliss of it all soured his stomach.

"Okay then," Karen said. "What is it?"

"You're gonna think I'm crazy, but hear me out."

"I already think you're crazy, Gordon. What is it? Chad and I are taking Maggie to the park here in a minute."

Gordon knew he must really be trying Karen's patience. She

purposely avoided bringing up Chad or their little girl whenever they spoke. She wasn't a gloater. Gordon had always appreciated that.

"I'll make it quick. I'm seeing a patient who claims he and his neighbor friend have the same dream."

"Well, that's not unusual, especially if they inhabit the same general environment," Karen said.

"No, the *same dream*, Karen. He told me that on several different occasions, they sleepwalked out of their houses at the same time and ended up in the same place with recollections of the same dream."

"Well, that's ridiculous. I think you need to switch track here and start to diagnose why your patient might be constructing this fantasy."

Gordon flipped through his journal again. He'd marked the cave dream with a sticky note. The entries to the front and back were smudged with thumbprints, but he was no closer to understanding what was happening in his twelve-year-old brain than he'd been when he first stumbled into the closet.

"Normally, I'd agree with you," Gordon said, bracing himself for his next words, "but what if I told you that I sort of had the same type of dream back when I was a kid?"

Karen didn't respond. Maggie's crying turned to laughing for a second. Gordon imagined Chad working to entertain the little girl, waving things or picking her up, tossing her above his head. He shut the image out. No good would come from going down that route.

"You're treating that Ethan boy, aren't you?" Karen asked. "The sleepwalker."

"He lost his case. They're sending him to Ditchfield unless they can get an appeal together, and that hinges on a clinical diagnosis and plan of care."

"Remember what I said about projecting? And remember why you left child therapy in the first place? Because you—"

"Get too invested, I know. But—"

"The boy isn't your kid, Gordon. None of them are your kids. They can't substitute. But you still try, and then when you can't help them, you think you've failed them. Hell, even when you can help them, you never think you can help them enough. You lose objectivity. You get obsessive."

Gordon looked at himself in the wall mirror opposite the closet. He was sitting on the floor amid the drifting dust of his past, surrounded by twenty little black books. Karen had a point. But she didn't understand. The similarities between Ethan's dreams and Gordon's own at Ethan's age were too strong to ignore.

"He had nowhere else to turn. I said I'd talk with him, see what he had to say, that's all."

"Well, maybe you ought to just keep it at that. Did it ever occur to you that maybe the child *should* go to Ditchfield? He did nearly kill his friend."

"I'm not so sure he did. At least, not in the way the court thinks he did," Gordon said. "And that's why I need to know, have you ever heard of anything like the exact same dream occurring in the minds of two separate people?"

Karen sighed heavily into the phone. Chad said something in the background, and Gordon could hear the heavy silence of Karen's hand covering the receiver. Then she came back.

"If I believed in the Jungian analysis of dreams—which I highly suggest you take with as much, if not more, of a grain of salt than the Freudian side of things because both of them will get you laughed out of a clinical setting—but if I *did* hold with Jungian analysis, I'd say that what you're describing is an example of an archetype of some sort, one of a set of several general themes or occurrences that have been found to inhabit the dreams of the majority of people of this earth. Things like being chased. Sinking. Flying. Certain colors. Jung would say that they trace back to an ancient response."

"How about an encroaching figure made of red mist?"

Karen snorted in laughter. "No. See, that is way too specific. That is why what Ethan claims happened cannot have happened. And if you think it happened to you too, maybe you ought to think about how easy it is to rewrite memories to tailor specific outcomes. Like wanting to find a connection to this boy, for instance."

Gordon shook his head but held his tongue. He wasn't tailoring anything, the proof was there, in those journals... until it wasn't anymore. Until the sleepwalking episode itself, of which he'd written nothing. And then thereafter, nothing.

"I'm sorry, Gordon, I really have to go," Karen said.

"Yeah, okay. Thanks for talking," Gordon mumbled.

"Take care of yourself, okay? I mean that," she said before hanging up.

Gordon sat for a long time on the floor, at first staring at nothing in particular, then flipping through journals again, finding nothing new in the entries but reading them through all the same.

Empty spaces in his memory. Nights when dreams flitted away from his grasp before he could journal them. And the same thing was happening to Ethan as well. *"I don't dream,"* he'd said. And now, Gordon had had two separate but distinct dream episodes wherein he'd revisited a place he'd thought his brain shuttered thirty years before.

Gordon wanted to run one more thing by Karen, but he decided to hold back after he got the distinct impression that she already thought he was going through a minor meltdown. Something was lurking in the recesses of Ethan's brain—something tied to the cave of Gordon's own dreams. A corner piece to the puzzle he'd found himself in a race against time to solve. So he'd wanted to ask Karen about her thoughts on the validity of induced REM sleep. If Ethan's brain kept forgetting, maybe Gordon could force it to remember.

The problem was, induced REM required more than just a willing patient. It required the use of specialized machinery, the likes of which existed only in a sleep lab.

But again, Gordon found himself availed of a window when he should be hitting a locked door. Johns Hopkins had a world-class sleep lab. Also, for better or for worse, Gordon knew someone who could get him access. If he was willing to be indebted, that was.

CHAPTER NINE

G ordon took up Caesar's offer of a cocktail before he'd even arranged his napkin on his lap.

"Full tumbler of ice, generous pour of scotch please. Nothing fancy. A blend is just fine."

Gordon couldn't be sure, but he thought he saw a knowing look in Caesar's eye as the waiter nodded and backed his way out. Gordon made a mental note to ask the man ten or so years down the line if he might be hired away as his mother's caretaker. Would he be ready for that? Could anyone be ready for that? Sure, Caesar looked like he had the patience of a saint, but it was one thing to serve the woman cocktails twice a month and quite another to be at her side daily. She had a way of making people feel as though they owed her without actually doing anything. And Gordon was there to actually ask her for a favor.

Caesar produced Gordon's scotch with a minor flourish, and Gordon let it sit and sweat for a bit in the noon heat of the patio. Even in the shade, the temperature had to be nearly ninety degrees, with enough humidity to swell a wooden door shut. He thought about his approach but was pre-empted by his mother's hooting hello to Caesar at the front door. *Too late.* He'd never been good with prepared words, anyway. He took a decent swig of his scotch and stood, waiting.

"My son! My son!" said his mother, and she hugged him and kissed him on both cheeks. "And a week before our normal lunch date? Have you been missing your mother?"

She waved off whatever response Gordon might have mustered. Her silver-and-turquoise bracelets clanked gently. She settled her linen pantsuit at the sharp creases as she sat and allowed Caesar to jump her chair in a bit. She set her earrings and gently adjusted her watch before clasping her hands before her and smiling kindly at him. *Happy as a clam.* She always seemed to know when Gordon was coming to her for help.

"How are things, Gordon?" she asked, pinching the stem of her chilled martini between two fingers and letting it hover over her mouth before sipping.

"To tell you the truth, Mom, I've been feeling a little odd lately."

Her brow furrowed, and she set her martini down. "Are you ill? When was the last time you had a physical?"

"A *physical*? I'd say probably the eighth grade, to clear me for baseball," Gordon said, rolling his eyes. "But it's nothing like that."

"This is why I told you to get that baseline lipid panel at thirty. Now, we'll be able to see if there's been any sort of—"

"Mom. Stop. It's this sleepwalking stuff. It started with the testimony, and it's got me looking at how weird my whole episode was and what I wrote about it and didn't write about it," Gordon said.

His mother snapped her fingers delightedly. "I *told* you that you'd look back at those dream journals. Didn't I? I said, 'Gordon, do not throw those out. You will regret it if you do—'" Caesar had appeared at the snap, and both of them watched him for a moment. "Oh, dear. No. I wasn't snapping for you. Good lord. I'd have to slap myself. I'm not that far gone. Escort me out the second I do, Caesar," she said, deadly serious as Caesar smiled and bowed himself out. She turned back to Gordon, but he cut her off before she could crow any longer.

"The boy in the assault case. Ethan Barret. He came to my office. His father asked if I'd evaluate him. It's his only shot at an appeal."

His mother paused then blew past all of the implications of her son spearheading therapy for a convicted criminal and instead asked, with a wry smile, "You're treating children again?"

"No. I mean maybe. Just this one. He reminds me too much of myself, and there's something weird going on here."

"That's wonderful, Gordon," she said and hooted once more before controlling herself. "It's about time you took another crack at child therapy. It's where your heart lies."

Gordon swirled his scotch and stared into the dripping amber. "Tell Karen that. She thinks I'm projecting. Says I get too invested, that I turn these kids into my own kids. The kids I can't have."

"That frigid bitch," she said offhandedly, "telling you you're projecting. What right does she have?"

"She's very probably correct, Mother."

"Of course she's correct. She's always correct. She's a brilliant psychiatrist. That doesn't make it a bad thing, though. People forget that *projecting* is just another word for *empathy*. Which is a concept Karen wouldn't understand if I beat her over the head with it." His mother waved a dismissive hand over the conversation as if that closed things. Gordon found himself smiling.

"The court gave Ethan thirty days," Gordon said. "And I've hit a bit of a brick wall." Gordon drained his scotch. "What I'm gonna tell you here might be hard to believe. Okay? But just hear me out."

His mother sat back, martini in hand.

"Ethan described to me dreams he was having around the time of the assault, dreams that sounded a lot like the kind of thing I wrote about in my journal with the cave before everything went blank. Ethan doesn't recall his dreams any longer, either. And just this past weekend, I helped Dana find a young girl who also sleepwalked. She was Ethan's friend, Erica, who Ethan said was having the same dreams too. When we found her, Dana asked if she remembered what she was dreaming about. Nothing. Each of us had the same type of dream, and then it disappeared. I managed to stop sleepwalking, but these kids are still doing it—and more dangerously. I think if I can monitor Ethan's dreaming, I can maybe figure out why. It could go a long way towards treating him. And maybe stop something horrible from happening to Erica too."

Gordon sat back and looked longingly at his empty glass for a moment before glancing at his mother. He readied himself for some sort of dismissal, not unlike the waving of hands that had put a nail in her previous point. His mother jutted out her lower lip in consideration.

"You're telling me," she began, her voice conspiratorial, "that you've been padding around with a girl named Dana?"

Gordon blinked. "That's what you got out of all that?"

"Who is this Dana? Is she single?"

"Mother!"

"Fine, don't tell me. Look, I'm just thrilled you're doing something outside of your apartment for once. And with a woman!"

Gordon looked plaintively for Caesar.

"I mean, even if it is chasing down some child's boogie monster. Have you told her all that you just told me? If she hasn't run off yet, she's probably worth looking at seriously. Even if she has run off. It's not like you're swimming in it."

"Wait, what exactly are we talking about here, Mother?" Gordon asked, his voice a sharp whisper.

"The girl of course. Dana."

"Officer Frisco," he said. "And no, I haven't told her any of this yet. I'm not stupid. I know how it sounds." But even as he said it, he felt fairly confident that while most people might run from him, Dana was not one of them. "She actually sort of got me involved in all this."

"I'm saying that if this woman believes there's something more here than meets the eye, and she's a cop with a decent head on her shoulders, maybe you're not completely insane," his mother said as if pointing out the color of the sky.

Gordon saw his opening, so he clipped his retort, "There's only one way I can think of to make sure I'm not insane. But I need your help."

Her eyes widened in mock surprise. She signaled to Caesar that she'd like a refresh on her martini and both of them would be having the usual meal. Gordon knew she was taking the time to enjoy her moment.

"What can I do for you, dear?" she asked after settling again.

"You're still an Elliot Society member at Hopkins, right?"

"Of course. It's what got you into the medical school."

Gordon looked at her sidelong.

"Oh, please. Of course you had the resume, too. But nobody gets into these places anymore without a little grease. Don't be naive. I kept it up because Maude from bridge club seemed to think an Elliot recommendation might get her oaf of a son into the undergraduate program."

"How altruistic of you."

"It is, isn't it? Maude also happens to be a councilwoman on the greater Bethesda zoning committee, which damn well better come in handy when I decide to put in a water feature out front that might be a hair against code. Just a hair."

"Ah, there it is," Gordon said. "Always a plan in mind. Well, you do whatever it takes. I don't care. What I care about is access to the Elliot Sleep Lab."

"For your boogie man?"

"Call it whatever you want. Can you get me lab time? I have to run tests on Ethan. I have some theories I need to confirm."

"And this poor child's parents are on board?"

"They're desperate, so yes. Does this mean you think you can get me lab time?" Gordon pressed.

She waved her hand again. "Of course I can get you lab time. Even if I wasn't an Elliot fellow. Keith Burback still runs that place, and he's always had a thing for me. We were in the same class, you know. He was too fat for my liking. Still is. But he's a good man."

Gordon sighed with relief. Maybe, just maybe, he'd be able to take a swing at this screwball of a situation after all.

Then his mother held up a finger. "On one condition, of course."

"Mom, please—"

"Oh, come off yourself. It's for your own good. You need to pursue this Dana Frisco. That's it. That's all I ask."

"Pursue her? She's not a lady-in-waiting."

"You know what I mean. I know you like this girl. Don't even try to dance around it. A mother always knows." She finished her martini with a delicate sip and set it aside to make room for the lunch, which arrived on cue.

Gordon couldn't say anything. He sat there with his mouth open, trying to form words. How did she know? Had he mentioned Dana before? It would be just like her to file away a casual mentioning for just such an occasion in which to corner him.

She took a bite of salad, even happier now than when he asked her outright for her help.

Gordon cleared his throat. "Fine. Yeah. I think she's... pretty great."

"Pretty great? What are you, twelve?"

It seems like it these days. He was dreaming the dreams of his twelve-year-old self, so why not bring back the twelve-year-old awkwardness as well? Or maybe it had never really left—he'd just managed to get married and divorced in the interim.

"She's got her own life, Mom. She has a daughter, and she's up to her ears in garbage just trying to do her job."

"I have no doubt. She's a police officer in Baltimore. There are worse places to do your job, but they require enlistment."

"Spoken like a true tourist. You have no idea what this city is really like. You haven't ever lived here. There's more to it than Waterstones Grille."

"I'm sure there is. I don't care to see it."

"My point is Dana is very busy, and she doesn't think of me that way."

"And my point is that she called you when she needed help. And you delivered. You helped find the young girl. That means something."

"That was luck. I had a hunch, and it paid off. That's part of the reason I'm hesitant here. Now, she thinks I can magic my way to an acquittal for Ethan. This is why you never set the bar high on your first day on the job."

"It wasn't luck, Gordon. You've never needed luck. You think when Karen left, she sucked all the talent from the room, but you're wrong." She set her fork down and dabbed carefully at her mouth, avoiding the lipstick. "Anyway, those are my terms. Do something. Anything. To let this girl know how you feel."

Gordon knew that if he protested vigorously enough, if he complained or bartered or bitched or sulked, his mother would pull the strings and get him in the lab anyway. Conversations were a kind of dance for her, but at the end of the day, she would help him however she could. In the end, he could either keep those lunches amicable or give her rounds and rounds of ammunition to go with her martinis, so he nodded. He would approach Dana. Because if he set aside all the banter and the snobbery, his mother was right. He was falling for Dana Frisco. He could be a twelve-year-old about it, or he could man up.

CHAPTER TEN

The Elliot Center for Sleep Disorders was located in the northeast corner of the Johns Hopkins School of Medicine campus. It was near the Welch Medical Library, where Gordon Pope had spent nearly a full quarter of his life, more or less, from pre-med classes all the way through his doctorate. He walked the campus grounds at last light, surprised by how hard the nostalgia hit him. The last time he'd walked around Hopkins was for his ten-year reunion, over ten years before, and then he'd had Karen at his side and a boat-load of chardonnay in his stomach. This evening, he was alone.

He'd told Andrew Barret that he would meet him and Ethan at the lab, but he wanted to make the walk himself. He was a sucker for nostalgia. That was part of the reason he kept calling Karen. He passed the library to his right and imagined himself there as he used to be, a loopy pre-med student, then a haggard med student, then a terrified resident, moving about the stacks, slamming cup after cup of coffee. He remembered sleeping there, waking there, crying there, and meeting Karen there. They'd even had sex there once, in the deserted journals section back by the microfiche machines at three in the morning, a nervous, clutching, sweaty, wonderful thing that lasted a quarter as long as Gordon had hoped it would. He could see himself through the glowing windows as he'd been then, a ghost moving from level to level. He doubted they even had microfiche any longer.

From the outside, the Elliot Center looked exactly the same as it had for decades—a square, Bauhaus structure two stories high, made entirely of brick on concrete. Not exactly the type of place that inspired a good night's rest, but then again, if you ended up there, you weren't sleeping right anyway. Rumor was the university was building a massive, multimillion-dollar pediatric sleep center that was supposed to be a bit softer, but as always, that was just a few years out. So the Elliot Center was it.

He met the student worker behind the desk and was ushered into the Elliot Lab without question. The Barret family was already waiting in the mauve appointment room. Ethan sat uncomfortably in a small chair in the corner, tapping away on his phone, a small overnight bag at his side. Andrew Barret stood and welcomed Gordon with a vigorous handshake, as if still afraid he might bolt. Gordon was surprised to see Jane Barret, Ethan's mother, also in attendance. She looked up at him with wide eyes resting on half-moon bags the color of storm clouds, her blond hair slightly disheveled. She gripped the arms of her chair as if it were moving and didn't get up to meet him.

After greeting them and waving awkwardly at Mrs. Barret, Gordon excused himself to ready the lab. He went through the double doors into a large, rectangular room with four beds that looked as though someone had tried very hard to make them appear as anything but rank-and-file hospital beds and had almost succeeded. He took in the room. It wasn't bad. It was painted a calming blue, and each bed had a different patterned bedspread. Framed pictures of calming desert and ocean scenes were spaced evenly along the walls. Still, it was very hard to make a hospital *not* look like a hospital. Gordon walked around the room, taking down several sterile-looking medical charts and unplugging every superfluous blinking machine he could. He took the pamphlets off the small table by the entrance and dimmed the lights. The corner bed would be best—it would feel the least like a dorm-room bed. Gordon fluffed the pillow and eased the hospital tightness of the sheets. He stood and crossed his arms. The place was still a medical lab, no bones about that, but it was far better than most, and it would do.

Gordon brought Ethan to the lab and showed him his bed. The boy stared at it numbly. He looked as though he hadn't slept in weeks, as though the room was yet another in a sequence of small rooms with strange people that would ultimately do nothing to help him. He sat down heavily on the duvet and kicked off his shoes. He was already in his pajamas.

"You sleepy?" Gordon asked.

"Yeah," Ethan said.

"When was the last time you got a full night of sleep?"

Ethan shrugged. If Gordon were to guess, he'd say the boy couldn't recall, it had been so long. That was written plainly on his face. He was terrified to give in to his exhaustion.

"Let me run all this strange machinery by you, all right? None of it will hurt you. But it is sort of weird to sleep with it all on."

Ethan looked blankly at the rig beside his bed through hooded eyelids, his phone hanging limply from both hands. Gordon had a striking impression then that the boy wasn't even fully with him there in the lab, that he was already half asleep, that his entire life now was battling against that liminal line of unconsciousness that presses and presses, more insistent the more it is denied. Still, Gordon went through the gear for the benefit of Ethan's parents watching behind a small, disguised panel of glass if for no one else.

"This is an EEG. This little guy will record your brain waves as you sleep," Gordon said, tapping a small tan box at the end of a clipped bundle of wires. "It has this funny hat that I need to put on you, okay? So just pop under the covers and lie like you normally would."

Ethan swung his feet up and kicked his way into bed, knocking the duvet off and scrambling the sheets. "Okay," he said quietly.

"Sorry about this, buddy," Gordon said, peeling off the backing of a ring of sticky tape at the base of what looked like a child's hairnet with little suction cups stuck in the webbing. "It's not all that comfortable, I know—unless you like sleeping with nets on your head. I have to get these electrode ends to touch your scalp, so I'm gonna root around here for a sec, okay?"

Ethan nodded his assent, and his eyes flicked from his phone up to the glass panel in the wall as Gordon settled the skullcap on his head.

Not so hidden after all. Gordon ran a baseline test on the output monitor several times, adjusting certain electrodes here and there until he got the readout he wanted. He was surprised at how intuitively everything was coming back to him. He'd done a fair amount of study in that lab, with older equipment. He was a little sad to see how little had changed in the field of sleep study. They'd had EEGs back when he was contemplating doing his doctoral thesis on sleep deprivation. What he was attaching to Ethan was sleeker and fancier, but it was the same thing.

When Gordon finished, he stepped back and checked the fit. Ethan looked as if he was trying to sleep while getting a perm, but it would give Gordon what he needed. The boy himself seemed remarkably nonplussed, almost drugged. He kept forgetting he held his phone, letting it fall and snatching it up at the last second.

"Last thing," Gordon said, holding up a little blue clip. "This monitors your heart. I'm just gonna clip it to your finger, okay?"

Ethan nodded, watching the two-way mirror as Gordon attached the clip to his forefinger.

Gordon followed Ethan's gaze back and forth. "Are you okay, buddy?" he asked, his voice a whisper.

"Are they gonna stay out there?" Ethan asked, his voice small.

"They can come in if you want. Sit by you while you try to sleep. No big deal. Whatever helps you get comfortable."

Ethan turned to Gordon and really looked at him for the first time that night. "No," he whispered, and his voice brought goose bumps to Gordon's neck. "They can't come in. Nobody can come in. Not even you." He rubbed with one foot at the ankle of his other, where Gordon had noticed a small rope burn as the boy was getting into bed.

"Ethan, you're safe here. Understand? This is a safe place. Nothing can get to you, and... and you can't get to anybody else, okay?"

"Promise me," Ethan said. "Promise me that they won't come in."

"I promise."

"You too. You can't come in either. Just look at the machines from back there. Behind the wall."

"I can't promise that. I may have to adjust things. Check stuff. Make sure you're all right."

"I'm not all right," Ethan said. "I'm just warning you."

"It's okay, Ethan. I've done this stuff before—"

"Be careful," Ethan whispered, and the genuine fear in his face brought back the goose bumps twofold. Gordon fought down a shiver. He needed to make Ethan feel as though the entire experiment was normal, which was a joke in and of itself. Nothing about it was normal. Normal seemed to have left the building of Gordon Pope's life as soon as he walked into that courtroom.

"Sleep tight," he said lamely. As if anyone could sleep tight while strapped to an electrode array and a heart monitor. But Ethan was already leaning back on his pillow. He tried to take the phone from Ethan's hands to set it on the nightstand next to the bed, but as soon as he grabbed it, Ethan held on.

"I need it to sleep," he mumbled. So Gordon let it be.

He flicked off the overhead lights at the door. The monitors were in sleep mode. A small floor light of soft blue allowed the attending doctors to see the sleeping patients if need be, but it was low, more of a night-light than anything. The room was as dark as it could get. He closed the door behind him and moved to the monitoring station behind the glass, where he sat down next to Mr. and Mrs. Barret.

"Ethan wants everyone out of the room," Gordon said, glancing at them out of the corner of his eye while watching the EEG output on the monitor in front of him. All receptors were active. The readout showed a line swinging in patterned peaks and valleys, slightly slower than a normally functioning brain wave, but that was to be expected given how exhausted Ethan looked.

"He thinks he's going to hurt us," Mr. Barret said, shaking his head. "It's ridiculous, but he won't let us near him at night. He locks his doors." He looked at his son in the bed, glowing faintly blue with the light of the phone in his hand.

"I noticed lesions around his ankles," Gordon said carefully, and as soon as he did, Mrs. Barret started to tear up.

"I swear to God I would never hurt him. You have to believe me. Not me, not Andrew. Nobody," she said, her voice quivering.

"I do. Otherwise, I would have called CPS the second I saw them. I've seen abuse, and I've seen abusers. You aren't them. But that leaves one alternative. He's giving them to himself, which means he's not only tying himself up, but he's also struggling enough against those restraints to burn himself."

She lifted a shaky hand to cover her mouth.

Mr. Barret looked at his son in utter confusion. "What is going on with you, my man?" he whispered.

"That's what I'm trying to figure out. He told me he doesn't dream. Everyone dreams, but not everyone remembers dreams. He was having no problem recalling his dreams up until the night he attacked his friend. Then his recall left him, for some reason. I'm going to try and get it back by inducing REM sleep."

They watched as Ethan fumbled to put his earbuds in, attached to his phone with a long white cord.

"He falls asleep to music?" Gordon asked.

"Sometimes. Sometimes to podcasts or video-game broadcasts. There are these people that broadcast themselves playing video games. All the time. He says he needs them to sleep. They're like his white noise."

Gordon watched Ethan in silence then turned to Mr. Barret. "When does he normally get up for the day?"

"He's up before we are, which is usually around seven."

That was completely medically unhealthy for a preteen. Preteens could comfortably sleep until noon without batting an eye. The only reason Ethan would be up at seven was if he wasn't really sleeping. Or sleeping in such short bursts that his body was neither here nor there subconsciously. That, ironically, was good news for the study because, even as Gordon watched, the boy was falling asleep. His brain waves settled into a regular rhythm of alpha waves. He was already tuning everything out. And if he hadn't slept for as long as Gordon thought he hadn't slept, he was going to sleep hard.

"Are you sure you want to be here for this, Mrs. Barret?" Gordon asked. He could hear the woman's rapid rabbit breaths, and they were making him nervous.

"Why?" she asked. "Is it going to be bad? Is he going to hurt himself?"

"I don't know what he's going to do. But my theory is that whatever it is, it's happening in or around the REM stage of sleep. REM sleep is like a bank. Every time you deny yourself REM sleep, your body remembers, charges interest. Then, when you finally do sleep, it hits you hard."

She watched him, horrified. Her husband squeezed her hand.

"Which is to say that whatever he's been doing to himself is going to come out here. Tonight. And you might not want to see it."

Mrs. Barret blinked away tears but shook her head resolutely. "It's in God's hands. Not ours. Not even yours, Dr. Pope."

Gordon watched the monitor. That was an odd thing to say, and it seemed to make Mr. Barret uncomfortable as they watched Ethan fight to stay awake in his bed. His head dipped again and again into his shoulder until it settled there. The phone dropped from his grip and slipped to the blanket. His mouth opened slightly, and his heartbeat regulated, then slowed. His brain-wave activity shifted to a steadier and more rhythmic pattern.

"He's in stage-one sleep right now," Gordon said, standing to get a better look at the boy over the monitors. "In stage one, we sort of rehash the day, but it's like a Dali painting. Disconnected images from our experiences, colors, snippets of thought—all of it floating around in our brain like a swirling pot of soup."

Ethan twitched his lip but offered nothing more revealing than that. Gordon sat back down, and the three of them waited in the low light of the monitoring station. At first, the Barrets couldn't take their eyes off their son, but as the night wore on, they settled into their seats and waited for Gordon to tell them of any changes in his condition. Mr. Barret sat with his legs apart, elbows resting on his knees. Mrs. Barret looked as if she was either sleeping or praying—Gordon couldn't tell which.

"He's downshifting now," Gordon said quietly, his eyes on the monitor where, here and there, a more severe peak and valley distinguished itself on the readout, "going into stage-two sleep."

Gordon stood again and watched Ethan. The boy had closed his mouth, and a small tapping sound began to come from the com system.

"What's that?" Mrs. Barret asked, her voice soft but high.

"His teeth," Gordon said. "He's tapping his teeth." Ethan was also moving his lips in the barest approximation of words. Gordon checked his watch and monitored the wavelengths. "Slower, slower. I'd say stage three now. He's progressing faster than normal, but that's to be expected."

"Is he dreaming?" Mr. Barret asked. "Can you tell what he's dreaming?"

"I think he's trying to dream," Gordon said. "But these waves are interrupted, see? Here." Gordon pointed to a staccato tightening in the rolling wavelengths. "He's fighting himself somehow."

Ethan settled again, his body slack. His phone slipped off his bed and clattered onto the floor, taking his earbuds with it. He didn't notice.

"We've broken two phones that way," Mr. Barret said.

Gordon nodded blankly, paying attention to the monitor, where the wave activity was now solidly delta. "This is deep sleep. Delta waves. He's either late stage three or early stage four. This is where sleepwalking typically occurs."

"Not in REM?" Mr. Barret asked.

"No. I have a theory that for some reason Ethan's body isn't allowing itself to get to the fifth stage of sleep. I don't think he's had REM sleep for some time."

Gordon's eyes flicked from the monitor to the boy, glowing in the low light. He watched as Ethan's legs moved, slowly at first, as if testing to see if they were still bound. His head rested calmly on the pillow, which made the independent movement of his limbs all the more alien. Andrew and Jane were silent. They watched Ethan as if they were strapped down and stunned.

"REM sleep is what heals us," Gordon said. "It's where we're free to spin the story of our lives on our own terms. There are theories, well-respected theories, which pin REM sleep to the development of consciousness itself."

In his bed, Ethan suddenly calmed.

"Without REM, we devolve. It's what separates us from beasts," Gordon said, speaking as if to himself, his hand pressed on the glass, his face inches from it, fogging it.

"Are you calling my son a beast?" Mr. Barret asked, standing to look through the window next to Gordon. His wife curled up in her seat, staring forward at nothing, gripping her hands together.

Gordon's reply was cut short when Ethan sat up smoothly in his bed, his eyes still closed. Both men froze, waiting for the anger, the rage Ethan feared, but it didn't come. He sat up, face forward, like a marionette. Gordon looked at the monitor.

"REM waves are erratic and rapid in their patterns. They look almost exactly like the neural patterns of a conscious brain," Gordon said, tapping the monitor. "These are not them. He's still in stage-four sleep. His dreams are not his own. He should be in the first wave of REM by now, but he isn't."

As if he'd heard Gordon, Ethan slowly turned his head toward them until it settled at the point where it faced directly at the one-way glass. Both men stood back involuntarily.

"He can't hear us, can he?" his father asked.

"No. This booth is soundproof, and he's deeply asleep," Gordon said, but his mouth had gone chalky.

Ethan's eyes were closed, his arms limp at his sides, his hands palm up and open, but Gordon would have sworn that somehow the boy knew what was happening, knew where they were. He relaxed by degrees until his head was fully rolled to one side, his mouth open. His teeth started tapping once more. Behind Gordon, Mrs. Barret started to mumble a Hail Mary. Mr. Barret bowed his head, but not in prayer.

"My wife," he said, taking no pains to lower his voice, "she thinks our son is possessed." The way he spoke showed how little he thought of her belief. But Gordon caught the fear in his voice, just a note of it, a tremulous crack in his stolid veneer, which had appeared when Ethan sat up. Mr. Barret looked toward Gordon out of the corner of his eye, but for reassurance or for refutation, Gordon couldn't say.

"Your son is sick, Mr. Barret. He is not possessed," Gordon said with far more vehemence than he felt. He had been raised Catholic, but his parents treated religion more as a social necessity and community obligation than a demonstration of faith. As for himself, he'd let God fall by the wayside around the time he learned his balls didn't work and he personally would be the end of a million years of striving and thriving ancestors. He couldn't square himself with a God that wasteful.

"Then what was all that about?" Mrs. Barret asked, suddenly behind him.

"I don't know, but he's fallen back into stage-one and -two activity. Hypnagogic imagery again, snippets of the day."

"So we start over?" Mr. Barret asked.

"Theoretically, yes," Gordon said. "A healthy sleeper will cycle through to REM about five times a night. Ethan tried once, and it didn't work. He's going to try again."

And so they waited.

Gordon noted as Ethan began his second cycle through the sleep stages. His teeth tapping turned to a grind at stage three. Five minutes later, he started to slide his feet, putting his knees up and down under the sheet. Gordon turned the microphone up, but not even a murmur came from the boy—no sound at all in the room other than the grinding of his teeth and the susurrous slide of his feet on the fabric.

"Stage four again," Gordon said. He marked the time—thirty-two minutes from stage one to stage four, faster than the last cycle. Ethan's body was rushing things, trying hard to reach REM, but again it was falling short. If anything, the sweeping patterns of his delta waves were even more consistent, less indicative of the rapid waking pattern that characterized REM sleep. The three of them watched through the glass side by side as Ethan sat up and threw his sheet off himself in one sweeping toss. His eyes remained closed as his hands probed the bed to either side of his body, his fingers snaking and then pausing in rictus forms. He tipped his head back and seemed guided by his nose like a hound, weaving and pausing, weaving and pausing. His hands gripped two fists full of the bed and started pulling in opposite directions. The bottom sheet stretched and stretched and then slowly ripped. Through the microphone, it sounded oddly like a plow through dirt. Then Ethan pressed a strip of sheet to his sweating brow, then to his mouth, licking it.

His mother turned away, crossing herself. Mr. Barret appeared to be blinking back tears. "People do all sorts of strange things when they're asleep," Gordon said, by way of reassurance. "Especially when their REM bank is dry. This isn't some demon. It's your son, and he's exhausted. He's acting out his hallucinations because his brain isn't producing the acetylene that paralyzes us in REM sleep. What should be going on in his head is going on in his body. That's all."

But even as he said it, he wondered if that really was all. Something about the movements Ethan made unsettled him beyond the obvious. They were far too practiced. He should be in the midst of a fragmented dream narrative, but instead he looked more like an animal who had woken up in a strange cage and was subtly feeling out his surroundings.

And then Ethan fell back to his pillow once again, jaw slack. "He didn't reach REM this time either. He's cycling through a third time," Gordon said.

Already, Ethan's brain waves had gone delta.

"Much faster now. He's already stage three again." Gordon flicked his eyes from the monitor back to where the boy lay. The tapping and grinding that had characterized the first hour and a half of sleep were gone. In its place was a steady, measured white noise, rising and falling.

"What is that?" Mr. Barret asked, cocking his ear to the speaker.

"Breathing," Gordon said. "He's breathing loudly." *And strangely.* The breaths were nearly unbroken, the rising and falling following one another instantly. It sounded more like panting.

Ethan sat up again, slower that time, more measured. Gordon would have thought

more aware if he believed that the boy was aware. But he didn't. He didn't think the child he'd sat with on the floor of his office was anywhere to be found right now. But *something* was aware. He felt that distinctly. Not a demon. Not a spirit. Nothing like that. He couldn't put it into words, not yet. He felt he'd need to sit in silence over about five fingers of scotch to figure it out. But for the time, all he could think to call this thing was *primal.* That word kept coming back to him, again and again. Stuck behind the one-way glass, he felt distinctly as though he was at the zoo.

Ethan began to feel at the wires attaching him to the machines. He started first with the vital-sign finger clip. He traced the cord gently to where it was attached to his forefinger, eyes closed. When he found it, he ripped it off. The vitals monitor flatlined, and a small, insistent beeping began, oddly quieted, as if not to wake the patients even in the case of a medical emergency. Gordon cursed. Ethan was starting to claw at his face. The EEG machine was already beeping an unsettled warning.

"He's gonna rip the EEG equipment off," Gordon said, pushing his chair back and going for the door. "Stay here, I'm going in."

Mr. Barret stood but acquiesced. His wife set a hand briefly on Gordon as if to bless him, but she seemed to think the better of it and turned toward the glass instead.

Gordon opened the door to the lab, and Ethan froze instantly. He was sitting upright on his bed, his eyes closed. One hand was wrapped around his sheets, the other already slipped underneath the mesh webbing of his hairnet. His teeth were clenched, but he was completely silent. Gordon could just barely make out the tinny sound of whatever Ethan had been listening to through his headphones, like the tapping of a bug scratching its way across the floor. Gordon started towards Ethan but stopped as the boy nosed the air and took a deep breath and let it out in stepped exhale. Gordon pointedly tried not to think of how Ethan had almost killed another person in just that type of state. It took the combined efforts of every professional bone in his body to start walking toward him again, but walk he did.

"Ethan, can you hear me?" he asked calmly, feet from the bed.

Ethan's face went slack. Then Ethan turned to Gordon and opened his eyes. Gordon nearly fell backward over the bed behind him. The boy's eyes were wide, too wide for his drooping face. His eyes were screaming, but his face was asleep. Gordon thought back to a case Gladwell loved to bring up in Psych 101, which was his wheelhouse back in the day, about a man in Canada who had driven fourteen miles along the interstate while asleep and managed to do it well. It was completely within the realm of medical science that Ethan could still be asleep right then. Still, Gordon had never before come face to face with anyone who slept with their eyes open. It seemed like something out of folklore. He wondered how many hysterical Hail Marys Ethan's mother was reciting back behind the glass. Admittedly, the situation was looking less and less like typical parasomnia—even less like extreme parasomnia. But Gordon was a medical man. He wouldn't brook nonsense like possession, especially when the boy's future was on the line.

And then Ethan spoke, and Gordon wondered if the hysterical Mrs. Barret might have the right of things after all.

"It is too late," Ethan croaked. They sounded like the words of a person who had just woken from a coma and hadn't quite recalled how to correctly push air through the vocal cords.

He's awake, then, was the first thing Gordon thought. Throughout their session together, Ethan had taken a nihilist tack, thinking he was doomed to his fate. So Gordon thought he'd simply awoken again and had jumped back on the defeatist train.

"It's not too late, buddy. Just try to get some sleep," Gordon said, checking the EEG setup.

"I am here now," Ethan said, interrupting Gordon's train of thought as surely as if it had slammed against a brick wall. Gordon turned toward Ethan, and the two of them stared at each other for fifteen seconds. Ethan didn't blink the entire time.

"Who are you?" Gordon stammered.

"The Red," Ethan growled. He bunched his shoulders and looked ready to spring off the bed. "I won't go away." He ground his teeth, and spittle flecked the corners of his mouth.

Gordon held up his hands, bracing for a bodily tackle, but then Ethan seemed to slacken. He slumped forward, eyes closed, sliding off the bed until Gordon caught him.

"Ethan?" he asked, picking him up and setting him back in bed. "Ethan!" He pressed two fingers against his neck and felt a racing pulse, but even as he stood there trying to count the beats, it started to slow and even out to something deceptively normal.

Enough of this. "Ethan," he said, speaking loudly and rubbing the boy's sternum with the knuckle of his forefinger. Ethan stirred, burrowed backward into the pillow, then opened his eyes, blinking. They were bloodshot but otherwise night-and-day different from the eyes that had been staring at Gordon moments before. He looked up and recognized Gordon instantly, then he grabbed his shirt.

"Did I hurt them?" he asked, his voice breaking to a squeak. "Mom? Dad?"

His parents burst through the door, his father with tears in his eyes, his mother sobbing. They came to his bed and knelt down, holding his hands.

"We're right here," Mr. Barret said. "Right here, son."

Gordon knew he had mere moments before the last remnants of whatever spell the boy had been under faded completely, like mist in the sun.

"Ethan," he said, breaking through his parents and standing over him. "What do you remember? Anything? You must think."

Ethan looked up at Gordon through puffy, tearing eyes. "Red mist," he said. "It was nothing but red mist. I breathed it, and it was hot. So hot. That's all I remember, the red and the heat."

Gordon stood back, leaving the boy to the soft words of his parents. "You can all go back home now," Gordon said numbly. "I'll take a look at what we've seen tonight and... and get back with you as soon as I can."

If the three of them heard him, they made no indication. Gordon backed away, out of the room, then returned to the monitoring station and sat heavily on the chair in front of the screens. Red mist. Again. And stronger that time. And he was breathing it. As if he had *become* it.

Before Gordon packed his bags to go, he had to check one more thing, just to make sure. He brought the EEG recording back to the last sleep cycle, the one where Ethan had spoken to him, eyes open. That was awareness. That was self-placement. That was situational comprehension. Lucidity.

But the records didn't lie. The delta waves were big and loopy and irrefutable. He'd never made it to the REM stage, the healing stage, but Ethan had been one-hundred-percent asleep the entire time.

CHAPTER ELEVEN

Gordon slept from six in the morning until two in the afternoon when he got back from the lab. His last thought before his head hit the pillow was that if he was lucky, all of that activity might spur some movement in his own dream. He wasn't lucky. He slept like a rock. When he awoke, he reached for his dream journal, newly installed on the dusty nightstand next to his bed. He held it for a moment then set it down, having recalled nothing.

He walked past his message machine—a chunky relic from the past he refused to part with—six times as he went about his morning routine before he noticed the message light was blinking. He stopped in his tracks, breakfast pastry in hand. The handful of patients he still had never called him. They'd been lockstep in their appointment times for months. On the rare occasions they needed to contact him, they e-mailed. The message machine was hooked to his business line, which had been gathering cobwebs for almost a year.

He chewed his pastry thoughtfully and pressed the playback button.

"Uh, yes. Hello. This message is for Dr. Gordon Pope. I got your name from the *Baltimore City Tribune* article about that Erica girl. I...

don't really know how to say this, so I'll just say it. I have a ten-year-old girl who is sleepwalking like crazy. Quite frankly, she's scaring the shit out of me. Excuse my language. I've called some other psychiatrists, but I don't think they get it. I thought maybe you would. Please, give me a call at…"

"Is this Jefferson and Pope from the article? 'Cause I'm trying to get hold of Gordon Pope? The guy who helped find that girl over in Tivoli? You're not gonna believe this, but my son does the exact same stuff as that little girl. It started probably five months ago, and it's just getting worse. My wife and I haven't slept in weeks. Call me back…"

"I hope this is the right guy because this is going to sound really crazy otherwise, but I'm looking for a psychiatrist named Gordon Pope from the *Tribune* article. It's gotta be you, right? How many Popes can there be? I think my son is gonna hurt somebody. He's sleepwalking just like that girl. I was terrified to call anybody because it sounds… well, it sounds insane. But every night, like, an hour after he goes to bed, he starts acting just… Listen, would you please call me back?"

The pastry dropped from Gordon's mouth. *Baltimore City Tribune* was the free local rag, the kind of thing that was at least seventy-five percent ads. Maybe three or four neighborhood beat pieces that read a bit like high-school book reports. The back page was chock-full of numbers for shady massage parlors.

And apparently somewhere in there was a piece about the Erica Denbrook incident.

Gordon walked around his apartment aimlessly, robe flapping open, orange juice in hand. Warren Duke had made it very clear that Gordon was to have no involvement in that search-and-rescue operation. He was quite sure the lieutenant had scrubbed whatever report was filed and made sure Gordon wasn't listed. He'd nearly been arrested for his trouble that night, so he had a hard time believing anyone down at the police department would willingly speak his name to a reporter, even if they'd been right there next to the dumpster with him when they found Erica.

Gordon gulped down his orange juice. So whoever had written the article likely got shut down by the BPD. Where would they go next? Well, if it had been Gordon, he would have tried to find other, similar cases, like the Ethan Barret case. Then he'd go to the courthouse, hang around, and ask a few questions. The reporters for the *Tribune* might be amateurs, but they were hungry amateurs. They were looking to write that piece that might get them a shot at a job at the *Sun* or maybe something that got the attention of the big boys in New York. They'd be annoyingly persistent.

And if they stuck around the courthouse long enough, they'd most likely run into Dana Frisco.

Gordon could picture the scene now. Dana Frisco would say she couldn't comment about the case at the same time she winked and nodded over at the parking lot. Then she'd say, off the record, exactly what happened. Because Dana was pissed off. No doubt, she'd seen the press conference just as he had. No doubt, she ground her teeth twice as hard as she watched Duke smile sadly in his navy blazer as he applauded his police force without naming any of them specifically, all while his own name scrolled constantly on the ticker at the bottom of the screen.

Gordon fished his cell phone out of the sagging pocket of his robe. He found Dana's number and hit the call button. She picked up after the second ring.

"Gordon?" she asked. She sounded as though she was walking somewhere, probably at the courthouse again. "Everything okay?"

"Dana, what did you do?" Gordon asked, but he spoke through a smile.

"Whatever are you referring to, Dr. Pope?" Dana replied.

"I have three messages on my business line. I haven't had three messages on my business line in a year. To be quite frank, I wasn't one hundred percent sure I still had a business line."

"Well, and this is strictly off the books, of course, but a plucky young kid from the *Tribune* was waiting by my squad car at the courthouse a few days ago. Said he had some questions about the Erica

Denbrook case that he wanted to ask me. Off record. Marty damn near had a heart attack, but he got over it after he made the kid swear not to mention him."

"Dana, you beautiful, beautiful woman," Gordon said without thinking. "You didn't have to mention me. I just did what I could do. I got lucky."

"Without you, Erica would be dead," Dana said flatly. She let that hang between them for a moment before saying, "Plus, Warren Duke is a prick and doesn't deserve one ounce of the praise he got."

"Well. Thank you. I mean it. Nobody but my mother goes to bat for me anymore," Gordon said. Speaking of his mother, her one condition for the sleep-lab deal came barreling to mind. Suddenly Gordon's mouth was dry.

"Were the messages for consultations? Maybe you can get some business out of all this?" Dana asked.

Gordon swallowed and felt that it sounded abnormally loud, like a fish gasping. He'd been just fine five seconds before but now felt like a gawky, two-stepping preteen at the school dance.

"Gordon? Did I lose you? Hello?"

"No, no. I'm here. The messages? Yes. The messages. They were asking about consultations. Believe it or not, there are other families out there having similar problems. Sleepwalking kids."

"No shit?"

"Yeah," Gordon said, and the full realization of that truth settled upon him, sobering him and washing the awkwardness from his mouth. "And that was just from the people who picked up that issue of the *Tribune*. Which means that this problem is bigger than Ethan and Erica. Maybe a lot bigger." Gordon stared blankly at his empty glass of OJ.

"Gordon?" Dana asked. "Is everything okay?"

He wouldn't lie to her. He would rather she think him crazy and never speak to him again than lie to her at that moment. The way she spoke, the weight behind the words, sounded as though she already had an idea that things weren't quite right in his head. She was the same woman who had gone along with the Chutes and Ladders idea. He owed her the truth.

"These kids are having the same dream. I'd bet my lunch that if I called back those parents and spoke with their kids, they'd all say the same thing. They'd have different names for it, I'm sure, but Ethan calls it the Red."

Gordon cringed, the phone to his ear, as he waited for Dana to dismiss him, waited for the moment Dana would become Karen, would coddle him out of pity but make it clear that he was delusional. *"Save it for the campfire, Gordon. You did a good thing finding Erica, but this is too much. This has got to stop. These kids are messing with you. Be reasonable."*

But reason had left the building. So far, Gordon was the only person who seemed able to grasp that. Even Ethan's parents thought the boy a one-off sickness, but Gordon was seeing a pattern. The problem was, crazy people also saw patterns. That was a hallmark of schizophrenia. So it was time for Dana to abandon him, too.

"Jesus," she said. "Really?"

"Wait. You believe me?"

"Gordon, I got a little girl of my own. Now, she's not sleep-walking or anything like that, but I can't tell you the number of times I've looked at my baby over the years and wondered if she's actually from the same planet as me. I love Chloe with the heat of the sun, but kids are weird. They do weird stuff. Sometimes they do scary stuff, too. So why not? What do I know?"

Gordon started laughing. He couldn't help himself. Relief swept away his fatigue, washed away his worry that despite what he'd seen the past night, he wouldn't be able to make sense of it. Somebody out there besides his mother believed in him.

And then his mother's one condition wriggled back into his thoughts. His heart rate picked up instantly—he could feel it. The truth was he liked Dana. A lot. More than even he had before, when he took way too many drinks from the rusty courthouse water fountain on the off chance he might run into her again. His mother had only given voice to what Gordon had been pussyfooting around for the past year. It was time.

He felt as though he was breathing obnoxiously into the phone, as though too much silence had passed since Dana had last spoken. Why was he being so weird about this? He was acting as though he'd never asked a girl out before, and a little voice in his head said, *Well, you haven't. You drunkenly made out with Karen in college, and that kicked off that whole disaster. Before that, you mostly read books and collected figurines.*

"All right, well..." Dana began. "I'm glad you got some press. Even if it is Podunk press. You deserve it, Gordon."

That sounded to Gordon a lot like a prelude to a sign-off. His window was closing. He was panicking. So he did what he always did when he panicked. He told the truth.

"Dana, I need your help."

He heard Dana's shoulder com crackle and then clip to silence. He dared to imagine that she'd shut it off for him. "What's up?" she asked.

"Are you busy tonight?" Gordon asked.

"Hmm. That depends. Is this personal or professional?"

"Definitely both."

"Are you asking me on a date, Gordon?" He thought he heard a smile in her voice.

Gordon thanked God they were doing this over the phone. His face was as red as a strawberry, and the OJ was audibly percolating in his gut. "Yes. But it's gonna be a weird date."

"Wow, take it easy, Casanova."

"I'm trying to get in touch with my primal side. But I need you."

Dana snorted. Her com buzzed again. In the background, a low hum of activity echoed down the marble courthouse halls. "Do I at least get dinner first?"

"How about Chinese takeout at the Elliot Sleep Lab at Hopkins? Say eight p.m.?"

"How romantic. I'm guessing this has to do with Ethan Barret."

"I thought so too, but now I think it might have to do with all of us."

In the prolonged silence that followed, Gordon felt irrationally terrified Dana was going to say no. So he didn't give her the chance.

"Please, Dana? If I'm right about this—and that's a huge if, but if I am—these kids don't have much time left before they all start acting like Ethan did that night."

"Who am I kidding? You had me at takeout Chinese."

Gordon almost collapsed. "Thank you. I mean it. Thank you. And be prepared, because I'm gonna keep you up all night."

Dana laughed, full throated and loud. "I'll see you at eight."

When she hung up, Gordon was still smiling. He wasn't any closer, really, to figuring out what the Red was. Ethan was still mere weeks away from forcible rehabilitation at Ditchfield. He now knew of at least four other kids, and probably far more than that, who were going down the same path. It was hot as sin in Baltimore and raining at the same time. He was groggy, exhausted, and still as broke as he'd been when he went to sleep.

But Dana had laughed, really laughed, and she was coming to the lab with him. So in that moment, none of the other noise mattered.

GORDON WAS ALREADY at the lab that evening when Dana arrived. He was waiting in the control room where he'd stood just a day earlier. Two folded boxes of Chinese takeout steamed on the desk by the monitors. Dana took off her raincoat and hung it from a peg behind the door. She was dressed in a linen skirt and purple rain boots. Gordon couldn't help but smile. He'd never seen her wearing anything but her police uniform. Just seeing her dressed like a normal person, he felt as though Dana had let him in on a secret, as if he'd earned the right to see her as something other than the authority figure she was day in and day out on the beat.

"You look great," Gordon said. "We should be out along the harbor. Someplace hip. Not in this old block of concrete."

Dana waved him off but smirked in a way that let Gordon know she pretty much agreed with him. "Is that from Great Wall?" She pointed at the food.

"You know it. Crab Rangoons in the bag there too."

"Nice. I love Great Wall."

"I wanted to bring wine. But you've got to stay awake for a while."

"Don't worry about it. I'm going through a beer phase anyway."

"Well, I've got Cokes. Coke is like beer for kids. It's close."

Dana snickered. "Where is the kid? Ethan?"

Gordon took a deep breath and sat on the desk and was suddenly absorbed in the food. He popped open his box of General Tso's chicken and doled out a generous glob onto a paper plate. "He's not coming today," Gordon said quickly. Then he took a big bite of crab Rangoon.

Dana crossed her arms. "Okaaay," she said. "So you really do think this place is a romantic first date then, huh? Maybe you need your own head examined."

"I think you're right on the money, there, but no, I need your help still. We're using the lab, but the patient is going to be me."

Dana stared at Gordon in silence for ten seconds while he crunched his crab Rangoon through puffed cheeks. Then she cleared her throat. "All right, Gordon. Enough bullshit. What is going on here?"

"Here," Gordon said, handing her a carton of Chinese food and offering her a seat in the swivel chair before sitting down himself on the same bench where Jane and Andrew Barret had sat last. "It's spicy beef lo mein. Their beef lo mein is a minor miracle. It makes everything easier to take."

Dana took the carton and started eating straight from it with a plastic fork. She paused after the first bite, looked down, and nodded in grudging approval. Then she crossed her legs, chewed, and waited.

"Okay, so you know how I said Ethan Barret and Erica Denbrook were having the same dream?" Gordon asked. "And how I said I'm getting calls now, from other parents, worried because their own kids are sleepwalking? And how I told you I think all of these kids are having the same dream? And then remember how after I told you all that, you didn't run away from me, screaming for a straitjacket?" He hoped she remembered especially that last bit.

"Yes," Dana said. "Although the more you talk about this, the more insane it sounds."

Gordon sucked at his teeth. "Well then, this next bit might really be the straw that breaks the camel's back."

Dana took another bite and watched him through narrowed eyes.

"What if I told you that I had the same dreams as these kids?"

Dana shrugged. "That's not too crazy. If a bunch of kids are having the same type of dream in this city, makes sense the adults would start to have it too. Maybe it's something in the water. Or maybe it's sort of a collective anxiety because Baltimore is slowly falling apart. Not the craziest thing I've ever heard. You should see some of the shit I dream about."

"Yeah, but I had the dream over thirty years ago," Gordon said. "And I lived in Bethesda at the time."

He let those words hang in the air and went back to attacking his food.

"Huh. Well. Yeah. That's a little bit weirder. A lot weirder. Makes it tough to pin it to something happening here, now. Not if you were dreaming it three decades ago."

Gordon nodded vigorously and started talking through a full mouth before stopping himself. He coughed and swallowed and coughed. Took a big swig of Coke. Wiped his eyes. "That's exactly what I'm saying! I think this stuff might be ingrained. An imprint, something ancient, something Jungian. Have you heard of Carl Jung?"

"No."

"That's okay. Forget it. The point is I had the same type of dream, but then they stopped. I want to know why they stopped. Because if I know why they stopped, I think I can help these kids stop their own dreams, and then maybe we can avert this entire train wreck before we have a hundred—or a thousand—Ethans."

Dana sat back in the chair and appraised Gordon. He knew he'd put a lot on her, but he'd tried to do it in stages, sort of like boiling a frog. The truth was, he wanted her alongside him more than anything. A sort of clarity came to him when he was by her side, a clarity that helped him come up with ideas like playing Chutes and Ladders.

Gordon expected her to scoff or laugh or set down the Chinese and pick up her coat.

What he didn't expect was when she asked, "Why do you care so much?"

She didn't ask it as if she thought it silly that he cared so much. She wasn't mocking him. The question was genuine.

"Do you know how many violent assaults there are in this city every day? Stuff like Ethan pulled, only these guys are wide awake?" she asked. "Hell, do you know how many people die in this city every day? How many kids are essentially doomed, one way or another, before they ever reach thirteen? No sleepwalking required?"

"I can guess," Gordon said softly. "But it'd probably be low."

"And yet here you are, two nights in a row, working your ass off at a sleep lab. You look like you're running on fumes, no offense, but you're still going. Why? Why do you care so much about these kids?"

He almost said, *"Because I can't have kids of my own. I'm a single white male in debt and underemployed. People like me have zero chance of adopting. And zero also happens to be the number of working testicles I have."* But he was prepared to heat the water by degrees, not flash-fry the poor woman.

"I like kids," Gordon said instead, simply and honestly. "And not in the way everyone assumes a forty-five-year-old single balding guy likes kids, either. Not the restraining-order kind of like. Don't worry."

"I know," she said, watching him carefully. She shook her head, but it was a soft, quiet kind of exasperation, and it struck Gordon as more the type of thing you'd do dug into a foxhole with a person than anything borne out of confusion. "And just when I get to thinking that there aren't any of us left." She took another bite. "All right, Gordon. What do you need me to do?"

AN HOUR LATER, his belly two pounds heavier with Chinese food he was vaguely regretting, Gordon sat on the middle bed of the lab in a threadbare Hopkins Medical T-shirt the school had mailed him fifteen years before, hoping for money they didn't get, as well as a pair of reindeer-patterned boxers that he'd sworn he would throw away three Christmases before. He was already rigged up with the brain-wave hairnet. Dana looked as though she was stifling a laugh the entire time he spoke to her.

"So you understand the waves, right? Because that is imperative. You have to recognize the waves."

"You wear socks to bed?" Dana asked.

Gordon blinked. "My feet get cold."

"It's summertime. It's ninety degrees at midnight."

"I have poor circulation of the feet," Gordon said before stopping himself. "Listen, Dana, you have to be able to recognize the patterns that indicate each of the five stages of sleep."

"I get it. You went over them five times. But I still don't get why you want me to wake you up all the time." Dana sipped her second Diet Coke.

"If you wake me up before I hit REM a couple of times, when I eventually do hit REM, it'll be that much more powerful. Like when you have a stiff drink after a week on the wagon. You wake me up during stage-four delta waves four times. Okay? Then in the fifth sleep cycle, I'll hit REM like a wrecking ball. If I'm lucky, I'll be able to bring back the cave dream as it was back then."

"Back when it was a nightmare that scared the pants off you," Dana said, nodding. "Sounds completely reasonable. You're actually hoping for a nightmare."

"If that's what it takes," Gordon said, swinging up into bed.

"Good thing I've got a food coma coming. Maybe I'll actually get to sleep. My mother always threatened me with these sleep labs when I couldn't sleep as a kid. Among other things."

"She sounds charming."

"You'd be surprised."

Dana turned and walked toward the monitoring room, but she stopped at the door and looked around. "Hey, be careful in that crazy mind of yours, okay?"

Gordon held a thumbs-up sign. "I'll see you in fifty minutes. Give or take."

Dana softly closed the door behind her, and Gordon stared at the ceiling while the noise-canceling machine played a steady stream of what sounded like an air-conditioning unit. His last waking thought was that he would never be able to fall asleep to that sound.

GORDON WAS WALKING along the wide perimeter of the back lawn of his childhood home. The grass was rough and thick, overgrown and sprouting seeds at the tips. Everything felt right. Normal. He was dreaming unaware and taking each set piece in its own right. He had a vague sense that he was there to do something, but it wasn't pressing and was quickly forgotten, like that last task left undone on a Friday afternoon. He was walking. Simply walking.

And then he was awake. Dana was shaking his arm gently as she said, "Gordon. Gordon, wake up."

He blinked, groggy, then jerked away from her, his place and purpose lost in a fog. His heart raced, then just as quickly began to calm.

"It's okay. It's just me."

Gordon nodded and yawned hugely then cleared his throat. "How long was I out?"

"Fifty-four minutes. You were just starting to leave the delta waves and settle into REM patterns. I got you as soon as I saw the change."

"Good. That's good. I feel like shit. Which is also good. It means my cycle was interrupted."

"What did you dream about?" Dana asked, rubbing her own eyes but otherwise looking as alert as always. For a split second, he allowed himself to think what it might be like to be awoken by her under other circumstances—say, if she was lying next to him in bed, for instance, in PJs of her own, not standing over him, looking vaguely concerned. He nipped that thought in the bud when the blood flow in his body shifted downward.

"Nothing. I mean, obviously something, but I can't recall, which is also good. Dream recall is at its strongest in REM sleep. If it all goes according to plan, I won't recall anything until you let me. How are you holding up? Bored out of your mind?" Gordon stifled another yawn and gauged if he should pee. He was okay, but he was glad he'd held off on his Coke.

"I'm fine. Reading a trashy romance novel. Trying to stop myself from finishing off the rest of the Great Wall. Sort of succeeding."

Gordon nodded, already groggy again. "Ready for round two?" he asked.

Dana said something that might have been *good luck*, but he already had his head on the pillow, fading, fading, and gone.

Gordon's dreaming from then forward slowly coalesced into something recognizable, like a gradually rising cake cooked for hours in the oven of his brain. He still paced the edges of his parents' estate, but the landscape was unrecognizable. He came upon things that had no place there but that still seemed normal to him as he dreamed unaware: his first car, a beat-up Chevy Nova that was pristine as he approached it then rusted and on blocks as he reached it. Next was the two-story sliding chalkboard Morty Gladwell had used in Psych 101, jammed with medical minutiae, the countless formulas that make up the balance of the human body and brain. He slapped it as if giving it a passing high five, still smiling. The grass of the lawn grew taller, around his knees. He accepted it as a child would and continued to walk. In a blink, he found himself walking through library stacks, the grass still underfoot. He knew Karen was close by—that was where they'd made love once. He felt a pulsing desire and a strange sadness at the same time. Of course he should be in those stacks, of course he should be with Karen. But something wasn't right. That was the first whisper in the corner of his mind that perhaps where he thought he was wasn't where he actually was. He paused and looked toward his feet, but they were swallowed in grass that was nearly up to his waist. Why would there be grass in a library? Why would there be a library in his parents' backyard? Could he be dreami—

His body was slack like a scarecrow as Dana shook him. He awoke slowly that time.

"Gordon," she said, louder, almost stern. "Gordon, you have to wake up."

He didn't jump back this time, no shock, no sense of displacement for Gordon—only an overwhelming exhaustion. His brain was sluggish. He mumbled something, distantly aware of the lab, of the experiment he was concocting on himself.

"This is it, Gordon. Are you ready?" Dana asked.

This is what? "What time is it?" he asked, not exactly what he meant to ask, but close enough.

"It's four in the morning. I've broken four cycles. This is it. Number five."

How could that be? It seemed he was checking his bladder a moment before. But all of that floated from him. His body was already falling back through the bed, back to the lawn. He heard a shuffling sound and smelled a faint waft of perfume. He felt a tickle of hair on his face.

"Good luck, Gordon," he heard. Or he thought he heard. And then a warm, soft pressing on his forehead. It couldn't possibly be a kiss. It felt too warm. It was like a kitten sleeping on his face. Or was it a kiss? He wanted badly for it to have been a kiss, but by then he was too far gone.

The slice-of-life imagery from earlier in the night disappeared, and Gordon found himself on the lawn outside his house, all alone in a vacuum quiet. Everything was in its place, yet everything had gone to seed. The grass had grown to his chest, and when he turned around, he saw the estate flaking, its whitewash peeling off the wood in sheets. The windows were broken, the doors missing. He placed himself within his mind almost instantly. *This is not my house. This is not my lawn. I am in a dream.* And just like that, he knew what he had to do. He wasted no time in pushing through the grass until he reached the edge of the lawn, where it met the undergrowth of the forest, which wasn't nearly as overgrown. He stepped over the threshold and into the forest, and then he waited. He waited for the pull that would drag him to the cave. He stood still, waiting, but felt no pull that time, either. No drag. No terror.

So Gordon walked.

The journey was tinged in sepia, and the forest seemed to disappear into black nothingness when he didn't stare directly at it. Dream time compressed and relaxed such that he was at the mouth of the cave in a blink while still feeling as though he hiked to it, and there he saw a snaking tendril of red mist float from the opening. He felt fear at first, but more than fear, he felt a sense of a job that needed to be done. He was here for Ethan. He was asleep in a lab right now.

The dream wavered, so he shut down that line of thought. He pictured himself as a child again, brought here countless times. He grabbed on to that fear he'd felt, making it his own again. The cave settled around him. The mist grew thicker. He walked forward, and it parted around his legs as he ducked inside.

Gordon immediately moved to the point in the cave where he'd been when the dream had broken over him thirty years before. He was finally in the REM stage he'd been denying himself, and it focused his sleeping brain like a natural amphetamine. The walls were clearer, the mist a deeper red. The cave closed itself off as it had all those years before, and when Gordon looked behind himself, he saw the stone was smooth again. No scratches.

Gordon sat just as he had then, and he covered his head with his arms. Gordon the boy had done it out of terror, weeping. Gordon the adult did it because it was what he'd done then to make the Red appear, but he didn't weep. He waited. He felt fear, surely, and anxiety as well, but that was because of whatever was happening in the waking world, outside his sleeping brain—because of the things he dared not focus upon, for fear his chance would collapse. His monsters were still there, but they had moved outside of the closet, and some small part of his mind knew that, so he was able to sit still as the mist tugged at him, brushed him, and moved over his closed eyelids and around his face, feeling like a blind man. His younger self would've screamed, *had* screamed, by that point, eyes squeezed shut. But Gordon bit his tongue and kept his eyes open.

He saw a figure in the mist, walking towards him. He did not claw against the cave that time, but he did press his back against it. He tried to grip for purchase on the floor and he had the rough, tearing sensation that the muted psychiatrist portion of his brain told him was night onychophagia: he was biting at his cuticles in his sleep. Then the figure walked out of the mist, and he stopped scrabbling, stopped pressing away, stopped everything.

He was looking at himself as a boy, and the boy was staring down at him.

Gordon's first inclination was to relax. *Where is the beast? Where is the horror?* But a whisper in the back of his mind told him to stay present, to stay alert. Gladwell's voice from another lecture, decades before, manifested like an errant note of the piano on the wind. *"The brain cannot self-actualize, Gordon. This is known. You cannot see yourself in a dream."*

This thing was not what it looked like.

The boy stared at the man still, as if it was as confused as the man was. Gordon marveled at it. He saw the scar he'd gotten over his right temple from when he and the neighbor girl had twisted the swings up until they spun like tops and then collided, only the boy's was still red, still fresh. He saw his chipped molar, a black gap in the boy's mouth. He would get it fixed the next year, just before his thirteenth birthday. He saw his mother's handiwork in the choppy way the boy's hair was cut. All those memories were correct, yet none should have been that clearly remembered. The psychiatrist in him sounded a warning.

"Are you what came for me in the mist?" Gordon asked.

The boy nodded.

"But... how? You're no monster."

"I am changed," the boy said. "You changed me." His voice was a crystal copy of Gordon's as it had been, even down to the tremulous breaking that hovered over each word.

"What were you before I changed you?" Gordon asked.

"You. But a different you."

Gordon shook his head. He'd tortured himself in a sleep lab for more riddles. The dream wavered. He shoved all worry of failure from his mind. Only when he gave up, when he sat with his arms draped over his knees, just as he had when he first spoke with Ethan in his office and simply watched this boy, did the dream settle over him again and solidify.

"This is madness," Gordon said, to the boy in his dreams, to himself. "I'm going mad."

A small smile pinched the boy Gordon's mouth. He stood straight, unblinking.

"Perhaps," the boy said. "Madness is one word for what I am. There are two parts to men. There is the part tied to the beginning and the part tied to the end. I am the part tied to the beginning."

"The beginning? You mean birth?"

The boy shook his head as if annoyed, and Gordon nearly reeled with an intense feeling of sympathy. He shook his head like that when he was trying to make himself understood to his family, his friends, when they just didn't get it.

"Before birth. Before even the knitting together in the womb. I am what you leave behind to go into life. The second you step into life, my grip on you begins to loosen." As he spoke, his face darkened, and the red swirled around him. "I hate it," the boy said.

Gordon saw violence in his eyes, a primitive darkness that he suddenly felt was probably similar to what poor Jimmy Tanner had seen in Ethan's eyes as he came for him—his friend gone, replaced by something else.

Then it was gone, and the boy straightened.

"Why do you come here again and again?" the boy asked as if he'd been watching Gordon for months, as if he wasn't a part of Gordon's subconscious at all but an alien observer. The psychiatrist sliver blared a red alert. Gordon closed it off, focusing on the cave, on the boy—anything to keep the dream together. "You must know that this place is empty for you," the boy said. "I lost you long ago. You are done with me, and I am done with you. Yet you pull me here. Why?"

"There is a boy. A boy who... who wants to be done with you as well. With his version of you."

"Ethan," the boy said, his eyes dark once more.

"Yes," Gordon said, fighting a stammer. His mouth was gummy, falling apart. He didn't have much time. "And a girl—"

"Erica. Yes. I know them both. I will take them both," he said, the cold finality of his words somehow made twice as unnatural by the boyish tone, like a child soldier utterly devoted.

"Why?" Gordon asked. "Why can't you let them go?"

"It's simple. They want the beginning more than the end. They cling to me. They may walk forward in life, but they look backward."

The dream wavered heavily, as if a fault line had snapped. Gordon knew he'd done it to himself. Speaking of Ethan and Erica was bringing his mind back toward the conscious world, and it was tipping the scale. He perhaps had time for one more question, and he wanted it to be *How did I beat you?* but he felt strongly that the boy, the thing, was proud and saw every child that slipped from its grasp as a loss not only for itself but for the child too.

"How did I lose you?" Gordon asked instead.

The boy's eyes glowed with blackness, the red mist swirled up and around him, and he faded, the cave faded, even as Gordon tried to grab hold of the walls of rock they turned to sand in his hands.

Only the boy's face remained, Gordon's from thirty years before, floating like the Cheshire cat, inches from Gordon.

"You decided to look forward," said the boy.

GORDON SHOT up from his bed. Dana was there already, sitting next to him on a small padded stool as if she was the doctor and he the patient. She leaned away and let him pant and blink and cough himself into awareness.

"It's okay, Gordon," she said, her voice calm, but when Gordon turned to look at her, her eyes betrayed her. Her mascara was blotted carefully, but she'd been crying. Still, just looking at her and at the way she looked back at him steadied his heartbeat. He could hear his vitals beeping through the walls, but they were slowing, normalizing. He brushed at his forehead and his gnawed fingers came away glistening with sweat.

"What time is it?" Gordon asked.

"Almost five thirty. I'd say you've been in REM for almost thirty minutes."

"You left the control room?" Gordon asked.

Dana looked away for only a moment. "You were a mess. Talking. Crying. Twitching. I didn't know—"

"It's okay, Dana." Gordon touched her hand briefly. "Thank you."

Dana looked at his forehead as if it was a million-piece jigsaw puzzle bunched in a box. "What the hell went on in there? Who were you talking to?"

"Myself. From a long time ago," Gordon said, already going through the conversation word by word, repeating it to himself in the manner he'd taught himself over years of journaling.

"Did you get what you needed? Do you know what to do now? For Ethan? Or any of these kids?"

Gordon took several steadying breaths and reached for his journal. "I don't know what to do to help Ethan," he said. "Not yet."

Dana slumped. Gordon looked up at her, pen in hand. She looked tired, burdened by a load he thought was his own but that she'd taken on with him. Her cute skirt and top were gone, replaced by floppy pajama bottoms and a jersey-cloth T-shirt. Her hair was pulled behind her head, bunched into a clip. She crossed her arms over herself as if embarrassed, but Gordon couldn't think of a single sight he'd rather see upon waking up from that cave other than her, right then.

Gordon grasped her hand again and smiled. "I may not know how to treat him yet, but I know what's wrong with him. And that's a hell of a start."

CHAPTER TWELVE

Andrew Barret no longer felt comfortable with his back turned to his son, but his wife was absolutely terrified of him. She spent the entirety of the day after the sleep study at St. Mary's Cathedral on Center Street, starting at six a.m. mass then staying through noon mass and evening vespers, and then she'd gone to her parents again.

Andrew was ashamed of his wife. Her newfound Christian zeal rang hollow. She was a lapsed Catholic. Before Ethan took a turn, she hadn't been to church outside of Christmas Eve in as long as he could remember, but now she insisted that nothing but God could help the boy. As if they lived in some sort of seventeenth-century village where the doctors were shunned as witches. He'd blown up at her in the car on the ride home as she muttered Hail Marys while Ethan stared out of the window through hooded eyes like a drugged dog. Once home, she'd immediately left again to "get her spirit right," and Andrew and Ethan were left together in the living room. The Orioles' game was on low volume, but neither of them was watching. Ethan stared at nothing, and Andrew stared at Ethan.

As much as he hated to admit it, in the silence of the living room as he watched his son pawing blindly at his phone while a low, rhythmic growl came from him with every breath, Andrew had a moment—just a moment—when he allowed that Jane's belief might not be as insane as he'd told her it was before she stormed off to a church she hadn't set foot in for half a decade. Either way, she was missing the point. For some reason, the child who sat across from him was no longer his son. But Andrew firmly believed, as he knew Jane did, that his son was somewhere in there. The question was how to get him back.

Thank God for Pope. Talk about possessed—the man worked feverishly. He'd called the house twice already to reassure Andrew that he was close to being able to treat Ethan and getting closer all the time. Without Gordon Pope, Andrew would've been as lost as Ethan seemed. He knew that Pope's insistence that Ethan's condition was a purely medical issue was keeping him scared *for* his son, not *of* his son, like Jane was.

Ethan picked up one of Jane's magazines from the coffee table and slowly started to rip the cover. The sound jarred Andrew even as he saw it coming, overwhelming the murmurs of the baseball game.

"Ethan, put that down."

Ethan looked in the direction of Andrew's voice but seemed to see right through him, as if he'd heard his name called in a crowd of thousands. He started tearing again.

Andrew stood. "Ethan!"

He took a step forward, and Ethan's eyes focused. He dropped the magazine. Andrew sat back down. He watched Ethan for a moment more, sitting, staring, and then took a glance at the baseball game—tied two to two. The heart of the order was coming up to bat for the Os—and then he heard a loud crash.

Andrew's eyes snapped back to Ethan. He'd punched through the glass lamp on the end table to his right. His fist was still inside the bulbous base. He stared at his arm as if it wasn't his own.

Andrew stood again, eyes wide. For a moment, he couldn't say anything.

Ethan slowly withdrew his fist, still clenched. A thin, steady stream of blood fell from his middle knuckle and splattered the wood of the end table. Andrew rushed to his son and grabbed his arm, still outstretched. A sliver of glass was embedded in the skin like an iridescent splinter.

"Here, hold it up," Andrew said. "I'll get the first-aid kit." He pushed Ethan's arm into an upward position, and Ethan held it there dumbly like a mannequin, his mouth open, his eyes unblinking.

Andrew walked toward the kitchen to turn on the sink. "Keep it away from the rug," he said, turning back toward Ethan. "Your mother will kill—"

Ethan was right behind him. A foot away. Standing still and bleeding. How the boy could have been that fast, Andrew had no idea. Ethan stared at him and started sucking at the cut on his fist. Even if Andrew found the words to speak, he doubted anything he might say to his son would register anyway.

When Andrew had been ten, his father got them a rescue dog, an unruly terrier that barked and barked and seemed not even to register a scolding, as if she went deaf whenever anyone raised their voice at her. One day, she took off out the open front door after the neighbor's dog and was tagged by a truck as she bolted across the street, oblivious to his screams. As Andrew faced his son, he was reminded of that dog for the first time in years. He reached out for him and grasped his shoulder, bony even by gangly preteen standards, and he directed Ethan in front of him and to the kitchen sink in a wordless exchange.

One hand still on Ethan's shoulder, Andrew reached up and took the first-aid kit from the high shelf above the refrigerator. He gently pried Ethan's fist from his mouth. His tongue lolled after it for a moment as Andrew put it under the running water in the sink. The glass was gone. Ethan must have swallowed it.

Was that to be their life from then on, his wife and son falling back into the Dark Ages while he walked on eggshells, trying to keep them all from breaking? He saw his son was clutching his phone still, white-knuckled. His son's addiction to the thing felt just as unnatural as his suckling mouth. He could see the screen. It showed that chat program he'd been on for months, the one he and Erica used to use religiously. Her name was on the screen but grayed out, unavailable. He looked back up at his son and found him staring back at him with glazed eyes that were as dilated as an owl's.

Ethan's waking life was looking more and more like his sleeping life. Whatever had plagued him in the darkness was creeping over to the light. And it was getting worse by the hour.

GORDON POPE SPENT a full half of his monthly booze-cash allotment to resubscribe to an online medical journal that he'd let lapse, but even after poring over the published literature on sleep disorders, which he noted was far less extensive than it should be, he still hadn't found anything resembling what he'd experienced the night before at the sleep lab with Dana. The research on shared dream imagery was annoyingly symbolic in nature. What Gordon had experienced, and what he believed Ethan and Erica were experiencing, was disturbingly specific, as if the same thing had appeared to all three of them.

He found countless articles on Freudian symbolism and repressed sexuality, but Gordon's dream wasn't sexual. He'd had plenty of sexual dreams before. He knew them. His life had been something of a repressed sexual existence recently. He would have recognized it. And anyway, professionally speaking, Freud served as more of an academic red flag than a primary source of theory. The new school of thought held that no shared symbols existed in dreams. The hip consensus in modern psychiatry was that people were individually weird, not collectively weird.

For years Gordon had bought that, but not anymore.

The one thing that did stick with him was an article by Crump and Lowe, titled *On the Validity of Freudian Limbic Theory*. The limbic system is the instinctive apparatus of the human brain, the primal part. The whole article read sort of like a backhanded compliment to Freud, but in essence it focused on how he was correct when he asserted that dreams were driven by primitive instincts. It was the word *primitive* that stuck with Gordon. He bookmarked the article.

From there, he went on a wild goose chase of reference hunting and two hours later ended up across the psychological line of demarcation with Freud's colleague and defector Carl Jung. One particular paper was a whopper, over a hundred pages of dripping academia titled *Jungian Analysis and the Evolution of REM Sleep* by Elsworth and Bortles. He read until his eyes blurred and was about to toss it when he stumbled across a sentence that made him stand up from his chair:

"Increasingly, it appears as though Jungian theory may have been correct insofar as the tenets presuppose that certain elements of dreams can reflect the collective experiential history of our ancient ancestors. The commonly occurring survival dream, for instance, in which we experience an intense fear of being pursued, might be said to emanate from a collective ancestral experience that is genetically coded."

It was dripping with *may*s, *might*s, and *insofar*s, but it spoke to Gordon. Could it be that Ethan was being overtaken by his primitive self? That Erica was in danger of being overtaken by her primitive self? Thirty years before, Gordon had made a stand against his primitive self, and he'd won out. They'd called the thing the Red, which made sense. Red was primitive. Red was ancient. Red was basic, like blood. Arguably, the pumping redness of the womb was the first thing a child could see. Medically speaking, these children weren't under attack from a physical red mist or a red monster, but Gordon had good reason to think they might be under assault from their own limbic systems.

As to why, Gordon had some ideas, each as harebrained and farfetched as the last. He couldn't afford to speculate on the why just yet. He didn't have enough time.

As for what could be done about it, Gordon was still in the dark.

But he had a medical definition of the problem, and that meant he could call Karen.

Gordon looked longingly at his empty liquor shelf, picked up his phone, and dialed his ex-wife.

ETHAN no longer recognized his bedroom for what it was. He *saw* his bedroom, and the things inside it, far more clearly than he ever had before, but he recognized only that they smelled of him and that they did not threaten him, so he assumed a type of possession by association over them, but they were not his anymore. If anything, he felt most drawn to his bed, but only because it smelled the most strongly of him, of his sweat and grease and urine.

One thing confused him: what he held in his hand. The word for it—

phone—was fleeing quickly down the dark corridors of his brain, and in its place another surfaced: *Erica*. It was his *Erica*. But it wasn't acting like his Erica anymore. It was silent when it used to talk. That made him grit his teeth and want to throw the thing, to wound it and make it wake up, but his Erica was delicate, he knew, so he held it as tightly as he dared and refused to let it go. And he sat on his bed, and he watched his father through his eyelashes.

He was lying in wait, like a snake in the grass. Because Ethan needed to leave. The Erica he held in his hand was only one part of Erica. The rest of Erica, the *meat* of Erica, was nearby. This part of her he held in his hand was broken, but the rest of her was not. This part of her wouldn't respond to him. Not to his touch or his taste or even to his squeeze. But the meat part would.

But first, he needed to leave this cave of his. His father was keeping him. Trapping him. Turning his cave into a cage. He sat in a chair across from his bed, but Ethan recognized neither the chair nor the bed nor the book his father was reading. He saw only the threat level that the man posed. Ethan could try to kill him. If he did, he could take the entire cave too. But Ethan knew his limits. The man was old, but he was still strong. Stronger than Ethan, unless Ethan used something—a weapon of some sort, something heavy or sharp. Even then, Ethan knew the old man was smart. He'd hidden most of his tools from Ethan.

No matter. Ethan could feel his strength growing. And the old man's strength was shrinking. That was the way of things in a pack. A time would come when he could kill his father easily. But not that day. So he was a snake in the grass.

He knew his father was tired. Ethan himself was beyond tired. He no longer needed sleep as his father needed sleep. Ethan slept by never existing fully awake or fully asleep. He slept like a shark. Parts of him were shut down, but others kept him moving forward always. Not so for the old man. The old man needed heavy sleep. Vulnerable sleep. Even his watch over Ethan, which Ethan knew was important to the old man, could not last forever for someone that needed heavy sleep. Trying to overpower him even if he slept still held too much risk. Best just to leave his cave.

Waiting, he watched his father fight against his sleep. He seemed to be asleep several times, and Ethan almost moved, only to find that the old man would snap awake again as if frightened. When Ethan finally rose from his bed, the night had truly come, the moon shining strongly through the window, and the old man hadn't moved in some time. He crept with a silence he didn't know he possessed, one born from a time when noise could get you killed or starve you by startling away your food. The normal distractions that plagued the mind of a young boy were gone. He made virtually no sound as he left his own room and then left the house altogether. He stepped out onto the front lawn, wearing a pair of basketball shorts and a large T-shirt that hung down past his butt. He carried only his phone. Stepping silently, he set off in the direction of the rest of Erica, but he stopped at the sidewalk. First, he needed to make sure that his part of Erica was truly silent and not just a snake in the grass. He took his phone in both hands and squeezed—squeezed as hard as he'd squeezed another member of his pack once before, when he was first waking up to the way of things and felt that he wanted to be head of the pack with only Erica at his side. He bent the phone until it cracked and shattered.

Then he dropped his phone in the grass. No, this part of her would not answer to him any longer, but the meat part would. He was sure of it.

GORDON POPE PACED his living room, seven steps each way. Karen Jefferson was on speakerphone.

"Again with Freud? Really?" she asked. "I thought we'd gone over this."

"No, no. Freud wasn't quite right. And Jung wasn't quite right," Gordon said.

"Well that's the first sane thing I've heard you say all this conversation—"

"But in a way, both of them were right," Gordon finished.

On the other end, Karen either made a sighing sound or perhaps just shifted her phone to the other ear. Gordon could hear the nonsensical chatter of Maggie playing in the background.

"So because you talked to your childhood self in a dream, you think you've had some sort of revelation with the ego and the id?" she asked.

"First of all, you know that studies show it is very rare to see yourself in dreams... if not impossible."

"What you saw was most likely an image of a boy. You made it into yourself."

"But the conversation, Karen. You have to admit it was way too prescient. Way too specific and driven. It was a *real* conversation." Gordon flopped down onto his battered recliner, and it popped ominously. He flipped though his journal, reading and rereading what he'd written about his dream in the lab.

"I'm going to be honest with you. You're sounding less and less like a medical doctor and more and more like a witch doctor these days."

Gordon picked up one of several EEG prints of Ethan's brain that were scattered around the base of the television. Much of the printout was dark—the outline of his skull looked like a hedge maze of black—but just beneath the cerebrum were bright white indications of activity, the limbic system.

"The limbic activity in the boy was off the charts," Gordon said. "That's undeniable."

"Now *that* I am more interested in. That is real. That is not normal. But it's hardly indicative of a primal takeover of the boy's brain, as if the limbic system is a virus of some sort." Maggie cooed next to the phone, and Karen continued in a baby voice, "The limbic system isn't a virus. Is it, Maggie?"

Maggie shouted, "No!"

Then Karen said, "That's right!"

Gordon felt a headache coming on. Or perhaps he'd had it for some time but just never noticed it. Say, for the past five years, if such a thing was possible without dying. He set the EEG prints on his head and let them slide down his face and to the floor. Karen was doing the baby talk thing on purpose in order to make him want to hang up, but he wouldn't give in.

"No, not a virus... All I'm saying is, isn't it possible that maybe there comes a point in everyone's life when a switch flicks in the brain —maybe in the limbic system, maybe not—when we, as self-conscious human beings, decide that there's no going back?"

"Back where? The womb?"

"Yes, but more to wherever we came from before the womb. The ether. The goo of oblivion." Gordon was well aware Karen hated philosophical mumbo jumbo, but he couldn't think of any other way for him to describe his theory. *Now we'll see who hangs up first.*

"Gordon, there is nothing before the womb. There is no ether. This type of nonsense should be hashed out with your priest."

Gordon ignored her tone and pressed on. "When I broke that

cave dream, back when I was a kid and I ended up actually sleep-walking to the place, that was a watershed moment for me." The words of the boy version of himself rang in his mind: *You decided to look forward.* "It was when my subconscious brain made a decision to grow up, something that very likely came from my limbic system."

Karen was quiet. Gordon took that as a good sign. Karen was only ever at a loss for words when she was struck by something that made her think.

Gordon pressed on. "We know the subconscious is guided by the limbic system. The most primitive part of the brain. The emotion system. It makes no differentiation between the future and the past, age and youth. It lacks the vocabulary. It's guided by something else, something ancient. Encoded in our genetics from the time when it ruled the roost. But it had to give way, at some point, to the waking brain."

"I'm listening," Karen said. "Skeptically. But I'm listening."

"And I think that if it doesn't give way, if it can't be bested like I somehow did in the cave way back when, it starts to exhibit itself more and more. The primal instincts it holds start to claw their way back to rule the roost again."

HOUSES AND TREES blocked out the silver moonlight, and Ethan kept to the shadows they made. He moved in bursts, pausing each time to look and to listen for a change caused by his passing. The night was just as deep, the sounds just as loud. Not even the ripping of the cicadas paused for him. He was as much a part of the night as the birds that slept nearby or the fox that ran silently to his right.

He recognized Erica's own cave by her smell. He hadn't realized he'd been following it until it hit him as he crouched under a wisp of an elm, newly planted and already broken by the heat of the concrete around it. He grasped the thin line of twine that staked it upright and watched the house in front of him. It was dark except for a blue light glowing from Erica's window. The light was low, but it still hurt

Ethan. His pupils stretched across his eyes by then, only rimmed by the barest hint of white. He walked onto the sharp cut of her lawn nonetheless and into the pool of light thrown from her window. Then he stopped. He squinted. He recognized that glow. It was the same type of glow as the phone he'd broken. It was her computer, her way of reaching him, as his phone was his way of reaching her. That was the way things used to be. Until she left his pack. Until she broke from him.

Ethan stood in the soft edges of light, faced with his own decision. He felt a strong urge to take Erica back. He knew it only as a need like his need for food or water. Erica was as important as those things. And as he saw her reaching out to others, joining another pack without him, the India-ink black and heavy silver colors of the night faded until all he could see was red.

ON THE OTHER end of the line, Gordon could hear Karen muttering to Chad.

"Just get her coloring book for her. I'll be in in a second... Yes, it's Gordon. I know what we said. Just watch her, and let me finish this conversation, would you?"

Gordon imagined Chad miming for her to cut the line with a clip of his fingers, and he rolled his eyes. He was running out of time. "Karen, this is serious," he said.

"So what you're saying is that this child is being taken over by his limbic system? Like he's undergoing some sort of human devolution?"

Gordon listened for sarcasm in her voice but couldn't find any. That didn't mean she was on board, but it might mean she no longer thought he was trying some sort of half-baked ploy to work through his own sterility or to get back to the way things had been with her. As for Gordon, he was positive it wasn't the first—not so sure on the second, but she didn't need to know that.

"Ethan is increasingly animalistic. Primal. He is losing all reason and acts on impulse. He has no regard for society any longer. He's increasingly sociopathic. That's the limbic system to a tee. If you could see this kid, Karen, you'd understand. The scans confirmed what I already supposed. The anterior cingulate cortex has gone silent, and the limbic system is lit up like a Christmas tree. He's lost his ability to reason."

Karen drew a big breath and let it out through her teeth. "And you think you were in danger of having the same thing happen to you at that age. Only you beat back this thing. But you don't know how you did it."

"That's right. And it's not just me and Ethan, either. I have about twenty messages from frantic parents on my machine, so many I can't even call them all back." Gordon looked over at his answering machine. The message indicator had been blinking red twenty-four hours a day. He knew what each one said, more or less. He also knew that if he could help Ethan, he could help all of them. And if time ran out for Ethan, it most likely meant it had run out for all of them.

"Why?" Karen asked simply.

"Why what?"

"Why is this happening? Why now? Kids have been sleep-walking for thousands of years. As far as I know, there's been no evidence of this extreme limbic activity. What the hell happened?" It was a question and a challenge. Gordon knew she wasn't on his side yet. She was a scientist even more than she was a therapist lately. In Gordon's experience, the more entrenched you got in the science of the brain, the less likely you were to make the leaps of faith you needed in therapy. But still, she sounded intrigued. Almost angry. Because scientifically speaking, this wasn't the way things were supposed to be, and it pissed her off. Gordon could see her, sitting at the kitchen table, leaning on her elbows, her hand massaging her temple, stray wisps of brown hair escaping her tight ponytail.

"I think it's this place," Gordon said.

"Baltimore?"

"Well, yeah, but also this place in time. You said kids have been sleepwalking for thousands of years. But think how vastly differently a child sleeps now from when they did then. Did you know that Ethan can't fall asleep unless he's on his phone? Unless he's listening to something? He chats with his buddies until his phone drops from his hand. And he's not the only one, I guarantee it. Light pollution. Noise pollution. Sensory inputs of all types. These are things that even kids a hundred years ago didn't have as prevalently as we do now, to say nothing of a thousand years ago. I bet if a kid from a couple hundred years ago saw what our night looks like, he'd think it was more like day. There's never a true night anymore. I think it's hindering the development of the anterior cingulate cortex, and the limbic system is compensating."

Gordon found himself shaking.

"And then there's Baltimore itself. I kept thinking, *Why would it be here?* If what I thought was true about Ethan, why would this mess start here? Then I picked up the *Wall Street Journal* the other day. You know what was on the front page?"

He waited for Karen to answer. She was quiet. He could hear her breathing, though, so at least she hadn't hung up on him.

"Okay, I'll tell you," he said. "It said 'Baltimore Grapples with Blight Problem.' Did you know that nearly ten percent of the houses here in this city are classified as unlivable? Ten percent! And then you got the houses that are livable but empty. Have been for years. They can't even get accurate figures on all of them, there are so many. The foreclosure crisis wiped out entire neighborhoods here, and nobody wants to come pick up the pieces and start again. Ethan lives in one of these neighborhoods."

That reminded him that he was supposed to be hearing from Andrew Barret soon. He'd told the man to call twice a day, once at noon and once at ten p.m., to update Gordon on the boy's status while he worked. His watch said ten forty-five.

"That doesn't mean the city is breeding monsters, Gordon," Karen said evenly.

"No, no it doesn't. But it does mean that parents these days aren't exactly keen on letting their kids run around and play. When you can't play outside, you play inside. The Internet is these kids' playground now. But it's a different sort of playground. It doesn't tire you out like the ones you and I had. It stretches different parts of the brain. Creates a different kind of exhaustion. Maybe even a different kind of sleep altogether."

Gordon stared at his watch as he spoke, and he got a sinking feeling in his gut with each second it ticked. He fumbled with his phone, with Karen still on the line, to check his call log. No missed calls.

"What are you doing?" Karen asked, her voice muffled and small as Gordon held his phone out in front of him.

"I gotta go, Karen," he said.

"Whoa, wait. Hold on just a second. You drop all this on me and ask for my help, and then you just *gotta go?*"

"I think something's wrong. I'll call you back."

"Wrong? What's wro—"

Gordon hung up and dialed Andrew Barret. He picked up on the first ring. His voice wavered as if he was barely holding back a lake of panic.

"He's gone, Gordon. I've been looking everywhere. I can't find him."

ETHAN WAITED, pressing himself down into the earth, until a cloud passed over the moon. Then he moved, crawling to Erica's window. He pushed through the bushes at its base, ignoring the thorns and pricks, until he pulled himself up inch by inch from the overhang of her window sill. His muscles ached, but he dared not move faster. Slowly, he rose until his bleeding forehead and then his eyes were at the base of the window.

Outside the soft glow of the computer, the room was completely black. But that hardly mattered to him. He was able to see more clearly in the dark than ever before. Erica wasn't here. His nose confirmed it as much as his eyes. The sense of smell that had brought him here also told him she had left. And he knew immediately where she'd gone.

A part of his brain wondered why he was here, at this window, sinking back down into the bushes, pushing through and flattening himself against the grass, waiting for the moon to disappear again. That part said that Erica was his neighbor. His classmate. His friend. But not *his to have.* That strangled cry in the back of his brain was enough to make him think for a moment about his pain and his weariness, and there in the grass, he almost closed his eyes to sleep. But that voice faded, faded, and was soon like a whisper. And as it faded, his eyes opened slowly, more and more, until they were pits of black again, and all of the times he'd spent sitting next to Erica in school, walking with her, laughing, watching movies, holding her hand when she cried, texting and messaging late into the night, then sometimes scrolling through everything she'd typed long after her parents made her sign off... all of that faded away.

He knew where she was. He would make her part of his pack again, under him.

He set off under cloud cover. The only eyes he felt watching him were those of the birds in the trees, who settled quickly again after he passed.

DANA FRISCO SAT in her idling squad car under the bug-swarmed halogen lights of a 7-Eleven parking lot that had seen better days. She tried to ignore the pattering of the moths and thumps of larger things on her windshield as she ate a microwaved hamburger she already regretted buying from the mousey teenage clerk inside. Marty sat in the passenger's seat, picking through a bag of home-mixed nuts and dried fruit and watching her unwrap the plastic.

"How can you eat that garbage?" Marty asked, crunching loudly.

"I didn't have time to pack a dinner before getting Chloe to her grandma's for the night." Dana lifted up the burger and inspected it. "Believe me, I'm not super happy about it. But after a night shift, you feel like shit no matter what you eat." She took a bite and shrugged. *Not bad. Better than squirrel food, anyway.*

As if Marty could hear her thoughts, he popped another generous pinch of trail mix into his mouth. "What you eat always matters. If you wanna stay sharp, stay cut, stay at the top of your game, it starts with what you put inside your body."

"Thanks, Dr. Oz."

"I'm serious. I know you've been trying to bust out of the beat, make detective and all, and—"

"Yeah, *that's* why I haven't made detective." Dana rolled her eyes. "It's what I eat. Thanks, rookie. I've been trying to figure it out for years now."

Marty was quiet. Dana closed her eyes. She'd overstepped. She never called Marty *rookie.* That was a shitty thing to do, a total cop-show thing, the exact type of marginalizing that she'd been fighting her whole career at BPD. They were supposed to be partners, for Christ's sake, equal. Plus, Marty Cicero might be a gym rat, but he was a sensitive gym rat. He put on the East Coast cop-swagger routine as good as any of them, but it wasn't him, not exactly.

"It's shit like that, you know, just like that. Acting like you know better than anyone else. Just going off on your own right in front of Duke's face." Marty jabbed angrily for a peanut.

Dana started to speak through a full mouth, but Marty stopped her.

"I know how it ended up. We found her, and then you got another red flag on your file. All I'm saying is, if you'd talked about it first, told me about Pope, maybe, then we coulda gone through Duke, found her, and you'd be closer to detective instead of sitting in front of a friggin' 7-Eleven at midnight, waiting for dispatch to send us to some domestic dispute or whatever."

The heat behind his words gave her pause. *"We coulda gone through Duke."* No partner of hers had ever said *we* like that before. But he didn't have the history with the department that she did. When God pushed the "cop" button on the great vending machine in the sky, he was the type of guy that popped out. She wasn't, but she felt called to the job, and the more it pushed back at her, the more she was determined to make it work. She didn't blame Marty. She'd been like him in her first year too. But he hadn't been squeezed by Duke for seven years—first, in their class at the academy together, her and Duke; then, on the beat at the same time; then, as he had been promoted on a whim to detective. Dana had taken years even to hit corporal, and that's where she'd stayed. Duke was a sergeant in four—lieutenant two years later. The rumor was that a phone call from his venerable father was all it had taken. Duke Textiles was a big supporter of the police union. And at every promotion, with every handshake, he looked at her. He found her in the crowd, just for a second. Not out of malice, either. Not quite. Malice she could deal with. The "Aw shucks" look that was somehow pitying and knowing at the same time was what got to her, as though he felt sorry for her that she would even question why he was where he was, with the big badge at his age, while she would still be in a squad car on a night beat, parking lot bound, with huge Maryland-summer bugs pinging off the windshield.

She wanted to snap all that off at Marty. He was caged there next to her, with nowhere to run. But she clenched her jaw and bit it back.

"Don't worry, Marty. You'll be right up there with all of them soon enough," she said instead.

Marty looked out the window. "That's not why I asked to be part-nered with you," he said quietly.

Dana paused midbite. She'd thought Marty Cicero had been paired with her just as the rest were: regretfully but with promises from up top that Dana Frisco's partners turned into some of the best cops in the precinct. She could hear Duke: *"Put up with her. We'll make it worth your while."* But Marty had *asked* to be put with her? She swallowed a mouthful of spongy burger and was about to ask him what he was talking about when her cell phone rattled in the cup holder. She picked it up, expecting it to be Chloe telling her good night, way past when Grandma knew she was supposed to be in bed... but it wasn't Chloe. It was Gordon Pope.

"Hey..." she answered tentatively. One day, she hoped, Gordon Pope would call her, and the sight of his name wouldn't drop her stomach an inch. But today wasn't that day.

"They can't find Ethan," Gordon said in a strained tone, forced into evenness.

Dana's stomach dropped another inch.

"Andrew Barret said he's looked everywhere in and around the house. He's gone."

"How long?" Dana asked.

Marty stopped munching and cocked an eyebrow.

"He's not sure," Gordon said. "But no more than an hour. Barret guesses thirty minutes. He was up with him in his room, watching him, but he fell asleep. When he came around again, Ethan was gone."

"Thirty minutes? Maybe he's just... I dunno... taking some air?" Dana asked, cringing.

"You haven't seen this kid recently, Dana. He's not the night-strolling type anymore. He's more the night-crawling type. We have to find him."

"We? Gordon, I'm on patrol right now." She looked at Marty pointedly. "If you want help from the BPD, you can call 9-1-1. Dispatch is all over the missing-kid calls these days. Duke says it's great publicity."

Gordon sounded as though he was working moisture into his mouth. "Ethan's on parole pending an appeal. If I call 9-1-1, he's going to jail. It's game over for him."

"Gordon, don't you think..." She paused and reworded her thoughts. "I mean, isn't it possible that Ethan might need to be some-where under twenty-four-hour care?"

"Twenty-four-hour care? That's the nicest way I've ever heard an insane asylum described in my life," Gordon said. "And the answer is no. I'm positive that Ethan does not need to be at Ditchfield. His limbic system is attacking him. You helped me figure that out at the sleep lab."

He wasn't accusing. He was pleading. Hearing it pained Dana because she did believe him. She didn't know what a limbic system was, but she'd have believed him even if she hadn't seen the way he struggled in his sleep that night, the way he seemed to be in a chess match with his own brain. She believed him because she trusted him. He wanted to help those kids more than anything. She could see that in his eyes when he'd woken up from that last sleep cycle and reached for his journal. But that was the problem. She didn't want to see him fail. He was unflagging and very bright, but he'd pinned his heart to the Ethan Barret case, and she knew his heart was brittle. He was one bad crack away from becoming a cynical asshole like the rest of the men she surrounded herself with, cops who'd seen too much, gotten hurt, and had no recourse but to think the only reason people messed up in life was because the world is garbage.

She wanted to say that the real reason she hesitated was that if Gordon tried and failed and fell and then gave up—if a man like him could give up—then she had no chance whatsoever to keep fighting her own battles.

"Nobody is giving this kid a chance," Gordon said, his voice husky. "His mother thinks he's possessed. His father is starting to accept that he'll never see his son again. And worst of all, the kid has given up on himself. Don't you give up on him too. Don't let me be the only one here, screaming at the clouds."

"God dammit, Gordon," Dana said, the curse coming out like a sigh.

"Is that a good 'God dammit' or a bad 'God dammit'?"

"What do you need from me?" Dana asked.

Marty narrowed his eyes.

"I need you to help me look for him, for one," Gordon said. "But more than that, I think this could get ugly. If Ethan is out there in the state I think he is, there's a good chance the cops are going to be called anyway. If they are, I need you to run interference until I can figure out what's going on."

Dana pinched the bridge of her nose but nodded.

"Can you do that?" Gordon asked.

"I'll do what I can," she said and hung up. She looked straight out the window as the silence in the cab fell heavily over them both. Then she cleared her throat and gripped the gearshift to go into reverse when Marty stilled her hand.

"What the hell are you doing?" he asked.

"Checking something out."

"With Gordon Pope?" he asked.

Dana stared at him. She knew she was going off the track again. She had no recourse.

"And I suppose you're not going to call this one in, either?" he asked.

"There's nothing to call in," she said. "The kid's been gone thirty minutes. Just checking up. That's all."

Dana could tell Marty didn't buy it. He was a lot brighter than he let on, not that she was exactly good at hiding things. He just shook his head, looking as though he wanted to say more, and she vaguely recalled wanting to ask him something, on a partner-to-partner level, before Gordon had called—something that felt important. But it had fled her mind when the phone rang.

"Are you with me?" she asked.

"Or what? I get left at the 7-Eleven for the night? I'm your partner, Dana." He plucked his hand from hers. "Like I could have kept you anyway," he said.

Dana backed up with force, the tires squealing faintly. The cashier inside looked up from his phone, his reaction time a full five seconds off.

"I'd just like to point out, though," Marty said, "for the next time you wonder why you're still bug-watching at the 7-Eleven parking lot, that while you may have a point of sorts vis-à-vis management at the department..." He was stumbling over his words, holding on to the *oh Jesus* handle above the window as Dana shifted into drive. "That at least *some* aspect of all this," he continued, "might be on *your* shoulders."

Dana smirked. That was about as antiauthoritarian as she'd heard Marty Cicero get in the eight months she'd been riding with him. She cut him off with a conciliatory raise of the hand. "Yeah, yeah. Buckle up."

She threw on the siren and peeled out onto the street.

CHAPTER THIRTEEN

Gordon Pope almost forgot to throw his car into park before jumping out into the Barrets' driveway. He had to skip back inside and jam the brake to keep the car from plowing through their garage. *Wonderful start. Why not just bring the whole house down?*

The neighbors were already skittish in the area. He could see dim lights and dark outlines behind ruffling curtains in the scattering of occupied houses around him. He'd told Dana to run interference with the cops, but he doubted even she could play gatekeeper for long if the neighbors got spooked.

Gordon trotted up to the front door. It was open a crack. He knocked once. It opened farther with his pressing.

"Hello?" he asked. "Mr. Barret?"

No answer. He walked inside. He stood in the small foyer of their ranch house. It looked quite similar to the Denbrooks' nearby, which he'd been tossed out of. Ethan's shoes were pushed haphazardly up against a shoe rack to his right. A small table stood to his left, strewn with mail. A leafed-through newspaper sat on a chair. A window AC unit sweated onto the windowsill, working overtime, still failing to beat the heat. The domestic trappings of the family home seemed so normal that, for a brief moment, Gordon thought maybe they'd found Ethan. Maybe the kid was just taking a long leak. Maybe he'd gone out to look at the stars and the fat orange moon. But Gordon knew better.

A strange murmuring sound came from around the corner, someone whispering in an unbroken string.

"Mr. Barret? Andrew? It's Gordon. Hello?"

No answer. Gordon walked inside. He'd watched the clock religiously on his drive over. Twenty-one minutes had passed between when Barret told him his son was gone and Gordon had shown up at his door—no time at all and an eternity all the same. Every situation had run through his head, from finding the boy asleep on the floor, to a bloodbath spreading over the tiles he walked on, to finding nobody at all. But he wasn't expecting murmuring.

Gordon turned the corner into the family room. It was a well-kept space, the type of place nobody ever went. It was just offset from the kitchen, where Gordon supposed most of the actual dining occurred. But it was here that he found Jane Barret.

He froze as soon as he saw her, and his mind stumbled over forming an apology at the intrusion, but she didn't even seem to notice him. She was on her knees on a small decorative pillow in front of what looked like an altar set flush against one corner of the room. A decorative sculpture of the Virgin Mary had been placed on a small desk there, surrounded by votive candles that put off a cloying vanilla scent. Different objects were scattered in front of the sculpture: a cup of wine, a gold medal on a blue ribbon that glinted in the firelight, a tattered leather bracelet, and a broken cell phone.

Gordon's first instinct was to back slowly out of the room, but then she spoke to him without breaking stride.

"I know you think me a fool, Dr. Pope," she said. "My husband does too."

Gordon nearly jumped. "I... I don't think anything, Mrs. Barret. I'm just trying to find Ethan."

"Ethan is gone. Andrew went after him."

"Where did they go?"

She stood from the pillow in a fluid motion. She took a votive candle in one hand and walked to Gordon. "Andrew thinks he's at the old theater. At the top of the hill. Ethan has always been drawn to it."

Gordon nodded and turned to go, but Jane grabbed his arm and turned him back around. Her eyes were wide and glassy, her makeup layered over dark bags beneath them. "Take this," she said. She poured a dollop of hot wax onto her fingers. It sluiced through and spattered red on the floor. Before Gordon could object, she swiped a cross on his forehead in wax.

Gordon tensed and blinked away the burn that she didn't seem to feel. He sensed her watching him for his reaction. "Okaaay" was the first thing out of his mouth.

"Save my son," she said, releasing him.

Gordon backed out of the house, nodding continually. Jane Barret watched him go to the door then turned back to the altar. Gordon flipped around and walked outside. He stood on the porch for a moment, wax on forehead, hands on hips, wondering what the hell had just happened. His first instinct was to wipe it all off, but he knew she was watching through the window. The medical professional in him scoffed at her. The frightened kid in him thought maybe it was best not to get cocky. He knew his mother would be appalled if she saw him. He could hear her now: *Act like a professional, for God's sake. You didn't go to fifteen years of medical school to have your face painted.* Which was another reason he kept the wax on as he took off at a run toward the upper neighborhood and the bleak skeleton of the half-restored theater that sat atop the hill there.

He followed the Chutes-and-Ladders path from before, starting with the sidewalk that led him past Erica Denbrook's house, but then he stopped. The milky moon was high in the sky, and most of the lights in the neighborhood were going off, but the lights were coming on in each of the rooms at the Denbrook house. He recognized Marcus Denbrook through a window. He was tearing through Erica's room. His voice was muffled as he threw open her small closet. He was speaking to his wife across the house. She was doing much the same thing, moving frantically from room to room, flicking on the lights. She moved to a window and looked out into the night, and for a moment, Gordon thought he'd been spotted, but whatever she was looking for she didn't find, and she turned away. Gordon knew then, recognized it in the frenzied, disbelieving look in her face, as if she'd just rebroken a bone in her body that she'd spent months nursing back to health, that Erica was missing again.

And Gordon had a very good idea of where Erica was.

If those dreams and those kids had taught him anything, it was never to discount coincidences. He turned to go down the first chute when a snippet of panicked conversation drifted through the window.

Marcus Denbrook said, "She's not here. I'm calling the police."

Gordon thought about barging in to hold them off. Maybe he could convince them to let him take care of things. He'd found their daughter once, and he could do it again. But then again, they most likely knew nothing about his involvement. For all they knew, Warren Duke had returned their daughter with the help of Officer Dana Frisco. Why wouldn't they call the police? What could he say to them? *"Your daughter is in danger of being swallowed up by her own brain. And she's most likely with Ethan, you know, the boy that tried to kill his friend Jimmy? The one you've been telling your daughter not to speak to? How do I know this? Glad you asked. I've been having a series of vivid dreams that I believe are connected to Ethan and your daughter and in which I spoke to the thing that is consuming them."*

What a wonderful conversation that would be. Very productive, shortly followed by Gordon asking, *"Who are those men in white, and why do they have a straitjacket?"*

No, he would have to leave the Denbrooks to Dana and pray that she could step in between the call and the dispatch. He felt a strange calm. He realized, to his amazement, that he had faith in Dana because Dana had faith in him.

He set off again, running as softly as he could in loafers and khakis toward the path that would take him up, up, up. Time was short, and he couldn't bear to let them down. Not Ethan, not Erica, and not Dana, either. Especially not Dana.

DANA CAUGHT the call just after Doreen—their dour dispatcher on duty—rolled off the address. The moment Doreen paused after the code, Dana chimed in.

"This is zero seven seven eight. We're out east already. We're on it."

"That was quick," Marty said acidly, but he left it at that.

Dana neither blared the sirens nor flashed her lights, ignoring Marty's brief but smoldering stare. She wanted to keep as low of a profile as possible. She knew the lights alone would bring out half the neighborhood... or half of whatever remained.

The place looked even more decrepit and shuttered than it had when they'd first visited only weeks earlier. The BPD was pushing a department-wide initiative called Broken Window Policing. The basic idea was that if a place looked like shit, it would attract crime. Fix up the windows, get rid of the dark alleys, whitewash the graffiti, and the theory was that less shady activity would occur. Dana didn't know about all that. In her experience, crime found a way, but as she drove up to Ethan Barret's house, her first thought was that maybe the policy had its merits. Tivoli Estates just felt bad. But fixing broken windows and power-cleaning a few fences was one thing. Fixing what was essentially an entire abandoned neighborhood was something else entirely, something the city of Baltimore had yet to figure out. An abandoned house couldn't be whitewashed.

"I knew something about that address was familiar," Marty said as Dana pulled onto Ethan's street. "It's the girl. Erica Denbrook. It's her house, not Ethan's."

Dana slowed the car to a stop and picked up her com. "Dispatch, this is zero seven seven eight. Say again on that Tivoli address?"

Doreen repeated the address, twice as droll. Marty was right. That was the girl's house. Again. Instantly, she knew the two were connected. The two kids used to play together. That they would go missing together made a macabre sort of sense. Marty picked up on her line of thought almost instantly.

"You're telling me both kids are gone?" he asked. He turned to look at Dana, and for the first time, his face showed open confusion. Not the rock-solid I'll-take-whatever-shit-this-city-can-throw-at-me look that rookie officers liked to affect. And she saw some fear there, too.

The man surprises at every turn. Dana opened her door and stood, settling her belt and gun. "C'mon. And let them do the talking. Say nothing about Ethan."

She knocked quickly on the door three times. McKayla and Marcus Denbrook opened the door as one. McKayla looked up at her, recognized her, and broke into tears at once.

"It's you! You can find her!" She grabbed Dana by the shoulder and started weeping.

Dana held her awkwardly, at a loss for words.

Marty stepped in. "Erica's missing again?"

Marcus nodded. His eyes were tired, his face sallow.

"No sign of break-in?"

Marcus shook his head. "It's just like last time," he said. "I thought it was maybe a one-time thing. The sleepwalking, I mean. I should have stayed up. I did, for two straight weeks. But I thought she was good. I thought she was all good." He seemed to be talking more to himself than to Marty.

"How long has she been gone?"

"An hour at most," Marcus said.

McKayla was still holding on to Dana for dear life.

"I went in to make sure she wasn't on her computer, like I always do," Marcus added. "She was gone."

Dana felt her phone buzzing in her pocket. She set McKayla standing again and took a step back while Marty jotted down information on his notepad.

"We'll start at the construction site where she was last," he said.

Dana pulled out her cell phone. The text was from Gordon Pope. *Theater. Top of hill. Meet you there.*

The theater was just past the construction site, along the same path. Dana considered that Erica might have been trying to get to the theater all along the first time and had just fallen into the construction site along the way. She touched Marty on the shoulder and nodded toward the door. "Mr. and Mrs. Denbrook, we have reason to believe that your daughter might be at the theater up top. Am I right in thinking that she occasionally went there?"

McKayla and Marcus gave her blank looks. Marcus shook his head. "That broken-down place? I don't think she's ever been there in her life. You think she might be there? Why?"

Never underestimate what your kid won't tell you.

"I need you both to stay here in case she comes back. It's important. We'll be in touch, okay? We're gonna find her." McKayla nodded while Marcus was apparently trying to reconcile that newest piece of information with what he knew of his daughter.

She pulled Marty out after her before either parent could think too much about her source of information.

"Top of the hill," she said. "C'mon."

She took off at a run. Marty was right behind.

BY THE TIME the hill leveled at the top, both Dana and Marty were huffing in the still air, their uniforms damp at the neck and drenched at the back. Behind them, the south end of Baltimore County glittered in spotty bits and pieces like bunches of glowing algae in a sea of black. In front of them stood the remnants of the Tivoli. It was a tattered patchwork quilt of a structure, a collection of several buildings that stretched back and out of sight down the far end of the slope. The original bones of the classic theater were still recognizable; extravagant concrete moldings turreted the top of the building, and old red brick ringed the bottom. The redeveloped accents and additions here and there—a big bay window on the second story, a large dome addition to the back—might have looked lovely, had they not been shattered and rotting. The whole place had been left for scrap, and when the scrap was stripped by tweekers, what remained was given to the birds. Dana would have liked a better look at the perimeter of the place, but as they stepped toward it, the one remaining streetlight in the area popped off as if to say, *"Forget it, cops."*

She thought Marty was reaching for his gun, but he clicked on his Maglite instead. Its beam was absurdly bright under the scattered cloud cover. "I don't know what the hell is going on here," he said, "but after this, if I never see this neighborhood again—or anyone in it —it'll be too soon. Understand?"

Dana heard the unspoken ultimatum in his words. Marty was saying, *"If this is how you're gonna operate, I'm out."* And she knew, also, that Gordon Pope was who Marty never wanted to see again. And she could have blown her top—railed at her rookie partner and told him to sack up and do his damn job, but she didn't have it in her. She felt sad and was surprised at the sadness, surprised at how it hit her. Forty-five minutes before, he'd been lightheartedly ribbing her about her choice of late-night dinner. Dana sensed a thunderhead on the horizon, one felt but not seen, and its looming silence was pulling the strings of her life until they were fraught with tension. One wrong step, one wrong word, and the strings would snap.

"All right, Marty. Just hang with me here, okay?"

Marty might have been expecting a lot of different responses from his partner, but not that. Dana knew it from his silence. Then he nodded. They walked toward the Tivoli, two sweeps of bright white in a sea of shadows and strangled moonlight.

"Gordon?" she called, tentatively at first, then full bore. "Gordon, where are you?"

No answer. A dog barked in staccato bursts somewhere below. She plucked out her cell phone. No service. *Naturally.* She wasn't surprised. The Tivoli felt like the kind of place that plucked every sort of call for help right out of the air. Nothing about this investigation came easy. The whole phenomenon, the sleepwalking, the dreams, it was all part of a thing buried deep. Digging was always hard work.

Getting inside the theater, at least, was not hard work. The front façade was entirely open air. Apparently, the plan had been to have big double doors flanked by bay windows, but none of it had materialized. Dana and Marty stepped over plywood and onto the trash-strewn concrete floor inside. *Better than rotted wood. Small miracles.*

Marty swept his flashlight from side to side, catching snippets of graffiti and the glitter of glass bottles and aluminum cans as he went. He lingered on a pile of rags in the corner for a moment. "Anyone here?" he asked, his voice booming.

Dana heard scurrying, then silence, then she heard Gordon's voice.

"Over here! Hurry!"

Both officers snapped their beams forward. The voice had come from the other side of the building, out of what was supposed to be the back doors. A courtyard was wedged there.

"Hello?" Dana asked, walking carefully but quickly through the bones of the theater out into the skeleton of a decrepit atrium. The plan might have been to cover it with a paned dome, but it, too, was unfinished and forgotten, stretched above them like a brittle honeycomb.

"Here!" Gordon cried, his voice coming from the courtyard's far side.

A dirt-strewn path led from where Dana and Marty stood down a shallow flight of stairs to a flat space that, in a better time, might have held a playground. Instead, it looked more like a massive, empty altar. Beyond that, the path reconvened near an exit tunnel. There she saw Gordon kneeling over what looked like a pile of clothes. Gordon waved them over. The clothes groaned. Dana took off at a run and spanned the atrium in moments. Gordon had his sleeves rolled up, his hands darkened with blood. He stepped back as they came. Dana bent down as Marty watched her back. The pile was Andrew Barret.

Dana dropped to one knee and checked his pulse, her light scanning him from head to toe. She didn't notice anything immediately wrong with him, and his heartbeat was steady, if a bit weak, but then she saw the dark red corona in the dirt under his head.

"Sir? Can you hear me? Hey, Mr. Barret. Andrew."

"He's been struck in the head," Gordon said.

His lips fluttered, but no sound came. Dana gently lifted his head and peered behind. A flap of scalp as wide as a baseball started to pull away from his skull at the back of his head. Marty saw it as soon as Dana did. He unbuttoned his uniform shirt and whipped it off then gently placed it under Barret's head, settling the flap just as Barret's eyes fluttered open... then closed.

"I found him like this. Maybe five minutes ago. I tried to call out," Gordon said, showing his mobile phone streaked with blood, as if he needed proof. "I got no service. And it's a shitty phone. So I've just been trying to talk to him."

"Mr. Barret, stay with me. You've got a concussion, buddy," Marty said. "You need to stay with me here." He rubbed Barret's sternum vigorously with the callous knuckles of his right hand.

Barret's eyes opened. He cried out and tried to move, but Marty's hand kept his head still.

"We're with the Baltimore Police," Marty said. "Can you tell me who did this to you?"

Barret's eyes were alert, but he kept his mouth closed.

"We're not here to arrest Ethan," Dana said, dropping all pretense. "We're here to help him. Did he do this to you?"

He looked into Dana's eyes for a moment then over at Gordon.

"It's okay, Mr. Barret. They're with me. Tell them what you told me."

"He hit me from behind with a rock," he whispered.

Dana could barely hear the man. "Ethan did? Sir, I need you to speak up. Stay alert, okay?"

Barret shook his head and winced sharply from the pain before Marty could brace him again. "Shhh," Barret said. "Be quiet, or he'll hear you."

Dana heard a heavy smack in the near distance and the scattered-sand sound of concrete chips falling from above. Both officers snapped their beams upward. Gordon crouched a little closer to Barret, as if to protect him. Dana found the brick, shattered and still dusting through the cold white of their flashlights. It had hit smack dab in the center of the open altar space. She traced her beam up to the top of the atrium, but it went through and out and caught only the scudding black clouds of the night sky. Had it been thrown?

"Ethan? Ethan it's me, Gordon. Why don't you come out, buddy?"

Silence. Gordon looked over at Dana and shook his head. Dana knew already, could tell by the flat tone of his voice that Gordon was under no illusions that the boy would walk back to them in his present state. If they wanted Ethan, they were going to have to go get him.

"Dana, I'm calling in an ambulance," Marty said. He glanced at Gordon, who was still scanning the broken ceiling. "I don't give a shit if it does mean the kid goes downriver. This man could die if he's not treated."

Dana almost argued, but she caught herself. When the medics arrived, they'd have to file a report, which might open up a case, which meant the jig was up. Marty was watching her carefully, and she knew he was testing her. He'd already said he was as much as gone after this case. Maybe how she answered would determine if he would be taking her down on his way up the ladder. How far was she really willing to go for the boy's sake? For Gordon's sake?

In the end, Gordon spoke up. "I'm not some sort of fanatic, Officer Cicero. I tried to call an ambulance myself before you arrived."

"What the hell is on your forehead?" Marty asked.

Gordon looked at him, puzzled, then seemed embarrassed and wiped at his brow. Dana looked closer. Dirt? A smudge? It looked like a cross.

"I'm not a fanatic," Gordon said again, less convincingly that time, still scrubbing.

Marty looked unconvinced. He pressed his com and calmly ordered an ambulance to the top of the Tivoli district.

Barret tugged at the crease of Dana's slacks. "He's in there still," he whispered while Marty gave details. "Through the tunnel. I heard him when I called. He cried at me."

Cried at me? The image gave her shivers. He wasn't just telling her. He was asking her. His eyes were pleading with her. His son had just brained him with a brick, but still he was pleading with her to help him. It brought tears to her eyes. If Chloe had been the one in there, Dana would do the same thing. Her daughter could literally shoot out both her knees and run off, and she'd still crawl after her.

Dana stood. She looked down the open tunnel in front of them, which appeared to lead to a second structure on the downward-facing side of the hill. It was as wide as a bus and sloped gently into darkness, wide enough to accommodate a crowd it would never see.

"Marty, stay with Mr. Barret," Dana said. "You too, Gordon. I'm going in after them." She hadn't forgotten about Erica, the little Houdini. She was in there too. Dana couldn't see the little girl's footprints this time, but she felt strongly that they crossed paths with Ethan's somewhere back there nonetheless.

"I'm coming with you," Gordon said at the same time as Marty. The men looked at each other.

"No way," Marty said. "No way am I letting you go in there alone. You're my partner."

She held up a hand and turned to Gordon first, only to find that he was already running toward the tunnel. "Gordon!" she called after him. She let her hand drop. "Shit." She turned to Marty.

"Are you serious with this guy?" Marty asked. "I mean, really? He's nuts, Dana. Nuts."

"He has a lot invested in this," Dana said. "But he cares about these kids. He really does."

"I know what you're gonna say. You're gonna say, 'Marty, I gotta go in after him. Marty, I gotta find them. Marty, I need you to stay here with Barret until the ambulance gets here.' Well, that's bullshit. Gordon Pope put himself where he is on his own. We should both stay right here. The kid can wait ten minutes."

Dana heard the slimmest crack in his voice and knew he was fighting to keep his composure. What he'd said to her back while they'd waited at the parking lot surfaced again in her mind. *That's not why I asked to be your partner.*

He'd asked because he cared for her. Maybe he was even falling for her.

She found tears in her own eyes and unabashedly blinked them away and down her face.

"Marty—" she started, not knowing how to follow up, not knowing if she could.

"No," he said, cutting her off. "No. Dana, I'm waiting until I know this man has the medical attention he needs. If you go in there without me, I'm walking up to Duke tomorrow and requesting a transfer." He looked away as he spoke. His voice was as quiet as she'd ever heard it.

Dana hung her head. "He's a brilliant man, Gordon Pope. He thinks he can save them. And I believe him because I think he has a bit of whatever insanity is going around already inside him, like a vaccine. It makes him do shit like that." She waved over at the tunnel through which Gordon had disappeared moments before. "But this isn't his pretty little sleep lab. This isn't his office stuffed full of books. This is real life, and the bricks are already flying—"

Marty shook his head like a dog pulling rope. "If you go through that tunnel without me, I'm going to Duke to—"

"He's gonna get himself killed," Dana said. She was horrified at how much she believed it.

"If you go through that tunnel—" Marty repeated, more loudly.

"This isn't about you, Marty!" she screamed.

Marty was silent. He held her gaze for a moment in which she was determined not to look away, then he dropped it, and she was ashamed. But she'd been crossing lines all day—for most of her life, really—and she wasn't going to pull back now.

"Call me on the com as soon as he's packed away," she said flatly. She couldn't even look at him. She knew how he was watching her. She was reminded of Chloe. Chloe hated vaccines, hated them more than anything on earth. It got so bad that Dana had to trick her to get to the doctor or else she'd work herself into a hyperventilating fit. One time, days before she would have had to delay starting first grade because she hadn't gotten a physician's approval, Dana resorted to saying they were going to McDonald's just to get her in the car. When she parked at the doctor's office, Chloe gave her a look. It was that look. That look was coming from a thirty-one-year-old man.

Dana couldn't deal with it. She took off into the downward-sloping darkness, and as she was engulfed, she understood a little bit of why Gordon had done the same.

Some things are better left unsaid.

CHAPTER FOURTEEN

A s Gordon ran down the tunnel, he thought how ironic it was that he was less afraid of whatever monster lay at the end of it than he was of whatever was going on behind him, between Cicero and Dana. He knew his presence had something to do with whatever beef was between the two officers, and he wasn't up for it—not right then. Better to turn tail and run. Not his finest moment, relationally speaking, he knew. But was running away from feeling things really cowardice if by running he actually was careening *toward* uncertain danger? Didn't the one cancel the other out? Wasn't there a case to be made for hightailing it? He'd have to run it by his mother. She had a good grasp of those things.

What awaited Gordon at the other end of the tunnel he could only describe as Chernobyl meets Barnum & Bailey. It was the lobby of the theater proper. The design committee for the Tivoli was clearly going for a vaudeville revival look: big marquee signs stuffed with lightbulbs the size of grapefruits, glittering mirrors, dramatic murals of exotic places, loud wallpapering in stripes of gold and black and red polka dots. The problem was that when vaudeville broke down, which it undoubtedly had, it left a funhouse-of-horror look.

Almost everything made of glass was shattered. The sharp moldings were either crumbling or never there to begin with. The wallpaper was molded and sagging. The murals were bloated with damp and chewed through in places. Gordon held up the weak light from his phone and panned the room, cursing himself for not thinking to bring a flashlight. The corners were still in darkness, but he couldn't see anyone. *This would make a prime crack den in a more lively area of the city.* But not at Tivoli Estates. Apparently, even the bums and the dealers didn't think the place worth their time.

Gordon heard the voices of Dana and Cicero behind him, yelling at each other, but he easily tuned that out. He'd had a lot of experience doing that as a kid. He thought he could hear something else... something softer but noticeable. He tilted his left ear forward. There it was again. A crying sound. It came from the back corner, an area that looked as though it was supposed to have been the ticket office. It'd been designed to look like a circus tent, set flush against the corner of the room. Two shattered windows gaped where pimply-faced teens might have sat, bored, punching tickets and giving change. An unfinished door led back behind. Creeper vines, the tough New England bastards that never went away, had come in through the unfinished ceiling and draped the ragged tenting like a frozen rain of green leaves.

The crying was coming from back there. He looked behind himself. Dana and Cicero were still going at it. He turned back to the ticket booth. Ethan's time was about up. He couldn't wait any longer. His shoes scraped on the debris as he walked forward, and the sound echoed like slips of sand down a canyon.

"Ethan?" he called, trying his best to sound conversational but failing. He coughed and tried not to think about the mountain of mold and asbestos he was most likely walking through. He peeked his head through the gaping ticket counter. Nobody. But the whimper was clearer there. It sounded distinctly like a girl's, too soft and high for Ethan, almost like a constant sigh. Between the rats' nests, he could see the outlines of two sets of footprints leading through the employee doorway at the back and into the darkness beyond. It looked an awful lot like a cave.

"Erica?" Gordon called.

The crying cut off abruptly, as surely as if someone had pressed pause on the girl. Gordon held up his cell phone and waved it around as if he was trying to catch a signal.

"Erica, honey, I'm over here. I'm here to help you, where are you?"

Silence.

Shit. Am I really gonna have to go back there? But even as he thought it, he was swinging around the outside of the ticket booth and walking through the doorway, generously overstepping the rats' nests until he was engulfed in darkness. No moonlight. No open sky. *Typical. The one part of this place they do finish is where we end up.*

When the light on Gordon's mobile doubled up and shone back on him in the form of another looming shadow, he nearly screamed. He clipped his shout to a yip as his brain registered his own reflection in front of him in a mirror, a big one. And not just one. As he panned the hallway, he saw it was lined with mirrors, many of them unbroken, resting at an angle against the walls, forgotten materials for construction. His dim light was reflected back at odd angles through the thick dust that coated each as he walked past.

His heart hammered so hard he was seeing the pulse of the veins at the back of his eyes. He nearly screamed a second time when he thought he felt a spider the size of his fist tickle the back of his head— or perhaps it was the first kiss of a brick from Ethan's hand. He swatted it away only to find his hand grasping a creeper vine. He yanked it out of frustration and heard an ominous tumbling sound. He scampered forward.

Gordon found himself in what he guessed was a storage room or, judging by the continuing echo, something more along the lines of a storage warehouse. An unholy storage warehouse. He pledged to himself that if he got out of there and somehow managed to get Ethan and Erica out too, he would stop bitching about the tax increases it would take to level all the shitholes in the city like the theater. Rip everything down and plant a whole mess of columbines or something. Gordon liked columbines.

He fully recognized that his brain was running at a breakneck pace to keep up with his racing heart. That was an old mental fail-safe Morty Gladwell had called "scattershot thinking." When the heart races, the mind often skips all over the place. That was some-times the precursor to a panic attack but also often the mechanism that kept the panic attack at bay. Gordon hoped for the latter. Dana was somewhere close behind, and the last thing he wanted was for her to find him crying right next to Erica.

He stopped. He could see the girl now... or at least what he hoped was her, a small bundle curled up on the floor near the center of the storage room. His low light picked up on the sparkles of her pink pajama top. He waved at her and saw his own reflection waving back again from the rear of the room. More mirrors. They were stacked side by side in front of a big, rotted canvas replica of a vaudeville playbill. It read OPENING IN PARIS! MILAN! MONACO! BALTIMORE!

Erica's face was streaked with tears and she held her arms around herself, but she no longer cried. She was staring right at Gordon.

"Erica, sweetheart, do you remember me? Are you hurt?"

Gordon started walking toward her but stopped when she held up one finger in front of her mouth. Her eyes grew wide with terror, and Gordon heard a strange pattering, fast, like many moths batting against a screen door at the same time, and before he could turn around, he was blindsided by pain. He staggered to the ground, too surprised even to cry out. His vision jarred, and after he felt the back of his head, his fingers came away wet and red. He heard another flurry of pattering, Gordon looked up again, still on his knees.

Ethan was standing with his legs spread over Erica, an old, rusted pipe in his hand. He was staring at Gordon, his lips pulled back from his teeth in a grimace. A low, constant growl came from somewhere within him. His face was streaked with dust, his hair white with it.

His hands were dark red with mud and blood, and his knees and feet were black with filth.

Gordon held out one hand to stop him, but the boy made no move to advance. He only watched Gordon, but not in any way Gordon had been watched before. The stare was purely analytical, weighing the cost of attacking again with the risk of getting captured or struck himself. He saw no recognition in Ethan's eyes—and not only of Gordon as his therapist but of Gordon as a human. Gordon hadn't realized just how much that spark of the eye meant, how much it softened a face, until he looked upon Ethan and found it missing.

"Ethan, it's me. You remember me? Gordon? Think, buddy. There's some part of you in there that knows this isn't right."

Gordon staggered to his feet again, which seemed to unnerve Ethan. He looked Gordon up and down as if sizing up his bulk, determining his threat level. He gripped the pipe again and tensed. Gordon realized the boy must be thinking he wanted to take Erica. More than that, to *claim* Erica. He was standing over her as though she was a possession he didn't want to lose. And in the next moment, he was running at Gordon again, pipe held above his head. He didn't growl or yell, and his odd silence made his charge all the more surreal and terrifying. It was business to him. He was eliminating a threat. Still shaky, Gordon shifted to try and take the blow and maybe catch the boy, but he was dizzy, and his neck was wet with blood. He held his hands up and winced, waiting for the pain, but Ethan stopped on a dime and jumped back, his eyes on the hallway behind Gordon.

"Don't move, Ethan," Dana said. She had her Taser out. The red button indicating a full charge glowed angrily in the darkness. Ethan didn't move, but Gordon didn't think that had anything to do with the Taser. He was simply reassessing. He looked back and forth between the two of them. On the ground, Erica saw Dana and did recognize her, and she started to cry, either from pain or relief or both, but when Ethan turned at the sound, she stifled it with her own fist.

Ethan backed up to stand over Erica again, watching them the whole time, but when he stopped over her, he also looked down at her and cocked his head. An awful thought struck Gordon. The way Ethan looked at Erica had a cold, zero-sum air to it. It was the look of someone who has been pushed to the ropes of a bridge, cornered with the loot—the jig is up, but there's still one option left: the nuclear option, taking the loot down with him.

"I don't want to tase him, Gordon," Dana said, her voice shaky. "But I will."

"It's okay," Gordon said, speaking as calmly as he was able. "I know. But not yet." Gordon understood her hesitation. He knew as well as she did that if the boy was hit by a Taser, it wouldn't go well for him. He was skinny to begin with, and his ordeal had hollowed him further. He was a reedy, feral husk of a boy, and Gordon had the distinct dread that fifty thousand volts at that particular moment stood a good chance of killing him. But he also knew Dana had a job to do, to protect the innocent, and if she had to make a choice between the two kids in front of them, one looked more innocent than the other.

Gordon's theory was that Ethan was living in a constant dream. He had a hunch that if the boy was hooked up to an EEG monitor, the readout would be deep delta. His mind had been denied REM for so long that it had settled into stage four functionally. The boy was sick, not a monster. He kept telling himself this in his mind, again and again, but doing so was getting harder, especially when the boy looked at Erica as he did, especially when he tightened his grip on the pipe. Ethan shifted his flat gaze to Dana, who Gordon realized was crying, yet somehow the red target dot stayed true on Ethan's chest.

And then the barest hint of hesitation crossed Ethan's brow. A tiny pinching of the eyes. Confusion. A distinctly human look.

"Wait, Dana," Gordon whispered. "Here, move slowly toward me."

Dana sidestepped toward Gordon, but Ethan didn't follow her. He still stared forward, past where she'd been, where his reflection was illuminated in the light from Dana's shoulder rig.

"He sees himself in the mirror," Gordon whispered. As soon as he spoke, his mind raced back to Gladwell's proseminar on "The Mind at Night."

Mirrors and dreams. They just don't mix.

They'd read a case study of a Vietnam veteran suffering from horrendous PTSD nightmares back when nobody knew what PTSD was. Gladwell himself wrote it. The man was terrified he'd fall into his nightmares at any second, so he kept cutting himself. He figured that pain was the only way he'd know for sure he wasn't dreaming. Gladwell had a better idea.

"Look in a mirror. If you see yourself clearly, you're awake. If it's hazy, murky, or swimming, you're dreaming."

The clarity of Ethan's reflection, of the boy that stared back at him, was throwing Ethan for a loop, making him realize he was in a real place, in real danger. Dana turned to follow his gaze. Her shoulder lamp lit up his reflection crystal clear, and Ethan staggered backward, along with his reflection.

"Ethan," Gordon said clearly. "Read the words on the canvas. Read them."

The faded marquee was just above the mirrors. And enough of Ethan had surfaced so that his eyes shifted to the words. His voice was weak, croaking—but he read. "Paris. Milan. Monaco... Baltimore."

He barely got the last word out before he dropped the pipe and then dropped to the ground like a stone.

Gordon stood in shock. Written words had the same effect as mirrors on the dreamer. He'd never been so happy in his life that he stayed awake for those first seminars.

Dana wasted no time getting to the kids. She knelt down, and Erica grabbed her around the neck, at the same time pushing feebly away from Ethan's body draped over her. Dana picked her up. The girl seemed all too ready to be carried, and she buried her head in Dana's shoulder, her nose pushing the com aside, tears cutting rivulets in the dirt on her face.

"Are you hurt, Erica?" Dana asked. "Did Ethan do anything to you?"

Erica coughed and responded, "He pushed me down. That's all."

"Did he bring you here?" Dana asked.

Erica shook her head, a small keening cry building itself in her chest.

"He didn't bring you here, Erica?" Dana asked again.

"I wake up here sometimes. But I always go back before Mom and Dad know."

Dana sagged a little at that, nodding. Gordon was relieved as well. Ethan hadn't physically stolen her away. That was something, at least. Gordon moved to Ethan and knelt down. He felt for a pulse and found it easily, hammering against the side of his neck, but his eyes were closed.

"Ethan," Gordon said clearly. No response. He pulled back the boy's eyelids and saw they were rolled back to the whites. "He did this before," Gordon said, turning to Dana. "It's whatever passes for sleep for him now, sort of an emergency shutdown. Last time he came out of it with some lucidity. I don't really want to wake him right now, not if I don't have to."

"We've got to get him out of here," Dana said. "Maybe we can still salvage this shitshow without writing him up for kidnapping and assault. Because this looks like kidnapping and assault, Gordon—even if she says she woke up here and all he did was push her down. There's no way around it. Not for a kid on ice this thin."

"I'll carry him. I had to practically slap him awake last time. He'll be fine. I mean, all things considered."

Dana shook her head, amazed. "That kid looked like he wanted to eat your neck five seconds ago. Now you want to carry him like a baby?"

"Well, yeah. How else should I carry him? Like a sack of potatoes? That's not good for his back."

"You are a piece of work, Pope. Get to it then."

Gordon gripped Ethan under the armpits and lifted him up then held him to his chest with one hand around his waist. The boy was terribly light. He didn't even stir. His head lolled onto Gordon's shoulders. Dana was already on her way out, her light bobbing steadily in front of him as he followed. He ducked under the dripping ivy and pivoted out of the ticket box, sweating a lot more than he was accustomed to. Ethan was breathing a mile a minute on his neck, which felt like getting blasted by a hairdryer.

They passed from the outer yard back under the bridge to the ill-fated atrium, and Gordon knew something was wrong. He could see the lights. When every streetlight is out for a block in every direction, swirling red and blue are hard to miss. Still, Gordon held out hope that the commotion was just the medical response to Andrew Barret.

Dana passed through the tunnel first, and when he followed, his heart sank. The only person not arrayed in a swirling arc of red and blue in front of him was Barret. His ride had come and gone, back to the hospital and, hopefully, to nothing more than a boatload of head staples. In his place were two more ambulances and the slowly mobilizing efforts of what he guessed, at first glance, were fifteen policemen. And one lieutenant, of course. One ever-present asshole of a lieutenant.

In front of him, Dana tromped to a halt and dropped her chin, her body sagging again, but not, Gordon guessed, from anything resembling relief. Not that time. Not as they were surrounded.

"Put the girl down, Dana," said one bull-necked officer.

Another tall cop didn't even give Gordon the courtesy, charging toward him with hands out. If a team of medics hadn't brushed their way past the police and taken custody of Ethan first, Gordon had no doubt the officer would have pulled the boy from him by force and then probably taken Gordon to the ground for good measure.

One of the medics that tended to Ethan, a young woman, looked Gordon in the eye and said, "We'll take care of him, Dr. Pope. I promise." Still, his hands had to be removed, and still, he gave Ethan up reluctantly, like a farmer carrying the best of his crop to town, only to be robbed on the road.

Dana didn't go so easily. She knew the officers personally. She spoke each of their names as they squared up to her, reaching for Erica.

"Don't touch me, Halloran. If you touch me, I'll break your goddamn arm. You too, Vick. Hey. Victor, yeah, Victor Garcia, I'm talking to you. You know me. Put your hands down. What are you gonna do with that Maglite? Huh? You gonna swipe at me, you chickenshit?"

Each of the men refused to meet her eye and then faltered. For a moment.

Then one young man, a big fellow with his hair buzzed within a centimeter of his head and his uniform still creased at the seams, grabbed her by the lapel and screamed, "Put her *down*, Frisco!"

Then others bucked up. Gordon could see it in their eyes. They wouldn't be outdone by the rookie. They moved in again, and the rookie gripped Dana harder, balling her uniform in his fist until Marty Cicero popped a clean hook right across his jaw. Then he was on the dirt and not moving.

"What the fuck is this?" Cicero asked, staring down at the man as if he was a drunk on the sidewalk, then addressing the rest of the policemen. "See, this is funny because for a second there, I thought you boys were treating my partner like a criminal. But I must have been mistaken, right?"

Cicero stared at each of them in turn. They backed up. Victor Garcia looked cagily back toward where Warren Duke was standing, holding back Erica's family. The fear in Garcia's eyes was clear.

"Right, Vick?" Cicero asked. "Am I right? Because if I'm right, then my hand sorta slipped there with Packman, and we can leave it at that. But if I'm not mistaken, then maybe my hand keeps slipping."

An older cop with thinning gray hair and a slight stoop stepped forward. "It's all right, Cicero. No harm, no foul." He looked down at Packman—who had rolled to his stomach and looked to be shaking some wits back into himself—as if the young officer was his neighbor's dog shitting in his yard. "We'll let Lieutenant Duke take care of

Officer Frisco and her friend. Meantime, let's run a preliminary sweep and button this up before even more press arrive. Chop chop."

The officers dispersed slowly. One shouldered into Gordon on purpose then held up his hands. "Sorry, guy." The older one stared Dana down as he passed her by.

For a moment, only Gordon, Cicero, and Dana remained with Erica. But the second team of medics was already moving in, flanked by Erica's parents. McKayla Denbrook was grasping for her child as if an imaginary rope could pull her more quickly to her side. Behind them all walked Warren Duke.

In the brief interim, Cicero turned to Dana. He looked furious. Gordon thought he looked even angrier at Dana than he did at Packman, who had to sit down about forty feet away and seemed to be rethinking his career. Cicero spoke quickly and quietly.

"I know you think this circus was me, that I called it in. I didn't. Maybe I should have, but I didn't. The Denbrooks lost it. Ran up here themselves. Woke the whole damn neighborhood. Someone called the cops—a couple of someones. There's only so much mess I can eat for you, Dana. Then it's *my* career on the line, *my* life you're fucking with, and I can't abide by that."

Dana's face slackened as surely as if she'd been punched in the gut.

"Keep it together in front of Duke," Cicero whispered. "You can sink your own ship if you want. Fine. Just do it away from me. If for no other reason than I put Packman on the ground for you, keep it together right now. We're in enough shit as it is."

Before Dana could muster a reply, the medics were there with a stretcher. The Denbrooks reached for Erica, her mother saying, "Baby, baby, baby" over and over again, and Dana let go. Only Erica didn't seem to want to let Dana go. The medics tried to take her, but she burrowed deeper into Dana's arms. It took her mother whispering and softly, shakily brushing her fingers through the girl's hair to get her even to look up. Warren Duke stood behind them, his hands clasped behind his back, the badge on his hip reflecting the flashes of red and blue. He looked annoyed with Erica's reluctance. Gordon had the feeling Duke was hoping the girl would spring from Dana's arms, screaming and pointing back at the three of them with confused horror. He got no such thing.

In fact, separating the girl from the woman who had twice come to her rescue proved so difficult that Duke stepped away, toward the medics who were still treating Ethan. He spoke with them briefly, and the young woman who addressed him responded as if confused. Duke spoke more forcefully, and the woman stepped back, her hands up. She shrugged and took out a four-point restraint rigging. The second medic prepped a shot that Gordon recognized as a quick-punch benzodiazepine.

"Whoa, whoa," Gordon said, stepping forward. "The boy is completely unconscious, deeply unconscious, and he will be for some time. Is that really necessary?"

He quickly regretted his words. Warren Duke turned toward him with barely veiled disgust. All he'd needed was an opening.

"Ah, yes. Mr. Pope. Here again."

"It's Dr. Pope, Lieutenant."

Duke nodded as if he could not care less while his tie, with its golden clip, stayed motionless. "I can't expect you to understand these things, no more than I could understand your..." He twirled his index finger while looking for the words. "Kiddie therapy or whatever it is you do. But this boy has proven to be a danger, and he is under arrest. Thus, the restraints."

Duke took the four-point rig from the medic himself and clipped them around Ethan's feet and wrists, looping the connector below the rolling gurney. He did it like an old pro. Ethan never moved, never gave any indication he felt a thing.

"The sedative there is in case he wakes up en route to the hospital and tries to kill any of these hardworking medics like he nearly did that poor Tanner boy. Or like he very nearly did to his poor girlfriend."

"He didn't try to kill Erica," Gordon stammered. "And he wasn't in his right mind when he attacked Jimmy Tanner."

Duke held up a hand and gave that same dismissive nod again, as if it was all the explanation he needed to offer. "They'll keep the restraints on and the sedative ready until the boy is safely in a holding cell at the city circuit courthouse. There he will stay until his appeal is... sorted out."

He might as well have said denied.

"You can't just take him like this. He's very sick."

"Mr. Pope, if I were you, I would be far less concerned with little Ethan here and far more concerned with yourself."

Duke turned toward Dana and Cicero. Erica had finally allowed her mother to take her and set her gently on her own gurney. The medics were smiling at her and trying to get her attention while they logged her vitals. Erica reached for Dana, and Dana almost reached back, but Cicero pressed gently on her shoulder and nodded toward Duke.

"Frisco, Cicero, get over here," Duke said.

Cicero led Dana over with a barely evident series of presses. Dana stared at Ethan, cuffed to the bed like a young Hannibal Lecter. She breathed carefully through her nose.

"Frisco, you're the superior officer here, so I'll ask you. You wanna tell me how you and Cicero showed up to this call well before your backup?"

Cicero started to speak, but Duke held up one finger and silenced him with a sharp stare. Then he settled back and looked at Dana.

"It was a non-violent disturbance call... sir," she added, as if she had to pull it from her own mouth. "I thought Cicero and I could handle it."

"It was a missing persons call—"

"Not even thirty minutes old, Lieutenant," Cicero said. "Book says check it out before calling in for—"

"*Fuck* what the book says." Duke leaned over at the waist directly into Cicero's face. "I *am* the book. And you both knew goddamn well what was happening here."

Dana started to speak up, but Duke held up a hand. For one terrible moment, Gordon thought he was going to slap her. But he wiped his lips instead.

"I don't want to hear it, Frisco. I've already called for a full internal review of this dispatch. Of this case. And of the two of you."

Duke dropped his hand and shook his head like a disappointed father. "I don't know what has gotten into you two. Frisco, I'm used to this bullshit from you, but Marty, I expected better. I don't know who pulled the strings here..." At that, he looked right at Gordon. "But I've got a guess. As to why? I cannot fathom."

He turned his back on them and walked past Ethan, trailing his hand on the metal rail of the gurney. His signet ring popped up and over each chain restraint.

"Sir, please. Marty had nothing to do with this," Dana said, calling after him.

"Both of you will cooperate fully with the investigation. They will take control of your desks tomorrow morning. As of now, you're on administrative leave."

He looked back at them out of the corner of his eye. "Paid, though. For the time being. So the three of you can enjoy a nice night out together. Maybe talk over your relationship. Because if internal affairs finds that either of you or your friend..." He pointed right at Gordon. "If *any* of you are found to have obstructed justice in any way, you two officers will be fired, and this clown is going to jail."

None of them had any response. Dana stared after Duke as if he'd taken her heart with him and still held it in his grip, trailing intermittent spatters of blood on the way to his black Suburban. Cicero dropped his head and propped his hands on his hips.

Gordon watched his patient, the patient that had brought him back to life even as his own hung in the balance, as he was carted away toward the ambulance. The medics pressed the rig slowly against the back of the vehicle, and the legs folded as the gurney slid inside. The medic that had spoken to him turned and saw him and must have understood something of the slow self-hatred he felt creeping across his face, his anger at his own failure. She gave him a sad smile. Then she slammed the doors shut, and Ethan was taken away from them in chains.

CHAPTER FIFTEEN

K aren Jefferson woke early. She always had, even when she was married to Gordon and lived in Baltimore, which she thought somehow seemed dreary even when the sky was crystal clear and the sun was shining. In San Diego, getting up with the sunrise was easy. She never wanted to miss a single one of them.

When Maggie had been born, her New Mom Circle told her to get ready for the frustration of sleepless nights and early mornings. She'd loved all of it, the sleepless nights and mornings both, because it gave her more time with Maggie.

Maggie was nearly four, and both she and Karen had fallen into a wonderful routine, one that got Karen up an hour before even Chad awoke. She used that time as her own with her little girl. She crept into her daughter's room while she still slept and carried her out to their living room, where she set her in her "happy corner" of their big sectional couch. She had her toys there and a second, identical version of her favorite blankie. She was soon fast asleep again, facing their big bay window with its view of the purpling Pacific Ocean. Then Karen poured herself a cup of steaming black coffee—just one —and either wrote, wrote, wrote, or revised, revised, revised while sitting on the couch next to her daughter. When she got stuck, she looked at Maggie, and her mind freed itself up again.

Lately, she had so much material already written that she was mostly doing revisions. She'd finished her largest research study four weeks before—two hundred days of intensive analysis of over one thousand children, aged five to twelve, who suffered from acute Obsessive Compulsive Disorder. Her theory was that OCD could be linked directly to what she called "achievement pressure," a term that was colloquially accepted but still hard to define medically. Karen believed she could define it as abnormal activity in the central amygdala of the developing brain and then link it directly to newly exhibited OCD symptoms.

The experiment was massive, one that required a detailed medical history and full workup for each child, along with an extensive OCD-barometer tool she'd developed herself along with three members of her UCSD team over the course of a year. That was the crown jewel of her Davis Grant, and it was going to make one hell of a journal article, but even if it didn't—though she knew it would—the Davis Foundation had already short-listed her for a continuation grant and a teaching position, should she want it.

She had her career, she had Chad, and best of all, she had Maggie. In short, Karen Jefferson hardly ever spared a thought for Gordon Pope any longer. Unless he called her. Which he did a little too frequently for her comfort and certainly too frequently for Chad's. But even when he did call, she was surprised by how *surprised* she was to be thinking about him. They'd been married for two years and engaged for two before that, and they had dated on and off for five years as they both went through school together. Shouldn't she be pining, even a little? Shouldn't she get annoyed at the things Chad did every now and then that Gordon had never done? Things like looking down his nose at her on the odd Tuesday when she decided to have another glass of wine. Or when he decided to eat nothing but blended kale and vitamin B for a week and then blended a week's supply of said kale at ten at night on Sunday when she was trying to put Maggie to bed. Shouldn't she have a wistful moment, at least?

Probably. Most women in her situation would. But not Karen. And she knew why. She'd thought she loved Gordon, once. She was wrong. She loved her child, a child that had been waiting to spring from within her and that Gordon could never do his part to bring forth. Her choice was black and white and couldn't have been easier. In her experience, when a choice was easy to make, she rarely revisited it.

No amount of subtle accusations or cold looks from their circle of Baltimore friends—truthfully, *her* circle of Baltimore friends that he also happened to inhabit alongside her—could persuade her otherwise. Not even Deborah, Gordon's mother, who was more of the overt-accusation type of woman, and for whom Karen still felt begrudging respect, could persuade her to stay. And she had tried. Then promptly sworn Deborah to secrecy about her trying.

The proof that Karen had made the right decision was there in front of her, sleeping soundly with her arms spread out above her head, her pony pajamas slightly askew.

Gordon and Deborah could say whatever they wanted about her. Gordon couldn't give her this. This moment. This feeling.

Gordon was a good man. They had been young and in what she liked to call "stupid love," but still, something might have come of it if Gordon wasn't sterile. Bottom line.

Maggie was waking up just then. That was a slow, droopy process that Karen loved watching. Maggie scratched at her mouth, changed her breathing, and rolled over on her side. Her eyes opened to slits then to half-moons. She stretched like a cat and smacked her mouth and then just lay there.

"Mommy," she said, smiling.

"Hi, honey. How'd you sleep?"

"I flew," Maggie said.

"Flew? Yeah?"

"Yeah. Jenny said she could fly in her dreams, and everyone called her a liar."

"Jenny Burgess? From school?" Karen asked, but her mind had already started to flit back to the spreadsheet she had open on the laptop in her lap.

"Yeah, they called Jenny a liar, but I didn't." Maggie rubbed at her eyes and looked out the window at the sunrise.

"That's good, honey," Karen said, somewhat absently. "You can't call people liars unless you know they're really liars." She highlighted a row and marked it red for *check source data*.

"So I tried and I tried to fly, and I couldn't for a long time. It was hard. I just couldn't do it. Like my head was..." She looked for the right word but couldn't find it. "My head said no."

Karen paused and looked at Maggie. "You had a lucid dream?"

Maggie was still looking out the window. She shrugged.

"Did you have a dream where you were flying? Or did you have a dream where you wanted to fly and then you flew?" Karen asked. She set her laptop on the coffee table.

"I dunno," Maggie said. "Both. But it took a long time. I had to practice. Like at my books. Because at first my head said no, you know?"

And that was when a thought occurred to Karen that brought her troubled ex-husband rocketing to the forefront of her brain so quickly that it startled her.

Maggie saw the change come over her mother's face, and she furrowed her small brow. "Mommy?" she asked.

"It's okay, honey," Karen said, her mind racing, her eyes unfocused. "You just gave Mommy an idea."

"What idea?"

Karen brushed Maggie's hair back gently with one hand while the girl dangled her legs over the couch. "An idea that you should have some breakfast. How 'bout it? Any cereal you want. Even the good kind because Daddy's still asleep and he'll never know. Sound good?"

Maggie smiled and hopped down to the carpet. She tiptoed to the pantry as quietly as she could. Karen stood and followed, but she paused at the edge of the coffee table, where her phone sat. She eyed it, thinking of her last clipped conversation with Gordon. God knew the poor man had his problems, but he had some good points too, especially that bit about the effect of rapidly changing sleeping conditions on a slowly evolving brain. That had been intriguing.

What the hell.

Then Karen Jefferson did a rare thing. She actually picked up her phone and called her ex-husband for once, instead of the other way around.

GORDON POPE TURNED his tumbler of scotch round and round on the table and stared absently at his Cobb salad. He'd very nearly slept through lunch. He'd considered bailing on it, but sitting around his apartment and staring at the wall was doing him no good either. He needed a distraction. From his job. From failing as Ethan's psychiatrist. From his life in general. Plus, his mother's drinking habits made him feel less guilty about having a scotch at eleven in the morning, and he'd never needed an eleven a.m. scotch so badly in his life.

"I don't think you've blinked since you sat down, Gordon," his mother said, eyeing him over a frosty martini glass.

"If I blink, I may fall asleep," Gordon said.

"Eat something."

"I'm not hungry, Mom. I just came for the scotch."

"And the company, of course," she said.

"Of course," Gordon replied, nodding wearily.

His mother stared down her nose at him, and he recognized the look. It was the one she used before giving Gordon a piece of her mind, the one she wore with one foot on the soapbox. Gordon stifled a sigh and tried to buck up. No need to ruin her day with his failures.

"I never said thank you for the lab time," he said. "It helped me to diagnose Ethan."

"You don't sound thrilled."

"I couldn't treat him in time. I was too late. He had another episode last night."

His mother set one manicured hand flat on the table, and her silver bracelets clinked gently. "Did he...?"

"He bonked his dad pretty good, but we were able to calm him before anything really terrible happened." Gordon tipped his drink back until the ice tapped his teeth. "I mean, nothing more terrible than him getting arrested after all and him being held at the court-house without bail until his appeal, which is in a week, which is essentially a formality now because it will be denied and he'll go to Ditchfield, where his life will become a living hell of four-point restraints, sedatives, and antipsychotics that he doesn't need and that will do him no good. So. Nothing more terrible than that. Oh, also, I may or may not be going to jail myself, depending on the results of an investigation into my involvement in this whole thing."

His mother drummed her nails on the wood. Gordon set his drink down with a smack that turned Caesar's head from where he was standing near the bar. He popped a questioning eyebrow, and Gordon nodded for another.

"Did you ever follow up with this Dana girl like you promised me?" she asked.

"Seriously? That's what you want to know? That's what's got you most concerned? Not the fact that Ethan is screwed? Or that I might be going to jail? Or that I have fifty messages on my machine, and I can't answer any of them?"

"So you *didn't* follow up with her. Like you promised."

Gordon held his head in his hands. Caesar gently slid a fresh scotch into his view and patted his shoulder lightly before sliding off. Gordon didn't even look up.

"I did," he said. "Even convinced her to help me with Ethan. Although it didn't take much convincing. She's a good person. So she was there. Front-row tickets to watch a psychiatrist fail his patient."

"Sounds to me like you saved the day. You de-escalated the child. You quite probably saved his life," she said.

Gordon couldn't help but notice she sounded an octave more chipper upon hearing the Dana news. His mother was a difficult woman in many ways, but in many others she was remarkably easy to please. He could be going to jail, but as long as he was dating some-one, that was okay in her book. Gordon took his glass and pressed it to the golf-ball-sized knot at the back of his head. He felt his long-simmering headache resurging.

"He's done for, Mom. Maybe it's good I can't have kids if this is what my help gets them."

Her right eyebrow arched so severely Gordon thought she might be able to chop his salad with a look. "First of all," she said, "I'm not going to dignify that with a response. Second of all, unless I'm much mistaken, you told me you still have a week."

"Mother—"

"You're my son, and you have a week."

"What's that supposed to mean?" Gordon asked but was distracted by a buzz in his pocket. He fished out his mobile phone, on its last gasp of juice. He'd forgotten to charge it when he'd passed out as soon as he got back from the Tivoli fiasco. He saw a missed call from Karen Jefferson, and she'd left a voicemail.

Gordon almost dropped the phone in shock.

"Is everything okay?" his mother asked, but Gordon was already listening to the message. "What did I tell you about those phones at the table?" she asked, but Gordon ignored her. She sat back with her martini, looking more intrigued now than angry.

"Gordon, it's Karen." She sounded perplexed, as if she was as surprised to be calling him as Gordon was to be listening to her voice-mail. "Listen, I was thinking about what you said last time you called, when you had to go. What you said about taking ownership of your subconscious. I don't want you to think that I was lying awake at night or anything, but... Maggie said something to me this morning. She said that she had a dream where she was flying, a lucid dream, although she can't know what that is. But what struck me was that she said she had to work for it. Now, I don't know if it means anything or if it'll do you any good, but I felt that I had to call you. Maybe there's something there. Maybe you ought to ask this Ethan kid if he's ever had a lucid dream. I dunno. Just thinking out loud. Wish I could be of more help."

Gordon stared at nothing. *Lucid dreams.* Most people lucked into one or two of them every now and then. They were very liberating. Gordon had had to deprive himself of REM and quite literally medically induce his last one, wherein he spoke to his child self in the cave. But before that? It had been years earlier, and it had involved sex. Most lucid dreams he had did those days. He'd been in a bit of a dry spell in real life, but on the rare occasion he was in control of his dreams... well. And that lucid dream had been with Karen, too. Some habits were hard to break.

So his last had been lab induced. But when had his first been? When he was very young, like Maggie? Or maybe Ethan's age? He couldn't remember. But what he did remember was a final paper he'd written years before for Gladwell. He'd sought to define the sensation that occasionally happens in dreams when one floats above one's own body. He'd submitted it and gotten a C minus. That he'd passed the class at all was more due to Gladwell's friendship with Gordon than anything, but that paper came back to him in a rush. In it, he'd done a study on disembodied dreaming that took into account dozens of documented doppelganger experiences where he'd found one common theme: When the subject was able to take ownership of the dream, the doppelganger experience ended, often with a violent, sucking sensation and a panicked awakening.

Taking ownership... What if that was the cure? And the only way Gordon knew of to take ownership of the Wild, Wild West that was the human subconscious, was through lucid dreaming. When he told his subconscious brain to do something, and it did it. If lucid dreaming could bring a floating brain back to a body, might it also piece Ethan's fragmented brain back together?

Gordon realized he'd been holding his silent phone to his ear for minutes. His mother had her arms crossed, waiting patiently with a droll look on her face.

"I have to go, Mom. I'm sorry. It's about Ethan."

She smirked, but it was a kind smirk. "What happened to 'He's done for'?"

"I... I dunno. Maybe there's one last bullet. But I gotta go now."

"Then go," she said. "Go, my son."

As Gordon passed from the pleasant music and temperate air of Waterstones out into the driving heat of late summer, he marveled not at Karen or at his own recall but at his mother. She never seemed to know when to quit.

And more often than not, she was right.

CHAPTER SIXTEEN

Ethan's dream of running free, of taking claim of what was his by strength, of rising to the top of his pack, was cut abruptly short. When he awoke, he was splayed out on a thin mattress, chained at his wrists and ankles to the short walls of his bed. He was not himself by any means, nor was he the thing he'd been the night before. That waking dream had fled, but another was already building in strength, and to Ethan, they were seamless. The night before, his vision had been entirely consumed by the Red. That morning, the Red was floating around the edges of his sight and his thoughts like a flitting shadow, but it was growing.

His first inclination was to lash out, to test the strength of his bonds, but as he tensed to snap, he heard voices. They were vaguely familiar. He stilled and feigned sleep.

"Of course I can," said one voice, coming nearer, already booming. "Check the ledger again. It's Thomas Brighton. B-R-I-G-H-T-O-N. Think illumination. Think awareness. I'm his attorney, Officer... Belmont is it? Where is Dana Frisco? She usually oversees this lockup. You know what? Never mind. Why would you know that?

You apparently are unclear about even the *basic tenets* of attorney-client privilege, which states that I should have been notified upon the boy's arrival as the appointed attorney in an ongoing case where my client is unable to act on his own behalf, which—"

Ethan could hear them right outside the bars.

"Good Christ. Is he in four-point restraints? Tell me he is not in four-point restraints."

"Lieutenant Duke made it very clear that the boy be kept under strict supervision."

"Oh, did he? Is that what Lieutenant Duke said? And I suppose that means 'chained like a dog' these days? My client must have resisted arrest then, to a violent degree. And you must have that on record. Or did Lieutenant Duke neglect to give that to you, to give to me?"

The officer cleared his throat.

"Give me the keys to the shackles. Despite what Lieutenant Duke thinks, in the eyes of the law, for at least the next week, Ethan Barret is still a twelve-year-old boy, not some sort of pig trussed up for slaughter."

Ethan heard a heavy sigh. "Fine. Here." A chime as the keys were thrown and caught. "But just you, not this guy. He's not any sort of lawyer."

"I should hope not. There are far too many of us in the world as it is. No, this is the boy's court-appointed psychiatrist. He will also be staying. If you have a problem with this, I suggest you find Lieutenant Duke, if you can pry him away from whatever press conference he's no doubt gargling salt water in preparation for."

The officer paused for a long moment. "Make it quick."

"We'll take as long as it takes," Brighton yelled after the man. Ethan could hear the slow, heavy steps of the officer receding down the hallway. Then silence.

"Is he out cold, or what?" Brighton asked.

Then a voice Ethan recognized. A friendly voice, one that awoke a calm part of his brain by nudging it ever so slightly. "I doubt it. I think he can hear us right now. He'd better be able to. If not, we're screwed."

Ethan snapped open his eyes. Both men were standing next to his bed, and both men jumped back a good foot, as if a mouse had scampered across their shoes.

"Gordon," Ethan said groggily, as if the name was mud in his mouth. And he winced because as he spoke, the Red perching at the edges of his vision screamed at him. He would have sworn the two men could hear it. They must have. But they were steady, peering down at him.

And Gordon was smiling. "Hi, Ethan," he said simply. "You remember me."

The Red receded, but it deepened, like a dug-in tick suffused with blood. Ethan knew it was furious, but it was also confident that it was going nowhere and that Ethan would exhaust himself again, and it would be waiting. Soon, he would live entirely within the Red. That's what it wanted. That's what Ethan wanted, too, when it had control of him.

"The keys," Gordon said.

Brighton looked at the keys in his hand and then handed them over, but with none of the bravado of before. "Are you sure this kid isn't going to... I dunno... go all silverback gorilla on us?"

"No, we've got a small window of time. He lives in a waking dream now, but it has stages just like any other. He's still in the dissociative part, stage one. But he won't be for long."

Brighton looked as though the medical description shot right over his head, but he couldn't care less. "You got that right. I filed a motion for dismissal and a few other tricks that'll keep them busy for a while but won't do any good, so I think you'll be able to work with him for a little bit, but they could yank us both at any time. Especially since you pissed off Duke. Everyone knows he's the prodigal son of the precinct." He looked at his watch, a big, glinting thing. "I gotta go. I got a hearing in twenty."

"Thomas, thank you."

"Don't go thanking me just yet. You owe me. And you might not be thanking me when I call your ass to the stand on the next whale of a case I get."

Brighton walked out of the cell then paused behind the bars. "Doc. Good luck, hey? This could be major for my career."

With that, he passed by and out of Ethan's view. Ethan snapped back to Gordon, watching him carefully.

Gordon moved to the restraints on Ethan's feet and clicked open the clasp there, threading the chain back through the cuffs until Ethan could freely move his feet. Then he moved to work on his hands, one at a time. The quietly screaming part of Ethan's brain told him the time had come to act, to overpower this man, to establish himself as above this man. But that part was still pushed aside for the time being. Instead, Ethan felt an odd fondness. The fact that Gordon seemed blindly to trust him when everyone else was afraid of him only strengthened the feeling.

"Why don't you try just sitting up, feet on the ground," Gordon said. "Gently."

Ethan pushed his feet over with a groan. He was sore everywhere. How had he gotten so sore? He put his feet on the ground and winced, seeing for the first time that they were covered in gauze. *This isn't real. This is a dream.* The Red in him grew.

"How do you feel, Ethan?" Gordon asked carefully.

"Like I'm sleeping," Ethan said.

"You're not. See that? What is that?" Gordon asked. He pointed through the bars at a wall clock the size of a dinner plate. It had two big black hands for the hours and minutes and a slowly ticking red second hand.

"It's a clock," Ethan said. His voice seemed far away, and his vision swam, but whether that was from this dream he thought he was having or from having sat up too quickly or from the mere fact that he could no longer place himself anywhere for sure, he couldn't tell.

"What time is it?" Gordon asked.

Ethan blinked, his head lolling about. It seemed heavy. He heard voices, strangely amplified.

"What time is it, Ethan?" Gordon asked, louder that time.

Ethan squinted. "Four fifteen." And just like that, the world snapped back into place. The Red faded to the edges again, where it pulsed angrily. He could see the veins of his eyes like tiny streaks of white lightning where it crept, but the rest of his vision cleared.

"That's right. Wanna know something funny about dreams? You can never tell time in dreams. Even if you're standing right in front of a clock, it never tells time. Look again."

Ethan did. "Four sixteen."

"That's how you know you're not dreaming. We're gonna use that test a lot, okay? In the work we have to do here."

"Where are my dad and mom?" Ethan asked. He felt as if he hadn't seen them in forever. The last time he'd seen his dad was... watching baseball, maybe? He had a vague memory of the drone of the play-by-play. As for his mom, he honestly couldn't remember.

"They're on their way here," Gordon said, but he looked away. Ethan knew he wasn't telling him everything. But then again, even if he did, Ethan had the feeling he wouldn't get it, the way a person waking up from a coma after a long time wouldn't get it if he was handed a cell phone.

"Where's my phone?" Ethan asked.

"You broke it," Gordon said. "You haven't been yourself lately."

That much Ethan knew for sure. He hadn't been right for quite some time. He remembered. He reached for the chain that had been around his ankles.

"You have to put these back on me," he said, feeling hot tears well in his eyes. "Forever. Understand?"

Gordon crouched down in front of Ethan so he could look up at him, and even though Ethan wanted to look away, he couldn't. Gordon's eyes kept following his.

"I'll put them back on you if you need it. But let me decide that, okay? And it won't be forever, buddy. Not if I have anything to say about it. And not if you work with me. If you work with me, there's a chance you might never feel like you need these again."

Ethan wiped away his tears with the shoulder of his shirt. "What do I need to do?"

Gordon sat next to Ethan on the cot and turned to him. "Have you ever been able to change a dream?"

"Change a dream?"

"Yeah, like, have you ever been dreaming and then realized you were dreaming and decided to change that dream up? Say, decide to fly or drive a racecar or talk to a pretty girl and be really good at it."

Ethan thought back. He recalled some times when he thought he might have realized he was dreaming, well before his long, waking nightmare fell over him, but as for changing it? Flying? He was pretty sure he'd remember something like that.

He shook his head. "I don't think so."

"I don't think so either. In fact, I'm about as sure as I can be that you've never had a lucid dream in your life. And we need to change that."

The Red twitched. It went the dark shade of heart's blood for a moment and tunneled his vision before receding. Ethan had to steady himself on the bed.

"You okay?" Gordon asked quietly.

Ethan found he was breathing heavily—panting, really. He had to force deep breaths to slow down his heart. He found his jaw clenched as well, grinding. He pried it open with effort.

"We don't have a lot of time," Ethan whispered.

"Story of my life," Gordon replied.

FOR THE NEXT FOUR HOURS, Ethan and Gordon played with a pencil.

Gordon started by dropping the lid to the open-air toilet in the corner of the cell with his shoe, and setting the pencil on the closed lid. He turned on his heel, walked back to the bed, and sat down next to Ethan. He wormed back on the bed until his back was against the wall and his legs kicked up. He motioned for Ethan to do the same. If anyone had come by, they'd have found a grown man and a young boy sitting on a prison bed, staring at a toilet.

"I don't get it," Ethan said.

"If we were in the lab, I'd have other tools, other things I could use to try and get you into a pattern of lucid dreaming. But we're not, so we gotta make do."

"With a pencil?"

"For the next thirty minutes, we're going to play a little game," Gordon said, setting his watch. "It's called 'Who can stare at the pencil the longest without blinking?' If I blink, you win the round. If you blink, I win the round. We'll keep score. For every round you win, I give you a buck."

"And every time I lose?" Ethan asked, a small smile on his chapped lips.

"You give me ten bucks."

"No way!" Ethan said and laughed once. The sound was so foreign to him that he was nearly startled.

"C'mon, I'm broke."

"A buck for a buck," Ethan said.

"Deal. Ready?"

Ethan set his hands on his thighs and got to staring as Gordon did the same to his left. "No cheating," Ethan said.

"I wouldn't dream of it," said Gordon, still as a statue. "Remember, stare at the pencil, okay? Not the toilet or the gross stains under the toilet or the wall or the gross stains on the wall—"

"I get it."

Ethan stared until his eyes watered, then he stared some more. He stared until he had to squinch up his mouth to keep from blinking, then he stared some more.

"Damn it, I blinked," said Gordon.

Ethan smiled and blinked and blinked and blinked. He still saw the pulsing Red at the edges of his vision, but he also saw an imprint of a bright white pencil on the inside of his eyelids.

"That's Ethan one, Gordon zilch."

"Nice," said Ethan.

"Again, ready?"

Ethan wiped the tears from his eyes and set his hands on his thighs. "You bet."

"Okay... go."

ETHAN COULDN'T REMEMBER the final score because at the end, a strange thing started happening to him. The pencil stopped being yellow and started becoming red. It stopped being a game, and Ethan started to focus on the bars of the cell. Then the bed. What was he doing here, again? And this man beside him... He knew the man, right? If not, if this man wasn't of his pack, wasn't under him, then he was against him, and Ethan needed to—

"Ethan, what time is it?" asked Gordon.

Ethan looked up at the clock, his face heavy, as if small weights hung from his cheeks. But he still saw the clock. He still saw the hands.

"It's four fifty-two," Ethan said.

The room popped back together. Gordon was looking carefully at him. After a moment, Gordon patted him on the back. "That's right, buddy. It's four fifty-two. And I owe you twenty-two bucks."

Ethan laughed weakly. They'd been playing a game. That was all.

Gordon stood up, walked over to the toilet, and picked up the pencil. He pulled a white piece of paper from his pocket and drew a big circle on it, then he propped it up against the low metal headboard of the cot, between the slack chains.

"I think we'd better stand up from here on out, okay, champ? You're getting a little tired."

Ethan nodded. He tried to shake the fuzz from his brain, and got it most of the way clear, but he noticed the Red had advanced. It no longer lingered in the periphery. It was pulsing in the side of his vision proper, pacing like a lion in a cage.

"Pencil," Gordon said. He tossed it to Ethan.

Ethan barely caught it.

"This is big money time. We're playing a fun little pastime I like to call Pencil Chuck. Every time you throw that pencil through the bull's-eye, you get five bucks. Every time I do, I get five bucks."

Ethan nodded.

"Thing is, you gotta stare at the pencil in your hands for thirty seconds before each throw. Got it? Them's the rules. You're up first. Start staring. I'll tell you when to throw."

Ethan liked that game. He pretended he was in a quick-draw competition—staring, staring, staring, then *snap*. He'd throw it like a ninja star. The first ten or so times each, neither of them got anywhere near the paper. Once, it nearly rolled outside the bars, but Gordon stopped it with his foot. Then, Ethan nailed the paper. It was a flat-sided strike, and it didn't go through, but he whooped anyway, and Gordon laughed. The next shot Gordon careened way high, hit the wall, and bounced under the cot. Ethan scrambled to grab it, barely noticing the pain from his bandaged feet, but once he was underneath, in the darkness, the Red surged within him. The smells and sounds of the holding cell assailed him. He could smell Gordon's sweat and his anxiety. He was putting on a good face, Ethan knew, but he was frightened. And frightened was weak.

"You okay down there, Ethan?" he asked. Gordon tapped his leg, and Ethan almost snapped at him. And Gordon knew it, too, because he withdrew. Ethan knew the man was wily. Ethan inched his way back out from under the bed, lying flat with his knees splayed, like a lizard. When he was backed out, he climbed up the bed until he was standing. Gordon was watching him carefully.

"What time is it, buddy?" Gordon asked.

Ethan looked at the clock. "Five fifty," he said, but his voice was flat and his eyes slits. The Red was expanding, as if it was taking in great big breaths and puffing itself out to cover everything in his brain. Very little of his vision was as it had been that morning. His memory of that time was distorted, as if he'd seen everything through rippled glass. The Red was so much clearer.

"A few more tosses then?" Gordon asked, his voice even. "I bet you could get up to fifty bucks."

Ethan nodded and held out his hand for the pencil.

"Stare at it for thirty seconds, now."

Ethan stared at it without moving, without blinking. Then he threw it right through the middle of the paper in one snapping motion.

Gordon looked at it for a second then turned to Ethan. "Nice work, my man," he said. But his voice was flat.

Ethan walked over to where the pencil lay and he picked it up. He walked back to the throw line.

"It's my turn," Gordon said, holding out his hand.

In a flash, Ethan struck at him with the sharpened point. He felt the pencil catch in Gordon's forearm, and he ripped down, nearly shuddering with the pleasure of the feeling. But then he stopped. He looked over at Gordon, who had jumped back and was holding his arm but, incredibly, had neither cried out nor fought back. He just watched.

"I'm sorry," a part of Ethan's brain said, some small part, getting smaller.

"One more time, Ethan," Gordon said, wincing, blood running down his arm.

"Okay," Ethan said slowly. He set his feet, rubbing the pencil until he felt it nearly splinter. Then he saw the target. It was red. He flicked out his hand, and the pencil ripped through the paper. Then he felt a ring of cold metal click shut around his ankle. He heard a clacking sound as it tightened, and Ethan turned to see Gordon stepping away, his face drawn.

Ethan growled at him. He tried to jump but fell face-first.

Gordon rushed in and then leaped back just as quickly because Ethan was already up again, kicking against the restraints. Heedless of his bandages. He could hear other noises from outside the cage. Yelling. Running.

"Remember the pencil, Ethan!" Gordon said.

Then the Red took Ethan under.

ETHAN WAS IN A STRUGGLE. He was caught like a coyote in a trap. He tried to gnaw his arm off, gnaw his leg off. He kicked and screamed until he couldn't any longer. Then he played possum, hoping to lure one of the men around him close, so that he could strike out with his teeth. Those men meant him harm. They were trying to dominate him, take his pack from him, take him under them, make him subservient. He would not allow it. He was stuck in their cage, in their cave, but that didn't mean he was theirs. Not yet.

But the men didn't get close. They were all wily, just like the bald one. Nobody came near his mouth, not until he felt a hot pricking sensation on his leg. Then his consciousness and his subconsciousness melted away. Then he remembered nothing.

Ethan awoke to a man speaking, a man he recognized again. Gordon Pope.

"None of this is gonna be worth a damn if they sedate him when he starts to go under. He needs to do things in his dream. He can't do things in his dream if he's in a medical blackout."

"I'm working on it, Pope." This from the other man, the slick man in the suit. "You never told me what a pain in the ass you were when I started billing you out for expert-witness jobs. You should have done that. It would have saved me one hell of a headache."

"We gotta stop the sedatives, Thomas. And I need a longer visitation."

"It wasn't the end of visiting hours that caused that circus last night. If I recall correctly, it was the boy trying to kill everyone."

"The cops were breathing down my neck the whole time. I saw them in the wings," said Gordon.

"I called in some favors. You'll have your time," Thomas said. He sounded weary.

Ethan wanted to see, but he also wanted them to keep talking. So he'd struck out at people? Tried to kill them? He remembered nothing properly after the staring game. Vague memories of throwing a pencil. Then the Red. He saw it now, and with his eyes closed, it was doubly apparent. It was halfway across his vision already and gaining ground. He hated it, but he loved it. He was torn. His brain felt creased in half, ready to rip. The Red was warm. Safe. Without a care for these people, he was free. More and more, it felt natural.

"He's very ill, Thomas. And we have very little time. Four days."

"That fact, and that fact alone, is why they keep letting you in here. If word got out that they refused a mentally ill boy his medical counsel on the eve of his parole, they'd all be strung up. So you got your time. What's left of it. Good luck, Pope."

The lawyer walked away. Ethan heard the tapping of his shiny shoes. The cell door closed, and someone grunted then clomped away. He heard Gordon shuffle in. Was that a sigh? He snapped open his eyes. He felt a strong urge to reach out to him, but when he did, he was cut short by the restraints. Gordon looked down at him, but Gordon was smiling, and Ethan could tell from Gordon's eyes that almost all of that smile was genuine while the rest was putting up a good front for his benefit. Then he saw the bandage on Gordon's forearm. He didn't remember doing it, but he knew he must have done it. That was his life now.

"I'm sorry," Ethan said.

"Forget about it," Gordon said. Then he pulled a pencil from his back pocket, the same in every respect to the one from the day before save one: it was unsharpened.

"What time is it, Ethan?" Gordon asked.

Ethan looked up at the clock. Saw the sweeping hand. Saw it true. "It's four fifteen."

"Good. Let's get after it."

GORDON'S VISIT on this second day seemed to Ethan like a living memory. He viewed it from afar even as it was happening. He was cold, distant, uninterested in the pencil or the games, but Gordon didn't care. Or at least, he acted as if he didn't care. He kept thrusting it into Ethan's hands. He kept a tally of numbers and dollars that was difficult for Ethan to understand now. They were trappings of a life he no longer cared to be a part of. Why had he ever cared? What mattered was freedom, and he was chained. If he ever hoped to get out and take charge of himself again, he would have to break everything: the bars, the doors, the people. Even Gordon. He would be easiest, Ethan knew, because Gordon felt a fondness for him. The Red said that fondness was weakness. The Red was right. It was as easy as that. The boy Ethan sank, and the Red rose.

The day ended the same as the one before, with Ethan in chains although this time, it came sooner. Ethan snapped the pencil, snapped it right in his fingers, like the delicate bone of a bird's wing. And just as soon, he felt the cold snap of the manacle around his leg. He lunged at Gordon, swiping at him with his fists and his free leg until he fell back on the bed. He cut his head and could smell the copper tang of blood stronger than anything else in the room. Stronger even than the rancid toilet.

Gordon rushed in to help him, and Ethan let him closer, closer, until he was within his grasp. Then he ripped at his face, his eyes. Gordon yelled and fell backward, away, but Ethan knew he'd hurt the man, and he laughed. Gordon was the agent of his capture, the reason he was caged. He was the one keeping him from his place with Erica. From his own cave. Gordon pushed himself against the far wall, but he reached out to Ethan as though he still wanted to be by his side. Why the persistence? Why did he care? Didn't he know how vulnerable this made him? How predictable?

Ethan heard commotion then. Noises. Others came permeated

with strong smells of alcohol and strange, unnaturally clean smells of bandages. Men that grabbed his free leg and both hands at once and chained him again. Then came one man with the strongest smell of all. Most of it was locked in a syringe, but some of it leaked from the razor point, dripping onto his hands. He gripped at Ethan's thigh, pinching a hunk of it between his thumb and forefinger.

"I certainly hope that is not what I think it is, good sir!" came a breathless voice, yelling but trying not to yell. A drowning part of Ethan's brain recognized the slick man. The lawyer.

The man who pinched him paused.

The lawyer waved a piece of paper around. "Because if it is, and you stick my client with that poison, you're gonna need a good lawyer yourself. May I give you my card?"

Ethan understood little. There was yelling, then whispering, and then, somehow, Gordon speaking to him.

"What time is it, buddy?" he asked. Ethan felt a drop of blood splatter from Gordon's face onto his own. It was warm and then quickly cold. Ethan turned toward the clock.

"It's..."

He looked at the sweeping hand, trying to see the numbers, but they were melting.

"It's..."

HE WAS BACK in his cave now. His own cave. The cave they'd ripped him from when he stood over Erica. The one he'd fought for. That he'd marked as his own. He remembered now. His Red memories opened like snap shades as his other memories closed. His body was chained, but here, he was free. He ran the perimeter of the mirrored room like a loping colt, stretching his legs and jumping. He stopped in front of one mirror and saw right through it. Not himself, of course, but what he was before he was forced to awaken into the world that had chained him. The mirror reflected a world where nothing that men built stood. Where there was no care in his mind but of survival and continuation. How freeing that was. How light he felt, staring into it. It was as it should be. He knew. Not least because it was dripping in red.

He would make his home here. With the mist. He would let it take him where it would. If chains were what awaited him moving forward, he wanted to fall backward. The mist seemed to understand this. It growled with pleasure and expanded around him, filling his mouth and his eyes and his nose. Ethan lay down in his cave and let it wash over him.

But something was wrong. Something was in his cave that shouldn't be. He sat up, breaking free of the red as he twitched left and right, looking for what did not belong. There, in the corner, propped up against a mirror.

Ethan stood. The mist protested, gripped him like tendrils of seaweed at the bottom of a lake, but it couldn't quite hold on to him, not yet. So Ethan walked. He stopped in front of the mirror. It still showed the red infinity, but Ethan didn't gaze into it again. He stooped down, crouched, to find his intruder. He grasped it in his hand.

It was a yellow number-two pencil.

Ethan looked back at the mirror, and he saw in its reflection a clock.

"FIVE FIFTEEN," said Ethan. "It's five fifteen." He felt outrageously weary, as if he'd been placed on a tilting table in the middle of an ocean. Stay awake and you can balance. You live. Fall asleep and you drown. Or perhaps he'd fallen off long ago and had been drowning this entire time.

Beyond the cell, underneath the clock, he saw his mother and father. His mother muttered prayers. His father had a bandage around his head, a bandage that Ethan knew hid his own handiwork.

"I'm sorry," he mumbled. That was all he seemed to say these days.

His father leaned in, gripping the bars.

"I'm sorry, Dad." He wasn't asking for forgiveness. Ethan knew now that he was beyond that. It was a goodbye. He had to stay away from them forever. He knew now that this was where he belonged. Alone and in a cage.

Except that he wasn't alone.

"You saw it," Gordon said, his face swimming into view, and he was smiling. "You saw the pencil. I heard you."

"It doesn't matter," Ethan said. "The Red is there. It's too strong. A pencil can't save me."

Gordon stood and walked over to his bed. He began undoing his shackles. "You're wrong, buddy. That's what you need to understand. Your Red, your mist, it's as strong as that pencil is. No stronger. The same brain that created that mist created the pencil. Get it?"

Ethan stretched his neck and turned back, only to find his parents had disappeared. He wondered if they had ever really been there. He shook his head. Gordon handed him a glass of water, and he drank it down in one go. "I don't get any of this," he said. His head throbbed. His vision was already clouded with red. His hands tensed. Part of him already itched to rip at Gordon where he was wounded. At his arm and at his face, which was striated with four raking scabs that he knew he'd given him.

Gordon knew it, too. Ethan could see in his eyes. But Gordon stood with him. That made no sense to Ethan. Any other creature would have put Ethan down long before or, at the very least, left him to die there in the cage. But not Gordon. It confused Ethan. It confused the Red.

Gordon chained him again, reluctantly. It must have been Ethan's eyes. He felt that they were red on the outside now as well as the inside, and maybe Gordon didn't want to take any chances. Ethan reached out to Gordon and pawed at him, gripping him. Gordon allowed it but pulled Ethan's hands away after he started squeezing, his fingers dimpling into the skin of Gordon's arm. Ethan felt an urge to keep him safe and to destroy him at the same time.

Gordon pushed him down on the bed. Slammed the pencil into his hand. Moved Ethan's head to stare at it. Held it there. Forced his eyes open until they swam with tears.

"Remember. The. Pencil."

ETHAN WAS BACK in his cave of mirrors. He was unsurprised. He transitioned seamlessly. It seemed to Ethan that he'd always been in this cave. The mirrors swam in red smoke. They reflected a host of seething images when he gazed into them as he walked his perimeter, but none of them were of Ethan himself. This didn't bother Ethan. All was as it should be. The cave shed everything from him that no longer mattered. The trappings of life sloughed off like dead skin. No need for any of them. All that mattered was ownership of this place. Of his cave. Of everything in it.

Except that damn pencil.

What *was* that pencil doing here? It felt out of place. Worse, it wouldn't go away, and every time he saw it, he felt he should do something with it.

It means nothing, said the Red. *It is of as little consequence as your things in the waking life.* And Ethan wanted to believe it. But he couldn't quite forget it. Something pricked at him.

The Red tried to cover it, to wipe it from the cave, to shroud it, but even underneath the mist, a glint of yellow could still be seen. It troubled Ethan.

It is a thing of the world you leave behind, said the Red. *Stop thinking of it as a pencil. Strip its name the way you have stripped the name of your mother and father. The way you stripped the girl's name when you took her. If you strip it, you can kill it.*

Yes. True. All good points. Ethan nodded. He even tried to forget it. He walked to the other end of the cave. He knelt in the mist, breathed it in and out, let it suffuse him.

But why was it here in the first place? The pencil?

Ethan stood, the mist falling from him.

What are you doing? asked the Red.

"This thing is out of place."

Don't touch it. Forget it, and it will go away.

Ethan tried to believe, but he couldn't. "It has to go," Ethan said, and he started to walk toward it.

And he awoke.

He sat up in his cot, and he saw Gordon. Gordon smiled at him. He crossed his arms the way he had the first time he met Ethan, when he was the only one who decided to help him.

"You did it," Gordon said. "You're free."

Gordon gestured around the cell, and Ethan found the cell door open. His father was behind it, on his knees, waiting for Ethan to come to him. His mother was there too, weeping with joy.

"Where is the pencil?" Ethan asked.

Gordon's face faltered. He blinked. And with his blink, a wisp of red leaked from his eyes. "There is no pencil anymore. Walk out and into your new life, Ethan. Take your place above your father. Take the girl as well. Everything you can take is yours now."

Ethan stood. There were no chains. His mother and father, smiling, prostrate with hands wide open, were also misting with red smoke. Ethan reached the cell bars and grasped them and they smoked in his hands. They felt more like sand than steel. He paused.

"I want the pencil," Ethan said.

Gordon screamed at him. It was an inhuman sound, and it took the shape of a plume of red mist as it came from his throat. Ethan saw why. The pencil was behind Gordon. Gordon wanted the pencil for himself.

"It's mine!" Ethan said, and he ran for it. Gordon exploded in a puff of red as Ethan reached through him to grab the pencil. But once it was in his hands, he had no idea why he wanted it so badly. It was just a pencil, after all. As for the rest of this place, it was mist. His life was mist now. He knew he could give the pencil back to the mist. It would take it, gladly. It snapped at it now. In the form of his parents, inching toward him on their knees with their hands out. In the form of Gordon, back together again, reaching for him. Smiling. Leaking red. It was all mist. Nothing more.

Except for this pencil. This pencil was something more. It meant something. Ethan looked from the pencil to his parents to Gordon and then, behind them, to the clock. It was four fifteen.

"See?" said Gordon. "The clock doesn't lie. Give me the pencil."

Ethan looked at the pencil. Then back at the clock.

It was midnight, on the dot. Ethan blinked. That was weird. He felt it important that he take a minute to think about the clock, but again Gordon was there, stepping in front of the clock. Ushering Ethan through the cage doors. Grasping for the pencil. Nodding eagerly, his eyes bright with mist. Gordon placed a hand on Ethan, and it felt as though it was fusing with him. A jolt of adrenaline pulsed through him. His vision darkened to a deep red, an ancient red.

Yes, said Gordon. *Yes.*

Ethan's heart raced. He felt himself grow stronger, more aware, as the connections of his frontal lobe, the noise that made everyday life every day, the noise that made life *life*, fell away from him. The connections between his parents, his friends, his house, his school, all started to break. He felt Gordon place a second smoking hand upon his shoulders, and it sank into him with the surety of a deep heat.

Yes, said Gordon. Although it wasn't Gordon anymore. Ethan cared less and less about Gordon. Less and less about the names and titles of anything. It was the Red that was sinking into Ethan now. And Ethan let it.

But now Ethan could clearly see the clock. And it no longer told time of any sort. That was not normal, was it? For a clock to tell two different times, and now to be a swirling fog of dripping numbers? Was that normal? And if not, what was happening?

The clock face dripped down the cell wall, and the numbers plopped in smoking red dollops right onto a bright-yellow number-two pencil. He'd thought it was in his hand, but the mist must have taken it. Everything around it was red, but nothing was red about the pencil. He remembered that pencil. How it felt, how it looked. He remembered it because...

Because he was supposed to.

Because he was dreaming right now.

The Red froze as if it physically felt when Ethan came to that conclusion. Its arms, wrapped partway around Ethan's brain, tensed. Waiting. Like an intruder in the corner of a dark room freezes when glanced at, in the hopes that the gaze will pass on, the door will close, and he can get back to work. But Ethan turned on the light.

"I'm dreaming," Ethan said.

I will not lose you, said the Red. *I have all the time in the world to claim you. Your waking mind will break soon enough.*

The cell began to melt after the fashion of the clock. Then his parents began to melt, like wax figures in the heat, smiling and prostrate all the while. Only the Red remained solid. Even the pencil began to melt. Even Ethan began to melt.

It's waking me up, thought Ethan. *It's kicking me out of my own dream.* And Ethan despaired. Because the Red was right. He was losing more and more of his waking mind with each moment his exhaustion deepened. If he left this dream, he might never understand when he inhabited another. His whole life would become one long, endless, red dream.

Unless he got that pencil. But it was behind the Red, and it was melting. It was almost gone, a puddle of yellow paint in his dreamscape of red, when one word struck him.

Spin.

Gordon's word. Not the red Gordon but the man who was trying to help him. The man who believed he could get better. So Ethan spun. He held out his arms and spun like a top, and at first, he tilted with the dreamscape, but then he righted himself. Faster and faster he spun, and the world around him pulled itself together like a centrifuge, filtering out the noise and returning the substance. His mother and father picked the pieces of themselves from the air and were patched together again. The clock ran back up the wall. The clock face still swam, but it swam with substance.

You can never tell time in a dream, thought Ethan. Gordon had told him that too. Ethan smiled now as he spun.

He smiled wider when he saw the pencil clump itself together, connecting to pieces of itself like yellow quicksilver until it stood practically shining yellow, right behind the Red.

But the Red glowered now. It seethed.

Come with me, child. I won't ask again, it said. *You want the world I offer. Of oblivion. Your connections to this life only bring you pain. When you don't know death, you cannot fear death. I am the beginning. I can spare you the end. You will never lose anyone if you never come to love anyone. Never know pain. Never know despair. You will be free. If you come with me.*

No fear would be nice. He'd been so afraid recently. And no loss? That would be nice, too. He knew these things came with growing up. He knew adults all dealt with fear in their own ways. His mom held on to faith. His dad held on to family.

But it would mean no Mom or Dad. No Erica. No Gordon.

"Give me the pencil," said Ethan.

The Red seethed in laughter.

"Give it to me!" Ethan commanded.

I will not. It is not mine to give.

No, of course it wasn't. That's because it was Ethan's to take. It was his dream. That was his Red. That was his pencil.

And just like that, the yellow number-two pencil was there in his hand. Ethan made it happen.

No! screamed the Red, and as it reached out to Ethan, a sucking sensation followed, pulling the Red back, vacuuming the mist from it in tendrils.

"My pencil. My dream," said Ethan, and with one sharp push of his thumb, he snapped the pencil in two. His dream world compressed, and his stomach dropped. The red mist was sucked entirely away, and Ethan found himself standing in front of himself.

Not himself shrouded in the red, just his own reflection. But he knew it was the boyhood version of himself, the part he'd just chosen to leave behind. The part attached to the beginning.

It held out its hand and smiled sheepishly. Ethan hesitated to take it.

The boy nodded understandingly. "You have made your choice. The Red has no power over you any longer."

"And you?"

"I am always a part of you, a reflection of your past, of the moment you chose to stop looking backward," it said. "But I am no longer you anymore."

Ethan tentatively reached out his hand, grasped its hand in his own, and with one final, ear-popping jolt, he shot up in his cot, in the Baltimore City Courthouse jail cell. He awoke so fiercely he jolted against his restraints, and he started to cry.

Only after his father placed his hand on Ethan's head and his mother grasped his sweating hands in her own was Ethan able to slow his hammering heart. He met both of their eyes, and what they saw there must have been good because they started to tear up as well. Then he searched the room for Gordon. He found the man standing away and behind them, peering around his dad, his hands balled into tense fists.

"I found the pencil," Ethan said. "And I took it."

Gordon wiped at his own face. He seemed to know already, and he nodded. "Yes, you did."

"And you told me to spin."

"You heard that?"

Ethan nodded. "It fought back. It wanted to break the dream. So I spun it back together."

Gordon nodded vigorously, tears streaming down his face.

"Why is everyone crying?" Ethan asked.

"Your eyes, buddy. They're as blue as the sky."

Gordon moved from legs to wrists and clicked open all the restraints. "I don't think you'll be needing these ever again," he said.

Then he rubbed at his face, checked his pockets for his things, grabbed his pad and pencil, and turned to go.

"W-wait!" Ethan cried. "Where are you going?"

"To get some coffee. And then some more coffee. You're better, Ethan, but you're still in jail." He checked his watch. "I got about eight hours to write down the plan of care I have for you that's gonna get you out."

CHAPTER SEVENTEEN

ONE MONTH LATER

Gordon arrived at lunch to find his mother smiling and waving. She motioned him back to the patio, martini in one hand, and Gordon watched as she nearly dumped it when she saw he was not alone. Gordon cringed a little, his palms sweaty. He let go of Dana's hand and wiped his own off on his slacks.

"Gordon, it's okay. She's your mother. This isn't a job interview," said Dana.

"There is a way we could do this, you know, without you ever having to meet my mother. It would take some scheduling, but—"

"Gordon. Stop it. It's gonna be okay."

His mother still stood, her slender, jeweled hand pressed lightly to her chest. She looked from Gordon to Dana and back at Gordon, as if he had grown horns.

Gordon cleared his throat. "Mom, this is Dana Frisco, the woman I've been telling you about."

His mother stared but smiled so widely that it jangled her earrings.

"Well, how about that. He wasn't lying," she said, extending her hand. "Praise the Lord. Dana, I'm Deborah Pope."

"Nice to meet you. Your son talks a lot about you," Dana said, smiling warmly. "It's obvious you mean a lot to him."

"Oh, phooey," his mother said, waving her words off and basking in them at the same time. Then she turned squarely to face her. "You know he's sterile, right? Medically. His testicles don't work right."

"Jesus, Mom. Can we at least sit down first?"

Dana reddened but didn't flinch. Gordon thought he saw the subtle upturn of a smile at the side of her lips.

"Yes, I do," she said.

"Good, because the last woman he was with couldn't deal with it. She was a bit of a bitch. Brilliant woman, but a bit of a bitch."

"Mom, enough. Caesar!" Gordon looked around, calling out desperately. "Drinks! More drinks. Please and thank you."

The three of them sat. Dana gave Gordon a look of complete understanding that settled him, a look he was increasingly falling in love with. The look said she got it.

"Gordon has told me," Dana said, "about his condition and his ex-wife. So we're all square there," she leaned in to his mother conspiratorially. "I already have one beautiful little girl. And one is plenty for me."

His mother leaned in to meet her. "Tell me about it," she said, nodding her head toward Gordon. "He's my one. He was plenty. Still is."

That settled, both women leaned back out. Gordon looked between them as if he'd seen dogs and cats curl up next to each other.

"I like her," his mother said. "Let's eat."

HIS MOTHER and Dana talked comfortably for the rest of the meal. His mother was engrossed in Dana's recollection of how they met, a story Gordon had told her himself several times, but she was riveted nonetheless. She even forgot about her martini for a bit. Gordon piped in every now and then, adding details from when Dana couldn't be there, like in the cell with Ethan.

The truth, however, was that the battle, such as it was, had taken part in Ethan's brain. He'd spoken to the boy about what he'd seen and done and so had a picture of it, but from Gordon's perspective, he'd sat watch over a tossing and turning and gnashing and growling young boy for three days and nights. He'd played games with him when he could and kept him safe when he couldn't. He'd told him to spin when Ethan started to mumble that the dream was collapsing. Spinning was another old Gladwell trick. He'd had no idea if the boy could hear him, or if he could help, but all he knew was that Ethan was thrashing one moment then sitting up the next, the red having fled from his eyes. Gordon knew in an instant Ethan had beaten it.

Gordon explained that after the ordeal in the cell, he went home and sat down in front of his computer. He spent the next six hours writing nonstop. He needed an official definition for the affliction. "Scary Mist Monster" wouldn't fly. Not even "The Red" was up to standards. What Gordon ultimately settled on sounded like it read right off a prescription bottle. Ethan had suffered from "cerebral self-aversion," an autoscopic phenomenon that manifested itself in a child's prepubescent years. Preliminary signs included violent para-somnia, particularly of a kind that involved sleepwalking.

Its root cause was as yet undefined, but Gordon laid out what he thought was a very compelling case that pointed toward radically disturbed sleep patterns in the modern era. Light pollution and noise pollution levels were drastically different from those under which the human brain had initially developed, and continuous neural bombardment by said pollution was the likely perpetrator. Not only were children not developing under "normal" sleeping conditions, but our society had changed to such a degree, and so quickly, that "normal" sleeping conditions were unattainable, perhaps gone forever.

In short, modern children were not developing their subconscious properly because what they thought was sleep wasn't sleep, not in the sense that humanity's ancestors knew it.

Gordon found the hypothesis compelling enough to include it.

That wasn't necessary for a plan of care, but it did give his case more presence. Karen agreed. She said so after he shared his outline with her and gave her a brief rundown of what had happened in the cell.

As for the cure? Lucid dreaming, which was simple enough in theory but a good deal more difficult in practice, as he'd found out. He could only speak to his experience with Ethan, but he outlined his yellow-pencil technique in detail. He called it a "carry-through symbol."

"A yellow pencil, huh?" Karen had said. "Very clever. Another Gladwell trick, perhaps? You always loved that old coot."

Gordon smiled then because that hadn't been Gladwell's at all, actually. When he was struggling to come up with a symbol Ethan might be able to carry through into his dreams, he remembered one late night in college when he and his roommate had played Tetris for almost six hours straight. That night, he'd dreamed of dodging a nonstop array of falling Tetris blocks.

The good news was that once the carry-through symbol appeared and the subject was able to actualize a lucid dream, the disorder had apparently disappeared completely. Poof. The Red was blown away. After that night, Ethan slept for twelve straight hours like a dead man, and his parents said that his eyes were flitting all over the place under their lids. Although he didn't have the machinery to guarantee it, Gordon was certain Ethan had finally fallen into REM sleep, working to balance a dreadfully empty bank and succeeding.

Since then, Ethan hadn't had any further parasomnia occurrences. His symptoms stopped just as Gordon's own had, years before. The difference was like night and day. He had normal dreams with normal themes thereafter. The Red was gone.

The plan of care he'd dumped on Thomas Brighton's desk fifteen minutes before the appeal was hasty, full of spelling and punctuation errors, badly formatted, and poorly footnoted. However, it had been peer reviewed, more or less, by Karen Jefferson herself, and she found it held water. Gordon believed in it wholeheartedly. Brighton seemed to have expected it. He looked down at it, shuffled through some of the papers, returned them to Gordon, and dusted his hands.

"Can you take the stand?" he'd asked.

"You better believe it."

ETHAN'S SENTENCE was reduced to six months of probation, and he was court ordered to submit to psychological evaluation once a month for the next year, after which the entire affair would be expunged from his record. The opposing council was stunned, not at the over-turning but at the revelation of the nature of the disease. Jimmy Tanner's father even came over to Ethan and wished him luck in his treatment. He said that Jimmy had woken up a week before and was recovering at home. He suggested that the best thing for everyone would be to close this dark chapter and go their separate ways. Andrew Barret hugged Gordon right there in the courtroom. Jane Barret flashed him a knowing smile, as if she'd always known the Big Guy Upstairs would come through in the end, and all He'd needed was a man like Gordon working on His behalf.

Ethan wept with joy when he heard the verdict. Gordon would have also, if he weren't focused as intently as he was on simply staying upright.

HIS MOTHER MARVELED at the story. With Dana to help tell it, it sounded remarkable even to Gordon, more the type of thing a spy or a mad scientist would go through, not a scruffy psychiatrist. Without her, he knew he'd be knocking on Thomas Brighton's door right now, begging for work, not filling his planner with consultations and appointments. Dana, who kept one hand resting lightly on his leg while she spoke to his mother. Dana, who didn't think he was nuts. Who never had, even from the very beginning. Dana, who had brought the entire Ethan Barret story to her plucky contact at the *Tribune* and then taken the ensuing article to Warren Duke's desk.

The way she told it, Duke's eyes practically crackled with fire and brimstone, and a purple vein pulsed at his tanned temple, but he smiled and politely congratulated her because the captain of police had caught wind of what had happened in Duke's department and had called him a day earlier. He'd suggested Marty Cicero be put up for a commendation and said that since Officer Dana Frisco seemed so good with kids, maybe they ought to put her in for one of the detective slots that would be coming up in the new unit, the one the mayor had suggested after all the sleepwalking hubbub. They were planning on calling it the CPI unit, for Child Protective Investigations.

Dana said Duke had told her all that through gritted teeth, then shook her hand limply. Outside, Marty Cicero was waiting by her car. She told him he was going to get a commendation, but he shook his head and said he didn't deserve it. What he really wanted to know was if she was getting a new partner since she was going to be a big-shot detective.

"They let me choose," she said. At that, Cicero nodded his head. He turned to leave, but she stopped him. "And I asked for you, Marty."

Dana said the big man had teared up then. He had shaken her hand and held it and looked as though he wanted to say something more, but all that came out was "I'm sorry."

Dana told him to shut that crap down right that instant. He was right to call her out when she was out of line. She hoped he would again in the future because she didn't doubt the day would come around again.

"One of us has to keep the both of us alive," Dana said.

Gordon had the feeling that she was leaving something out, something about the moment the three of them had outside of the tunnel. Gordon suspected Cicero had other reasons for wanting to be Dana's partner, not all of them professional. He liked Cicero, even if Cicero didn't like him. He thought Cicero was good for Dana. Still, Gordon envisioned a storm in the distance on that front, but a storm for another day.

Over the last of their Cobb salads, Gordon told his mother and Dana how Ethan had visited him earlier that week for the first time since the appeal. The boy that he saw was nothing like the one he'd treated four weeks before. Compared to the new Ethan, the pallid, frightened Ethan that Gordon remembered from the cell was nothing but a shade. A shadow of a memory. More like the mist he'd chased away than anything. The new Ethan's smile, along with the way he hugged Gordon, was weighty. It had heart.

Ethan had said he'd told Erica about the pencil, and she'd found it herself not long after. They were hanging out again. Both of their parents were there the whole time, but they were together again. Bit by bit, things were getting back to normal. And then he gave Gordon a pencil of his own, a bright-yellow number two with the words *World's Best Doc* engraved on it. Gordon kept it balanced carefully on the top of his computer monitor, where he could see it every day.

Since that visit, he hadn't heard from Ethan. He doubted he would until Gordon evaluated him for his next monthly review. Then Gordon guessed there would be more radio silence until the next. After a year, it was Gordon's strong hope that he'd never see Ethan again. That would mean he was healthy, and Gordon believed the boy was indeed healthy.

"So that's that," Gordon said, as Caesar cleared their plates.

His mother sat back and took a sip of her martini, cooled in a frosty new glass. She appraised both Dana and Gordon. "My son once told me that if he couldn't save that young boy, if he let him down, then maybe it was good that he couldn't have a child." She looked pointedly at Gordon, who looked down and spun his cocktail tumbler slowly. "He seemed to think that he didn't deserve a child."

Dana squeezed his leg.

"What I believe," she continued, "and what I should have told him then but didn't, was that I think the reason he is not able to have a child, unable to care for his own child, is because he was meant to care for hundreds. For thousands."

Gordon looked up when he heard her voice break slightly. His mother was a loving woman, but she wasn't exactly *caring*. Gordon believed that was perhaps the most heartfelt thing he'd heard her say.

Then she waved her words away and finished her drink. "That's what I think, anyway." she said, as if she'd been speaking of nothing more than when the leaves would change color.

"Me too, Deborah," Dana said, squeezing his knee again. "Me too."

THAT NIGHT, Gordon Pope put the finishing touches on his journal article. It was titled "Violent Parasomnia and the Preteen Cognitive State," and it was based largely around Ethan's plan of care. He'd already submitted the abstract to several journals. The Johns Hopkins University Press had picked it up in short order and slated it for publication in the journal *Philosophy, Psychiatry, and Psychology*. He hadn't told anyone other than his mother, who promptly asked him why he hadn't waited to hear back from the *New England Journal of Medicine* first but then congratulated him nonetheless with a big kiss on the cheek and another round of drinks. He wanted to see it in print first, to really know it was there, with his name on it, before he told Dana. Part of him still believed it didn't exist. He'd stared too long at a blank screen, deleted too many words, and crumpled up too many outlines in disgust over the years. But that was before he'd stumbled into a court case involving a troubled young boy, looked in his eyes, and seen a bit of himself where everyone else had seen a monster.

He printed out the final draft then e-mailed the digital copy to the *PPP* editorial board and sat back in his chair, threading his hands behind his head. He hoped others would be able to see the warning signs in their own young patients and craft similar plans of care. Maybe those kids could start to sleep soundly again.

Because he had messages.

Oh boy, did he ever have messages. He was booked solid for the next two months. He actually had to go out and get a new kids' chair and a couple of new pairs of pants. He realized how unemployed he looked when he'd gone through his closet the week before and thrown out everything over five years old and found he had nothing left.

He'd also finally been able to replenish his scotch collection. Or lack of a collection. He had a nice array. Nothing crazy. He wasn't a huge fan of the expensive stuff. A simple, good old-fashioned sipping blend had always set him right. He poured himself one then, a cele-bratory dram, as he pressed the play button on his simple, good old-fashioned message machine. He sat back down and took out his pad to write down numbers.

Three messages awaited him that time, two from Baltimore residents. They'd heard about the Ethan Barret case. They were desper-ate. He'd call them back. Gordon lifted his tumbler for a big tipple when his business line actually rang. He decided against answering. They could leave a message too. That day was for relaxing. For cele-brating. The machine picked it up, and Gordon took a sip as it recorded then started to play on delay. When he heard it, he paused with the glass to his lips.

The caller was a woman, and her voice had that strange, high-pitched timbre that only came out when someone was fighting to keep their voice in control, to hide how frightened they actually were. He knew that tone well. He'd been speaking with it for some time, up until recently.

"Dr. Pope? Are you there?"

Gordon paused. She was waiting for him to answer still.

"No? Please. I know you're extraordinarily busy, but if you're there, please pick up."

Still Gordon paused. He had the distinct feeling that if he picked up that phone, it might flip the switch that shifted the train track of his life. He'd only recently hit a straightaway, one that promised easy work, decent money, and modest rewards. The Ethan Barret case was a once-in-a-lifetime thing for a psychiatrist. Something you could coast a career out of. Gordon had to understand that. Didn't he?

He was at the phone in the blink of an eye. "This is Gordon Pope."

The woman let out a gasp of either shock or relief. "Thank you so much for picking up."

"What can I do for you?"

"It's not me, it's my daughter."

"Is she sleepwalking?" Gordon brought his pen to his pad again. He was almost relieved. He wasn't quite sure what had first spooked him about the call—maybe the way she had sounded initially on his machine, that was all.

"No, no. She sleeps just fine."

Gordon stopped writing on his pad.

"Well, then what... what's wrong?" It sounded harsh, but he was caught off guard. He knew he shouldn't be. Sleepwalking wasn't the only thing afflicting kids, after all. Maybe she had an anger issue. Maybe she was OCD. Maybe she was getting things pierced and wearing too much black for her mother's taste. It could be any number of those completely ordinary, completely explainable things. The straightaway tracks.

"It's hard to explain." She laughed, high and nervous. "To be honest, I don't think you'd believe me if I told you."

No straightaway then, it would seem.

"You'd be surprised at the things I would believe," Gordon said.

"I know. I've heard. That's why I called you. It's just that... Listen, I'm staying at the Marriott on Center Street in town. Both of us are. I was really hoping you might just be able to come over and see for yourself."

Gordon found himself caught in a moment in time that seemed heavy, thick with portents. Another turning point. He'd picked up the phone and started the fuse, but all he had to do was set it down again to tamp it out. Straight and narrow. Decent income. Modest recognition. Pleasant life. He finally had a girlfriend, for God's sake.

And what would Dana say about this?

"When can I see her?" Gordon asked.

She thanked him again and again. She gave him her number and told him she'd meet him in the lobby. Gordon wrote it down and hung up, and all of a sudden, the fuse was burning bright. Snaking into the unknown. He looked at his scotch, still on his desk. He took it to the sink and dumped it out.

Straightaways were well and good, and Gordon knew they had their time and place. Just not then and there. As Gordon picked up his keys, he could almost feel the ground shift under him, but he stood tall. He smiled. It was time to get back to work.

MIND GAMES

A
PSYCHOLOGICAL
THRILLER

B. B. GRIFFITH

CONTENTS

To Jay, who is always an inspiration.

"Sometimes I think people take reality for granted."

—Alex Ridgemont
Made You Up by Francesca Zappia

CHAPTER ONE

Sophie's walk home from school was starting to scare her.

Most of the kids at Merryville Preparatory Academy didn't walk home from school. Most kids she went to school with had parents or chauffeurs pick them up, but Sophie's mom was very busy writing her book in the afternoons and often forgot about her. So Sophie walked.

Most of the time, Sophie's walks were uneventful. She knew five blocks shouldn't be a problem for a girl to walk. Especially a girl just turned twelve. She'd be a teenager soon. Teenagers were supposed to do things like walk here and there alone and not be scared. Especially in Merryville. Sophie knew bad things sometimes happened to girls who walked alone in Baltimore, but not in Merryville. Merryville had gates. Merryville had guards. The families that lived in Merryville paid a lot of money to stay safe and quiet and keep those bad things outside.

Sophie told herself all of those things over and over again. But something still followed her. What stalked Sophie seemed to walk through gates and couldn't care less about guards. What stalked Sophie was already on the inside.

How he'd gotten on the inside, she couldn't say. He was the exact type of person that the gates were built for, that the guards were paid to guard against. His name was Mo, and Sophie knew him well. She always knew when he was nearby. She got a prickly feeling of anticipation—like when the towering trees above her rustled with a cold autumn wind she couldn't feel yet but knew would hit her soon. That was Mo. A distant murmuring that made her stomach twinge. A soft muttering that grew stronger with every step she took until Sophie could practically hear his words, which were always the same.

All Mo talked about was fire.

Sophie's house was at the end of a softly curving street called Long Lane, where the addresses all had single digits. The street was wide but empty, the sidewalks pristine and white, as if the leaves themselves avoided them in their falling. As she walked, she kept hoping for a car to come or a dog to bark or a door to slam—anything to make her feel like just a normal girl walking home from school in a normal neighborhood, back to her normal home and normal mom. But no cars came, and no dogs barked. Merryville was as quiet as always, except for the murmuring trees and the scattered-sand sound of the leaves bumping down the street behind her.

The autumn wind she'd heard in the distance finally caught up, gusting her long blond hair forward and twisting it about her face as she was swirled in a tornado of fallen leaves the color of flame. She brushed them from her hair and plucked them from her plaid dress uniform as she walked. She wiped her hands instinctively on her bony hips. Leaves were dirty. They'd been lying on the street, and the cars rolled on the street, and the tires on the cars had been all over—even into the parts of Baltimore where bad things happened to girls who walked alone—and they brought their dirt from the bad parts past the gates and into Merryville. Onto the leaves. And then into her hair.

Sophie felt her heart racing. She focused on stepping over the cracks on the sidewalk. She focused on taking the same number of steps between each crack. She focused on counting.

A shadow flitted across the street. Sophie forced herself not to follow it with her eyes. She tucked her thumbs more tightly around the straps of her backpack and kept counting and kept walking—faster but not too fast. Too fast, and Mo would notice her.

She told herself the shadow she'd seen was a tendril of cloud skittering in front of the weak autumn sun. It had to be. It just had to be because her mom had told her time and time again that Mo wasn't real. Mo was imaginary. Mo was an imaginary friend that had lived in Sophie's mind for years.

And maybe that was true, once. Back when Mo had tea parties with her. Back when Mo played the guy dolls so Sophie could play the girl dolls. Back when Mo would help her hide in piles of stuffed animals when her mom and dad screamed at each other. Back when she was a little kid that cared about tea parties and dolls and stuffed animals and was scared at how quiet the house was after her dad moved away. But then she became twelve, which is almost thirteen. She was used to being alone now. She was used to having a mom that was busy writing her book. That's when imaginary friends are supposed to disappear. The funny thing was, in a lot of ways, Mo *had* stopped being imaginary. The not-so-funny thing was Mo didn't feel imaginary anymore because he felt more real every day.

Another flitting shadow, and not a cloud in the sky. The breeze was heavier in the canopies. The leaves clattered against the looming red-brick façades of the houses she passed, and they stuck like swarming bees in the hedges that separated the estates. Her plaid dress strained at the boxy outline of her coltish frame. For a moment, all she heard was the roar of the leaves, and all she saw was the blond explosion of her own hair, but then she heard something else.

You're all alone, Sophie.

A soft press on her back, between her shoulder blades.

She whipped around, the wind blowing her eyes clear once more. Nobody there. But Sophie knew better.

The tricky thing about Mo was that he was fast. She rarely saw him, but she could hear him. When he decided to speak up, she could hear him anywhere. Mo was especially fond of sewers. That was why Sophie sprinted over every storm drain and eyed every manhole with her knuckles white around the straps of her backpack.

A gleaming black sedan came around the bend. Sophie recognized it as belonging to one of the chauffeurs from school, and she thought about crying out and asking for a ride, just for the next three blocks. But she couldn't risk the driver talking to her mom and her mom asking why Sophie seemed incapable of walking five blocks from school.

Her mom, Dianne West, could never know that Mo might be creeping around again. That, as she liked to say, "just wouldn't do. Not for a girl your age, Sophia Alexandra West. Not any longer."

Sophie thought she saw the brim of a baseball cap dart back down behind the iron gate of her neighbors' drive. She froze in between cracks on the sidewalk, then against her better judgment, she craned her neck for another look. The gate was swathed with ivy in an explosion of fall colors, and she couldn't make out anything on the other side, but something rustled. She backed away, not realizing how close she'd come to the storm drain until it was too late.

Nowhere is safe, Sophie.

Sophie managed to clip her scream off at a yelp then took off at an awkward lope along the far edge of the sidewalk. Her heart raced, and the sound of it hammering in her chest mixed with the rattles of the leaves, and in that instant, she heard Mo all around her.

Burn it.

Burn it, Sophie.

Burn it all down.

His words hissed with the wind, rolled together in one long whisper.

"You're not real," Sophie said, gritting her teeth through tears that were blown dry as soon as they trickled down her face. "Mom says you're not real."

But even as she spoke, she could feel Mo beneath her, dashing along through the pipes. She could picture him: the laces of his sneakers untied and flopping and the cuffs of his blue jeans trailing in the muck. His white T-shirt would be grubby, as always, and his black baseball cap, a size too big, plunked down low so the brim shaded his eyes and all she'd see was a full set of grinning teeth. He was straining toward her from below, running along the far right side of the pipe so as to be right under her, step for step. She just knew it. Even though her mom said it couldn't be.

Sophie saw another storm drain ahead and stopped. Only a block until home—but it might as well have been a mile. Mo was getting louder—louder than he'd been in a long time, in years and years. Only one other time could she remember Mo having been so loud. That time, he'd gotten her in a lot of trouble. That was how she lost her tree house to the flames. And the big backyard tree to the flames. And almost the entire west wing of the house to the flames.

The wind died down, and Mo's voice went with it, but Sophie knew better. She stared at the dark slot of drain, her shoulder muscles shaking, her scuffed white hush puppies pigeon-toed under knees that felt like giving out. The longer she stared at the black of that place, the more she saw. First, a little wiggle of movement in the dark. Then the black swirled into different shapes. A body? A ball cap?

Sophie shook her head violently. Kids don't hang out in sewers. Not real kids, not imaginary kids. Nobody hangs out in sewers. It was impossible. All of it was impossible. She set herself, pushing her back straight, the way her mom had always told her. She held her chin high. She swallowed hard and started forward. The gutter loomed. She wanted nothing but to run to the middle of the street, but that would be the final straw. That would be admitting he was back. Her skinny ankles passed within a foot of the drain. Her arms puckered with gooseflesh, but she forced herself to walk at a normal pace. One step. Another. She sagged with relief. She was imagining things after all. Mo was gone. She turned away from the grate. She'd been staring at the dark slot with such force she felt her neck crackle with tension.

She could finally swallow. She saw the gate in front of her own drive. It was already open, beckoning her home. He was all in her mind, just like her mom said.

In her haste to get home, she stepped on a crack. She could feel it soil her like gum on the bottom of her shoes, and she shuddered. She wiped her shoes on the lawn nearby, stepped back to just past the previous crack, then counted off again… and when she looked up at her house, Mo was standing in her driveway.

He stood like a skinny superhero with a gaunt grin. Hands on hips. Chest puffed out. His mouth never moved from that smile, but over the years, Sophie had learned to recognize his mood from the expressions of his eyes. Back when Mo was her friend and didn't scare her so much, his eyes had laughed. Not anymore. Now his eyes were screaming.

His voice rang loud and clear in her head. *The only way to stay safe is to burn it all.*

Sophie grabbed her head in her hands, wrenching it back and forth, and the wind roared down the wide street of her block, raking empty sidewalks, buffeting against closed gates, and screaming past enormous locked doors. She ran toward him, toward her bedroom in the house behind him, where she would be safe. She expected to run right into him, but she never did. She managed to look up, blinking through tears, at the point at which she thought she'd hit him, but she found nothing. No sign of him. No sign of anyone. Nothing but the wind.

Long after she slammed the front door behind her, long after she shed her backpack in the anteroom, long after she ran up the first flight of stairs and threw herself, moaning, onto her bed, the wind still carried his voice.

Burn it, Sophie.

It's the only way to stay safe.

Burn it all.

The worst part, the part that struck at her with more raw fear than even that moment where her exposed ankle had been inches from the gaping darkness of the sewer, was that she knew he was right. In her heart of hearts, she knew Mo was right. She had to burn it. That was the only way to stay safe, to keep her mom safe, to keep everyone safe. Everything was so *dirty*. It all had to go.

For Sophie, it was burn or die.

CHAPTER TWO

Dianne West did not recognize the shrill scream of the fire alarm at first. She thought the sound might be some sort of ludicrous bird gone completely off its rocker on the balcony. She even looked out of the window of her study, left and right, and searched the trees for a few moments in a bit of a stupor. She got that way when writing her memoirs—hard to bring back. Her writing was like a deep dive, and she needed to come back in stages.

With another span of steady bleating from the hallway, she came to her senses. No bird sounded like that. She recognized the cacophony. She hadn't heard it for some time, but she had heard it before. She shot up out of her seat, shut the window so the neighbors wouldn't hear, saved her work, and started running. She ran out of her bedroom, her slippered feet slapping softly against the runner carpet in the great hallway of the second floor, all the way to the stairs, where she found the keypad. She'd marked where the keypad was affixed two years before, under similar circumstances. She knew those systems called the fire department outright after sixty seconds if you didn't key in an all-clear code. The fire brigade was the last thing she needed.

She flipped open the terminal, keyed in the code, and waited with bated breath for a half second until the alarm silenced. She sagged against the wall in momentary relief. Step one accomplished.

Now to find the fire.

Dianne followed her nose. She sniffed around the hallway overlooking the foyer then took a few steps down toward the landing between the ground floor and the second after tightening her robe around her. She smelled nothing downstairs. She turned around, stepped up, walking faster, her nose in the air. She didn't call Sophie's name. She knew that would have no effect at that point or might actually make things worse. She had to find her daughter herself.

Dianne walked past her bedroom chamber toward the library. There it was. There was the smell. The steely tang of struck matches, then below that smell, something sweeter. Almost like tobacco. Dianne stopped at Sophie's room. The door was closed. She threw it open. The air there was slightly hazy but with no sign of fire. No sign of Sophie, either, beyond her meticulously ordered art supplies and the rumpled spot on top of the comforter. Of course she wouldn't set fire to her own room. That was the only place she seemed not to mind going those days. But she was close.

Dianne set off down the hall again, testing doors at random, most locked. Some opened into the stuffy blackness of curtains long drawn. Smoke that had merely blurred the edges of the room now stung her eyes then became a fog. Dianne knew what was burning. No more testing of doors. She quickly padded her way down the hall toward the library, and there she found the fire. It was a pile of old books set carefully in the center of the wooden floor. Beneath them, a pile of fallen leaves had burned to crinkled ash, which was already floating in the air. The books were fully engulfed, the flames half Dianne's height already. The fire was the second most substantial that Sophie had set... that Dianne knew about, anyway. Thankfully, it was still confined to twenty or so books in the middle of an otherwise empty room, one that, if Dianne were being frank, she hadn't entered in months. The wood would have to be refinished, of course. But the room—and the west wing—would air out. If she could put it out.

She eyed the curtains. She'd brought in the velvet from Cairo specifically for the library. Tough loss. She ran over to the nearest and yanked down hard. Dianne was a slight woman, shorter than her daughter since Sophie seemed to have shot up like a reed, and she'd neglected her personal trainer recently in favor of the memoir, but she still had wiry strength. After hanging on the velvet for a few moments, she heard a pop and saw a fastener shoot off into the haze. More pops, then a snap. The curtain fell over her. She threw it off herself, the first real notes of panic striking her, until she was free once more. Then she dragged it behind her like a royal train. She bunched the curtain in both fists and heaved it over the burning pile, then piled it on top of itself until it looked like a huge velvet beehive. The fire had grown by then, but it was no match for the heavy curtain. Dianne slapped at it with her slipper, crunching the burned books and ash and half-burned leaves underneath until it was spread out evenly under the curtains and the smoke creeping out from the sides guttered then quit.

Dianne peeked under the curtain. A waft of smoke caught her in the face, but it was dead smoke, dark as the ashes underneath. She let the curtain flop and nodded in admiration at the velvet. Looking at it from on high, one would never know it had burned at all. She'd get the exact same style. And clean the opposite curtain. And the upholstery. The smell just wouldn't do. Not even a hint of it. If there was even a hint, she'd throw everything out and redecorate.

Dianne opened the windows, wiped her brow, and turned around. Second objective accomplished. Next, to find her daughter.

Dianne checked in the gap behind the sofa against the far wall but found nothing. She eased onto her knees on the hardwood floor and looked low. Nothing. She shook her head and bit her upper lip. Sophie wouldn't be there, by the fire. When she was under one of her spells, she followed a certain pattern.

Dianne stepped out into the hall and straightened her back. She already felt better. If she could compartmentalize issues, setting them in little boxes in her mind, she could tackle them. The alarm settled was one compartment, set away. Next, the fire was set away. She would find Sophie too and set that away. Then she would get back to her memoir and eventually, when it was perfect, set that away too. The fire was a minor setback. That was all.

Dianne moved over to the wallpaper, a felted white fiber blend imported from Chamonix, raised at the fleur-de-lis patterning. She ran her fingers along it, her eyes peering until she found what she was looking for: a faint line of colored pencil, left as if an afterthought, like someone lazily trailing a finger in water.

That time, the color was orange. Dianne followed the thin trail as it bumped on and off and in between the raised fleurs-de-lis, out of the room, around the corner, and down the hall. Soon enough, she didn't need the trail any longer, for she could hear the whimpering— more than whimpering, actually. Something in the timbre of the sound reminded Dianne more of full-blown crying, only muffled, as though Sophie was sobbing, but into a pillow.

The end of the hallway rounded off into a circular sunroom ringed with windows that let in the final slanted rays of the hollow afternoon sun, all light and no heat at that time of the year. The windows had seated window wells with matching cushions, and in the leftmost window well, she found Sophie, crying into her dress. She'd pulled it up and over her head and stuffed a ball of the fabric into her mouth. She lay on her side, her skinny legs pulled up into her chest, her long, bony back exposed to Dianne. She was rocking slightly on her side. The orange pencil lay on the floor below the seat.

Dianne covered her mouth to stifle her disappointed cry. She'd seen Sophie in the midst of her episodes before, but never as bad as that. She'd been prepared to find her daughter wandering, maybe sitting dazed on the floor, legs crossed, back slumped, as she had been after the tree-house fire. But this... this looked as if she was in physical pain. This was a definite regression.

"Sophie? Sophie, honey. Can you hear me?"

Nothing. Muffled sobs. Steady rocking.

Dianne moved over to her daughter and gently put her hand on the small of her back. Rather than calming her, that seemed to shock Sophie. She spat out the fabric and wailed from underneath her dress.

"It's the only way! If I don't burn it, they'll come in! They'll take me! They'll murder me! They'll murder everyone! Mo told me! Mo told me! Mo told me!"

Dianne jerked her hand back as if burned. Sophie grabbed a fistful of fabric from under her dress and jammed it into her mouth again, as if it was a leaking faucet she was helpless to stop.

So Mo was back. Dianne had been afraid that might happen. She'd suspected something along those lines ever since Sophie started talking to herself again. Not in public, of course, but here and there. Walking past Sophie's bedroom, Dianne would catch snippets of conversation. She kept the house silent when she wrote. Sounds traveled.

But what to do? Dianne absolutely would not brook a hospital. No emergency medical care of any sort. An ambulance rolling in through Merryville to pick up her raving daughter would be even worse than the fire brigade. At least with the fire brigade, she could come up with some other excuse, a faulty fuse or the cleaning people accidentally turning on a burner or something. Much harder to explain away an ambulance.

But Sophie needed help. The sounds she was making struck Dianne to the core. No daughter of hers should be in that much distress. She wouldn't stand for it. If only she knew of some way to mollify her, to reach her child in the depths of whatever hell she'd fallen into and pull her back. Clearly, Sophie was undergoing a mental break of some sort. What the girl needed more than anything, more than a hospital or an ambulance, was a psychiatrist.

Dianne narrowed her eyes in thought. Hadn't she read something about a child psychiatrist? Maybe she'd seen it on the news, briefly, as she watched television in bed, trying to rouse herself after one of her marathon writing sessions, perhaps a month before. The details were coming back to her. She could picture him in the awkward local-news interview. He was a sort of sad-looking fellow—handsome in a weary way, a little soft about the waist, with wire-frame glasses and more scruff on his chin than he had on the top of his head. He'd spoken all of ten seconds or so before they cut to some sports news, but he'd had a calm, steady voice, talking about... sleepwalking. That was it. Kids sleepwalking in East Baltimore. Dreadful. But he'd been up to the challenge. What was his name, again?

Dianne took a long look at her daughter, her eyes softening.

Pope. That was it. Gordon Pope. A compassionate last name. Maybe he could help. She reached into her dressing gown and pulled out her phone.

CHAPTER THREE

In the palm of his hand, Gordon Pope was spinning a large novelty pencil that read "World's Greatest Psychiatrist" while staring at his office clock, waiting for it to strike five. Cocktail hour. No scotch before five. That was the rule, although where that was written—on what sacred stone—Gordon couldn't say. Four was just as good as five, as far as he was concerned. But therein lay the slippery slope. A month before, he'd have fudged it to four. Three months before, he hadn't had a clock in the office, which meant it was always five o'clock. But that was when he'd been in the depths of the sleepwalker case and hitting a lot of personal lows. *Lows* was actually being generous. He was broke, heartbroken, chasing the past, and drinking heavily. Since then, things had changed.

Gordon had a girlfriend. Dana Frisco. Detective Dana Frisco. A picture of her sat just to the right of his computer, taken at Waterstones, a swanky bistro near the inner harbor just the previous month. Dana was leaning forward slightly, always eager, always engaged. Her shining black hair settled over her darkened shoulders. Her smile was fierce but friendly, and Dana could be either. Depending. Gordon's eyes were wide in the picture, and he looked nervous, as if he expected someone to jump out of the bushes to pinch him and wake him up. He'd thought of himself as *divorced* for so long that he occasionally still caught himself staring at the photo in shock, as if he was looking at another Gordon in a parallel universe.

Prior to the Waterstones photo, the only photograph in Gordon's office was a large portrait of him with his arm rested awkwardly upon the wingback chair in which Karen Jefferson, his ex-wife and still half of the nameplate of the Jefferson and Pope practice—although only in name—sat primly with her ankles crossed. Well, that picture and a yellowing four-by-six of him and his mother, Deborah, taken the last time she'd dragged him to her Laguna Beach time-share. He'd pinned it to a corkboard by the computer with other odds and ends. She looked radiant and trim at seventy-five. He looked pallid and a little ill at forty-five.

Another new addition: better reading material on top of the john. After the divorce, when Gordon was forced to give up the condo and move into his office full time for cash reasons, he took all that he owned and stuffed it into various places willy-nilly. In a fog of depression, he'd put a stack of old newspapers in the bathroom as if the prior year's *New York Times* was entertaining reading. Now, he had the most current medical journals on rotation. Probably not much better, from an entertainment standpoint, for anyone outside the profession. But at least they were current.

The new business had helped spiff up his wardrobe, replenish his scotch collection, and bring him back from the financial brink to mere low-level financial discomfort felt by the majority of single-income private-practice psychiatrists. But Dana Frisco was the real reason he'd picked himself up. She made him consider things he thought he'd never consider again after Karen—things that made his stomach do little loops that were both uncomfortable and oddly exciting, like a roller-coaster ride. Both of them were strapped in, listening to the *tik tik tik tik* of the climb—the classic kind of coaster that clacked and shook your teeth and was built on old bones. When you were on it, always in the back of your mind was the very real possibility that the entire structure, planks and nuts and bolts and all, might crumble to the ground on which it stood. Their relationship felt new and old at the same time, and it thrilled him.

But even thoughts of Dana couldn't make the clock tick to cocktail hour any faster. Nor could spinning a pencil in his hand. The only thing that could speed up that clock was creating a reason to celebrate, and Gordon had one. He'd just submitted his final approvals for his article in the fall quarterly of *Philosophy, Psychiatry, & Psychology*, Gordon's sole published contribution to the field of psychiatry to date—the result of a tireless effort to save a young boy in East Baltimore from himself. The case had changed Gordon's life and given him a burst of clients. For a man that took any excuse for a celebratory swig, that was plenty.

He popped the cork top of a very decent single malt. No more plastic bottles for him. He smelled the bouquet as he poured—a wildfire of peat that nearly made his eyes water and definitely made his mouth water. He lifted the glass to his mouth.

The phone rang. Gordon blinked in annoyance. Jefferson and Pope was closed. No calls taken after hours. For the first time in five years, Gordon could say he had a halfway decent business, so "operating hours" finally meant something. He waited out the rattling ring of his old landline then lifted his glass again. The answering machine kicked on while he took a long sip.

"Dr. Pope? Are you there?"

Gordon paused, pursing his lips, scotch between his teeth. Something in her tone of voice turned the sip sour in his mouth and pulled at his gut, not unlike a big drop on that old wooden rollercoaster.

"Please... please pick up."

And that was all it took to get Gordon to forget about the scotch. He swallowed the one sip and forwent the rest. He was almost powerless to do anything else.

That was how he found himself driving to a Marriott on Center Street with the words of a woman named Dianne West ringing in his ears: *"It's my daughter. It's hard to explain. To be honest, I don't think you'd believe me if I told you."*

GORDON SPENT ten minutes driving up and down Center Street looking for an Extended Stay Marriott, but he had no luck. He was in a swanky area of town—nothing Extended Stay about it. Then he saw the JW Marriott: sleek black marble with a glittering chandelier above the valet. Carpet on the sidewalk. Gordon wasn't about to hand over his beat-up two-seater to a place with carpet on the sidewalk. He had no cash, for one. He was making ends meet, but not *valet* making ends meet. Plus, on that block, he was fairly sure the valet just rolled cars like his into the harbor.

Fifteen minutes to find a parking spot and five more to walk. Gordon's scuffed oxfords clacked across the black marble entryway of the JW half an hour after he'd hung up with Dianne West. He nodded at the valet as if he hadn't just driven off to avoid him, and he pushed his way through the revolving doors. Two desk clerks looked up at him in unison, half smiling.

"I'm here to see a Mrs. Dianne West. My name is Gordon Pope."

The smiles became a good deal more gracious.

A trimly dressed manager seemed to appear from nowhere. He placed a brief hand upon the nearest clerk's shoulder to still her typing and said, "I'll take it from here. This way, Dr. Pope."

They walked through the marbled lobby and past the elevator bay, turned right, and walked down another, shorter hallway until they stood in front of a single elevator that opened as soon as the manager pressed the call button. Inside, he swiped a keycard and hit the top floor. They rose in silence.

When the doors opened, the manager held them with a soft press of his hand and gave a brief bow as Gordon exited. "Last on the left, Dr. Pope."

The elevator doors closed behind him. The hallway was long but had only four doors on each side. At the end was a large, rectangular window overlooking a busy intersection, yet Gordon heard nothing of the city outside. His shoes made a soft pressing sound as he walked, barely louder than kneading bread.

Gordon stopped in front of the last door on the left. He brushed his head free of the dampness that seemed to crown it every time he found himself in one of those situations, where he didn't know what was behind the door. He wiped his hands on the seat of his pants and pulled at the cuffs of his shirt. He knocked once then twice and went for a third, but the door opened with a jerk, and Gordon swiped at air.

"Dr. Pope. Thank you for coming. Dianne West. Inside, please."

A short, trim woman with a blond bob and a sharp glint in her eye grabbed his shoulder with surprising strength. Gordon was practically pulled inside. As his eyes adjusted to the low light, he saw the room was but one of several attached, a suite that sprawled to his left and right. The door closed behind him, and the first thing Gordon heard after the click and slide of the lock was a rhythmic whining, as if someone was trying to lift something heavy and failing, again and again and again. Gordon knew better.

Gordon moved immediately toward the door on the right, where the sound was coming from, but again he was stopped, spun around by Dianne.

She assayed him keenly, unblinking. "Before I let you go in there, I must be assured of your absolute discretion, Dr. Pope. I appreciate how you helped the sleepwalking children, but I heard of it from the news. I cannot have anything in the news. Understood?"

Gordon had dealt with controlling families before. He knew the only way he was going to see the girl was to agree. The rest could be sorted out later.

"I assume you're her legal guardian?" Gordon asked.

Dianne nodded.

"Then unless she's being abused, what you say goes."

Dianne still held his bicep, her eyes running over his face as if she could read it like tea leaves. Whatever she saw, it was enough. She nodded.

"Her name is Sophie. She's prone to... episodes."

Gordon turned again and walked toward the strained cries. He passed through an interior doorway into a second bedroom, and Sophie immediately went silent. Gordon looked about. He'd expected to find the girl in bed but couldn't see her anywhere. The bedspread was military tight, the glassware still covered in paper doilies. One mint rested on each of the enormous feather pillows on pillows on pillows. He glanced toward the bathroom. The sink was running, but the lights were off. Gordon made a move that way when a soft scratching on the carpet to his left gave him pause.

"Sophie?"

A single, soft moan. Clipped quickly that time. Gordon stepped past the dresser and minibar and flat-screen television and stopped at the foot of the bed. Sophie West was on the floor between the night-stand and a four-corner desk set against the wall. She had the same blond hair as her mother although hers was much longer and had a glistening, unwashed look. Her eyes were the same color of blue as well, staring straight up at Gordon. She'd stretched her plaid dress over bony knees. Her right hand was hovering over her shoes, scuffed white hush puppies. She held her fingers over the right shoe as though contemplating a chess move. The other hand she had balled into a fist, stuffed halfway into her mouth. Her backpack was open on her other side, and a set of high-quality colored pencils lay propped carefully against it, organized by color.

As soon as she saw Gordon, she started to keen continuously again. Her eyes darted to Dianne, who had followed a step behind Gordon, her hands wringing.

"Now Sophie, stop that," she said. "Can you hear me? Sophie, look at me now. This is Dr. Pope. He's here to help you."

Sophie remained unchanged. Dianne moved in toward her, but Gordon stilled her with a firm hand on one shoulder.

"Mrs. West, I have a policy," he said. "I work with children. Children alone. If you want my help, I'm going to need to work with Sophie one-on-one. Which means you out of the room."

Gordon watched her steadily. That was always a pivotal moment in patient treatment—the parental buy in. Gordon didn't need Dianne West to tell him that Sophie was having a break of some sort. That much was evident when he walked into the room. The question was: Had she called him in order to really help her child or because she thought he could give her a quick fix and get them on their way out of the private exit from the five-star hotel.

Dianne West looked at him carefully, and Gordon could tell by the tightness in her face, the way she held her jaw apart behind her closed lips—as if she wanted to scream but was keeping it in—that she was afraid. She was afraid of what was happening, and she wanted her child helped long-term. Not quick-fixed.

She nodded, turned around, and went to the door. After giving him one last look, she closed the door behind her.

Gordon let out a breath he hadn't realized he'd been keeping in. The young girl had just gone from a simple evaluation to a patient. And good thing, too, because Gordon wasn't a quick-fix type of doctor. To Gordon, patient care was either all-in or fold.

He took a seat at the foot of the starched bed, a good five feet from the girl. She whimpered softly, her eyes rolling.

"Sophie," Gordon said, clearly and calmly.

Her eyes moved to him. So she was in the room at least, not completely inside her head. She shifted her fist in her mouth like an awkward bit of an apple. With her long, skinny legs bunched into the corner, she looked very much like a spooked animal.

"You can say what you want to say, Sophie," Gordon said. "Whatever it is, you can say it to me."

She popped her fist out, said, "You aren't safe. Nobody is. Get away from me. I'll kill you," and slammed it in again with such force that Gordon winced.

"I am safe," Gordon said. "Wherever I am is a safe place for you."

Sophie looked at him in intervals, like a bird. He could tell from her eyes that she saw him not as a stranger as much as someone who had the misfortune to be caught up within her mind.

Gordon waited patiently, his hands clasped between his knees.

Sophie dropped her hand to the floor. "Mo's back," she whispered. The girl was going through her own private emotions: her face fell, her mouth half open, her eyes sad half-moons. Then she turned to her shoes and flipped them, one over the other. She set them just so, inching the right in with her pointer finger a millimeter at a time until the backs stood perfectly aligned with each other. She popped up to standing in an instant and walked around Gordon toward the bathroom.

Gordon stayed seated. He knew that the less he moved during that type of situation, the better. Without any knowledge of Sophie's prior medical history, the best course to take would be to create a safe space and minimize sensory input. So he watched her quietly.

For the moment, Sophie seemed to have completely forgotten about him. She turned the right and left faucets of the gleaming sink to exactly the same degree. She wet her hands, nodding her head, as if keeping time in her head. She took the bar of soap and rolled it over in her hands seven times. She set it down on the dish and washed her hands free of suds for another seven nods. She carefully removed a rolled washcloth from the basket set against the mirror and patted her hands dry. She left the sink running and proceeded to touch the top of everything on the countertop one heartbeat at a time. She turned back to the door, moved into the bedroom again, and clicked the light on and off seven times until the room was dark again.

Sophie walked around Gordon, giving him a wide berth without looking at him. After sitting down in her corner once more, she looked at her fist and set it down in her lap. She sighed. Her eyes darted at the four corners of the ceiling.

"Who is Mo?" Gordon asked, as if none of her cleaning had happened.

"He's my friend. My twin. His name is Mophie, like I'm Sophie.

He's also not real. He's not real. He's not real." She repeated herself like a child confronted with what she refused to believe.

"Is Mo here right now?"

Sophie shook her head. Gordon was surprised to find himself relieved. The intensity of the girl's fear was contagious.

"His voice is, though," Sophie whispered, looking at the four corners of the room again.

"What is his voice saying?"

Sophie shook her head. Her eyes welled with tears and wandered until she could blink them back in line again.

"It's okay, Sophie. You can tell me anything. It's just you and me here. No Mo—nobody else."

Sophie grabbed her knees and tucked them close then spoke into her lap. "He says the only way to keep me safe from this place is to burn it."

Her voice was strangely calm. No waver at all, as if she were reading off of a menu in her lap. Over a decade of treating children across the spectrum couldn't save Gordon from the shiver that inched up his spine at how defeated she sounded.

Sophie swapped her shoes again, inched them forward until they were exactly even, then popped up and moved back to the bathroom. Gordon simply watched her and stayed still.

Twenty minutes and five washes later, Gordon left Sophie in her corner of the bedroom to exit to the main parlor. Dianne West was so close to the door that he bumped her upon opening it. She didn't even try to hide that she'd been eavesdropping. Gordon eyed her blankly, too lost in his thoughts to comment, then moved over to the plush couch opposite the television and sat down. His head was jammed with years and years of case studies, and in many ways, what was afflicting Sophie found precedent there. But in other equally important ways, what he'd just seen in that room stood alone. Every time he ran down a mental checklist for a surefire diagnosis, he came up lacking. She checked boxes of several conditions but left other integral boxes unticked.

Dianne did not sit down. She stood in front of him, her arms crossed, as if urging him not to get too comfortable.

"Your daughter suffers from acute obsessive-compulsive disorder," Gordon said, starting with the easiest. "That much is obvious. And I'm sure you're already aware of it."

Dianne nodded. "The hand washing, the organizing, the counting of things. She's been doing that in some form most of her life. It's actually what usually gets her out of these messes. She... counts herself calm. It's never taken this long before."

"When children exhibit obsessive-compulsive behavior, it's often because they feel as though their lives are out of control in ways that they cannot help. So they turn to controlling whatever they can. Counting. Washing. Organizing things in their vicinity. It can become crippling, and it often worsens if left untreated. Can you think of any reason why Sophie might be feeling out of control?"

Gordon left that in the air. He stopped short of suggesting that, in almost every case, that feeling of chaotic helplessness stemmed from disruptions in the home. Dianne grasped his meaning. She pursed her mouth as if deciding whether to take offense, but a soft shuffling sound from the back room seemed to remind her that her daughter, while slightly calmer, was still not well.

"Divorce," she said simply. "My ex-husband, Simon, ran off with his personal assistant. After twelve years of marriage. But the divorce was finalized over a year ago. He's been out of the house ever since. Could that really be it?"

Gordon shrugged. "Perhaps. The mind processes trauma in its own time. Wounds can linger. And divorce, especially after such a long time, is a big rip in the fabric of what binds a household." Gordon knew firsthand how big a tear it could be. He'd been divorced after five years and it punched a huge hole in him. The stitches were only just holding, and that was less because of him and more because of Dana.

He tapped his lower lip in thought, wondering whether a divorce in the family alone could cause Sophie's behavior. Perhaps. That was certainly a piece of the greater picture, but Gordon felt it wasn't the whole. It fit, but it didn't *click*, like jamming a puzzle piece into the wrong place.

"Is that when Mo appeared? Around the time of the divorce?"

"No," Dianne said, sighing heavily. "Mophie has been around since Sophie could talk. I thought we were rid of him a year ago. But he came back."

"Around the time of the divorce," Gordon said to himself.

Dianne tapped out time on her fingertips then nodded.

"Was it a particularly *bad* divorce?"

Dianne moved her jaw back and forth behind closed lips. "It wasn't *pleasant* by any means, but as far as these things go, no. It was quick and clean. Simon wasn't abusive, just thoughtless. He's moved on now. Doesn't seem worse for not seeing Sophie but once or twice a year."

The textbook answer was that Sophie had created Mo as a stand-in for an absent father and developed OCD as a result of shifting terrain at home. There it was. Right there. Page one of Psychiatry 101. Except that Gordon felt no click.

"I've never had an imaginary friend come back," Gordon said thoughtfully, scratching at his scruff.

"Excuse me?"

He looked up at Dianne, who stepped closer to hear him. "I've treated plenty of children with imaginary friends. And many who acted out through those friends in violent ways like burning or cutting. But once the friend goes away, I've never had one come back."

Dianne cringed. "So she told you, then. About the burning."

Gordon nodded and watched Dianne quietly. One of the most powerful weapons in his arsenal was the silent wait-out. Gordon could wait quietly better than anyone he knew. A pregnant pause made people so uncomfortable that they often offered up more than he ever could have pried from them—all of their own accord.

"We had an... incident. Some years past. When Sophie was ten.

She set fire to a good chunk of the estate, claiming Mo told her to do it."

Gordon sat back on the couch and watched Dianne carefully. "That would have been before the divorce," he said. "So Sophie has been exhibiting concerning behavior for some time."

Dianne nodded and looked away. "My daughter is recently worse. But she was... always a little off."

"Mrs. West, if I'm going to treat Sophie, I need complete honesty from you. Do you understand?"

"So that means you'll fix her?"

"In psychiatry, there are no quick fixes. Especially with children. And especially if the parents of those children aren't straight with me."

Dianne reddened and picked at the arm of the couch. Embarrassment? Anger? Either way, Gordon could tell she wasn't used to being spoken to in that way.

"I'm sorry," she said primly. "It's just that my family..." There she trailed off, carefully measuring her words. "My family is in politics. And the Baltimore political scene is notorious for taking everything they can and throwing it against you. In other cities, in other states, children would be off-limits, but not here. Do you understand what I'm saying?"

"Are you concerned for your daughter's health or your reputation?" Gordon asked, struggling to keep his voice level.

Dianne squared to Gordon. "Both," she said unabashedly.

Gordon couldn't help shaking his head. Of all the times to think of oneself...

"Can't it be both?" Dianne asked. "I promise I'll be up front with you however I can. Will you help her?"

Gordon stood. He walked to the door, but in the interval caught a glimpse into the bedroom once again. He saw a meticulously placed pair of scuffed white hush puppies and, just poking out from the corner, the toes of Sophie's stocking feet. They were curled tightly into the carpet.

Gordon was fairly sure he didn't like Dianne West, but that was nothing new. He quite frequently butted heads with the parents of his patients. Gordon wasn't going to help Sophie because Dianne asked. He was going to help her because Sophie herself couldn't ask. She was right there, but she couldn't ask. She was frightened. And she needed help.

"I'll clear my schedule," Gordon said. As if his calendar had been jammed for years and not just respectably cluttered for a matter of weeks.

CHAPTER FOUR

Dana Frisco and her daughter, Chloe, watched Gordon chew thoughtfully as he sat across the table. He cut his pork loin slowly, his eyes off in the distance. Chloe turned to her and rolled her eyes hugely, nodding at him. Dana gave a lot of credit to Chloe. Other eight-year-olds might have made a scene if their mom's eccentric new boyfriend ate his dinner without speaking. She knew he wasn't deliberately being rude. His mind was just elsewhere. He ate like a placid cow. An enlightened placid cow, but a cow nonetheless.

Dana cleared her throat. "Earth to Gordon. Are you with us, Gordon?"

Gordon looked over at her. "Hmm?"

"The salt, big guy. Chloe asked for the salt. Three times."

"Oh." Gordon fumbled to set his knife and fork down. Then he fumbled again with the salt, spilling a cascade Chloe's way, which elicited another eye roll that would have held its own against even the most jaded teenagers. Dana would know. As one of two detectives in the newly formed Child Protective Investigations unit of the Baltimore Police Department, she'd been dealing with a lot of teenagers lately. She'd found, even in the month she'd been assigned the detail, that teenagers rolled their eyes at just about everything, good or bad.

"Chloe, keep your eyes in your head," Dana said.

By all rights, her daughter should have another four years before the serious cynicism set in. Then again, Chloe had always been ahead of her class. And really, she couldn't blame the girl. Gordon was awkward around Chloe in the best of circumstances. He seemed to settle right in with all the new kids he was getting as patients, but you'd never know it the way he acted around her daughter—which was a bit like an awkward butler.

Gordon set about muttering apologies and gathering the salt with his palm until he accidentally dumped all of it down a seam in the table. He paused as it hit the floor. Beets, her mother's Boston terrier, was there in a flash, tongue to wood flooring. Gordon gave up and handed Chloe the salt. She managed not to shake her head as she put a tad too much of it on her mashed potatoes, which Dana chalked up as a parenting victory.

"Where's your head at today?" Dana asked.

"It's here. It really is."

Dana gathered a bite on her fork. "Work gets to me too. It's okay."

Gordon cleared his throat. "A tough patient came in. A strange case. Very strange."

"Strange?" asked Dana.

Gordon glanced at Chloe, who was watching Beets go to town and looked like she couldn't care less.

"Strange behavioral markers. There's an obvious obsessive-compulsive diagnosis, but... it just doesn't fit well. It's hard to explain."

Beets ran his bulk into Gordon's shin in search of more salt.

"Hey, Chloe..." Gordon said.

She looked up in wary surprise.

"Did you ever have an imaginary friend?"

Chloe thought. "No."

"What about Bun Bun?" Dana said. "Remember Bun Bun?"

Chloe reddened a hint. "That was nothing. Just me talking to my Bun Bun stuffed animal is all. I don't do it anymore."

"Why not?" Gordon asked.

The genuine, almost childlike curiosity in his voice seemed to give Chloe pause.

"I dunno. I got real friends like Alex and Catelyn. Not so much Catelyn. But for sure Alex."

Gordon nodded absently, clearly lost in thought once again.

"I still like Bun Bun, though," Chloe added, as if she felt guilty. "Even though I don't play with him anymore. He's on my favorite shelf and stuff, still."

Dana heard a telltale shuffling sound from just downstairs, where her mother was supposedly "watching her shows." Dana's house was small, but she knew the downstairs television was farther away than the base of the stairs. She heard her mother clear her throat and barely stopped herself from rolling her own eyes.

"Yes, Mama?" Dana said loudly.

"Chloe, it's time to finish your schoolwork," Maria Frisco said loudly, as if Dana hadn't spoken.

Chloe looked at Dana with all her might until Dana eventually nodded that Chloe could be excused. She jumped up and clattered her dishes to the sink, where she stood on her tiptoes to run some perfunctory water over the lot before setting them loudly in the basin. Then she shot off down the stairs.

The dining room was quiet.

"She has candy down there," Dana said.

Gordon picked morosely at what was left on his plate. "Candy?"

"Ma keeps a huge jar of Starbursts in her room. She's been spoiling Chloe since she could walk. It's nothing personal. Plus, her toys are down there."

"So she's not really doing homework."

"I doubt it."

"So not only does Chloe think I'm weird, but your mom doesn't want me around her to begin with."

Dana let out an even breath. That was about the whole of it. She wouldn't lie to the man. Gordon nodded. She could see he was trying to shrug off the double dismissal as no big deal but only partly succeeding.

"I get it. And I know I don't have a lot to talk about with Chloe. I just... I think I'm still trying to figure all this out, and kids always know."

"What are you trying to figure out?" Dana asked, a hint of worry tingeing her voice. She knew he cared for her, but she sometimes wondered if all this—her daughter, her mother, her job—could ever find space in the brain of a man like Gordon Pope. A brain that was already filled to the brim.

"I'm terrified that all this could fall apart, at any second," Gordon said. "It's all so fragile. Everything is. You see some of the kids I've seen—you see how they're shattered. They're just shattered." His face dropped, and he was clearly thinking of something recent. Something fresh. Something today. "And they don't know why, you know? You can break inside even if you don't know why. Your brain doesn't care if you understand why it's falling apart. If it's gonna fall apart, it'll do it regardless. Sometimes the deck is stacked against you no matter what you do. And sometimes I get afraid the deck is stacked against me too. Against us."

Dana stood and walked over to him and plucked him up from his seat by the crook of one arm. She turned him to face her.

"Gordon, the reason you're good at what you do is because you get in the heads of these kids. You become them. But these kids are damaged. Don't forget that. Don't let them damage you."

Gordon wasn't tall, but she was shorter. Still, she pulled him close. He came reluctantly at first, like a teen being dragged onto a dance floor. Eventually he nuzzled low into her neck and hung there.

"Your mother hates me," he said.

"She's old-school Catholic. She saw what it did to Chloe and me when Brett left. Right now, she hates everyone not me or Chloe. And occasionally, just everyone not Chloe."

He let her hold him for a time, fully there with her at last, before saying, "I should go."

"I'm on night shift, but I'll try to come over late night."

Gordon nodded, already falling back into his own mind again, as he had with the last "strange case" he'd come across. The sound of Chloe laughing downstairs gave Gordon a brief, bittersweet look. Dana knew that every attempt he'd made at getting Chloe to laugh had fallen flat—nothing but eye rolls in return.

"Her toys are all down there..." Dana offered, again.

He shrugged on his jacket and placed a hand on her shoulder. "It's okay. Kids come around in their own time," he said. "If they think it's worth it."

She watched as he pulled away in that rattling car of his, one brake light out, some internal belt whining softly. His off-key horn bopped twice in farewell.

That night, Dana went through her open cases file by file while her mother watched a movie with Chloe—the same Disney movie she'd watched earlier that week, by the sound of it. And several times the week before. Chloe's voice squeaked in off-key beauty, every word on cue as if she was reading from a karaoke machine. Her grandma would be bobbing along, clapping her hands softly on her knees. The thought made Dana smile, which was good. It almost offset the melancholy that settled over her every time she cracked a file folder recently.

She'd thought making detective would change everything, and in many ways it had. She made more. She got the badge. She got off the beat and into a new department she thought would be the perfect fit. But the more things changed, the more they stayed the same.

She thought the detail change meant that she'd also leave her old boss, Warren Duke, behind—that she'd be able to start fresh in a department not run by an entitled, blue-blooded lieutenant hell-bent on keeping everyone not in his inner circle "where they're best suited." That, in her case, meant *in her place*.

She should have known better. CPI didn't fall under Lieutenant

Duke's jurisdiction. However, it did fall under *Major* Duke's jurisdiction. A district is a lot of territory—hard not to fall inside that. Too much to hope that she'd be promoted out. She'd helped crack a major case. With police, the shit rolled downhill, good and bad. When she was recognized, he was recognized too.

So there went that. Exit plan foiled. Window slammed shut. The thought made her throat itch, as though she'd swallowed a pill wrong and a little piece of it had lodged somewhere below her neck and above her lungs.

As if being under Duke's thumb wasn't bad enough, the work itself in her new detail was completely underwhelming. She thought CPI would put her in the middle of cases with teeth—things like abductions, gang recruitment, trafficking, abuse—but the cases she saw came from Duke, and she and Gordon had beaten Duke at his own game with the sleepwalkers case. She quickly learned Duke didn't take well to getting beaten at his own game.

Dana flipped through her tabs again, each finger-worn by then. She had twelve open cases. Six of them were repeat truancies. Four were petty vandalism. Two were social-work assists—validating food stamps. Never one to sit and take it on the chin, Dana had already spoken to Duke. As one of two detectives in a new unit commissioned by the mayor himself, she could still do that—go to the major and act while she still had favor on her side. So she asked for any one of the myriad of cases she knew were out there in homicide or CSI involving youth. Cases that might be better served with her.

Duke never even looked up from his paperwork when he told her to "enter the pool slowly." So there went that.

Chloe warbled out a verse of song from the basement that broke Dana's melancholy. She eased her grip on the file in front of her, which she'd been subconsciously crushing. Truancy cases only got so much traction—kids who didn't want to go to school wouldn't go to school. What Dana wanted was a case where a kid wanted to go to school but couldn't. Those existed, she was sure of it. But in the BPD, you tackled the case that crossed your desk, no matter what department you were in. Dana rubbed her eyes and checked the clock—well past Chloe's bedtime once again.

She took Chloe through her bedtime ritual with as much vigor as she could muster. Chloe had a singing toothbrush on its last legs that sounded a bit like a phone call under water, but Dana sang along nonetheless, brushing side by side with her daughter. She read her favorite bedtime story to her for the third time that week, about a teddy bear named Mr. Buttons, who loses his felt nose.

"Mr. Buttons walked a long path through the forest every day. And every day, Mr. Buttons tapped the trees with his felt nose so he could find his way..."

She turned on Chloe's night-light. The mobile of stars above her bed lit her small bedroom glowworm green. Then Dana went to her own bed and lay down fully clothed on top of the puffy duvet she ended up kicking off every night, feeling vaguely disappointed in everything without being able to pinpoint why.

Dana shot awake in darkness—she froze, disoriented and with a ringing in her ears. Many hammered heartbeats later, she was finally able to place herself: on top of her bedspread, still in her clothes. She must have fallen asleep where she'd lain.

Her neck was damp around the collar, her pants bunched at the legs. The ringing persisted. She shook her head to clear it, to no effect, until she realized it was coming from her purse. She stared dumbly at the glow of her phone while she pulled it out. Its screen lit the entire room and read "Marty Cicero." Her partner.

"Hey Marty," she answered, trying to sound alert.

"Wakey wakey," Marty said, his shipyard east-coast accent punching through the phone. Eighties hair metal was blaring in the background: Marty's unique way of dusting his own cobwebs. "We got a crime scene."

Dana and Marty had been partners before CPI. They were assigned together to the beat by Warren Duke, who often threw hard-case cops at Dana like a kid lording over a science set, just to see what came of it. To see who survived. In the end, Dana was always standing. If surviving meant staying right where she was while the men who sat beside her in the cruiser moved out and up, then she was the definition of a survivor, but that's all she did: survive. Then Marty came around, the first beat partner she didn't immediately want to throttle, despite how he sometimes came off like a gym rat. Since then, she'd had plenty of opportunities to see that he was much more than his meathead exterior. He was fiercely loyal and more perceptive than anyone in the department, save herself. They'd become friends and developed a strong rapport. She knew Marty wanted more, a partnership of a different kind. He'd all but confessed himself to her when they broke the sleepwalkers case, but so far she'd been able to avoid the topic directly. The new detail helped. Both of them were still trying to tread water, finding their place again. That took up most of their time. Eventually, however, she knew they'd settle in, and things would need to be addressed.

Marty knew she cared deeply for Gordon, but he was also stubborn, refusing to back down even in the face of defeat. She wanted desperately to keep things working between them. And between Marty and Gordon, who had a frosty relationship, to say the least, although Marty was most often the antagonist. Gordon was too oblivious in many ways—too single-minded in others—to have much of a frosty relationship with anyone. Except when people stepped between him and his patients.

So much for seeing Gordon that night. He would understand.

From what Dana had gathered on the phone, the case was their first big one. Felony destruction of property was a big deal. She felt more and more like a police detective as she dressed. Then she tried her best to tiptoe past Chloe's room and left a note under Maria's door. They knew the drill. Back on the beat, Dana was often out more nights than in.

She felt strange driving to a crime scene in her minivan, but she didn't have time to report to the station. The van was a relic of the old days with Brett, back when she'd thought Chloe would be one of at least two, maybe three. Maybe even four. If things kept going the way she thought they were going to with Gordon, Chloe would likely be her last. She didn't know the first thing about adoption, and Gordon was sterile. The minivan had a lot of empty seats. Sometimes, when she looked in the rearview mirror, she felt as if she was looking into a bare closet, and she was nudged by a hollow sadness. But it was a good car. It was as sturdy as a tank, and it just kept running, so she ran with it—empty seats and all.

She plugged in the directions Marty had given her and took off, cruising north past the city, then past the suburbs, into neighborhoods that looked less like neighborhoods and more like well-kept hedge mazes with houses hidden inside. Her tires hissed down a newly paved two-lane road, and she slowed to the speed limit only when she saw the turnoff in the distance. An enormous ivy-clad gate met her at Merryville. Not Merryville Estates or Merryville Place or Merryville Manors—just Merryville. The name was written on an oxidized brass plaque attached to a redbrick guard station. An attendant stepped from the station at the sound of her approach—an older man in a maroon jacket and slacks with a green tie. He carried a clipboard and watched her benignly over spectacles perched on the tip of his nose. The clock on Dana's dash read 2:08 in the morning.

"May I have your name, ma'am?" the attendant asked.

"Dana Frisco. Detective Dana Frisco," she added, after a moment.

"May I see your badge, please?"

Dana unclipped her shield from her hip and brought out her identification. The attendant looked at both carefully. Back up at her. Back to the pad. Then to her badge again. Dana tapped the side of her car and looked beyond the gate. Somewhere in the distance, lights were flashing silent red and blue, a lot of them. But the trees were too dense to figure out where.

"Straight ahead, ma'am," the attendant said. "Just down Long Lane." He handed back her badge. The gate swung open smoothly.

The moonlight caught the ivy as it moved, the leaves fluttering briefly in the still night air. They'd turned yellow and red in a swath on the diagonal, like flung paint.

Dana drove in silence down a wide avenue flanked at even intervals by towering white oak trees. The houses she saw beyond the trees sometimes spanned half a block. Each had a big main, often an imposing plantation-looking building, but most houses had other houses—at least one, maybe two. Like ducks in a row. She saw lights on in some of the windows, despite the hour. Faces in silhouette, like small black dots, peeked out. One man in a long robe stood boldly on his front porch, eyeing her. *They must not see a lot of flashing lights here.*

She crawled by—even if she'd had lights and sirens, they would be off and quiet. She was part of an investigatory unit, so Dana and Marty arrived in the aftermath now. They pieced together the scene after others had put out the fires.

The moon dappled the road through the leaves as Dana rounded a soft bend, then slowed.

Unless the "fire" is actually a fire.

A stalwart-looking redbrick structure was belching smoke darker than the night from its ground-floor windows. Dana couldn't see any flames, but the building still glowed an angry red inside. Two firefighters were handling a hose to keep a steady stream of water jetting into the nearest window. Six or seven others milled around, speaking to each other, standing with arms crossed. By their relaxed body language, Dana could tell the blaze was under control. Time for the detectives, which begged the question: Why call CPI?

Marty was waiting behind the trucks, leaning against his Charger and munching on his ever-present bag of almonds like popcorn at the movie theater. He wore a polo shirt that looked painted onto his broad frame, dark denim jeans, and high-top basketball shoes. His badge hung from a dog-tag chain around his neck and rested between his pecs. He looked as fresh as a morning bird. Dana looked briefly down at her own clothes, workout pants and whatever T-shirt had been on top of the pile. She made a mental note to put together some sort of outfit for times like that and set it away on top of the dresser. She needed to look like a cop, not a harried mom trying to squeeze in five minutes on the treadmill.

Marty held out the almonds to her as she approached. "Brain food," he said. "Low calorie, high payoff." He looked her up and down and smiled but kept quiet.

Dana yawned and took a handful. She leaned back on the gleaming hood next to Marty, and both of them took in the scene. Two uniformed police walked the perimeter, speaking with curious neighbors as they approached, keeping others away.

They crunched almonds in comfortable silence.

"I don't get it," Dana said. "Why call us in?"

Marty pointed at whitewashed wooden lettering sticking out from a flowering hedge across the road, just offset from the building: Merryville Preparatory Academy - Est. 1893.

"I get that it's a high school," Dana said. "We got that much from dispatch."

"Everything school," Marty said, his accent pinging off the words. "One of those baby-kids-through-high-school deals."

"Baby kids?"

"Yeah, like two, three years old. I asked."

"So day care through high school. You work for a child-protection unit, Marty. You gotta talk shop."

Marty shrugged. "Eh. They're all kids to me," Marty said, not unkindly.

Dana was still trying to figure out precisely how Marty felt about kids as both of them settled into their new jobs. He had none of his own, and at first glance he was the type of guy who might hold out a baby at arm's length, blinking dumbly, traps bulging. But he'd surprised Dana with how comfortable he was around Chloe. The few times they'd met, he spoke to her like an old friend, getting down to her level. Chloe still talked about the time he'd given her a handful of confetti poppers at the barbecue Dana hosted to celebrate their promotions.

"They think a kid did this?" Dana asked.

"I think they want to rule it out. Although I'm not too sure what they think we're gonna find after it's been hosed down and picked through by the first responders."

Marty nodded toward where two other policemen were listening patiently as a group of men and women were all trying to speak over one another.

"I think this might be one of those 'call in the cavalry to shut up the rich people' type deals." He popped another almond in his mouth and chewed around a smile. "They had to punch through a Land Rover to get to the hydrant across the street. Ran the hose right through the windows and over the steering wheel. It was awesome."

Dana suppressed a smile. "Let's start at the back. Away from those people."

One of the uniformed police—a sleepy-looking young guy from nearby Bolger station—told her the easiest place to start was with the head of janitorial services. He pointed out a slightly stooped older man in an oil-stained canvas jacket and sharply creased work slacks. Dana flashed him her badge and pulled him from the minor scrum forming near the hamstrung Land Rover. He didn't need much persuading.

"Security cameras show somebody coming in from the west entrance just before the fire." He handed Dana an eight-by-eleven print, in black and white, time-stamped at 12:17 a.m., barely two hours before.

The picture was grainy and off-center, taken from above. It showed a small person walking down a darkened hallway, not much taller than the surrounding lockers. The figure wore light pants—probably jeans—and a white T-shirt. A black baseball hat obscured the face and head.

"This is all we got," he said. "The kid kept away from the

cameras, which is why we think they knew the place. That and it's a pretty private neighborhood. Not a lot of outsiders."

"West side's as good a place as any to start," Dana said.

The janitor talked as they walked, in a voice that sounded scratched by cigarettes. "West side is the main entrance. The school was a manor house for most of the eighteen hundreds. Way too big for its own good. East side was added later. It's where the science labs are. That's what was torched."

They followed the man down an immaculately kept walkway that wound around the building to the west.

"How much does this school cost for a kid?" Marty asked, his head on a swivel.

The janitor sniffed and shook his head slightly. "Twenty thousand a year, to start."

Marty laughed. "Twenty thousand a year for high school?"

The janitor shook his head. "No, son. Twenty thousand for elementary. To start. High school is thirty-two thousand a year. And going up. If you can get a spot. And you don't need to tell me how crazy that is. I already know."

Marty whistled. With the way the janitor spoke—the shake of his head—if Dana were to guess, she would say he made about as much for a year of work as one of these high-school kids paid to attend. Maybe less.

"Here you go," he said as they came upon wide wooden double doors under darkened metal sconces. He unlocked the doors and heaved them open, ushering them inside the main foyer. At that end, the school was silent. Their shoes squeaked softly on the floor, an enormous tiled mosaic of the school crest, which depicted a flaming torch over an open door surrounded by Latin. The janitor stopped them at the center and pointed at a gleaming glass eye nestled in an upper corner of the ceiling, pointing down the right hallway of lockers.

"That's the camera that caught the kid. He went down the hallway there, toward the east wing. And this is where I'll leave you. I suspect I gotta start cleaning what they'll let me on the east side. We're already gonna be shut down long enough as it is. Let me know when you're done. I gotta lock up again. Fire or no fire, I gotta lock up."

Dana thanked him, and he nodded, already looking distracted by his own thoughts as he walked back out. The heavy double doors softly clicked shut behind him.

A single line of emergency halogen lights buzzed overhead, snaking from all directions toward the various exits. The fire-alert strobes still pulsed even though the alarm had long since been silenced.

"Hello?" Marty shouted.

Dana winced involuntarily as his voice echoed down the halls and off the lockers. She looked at him skeptically.

Marty shrugged. "Never hurts to check."

They both set off down the east hall, toward the fire, following a path already tracked and slightly wet from the firefighters. They walked slowly and in silence, and with each step away from the main foyer, the air seemed to darken. Dana found herself squinting to make out the locker numbers and was patting at her pockets for a light when she heard a soft, metallic tap and ring, like the sound of a dropped coin that then rolls.

Both detectives froze.

The sound had come from somewhere ahead of them, beyond the safety lights, in the pitch blackness.

"You heard that, right?" Dana whispered.

Marty nodded.

She strained her eyes but saw no movement. The hall gaped like a long, empty highway under a covered moon. Dana's hand ventured to her gun, in a holster under her arm, but she hesitated. Drawing a gun in a school felt wrong when a kid might be on the other end of it. "You bring a flashlight?" she asked instead.

Marty let out a sigh just loud enough for her to hear then put a small Maglite in her hand with a wry smile. He turned on his own massive Maglite.

"What would you do without me?" he asked.

"Walk around in the dark in peace." She rolled her eyes.

Together, they made their way slowly down the hall, beams of light sweeping the floors and walls, reflecting off the glass windows of the closed classroom doors. Several steps later, Marty pressed lightly on Dana's arm. His beam fell in an expanding line down the left-side lockers, blocks of dull green metal, each shut as tight as the next —save one.

They watched the open door of the locker for a moment. Dana could have sworn it was moving when the beams first caught it, swinging halfway closed. It occurred to her that if it had swung open and into the next locker door, it might have sounded something like a dropped and rolling coin.

Dana called out, "Hello?"

She strained her ears, listening for anything, which meant she heard everything—the revving of the fire trucks' diesel engines as they moved about, the ringing of the halogen safety lights above—but also things that might not be there, that might be her brain tricking her. The distant hum of traffic or a scampering down in the darkness? The first responders talking back and forth somewhere outside, or a muffled laugh, small and childish? Dana shook her head as though she had water in her ears. She couldn't be sure what she heard.

Marty walked over to the open locker, gave the door a perfunctory swing until it tapped the one next to it. The sound was remarkably similar. He lit up the inside. All Dana could see was trash. Lined notebook paper crumpled into balls, maybe ten of them, lay at the bottom. He sifted through them with his flashlight then moved to the small cubby up top, and there he stopped.

"What is it?" she asked.

He moved aside, his face vaguely confused. "Take a look."

Dana stepped in, shining her light. There, in the otherwise empty cubby, was the only flat piece of paper in the locker. Dana started to reach for it before she saw it was a picture drawn in colored pencil. She turned her head to match the orientation. At a glance, it looked like a black dinner table surrounded by fire. Three people crouched underneath the table, out of the flame, their knees drawn to cover their faces. The artwork wasn't exactly crude—the figures were defined and shadowed and the fire well blended—but it still held an air of childishness to it, multiple lines to sketch the bodies, the coloring uneven and scribbled at the edges.

A boy stood on top of the table, legs spread, hands on hips as if it was a podium and he'd just won gold. His smile was a half-moon sliver slit with lines for teeth. A black baseball cap's brim poked out at an odd angle from his head

"We oughta bag this," Dana said quietly.

A year before, Dana knew that Marty might have second-guessed her. Procedure was to take in the scene, establish your fundamentals about how things should be, then look for things that didn't fit. A bunch of scribbled trash in an open locker? He'd have said it was no big deal. But that was then. Now, Marty took out a bag. He picked up the drawing with a pinched kerchief from his pocket, sealed it, and carefully tucked it flat in his back pocket. After a moment's hesitation, he picked up a crumpled piece from the bottom and unfolded it.

"Same picture, more or less," he said.

"Leave them. If they mean anything, we'll come back. They'll keep."

Dana noted the locker number, 210, then moved on down the hall, Marty close behind. She stepped carefully and quietly and replayed her first glance down the hallway in her mind, along with the sound she'd heard.

"Did you see anyone?" she whispered.

"No. But I definitely heard something."

They reached the end of the hallway, where it formed a T at what looked to be the library, locked tight. To the right were more darkened lockers and a double-door exit, barely illuminated. To the left, the hall sloped slightly downward, toward the fire. Dana cocked her head in the direction of the darkened exit and focused on listening. She shone her light down the hall, where its beam died twenty feet out. The red exit sign glowed like an evil eye. Not a sound that way. She turned around. Marty was flashing his light perfunctorily through the windows of the locked library, where it refracted and scattered around the cut glass.

"C'mon," she said. "Let's get to the scene."

When Marty swung his light to the left, something caught Dana's eye. The light-blue walls of the school were painted with a racing stripe of the school's colors, crimson and white, but the white was marked. The effect was faint, especially in the low light, but it was noticeable. An erratic scribble of orange leveled out into a dragged streak, as if someone had walked alongside the wall with a pencil stuck out at their side.

Dana followed the orange down the hall as it leveled out into the east wing, and the smell of old smoke tickled her nose. Marty followed her in silence, adding his light to hers. The pencil wasn't hard to follow, a steady streak of orange, sometimes darkening with what appeared to be a nearly gouging force. Something about the colored streak reminded Dana of breadcrumbs and dark forests, as if they were meant to follow it.

In the stories, Hansel and Gretel nearly ended up in an oven. Had Dana and Marty followed the orange a few hours earlier, they would have ended up in an inferno of a different kind. As it was, their path led into the waterlogged science wing, the walls still flashing blue and red. Everything reeked of soaked ash. The orange mark looked to have been blown off by a strafing of the fire hose that broke the floor-to-ceiling windows separating the labs from the outer hallway. She could see all the way through the labs and out the big double doors in the back, which had either been removed or broken off. A fireman just outside looked at her questioningly until she flashed her badge, then he nodded and continued straightening the main hose, prepping it for rolling up.

Looking at the lab, Dana was taken back to her own high-school science classes. High black-topped tables were spaced evenly about, each with silver gas spigots to attach Bunsen burners, the only things still standing where they should—and only because they were bolted down. The cabinets for equipment that ringed the room were shattered, their contents strewn. Beakers and mixers and boxes of pipettes were scattered on the ground, their delicate glass shattered as easily as broken light bulbs. Stools that had likely ringed the tables during class were instead blown over and pushed back, even into the hallway in some cases, all casualties of the hose. Dana had responded to many fires in her time. Fire damaged. Water destroyed.

She noticed the gas levers were all turned to different angles. The air still smelled vaguely of rotten eggs, underneath the wet ash. "The burners started the fire."

Marty nodded. "What a mess," he said. "What the hell are we supposed to do with this? Read the ashes?"

Marty was right. Whatever clues the kid may have left were washed away. "We're not getting anything else from this room," she said.

Dana turned back toward the hallway they'd followed, looking at where the orange pencil stopped. Perhaps it wasn't leading inward at all. After Black Hat turned on the burners and sparked the fire, maybe he drew a trail behind him on his way out.

"Let's get some fresh air," Dana said, stepping carefully around the shattered and dripping classroom. She walked through the broken doors at the rear, joining the first responders once again. She continued past the noise, past the lights, past the bickering neighbors, all the way to Marty's car—a full loop. Both detectives leaned against the driver's side door. Marty took out his almonds. Dana let out a small sigh. She tried to piece together some sort of narrative that might fit with what they'd found in the locker, but she couldn't. She felt the picture was important, though. She felt it was something that mattered.

A man in a rumpled suit spotted them from the small crowd still near the Land Rover. His eyes settled on Marty's badge. He excused himself from a spirited debate about when the school would reopen and trudged over to them with weary, dragging steps. "Detectives?"

Dana nodded. "Dana Frisco." She extended a hand. "This is my partner, Marty Cicero. We're with the Child Protective Investigations unit."

"Jack Pence. I'm the principal." As he moved in to shake their hands, it became clear that his blue blazer was on top of pajamas. "What a mess. At least nobody was hurt. I saw you take a walk through already. Anything stand out?"

"Maybe," Dana said. "What can you tell us about the kid in the hat?" She held up the security still.

Pence nodded as if he'd stared at it for hours already, to no avail. "Already told the police and anyone that would listen. I have no idea who that is. Nobody could tell with the hat and whatnot. We have uniforms here. Nobody wears jeans and T-shirts."

"Maybe you could start from the beginning. Who called in the fire?"

"Our groundskeeper lives on site, in a small cottage in the south fields. He was the one who first saw the flames, he says around one in the morning. I got the call not long after. Probably the same time as you. That's all I know. I've been fielding questions from parents ever since. All of them are convinced this is going to throw off the graduation schedule and impact their precious snowflakes' chances at Harvard. Meanwhile, half the damn school is on fire." He pinched the bridge of his nose as if to calm himself. "I'm sorry. I wish I could be of more help."

"Any of the neighbors see anything weird?" Marty asked.

"This is a reactionary neighborhood, Detective. They wouldn't take well to seeing that picture you're holding. It means their gates and hedges aren't as bulletproof as they like to believe. Please tell me you've found something, anything, that can close this as soon as it was opened."

Dana nodded to Marty, who took the bagged drawing from his pocket.

"Anything about this strike you? We found it in an open locker. There were more like it balled up at the bottom."

At first, Dana thought Pence might dismiss the drawing. In truth, she could count on both hands the number of cases she'd investigated so far as a detective with CPI. She was still in that hazy, treacherous no-man's-land that came with a new position. If Pence laughed the drawing off as ridiculous, she'd probably believe him. That vulnerability annoyed her. Dana wanted to be good at her job right then, as good as she'd been on the beat.

"What locker?" he asked instead. He turned the bag at different angles in the light of Marty's flashlight.

"The wing of lockers just to the right of the foyer. We're going to need to know who has locker two hundred and ten."

"The two hundred block? That can't be right. Those lockers have all been cleared. We're refinishing that entire wing. A gift from the graduating class. They've been empty for two months."

Dana leaned back wearily against the car. No answers. More questions. The case hung open and swinging, as surely as locker two hundred and ten.

Pence turned his head toward another gathering clump of neighbors, and his slight sigh betrayed his annoyance.

"If you'll excuse me," Pence said, "this looks like it's going to be a long night, and it's only just started."

Dana was thinking the exact same thing.

CHAPTER FIVE

S ophie looked completely worn out. Gordon knew that after an attack of mania often came depression, or bone-weary exhaustion, as if the body had been drained beyond health—similar, in many ways, to what amphetamines did to the brain, firing dopamine receptors beyond their pay grade and going negative in the vacation bank. She seemed sore. She kept rolling her neck, tapping her sneakers on the shaggy rug of his office, and jiggling her bony knees as if trying to keep herself awake. Gordon tried to remember if her knees had been so bruised two days ago at the hotel. He couldn't recall.

"Do you remember when I came to visit you in the hotel room, Sophie?" Gordon asked.

"A little," Sophie said.

She looked at him in fits and starts, like a bird. She sat in his small chair, an exact replica of the one Gordon himself sat in across from her, just slightly diminished to fit his clientele. She smoothed the thick rug beneath her feet with the toe of one shoe after disrupting it with the other. Smoothing, then disrupting. Smoothing. Disrupting. When she wasn't looking at the floor or sidelong at Gordon, she looked toward the closed door to the waiting room beyond, where

Dianne sat, coughing every now and then in what Gordon thought was a conspicuous manner, as if she wanted to let him know she was still there. Still a part. Still the one that had the final say.

"You were organizing some stuff. And washing your hands. Remember that?"

Sophie nodded. "I do that," she said. "Mom tells me it's silly. After a while."

Gordon noted that but didn't respond to it. "What's going through your mind when you're washing your hands and organizing your shoes? How do you feel?"

"Like if I don't, bad things will happen. Like I'm keeping bad things from happening."

"What things?"

Sophie shrugged and rolled her neck. "Dying. Getting taken. You know, bad things. They can happen to anyone. To me. To Mom. Especially girls."

"And organizing, cleaning, putting your things away the right way, these keep the bad things at bay?"

Sophie looked at Gordon for her longest stint yet. She nodded. "That and drawing."

Gordon remembered the colored pencils at her feet in the hotel room, organized by shade of color. "And what about fire?" he asked.

Sophie looked away again. Outside, Dianne cleared her throat. Gordon made a mental note to put the waiting-room furniture away from the shared wall. He felt as though Dianne had an ear pressed to the door.

"Fire's when nothing else works. Fire works then."

"Fire works for what?"

"When nothing else will save me or Mom or anyone else. Fire will."

"Save you from the bad things? Like dying or getting kidnapped?"

A sinking feeling had settled in the pit of Gordon's stomach ever since he'd left the hotel room. As Sophie spoke, it threatened to creep up and sour his throat. He cleared his throat to fight it back down, but he still couldn't shake it, and he was starting to see why. He'd assumed the fire starting was a result of the OCD symptoms, that when one of Sophie's patterns was broken, she set fire to the whole thing to "clean" it. Lashing out in that way had plenty of precedent in literature, but it wasn't a diagnosis that sat well with Gordon, and he thought he knew why.

Gordon was beginning to believe that both the fire starting and Sophie's OCD were symptoms in and of themselves, of something much more problematic.

"Sophie," Gordon said, stirring the girl, who seemed almost asleep. "Can you talk to me about Mo?"

Sophie blinked as if trying to force herself back awake. Gordon noticed, unsettlingly, that her eyes flitted to the four corners of the room once more before settling on him again, just as they had in the hotel room.

"He doesn't exist," Sophie said, as if reading a script.

"Maybe not with you and your mom. But with you and me, if he exists, he exists."

Sophie took her shoes off and set them carefully underneath the chair before tucking her feet underneath herself. She sized Gordon up as if for the first time. In Gordon's experience, first visits with kids often went in the same initial direction. They viewed appointments as a chance either to get away from their parents and act out in a new environment or to be extremely bored and sleep—until something sparked them and they realized that Gordon wasn't a babysitter. That he was, in fact, there to try to figure something out *with* them.

"He doesn't exist," Sophie said again, but her eyes said otherwise.

"Okay," Gordon said, playing along. "So he doesn't exist now. But maybe you could tell me about the first time you met him? Way back when."

Sophie rubbed her eyes, and they opened a shade brighter. "I don't remember the first time I met him. He was always sort of there. I just remember the first time I talked to him."

"Yeah? What did you guys talk about?"

"I was seven." She looked up, thinking. "No, eight. And I was feeling bad, you know. Just like something bad was coming for Mom and Dad. They were fighting and stuff before they got divorced. But that wasn't it. Even before they started fighting, I felt it coming. Just, like, I knew something bad was gonna happen, and Mo and I used to play this stupid hide-and-seek game. Which was basically me just hiding and playing with myself." Sophie shook her head, as if ashamed.

"A lot of kids have imaginary friends, Sophie. It's nothing to be ashamed of."

Sophie wasn't buying it. Her porcelain complexion was reddening. She might as well have been talking about wetting the bed. She was at an age when kids tried their hardest to distance themselves from everything that makes them kids. But Sophie couldn't distance herself from Mo.

"I'd hide, and Mo would try to find me," Sophie said. "A lot of times, I'd hide, and he'd never find me because I had a place in the basement, underneath this table, that he didn't know about."

Gordon searched for fear in Sophie's voice, but all he heard was an edge of competitiveness, almost like a sibling rivalry.

"The first time he talked was when he found me there. I was hiding where it was dark. Quiet. I felt like things weren't pressing down so much on me. Then I heard his steps. They were always light, barefoot. But I could hear them."

Gordon furrowed his brow. That was a strangely specific detail for an imaginary friend to exhibit.

"It was totally dark, but I could hear Mo moving around, giggling. Which was weird, because he'd never giggled before. And I didn't like it. So I moved to the back of the wall, but I think he heard me. Everything in the basement was real quiet, and I could hear the pipes ticking and stuff, then he stuck his face down from up top. Everything sort of caved in on me. It felt like everyone was about to die. I was about to die, too. So I curled up and closed my eyes, and that's when he said, 'Burn it.'"

"And that was the night of the fire?" Gordon asked, keeping all judgment from his voice.

Sophie nodded. "I don't remember setting it. All I remember is waking up in the hospital. Just like waking up at the hotel room."

Gordon nodded. A new diagnosis was forming. A flimsy one. Gordon wasn't happy about it—he didn't like flimsy—but it held up if what Sophie was saying was true.

"What's Mo like?" Gordon asked. "What does he look like?"

"He's just like me, but a boy. He wears dirty jeans and a messy T-shirt and stuff like he just got back from playing tag for hours, and he doesn't wear shoes. And he wears a black hat. And he smiles all the time."

Gordon's diagnosis took another whack. Those details were remarkable.

"And does he still talk to you?"

Sophie looked into her chapped hands, seeming suddenly weighed down. She'd been remarkably engaging so far, given what she'd gone through. That was a good sign—it meant she knew she had a problem and wanted it fixed—but it also took a lot out of her. He felt he didn't have much time left with her that session, before she sank under again.

"He still talks," she said. "He talked in the hotel room."

"He was in the hotel room?"

"After you left. He came. He doesn't like you. He wanted to play hide-and-seek again. But I felt better after cleaning up and stuff, and I could ignore him."

Flimsier still. With each answer she gave, he had more questions. But the bones of his diagnosis still stood.

Sophie was looking at the four corners of the ceiling again, as if the voices she heard came from there. Her slim fingers were gripping her bruised knees with force. She seemed to be trying to back into the corner of her chair.

"Sophie, this was tough for you. I'm very proud of you."

She looked at him fleetingly. She was fading fast. He wished he could reach into her brain and hold it still, keep it from getting swallowed in her sickness. Because while Gordon still had his questions about specifics, he felt strongly that Sophie West was schizophrenic. Her condition manifested itself in the form of delusions—hallucinations and voices. As he watched her worsen by degrees, it ripped him to pieces that all he could do was sit in his chair. He refused to show the dismay he felt. He steeled himself.

"We're gonna figure this out, Sophie," he said, trying his best to keep authority in his voice, even as Sophie let out a soft whine.

As if on cue, Dianne West knocked perfunctorily on the door and then opened it a moment later. She had a blanket that looked worn, most likely a comfort object from Sophie's childhood. She went immediately to her daughter and put it around her, tucking it rather tighter than necessary, almost as if she were willing her daughter to keep herself bottled up and pulled together. Sophie buried her head into her mother's shoulder.

"I think that's all for today," Dianne said, annoyance in her voice. "If she can manage it, we'll be back tomorrow." Dianne pointed at a tattered piece of notebook paper she left on the couch. "Things are... devolving. I found that in her room."

Gordon looked at it dumbly. He couldn't quite make it out. When he turned back to Dianne, she had helped Sophie to stand and was already moving across the room to the door.

Gordon watched from the steps as Dianne looked up and down the street, keeping near the building with an arm around Sophie until her driver arrived. The driver pointedly looked away as he held the back door of the sedan, and Sophie was ushered in as if being chased by paparazzi. They drove away without another word to Gordon.

GORDON PULLED into the parking lot at Waterstones, still distracted by Sophie and her story of Mo. He wasn't in the mood for idle, subtly

probing chat with his mother about his social life and new relationship, not even over scotch and a delicious Waterstones Cobb salad.
Nor did he want the inevitable Deborah Pope diagnosis when she
picked up on his mood, which she always did. His mother was
retired, but she was always the first to say that there was no such
thing as a retired psychiatrist. She would ask him to talk out his frus-
trations, which was the problem. He couldn't explain what was
nagging him about Sophie's case, other than the fact that she was a
schizophrenic that didn't quite fit the mold. But his mother set her
watch by those bimonthly lunches. Not attending had far graver
consequences for his long-term mental well-being.

His phone rang as he put his car in park. The ID read Mother.

"Hi, Mom," Gordon answered. "Sorry I'm late. I'm just parking,
I'll be right in."

"Don't bother, honey," his mother replied. "I'm afraid I'm going
to have to cancel lunch."

Gordon nearly dropped the phone into his lap.

"Hate to do it," she said sadly, as if reluctantly turning down that
second martini. "It's just that I'm in the hospital."

That time, Gordon did drop the phone. He smacked his head on
the steering wheel as he scrabbled for it on the passenger-side floor,
and the car horn gave a weak bleat.

His mother was already talking when he corralled it to his ear,
but he interjected, "Mother. Mom, can you hear me? Are you hurt?
What happened?"

"Oh, I'm at Hopkins in general inpatient. I lost a bit of time.
Woke up on the floor of the kitchen. But no, I'm not hurt."

Gordon finally gathered a breath. He steadied himself against the
car door, as if his rusty coupe was a boat at sea. His mother was
tougher than anyone he knew, save maybe Dana, but she was still
seventy-two years old. A fall was a fall. He felt as if he'd dodged a
bullet.

"I might be dying, though," she added, almost as an afterthought.

~

GORDON WALKED into Johns Hopkins Hospital in a daze, his mind tripping over itself. He punched the down button on the elevator when he meant to go up. He got off on the wrong floor. He'd done countless hours of clinical rotations at Johns Hopkins, yet he had to ask two different people where to find general inpatient. He was told Deborah Pope was admitted at the suite level. Naturally. He felt as if he was falling with every step, as if he'd leapt from a building in a dream and just never hit the ground to wake up.

His mother looked fresh as a daisy. She was dressed in silk two-piece pajamas, legs crossed, reading the *New Yorker* on top of a queen-size bed that would look at home at the Inner Harbor Ritz. Classical music played softly. A big double-paned window was opened outward to catch the last of the sunshine. A glass of iced tea sweated on a wooden table at her right. The suite level was pay-to-play, and the pay was steep, but the amenities were excellent.

She looked up at Gordon and smiled, and there he saw just a hint of the fatigue he'd always feared seeing in her—in a woman never before weary. He wanted to hug her, but he'd only ever hugged her in greeting for so long that he felt as though hugging her then would be admitting some sort of defeat. Instead, he sat down awkwardly in a leather chair by an enormous bouquet of flowers.

"Caesar sent me those. Isn't he sweet?"

"The waiter? From Waterstones? Are you serious? He knew about this before I did?"

"Oh, by moments. I called to tell them I'd be canceling the reservation, one thing led to another, he sent me flowers immediately. Such wonderful service there. Wonderful people."

Gordon flopped his briefcase on the ground and leaned back heavily. The leather puffed out around him.

"What the hell, Mom?" he said, more of a statement than a question.

"It's true. Breast cancer. Stage three. Not good." She folded down her page in the *New Yorker* and turned toward Gordon.

"Are you kidding me?" Gordon took off his glasses and rubbed his eyes. He suddenly felt as though he could fall asleep right there, which he thought was a strange reaction to trauma. Very possum-like.

"Is this why you blacked out?"

"No. I actually found out about it several weeks ago. I was trying to find a way to tell you. I had my first round of radiation therapy earlier this week. Sapped me a bit more than I'd expected."

Gordon could only blink at her. "You've known about this for *weeks?*"

"I was trying to find a way to tell you—"

"How about 'Gordon, I've got cancer.' That would have worked. Three weeks ago."

"Get a hold of yourself. This is a private floor. No hysterics up here." His mother stared sternly at him until he closed his mouth. "We both know you're quite busy these days. Getting the practice up and running again and whatnot—"

"No no no." Gordon waved her off in much the same way she often preempted others. "Don't you dare throw this back on me. This is about you thinking you can go it alone. Not wanting to seem vulnerable."

She looked down her nose at him. "Thank you for the insight, Dr. Pope. You can mail me the bill."

"What are we gonna do?" Gordon asked, feeling very childish, as if all he could do was throw a tantrum. When his father was on the verge of death, after a heart attack at sixty, he'd felt a calm sense of impending loss. No panic. But his father had been distant, more than a bit of a drinker, and unfaithful. His mother was smothering, more than a bit of a drinker, and faithful as the day is long. She didn't deserve to be sitting in a hospital.

"You don't deserve this, Mom," he said helplessly, the words pouring forth.

"Cancer doesn't care what you deserve, sweetheart," she replied, smiling sadly. "And we're going to keep at it," she added, as if pointing out the obvious. "I'm going to radiate the tumor to operable size and then get a double mastectomy."

Gordon choked on his own spittle, coughing loudly. His mother marched on.

"And you're going to keep treating your new patients. What are you working on these days? Your papers spilled out all over the floor."

"A double mastectomy?"

"Yes, honey. It's already scheduled. Now, tell me about work. I like hearing about your work. Now that you have a bit of it. Is that drawing yours? If so, I'd stick to psychiatry." Deborah pointed at the paper-strewn floor, her silver bracelets jingling gently.

Gordon followed her dumbly. She was pointing at Sophie's picture: a family huddled under a black table surrounded by fire— and a grinning boy standing atop, crude, but visible—a childish drawing, most likely done in the depths of one of her psychotic breaks.

"I think it's a bit of a family portrait. A drawing from a new patient I took on," Gordon said. "A very troubled young woman who sets fires that she can't remember starting. Still a girl, really. Just twelve. I'm having a bit of trouble with her diagnosis."

Just talking about something else—anything else—shattered the bubbling panic that crept up Gordon's throat like bad booze. The spinning roulette wheel of his mind settled upon the category of *work*, a well-worn groove, and he found himself able to take his first clear breath since arriving. His mother smiled briefly at him, as if she had known all along just how to bring him around.

"Is she the one grinning like an imp?"

Gordon shook his head. "She's under the table to the right, the blonde with her head down. But the one grinning like an imp set the fire."

"A brother?"

"Her imaginary friend. Mo."

His mother sucked in a breath through her teeth. "A twelve-year-old fire starter who blames her imaginary friend. And here I thought things might get easier for you after the sleepwalkers."

Gordon traced the figures in the drawing lightly with his fingers, and for a moment he forgot he was in a hospital. He might have been across the table from his mother at Waterstones, waiting for a refresh of his cocktail.

"There's more. She's getting external impressions of dread, existential dread that she ties to an impending and unavoidable abduction and assault, maybe a rape. Both of her and her mother. Her imaginary friend tells her the only way to stay safe is to burn."

"You think she's schizophrenic."

"I think so, yes," Gordon said before tilting his head in reconciliation to his own doubts. "Maybe. Maybe not."

Gordon hadn't had a chance to take a good look at the picture yet, in his hurry to get to the hospital. The way Dianne had pointed to it was unsettling, as if she wanted to be gone by the time he looked at it. He found Dianne in the picture, underneath the table, to Sophie's right. She looked just as haunted as Sophie did. The man to Sophie's left was likely her father, Simon. His eyes looked neither sad nor scared, nor wide and manic like Mo's. His were hollow black circles.

"That was three answers, Gordon," Deborah said.

"When I first met her, she was recovering from some sort of episode in a hotel room. Her mother is very protective, both of Sophie and of their family reputation."

Deborah nodded. She understood well about the importance of neighborly reputation. In that, at least, Deborah Pope and Dianne West would find a lot of common ground.

"She was organizing herself out of it using an obsessive-compulsive routine."

"OCD is an indicator of deeper trauma. And a symptom of full-blown psychosis," his mother said.

She'd moved to the side of the bed. If Gordon squinted, he could almost make himself believe that she was across a table adorned with two chilled bowls of Waterstones' Cobb salad.

"It's also a common indicator of extreme anxiety. Not necessarily a full psychotic break," he replied. "I don't feel great about the light benzodiazepine routine I put her on, as it is. But her anxiety is through the roof. I hate diagnosing schizophrenia because..."

"Because once you do, there's no going back."

Gordon nodded. The soft beep of her vitals machines brought him back to the room. The weight of Sophie's problems, coupled with the reality of his mother's diagnosis, dragged him down in his seat. His world seemed to visibly darken.

"Schizophrenia has no real cure. Only management. It's lifelong. And the medicine is brutal. And she's so young. Schizophrenic breaks don't usually happen to women until their twenties." Gordon rattled each fact off with a flick of his finger.

"You sound like you're making excuses. Like that's what other people might say to you to convince you otherwise. What do *you* feel, Gordon?"

Gordon dropped his head back on the chair, gazing at the ceiling. A particle-board ceiling. A hospital ceiling. All the fancy lighting and queen beds and fresh linens in the world couldn't change that. Couldn't change what his mom was facing. What Sophie was facing.

"It comes back to Mo. The problem is the specificity of him. He's too well-defined of an entity for a schizophrenic. Even one that is delusional. Or hallucinating. The literature describes voices without faces. Orders without origin. Schizophrenics may feel compelled to do things like burn, but I can't think of a case I've come across, or even read about, where a delusional patient so clearly understands the source of the voices."

"Mo."

"Mo." Gordon nodded. "He's a teenage boy. He wears jeans and a dirty T-shirt and pads around shoeless. Sophie can describe the sounds of his feet." Gordon pointed to the picture again. "He has a big Cheshire grin and wears a black ball cap down low over his face. And he tells her that burning everything to the ground is the only way to stay safe in Baltimore."

"I know a fair number of people who might agree with little Mo," Deborah said drolly.

"Mother."

"Metaphorically, of course," she added, holding up her hands. "But either way, it sounds like you've got a lot on your plate."

Gordon met her eyes and thought he saw a smile there, a measure of delight in the mountain Gordon had in front of him. And pride. Deborah Pope's own special brand of pride, only given when the whistles blew and her son was faced with the moment when he had to go over the top and charge the hill. He scrunched up his nose a bit to keep the water from his eyes. She looked like someone watching her child wave from the front step of the school before she was forced to turn away from him—maybe for good.

"Mom, I'm gonna stay with you here. I'll sleep in this chair."

"Nonsense. Their care is fabulous here. The chair would only give you back problems."

"Well then, I'll have them wheel in a bed. For whatever you're paying, they can wheel in a bed."

"Gordon—"

"I'm gonna be here, Mom. I'm gonna be with you through all this. Right here."

"Gordon, enough," she said kindly.

Gordon cleared his throat and dropped his head. The lump was painful in his throat.

"Here's what is going to happen. You will live your life. You will treat your patient. You will do what you have to do. And so will I. Now go home and get some rest. You're no good to anybody sleeping in a chair and waiting for your mother to go under."

Gordon coughed. "Mom!"

"The knife, Gordon. Under the knife. My heavens. Don't be so morbid." There, a little more of the old twinkle in her eye.

Gordon felt ashamed that he'd ever thought to skip lunch. What an ass he was. Spoiled. He'd been spoiled. And the other shoe had finally dropped.

His mother seemed to see the swelling of his guilt. Perhaps she felt it in the pregnant pause between them—Gordon had learned everything he knew about listening from his mother. She placed one disturbingly thin hand over Gordon's, stopping whatever confession he'd felt bubbling up.

"Trust me, honey, there will be plenty of time to wallow later in life. Not now. Go."

So Gordon went.

GORDON DROVE AROUND IN A FOG. He hardly registered the liquid sunset that brought the burnished trees to life and set brief fire to the hundreds of office windows lining Monument Street. His mind was awash with worry, for Sophie and for his mother, to the point where he felt as if he was no longer struggling to stay above the churning waters but instead had found some sort of numb stasis within them— not drowning but not really breathing either. He didn't realize where he was going until he was nearly there.

He knocked on Dana's front door, staring blankly at the thatched fall wreath of yellow leaves and red berries hanging in front of his face. Chloe opened the door, with Maria close behind, watching. Chloe gazed up at him through beautiful brown eyes that looked a hair too large for her face. Her mother's eyes. She was dressed in a shiny bubblegum-pink tracksuit. She thrust both her hands in the pockets like an adorable little gangster.

"Hi, Chloe." Gordon tried not to sound as though he'd been on the verge of sobbing most of the afternoon.

"Hi, Gordon," Chloe said.

"That's Dr. Pope, sweetheart," Maria said.

Gordon knew Maria was being polite, but he couldn't help but feel that she also liked the distance of the *Dr. Pope*. Dr. Pope had just started seeing her daughter. *Gordon* was a step along the way to *Gord* or even *Dad*, neither of which either Chloe or her grandmother seemed particularly enthusiastic about right now.

"I like your pink suit," Gordon said.

"Thanks," Chloe said. "I got it from gymnastics."

Gordon was about to ask her more. About gymnastics. About school. About her life. About anything. He thought too hard about where to start, and in the awkward silence, Chloe jumped in.

"Are you looking for Mom? She's at work still. She works all night tonight."

Gordon nodded. He should have called first. He wanted to tell Chloe that he wouldn't mind hanging out with her for a bit. Maybe between them, they could find a way to make it so he didn't feel like such a dope around the family. He'd never been around Maria and Chloe without Dana as a buffer. He wanted to, at some point, but just then, it sounded exhausting. Instead, he nodded and turned to go.

"Will you tell her I stopped by?" Gordon asked, pausing.

"Sure." Chloe nodded vigorously.

"Bye, Chloe," Gordon said. Then he craned to look behind her. "Bye, Maria."

Maria smiled benignly. "Goodbye, Dr. Pope."

In the silence of the car once more, he decided to call Dana. He plucked his phone from his pocket but paused when he saw his voice mail had logged twelve missed calls from a number listed as Unavailable. He had five voice mails. At first, he thought they must be from the hospital earlier, trying to get hold of him to tell him his mother had been admitted. The first message was a quick hang-up, mere seconds. So was the second. Odd, but Hopkins had HIPAA regulations against what could and couldn't be said on an answering machine, so perhaps they were waiting to speak to him personally. The third was similar but slightly longer. He heard a soft intake of breath, as if someone was about to speak, then the click of disconnecting.

Gordon furrowed his brow and pressed Next.

That time, someone was definitely breathing, soft and steady. It went on for ten seconds. By then, a strange feeling of dread was skittering across the back of Gordon's neck although he couldn't say why.

The fifth was the longest yet—twenty seconds of soft, steady breathing, a bit faster than his own. Childlike. As was the voice that spoke in a whisper.

"Leave us alone."

Click.

Gordon took his phone from his ear and stared at it as if he could read more from its blank screen. He played the message over and over again, trying to discern anything from the background during the soft breathing, but he could hear nothing. He had the feeling that whoever was on the other end was thinking hard about whether to speak.

"Leave us alone."

Gordon thought it sounded like a boy. A young boy. However, it could just as easily have been a girl. The voice had yet to fall into either category over the phone. When Gordon had been in his early teens, he was mistaken for Deborah Pope over the phone more often than not—enough so that he stopped answering, enough so that when his own voice started to crack, that was actually a bit of a relief.

He knew, with a certainty that he had no medical basis for but that was nonetheless undeniable—as sure as the slow shiver that now traced its way down his spine like a single drop of sweat—that the voice belonged to Mo.

Somehow, Mo was talking to him through Sophie. Somehow, she'd gotten his personal number and let Mo take over. His diagnosis was thrown to the wind. If Mo was able to call Gordon, that meant he was enough of a presence within Sophie that he actually existed. He had his own personality.

Perhaps Mo was a separate and distinct personality within Sophie. Perhaps the young girl was suffering from Dissociative Identity Disorder—multiple personalities within one. He'd been given another piece of the puzzle, but again it seemed to have no true home in the overall picture—as if three sides had clicked but the fourth still stuck. Sophie said that she remembered Mo's steps. She heard his voice. She saw him as separate from herself. Those who suffered from multiple-personality disorders often functioned for years without being aware of their separate selves. Many had no idea they were afflicted. Those that were aware of their other selves considered them a part of a whole, as living within. Not Sophie. Sophie saw Mo in front of her. Around her. Outside of her.

Whether Mo was Sophie's delusion or, as was looking more and more likely, a part of Sophie herself, Gordon couldn't say. It seemed like both, which didn't fit cleanly into either. He found he was grinding his teeth. He checked the time on the message. As recently as forty minutes before, Mo had been out in full force, which meant he had to get to Sophie before she hurt herself or others.

His phone buzzed again. At first, he thought it was another voice mail, perhaps from Mo. Anything from the entity himself might serve as a tool he could use to help secure Sophie's mind, to bring her back from mania without delving into the deep end of antipsychotics. If he worked quickly enough, perhaps he could exorcise that delusion and help her to realize a life apart from Mo so she could become her own woman without that shadow hanging over her.

No voice mail that time, only a text message from Dianne, but it confirmed his worst fear. It read, "Sophie has gone missing."

CHAPTER SIX

The smell of old smoke hung in the air, the same way that an unpacked tent can throw an invisible dusting of campfires past into the air. Whoever had turned on the gas and sparked the science lab had set one heck of a fire, but if their aim was to torch the whole school, their job was unfinished. Dana was counting on the fact that, in her experience, arsonists hated unfinished work.

She panned the east wing of the school from where she and Marty sat in the minivan. She saw no movement other than the quiet flutter and twist of a wide swath of police tape that cordoned off the burned area. The moon seemed to have fled the scene as well, casting only intermittent light from a great distance. The only person talking within half a mile was Marty.

"It's roomy. I'll give it that."

"What?" Dana replied absently, eyes straining.

"The ol' family wagon here." Marty thumped the roof with his fist. "You could fit a whole day care in this thing. I thought you only had Chloe."

"When I bought it, I'd planned on more," Dana said flatly. She was tired, on her second straight night inside Merryville without much to show for it. All she had to go on was a bunch of creepy draw-ings and a hunch. Meanwhile, her new boyfriend was walking around with his head in the clouds, proving her mother right with every visit. And right then, she didn't feel much like talking.

Marty dropped his hand and softly cleared his throat, nodding and looking away. She felt guilty. Her problems weren't his fault.

"It's all right, Marty. That was then. All that's left of that me is this car."

That had been her line for a long time. Recently, however, she felt less force behind it, which concerned her. Thoughts she'd packed away long before were bubbling up again, like what it meant that she'd never feel the sure swelling of her belly again, and what a good big sister Chloe would make. She shoved those thoughts to the back of her mind. She'd hated being pregnant at the time, found the sensa-tions that came with growing a child more annoying than inspiring or beautiful. She hadn't cared to repeat the process for years and years—thanked God repeatedly, in fact, that she had only Chloe to care for after the divorce. Then she fell for a man that couldn't give her a child, and all of a sudden, her hormones were going haywire. She was forty years old, for God's sake—hardly the time for her body to start waxing nostalgic about pregnancy.

"What I meant to say was not all of us can drive souped-up muscle cars. I gotta strap in more than my gym bag." She put a smile behind the barb that brought Marty around again.

"My baby's not just any muscle car," Marty said, perking back up. "She's a Dodge Charger. Hellcat edition. Stupid fast. Seven hundred horsepower..." He trailed off. He'd gone full car mode with Dana before and knew it went right over her head. "How's Chloe doin', by the way?" he asked sheepishly.

"She's still a little weirded out by me and Gordon," Dana said truthfully. "She's been singing along to her cartoons louder than usual when he's around."

"What, she doesn't like him?" Marty asked, a gleam in his eye. "I thought he was supposed to be a wizard with kids."

"Yeah, well. He is... with his patients. He's sort of like a fish out of water with Chloe." Dana shook her head. "Or maybe all three of us are flopping around a bit."

Marty leaned back and crossed his thick arms, "You two, maybe. Not Chloe. That girl kicks ass. Maybe he's intimidated."

Dana snorted a laugh. She thought of Chloe in her pink tracksuit, dancing around to her cartoons, her shoes sparkling up a storm. Very intimidating stuff.

Dana gestured out of the windshield with a tic of her head. "How about you just keep an eye out for the kid we should really be afraid of."

Marty tapped the top of the car above the open window as he watched the darkened school. "You really think the kid'll come back?"

Dana nodded slowly. "The far side of the lab was torched, but the side nearest the doors was only singed. Soaking wet paper everywhere, only half burned. He set kindling on both sides, but only the near side caught. Arsonists tend to be perfectionists, no matter what age. At the very least, they might come by again to check it out."

So Marty and Dana settled in and waited.

And waited.

And waited.

DANA FELT a tapping on her shoulder. She shot up and felt something firmly pressing her back down at the sternum. She almost screamed until she placed herself. Still in her car. Still with Marty, who had his arm barred across her, like a burly mother holding her child back during a hard stop. With his other hand, he pressed a finger to his lips.

Marty pointed out toward the school. After Dana's heart stilled, she could focus long enough to see the dark windows, as gaping and empty as they'd been when she first turned the car off to sit and watch. She shook her head, unable to see anybody.

"By the big tree," he whispered.

The cicadas had long gone to sleep, their roar replaced by the soft chirp of crickets. She looked at the clock and flushed with embarrassment. Marty had let her sleep until nearly three in the morning. She frowned at him, but he pointed again.

Dana watched the big tree they'd walked under with the janitor the day before, an enormous white oak that silently dropped leaves at a steady rate. All she saw was its dark mass, weakly lit in passing by the cloud-covered moon.

Then her eyes caught something, not much more than a flickering of shadow but visible in the harsh relief between the tree and the lighter fields beyond. She held her breath. The flickering pulled back behind the tree until she'd nearly convinced herself it was a trick of her imagination. Then a figure emerged, one limb at a time. Slowly. Like a shadow peeling itself from the wall until she could see its outline clearly in the space between.

He was small and thin, definitely child sized, possibly adolescent. He stood with his hands on his hips like a skinny superhero surveying his domain. No cape, but he did have a hat, a baseball cap, brim slightly to the side.

"That's our guy," Dana whispered. She felt it was a him. Something in the challenge of the stance said *boy* to her. He looked like a boy out on a dare. She could almost see his grin.

For a moment, she thought he was looking at them. They were at least a hundred feet away from the tree, one of several cars parked on the street outside the school, including the busted Land Rover—so she doubted he'd seen them. Still, the featureless outline of his shadow gave the illusion that he was staring at them in silence. Even the crickets had paused.

After several frozen moments, all three of them stock still, he clearly stepped away from them until he was lost in the shadows of the building at the cordon. The tape fluttered then went still again.

Both Dana and Marty slowly opened their doors, stepped out, then shut them with the barest push and click. They crossed the street like thieves. Dana felt strongly that direct confrontation would go badly for them. The boy's movements had been sure, quick. She could picture him bolting and disappearing into the night, their chance missed. Marty seemed to know that as well. He was good. And she owed him, no matter what came of this night. She was the one driving the stakeout, having told him to give up his Saturday night to sit there. She knew he looked up to her. Dana made a mental note to get more sleep. Senior officers did not fall asleep on watch. It was unlike her.

No matter how tired she had been, she was wide awake the second she stepped out of the car. Dana keyed in to every sound, every movement. Ahead of her, the desks had been taken out and arranged in rows under the broken moonlight and the reaching canopy of the massive white oak, each dusted lightly with fallen leaves. More leaves fell upon the detectives as they walked underneath, each floating down in silence, one after the other like lemmings at a cliff.

Dana thought she'd seen the boy go under the cordon, but she wasn't sure. Under the filtered moonlight and amplified silence, everything seemed so dreamlike. She was starting to second guess that she'd ever seen the boy at all. She turned to Marty and shook her head, but then her nose flared with a smell, an acrid, unmistakable scent that drew her in and repelled her at the same time. Gasoline. She nosed about, but the scent left her with a puff of the night breeze.

Marty pointed to his ear. She heard it, too—a whisper like the soft roiling of water in a pot.

Glugluglug.

It was coming from inside the burned-out lab.

Gluglugluglug

Dana dropped all attempts at silence. She took off running, rounding the desks at top speed with Marty beside her. With each step, the smell of gasoline grew stronger until she felt permeated by it. Then she saw him, a single figure standing like a sprinter on the blocks less than fifty feet from her on the edge of the grass outside the broken doors. He had on a black hat, which shadowed his face almost entirely—only his bright-white teeth shone in the night. He wore baggy jeans and a loose T-shirt that hung past his rear. His legs seemed bony and his shoeless feet oversized. He let out a brief, bubbly giggle before covering his mouth. Then he struck a match.

"Race me," he whispered harshly.

Dana could only wave her hands, as if she could blow out the match from a distance. She didn't even have time to utter a cry as he dropped it on the trampled grass and took off at a tear toward the black maw of the burned-out lab.

The world seemed to freeze. The police tape that surrounded them no longer fluttered. The weak wind died. Dana froze in shock, her hands out. Marty was caught with his mouth open. Only the strange boy seemed able to move, the strange boy and the line of fire that followed him—the boy with a giggle, the fire with a low hiss.

When time snapped back to her, Dana ran after him, not even thinking. She ran as if compelled, as if the fire were pulling her along with a crooked finger of flame. The boy was fast, and he had a head start. Already, he was jumping the larger debris before the outer wall. Dana vaulted it seconds later, but by then, he'd shot through the broken doors, feet slapping the charred linoleum inside, and in an instant, he was swallowed in darkness as surely as if he'd dropped down a hole in the earth. The hole was so black it caught Dana up for a moment, much like a driver instinctively slows before a tunnel. An ancient, ingrained response was telling her *Do not enter that cave. You don't know what is back there.*

Marty was yelling something: *Dana* or perhaps *Don't.* She heard his heavy steps slamming behind her. And she almost did stop, until the snake of fire shot inside the cave ahead of her, and its light, no brighter than a hurricane candle, was still enough to show the glittering teeth of the child just below the brim of his hat, head turned, midstride, eyes aimed at her.

Dana shot along the burn line, chasing the flame. She could smell charred plastic and ash and wet wood. She seemed to dive through each scent, one after the other.

Ahead of her, the boy careened around the aftermath of the fire as if it was his own bedroom, ducking the bolted tables with ease as they appeared. He was swallowed in darkness in a matter of moments, and at the same time Dana broke through into a new, overwhelming smell of straight gasoline. Then she really did stop. She held up her hands as if she could part the heavy curtain of fumes that watered her eyes and caught her breath in her throat.

Marty started screaming for her.

Dana blinked her eyes against the fumes. She saw the fire crawl forward through a watery haze in the air, and it seemed to her like a burning comet in the darkness of the room,

hurtling with massive speed at the same time as it crawled along across the horizon. Soon, she saw what Marty was screaming about. A spilled canister of gasoline was illuminated by degrees. Then another next to it. And another. And the comet was on a collision course—too far for her to stop it, too close for her to run.

She felt the explosion before she saw it, like the first step into a sauna. A heavy, powerful heat pushed at her with an open palm to the chest. A bloom of fire followed, and it seemed to Dana that the bloom passed through every color of the rainbow before ending in an all-engulfing white. She heard the explosion last of all—a basso thud that felt as if it thrust upward from the ground into the base of her lungs as she was yanked from her feet and out of consciousness.

CHAPTER SEVEN

Gordon creaked to a stop outside the iron-and-ivy gate of the Merryville neighborhood in his whining coupe. He frowned, checking the address Dianne had given him. Everything matched, but he wasn't expecting to be stopped at the gates. He'd known Dianne was wealthy, but Merryville looked like its own little fiefdom, outside and above the world around it.

His brakes roused the attendant from his novel. The man straightened his jacket and stepped from the booth with his clipboard.

"Can I help you, sir?"

"Is Long Lane down this way?" Gordon asked.

"It is. Are you Doctor Pope?"

"I am."

"May I see some identification?"

He looked at Gordon's license over the rims of his spectacles and jotted down its number on his pad, checking his watch to note the time. Gordon glanced at the clock. If one in the morning was an unusual time for visitors, the attendant didn't let on.

He handed back the license, nodded, and said, "Number eight Long Lane. Straight ahead."

The gate swung open noiselessly. The road ahead was dark and lined with trees like ancient sentinels. Gordon was uncomfortably aware of the slap and whine of his fraying engine belt as he drove forward.

Number eight Long Lane would have taken up one through eight in any city neighborhood. He'd never seen an estate so large that close to Baltimore proper. It looked like something more suited to Bethesda, where Gordon had grown up and the lots had rounded driveways and the occasional horseback rider could be seen cantering through the faraway fields.

The house itself consisted of three parts: a center structure of white stone and columned wood and two redbrick wings, each with a glittering slate roof lit at intervals from the ground. Every window was flanked by whitewashed shutters, every edge sharp, every tree trimmed for full fall effect. The lights were on inside, illuminating the windows at intervals throughout, but Gordon saw no movement behind them.

Gordon squeaked to a stop and parked on the street. He took the long walk over heavy flagstone to the front door, where he cleared his throat and rang the doorbell. A brass chime rang through the entire house like an echo in a canyon.

Then silence.

Gordon frowned. He tried knocking on the heavy door but felt as if his rapping barely penetrated the wood. He rang the doorbell again.

Silence.

Gordon pulled out his phone and tried the number from which Dianne had texted him. It rang. And rang. And rang.

Gordon dropped his hands to his side. He let out a slow, steady breath. The ringing continued. He cocked his head, listening. The sound jumped from his phone through the door and inside the house. Dianne's phone, at least, was nearby.

"Dianne?" Gordon stepped forward and placed one hand on the door, the other on the knob. "Dianne, are you there? It's Gordon."

It can't possibly be open. Not after the gate and the guard and the clipboard and signing in...

The front door opened at a turn of the brass knob. It swung in as if on oiled bearings. The house smelled orange-scented clean. It was lit in the manner that an empty hotel corridor is lit—at intervals and by lights that Gordon doubted ever turned off.

"Hello? If anyone is here, I'm coming in." *Please don't sic the hounds on me.*

He flicked his phone out again and redialed. He listened, eyes wide. He almost jumped back out onto the porch when Dianne's phone buzzed to life straight ahead of him. As it rang, it spun slowly like an angry, wounded wasp on the floor, dead ahead. He walked forward, through the gleaming marble foyer and into an expansive great room of dark wood, the nexus of the house. A dimmed chandelier hung above him, drawing his eye up the staircase ahead and along the balustrades of three floors of rooms. Pastoral artwork hung on the walls in burnished wood frames. A lacquered black grand piano sat near one corner, top open, ready for play. Dianne's phone buzzed at the base of a brass sculpture of an angry-looking buffalo standing just to the left of the stairway. Afraid to pick it up, he stared at it until it quieted.

He looked up the stairs and grimaced, his hands on his hips. Going up there seemed somehow more of an invasion, as if there were degrees of penetration. In the great room, with the foyer just behind and the door still open, he was barely in the house. He could still bolt. But up there? Up there, he was in it.

Gordon's eye was drawn toward movement from behind the stairs, toward the back of the main level. A white lace curtain fluttered out like a woman's dress in the sparse wind coming through wide-open double doors leading to the back patio and darkened lawn beyond.

Gordon walked toward the open doors. That he could pass right through, in and out, as if he had never been there, gave him some small measure of comfort. He pawed down the billowing curtain and pushed it behind heavy purple drapes nearby before stepping out.

Two floodlights slammed on, and Gordon threw his arms in front of his eyes. He stood still, hands up, until his hammering heart subsided. He waited for the shouts and accusations, but as his breathing steadied, the lights shut off again. *Motion sensors. Of course.*

"Dianne?" he called into the blind darkness. "Sophie?"

The last locusts of the season clicked softly in halfhearted response, their sleep disturbed. The crickets quieted.

As his eyes adjusted, Gordon saw in the near distance a small shed by a fledgling tree, which looked out of place surrounded by such grand compatriots. A new tree. He recalled the story of the fire. Dianne had said Sophie had started it in a tree house and it spread to one wing of the house. Gordon couldn't see any damage to the house from where he stood, but the fire had been years before, and houses like that one were quickly and spotlessly repaired. Old-growth trees, on the other hand, were not so easily replaced.

Gordon walked across the lawn, shading his eyes as the lights clicked on again at his movement. He saw that the shed was more like a small house, a beautiful little wooden playhouse complete with little windows and little shutters and a little hanging basket with live flowers. The door said Sophie's Place in painted white stencil on a miniature mailbox outside a small door that looked remarkably similar to the front door of the house proper. That, too, was open.

Gordon crossed from grass to a fresh cedar-chip flooring, and he felt confident he was standing where a large white oak tree had once stood before its charred remains were ground from the earth and Sophie's Place built anew. *The next best thing to a tree house if you no longer have the tree.*

Gordon pushed the little door open farther. It cut a track through a layer of dust on the floor of the single room inside. The floodlights shut off, and he was plunged into darkness. He pulled out his phone and used it to light what he could, which was almost everything. Glittering flecks of dust floated slowly in the air, nearly still. He guessed Dianne and Simon had had it rebuilt immediately after the fire two years back, perhaps thinking their troubled child still needed a place of her own. Perhaps she'd sat a handful of times in those small chairs, shoved to the far wall and stacked atop a small table like a little shuttered restaurant. No longer. The place felt forgotten, which made the footprints Gordon saw all the more out of place.

The small divot of the ball of a foot and five little tufts of toes, like instructions for a child's dance routine, repeated itself along the perimeter of the room. After years of neglect, someone had recently been in there—tiptoed or pranced on bare feet.

Gordon recalled Sophie's feet sticking out from the corner of the bed, her shoes neatly placed one way, then another, then back again after each of her washings. He knew the girl didn't like to wear shoes in the depths of her attacks.

Gordon followed the prints with his light, and they took him on a mad waltz around the little playhouse. The trail ended at a neat row of colored pencils, organized in shades in their open box, placed flush against the corner opposite the door. They spanned the color wheel from black to white, each the same sharpness, each the same height, which made the single missing color as obvious as a gap tooth. The pencils skipped from yellow to red. No orange among them.

Gordon heard a soft thump in the distance, and he flinched down. The sound unsettled him in a primal way, like a car wreck or a muffled scream. His gut told him he'd just heard an explosion and it was nearby.

Standing in that playhouse marked by a sick young girl who in all likelihood was very recently not in her right mind—who was likely following the voices in her head—in that moment, surrounded by floating specks of the past and ill portents of the present, Gordon knew that the explosion he'd heard was because of Sophie.

He rushed from the playhouse, and the lights snapped on again. He spun in a circle, looking for anything that might tell him where that awful *whump* had come from, but the lights were too bright and the trees too tall. The sky was nothing but a patch of black seen straight up from the bottom of a well.

He started toward the back doors again, planning to follow the sound out front, in his car if need be. It couldn't have been that far away, a quarter mile at most—not that Gordon had heard all that many explosions in his life. He tried to think of what the fireworks shows at the Bethesda Country Club had sounded like from Windmill Hill, where he'd sat as a child. That had been about a quarter mile—

Someone was in the house.

Gordon dropped to the ground and froze. He'd caught only a glimpse, but in that second, he'd seen a man in the house. Tall and broad. Gordon flattened himself in the vast expanse of the floodlit lawn like a petrified rabbit and tried not to panic. Anybody who even glanced outside would see him plain as day.

So he started rolling. He rolled like a log, over and over himself, staining his khakis while his brand-new shirt, one of two, came untucked and billowed around him like a sheet until he hit the metal edging of the perimeter. He smelled cedar and, underneath it, the barest scent of burned wood. At first, he had the absurd thought that he'd somehow run into the burned wing of the house, but that was long covered over. He smelled new burn on the weak wind, although in a way, the new burn was just a continuation of the old. Another entry in a long story of fire that seemed dedicated to this place.

All Gordon could do was lie still, dug in against the wood chips, as the man walked around slowly inside the house. He could hear his footsteps pick up then pause. The man was looking for something. Or someone.

"Sophie?" he said, gruff and demanding. An order.

The sweat Gordon had worked up in the rolling and the hiding froze on his brow as surely as if he'd walked into an icebox. He recognized that voice.

"Dianne? Are you here?"

The way he spoke their names sounded as though he was familiar with them, but his tone was harsh and clipped, annoyed. An underlying vein of anger was barely concealed. He stepped to the open back door and paused before stepping fully outside, where Gordon could see him. Warren Duke pondered the floodlights then turned his gaze to the playhouse. Gordon didn't dare breathe. The lieutenant, now major, had never liked Gordon. To say the least. *Hated* Gordon was much more accurate. Gordon had his theories—maybe because he refused to be pushed around by the man, maybe because he was a "civvie" inserting himself in police matters, maybe because he'd created quite a bit of paperwork for Duke's district recently—but in the end, he had no real answer. Perhaps Duke simply didn't like the look of Gordon's face.

Whatever the reason, if Duke spotted him, it would end badly for Gordon. Jailed for breaking and entering at best. He'd tried to arrest Gordon before. That Gordon wasn't in jail right then was due purely to the good press he'd given Duke when he broke the sleepwalker case. But good press was fleeting, and there Duke was, somehow, improbably walking out of the back doors of the house of yet another of Gordon's patients as if he owned the place. He was in his official uniform, his preppy jacket and pink oxford gone in favor of the dress blues of the BPD that showed his new rank in the bars on his collar and the bars on his arms. He held his cap in the crook of an elbow with one hand and shaded his eyes with the other. His signet ring flashed brilliant gold in the floodlights. He looked as if he was born into the rank, which Gordon knew wasn't far from the truth. The Duke family ran a textile empire out of the docks—had for generations. Other blue-blood east coasters were born with silver spoons in their mouths. Duke had the whole silver knife set. He was the type of man who could ruin you in Baltimore with a single word to his people, and that was *before* he'd become a major.

He was perhaps twenty feet from Gordon. Close enough to see the pulsing vein in his tanned temple. Gordon was sure he'd be able to smell the man's cologne if the growing smoke smell hadn't been so strong. If Duke made a half turn to his right and took a second to peer into the dark circle just outside the lights, he'd see Gordon sprawled out like a drunk on the lawn. Gordon's panic was real, but it was secondary. His mind was too busy tumbling over itself, trying to piece together what, exactly, Warren Duke was doing there.

He couldn't have followed Gordon. The two of them had stayed as far apart as possible for a month. More accurately, Gordon tried to stay as far from Duke as possible, which wasn't a problem. They didn't exactly run in the same circles. Maybe Duke was simply responding to the explosion. *But why stop by 8 Long Lane first?*

Perhaps he knew about Sophie and Mo and the Merryville fire. Perhaps he'd put everything together.

As Duke panned the backyard, Gordon realized he'd have the unfortunate chance to ask the man himself, in another couple seconds—right before the cuffs went on, most likely.

But then Duke froze, and a heartbeat later, Gordon heard why.

Sirens. Several of them, coming their way. Sirens at night in a neighborhood like that meant something had gone terribly wrong— the explosion really was as bad as Gordon feared. Duke turned around and looked through the house, back out front. Gordon heard the passing of two blaring police cruisers followed by the low whine of a fire truck and the telltale two-tone of an ambulance.

Duke pulled out his phone, glanced at the screen, shook his head, and tucked it back into his breast pocket, muttering a curse. He turned around and walked inside again, closing the glass doors behind him with a locking click.

Gordon lay still, his mind reeling. Only when the lights shut off again, when he was plunged into darkness like a cold pool, did he come to his senses. The bizarre voice mail, the strange house, the explosion, Duke's appearance—he needed to think things through. With Dana. And scotch. Lots of scotch.

He inched his way deeper into the hedges at the edge of the property until he was behind enough shrubbery to stand unnoticed. Then he worked his way to the perimeter of the lawn. The iron gate there was more ornamental than functional, just about shoulder height. He grabbed hold of the blunted top and, after a solid five minutes of scrabbling and huffing, positioned himself to fall down on the far side, directly on the car keys in his hip pocket. He sucked air through his teeth, pushed himself standing, and rubbed his hip vigorously as he looked to see where he was—in a small greenbelt between properties. The street was to his right. He walked until he saw flashes of blue and red dancing off the leaves and vines all around him.

The lights came from his left, around the corner. With his back to the iron gate, he peered around, staying out of view.

He needn't have bothered. Gordon counted three police cars, one fire truck, and one ambulance, but all attention was being paid to the ruined front face of what looked to Gordon like a fancy school. Great gouts of smoke billowed out and up from flashes of lashing flame. But that wasn't what held his focus.

Gordon squinted to better see the work of the medics. Two were kneeling on the ground to either side of someone, and Gordon realized he was fully expecting to find Sophie between them. He prayed he wasn't too late and pushed off the gate. As he walked slowly toward them, his mind raced with how he might explain himself, especially to Warren Duke, who stood as stark and sharp as a marble sculpture by the side of the ambulance, watching as the medics worked.

When he saw Marty Cicero, he thought he was hallucinating. Marty should be off with Dana, at work. Not leaning heavily against the ambulance as if it was the only thing holding him up. Duke held an air of detachment, but Marty seemed tethered to the victim with an almost visible line of emotion, so strong it nearly pitched him over.

One of the medics moved. Gordon saw a gloved hand glistening with blood. Everything slowed for him in that instant, and he saw Dana very clearly—first her ink-dark hair and a sliver of her face, eyes closed, tipped gently to one side. Her mouth was slightly open, as if she was doing nothing more than napping. After only an instant, the medic shifted again and hid her from view, but Gordon knew he would remember that moment as clearly as if it was painted on the back of his eyes.

He ran. Warren Duke turned toward him, and some small part of Gordon's mind registered the look he gave—a look that said he knew he'd be there, knew he had likely been at the house on Long Lane, too. A cold fury fell over Duke that hardened with each step Gordon took, but Gordon didn't care. He pushed past everything and everyone until Marty had to collar him and pull him away, but he couldn't stop Gordon from calling Dana's name again and again and again like a lost child at the supermarket, louder and louder until the medics closed the doors of the ambulance and rocketed away from the broken and billowing schoolhouse, and even then, he still called for her, but the blaring siren drowned out his cries.

CHAPTER EIGHT

Marty's Charger ripped down Highway 83, drafting just behind the ambulance. The engine of Gordon's coupe was screaming just to keep him in sight. Gordon rarely pushed his car past sixty-five. He had little cause to. Most of his life played out within the city limits. Normally, he would be terrified the entire car was going to fall apart around him, but just then he was grateful for the white-knuckle distraction. It kept him from thinking about what was happening in the back of that ambulance, from thinking constantly about that bloody glove and about the way her mouth had been slightly open.

Hopkins was churning, even at that late hour. The hospital never slept. Gordon left his car running in the roundabout. If they needed to move it, they would. Or they'd tow it. He hardly cared. He met Marty as he was flashing his badge at the emergency admit desk. Gordon drafted behind him again into the guts of Hopkins emergency care.

Gordon was hit with déjà vu. It felt to him as if an eternity had passed since he'd been there, but in reality, he'd taken those elevators hours before. The two most important women—most important people—in his life were both at Johns Hopkins Hospital. That his mother and his girlfriend would be admitted within a day of each other struck him as particularly cruel, as evidence of some greater mechanism out to destroy everything good he'd scraped from the barrel of his life.

Both Marty and Gordon were stopped at the door to the surgical floor. Marty spoke with the receptionist at the front desk briefly, his voice remarkably calm when Gordon wouldn't have trusted himself at a whisper. They were told she had gone straight to surgery. The receptionist at the front desk gave them each a color-coded card with a number on it that had been assigned to Dana. They were told to watch the monitors in the waiting room. Dana's number would cycle through from surgery to post op to recovery when visitors were allowed. Purple to green. No reds, of course—nothing that might indicate *how* things were going. Only neutrals.

At some point during Gordon's slow, shell-shocked pacing of the waiting room and hallway beyond, he realized he was alone, and he remembered Marty telling him he was returning to the scene to file a report. He checked the clock and saw he'd been there for nearly two hours and Dana's number was still firmly purple. The frightened hush of the waiting room grated on him, as if the air itself was pulled tight, near to breaking.

Gordon stepped out to the hallway and found himself at the elevators. He glanced at the time again—nearly five in the morning. His mother was an early riser, but she was recovering from her final radiation treatment before she went purple herself, and God knew she had enough on her plate as it was.

Still, he'd never wanted to drop in on his mom so much in his life. It took all he had to pull his hand away from the call button and turn from the elevator doors. What would he say to her anyway? *"Dana's hurt, and it was my patient that hurt her."* Marty had said they were chasing someone. A kid. In a black hat and jeans. Shoeless. They couldn't make a positive ID before the explosion, but it all lined up. Sophie was gone, and Mo had come out. The evidence that the two were one and the same was overwhelming. Yet Gordon's diagnosis still scratched at him like a sharp pebble in his shoe. He could practically hear his mother in his mind. *"You can't force yourself to believe your own diagnosis, Gordon. It's either right or it's wrong."*

True, but you *could* look the facts in the face. And the facts were that his girlfriend was quite possibly on the brink of death, and he was almost positive he knew who'd brought her there.

"Almost positive? Almost isn't a lot to hang a little girl's life on."

He looked up at the nearest monitor for what felt like the thousandth time. Still purple. The woman he loved—for he was sure of that now, he did love her, a pain that acute at the threat of losing her could stem only from love—had been turned into a purple number on a screen.

He was set to meet Sophie in five short hours for their scheduled therapy session. He stood up and took a deep breath. He could do nothing more for Dana in the waiting room. They would call him if her status changed. He fingered the card Marty had given him before leaving.

Marty Cicero
Detective, Baltimore Police Department
Child Protective Investigations

His number was blazoned on the bottom.

Gordon decided he would go home. He would prepare to meet Sophie. And if things went the way he thought they would, he'd be calling the police and placing her in rehabilitative care whether Dianne liked it or not. He didn't feel good about it. He felt as if he was forcing the puzzle, but only because Sophie had forced his hand. He knew Dana might tell him to step back, think rationally, but Dana was a purple number on a screen now, and Gordon's heart was breaking. He had to do *something*.

. . .

By the time of Sophie's appointment, Gordon had been notified that Dana was out of surgery. Marty relayed the details with clinical detachment that Gordon instantly recognized as the big man's way of coping with the terrible: second-degree burns on her arms and face and third-degree burns on her hands. The real kicker, the boot to the gut, was that a piece of metal, most likely from one of the canisters of gasoline, had struck her just above the temple. They'd worked for two hours to extract it. Her brain had swelled dangerously. She was in an induced coma until the swelling receded. They didn't know how long that would take—anywhere from one day to one week. Or never.

Gordon needed a hefty swig of scotch before he was able to stop himself from shaking enough to answer the door when Sophie and Dianne rang. He stood, smoothed his blazer and eased his jaw, then opened the door. The afternoon rains that often bookended Baltimore days during fall had just started, and Gordon expected to find daughter and mother in huddled disarray—Sophie unable to meet his eyes, her fingernails black with soot, and Dianne frantic, her perfectly bobbed hair at odd angles.

Instead, he found the two of them as he always had—Dianne eager to begin and to get out of the street, and Sophie with a rumpled look of exhaustion edged with panic. Her backpack was still on, her back bowed, her hands chapped. Gordon couldn't help but look at her nails as she gripped the straps of her pack. No soot to be found.

"Hello, Sophie," Gordon said with effort. "Dianne."

"Hi, Dr. Pope," Sophie said softly before moving aside and past him, toward the back room where their chairs sat. Gordon waited at the door another moment, facing Dianne and waiting for her to speak, to explain why she hadn't been where her phone was when he'd answered her call for help. But she looked at him questioningly.

"What happened last night, Dianne?" he whispered, unable to keep the edge of anger from his voice.

"What do you mean?"

"The text? The *fire*?" Gordon strained to keep his voice low. He had always suspected Dianne was a neglectful parent, but he didn't want to overplay his hand before Sophie could explain herself.

Dianne shook her head slowly. "I was at my writer's group all night. I never texted anyone."

Gordon's head swam. He felt like slamming the door in her face and going to bed. He pulled his phone from his pocket.

"I received several strange voice mails last night from a blocked number. And one text from you. 'Sophie has gone missing.'"

Dianne looked at the text Gordon showed her, but she didn't seem to register his words. She felt her pockets but came up short. She dug in her purse to no avail. Dianne opened and closed her mouth several times. He could see the wheels of her mind working, spinning furiously.

"You don't have your phone, do you?" Gordon asked. He pictured it where he'd left it, on the floor by the statue. He thought about telling her but stopped himself when he felt he wouldn't be able to answer the questions that followed, questions like "What were you doing in my house, and why did you waltz on in when I didn't answer the doorbell?"

"Somebody must have stolen it. But nobody knows you're treating Sophie. Unless..."

"Unless it was Sophie," Gordon said.

Dianne worked her mouth in silence. Gordon thought about dropping another bomb on her while her mind raced to catch up. He knew of at least one other person that seemed familiar with what was happening on Long Lane: Warren Duke. But if Duke was involved and Dianne knew it, that meant she was purposely hiding it from Gordon for some reason. She was crafty and would deflect if asked directly, but perhaps Sophie could provide answers. He checked his watch. Time to get on with the session. He invited Dianne in and helped her to her seat with a glass of water. He left her to her own thoughts as he went to Sophie, closing the door between the rooms.

He could feel the weight of Sophie's eyes with his back still turned. He felt tired, as if his shoes adhered to the floor with every step, just enough that it took an effort to move, just enough to make him weary, as if he was wading through sand. He forced himself to straighten, but that took effort. It occurred to him that he hadn't slept in over twenty-four hours. He was wallowing again. Wallowing did nothing. He'd wallowed for five years before he met Dana. He'd already wallowed once today, and he wasn't about to start again.

He'd meant to move right into things, to greet Sophie as he sat down, hands on his knees, leaning slightly forward and saying, *"So, how have you been?"* the same as every other session. Then he would sit quietly and wait until she felt uncomfortable enough to explain herself, press only where he needed to, and call Marty when he had to.

When he turned to her, he couldn't find the girl he wanted to hand over to the police, the one who delighted in fire. What he found was a girl meticulously plucking at her colored pencils, setting them just so in their case, turning them one at a time so the embossed lettering was out, carefully closing the box, then opening it and doing it again. Her hands were raw, but not from any burns that Gordon could see. They were raw from washing, chapped and cracked, her cuticles bitten to the quick. Little red dots of blood framed each stripped nail. She looked down intently, focusing on her organizing. He noticed that she seemed hung up on one pencil that seemed shorter than the others—the orange one. It was back.

"How are you feeling, Sophie?" he asked. He'd been worried about sounding angry, but instead he was worried about sounding sad, as if he was grieving. That he'd been within a hairbreadth of arresting this girl shamed him. As if taking her away would somehow bring Dana back. That was not the Gordon Pope Dana would be proud of.

"Bad," she said softly. She scratched at her chapped hands and winced. She rubbed her tired eyes with her forearm. She looked like she didn't want to contaminate herself with different parts of herself.

"You've been doing a lot of washing," Gordon said carefully.

Sophie nodded, embarrassed. "I'm trying to remember what happened. It helps me remember what happened."

"What happened when?"

"Last night. And other times too. When I forget things."

"You don't remember what happened last night?" Gordon asked, keeping his voice steady.

Sophie shook her head. "I try to sleep, but I can't because I hear the voices. Then they get so bad that I forget everything. I wake up different places. The back lawn. The library. Downstairs. But I don't think I ever really sleep."

"Does Mo talk to you?"

Sophie nodded. She picked up her colored pencils again and began to pluck each in order, sliding it up a half inch, inspecting the point, resting it down and turning the embossed side out again.

"So Mo talked to you last night, then you can't remember what you did?"

Sophie nodded, plucking, setting, turning. Gordon noticed a small tremor in her hands. He realized she was afraid. She wasn't a girl who delighted in fire. She was a girl who wanted to feel safe, a girl who was doing what she could to feel safe the only way she knew how. By purifying. By scrubbing and by burning. When Sophie couldn't do the burning, Mo did it for her.

"Have you been taking your medicine?" Gordon asked.

Sophie nodded again. "Mom makes me take the pills every morning."

The benzodiazepine should have built up a solid base in her system by then, but she seemed as anxious as ever—more so, even. He'd hesitated to prescribe full-blown antipsychotics—the side effects were often severe and long lasting, and they included things like breast cancer and blindness and were especially potent for adolescents—but his hesitation might have very well cost Dana her life. He wouldn't make the same mistake twice.

He pulled out his prescription pad and tapped his pen on it. He recognized the power of drugs, but he always had an aversion to medicating a symptom into submission as a first line of defense. It felt like giving up. If only the damn puzzle pieces fit together better...

"Sophie, do you remember calling me last night?"

Sophie paused in her ordering and bit her lip. Gordon could see she was trying, really trying. Her eyes wetted lightly with tears of frustration from how hard she was trying to remember, but she shook her head.

"What about sending a text? Do you remember sending me a text from your mom's phone?"

Gordon showed her his phone: "Sophie has gone missing," but Sophie shook her head, her eyes rimmed with red. She sorted faster, faster, until one of the pencils caught and tumbled the entire box from her hands. The box struck the floor and threw its contents all over the rug, and for a moment both Gordon and Sophie froze. Sophie's shaking hands moved slowly to her mouth.

"It's okay, Sophie," Gordon said, holding his own hands out to her as if he could dampen her panic. "It's okay. We can gather them up again. Look." He moved toward the pile until she started crying softly —a sound so desperately sad and broken that Gordon imagined it was similar to the sound dogs made in strange kennels in the dead of night. He sat back down without another word.

Dianne shot into the room with her hands out as if prepared to tackle someone. She saw Sophie and Gordon, and her eyes measured the distance between them.

"She dropped her pencils," he said calmly but clearly, yet his voice was overrun by Sophie's one long wail. Dianne moved over to Sophie and grasped her shoulder, shaking it. "Sophie, this is your mother. Get a hold of yourself this instant."

Sophie didn't even seem to register Dianne. She slid to the floor and began to gather her pencils furiously, holding out the hem of her plaid skirt and piling them on as if the floor were poison to them, and to a child with severe OCD, it likely was. The pencils were contaminated now. She would have to clean them in her own way. But that would take time, and from the way Sophie's eyes rolled continuously to the four corners of the ceiling, he knew they didn't have time. The voices were beginning to call to her. Mo was beginning to call to her.

Still, Dianne shook her, calling her name over and over again and shushing her.

"Dianne, you have to let her gather them herself," Gordon said.

Dianne didn't seem to hear him. She looked close to a panic attack herself. He wouldn't touch Sophie—that broke protocol, especially considering her condition—but he could remove Dianne. In one swoop, his grabbed her by the shoulders, stood her upright, then stepped between them.

"Dianne," he said flatly. "Enough. Let her go through her own motions. It's the only way she'll calm down."

Dianne breathed heavily through her nose and held a balled fist to her front teeth. She looked furious and dismayed at the same time. Her eyes flitted to the window Gordon had opened earlier to hear the rain. She was worried about sound carrying out to the street, worried about her daughter causing a scene again. She couldn't catch a deep breath. She seemed embarrassed and a bit ashamed, both of Sophie and of herself.

As Sophie gathered all her pencils onto her dress, she calmed from a cry to a mewl then a whimper, but her eyes still panned the ceiling above. Dianne watched her daughter with wringing hands, her head tilted forward as if she wanted to rest it on Sophie's shoulder. Gordon dropped his hands to his sides and rolled his neck, his exhaustion redoubled. He'd gone from blood boiling to cold weariness too many times already that day. He felt raw and frayed, as if he'd been turned inside out.

"Dianne, it's my professional opinion that your daughter is in the middle of a psychotic break. If she isn't hospitalized soon, she may spiral downward, and she may hurt herself... or others. If she hasn't already," Gordon added, regretting it immediately when Dianne's eyes flicked to his in a heartbeat.

Gordon went no further, but he knew Dianne had caught his meaning, and he knew from her silence that she understood. Dianne was a strange and distant woman, but she wasn't stupid. She'd dodged his question about the fire at Merryville Prep earlier, but that didn't mean she was ignorant of it. She could put two and two together.

Then she shook her head.

"Absolutely not. She needs to recuperate at home until this passes, just like it did last time."

"When she nearly burned down the house, you mean," Gordon said quietly, gesturing Dianne aside as he spoke. He watched Sophie carefully, unsure of what he should and shouldn't tell her directly at that time, unsure of what she would understand even if he did.

Dianne crossed her arms in front of her small frame and pierced Gordon with the flat, off-center gaze of a dug-in mule. "Houses can be repaired, trees replanted. Those are just things. We're talking about her life, here. Her reputation. This will pass just like it did last time." On the ground behind them, Sophie began meticulously placing her pencils in the box, at an angle, as if constructing a ship in a bottle. Her crying had stopped entirely, but her eyes still raced across the ceiling, and now and then she flinched, too. Whatever she was hearing, it was getting louder.

"When she burned the tree house down, it was what we in psychiatry call a prenode, a quick surfacing of psychosis that often foreshadows the full-blown disease. It can happen in young women her age, and while it often passes quickly, when it comes back, it comes back with a vengeance." He nodded toward Sophie. "This one isn't going to pass without medical help."

"Fine, then we'll bring the hospital to her. You can come stay with us. I'll pay you double. Triple."

"Dianne—"

"You'd have your own living quarters, an entire wing of the house. Your only job would be Sophie."

"I can't do that. I want to do everything I can for her, but—" He thought of his own practice, just beginning. He thought of Dana and what she might need in terms of the future if she pulled through. He thought of his mother and what she might need. Suddenly, he felt a little ill himself, as if the corners of the ceiling that Sophie so feared were also closing in on him, and it must have shown on his face because Dianne dropped her head, resigned. "She needs around-the-clock medical care right now until she's able to come up from this, then she'll need careful management. This is a disease, Dianne. She's going to have to manage it for the rest of her life. And so will you."

Dianne laughed sadly, her mouth cut into a grimace. "Careful management. Our family has always been good at that. It's what we do. Carry on as if nothing is ever wrong."

"That's not what I mean at all—"

"No hospitals. That's my right. I'm her legal guardian. I'm the final say. That's it. I'll care for her at home myself until this passes."

She was right. A child psychiatrist could only advise a path of treatment. He couldn't have anyone committed against the wishes of their legal guardians without tangible evidence of intent to harm. He didn't have that. And as much as he ground his teeth, he couldn't even hate Dianne for her decision. Gordon despised mental hospitals. Even the most luxurious of them treated the symptoms, not the cause. The more expensive the care, the more daintily they approached the root of the problem. Hospitals were businesses first and foremost.

But Dianne still didn't get that what Sophie had wasn't going to "pass." He didn't want her taking Sophie in her current state. He imagined she had looked very similar before she set fire to the tree house and before she disappeared last night—before Dana ended up on the grass, blood in her hair, her lips parted with eyes closed...

All Gordon could do was watch as Dianne gathered her daughter. Her touch was gentle but firm, and Sophie responded to it in her daze. He thought of Sophie and Dianne, alone in that massive house. He'd come to his senses about handing her over to the cops, only to watch his patient be carted off to a prison of another kind. Desperate, he took another tack.

"The police are already involved, Dianne. The explosion last night badly hurt an officer I care about. Her superior is directly involved, too. A man named Warren Duke."

Dianne paused. Gordon watched her carefully. She brushed Sophie's damp hair from her forehead, trying to catch her daughter's rolling gaze with her own direct one. Gordon waited and listened, but Dianne was in no rush to explain herself.

Gordon chimed in again. "I've run across Duke in the past. He can be a... difficult man."

Dianne nodded but offered nothing more. Instead, she set her mouth in a prim line and helped Sophie to stand. When she looked at Gordon again, she was composed, as if she knew she had the upper hand.

"You care for my daughter. You want to see her well. I know it. So you'll have to work within the rules I've set. And you will. I know that too. That means no hospitals. No clinics. No outside opinions. Nothing without my say. I will call you when Sophie is well enough once more to continue her sessions."

Gordon moved aside as Dianne herded Sophie through the office and out the door, covering her with her own jacket to keep the soft but steady rain off her head until she disappeared once more into their waiting sedan.

After they left, Gordon poured himself a drink and sat on the floor with his back against the patient's couch. The clock ticked. The rain fell. Traffic hummed distantly. The day continued into night, and the full weight of what had occurred pressed upon him with slow, relentless pressure. His head felt heavy, but his eyes remained open. They followed along with the steps of his thoughts as he recounted each session he'd had with Sophie. He looked for missteps he might have made, missteps that had ended up with Dana in the hospital. He badly wanted someone to blame—might as well be himself.

But he couldn't see where he'd gone wrong. He'd done everything by the book. No psychiatrist he knew would have diagnosed schizophrenia right off the bat. Her symptoms were indicative of a psychotic break in some ways but atypical in others, especially Mo. Mo was in line with dissociative-identity disorder, which was very different from schizophrenia. Moreover, she wasn't responding to the benzos. The pills should have been enough to calm her by then.

He'd done the best he could with what he knew as he knew it, but he still felt that he hadn't acted quickly enough, that he *still* wasn't acting quickly enough to stave off the next disaster. Instead, he'd handed a very sick girl off to her mother, who sometimes seemed to value her family name more than her daughter. Gordon did believe that Dianne loved Sophie, in her own way—his own mother had strange ways of showing affection, too—but Dianne seemed willfully ignorant of her daughter's situation. She had managed to let the girl sneak out twice, and twice things had ended in flames—three times if you counted the tree out back.

Gordon picked up his phone and dialed Marty.

"You want me to bring her in?" he asked, first thing.

"No."

Marty was eating something—probably those damn almonds again—but he paused. "You're kidding me, right?"

"No. Something else is going on here. Sophie is too fragile. I can't risk being wrong."

"Then we figure out what else is going on while she sits in a holding cell, away from the matches. We hold kids all the time. You shoulda seen some of the goons I brought in from working the corners. It's no big deal."

Gordon could tell that Marty was still fired up. He knew Marty was the type of guy that went ice cold to deal with the moment and make a level decision, but he saved his anger for afterward. To keep himself going. To finish the job.

"She's not a drug dealer, Marty."

"She could have killed Dana," Marty said, popping each word.

"You think I don't know that?" Gordon asked, surprised to find himself yelling. "You think that wasn't on my mind the whole time she was here? But nothing about this case fits. When I was at her house, responding to the text, I saw Warren Duke there."

"Duke? You never told me that. Did he see you?"

"No. I don't think so. The explosion caught everyone's attention first."

Marty crunched another almond, slowly that time, as if in thought. "Warren Duke. What the hell?"

"I don't know. I'm not sure that Dianne knows, either. But she didn't seem worried when I told her he was involved. This goes beyond Sophie."

"So we just let her go about her merry way, then? Until she lights the whole frickin' town up?"

"No. I had to let her go with her mom, Dianne. And between you and me, I think Dianne's parental priorities are all out of whack. I see this quite a bit with parents in her tax bracket. Bottom line is I don't trust her to keep an eye on Sophie. The girl has slipped out three times now under Dianne's watch. I think we need to take over." He came to the decision as he spoke. He drained his scotch and found himself standing. Sleep would have to wait.

"Take over?" Marty asked.

"Yeah, we need to, ah..." Gordon searched for the right word, the cop word. "Case the joint."

Marty snorted.

"If we're right and she really is going to the school at night, our best chance to catch her in the act is to nab her as she leaves home, right? Then I can walk her into round-the-clock care myself. With proof, what I say trumps Dianne. As a matter of fact, maybe you can arrest Dianne for criminal negligence while we're at it."

"Now we're talking," Marty said. "We use my car. I'll be over in twenty."

CHAPTER NINE

Gordon sat in silence with Marty, the two of them watching the house on Long Lane from the front seats of Marty's car. With the low rumble of the engine gone, the distance between the men seemed tangible. The name of that distance was *Dana*, but neither of them had addressed it yet.

Outside, the light was already starting to fail, and it seemed to lean heavily on everything it touched on its way out. The gold and red leaves hardly stirred on the trees. Those strewn upon the expansive grass lawns of the estates around them stuck there as if glued. Nobody walked the streets. No dogs barked. Gordon felt as if the entire neighborhood was standing in shock for the burned school five blocks down. He was reminded of the sleep laboratory at Johns Hopkins. The walls and ceilings of the control room there were covered in a strange, webbed material that caught and trapped all sound. He would have to take periodic breaks from the room when working because of how unsettling and heavy it felt.

"I meant to stop by Dana's place," Gordon said, clearing his throat, speaking for the sake of breaking the silence. "Check on Chloe and Maria."

"I already did," Marty said, his hand hanging out the window, brushing the outside of his door. He didn't look at Gordon as he spoke. His eyes were focused intently on 8 Long Lane even as Gordon turned to look at him. "That a problem?" Marty asked. "I'm her partner. It's what partners do."

Gordon couldn't tell if he was trying to get a rise out of him or if he was just stating facts. Everything that came out of Marty's mouth sounded a bit like a challenge. Gordon wasn't one for confrontations. He preferred to nip things in the bud if they were awkward, to keep them from growing more so. So he said the first thing that came to his mind.

"It's a bit of a problem. Because I think you're in love with her."

Marty coughed. Gordon felt his face getting hot. The words had leapt from him before he could stop them. And more came behind.

"Chloe really likes you. I've seen it. At the promotion party, she practically jumped into your arms. And she hardly talks to me. Even though my job is talking to kids. Which tells me two things. One. Maybe I'm not as good at talking to kids as I think. And two, since I know Dana's a good person, odds are very high that Chloe is a good person, and if Chloe likes you, that means you are a good person. Kids can always tell. You're a good person, and you love my girl-friend, and you get to spend a lot of time with her. More than me. That doesn't bode well for me."

The silence that fell then was a palpable thing. Gordon cleared his throat to try to break it again, but it wouldn't be broken that time.

Whatever Marty had been expecting, it wasn't that. He creaked back in his seat. "Wow."

"Well, you asked me if I had a problem."

"Does all that"—Marty spun a finger near his temple—"go on in your head, like... all the time?"

"That's about a third of it, I'd say."

"Jesus."

"That's all you have to say?" Gordon asked. He gestured back and forth along the space between them. "Marty, we both are a big part of Dana's life. We've got to figure this out."

Marty's grip on the steering wheel tightened. He looked as though he was about to say something, but then he tensed suddenly and leaned forward, eyes intent.

"What is it?" Gordon asked.

Marty shoved a quieting hand in his face without looking and pointed down the curving lane. Gordon peered around his bulk, and there, at the very end, he saw a solitary figure in a plaid dress. The light from the street lamp above reflected dully off her long blond hair. Her arms were clutched around her chest, her back and head bowed, and she scanned the gutter as she walked, occasionally shaking her head.

Gordon muttered a soft curse.

"That's Sophie?" Marty asked.

"That's her."

"She looks awful," Marty said quietly.

"She feels awful."

They watched as Sophie sat down on the expansive front lawn of her neighbor's house, grabbed her bony knees, and started rocking. Gordon felt a physical pain in his chest at seeing her. As if his stomach was turning in slow knots. He wanted to run to her, console her, and give her a time and place and person she recognized in an attempt to ground her mind in the present. But if she was going to the school, on her way to burn again, they needed to know.

She was close enough that they should have been able to hear her if she'd been crying. Gordon listened intently until he realized she was being completely silent in her torment, as if she was trying to hide from the voices. From Mo.

"She doesn't look like she knows what planet she's on," Marty said. "Much less how to start a fire."

For five interminable minutes, they watched Sophie West spiral downward until she was practically flattened against the grass with the silent weight of her delusions. She never even made it past her neighbor's mailbox. Five minutes was all Gordon could take.

"This isn't helping anybody," he said, opening the door, ready to throw off Marty as best as he could if the big man protested.

Marty got out of the car after him, but to Gordon's surprise, he looked across the hood and waited. "She's in a nightmare right now. You just gonna stand there?"

Gordon tucked in his shirt and started walking. He felt beset on all sides by fears and insecurities—Dana and Marty, his mother and her cancer, his fledgling practice. In many ways, the cornerstones of his life were crumbling. But he could still help Sophie. This was what he did. This was his domain—maybe his last, but it was still his. With every step he took across the street, he stood a shade straighter. Marty seemed to understand as well. He followed several paces behind Gordon, giving him the lead.

Gordon took even and sure steps until he was able to sit down in front of Sophie on the grass. He did this without speaking, and he kept a relaxed and receptive look on his face, as if nothing was remotely odd about the two of them sitting on a freshly cut lawn in the chill of an October night.

Sophie looked at him in stride. She didn't jump or shy away, but she didn't recognize him either. Gordon knew that by then, Sophie most likely had built him into her delusions in some way. Whether they were in the patient's chair or on the front lawn hardly mattered to her.

"Hi, Sophie," he said.

"You're here to kill me."

"No, Sophie. I'm here to help you, like the other times."

"Then I'm here to kill you," she said, nodding slowly to herself.

Gordon fought against a shiver. "Nobody is killing anyone, Sophie," he said calmly. He purposely repeated her name again and again, to remind her of who she was.

Sophie shook her head pityingly. "If I don't, everyone dies worse."

In pain forever. All the way down the line. Burning now saves them later. Except..."

Gordon waited, but Sophie seemed to have lost her thought. "Except what, Sophie?"

"Except that I can't do it. I can't save you." She sobbed quietly, rocking again.

"That's okay. I don't need to be sav—"

"But Mo does what I can't," she whispered, staring at him with cold, wide eyes that froze the words in his mouth. "Mo can save you. Mo can clean you."

Gordon saw his opportunity. "Does Mo want to talk to me right now?"

Sophie looked around rapidly. She checked the shadows carefully and listened to the sky. "Later," she whispered. "He'll come for you later."

Gordon nodded, but he was troubled. Her symptoms had danced around one another like waves in a stormy bay, but they were violently colliding, and Gordon couldn't parse one from the other. All was one wave.

Sophie was shivering. The wind picked up and kicked tiny locust leaves in a swirl around her. They caught in her hair and rattled down the concrete like scattered toothpicks.

"Let's go home, Sophie," Gordon said.

Sophie nodded, but she stayed in a ball until Gordon gently led her to stand, with a sure grip on her elbow. Protocol had gone out the window some time before.

Marty followed at a distance while Gordon took Sophie up the winding flagstone front path of 8 Long Lane. He found the door open and didn't bother knocking.

"Dianne," he called from the foyer, working with effort to keep his voice steady and even. "It's me, Gordon Pope." *Again.*

Silence.

"I found Sophie. She's right here. She's okay." He turned to

Sophie and found her already staring at him, not in alarm, but with intensity. "You're okay," he repeated to her.

The house was as silent as when he'd first visited. All he heard was the ticking of an enormous grandfather clock he couldn't see and the soft whistle of his lungs pulling air as he tried to keep calm.

"Sophie, is your mom here?"

She still stared at him like an infant, offering little. He felt she was hardly daring to breathe, as if any movement might betray her location to Mo and the voices she thought were chasing her.

He turned around and found Marty watching him carefully as well, from just outside the door, with an intensity of a different sort.

"I'm gonna find Dianne," Gordon said.

"Open door's an open door," Marty said quietly. "And I've had about enough of this shit. But let's make it quick." He moved around Gordon with an eye to the hallways on the ground floor and the kitchen beyond.

Gordon led Sophie to the stairs. She needed a safe space, a place she'd already cleaned and ordered—her bedroom—and he guessed that was somewhere upstairs. She moved in quick, birdlike jerks, and a subtle whine gathered at the base of her throat. He picked up the pace but stopped at the bottom step. Hand-drawn pictures were strewn about the stairway from top to bottom, perhaps twenty of them, some flat, others crumpled, some at odd angles against the banister. One hanging precariously from the carpeted runner three steps above fluttered down to the ground at Gordon's feet as if disturbed by a ghost's passing. A quick glance showed the same table-on-fire pencil drawing as the one Dianne had given him.

"Did you do this, Sophie?" Gordon asked, picking up the nearest drawing.

She didn't seem to see any of them or much of anything in front of her. She was muttering to herself in sibilants, soft hissing sounds that reminded Gordon of hidden pockets of air escaping burning logs. Marty came back in from the kitchen and found Gordon's eyes. The big man shook his head. Nobody was on the first floor. So up they went.

Gordon picked up the pictures at each step, gripping them in a tattered portfolio with his free hand. He could hear Marty following several steps behind, his heavy work boots pressing the carpeted runner as he walked.

"Dianne!" Gordon called again, as loudly as he dared with Sophie on his arm.

He listened, and then he thought he heard something. Steps. Small steps, pattering in a quick run and then stopping. So fast he almost couldn't be sure what he'd heard. He turned around and found Marty listening with his head cocked. He'd heard something too.

"Dianne, it's Gordon, I've brought Sophie. I'm here with a... a friend." Gordon stepped faster, reached the landing between floors and then turned toward the second floor. At the top was a bedroom with double doors wide open. As Gordon crested the stairs, he saw quick flashes of light coming from a television there, staccato bursts that lit the darkened room like a strobe, and in the glimpses he was given, he saw a lump of bunched blankets, and from the lump a hand draped, fingertips trailing nearly to the ground.

"Dianne?"

No movement. Gordon stepped quickly to the doors and paused. Dianne West was sprawled out on an enormous bed, the covers bunched oddly around her body and head. For a horrible span of seconds, Gordon thought she was dead, but then she unleashed an enormous snore that made him jump, almost yanking Sophie back. Even Marty flinched, waiting back at the stairs.

"Dianne, get up," Gordon said.

He slowly let go of Sophie, and once he was convinced she could stand on her own, he shook Dianne gently at the shoulders. She breathed heavily but wouldn't wake up. At the nightstand to her side was a fifth of vodka, three quarters empty, and a bottle of prescription pills. Sophie's prescription pills, the benzos. Gordon picked up the pill bottle, and its white cap fell right off. He feared the worst, that Dianne was in the process of trying to kill herself as they stood there, but the bottle was nearly full. Perhaps two or three pills were gone at most.

His initial relief was replaced quickly by a hardening anger. Dianne had never given Sophie her anxiety medication to begin with. She was stealing it herself, popping one or two at night with four or five shots of vodka as a sleepy-time cocktail. No wonder Sophie got the run of the neighborhood. Dianne was maybe a hundred pounds soaking wet. A stampeding elephant wouldn't wake her at that point.

"In what world can I not have kids but you can," he muttered. He turned back to Marty. "She's been self-medicating. With Sophie's prescription."

Marty nodded, but he seemed distracted. He had one ear down the hallway. "You heard those footsteps, right?" he asked, his tone low, as if speaking to himself. "Somebody else might be here."

"There's nobody else here, Marty. This place is an enormous tomb. It could have been anything that we heard—a floorboard, the furnace, the pipes. But if I don't get Sophie to a safe place soon, the damage could take years to mend."

Sophie's fluttering heartbeat was visible through the pale white skin at her temple. She looked at him with pleading eyes. "You must be quiet," she whispered. "You must be quiet. Everyone be quiet. Everyone be quiet. They'll hear you. They'll hear you."

Repetition. Delusions. Not long now. Gordon rolled a pill into his palm and walked over to Dianne's work desk in the corner, where her computer idled. There, an empty glass stood next to a full pitcher of water. He smelled it to make sure then poured Sophie a glass and brought it to her. He was expecting her to fight it—no telling what she was seeing then or what she thought the water might be—but she took the pill down and the entire glass of water in a series of long gulps.

She gasped for breath at the end. "Will they go away now? Will they go away now?" Her voice wheezed.

"They'll go away soon."

The jostling of the desk snapped Dianne's computer awake, and it flicked on with a brightness that made Gordon squint. A wall of unbroken text appeared on the screen. Dianne's precious memoirs. He turned back toward her, motionless and snoring loudly through everything. He shook his head in disgust. *How can she possibly have so much to say?*

"C'mon Sophie," Gordon said, "let's get you to bed."

But Sophie had already settled into bed, on the opposite side of Dianne, curled up in a ball, staring at her mother across a space big enough to fit another two Sophies. Her muttering stopped. She seemed catatonic, but at least her breathing was calming—slow, exhausted gulps instead of panicked rabbit breaths.

"I want to take a quick look at the rest of this landing," Marty said slowly. "I swear I heard something—"

A sound came from downstairs, a slow, soft *whoosh* of air accompanied by the sure turning of oiled hinges. The front door was being opened again. Both men froze, staring at each other, then moved quickly and quietly to the banister over the landing.

Warren Duke took two sharp steps into the foyer. The clean clicking sound his gleaming oxford shoes made on the wood seemed to echo around the entire house. Gordon stared like a cow over the railing until Marty whipped him back out of view.

"Dianne," Duke said, his voice clear and commanding. "Sophie, get down here."

Gordon turned to Marty dumbly, mouth working in silence, until the big man's crushing grip on both shoulders steadied him.

Marty leaned in close and whispered, "We have to find another way out."

Gordon looked to his left and right. He looked up, to the darkened third floor. He looked behind him, to the room where Dianne still snored and the manic light of the television played off Sophie's unblinking eyes as she stared at her mother. Nothing looked like an exit.

"Dianne, if I have to come up there, it's not going to go well for you or Sophie," Duke said.

Gordon heard two more sharp steps toward the base of the stairs. He looked at Marty and shook his head, helpless. His bowels felt loose and roiling. He was sure Duke could hear his stomach, even over Dianne's snoring.

"Goddammit, Dianne!" Duke said. "Do you want the police to take Sophie?" Another sharp step, then a soft step. The first stair. Another. Faster. He was coming up two at a time.

Gordon pulled Marty in that time. "Hide," he whispered. He pushed Marty away from him, down the hall, then turned and stepped as carefully and quickly as he could the other direction. Gordon crept until he found the library, darkened. It smelled oddly of campfire—or perhaps he just had fire on the brain. He contemplated closing the door but knew he had no time to hide the click of the lock. Across the hall, Marty stepped into what looked like a linen closet, large enough to be a bathroom. Marty swung the door closed behind him, stopping at the latch, just as Warren Duke stepped onto the second-floor landing.

Gordon had a bull's-eye view of the man from where he stood in the darkness. He was dressed in gray slacks and a navy sport coat with golden buttons that gleamed even in the low light. He was tanned to perfection, his salt-and-pepper hair cut short, just a shade longer than a military buzz. His jacket was trim and fitted, save for a slight bump under the right armpit, a gun.

As soon as Duke had walked through the front door, Gordon's mind fled down the path of every worst-case scenario he could think of, from getting thrown out to getting in a fistfight with the major, even getting arrested. Seeing the gun reminded him that things could always be worse. If things went really south that night, he could end up dead. His stomach squeaked again. Duke didn't notice. He was looking into the open bedroom, and his eyes were angry slits. By then, he'd seen the bed, but if he felt shock or dismay, he didn't show it—only sneering disgust.

"Sophie," he said. Another command. He put his hands on his hips, as though he was scolding an unruly dog. He took a step toward the bed, almost out of Gordon's line of sight, when the closet Marty hid within suddenly clicked. Nothing remarkable. Not an opening. Not a closing. Just a latching, as if the tongue of the handle had finally decided to shoot into the lock.

But Warren Duke heard it.

Duke rocked backward on his heel, looking down the hallway toward Marty.

"Who's there?" he said, low, growling. His eyes fell on the closed closet. He turned toward it and slid his handgun from its shoulder holster with the sound of metal on leather.

Without knowing quite why, without any real reason, other than the knowledge that things would go much worse for Marty, in the long run, than they would for him if one of the two of them were caught, Gordon stepped forward from the library into the light.

"It's me, Duke. It's Gordon Pope."

Duke spun around in an instant, and Gordon grimaced, waiting for the roar of the gun and the ripping of bullets. Two of them. Maybe three, tearing his stomach to pieces—at least it would shut the growling up. But no shots came.

When Gordon opened his eyes again, he saw a strange thing. He saw a hint of fear in Warren Duke's face, but the gun never wavered. And Gordon knew that the only thing more dangerous than a furious man was a frightened furious man.

"I've been treating Sophie," Gordon said slowly, his hands out and up at shoulder height. "I found her outside, wandering alone. She's having an attack. I believe that she's schizophrenic and that there's a good chance she's been setting fires, listening to the voices in her head. I just wanted to make sure she was safe in here and not... out there."

Warren stared at Gordon the entire time he spoke. The vein at his right temple pulsed. When Gordon finished, Duke stayed still.

Only a brief twitch of his right eye betrayed that he'd processed Gordon's words at all.

"Are you alone?" Duke asked, his voice a low growl.

"Yes," Gordon said, making a huge effort not to glance behind Duke at the closet. "And now that you're here and you can take things over, I'll leave. Like I said, I just wanted to make sure she wasn't..."

"Lighting fires," Duke said evenly. "Like the one that nearly killed Detective Frisco." His face was hard and his eyes flinty, showing no remorse—certainly not for Dana personally, but also not even for a fallen fellow officer. Not for anything.

"You can put the gun down, Duke. I'm not gonna hurt anybody."

Far from putting the gun down, Duke walked toward Gordon slowly. "I can't be sure of that," he said. "I get a message about a little girl wandering the neighborhood, and I find you hiding here with her. I don't know what your intentions are."

He stopped with the gun inches from Gordon's forehead. It seemed to suck in the weak light from the hallway, its dull black gleam fading into the darkness around them. Gordon could smell Duke's cologne and hear his even breathing.

"You can ask Dianne—"

"Don't talk about Dianne!" Duke snapped, stunning Gordon into silence. "Why is it that every time there is an issue in my district that requires my attention, I find you feeding in the mud at the bottom of it?"

"I don't know," Gordon said honestly. He was wondering that himself. He'd been thrown into a cage with Duke twice now in a span of as many months. That didn't seem fair to either of them.

"Do you think I need help doing my job, Pope?"

Sometimes. But he bit off the reply and shook his head vigorously. "Nope. You do your job, and I do mine."

"What was *your* job—Sophie and her episodes—is now *my* job. Mine alone. Do you understand me?"

Gordon backed up a step, eyeing Duke sidelong. "Are you telling me not to treat my patient?"

"This is police business now. You can either turn it over to me, or I can make you turn it over to me. Are we clear?"

"Not really. I'm treating Sophie at Dianne's request, not yours—"

Duke stepped in to Gordon, closing the space between them quickly. He wrapped Gordon in a bear hug with his free arm and shoved the barrel of his gun up and under Gordon's chin, digging into the soft skin there until he almost choked. Gordon saw a flutter of movement from the closet beyond and shook his head quickly. The door paused.

"I understand now," Gordon said, his voice thin and strained, his Adam's apple bouncing off the cold steel of the barrel. "I understand," he croaked again.

Duke stepped off, holstered his gun in one deft movement, then picked at the cuffs of his light-pink oxford until satisfied with how far they protruded from his jacket sleeves. He smiled wanly, as if he'd never attacked Gordon at all.

"I'm going to escort you out of this house now, Pope, and if I ever see you near Sophie again, I'm opening a sex-offender investigation. It will follow you around your entire life and destroy what little practice you have. Not many people want to trust their children with a sex-offender psychiatrist."

"I'm not a sex offender, Duke," Gordon said, surprised at the growl in his voice.

"Oh, I know that. You're a third wheel, a thorn in my side. You take real police off of real work, and you insert yourself where you're not wanted. Constantly. But I'm fairly sure you're not a sex offender. That hardly matters, though, does it? Once the claim is made, the taint is on you regardless."

Gordon swallowed hard. He knew Duke was right.

"I see you do understand. Now, then. You first."

Duke walked behind Gordon as they descended the stairs. Gordon took his time crossing the great room, hoping that Marty would find that back exit they'd been looking for before Duke came back up.

Duke shoved him in the back. "Move it."

After another shove, Gordon was out of the house. The big door swung shut behind him and locked. Gordon shivered, his sweat-soaked collar and brow chilled in the cold night air. He walked down the winding path and across the street before he turned to see the house again. The center-front window on the second floor was for the master bedroom. He watched the distant flicker of the television as he tried to piece together what had just happened. Duke had come on strong—so strong he'd nearly shot him, which was very unlike Warren Duke. That would've created far too messy a cleanup, even for a major. The slow ruination of Gordon's life with a false sex-offender accusation was more Duke's speed, maybe with a pistol whip thrown in there for good measure. Either way, one thing was for sure: something about this case meant an awful lot to Warren Duke. Gordon recalled the flash of fear in his eyes. *What about Sophie could possibly scare a man like Warren Duke?*

After a few minutes, the light in the master bedroom went on, and Gordon saw Duke from the waist up. He moved over to the bed and shook someone, hopefully Dianne. He was not gentle.

"You weren't kidding," Marty whispered from nearby. He was walking down the sidewalk toward him, breathing heavily and edging toward the lawn.

If Gordon had had any adrenaline left, he might have yelped and brought Duke to the window. He'd given Marty little to no hope of escape, fully expecting to see the major screaming at the detective through the window next.

"Duke is elbow deep in all this," Marty said.

"Jesus, Marty. After all that, you think it's a good idea to sneak up on a guy?"

"You'll live."

"How'd you get out?"

"Through the bedroom. It's a huge his-and-hers deal. At the back, there's a door to that porch and a fire escape on the far side." Marty pointed to the right of the second story, where a whitewashed porch wrapped around the far edge.

"Good thing."

"Yeah. Good thing. Listen, I, uh..." He struggled with his words and cleared his throat softly. "Thanks for saving my ass in there. You didn't have to do that. Not after all I said about you."

"What did you say about me?" Gordon asked.

"You know, in the car. And... other stuff. I'm just sayin' you didn't have to." His voice was soft. Marty had spoken quietly before, but never softly.

"Yeah, well. Duke actually has to go a step out of his way to ruin my life. He can ruin yours in his sleep."

Both men watched as Duke helped Sophie to sitting. They could just barely see the top of her head as he sat next to her. She was bobbing, looking toward the ceiling, and he turned her face back to his again and again as he spoke intently. Gordon took some small comfort in the fact that at least she seemed remarkably unperturbed at seeing Duke.

"He's kind of a piece of shit, isn't he?" Marty said softly. "The major."

"Yes, he is, Marty. Yes, he is." *And I wish I knew why.*

Back in the library, Gordon had had his stomach in his shoes and his hands in the air with Duke's gun in his face, yet he still couldn't quite believe he was seeing the man. Duke was right: they kept running into each other. And each time, Duke seemed more disposed to hate him. He'd claimed Gordon was meddlesome, but nobody holds a meddlesome man at gunpoint. Duke was another puzzle piece. Part of the greater picture. Gordon was determined to figure where he fit.

In the quiet silence, as both men watched Duke try and fail to put Sophie straight, Gordon thought for the first time that while he and Marty would never be friends, maybe they could help each other figure out the common thread.

Marty turned his head a tick to the right. His eyes were intent again, like an elk catching a sound.

Gordon followed his gaze to the second level, just outside the master bedroom, where the porch wrapped around the second deck. "What is it?" he asked.

"I thought I saw something," Marty said, all softness gone, his voice slate again.

"Where, on the porch?"

"Shut up."

They watched for another half minute. Nothing.

"I don't see anything, Marty." But as he spoke, his words died in the air.

A small figure in a white T-shirt and a black hat appeared on the deck with exaggerated, prancing steps, and as he did, Gordon was struck by how wrong he had been about everything he'd assumed. Flat wrong. As wrong as he could be.

Gordon drew a singular line of sight from where Warren Duke was still speaking to Sophie on the bed where Dianne snored, to the outside of the window, across the second story, to where Mo stood with his hands on his hips, grinning hugely in the moonlight. He saw them looking. He looked right back and put one finger to his lips.

Everything went out of the window. In more ways than one.

"Son of a bitch," Marty said, bewildered.

If Gordon could speak, he would have agreed.

CHAPTER TEN

D ana hovered in a world in between. She felt as if she were in several places at once—some small part of her knew she was in a hospital bed, attached at the arms and hands and mouth to tubes and machines, but she was not there on the inside. She had no sense of time. She felt no pain. In the place her mind inhabited, the touch of the thin hospital sheets lay upon her with as much presence as shadows. The rhythmic hiss and beep of the machines were like white noise. She was in a hospital bed, but she was not *mostly* in a hospital bed.

Dana was *mostly* walking back and forth over a well-worn path in her brain: the minutes leading up to the explosion that had burrowed a piece of gas-soaked metal into her brain just above the temple. At first, she was running up and down that path, and she was helpless to stop herself. She relived the explosion again and again, each time recognizing her fate too late, seeing that the trail of flame she followed led to a pile of stinking gas canisters, which exploded again and again and again in a flash of white heat that obliterated her and put her back at the beginning again, on the lawn outside the lab, in the dead of night, tracing a snaking trail of fire.

She felt no pain when she was obliterated, only panic. The experience repeated itself faster than she could sort it out properly in the compartments of her brain. She felt like a woman picking a single apple from a tree, only to find another behind it, then ten, then a hundred more falling around her.

For all Dana knew, she relived the explosion for years. Or perhaps just for moments. Time had lost all effect upon her. She lived in a vacuum of personal tragedy until one time, when she was deposited at the start again, instead of running after the flame as she had forever, she walked.

The snake of flame didn't run away from her. It kept pace just ahead. She couldn't stamp it out, nor could she dash to catch it, but she found she was able to conduct it, rewinding and playing and fast-forwarding, as if she was at the controls.

Dana no longer felt panic once she was at the controls, but she did get angry. The damn fuse was always out of her reach, like a carrot in front of a donkey. She swiped, spat, and screamed at it. Nothing worked. Sometimes, she became so infuriated at her impotence that she sped everything up again and took off running as she had in the beginning, just so she could explode along with her frustration.

She always ended up at the beginning. On the lawn, in the moonlight, the fuse just out of reach.

Other times, Dana sat on the grass of the darkened schoolyard right at the beginning and did nothing but watch the flame. When she stood still and it stood still, the fuse looked less like the instrument of her demise and more like a candle in a dark window.

She might have sat for moments. Or for years. Or forever.

Only one other person joined her on that well-worn path of her brain: the fire starter. The one who lit the fuse. And whoever he was, he inhabited the farthest edge of what had become her world. Just close enough to exist. Mere steps from falling off the map.

Dana spent swaths of what passed for time in that place watching the fire starter. He moved just like the fire, locked on a predestined path, in perfect timing with everything else. At first, she thought he'd never be more than a mirage in the distance, but after a time,

Dana found a single frozen moment along the inevitable path to her explosion where she could see his eyes. That frozen heartbeat was very near the end, very close to the obliterating whiteness. She was fully inside the darkened, hollowed science lab, but the fuse hadn't yet reached the canisters. In that frozen moment, inches from oblivion, the boy stood nearly visible. The brim of his hat still obscured the top of his head, and the shadows obscured the bottom half, but his eyes were visible in a single stripe of light from the fuse, like a superhero's mask. That was when he'd looked back at Dana. That was when their eyes met, just before the explosion.

The fire starter was frozen, crouched to run, shoulders thrust forward. He looked eager to go but torn on which way to run. Half of him was set to flee the blast, but the other half looked as though it wanted to run toward it, as if he wanted the oblivion too.

In the fey light of the fuse, Dana couldn't tell the color of his eyes, but it was obvious that they were in pain. Floating as they were, between two strips of shadow on his face, Dana was able to take them out of that well-worn path entirely—away from the fire and the white that followed—and when she did, when she focused only on them, she thought they looked more afraid than triumphant, more tormented than pleased.

Dana wanted desperately to know more. She felt very close to understanding the child, very close to knowing who he was, but her brain had offered all it could in terms of the past. Already, it was growing restless with itself, changing things Dana knew for fact with machinations of its own. Toying with her. The fire starter's face became Chloe's. Then her mom's face. Gordon's. Her own. Each more silent and staring than the last, until she couldn't take it anymore and ran into the blinding white explosion again

The loop was enough to make anyone crazy. She felt herself spiraling slowly downward into a place of no return. She knew of a way to make the white at the end last longer. To jump the well-worn path altogether. It involved giving up, no longer caring what was beyond where she was trapped. Easy enough to do. She supposed, although she dared not dwell on it, that she could fall *completely* into the white—leave the loop, and everything else, forever. She admitted to herself that the notion held appeal. Like when she caught herself falling a touch too far into a daydream. It would be so easy, like falling backward. All she had to do was decide to do it. And since in that place, dwelling upon the white was the same as inviting it in, she suddenly found herself walking to the explosion. Pausing right before. Turning around, closing her eyes. She held her arms out, ready to fall into the whiteness forever...

Then she heard Gordon's voice.

"We're on the same case again," he said. *"You and I. I thought you might want to know that. Your fire starter is my patient's imaginary friend. Maybe if I told you at dinner. Talked more. Was present more. Maybe we could have figured out that we're on the same road and could've tackled this together. Maybe then I wouldn't have been so sloppy."*

Dana dropped her arms to her side and retreated from the explosion. The flame backtracked with her. "We still can, Gordon. I'm here. I'm right here."

"I owe it to Sophie to figure this out. And I owe it to you, too."

"You don't owe me anything, Gordon," she said, speaking to the black sky within her mind. "You've already given enough. Maybe too much."

"So how about this? How about if I don't give up, you don't give up. Deal?"

"Deal."

Gordon sighed, and it sounded like the wind whispering through the giant tree under which Dana found herself sitting once more.

"Now I just gotta find an imaginary friend that starts fires," she heard Gordon say. He sounded heartbroken. He sounded the way the fire starter's eyes looked, which was how she came to understand.

"Look for loss, Gordon. Look for loss and for pain, and you'll find your imaginary friend. You'll find your fire starter," she said, but her words were carried away into the blackness above.

"Remember our deal, now. Okay? Please?"

"I'll remember."

GORDON WATCHED Dana carefully in the silence, not expecting any answer, of course, but willing to at least give her a chance.

Nothing.

Nothing but the slow hiss of the ventilator and the continuous beeping of her vitals. Gordon had been by Dana's side for only ten minutes, and the sounds were already driving him crazy. *If anything gets through to her, it's gonna be that damn beeping, not me.*

He sat back on the couch, rested his head on top of its back, and stared at the mauve ceiling. Mauve walls. Mauve floors. Even the couch he sat on, the kind that was halfway between couch and awkward single-sleeper bed, seemed different shades of mauve. Gordon started to drift in a sea of mauve. He'd been awake for almost two days straight. He felt the autumn sun drifting through the window and draping across his face like warm lace. He didn't want to look at it. Another morning had come, and he was no closer to figuring out how to help the people he was supposed to help—farther, in fact. Dana might just sleep forever. And if she did, he was resolved to sleep forever too. Maybe they'd run into each other somewhere out there, forever sleeping.

GORDON AWOKE TO A TAPPING, light but insistent, on his knee. Pain shot through his neck, and his mouth felt gritty, his tongue foreign. He rolled it around his closed mouth to no avail as he righted his eyeglasses and realized with a sinking feeling that he was still in the hospital. Dana was still motionless in the bed in front of him. Everything was the same except that Chloe was at his side, tapping his knee.

Gordon coughed to clear his throat and scooted quickly to make way for the girl. He checked his watch—just past eight in the morning. He'd conked out for almost two hours, just long enough to feel terrible when awoken.

"Hi, Chloe," he said hoarsely.

Maria stood at the foot of Dana's bed. She glanced at him but didn't seem to see him. She was completely absorbed by her silent and still daughter, as if she was seconds from collapsing onto Dana's bed herself. She had the heartbreaking look of the elderly in grief, as if all of the strength she had stored up to face her own end had to be used prematurely to face another untimely end. She was pallid and gray, years older than she had been two days before.

Chloe was different. Gordon was all too familiar with the unique ways children dealt with grief. Kids played the hands they were dealt. They knew no better. Adults complained about the hand while kids figured out how best to play.

"Did you sleep here all night?" Chloe asked. Her face was streaked with tears, but they were old tears, and they clashed oddly with her bright eyes and casual tone. She made no move to sit next to him.

"Not all night. Just for a bit," Gordon said.

Chloe nodded understandingly. "I try to sleep here, but Gigi says it's not good for me." She looked conspiratorially at Maria, who had moved over to Dana's other side and was gently massaging her right hand.

"Do you talk to Mom?" Chloe asked.

"Yeah."

"Me too. Did she answer?"

"No."

"Me neither."

Chloe held her favorite book at her side, the one Dana read to her nightly. *Just in case,* Gordon thought. Chloe stood in stark contrast to everything in that room. Optimistic. Inquisitive. Awake. Even her bright-pink tracksuit seemed to push back against the mauve and fight against Dana's coma in some subconscious way. She watched her mom carefully, and those bright eyes turned brighter again with unshed tears, but Chloe didn't fight them or wallow in them. Perhaps she had, at first, but since then had learned that tears had no better chance of waking her mother than dry eyes.

Maria busied herself tidying a room that didn't need tidying, plucking a few dead stems from the single vase of flowers at the sink, which looked hospital standard. No other cards sat nearby. No other flowers. No teddy bears holding little hearts that said Get Well Soon! Cops nearly killed in the line of duty got national news, an outpouring from the department and community, but all that was missing, and although Gordon didn't know *how*, he was confident the strange hush surrounding Dana was due to Warren Duke. He could almost smell the man's cologne underneath it all.

"That tube is helping her breathe," Chloe said knowingly. She took a few deep breaths, as if to prove to herself that she still didn't need one of her own.

"I'm sorry, Chloe," Gordon said suddenly. His role in all of this, in Dana ending up there, hung on him like the invisible film of a bad hangover. Maria stopped her plucking, and by the slight turn in her head, Gordon knew she was looking for someone to blame, too... and finding him. Gordon understood. In the few months he'd been dating her daughter, she and Dana had gone from the frying pan to the fire. He felt as though he were sinking down in the couch with the weight of her eyes.

Chloe tapped him on the knee again, concerned, not for Dana but for him.

"It's okay. You didn't hurt Mom," she said simply—a mantra, perhaps one Maria taught her as she was trying to explain tragedy to the little girl, and she had given it to Gordon.

Gordon found it incredible that Chloe would even acknowledge him when her mother was on ventilation three feet away, much less try to cheer him up. He smiled, and a bit of the weight that had settled on him shifted off, dropping to the floor.

"Do you know who did hurt her?" Chloe asked, and the evenness in her voice, the sudden and slight distance, hammered home to Gordon that the young girl really was her mother's daughter. She wanted justice.

"Sort of," Gordon said. That was all he could think to truthfully say.

Chloe nodded again, as though the two of them were on the case. Just talking to the girl made Gordon feel better by the minute.

"Are you gonna get them?" Chloe asked quietly. "You and Mister M?"

Mister M was Chloe's name for Marty. She thought he and Marty were a pair, which made Gordon smile and made him miss Dana all the more acutely, like a stitch in his side. Dana was trying her best to bring Gordon to Marty's level in her daughter's eyes, and it seemed to be working.

"I'm gonna try," Gordon said. He didn't know how and wasn't even confident he could get himself through the morning, but he would try.

Gordon stood and picked up his briefcase. He stretched his neck again and walked on pins and needles to the door. He paused by Maria, and she nodded farewell, eyes downcast. She closed the door softly behind him, and he was left in the hushed hallway. He walked without direction down the halls, around corners, through heavy double doors—walking just to walk, walking to wake his brain. Soon enough, his mind fell back to the facts, the puzzle pieces.

Sophie was not Mo. Mo was not Sophie. That meant Gordon had to figure out who Mo was. Obviously, he was someone with ties to Sophie. Someone that knew the house on Long Lane or had access to it. Someone who had known Sophie for a long time. Mo had been a fixture of Sophie's life since she was a little girl. Gordon wondered if he'd always been real. If he had, more questions presented themselves—like how he could remain a boy for over a decade. And how the rest of the family could have missed him for all those years.

Gordon checked his watch. Time to make a family visit of his own.

When he walked into his mother's room, she was already awake. Her gauntness pained him. She looked off-color as well, and he could tell by the slight pinch to her mouth that the radiation therapy of the day before was making her ill, but she still smiled at him. "It's my son!" she said, as if he'd flown in from out of town.

The *Sun* was already read, set on the chair, and she was halfway through the *Wall Street Journal*. She turned down her page and set the paper to one side, looking at him squarely.

"How are you, Gordon?"

"Not good. But you're worse, and I feel like an ass talking about me."

"Oh, nonsense," she said, waving his comment away. "Aside from the cancer, I'm just fine."

He was acutely aware of a lack of soft chiming to her movement. Her usual jewelry was off and away. She had a plastic ID bracelet instead, flush to her wrist and comically small. He badly missed her chimes.

Gordon dropped his briefcase to the floor and sat on the couch opposite his mother's bed. He felt he was living out of a briefcase those days, from couch to couch. He couldn't help noticing the couch in his mother's room was a lot plusher and a lot less plastic than the one in Dana's. And more brightly colored. Mauve had no place in the out-of-pocket suites. The beeps and hisses of the machines were hushed there as well, hidden behind walls and curtains, away from view.

"Can we get Dana up here?" Gordon asked.

"Would it matter to her?" his mother asked.

Gordon scratched at the four-day-old growth of beard beginning to itch his neck. "No," he said, "I suppose not. She'd say she was just fine with the rest of the world downstairs. If she could."

His mother folded her hands in her lap and waited for Gordon to speak. The bed was folded tightly around her, but the only evidence of her bottom half were the two small points of her knees. She seemed to be shrinking by the hour, which wasn't good, going into a major surgery. Ideally, she would be hale and hearty. Ideally, the surgical team should be worried about giving her enough anesthesia to knock her out. Instead, Gordon was sure they feared the opposite: that they would give her too much and she might not awaken.

"What happened?" she asked after half a minute, during which Gordon didn't take the bait. "You only stare at the ceiling like that when you're feeling more forlorn than usual."

"You know Sophie's imaginary friend? The voice in her telling her to start fires?"

"Yes," Deborah replied, playing along.

"Turns out he's not imaginary after all."

He waited for the gasp, the theatrics. Instead, his mother laughed delicately.

"So you were right, after all," she said.

"What? No, Mother. I was about as wrong as you could be. Mo isn't Sophie's psychotic delusion. Nor is he some personality of hers. He's as real as you and me."

"Forgive me. I thought you were trying to diagnose your patient. You know: do your job, not figure out who this Mo is."

Gordon didn't follow. "The two go hand in hand."

"Oh, so I suppose that now you know this Mo is a real person, everything is fine with your patient, then. She's back in school, is she?"

Gordon thought of Sophie checking the ceilings. Babbling. Washing. Her near catatonic state on the bed.

"No. She's very sick. And now that I think we can safely rule out dissociative identity disorder..."

"Your initial case for schizophrenia is that much stronger. Congratulations. Looks like you were correct. You have a full-blown schizophrenic patient with an impish firebug of a friend."

His mother was right. Sophie's symptoms exhibited themselves despite Mo, not because of him. He'd been so focused on catching

Mo for Dana, and for himself, that he'd lost focus on helping Sophie. Mo wasn't his patient. Sophie was.

"So I was right about the schizophrenia. I left her worse off than when I started treating her. Forgive me if I don't break out the champagne on a correct diagnosis."

"You should break out the champagne anytime you have champagne, Gordon, but that's beside the point. The point is you're still thinking of this Mo person as part of Sophie's diagnosis. He's not."

Gordon opened up his battered leather satchel and took out the collection of drawings he'd found scattered along the stairs of the house on Long Lane. He eyed the topmost, taking in the table and the manic grin of Mo standing high atop the family.

"What is he, then?"

"Part of the treatment. Of course."

His mother's words seemed to cause a subtle shift in the ground under Gordon, as if by turning the puzzle upside-down, he might better find a place for the errant pieces he still held.

"She'll never have a cure. Schizophrenia carries with it a lifetime of symptom management," Deborah said. "She'll always be striving for balance and understanding of what triggers her breaks, what brings on episodes, what causes her anxiety. You said yourself Sophie and Mo are connected somehow, and as long as Mo is still out raising hell, she'll never be able to manage her condition. But if you straighten out Mo, it will go a long way to straightening out Sophie."

The shift grew more pronounced. His mother's words rang true. They also ran right up against Warren Duke's threats.

"Warren Duke wants me off this case. He threatened me with a phony sexual-assault inquiry."

"That man again?"

"Said he'd shut down my practice. He *really* doesn't want me to dig any deeper in this."

"I see." Deborah seemed to weigh sides in her mind, tilting her head this way and that. "And how does that make you feel?"

"Like I must be getting close to figuring out the whole picture," Gordon said, grinning.

"So you'll keep walking, then?"

"I'd never forgive myself if I stopped."

"Wonderful! You've moved past diagnosis and are now in treatment," she proclaimed, adding a little clap at the end.

Gordon flipped through the collected drawings, his mother's words still reverberating in his head. He felt lighter, so he stood. He took the drawings over to a two-seat table near the bay window and laid them out, end to end, as he might a CT scan of a brain, which in many ways, they were.

All day, he'd been looking for similarities between the pictures, but he decided to turn the puzzle upside-down. Now he noticed differences. Consistent differences.

Always Mo, standing above the table—always Sophie, crunched between her mother and father below the table. But half of the pictures looked like art, and half looked like sketches. The difference between the more finished pictures and the rudimentary ones was obvious. He sorted them into two piles with ease. He brought out the drawing Dianne had given him in his office and measured it against the two subsets. He settled it with the finished half.

The finished drawings had contour and shade and range of color. They were well composed and cleanly drawn. They also were very similar. Sophie sat between Dianne and Simon, all three of them under a black table. Mo stood triumphantly above them, with flames all around. After several minutes of studying those, Gordon stacked them and set them aside. The rudimentary set of drawings was what interested Gordon more. Those varied from page to page. In most, Dianne had short hair, but in three, it was long. In one, she was blonde, in the other, brunette. The differences were subtle, but knowing how precious Sophie's colors were to her, Gordon doubted any variance in her drawings was taken lightly. And Simon, to her right, was bald in half of them, his head a horseshoe shape. In the other half, he had long, curly hair. In some, he had a moustache, just a faint line, in others, he had a full beard. The only thing that stayed consistent in those drawings was Sophie and Mo—Sophie a ball of limbs between them and Mo a glorified stick figure, grinning up top.

Gordon found himself drawn to the depictions of Simon. His eyes were covered. If the three of them under the table were like the wise monkeys, Sophie was Hear No Evil—head down, hands scribbled over her ears. Dianne was Speak No Evil—her mouth a thin line throughout, even as the rest of her changed. Simon was See No Evil. His hands often covered his eyes.

In the childish drawings, Simon wore a rich gold wedding ring on his ring finger. In the finished set, his hand was bare, another detail from Sophie's mind that Gordon felt was intentional. Sophie drew her father covering his eyes twenty-five times. *What don't you want your father to see, Sophie?*

Duke had Sophie and Dianne at the moment. Gordon had to wait for things to cool before he approached either of them again, but perhaps Simon could shed some light on the big picture.

Gordon stood back and turned to his mother, who was watching him patiently and seemed to be enjoying herself.

"What are the pictures telling you?" she asked, ever the psychiatrist.

"That perhaps I need to pay a visit to Sophie's dad," Gordon said, and he pulled out his phone. He was about to pull up Marty's phone number but saw that he'd already missed a call from him sometime during his two-hour nod-off. He smiled. He figured that Duke's threats wouldn't be enough to slow Marty down either.

The temporary truce between Marty and him felt tenuous, like soldiers pausing on Christmas day, knowing that in the end, only one of them would be left standing. He knew that when it came to Dana, someone was going to have to back down. Gordon knew it wouldn't be him, but he was sure Marty thought the same.

Still, a truce was a truce, and right then, Gordon needed all the help he could get. So he hit Redial.

Marty picked up on the first ring. "I been tryin' to get a hold of you."

"What do you know about Simon West, Sophie's dad?" Gordon asked.

"Funny you should ask."

CHAPTER ELEVEN

Gordon stood in the valet roundabout of Hopkins until Marty rumbled through in his Charger. Its growl reverberated under the carport, eliciting scowls from the discharged patients and nods of approval from the valet. After Gordon buckled in, Marty pulled out and then promptly in to the gas station across the street. He tapped his hand on the center console between them, palm up and open.

"Twenty bucks," he said. "You put in twenty. I put in twenty."

Gordon felt around in his jacket for his wallet. "Forty bucks for gas? What's this thing get? A mile to the gallon?"

Marty plugged in the spigot and pressed Premium. "Sixteen to the gallon, highway. But Lancaster, PA is an hour and a half away. Maybe your car gets better gas mileage. Maybe it also leaves us stranded on the state line."

Gordon nodded. Marty had a point. While the meter spun on the gas pump outside, Gordon watched the clock on the dash tick inside. Two weeks had passed since Dianne West first called him about Sophie. Four days since Merryville Prep had first burned. Three days since he'd last spoken to Dana—a dinner he could barely remember attending. How he wished he'd watched her with even half the focus he'd had on Sophie's case that night. What he'd give for one more dinner. He'd ignore everything else but what was right in front of him. *Who* was right in front of him.

Time should have stopped the moment Dana stepped out of it. But time went on. Just about twenty hours were left until his mother stepped out of time herself to remove the cancer in her breast. Two hours after that, she would step back in, God willing.

And one and a half hours to Lancaster, Pennsylvania, where they'd find Simon West and hopefully some answers.

GORDON HAD no desire to force conversation as they drove, and Marty seemed content focusing on the road. After a time, Gordon closed his eyes, not actually intending to fall asleep. He should have known better.

A loud buzzing awoke him, and he popped his head up with a disconcerting crunch in the neck. He was dreaming of alarms going off in Dana's hospital room, and it took him a good ten seconds to realize that the whining buzz he heard was Marty going over the sleep strips on the highway, wide awake.

"You were drooling on my seats," Marty said.

Gordon wiped at the corner of his mouth and did find a bit of a pool there. He wiped more vigorously, muttering an apology.

Marty ignored it. "I been thinkin' about Sophie," he said and left the words hanging in the car.

"You could have just tapped my shoulder if you wanted to talk," Gordon said, his voice gravelly. "Where are we?"

"Near York. You've been out for like an hour. I think Sophie's got the major in a corner." Marty rattled all that off as if it was related.

Gordon rubbed at a knot in his neck that seemed to have checked in permanently. "Duke? In a corner?"

"Yeah. She's got him pinned in a bad spot. I think he's afraid of her or something. Why else would he be there? Duke doesn't care about anything that doesn't affect his bottom line."

"I don't know," Gordon said skeptically. "He didn't look afraid. You saw the way he talked to her. If we weren't driving to see her dad, I'd say he was scolding her like an angry father."

"I went back to the station to look up the Merryville fire file while you... checked in on Dana." The pause was noticeable but just barely. "You know, to double-check what I'd put in my statement."

"And?"

"And it wasn't there."

"What do you mean it wasn't there?" Gordon adjusted the seat-belt off his collarbone. He felt as though he was losing weight again and bones were showing on him. The new khakis fit almost as badly as the old khakis had, back when he was living on ramen heated in a coffee pot.

"I mean it wasn't there. Not in the paper files. Not on the server. Not anywhere. I know I filed it. I've never misfiled a report in my life."

Gordon was quiet, digesting that most recent puzzle piece.

"I don't misfile," Marty said again, vehemently.

"I'm not saying you did." Gordon held up his hands.

Marty plowed on. "Every case is assigned a lead detective. Every lead detective is assigned to file. Dana..." Marty cleared his throat and focused twice as hard on the pavement in front of him. "Dana gave me this case. Merryville was my first as lead detective. My name was on top of the paperwork. I was the one in charge of the file."

Marty squinched up his mouth for a second. "I didn't misfile it," he said again quietly.

"I believe you. But you know what that means—"

"That means someone deleted it." Marty nodded deeply. "And very few people have admin access to case files. It's a rank thing."

"Rank like major."

"Bingo."

"So you're telling me that there is no record of any suspect in the Merryville fire?" Gordon asked.

"That's what I'm sayin'," Marty said, emphasizing with a thump of his thumb on the steering wheel.

Gordon rested his head back and closed his eyes, picturing Maria tidying up a hospital room that didn't need tidying, that was bare to begin with. "She had no flowers. No cards. Nothing from anybody at the station or anywhere else."

Marty gripped the steering wheel with such force that his shoulders tensed. His eyes hardened under his rock shelf of a brow.

"When I showed up at the station and everybody was going on like nothing happened, I thought they were disrespecting her. I was about to clean house. Then this one guy from the western district that I used to double with sometimes comes up all hushed like, and he asks how Dana's doing recovering from the wreck. He said he'd heard she was in a car wreck. And that booze was involved."

Both men were quiet for a time then, as the Pennsylvania countryside flew by. The October sun had already come full swing into the windshield and the clock had barely struck four. They'd be driving back in the dark.

SIMON WEST LIVED in a cookie-cutter neighborhood in a suburb on the outskirts of Lancaster, called Centennial. Marty followed his GPS through four-way stop after four-way stop. Gordon could see every house from every other house. The trees were barely higher than the stop signs in most places. Four or five of those trees stacked top to bottom might reach the height of one of the old-growth white oaks of Merryville.

The address Marty had plugged in was coming up on the right: a small ranch house with overgrown fitzer bushes out front covered in fake cobwebs for Halloween. A single string of orange jack-o-lantern lights was hung across half of the front window. Marty parked along the street in front of an unhitched camper covered in fallen leaves, its towline resting on cinder blocks.

Marty shut off the car. "This is it."

"I suppose he knows we're coming."

Marty popped open his door and heaved himself up with one hand on the roof. "Nope. I want to see this guy without him preparing."

"Aren't you supposed to have a warrant?" Gordon crunched his way up the cracked sidewalk behind Marty. "Or some paperwork or something? That says we can be here?"

Marty turned around, and Gordon nearly ran into him.

"We're just talking," Marty said in a way that sounded as though, if it came down to it, Marty would do nothing of the sort.

A ratty-looking plastic witch by the front door chattered like a set of novelty teeth when the men approached. Marty watched it skeptically as he rang the doorbell. Both men stepped back and waited.

Gordon listened for movement but heard none. So when the door opened suddenly, he couldn't cover his surprised yelp. Even Marty tensed. The man who stood behind the screen door was short and compact, with small, sharp features. He wore a tight-fitted workout shirt, of the type a cyclist would wear, tucked into his jeans. He was muscular in a small, quick way, not unlike Dianne West. He wore a black-and-orange Orioles hat low on his head, with a brim so curved it was almost as if he was surveying them through a spyglass.

"Simon West?" Marty said.

"Who's asking?" he replied, not rudely but straightforward.

"I'm Detective Marty Cicero, with the Baltimore Police." He held up the badge that hung around his neck. "This is Gordon Pope. We were hoping to speak with you."

Gordon fully expected the door to close again. Instead, the man looked closely at them both in a way that Gordon couldn't help but think was quite brazenly childish then nodded rapidly.

"I'm Simon," he said. "I was wondering when you'd come by. Let me guess. This is about my ex-wife."

"Close," Gordon said then paused. No need to play his hand needlessly.

West furrowed his brow for a split second. A small exhale through the nose. "Sophie?" he asked, a shade more quietly.

Gordon nodded. "May we come in, Mr. West?"

West took in a big breath and held it there, pondering. He removed his hat and scratched at his head in thought. He was nearly bald beneath. What hair he had was trimmed neatly to within a centimeter of his head.

"I suppose you should," he said.

Soon, Dana would have to make a choice. She felt it with an undefined sense of foreboding as she sat under the tree in her loop. The foreboding was not unlike the constant, low-level fear that one day, her child would grow up and leave her. One day, her mother would die. One day, she'd realize, as all police do, that the time had come to hang up her shield. She knew she was reaching some final ultimatum on that well-worn path of her brain because the fire starter at the edge of her world was becoming clearer to her.

The part of Dana still tied to the outside world knew how important it was to ID the fire starter, knew that people dear to her were tied up intimately with it, including Gordon, whose voice still echoed in the chambers of the loop. She was desperate to see the fire starter as he truly was, and she knew she could. If she made the choice.

But it meant going into the white explosion forever.

Dana didn't know what that meant, not entirely, but she knew it was a final thing. She'd know everything, but it would cost her everything.

So she sat and watched, and the time for her choice neared. The fire starter's face was no longer one she knew, no longer a trick of her mind. It was real. The face taking shape was the one she'd seen in the seconds before the explosion. She'd walked the well-worn path in her brain long enough to uncover the truth... but he was too far away to see.

The urge to get closer was almost maddening, like an itch lodged at the back of her throat that wouldn't go away. An ID meant a suspect. A suspect led to conviction. A conviction closed a case. Closing cases was her job.

She found herself on her feet again, behind the static burn of the fuse, as she had been countless times before. She walked closer to the fire starter, but that time her walk felt different. She knew that going into the white that time meant going away from Chloe and from Gordon forever.

But that itch. She gagged with the persistence of it. Each step toward the whiteness gave her a tiny reprieve. That time, the flame of the fuse didn't jump ahead of her. It waited for her until they were side by side, and it burned next to her, step by step. Its meaning was clear: *"You can finally see the truth, but then I take you."*

She almost turned away again to go back to her spot under the tree, but then she saw how close she was to the fire starter, how tantalizingly close. Already, she could see something more, the hat, the ears, clearly delineated, pushed down at the bill but up at the back—and there, no hair.

The fire starter was bald.

Still, Dana could only half place him. With every revelation, the urge to move forward grew until it was a hair shy of unbearable, and she found herself in step with the fuse again, inches from the cans.

Another tantalizing revelation: the fire starter was not a child. He was short and trim but not a child. She couldn't say how old, only that from a distance, his features appeared childlike when they were not.

With another movement, the fire starter would be hers, but so would the white. Her choice had come. She started weeping with the pain of indecision.

Then she heard a voice.

"Dr. Pope said I can talk to you as much as I want, and so I will."

Chloe.

"Mr. Buttons walked a long path through the forest every day. And

every day, Mr. Buttons tapped the trees with his felt nose so he could find his way back."

Her book. She was reading to Dana. She was... out there.

Dana took a step back. The flame followed, but it flickered and flared as if angry. Dana looked at the fire starter, almost congealed, almost complete, his eyes ever frozen upon her.

"Mr. Buttons was never lost. Until one day, walking through forest frost, he sneezed and found his nose was tossed into a mound of snow."

Her voice danced across the rhymes with confidence. The itch was numbed.

"Help! cried Mr. Buttons as he sat down upon the ground. And he sniffled and he whimpered until he heard a digging sound."

Dana spoke along with her daughter the words she knew by heart: "And up popped Mr. Velvet Mole, who came to him and said: I heard your cry, and here am I, to calm your worried head. I find things for a living. I've really got the knack. Stick with me, and you will see you can find your way back."

"Find your way back."

Chloe's words echoed in her mind until something subtle but definite popped back in place within her. She realized for the first time that she was in a coma. And in that split second of realization, she broke the coma—broke the loop—and slipped upward into a dream where frozen things were no longer frozen.

The fire starter blinked and widened his grin monstrously, all true resemblance gone, until he was a creature made mostly of teeth, with hollow black pits for eyes. After a lifetime of staring at what was essentially a still-life painting peppered here and there with hints of movement, seeing the fire starter break free of his frozen position and turn fully toward her made her scream out in silence.

Dana turned and ran, and the fire starter followed. She heard the susurrant scampering of tiny feet behind her, like the sound of a cockroach dashing on kitchen tile. The two of them were in a footrace once again.

Dana ran to the edge of her world. She felt fingers of fire reach for her, their heat searing her back. She flung herself off the edge of her mind, and she fell.

DANA FRISCO WOKE UP, not with a shout or a jolt—she was too stiff for that—but with a single squeeze of Chloe's hand in hers.

Her daughter met her eyes, dropped her book, and threw herself on top of her mother, tubes and attachments and bandages be damned, until Dana's mother pulled her away. At first, she scolded Chloe. Then her eyes met Dana's, and her tears joined Chloe's as she fell to her knees.

Movement was agony for Dana, but she could do it. She wiggled her toes and squeezed her daughter's hand again and again. She felt a terrible blockage in her throat and realized it was a ventilator. She fought off panic as the room screamed with alarms. She scrabbled weakly at the mask and might have attempted to rip the tube from her throat herself if Chloe's hand hadn't kept her still while the crash cart came in. The staff was clearly expecting to see a dying woman, and the doctor in the lead nearly dropped the defibrillator paddles when he saw her looking back at him. She waited for another eternity while they tended to her, pulling things from her with sickening pressure on the inside and outside, where no pressure should ever be felt.

All she wanted to do was work moisture into her mouth. All she wanted to do was tell Gordon what she knew to be true about the fire starter, what she'd seen before the coma broke.

She prayed she wasn't too late.

MORE FAKE COBWEBS festooned the banister just inside the house of Simon West. An empty plastic bowl sat on a small end table offset from the base of the stairs, awaiting candy. A plastic skull grinned beside it with fake tea-light candles that glowed orange inside its eye sockets. West walked ahead of them under a line of plastic bats hanging from plastic strings.

"Watch the bats. They get tangled," he said, not looking back. Both men ducked under.

"You're pretty into Halloween, Mr. West?" Marty asked.

"You have to be, with a ten-year-old. It's a prime Halloween age. Sophie never much cared for it." West gestured at a plastic tarpaulin with two dancing skeletons taped to the patio door. "I suspect she had enough of all this in her own mind. But Dustin's different. Loves all the ghoulish stuff. Can I get you men something to drink? Water? I think I might have a beer somewhere in the back of the fridge." Simon spoke in flat monotone, and quickly, as if his mind was a sentence or two ahead of his mouth.

"We're fine, thanks," Gordon said.

West paused briefly and nodded then sat down at the table, gesturing at the chairs. "So what did Sophie do?"

"Not so much Sophie, Mr. West. It's her friend. Mo."

West held Gordon's gaze without blinking. "Her imaginary friend. Yes. She's caused quite a bit of trouble with her imaginary friend. Don't tell me she's starting fires again."

"She's not. As a matter of fact, I don't believe she ever was," Gordon said, leaning forward and crossing his arms on the small dinner table. "But Mo was. Because Mo is real. And Mo has been real for a long time. We saw him ourselves, on the deck of 8 Long Lane."

West still hadn't blinked. Gordon felt as if he was in a chess match with the man. The opening move was when he'd invited them in. Gordon was struck by how little surprise the man showed. It said something without saying anything at all. It said that West knew—in some form, at least. He knew that Mo was real. And he was keeping it to himself.

Marty was unabashedly casing the house. He craned his neck to see around West to the far wall, where family pictures hung in a neat row. In one, Simon West stood with his second wife, a kind-looking young woman in a conservative dress with green eyes framed by herringbone eyeglasses. Their son Dustin sat between them, lodged comfortably between the pockets of their shoulders.

"I can just bring the photo over to you, Detective. If you want to know what Dustin looks like."

Simon seemed oddly at ease with two strangers in his house—one of them a cop snooping around his family—almost as if he'd been preparing for that day. He stood and walked to the pictures, and as he panned them, Gordon caught a half smile, as if even then West was reliving those moments. He plucked the largest from the wall, a framed portrait the size of a sheet of paper of the three of them outside a carnival game, the kind where you shoot a squirt gun in a hole to fill up a balloon until it pops.

"My wife, Sally, and our son. This was taken six months ago."

Gordon saw Marty's face fall as he looked at the picture. Marty had hoped to find their fire starter, but the child in the picture was in a wheelchair. When Gordon looked up again, he found West watching him carefully.

"Dustin has a mild form of cystic fibrosis. It occasionally happens with high-risk pregnancies. Sally was forty-two when we had him. As you can see, my son isn't the type to light fires and run away."

His eyes showed no triumph, and his tone was assured but not gloating. If he felt he'd caught both men out, he wasn't showing it.

"You were granted no custody over Sophie at all?" Gordon asked.

"On paper, I have limited custody. If Dianne were to bring Sophie here, I could watch her, be her father again. Dianne has not. So I haven't. Dustin and his half sister are strangers. They've seen each other perhaps three times in their lives. I wanted it otherwise, of course, but the custody battle saw to that."

Gordon had been involved in more than his fair share of custody battles. When he was first starting out, he had seen many patients with parents spiraling quickly toward divorce. He often was called in to testify on behalf of a child in court. Gordon prided himself on being able to tell very quickly where best care lay. He'd seen firsthand what Dianne West did with her time, and while Simon West set him ill at ease, the impression he gave wasn't any worse than what he got from Dianne.

"Seems strange to me that you wouldn't be granted any custody at all," Gordon said.

"It does, doesn't it?" West replied. "Dianne is a drinker. Dianne dabbled in pills. Just sleep medication, at first. But I knew she was going harder when I wasn't looking. On paper, it's a no-brainer to give custody to me."

"On paper," Gordon said, waiting.

"In reality, there's Warren Duke." West looked at both of them as if they had known all along. When they remained silent, he furrowed his brow, but only slightly. "You do know about Warren's involvement, don't you? I assumed so, given that you're police."

Marty turned slightly to Gordon, met his gaze briefly, and shrugged. Gordon nodded. He was as tired of charades as Marty. They could play Battleship in the dark or try to get to the bottom of things. Time was running out for every player on the board.

"We know Warren Duke is involved. He was at the house on Long Lane the night we saw Mo. But in all honesty, we have no idea why. We were hoping you might shed some light on that."

West smiled grimly and sat back in his chair. "I don't know who you think you saw on that veranda, but I can tell you this: I'd stay out of it. Sophie could set half the city on fire with Mo dancing behind her the whole way, and she'd still never see the inside of a mental-health facility. Warren Duke wouldn't allow such a dark mark on the family name."

Gordon slumped. The puzzle piece fit, but it darkened the picture as a whole. "The family. Of course."

"Warren Duke is Sophie's uncle. Before Dianne was Dianne West, she was Dianne Duke."

West kept speaking while Gordon's mind reeled. So Warren Duke was in the family. He was protecting the family name or, as was more likely, the upward trend of his career. After major came deputy director then director—all positions that were highly vetted and extremely political. Who actually had set fire to the school—whether it was Mo or Sophie—didn't matter as much as how it looked. And it looked as though Sophie had set the fires. Committing her would all but confirm her guilt. Men had lost appointments to deputy director for far less.

"His relationship to Dianne, and to Sophie, isn't something he speaks of," Simon continued. "He's quite guarded about it. Fiercely so. He was as thrilled as I've seen him when the divorce was finalized and I moved out here. He thinks Sophie's mental troubles come from my side of the family."

"Do you agree with him?" Gordon asked. "I mean, have you ever been evaluated, or anyone on your side..."

"No. I refuse even to brook the argument. Not from Dianne, not from either of you, but especially not from Warren." He spoke with an abrupt ferocity before calming himself visibly with a deep breath. The silence around his exhalation was palpable. West tapped the table lightly with his knuckles. "And now, if you men will excuse me, I have a dinner to make before Sally gets home with Dustin."

Gordon knew they had no precedent to stay longer. He stood first. Marty followed, slowly, none too happy. Gordon could tell Marty didn't like Simon West and didn't trust him one bit. He knew that flinty look well enough. Marty often looked at Gordon that way.

They walked silently to the door. The sun was on the far side of the day already, and the temperature was dipping quickly, the first freeze of the year just around the corner. As Gordon buttoned his jacket, and before West could close the door behind him, he decided to throw caution to the wind.

"Can I ask you why you and Dianne separated? Or was that because of Duke too?"

"Warren's reach is long, but not that long," West replied flatly. "Dianne's an addict. I didn't want to spend my life picking up after her. Although neither side was too hurt to say goodbye. That's how you know. When it ends without much of a bang, you realize it never had any power behind it in the first place."

"Why does she do that to herself? The pills, the booze?"

"For that, I think you'll have to ask her."

Gordon nodded and turned around again, but Simon spoke up once more.

"Try not to hold it against her. Suffice to say that she had a hard time watching Sophie grow up. A hard time letting go. That house was meant for a huge family. Soon, it will just be her."

GORDON WAS LOST in his own thoughts as Marty drove them back to Baltimore. An expectant quiet gathered in the car as both men tried to make sense of what they'd learned.

They were nearing the halfway point when Marty muttered, "Do you think it was him?" His voice was so low that Gordon almost missed it.

"Him? You mean Simon?"

"Do you think it was him that started the fires?"

Gordon pondered the thought. If he was honest with himself, he was trying harder to fit Warren Duke into the role of fire starter than Simon West. Duke would never touch the match himself, of course—he'd have some paid thug to do that... but no. As much as Gordon wanted to paint Duke the villain, he knew the man was trying to shove Sophie under the rug, not bring her out into the light by drawing attention to the family with flame.

"I don't know," he answered. "Could be, I suppose."

"He has the build. Think about it. We've been thinking all along it's a kid Sophie's age, but none of us saw him up close. Maybe Mo is man. A small man."

Gordon pictured Mo in his mind. Manic grin. Hands on hips. Finger to his lips. "Shhh."

Marty gripped the steering wheel with both hands as if he

wanted to rip it from the dash. The car accelerated, ripping down the highway as Marty opened up.

"I mean, think about it, right? Dude gets shut out of his kid's life? Has a grudge against his wife's family? Maybe the only way he can see his daughter is by following her around like her imaginary friend, raising hell for his ex-wife as he goes."

Gordon was pressed gently back in his seat again. He checked his seat belt was fastened with a quick touch and settled it flat across his chest.

"It fits, yeah," Gordon said, "but why tell us all that, then? I mean, why let us in at all? To gloat?"

Marty didn't slow down at the city limits, only switched lanes more aggressively, lost in thought. Gordon didn't dare speak to him. Any break in Marty's concentration might end up breaking them both in two.

They were just past the 695 interchange when Gordon got a text. He pulled his phone from his pocket and read it before looking at the sender:

Am awake. Can't speak. Slowly putting myself together. They will allow visitors in three hours.

It was from Dana.

Gordon forgot all about how fast they were going, forgot all about Simon West. All thoughts about Dianne and Sophie were blown from his mind. He braced himself with one hand on Marty's massive shoulder and whooped until Marty was forced to slow.

"It's from her! She's awake! She's awake, man! We can see her later tonight!"

Marty's mood broke. A smile cracked his face like a single ray of sunshine beaming through a thunderhead. "Thank Christ," he said.

Dana sent a second text quickly afterward: *Fire starter is old. Adult. And bald.*

Gordon's silence piqued Marty, who asked, "What is it? What's wrong?"

Gordon read him the text hesitantly. Marty's face fell. Gordon knew what he was thinking. Simon West was old. And Simon West was bald. They'd seen it when he removed his hat briefly.

"I knew it," Marty said, deadly calm.

"Now, just hold on a second. Let's try to make sense of this."

Marty shook his head, gripped the wheel tighter, and made a nearly suicidal exit, scattering debris across the median and nearly running a camper off the road.

"I'm going back," Marty said, reading the signs for directions back to 83 North. He was approaching a stoplight at an alarming speed.

"What are you gonna do? Just drag him out of his house?"

"That's probable cause in my book," Marty said, ticking his head toward Gordon's phone, still in his hands. "Shouldn't have a problem at the station, not for a man within a hairsbreadth of being a cop killer."

"Nobody at the station *knows anything*, Marty. We'll see her in a couple of hours, and we can clear all this up." Gordon tried to talk him down like one of his patients, but that only seemed to rile him further.

"Oh, I'll see her, all right. With a nice present. Simon West in cuffs."

Gordon saw a way out. The signs ahead were for Towson. Merryville was just past Towson, perhaps ten minutes away.

"There's another way. Let's go to Long Lane. We can confront Dianne directly about Simon *and* Duke. Maybe get a warrant."

Marty said, "There's another reason people talk so freely like Simon did. It's 'cause they think they can't get caught. You go talk to Dianne if you want. It didn't get us far last time, and it won't this time. I'm going to talk to Simon West."

So it was that Gordon found himself in front of the Merryville gate once more. The leaves on the iron seemed to have turned bloodred just in the past forty-eight hours. The deep-earth rumble of Marty's Charger faded in the distance as the quiet, bespectacled attendant stood and set his battered paperback down spine up, waiting patiently while Gordon approached.

"Dr. Gordon Pope, here for Sophie West."

Gordon prayed he had a standing invitation as the attendant scanned a list on his clipboard with a single finger. The man nodded, and Gordon did his best not to sag with relief. "I suppose you know the way by now, Doctor?"

"I do."

The gate swung open, and Gordon walked in.

AFTER TEXTING GORDON, Dana was hit with a wave of exhaustion. What mattered next was recovering, finding full movement again, regaining normal speech. The face of the fire starter was already fading, in the way that dreams do. The revelation that he was not a child at all, that he was suffering, himself—those things seemed to matter less and less by the moment as she hugged her daughter and was held by her mother and worked her swollen tongue into shape once again. The worry and fear that gripped her upon first opening her eyes faded. Soon Gordon would be with her, and Marty as well. Together, they could tackle the case in good time. The realness of the world around her was what mattered—the true and changing light and sound and feel of the place she had awoken into once more, along with the solid presence of her daughter by her side.

Then Deborah Pope was at her door, and she was smiling warmly, if a little sadly. Dana was confused. Deborah could not possibly have known she was awake yet. And Deborah looked terrible. She was drained and weak, standing only with the help of a harried-looking attendant. Then she noticed the loose gown and the plastic bracelet, and she knew. She knew immediately that something was eating Deborah Pope from the inside. Only cancer could bring a woman like her to such a state.

In her hand, she held a stack of papers.

"Hello, sweetheart," she said, with a fondness that brought tears to Dana's eyes. "He'll be so happy to see you." She glanced behind her at the staff accompaniment, who tapped his watch. "I wish I could be there for the reunion. But I have no time left. The surgery team is already assembled. So it's up to you to tell him." She held up the papers. "He rushed off looking for the wrong person and left these with me. I've been studying them for some time. There is a pattern to these drawings, a very sad one, and I think my son has put himself in a great deal more danger than even he knows."

CHAPTER TWELVE

Long Lane was silent. No cars passed Gordon as he walked. The street and sidewalks were cold and hard and clean, as if every leaf that fell from the dwindling canopy above was snatched in the air before it even hit the ground. Hedges and solid brick fences loomed to his right and left, blotting out what little light there was from the houses themselves.

He wondered if perhaps he should have gone with Marty after all. Then he heard the quiet click of the gate closing shut behind him, and he knew his decision was made. He pictured Sophie walking back from school in the dark like that, a troubled girl trapped in her own head, worrying about things no child her age should worry about, so secluded from the world that she became terrified of what lay beyond the walls of her own neighborhood. And when her condition gave voice to her fears, she felt she had no choice but to burn everything clean again. Like cauterizing a wound.

She couldn't bring herself to start the fires, but she'd found someone who could, someone who turned her psychosis into reality, who knew her sickness as deeply as she did herself, and who was unafraid to light it up. Someone older. Someone balding. Possibly

Simon West, although Gordon wasn't as sure as Marty. West was off, true, and strangely intense, but he was also guarded and private. He didn't strike Gordon as the type of person to stand grinning over his work like Mo, hands on hips. Mo smiled every time anyone had seen him—unrelentingly, almost as if he was stricken with rictus. Simon West hadn't smiled once.

Their biggest problem was that if Simon West *wasn't* Mo, they were back to square one with no more leads.

Gordon came upon 8 Long Lane, rounding the soft bend of the street until the whitewashed-wood-and-brick façade came into view. The house was stunning in the sunset, well-kept and proud. Any passerby would have no idea how empty it was inside. He hoped that at least one of the two inhabitants had the wherewithal to answer his questions.

The wide-open front door and darkened anteroom suggested otherwise. *For a family so concerned with their secrets, they sure don't care for locks.* Or, as was more likely, Sophie was wandering again.

As he approached, he couldn't help but remember that all the previous times he'd come, the door had been closed—unlocked but closed. That it hung open seemed more like an invitation. The door might have been wide open for some time—hours, perhaps most of the day, waiting for him.

Gordon pulled out his cell phone and thought to call someone. Anyone. But he had nobody to call. At the threshold before the darkness, he was struck for the first time with the reality that his mother was now in prep for surgery. The enormity of that hit him like a surge of cold water in the open ocean, and he found himself leaning against the doorpost. She'd made him promise to stay away, but it still felt like a betrayal. He could call, but she was beyond picking up.

Might never pick up again.

He shook that dread thought away. He could call Dana, but she wouldn't answer either. She was going through the long, aching process of coming back into the world. A body paused doesn't easily start again. She couldn't even speak.

So he was alone. Still, he refused to enter without some note of his passing, so he texted Dana.

Marty went to follow a lead in Lancaster. I'm asking questions at 8 Long Lane.

He sent it, stared at his phone, and typed again.

I think I need more friends.

Sent that, too.

I miss you terribly. Can't wait to hold you again.

Sent.

Gordon took a deep breath and told himself to put away the phone. He sometimes got that way. He had with his ex-wife. He didn't need to start with his girlfriend as well. He pocketed the phone and took a step inside.

The marbled flooring of the foyer seemed electric with the moonlight that cut through the large slot windows above the front door. Gordon hardly spared a glance to his right or left as he walked through to the great room. He was sure he would find nothing out back tonight, either. If they were around, Dianne and Sophie would be upstairs, where he already heard the tinny, frantic buzz of the television on low volume. The great room was so dim that Gordon could see the television's light from where he stood on the floor below—flashes of white that crept around the open double doors leading to Dianne's bedroom.

Gordon called their names as loudly as he could, in part so his voice might rouse one or both of them, and in part to dispel the strange dread that drifted over the place like low-lying mist.

"Mo?" he added.

Nothing. Gordon walked to the stairs, pushing forward one step at a time, all the way up. He decided against further calling and instead listened, trying to hear the telltale patter of feet or the quiet moaning of Sophie hidden away somewhere, but all was quiet.

Gordon expected something awful when he turned the corner to see the bed. He wasn't sure what—a grinning man-child, perhaps, or a book of matches in a speckled swath of blood where Dianne should be. Instead, he found Dianne again, eyes closed, breathing deeply. One arm was flung wistfully over her forehead, the other draped partly off the bed, her covers strewn.

Gordon was almost disappointed. He looked for the pills briefly but couldn't find them on the dresser or in it. He smelled the full glass and pitcher on the nightstand to her left. Water. No vodka bottles to be seen. Gordon thought that odd, but perhaps she'd medicated downstairs, watching the darkened playhouse out back, and only made her way up when the world was comfortably numb again and she could collapse into sleep.

A second source of light shone electric blue from the corner, her computer. It was awake, which was also odd. Gordon put off the awkward decision of how best to rouse Dianne and instead walked to the desk and sat in the small chair there, still warm. He looked back at Dianne. She must have only recently passed out, which was good because she would be easier to rouse.

So this was the book—Dianne's memoir, the magnum opus she sometimes seemed to care more about than her own daughter. At first blush, it looked like Dianne had been suffering some sort of odd writer's block. The page was black with words, paragraph after paragraph, but each was simply a repetition of one word, a name. The first was *Sophie*, repeated two hundred or so times. The next paragraph was her own name, *Dianne*, repeated another two hundred times, maybe more.

Another break. Another name. *Ashley*. Again and again. Then *Peter* followed by *Sarah* and *Andrew*. Each their own block of text.

After Andrew came *MOMOMOMOMOMOMOMOMO*. No breaks. At first, Gordon thought Dianne had written *Mom*, but as he scrolled, it dawned on him that she had written *Mo* for almost twenty pages. Gordon ended up scrolling faster and faster and thought perhaps all of the document—all four hundred pages of it—was *Mo*, but at page seventy-five, it started over again with Sophie. Then Dianne. Ashley. Peter. Sarah. Andrew.

MOMOMOMOMOMOMOMOMOMOMOMO
MOMOMOMOMOMOMOMOMOMOMOMO
MOMOMOMOMOMOMOMOMOMOMOMO
MOMOMOMOMOMOMOMOMOMOMOMO

Gordon's breathing quickened. He'd found the right piece of the puzzle at last.

A rustling and a creak came from the bed. Gordon turned and found Dianne sitting up stock still, with her hair over her face. He was too startled to react, sitting in her desk chair, one elbow up on its back, watching her with blank horror, as if a foul ball had been careened off right at his face and he was powerless to duck.

"Dianne?" Gordon whispered because he was no longer so sure.

Her bobbed blond hair hung over the front of her face, backward and askew, like a poorly groomed show dog, but it had to be Dianne. Her trim arms and sharp fingers reached up and parted the hair in front of her face, and beneath it was a grinning set of white teeth and manic, swimming eyes—eyes that were Dianne's but also were not.

With one hand, Dianne pulled off her wig, and beneath it was a patchy, scabbed mess. Her head was shaved to bleeding across the front and tufted in the back, where it looked as though clumps of it had been pulled out by her own hand. She grabbed the crystal pitcher, her fingers snaking around the handle with a solid grip. Gordon saw it happening but couldn't take his eyes off her face.

There it was, the black hole in the picture where his puzzle piece fit. Gordon was looking at Dianne, but he was seeing Mo. He waited for it to make sense, for his brain to catch up with himself, but it didn't. He felt no satisfaction in finishing the puzzle just to find the picture a jumbled horror show.

In the time it took for Gordon to stand up, Mo had sprung to his feet and flung the crystal pitcher with surprising speed and accuracy at Gordon's head. A glittering arc of water left the pitcher as if jet propelled, and he thought it was quite beautiful, spinning slowly, like a constellation of stars.

He felt the water hit him first, just a few splashes, like rain on his face. Then the pitcher connected solidly with the side of Gordon's head, and everything went black.

Marty Cicero was already halfway to Lancaster, teeth gritted, knuckles white on the steering wheel. He drove in near silence, his mind on Simon West but also on Dana. He ran scenarios through his head, of how grateful she'd be when he could show up with the case closed. The man who'd put a piece of metal in her head would be safely behind six inches of solid metal himself, for the rest of his life. She might even smile that stunner of a smile, made all the more powerful on account of how rare it was. He hoped she could still smile. The blast had spared her face, so there was a good chance. Almost cost her an arm, but they could work through that together. Rehab it. Get her back in fighting shape. More than anything, he wanted to make her smile again.

The buzz of his phone in the cup holder jarred him back to the road and the speed he was going—damn near 105. He had to get his driving under control. He hadn't meant to let Pope see him like that. The only place he could blow off steam was in his car, and he took advantage, but from the way Pope triple-checked his seat belt, Marty was pretty sure the man was never getting in his car again.

Fine. He'd never asked for Pope's help. Never once. Didn't need to.

He snatched the phone up and looked at it and saw *Dana Frisco* on the caller ID and involuntarily hit the brakes so that he fishtailed a little before he could get himself under control. His face was flushed, and his mouth went dry.

"Dana?"

Her voice was scratchy, as if she was speaking through an old radio, but it was her. "Marty, listen. Mo is Dianne. Dianne West. Do you hear me? Where are you? Please tell me you're with Gordon. I can't get a hold of him."

"I'm..." Marty blinked. The flush that hit his face crept down his neck. From nervous to embarrassed in an instant—and when Marty Cicero was embarrassed, he got mad to cover it up.

"Well, it's nice to hear from you too, partner. You know I've been doing nothing but worry myself sick over you for the past three days?"

"He's not picking up his phone," Dana said, plowing forward as if Marty hadn't spoken at all. That, more than her words, made it eminently clear to him where her heart lay. He felt as if someone had just landed a blow to his sternum.

Marty swallowed hard, forcing his head to clear and becoming a cop again. "I left him in Merryville to follow up a lead," he said, and perhaps the frost that flattened his voice gave Dana pause, or perhaps she was dreading the answer he'd given, because she was silent on the other end of the line. "It was a good lead—"

"Marty, listen to me. You've got to get back there now. She'll kill him. She thinks... It doesn't matter what she thinks. All that matters for you is that you get there and get him out." She was already losing her voice. She sounded exhausted. "I'm gonna call it in now, send the squad if I can, but Duke might interfere. I know he's involved in this. So it's probably gonna be up to you."

"Dana..."

"Save him, Marty," she said, her voice a pleading whisper. "Please. Don't let him die."

She trailed off and hung up. Marty dropped his phone into the cup holder in the console. He did not stop. He did not turn around. Marty continued on like that for another three miles, listening to the engine. Part of him contemplated continuing on forever, ripping up the road ahead and never looking back, but he couldn't outrun what he felt for Dana, just as surely as Dana couldn't hide what she felt for Gordon.

What eventually got to Marty—what made him slam his open palms against the steering wheel and take risky advantage of a half-paved emergency access road to flip around and gun it back the way he'd come —wasn't actually Dana. It was Gordon and the picture Marty had in his mind of Gordon coming out from the library, Warren Duke's gun in his face. Gordon Pope had subtly waved him off, kept him hidden, and saved his job. Gordon had done all that for him despite knowing damn well that Marty Cicero did not like him and probably never would.

Gordon was a huge liability from a professional standpoint for both Marty and Dana. He'd stolen away from Marty any chance at a different life with Dana—a life of love returned—but he was also a good man. And good men deserved help if they needed it.

Marty squealed into the far-left lane, thick tires spinning. He floored it again, muttering every filthy word he could muster from years as a cop and decades of living through everything Baltimore had thrown at him before that. When the muttering didn't make him feel any better, he roared right along with the engine.

GORDON WATCHED his mother on the operating table. He stood in an observation room of some sort, separated from the doctors by glass. They moved around her like wraiths with steel teeth flashing as they cut. Gordon pressed against the glass to see as best he could, but his mother was shrouded in a blur of blue-clad men and women in white masks. He pressed harder and harder, and the side of his face ached terribly with the pressure, burned with it. The sea of blue and white parted for a moment, and he saw his mother staring right at him even as they cut her with terrible tugging motions. The steady, unblinking force of her gaze staggered him back from the glass, but the awful burning pain remained. Her mouth opened, and she spoke his name in silence. Gordon couldn't respond, but to his right, he heard a soft, subtle creaking sound that struck him as terribly familiar, like a woman sitting up in a bed, and when he turned to look, he found

Dianne, head shaved, scabbed, tufted, and bleeding. He almost screamed until he realized she was paying him no mind. She was reaching out to the operating room with the same yearning as Gordon had before, and when Gordon followed her grasping hand, he saw that his mother had been swapped out. Now, Sophie lay on the operating table.

"*Sophie,*" Dianne croaked. "*Ashley. Peter. Sarah. Andrew—*"

Dianne burned. She went up in flames without the cry of *Mo* on her lips. Gordon could smell it. The char was overpowering...

GORDON COUGHED himself awake and immediately regretted it. He felt each hack tap on his brain like an icepick. Jagged explosions the color of rust and blood erupted behind his closed eyes. He grabbed at the nucleus of his pain and immediately regretted it again. His hand came away wet with blood. He couldn't see it, but he felt it.

He couldn't see much of anything. At first, he thought that he'd gone blind, that someone had stolen away his sight before leaving him on a hard floor in a hot room filled with smoke, but as his eyes adjusted, a crack of white light materialized before him. Gordon pawed at it and found slatted wood. The wood gave, and the crack of light grew. He kicked out at it, and the wood gave completely. A door. He was in a closet. As it swung open, a wave of smoke poured in, and Gordon reeled, nearly vomiting. He covered his nose with the crook of his arm, squinted his eyes against the burn, and scooted out of the very same linen closet that Marty Cicero had concealed himself within a day earlier.

Out of the hazy darkness, he emerged into a raging inferno. Arms of reaching flames spread from Dianne's bedroom, belching gouts of smoke that billowed upward and piled upon the ceiling like a deadly thunderhead around the chandelier.

More smoke poured in a thick and steady stream from the library across the hall, and a loud crackling sound told Gordon the books were going up in flames. Gordon grabbed a silk fitted sheet and draped himself in it then scampered by the fire in the bedroom. If Dianne was in there, she was a goner, but Gordon doubted she was. She was Mo, after all, and Mo never got caught in his flames.

What worried Gordon was that Sophie was still unaccounted for. The events leading up to the attack all fell into place, and Gordon despaired to find she had no part in them. The fires would likely trigger an attack. If she was already in a manic state, they stood a good chance of elevating her to a catatonic state. She could be paralyzed somewhere.

He tried to check the library. The flames hadn't yet reached the door, but the closer he came, the more intense was the heat, and he had to turn away. He looked beyond the linen closet to where her bedroom would be, but as he did, a crack resounded as a ball of fire erupted from Dianne's room, expanding out to char the hallway. If she was anywhere on the second floor, she was gone. And if Gordon didn't get out soon, he'd be gone too.

He ran for the stairs, and there he saw a jagged swath of color, as if someone had dragged a fistful of colored pencils against the pristine white wallpaper leading down the stairs. It was unmistakable. On purpose. A sign that said, "Follow me."

Gordon needed no convincing.

The rainbow trailed downstairs, jumped the banister, and picked up again on the floor of the great room behind the buffalo. From there, Gordon hoped it might go out the front door into a crisp autumn night, but it didn't. It went behind the great room toward the kitchen.

Gordon paused at the front door. He had a chance to get away and stay alive. He could stand at the perimeter and watch the house get consumed, praying that Sophie and Dianne had somehow gotten out.

The problem was Gordon didn't believe that they had. He believed the rainbow mark was more than a trail—it was a cry for help. At the end of it, he would find Sophie. If he hurried, he could get her out alive.

He turned from the door and followed the rainbow deeper into the house. The fires were upstairs, but they wouldn't be for long. Already, the smoke was muddying the light on the main floor. The chandelier above looked like a foggy lighthouse seen from a distance. Gordon followed the lines of colored pencil with his fingers as well as his eyes. Sophie had dug deep into the felted wallpaper, ripping it as she went. The rainbow wrapped the backstop of the great room, and for a moment, Gordon thought he'd lost the trail. He spun in a slow circle in a near panic, and he froze when he saw what looked like an enormous orange slug crawling out of the stove.

He squinted through the smoke until he recognized the lace curtains from the back door, the ones that had billowed in the wind what felt like a lifetime before. They were bundled blobs of flame, dragged from their hangers and jammed into the oven, set to broil. He ran toward them with a mind to pull the sink sprayer out, but when he was feet away, they went up with a *whoomp* he could feel in his gut. He staggered backward. No more distractions. *Follow the rainbow, follow the rainbow, follow the rainbow.*

Coming back from the kitchen, he was able to spot the rainbow again—on the whitewashed walls leading downstairs.

"Stupid, stupid, stupid," Gordon muttered as he rattled down the stairs, barely touching each, burying himself deeper in the flaming house.

He came upon the main basement, which looked finished and pristine, with a massive projection television and several rows of plush leather viewing chairs, but the rainbow didn't stop there. It went deeper, and Gordon followed until he found himself another floor down, in a large unfinished cellar. The front half was entirely taken up by rack upon rack of wine. The light from the hall died ten feet in. The smoke hadn't found its way there yet, but Gordon knew it was coming. Already, he was sweating profusely. His shirt was drenched, and his brow was wet. He wiped down the front of his face and reset his glasses, but that was like turning on the wipers in a downpour. He couldn't keep up.

"Sophie! It's Gordon!"

The roar of the fire was muted there, replaced by an eerie hissing and a subtle moan—not of a frightened little girl but of cool air escaping out around his legs. On the floor far above, something heavy fell with a reverberating boom. Time was very, very short.

He flicked the light switch several times, to no avail. He pushed through his fear and walked deeper into the cellar, looking for the rainbow, but the rainbow had stopped. When he reached the first row of bottles, he found a handful of colored pencils scattered on a small table, next to a solitary glass of wine, a cigar box full of corks, and a small penlight.

Gordon clicked the penlight on. It would have been perfect for a better look at the labels deep in the collection, had the house not been on its way to collapsing around him in a blazing inferno. The light did little aside from illuminate what was right in front of his face, and what he saw was smoke. He coughed violently, as if in the seeing he finally believed. He figured he had five minutes to get up to the basement proper and find a recessed window to climb out of. He'd seen one when he was rolling around on the lawn a lifetime ago. Not much time, but five minutes was still five minutes. He had a chance to find her.

He noticed that while the bottles were mostly caked in dust, one row of wine looked as though fingers had brushed a swath along a line that led deeper into the cellar. He hunched over and followed it, blind to everything else. Soon he was quite far back. He guessed the collection had well over a thousand bottles, untouched for years, except for that brush of a hand. It bounced over each in turn... until Gordon reached the end.

The wine rack went on, but the wine stopped. He guessed he was near the back wall, although he couldn't be sure. That eerie hissing was louder, the air less smoky but thickening by the minute.

"Sophie?"

No answer. Gordon stood on his tiptoes to look over the racks, but he was just a hair short. He crouched down, peered between the racks, and saw that the collection hadn't really stopped, that in fact at least one more bottle was jammed farther back in the rack, almost out of sight. He reached in and felt for it, but what he pulled out wasn't a wine bottle. It was a mason jar, small, half the standard size and filled a quarter way with red liquid. He turned it slowly until he found a piece of paper tape on its back side. On the tape was the name "Andrew."

Part of Gordon understood what he was seeing because his hand started to shake slightly. The reverence with which he returned it to its spot indicated that his body, at least, understood, even if his mind was running behind.

He moved down the line and shone the light into the next slot. There he found another jar the same size, and he pulled it out and turned it over, an inch of liquid rolling viscously inside. On its lid was another piece of tape that read "Sarah."

Gordon cocked his head as if he still didn't understand, but he was lying to himself. His body betrayed him further—his hand trembled fully. The jar clacked softly upon the wood as he replaced it.

Gordon moved mechanically to the next slot. He could do nothing else... until he saw another jar. A large jar.

The fire and smoke were pushed to the back of his mind, but they were very much at the front of his senses. The acrid, overpowering forest-fire scent of roasting stone and sizzling wood had been turning his stomach without his knowing. Seeing that jar brought the pique to full. His mouth filled with spittle, and his stomach surged, but he fought it down. He refused to vomit. He felt it would be disrespectful to the jars, to what they held.

The large jar was the size of a flower vase. It was marked "Peter" and "Sarah" on two separate pieces of dry, yellowed tape. In the smoky haze of the penlight, he saw two very small floating figures within a sea of red, barely defined, more like clumps of twisted sticks than anything recognizable. But Gordon knew. He turned away, fell away, pushed himself back against the far wall. He was in shock less because of what he'd seen and more because of how he'd missed seeing it all along. He only stopped dragging himself against the concrete when his backside slammed squarely into a workbench set flush in the most distant corner of the house.

He turned to feel his way around it, shining the penlight in vain. All he could see was a slow, sinister roiling of smoke in the shallow cone of its light. The tabletop was made of stone and still quite cold. He had no idea how big it was and tried to walk around it. He took in a big breath to call out for Sophie again but ended up with a lungful of smoke. He coughed violently, his head splitting again, sickly orange stars everywhere.

A hand shot out from the blackness and grabbed him around an ankle. Gordon would have screamed if he wasn't coughing. Instead, he braced himself on the cold black table and dipped low, ready to grab hold of whatever was grabbing hold of him.

He grabbed Sophie. Even though he couldn't see her face, he recognized her plaid uniform. He collapsed to sitting, coughing still. He felt as if he was trying to breathe while buffeted by waves. Perhaps one in five breaths actually got where it was supposed to. The rest were blown right back out.

What eventually stilled him was the look on Sophie's face as she shot out from the darkness, inches from his nose, with a single finger over her lips. "*Shhh.*"

Her face was manic, eyes wider than was natural, in snakelike focus. She didn't blink, despite the smoke, her mouth open slightly. She looked pained, as though it took an enormous amount of initiative just to move, much less grab hold of Gordon. She leaned back against the concrete wall beneath the black table and looked forward again as if Gordon wasn't there. He leaned back too. The concrete was blissfully cold, the kind of cold that made him desperate to dive into snow or stand under a hose or sink deep into a lake.

His shoes slipped on what Gordon thought were scraps of paper, rolled scrolls, but as he slapped at one, his hand stuck to it. He peeled it off and brought it to his face and saw he was holding a sheet of uncut photographs, one of many that lay scattered around them.

They looked like pictures of a grainy eclipse, but Gordon recognized them as ultrasound prints. They were dated twelve years before and clearly marked with pen on top:

West, Dianne M.
Day 78.

Two granulated blobs were circled. Twins. Over the left fetus, the word *Sophie?* was handwritten in cheerful script. Over the right was a smiley face and a series of excited question marks and exclamation marks.

Sophie's twin. Gordon set his tired head back against the concrete and closed his eyes. Understanding washed over him again and again, and it was bitter and salty, and it burned. He knew, finally. He knew, and it felt nothing like he'd thought it would. The puzzle had hollowed him.

Sophie gripped Gordon again, around the arm, and Gordon opened his eyes. Across the room, along the perpendicular wall, was the source of the loud hissing. Three enormous gas furnaces were illuminated weakly by bare bulbs, as if each was being interrogated. A figure moved quickly across the path of light, a moving shadow that Gordon recognized.

Mo was hacking at the base of the nearest furnace with some blunt instrument, pummeling the metal with wide, swinging blows, trying to rip it open like a cooling vein of lava to expose the slow-burning heart. The hissing was the gas pouring out, bleeding like sap. If the smoke wasn't masking it, he was sure the whole place would smell like rotten eggs.

"Sophie, we have to go," Gordon said, but he was surprised and terrified at how calmly he said it, as if muttering in his sleep.

Sophie held him fast as they watched the fire at the heart of the farthest furnace grow before their eyes—it caught the gas as it leaked and puffed up like a beating heart filled to the brim. Mo turned around and ran back toward them quickly. She hopped up on top of the table, and Gordon could hear the creaking, feel the tremor of it. He imagined her, hands on her hips, surveying her work with that hollow and weeping grin.

He coughed heavily. His lungs wracked and scoured. He spat on the floor.

Dianne's head shot down from the top of the table, as if hung upside down. She stared at Gordon with screaming eyes, but her mouth was silent, split in an upside-down grin.

Gordon didn't scream or crawl away. He looked right back at Mo. Gordon had no fear, only terrible understanding. He saw Dianne there, hidden behind all the pain. And Dianne wasn't a monster. She was a broken mother who'd shattered her psyche to deal with extraordinary loss. Nor was Mo a monster. Mo was the brother that Sophie would never have, the brother that was Dianne's fifth miscarriage. Sophie's twin in the womb. When he never opened his eyes, Dianne took it upon herself to open his eyes for him, to become him. Mo was a personality Dianne created to protect herself and Sophie—the way a big brother ought to.

Mo *had* been watching over Sophie ever since she was born, an imaginary friend that wasn't so imaginary, flitting in and out of Sophie's very real psychosis as often as he flitted in and out from behind her mother's eyes.

And there Mo was, standing above them, trying to protect her still. Gordon had no doubt that Mo was trying to protect Sophie by burning the house down. He didn't know how, but that table, that place, held some sort of talismanic power over Dianne. In all the pictures, it stood safe from the flames.

But pictures were one thing. The reality was that all three of them would die if Gordon couldn't get them out.

Gordon heard a heavy clunk as Mo let the big pipe wrench he'd been swinging fall to the ground in front of them, then he hopped down. Gordon realized that while Mo was perfectly willing to protect Sophie, he didn't care for Gordon at all. In fact, he probably saw Gordon and Dana as trying to part him from Sophie. Most likely, that was why he'd lured Dana almost to her death at the school. Gordon reached for the wrench, but Mo snatched it away, and when Gordon scrabbled toward it, he was baffled by how weakened he was from the smoke. Clumsy. Dizzy. Sleepy.

Mo sidestepped Gordon's grasping hands easily and swung the pipe wrench squarely into his shoulder blade.

The pain was blinding then instantly numbing, but Gordon still could have fought back if he'd wanted to. He saw how weak Dianne was behind Mo's rictus veneer. She was clearly exhausted. She dragged the wrench back to herself slowly, but Gordon couldn't bring himself to hurt her. She'd been hurt so much already. He held his hands out as if to hold her when perhaps he should have lashed out with a kick to bring her low. She scrambled back in a burst, quickly out of reach.

"I'm so sorry," he said. It was all he could say.

Even as he saw her wind up hugely with the wrench again, that time aiming for his head, all he could do was reach for her, as if to hold her hand... and close his eyes.

He waited for the crushing blow. He felt a rustling instead, against his legs, and when he opened his eyes again, he saw Sophie sitting in front of him, between him and Mo. Her legs were clasped to her chest, wrapped by her arms, much the same way he'd first seen her, when she hid beside the hotel bed and he talked her down from her mania as she washed—such a vulnerable child, diminished, yet perhaps the only thing that could give Mo pause.

Mo screamed, a horrible sound, like a newborn animal that finds its mother dead. Gordon was almost relieved when the hissing over-took it... until the furnace exploded.

Mo was thrown forward into Sophie and Sophie thrown back-ward into Gordon, and all of them were forced back beneath the table, which was swept at the legs down and on top of them, nearly crushing Gordon with its weight as it rolled.

The table saved the three of them from the roiling wave of flame that passed overhead. When Gordon could shrug it aside, he pressed his cheek against the floor and sucked in what he could only assume was the last clean breath of air in the entire house. The furnace was roaring outside of itself, engulfed in a stream of blue fire coming from the valve at its base. The other furnaces were glowing angry red, sagging in the middle. They would ignite soon, he knew. But the effort of moving the table off himself was proving too much. Sophie was pressed against his chest, unmoving. He felt Dianne at his back, also still—all of them in a row. Gordon tried once to move but fell back. The relentless weight of the table began to slowly crush him again.

He realized with shocking clarity and remarkable calmness that they were all going to die there, and none of them deserved it. Certainly not Sophie, but neither Dianne nor him. He might have been too late to save them, but he'd given it everything he had. He'd turned toward the darkness instead of away. His mother would be furious with him for running into the fire, but his mother would understand. And Dana would, too.

He felt a lightening, a freedom. *This must be what dying feels like.* He could finally breathe again, so he took one last breath. Smoke be damned.

CHAPTER THIRTEEN

SIX MONTHS LATER

Dianne West looked at the psychiatrist's chair across from where she sat, waiting patiently. She still hadn't gotten used to her appointments and doubted she ever would. She'd only recently gained the confidence to drive herself to them. She still wore over-sized glasses and often a silk scarf, wrapped demurely around her head. The scarf was to cover her short hair—still patchy in many places but growing in better than she had expected—but also to cover her self.

After the fire, all three of them, Dianne, Sophie, and Gordon, had been rushed to the hospital. Sophie was the first to leave, the least injured. She was placed in a private care facility to recuperate, under orders of her father, who legally still had partial custody. Dianne was still in the depths of her disorder at the time she was taken away. Another two weeks passed before she could walk under her own power, another three before she could go an hour without coughing. Then she had to face the aftermath.

That first week, she had her driver roll slowly past the ruins of 8 Long Lane. It was totally destroyed. The burned-out bones of her house jutted here and there like some ancient buried beast slowly exposed by the erosion of time. She told the driver to stop and stepped out. The smell was still strong, the earth still black. That the fire was contained to her lot said less about the ferocity of the blaze than it did about the outrageous size of the Merryville plots. In any other neighborhood in the city, an entire block would have gone up.

No charges were filed—the work of her brother, no doubt. Since the fire, she'd heard that for such a large and consuming blaze, it received little to no attention in the press, either, which she was sure had something to do with Warren as well.

She was a pariah, shunned by her neighbors and whispered after wherever she went in Merryville, so she left. She leased an apartment north of the city in a quiet neighborhood near Druid Lake, where nobody knew her and nobody cared. Then she made the momentous decision to call a psychiatrist.

Only one person would do, but she doubted he would ever be able to see her. She wasn't sure, in fact, if he even had the capacity to see anyone any longer. But she called.

That had been four months before. Today was her twenty-fifth appointment. She heard him coming, clacking down the stairs in his slow way, and she smiled.

GORDON POPE PUSHED OPEN the door to his patient room with his rear and caught it open with the butt end of his cane. He shuffled in and righted himself, smoothing his jacket and coughing lightly into a silk kerchief Dianne had given him on their fourth appointment together—when it became apparent that theirs was, in fact, going to be a long-term professional relationship. He steadied himself. The stars were lessened now, but occasionally they came back. Dianne stood to offer him an arm, but he waved her off.

"I'm fine," he said. "Thank you. Just a bit too much activity."

He walked with three soft clicks to his chair and sat heavily, sighing with contentment as the leather settled around him. Seeing Dianne, an adult, sitting across from him on the small chair built for children still struck him as odd. Then again, she was a small woman, the size of her daughter, easily mistaken for a child from a distance. Nor was Gordon technically going back to adult clients. Dianne was paying the bills, but he was not treating Dianne.

"Are we ready to begin?" Gordon asked.

Dianne nodded.

"Okay, then. I want you to close your eyes and picture yourself under your table again. In your safe space. The only place you feel as if you can be anyone you want to be. It is warm there, and dark, but the stone is pleasantly cool. You rest your head on the stone. You take deep breaths, slowly, and you count back from one hundred..."

Dianne got no further than seventy-eight that time. She was slipping into hypnosis with ease, which was to be expected. The more times she went under, the easier it was to achieve the hypnotic state. They'd worked diligently at that together for a solid month.

"Who am I speaking to?" Gordon asked, his voice calm.

Dianne, eyes still closed, body slack but sitting, replied, "Hi, Dr. Pope. It's Ashley."

Gordon smiled. Ashley was the oldest. As far as Gordon could tell, she was around seventeen. She was the first personality to make herself known to Gordon during their therapy sessions. She considered herself the big sister of the other four and often surfaced when Dianne was incapacitated, either through alcohol or pills. She liked Gordon and recognized Dianne's need for therapy. She knew that the others sometimes ended up hurting Sophie when they were trying to help her.

Ashley was the one who'd drawn the rainbow that brought Gordon downstairs.

That Sophie had never actually drawn any of the pictures was one of the first surprises he learned in treating Dianne's multiple personalities. All of the artwork was done, at various times, by either Ashley, Peter, Sarah, Andrew, or Mo, a pattern that his mother had picked up on after he'd gone rushing to find Simon West.

"Hello, Ashley," Gordon said. "How is it under the table today?"

"It's a bit of a mess. Sarah and Andrew are fighting again. I had to promise them ice cream to shut them up."

"Ice cream usually works," Gordon said.

Dianne ate the ice cream, of course, but it sated the twins. Gordon still had dreams where he came upon their jar. In them, he often had a fear that the contents, their preserved fetuses, would speak to him. They never did, but their silence was more horrible. They were Dianne's third and fourth miscarriages, late enough to cause her great pain. Ashley told him that Dianne had to go downstairs to the cellar, under the table, where she passed both of them on the concrete floor like a frightened animal. Ashley said Dianne wrapped a towel around herself when it was done, jarred them both in memoriam like the first two, and went up to take a shower. She was at a society dinner that night.

Gordon suspected that the passing of the twins was when Dianne's mind cracked, but she'd been trending that way for years. Keeping evidence of a miscarriage wasn't in and of itself unhealthy, but the attachment she'd formed to each was taking her down a dark path. When she became pregnant with twins again, her joy temporarily masked the cracks, but they were there.

Sophie's twin came out first. He never drew a breath. The umbilical cord was wrapped tightly around his tiny neck, and he couldn't be revived. At the time, Dianne thought she'd lost both twins and the horror of Sarah and Andrew was happening all over again. By the time Sophie came, wailing loudly into life, Dianne was already broken even as she wept with joy over her new daughter. The jars started talking to her shortly afterward.

"And how is Peter?" Gordon asked.

"Perfectly quiet," Ashley said.

Gordon had met Peter for the first time the previous week. Peter was shy and rarely came out. He was the one that pranced around the playhouse just before Gordon arrived. He watched Gordon trace his steps around the dust of the playhouse from a special place he knew of on the lawn where nobody could see him, not even the lights. He often slept there, under the trees, for hours and hours and hours, away from everyone. He was a moody fifteen.

Each of Dianne's personalities came out in its own time. Gordon was never sure who would show up. Ashley did most of the time, but sometimes the twins, too. One was never far from the other. They often answered each other's questions. Dianne had a remarkable way of slightly modulating her voice. Andrew spoke faster than Sarah, and Sarah had a minutely higher pitch. Unlike Ashley and Peter, the twins didn't age with time. They stayed the age they would have been on the day that Mo passed. They were frozen in time at four years old.

The only one he had yet to meet again was Mo. Ashley preempted his next question with a surprising answer.

"Mo says he wants to meet you now. For real this time."

Gordon straightened. His goal for months had been to bring Mo out in a safe environment. Since the fire, he'd taken all of his rage and walled off his area of the table. Ashley said it was getting "weird under there." Gordon knew the longer he remained shut away, the greater the chance he would explode forth again, looking to burn.

"Is he sure?" Gordon asked.

"Yeah. But..."

"But what?"

"If I hand off to Mo, I don't know what's gonna happen. Dianne told me to never let him out."

"This is a safe place. Mo can come out here. I have to talk to him if I ever hope to get all of you up on the table."

Up on the table was code for integrating the personalities. Ashley understood it, and so did Dianne, and both were on board, but the twins were scared to leave their nook underneath the table, and Peter liked being alone. Gordon was still working on the three of them but was confident that they would go along with the plan in time.

Mo was a different story.

Ashley let out a big sigh. "Okay," she said. "I'll get him."

Dianne dropped her chin and breathed deeply. All was still. The ticking of the clock was the only sound. Then, very slowly, Dianne's mouth split into a wide grin. She opened her eyes, which was something she'd never done before under hypnosis, and slowly raised her head again until she was staring straight at Gordon.

Gordon remembered the pipe wrench. It took a great deal of personal will to stay rooted to his seat and not shuffle quickly out the door.

"Hello, Mo," Gordon said. His voice wavered a little.

"You took her away from me," Mo whispered, a harsh sound that reminded Gordon unsettlingly of the hiss of the leaking furnaces. He never broke his grin as he spoke, his whisper forced through his teeth.

"Who did I take away?"

"My sister. You took my sister away from me."

"Sophie is safe, Mo. She is sick but getting better every day. Soon, you'll be able to see her again. If you can behave."

Mo gripped the edges of the small chair until his nails bit into the leather. "She needs me," he said. "Nobody else will keep her safe. Who burned the tree house after she fell from it, so that she'd never fall again? Me. Do you think it was Dianne? No. Dianne came to me, frightened and weak, and told me how Sophie was ridiculed at school for her counting and washing, brought to tears in front of everyone in the science labs. Who made sure she'd never get ridiculed at school again?"

"You did," Gordon said.

"I did. I do what nobody else can. And when Sophie gets older and the real horrors of life begin, who do you think will keep her safe then? *Ashley?*" He said his alter personality's name with derision. "She's too busy wrangling the twins. Peter? He's too busy moping around under trees. Dianne can hardly hold her head up with the drinking and pills. So it'll be me. I'll make sure she never gets hurt."

"Dianne is working on the drinking problem, Mo. And the pills. Ashley tells me she doesn't do them anymore."

"Ashley doesn't know everything like she says she does. Peter's started to drink recently."

Gordon took in a slow breath. He'd have to speak with Dianne about that. Wrangling a drinking habit was hard enough when you just had the one personality to deal with. He tried not to let his disappointment show. Integration was a complex process, and they were bound to encounter setbacks, but he knew that most of Dianne's personalities seemed in it for the long haul.

After his outburst, Mo relaxed a bit. His hands eased their grip on the chair, and his smile seemed less manic.

"Why do you smile, Mo?" Gordon asked. "You don't seem happy, but you always smile."

Mo's eyes softened, but his grin hardened.

"I was, once."

"When?"

"When Sophie was born. That was the last time all of us came out at once without fighting or running into each other. Dianne said we were going to lose Sophie. We had prepared for it, prepared to find her under the table, like us. But when she came out and Dianne held her, I was happy she didn't end up under the table with us. I was happy she was forever up top. I was happy then, for a moment."

Gordon took mental note of a powerful insight. Despite Mo's violent words, the only time he'd been happy was when he realized Sophie would live outside of Dianne—would be forever up top.

"You can be up top too, Mo. All of you can be like Sophie if you'll work with Dianne instead of wall yourself off underneath."

Mo was silent, eyes downcast. "I'm going back now," he said after a moment.

"Thanks for talking to me, Mo."

Dianne had already dipped her head. Her smile faded. When she looked up again, Gordon recognized the scared, tired eyes of Dianne herself. She looked exhausted. The sessions took a lot out of her.

"Did we make any progress?" she asked.

"We did," Gordon said. "I'll see you at the same time next week."

. . .

AFTER DIANNE WAS GONE, Gordon wrote down all his thoughts from their session. He had a folder for each personality, and most of them were quite substantial, but until then, Mo's had been empty. Gordon finished printing the debrief and slid his first sheet of paper into the folder then sat back. At times, the amount of work he knew was ahead of him with Dianne was overwhelming. But in moments like those, when he could hear the sound of his breakthrough as it settled in the folder, when he could see it with his own eyes, everything was worth it.

He looked at his message machine, an ancient plastic relic from the past, and found it was blinking red. He pressed Play.

"Hello Dr. Pope, this is James Cohn over at Brookhaven Clinic. I'm Sophie's attending physician. You wanted me to call you when the next payments came through, and I can confirm that they have, and I can confirm that they are indeed courtesy of a Mr. Warren Duke. So Sophie is all set. She's progressing nicely although we still think it'll be some time before she's able to check out. As always, you're welcome to follow her notes on our shared system, as her primary care provider. Give us a call with any questions."

Gordon smiled. *So Duke had caved.* Gordon had thought he might. All he'd had to do was figure out why Duke hated him so much. Why they kept crossing paths. And he'd used it to his advantage.

After he was released from the hospital, Gordon went directly to the police department and said he wanted to clear up some miscommunications surrounding the injury of Detective Dana Frisco. He told a slack-jawed member of the arson unit that the Merryville Prep fire was actually intentional. He knew who set it, as did Dana Frisco, who'd risked her life and was injured on the job and would be needing full pay and extended leave to recover.

That got Duke downstairs really quickly.

He took one look at Gordon, taking in his cane and his cough, and the vein at his temple started flickering like purple lightning.

"Would you join me in my office, Dr. Pope," he asked with a

forced smile that would have made Mo proud.

Once behind closed doors, he dropped all pretense, and Gordon could see that if the two of them were under other more primitive circumstances, Duke wouldn't have hesitated to kill him—his hate was that strong. And after almost a solid month of grueling rehab, where all Gordon had had to keep him occupied during the pain were his own thoughts, he'd finally figured out why.

Simon West eventually showed him the obvious, what he should have seen all along. When Simon took Sophie under his wing and checked her in to Brookhaven—which even Gordon had to admit was an excellent facility for young children with mental disorders of her magnitude—and he paid for the initial treatments out of his own pocket while Dianne was still in the depths of her psychosis—which was *not* cheap—Gordon ended up marveling at the man. At first, Gordon thought he might have a condition of his own—he'd come off as eccentric and strange—but in the end, he was the sanest of all of them.

That meant that a propensity for mental disorders ran solely through Dianne's line of the family.

The most overlooked aspect of acute psychosis was also perhaps its most damaging: it ran in the family. Not content to destroy the lives of one or two individuals, it tended to attack entire branches of family trees. And Warren Duke was one of those branches.

"Don't sit down," Duke said, first thing. "You're going to go back down there, say you'd had too much to drink, and walk away before I pick up this phone and end your life forever. Do you understand me, Dr. Pope?"

"I'm not going anywhere, Duke," Gordon said, and he sat down.

Duke sneered at him and started dialing.

"How long have you been hearing voices, Major?"

Duke stopped dialing and slowly hung up the phone.

"Not long, I'd suspect, given how high functioning you are. But they're getting louder, aren't they?"

Duke's silence told Gordon all that he needed to know.

"If it's still early enough, it's easier to treat. But you have to stop fighting against it, projecting your weakness onto your sister and her daughter, and you have to stop taking it out on me."

Duke remained frozen, as if his system was rebooting.

"So here's what's going to happen. You're going to commend Detective Frisco for bravery in the line of duty and grant her full pay while she recovers from her injuries. Then, you're going to commend Detective Marty Cicero for the same, personally. In fact, you owe Marty three times over. When he lifted that table in the basement, he saved your sister, and he saved your niece, and he saved me. And I'm the one continuing to save your sister. That's three favors you owe him. Do you understand me? I'm gonna keep track of them. And last thing: You're paying for the rest of Sophie's treatment, for her life. Do you hear me? And so I know I got through to you, I want you to make your first payment courtesy of Warren Duke."

Still no movement from Duke, but Gordon thought he'd made his point. He stood to leave. At the door to Duke's office, he paused and turned around. Duke was taking shallow breaths but was otherwise still.

"When you decide you want to take control of your condition, give me a call. I can refer you to some psychiatrists who just might put up with your bullshit long enough to work with you."

He'd left without another word and begun the long process of rehabilitating Dianne West. And sitting there with Mo's file still in hand, a grin on his face, he felt better than he had in a long time. Apparently, he and Warren Duke had finally come to understand one another.

Gordon closed his eyes and leaned back in his chair. His recovery from the fire was a slow process, just like everything in his life those days. The table had torn his ACL and MCL and shredded his meniscus when it hit him, and the doctors said even when fully recovered, he might always walk with a bit of a limp. He was learning to live with it. He just needed a little longer to get places lately, but the good things, the things that mattered, would keep.

Three sharp beeps of a horn woke him from his nap. He checked his phone and found that he'd missed three calls. He checked his watch and cursed. He stood as quickly as he was able, wincing as his knee eased into position underneath him. Then he grabbed his coat and keys and locked the door to his office behind him. Dana's minivan was already at the curb.

"Why don't you *ever* answer your phone, Gordon? We really need to work on this."

"Sorry," he said sheepishly. "I'm taking it off vibrate as soon as I get in the car."

He opened the passenger's side door and found his mother sitting primly in the seat already.

"In the back, dear," she said.

He nodded. "So this is how it is now, huh?"

"Yes, honey. This is how it is."

Gordon pulled open the sliding door with effort but was helped from the inside by Chloe, who opened it the rest of the way.

"Hi, Gord," she said, smiling. "You can sit next to me in the back, 'kay?"

Gordon looked into the far back of the van. It was like spelunking in a cave.

"All the way back?" he asked.

Maria leaned over to him and offered a hand from the captain's chair in the second row. "Here, Dr. Pope, I'll help you up."

Gordon reached for it, and she pulled him up and in. "You don't have to call me Dr. Pope, Maria. You can call me Gordon. Or Gord. Or Gordo. Or anything."

"I like Dr. Pope," she said, smiling.

Several minutes later, Gordon was settled in and buckled up next to Chloe in the far back of the van. He saw Dana's eyes in the rearview mirror. She winked at him.

His mother chimed in from up front. "Now then, all that's settled. Shall we go eat? I know the perfect place."

SHADOW LAND

A
PSYCHOLOGICAL
THRILLER

B. B. GRIFFITH

CONTENTS

For Lee Z., who doesn't have an ounce of quit in him.

"It's Baltimore, gentlemen. The gods will not save you."
—Commissioner Ervin Burrell, *The Wire*

CHAPTER ONE

In the Maryland hill country at the foot of the Patapsco mountain range, night came early—especially in the bone-cold month of February. When the sun dipped below the jagged mountains to the north of Ditchfield Juvenile Correctional Facility, the five buildings making up the property were plunged quickly into darkness. The repurposed manor house-turned-administration center looked like a part of the craggy valley itself, a grand building crafted from soot-colored stone with brickwork the same dried-blood black of the surrounding rock.

Veteran correctional officer Andy Bagshot liked Ditchfield best at night. He requested night shift whenever he could. Darkness suited the old estate. Fewer eyes were watching his every move. Plus, it paid better.

Andy started his nightly rounds for bed check at 8:00 p.m. If the inmates cooperated and signaled during roll call the way they were supposed to, he could usually do it in thirty minutes. Sometimes, the inmates didn't cooperate with the other guards, which dragged things out. They always cooperated with Andy, though, because they didn't want what would come to them if they made his job difficult.

He started on the south side of the property at Pod A, a housing block for the "low-risk" kids. He walked around the outside of the squat brick building and gave every window and door a perfunctory check. He scanned the exercise yard and picked up a basketball blowing slowly across the empty court in the freezing night air. He tossed the ball into the nearby rec basket and slammed the cage shut. A lot of kids on the south side—in Pod A or Pod B—were still allowed to play basketball. They were the warden's favorites.

Andy didn't think any of the little shits should get to play anything, no matter what pod they were locked up in, but that wasn't his call.

Kids on the north side were different. Pod C and especially Pod D housed the crazies, kids that went through life getting *stuck and stowed*—a lot of solitary confinement and a lot of prescription drugs. Many of the guards hated working Pod D in particular. The general consensus was it creeped out the staff—but not Andy. He liked Pod D the most.

Unfortunately, the warden had taken Andy off north-side rounds after a little incident in the fall in which his nightstick happened to pop the orbital bone of one of the Pod D kids. He probably should have lost his job, but the warden and Andy understood one another. Sometimes nightsticks slipped.

He pressed his key card to the reader beside the front door to Pod A, and the lock snapped back like the sound of muffled gunfire. He swung open the door and was greeted with the musty, dirty-penny smell of teenage boys—forty of them—criminals, every one bad enough to get the Ditchfield treatment, which usually required committing a violent crime or repeat offense. Assault and theft ended up in Pods A and B, mostly. But Pods C and D housed juvies sent up for aggravated crimes, including attempted murder and in a few cases straight-up murder, things that would get them sent away for twenty plus at the Chesapeake supermax prison in Baltimore but, because they had the dumb luck to be under eighteen when they committed them, had landed them here instead.

As far as Andy was concerned, a criminal was a criminal. Age didn't matter. They were all lost causes. Almost all of them would end up in Chesapeake anyway, one way or another, whether for the crime that got them here or for the crimes they would commit in the future.

"Up against the wall," he said, his voice carrying.

All the routine nighttime shuffling about and side conversations ceased. The boys were already in their cells because they retired straightaway after dinner, but now they backed up against the far walls of their cells. At Ditchfield, each kid got his own cell. The pods were always at capacity.

Andy would just as soon double them up in the cells. Free up more real estate for new arrivals and transfers both. *Pack 'em in and let 'em break each other down.* But again, that wasn't his call.

"Roll call," Andy said and started walking. When Andy walked, his arms stuck out a bit, like a bodybuilder's, although Andy came by his bulk naturally. He had a big frame and a gut that filled it almost to overflowing. He wasn't much predisposed to exercise of any sort. He liked being big. In his line of work, having some weight to throw around helped.

First, he did the cells on the right side. Each boy said his last name as Andy walked past. When one muttered, Andy stopped and told him to repeat himself clearly. The new kids still required some teaching. The day before, the boy in Cell Ten had been up against the bars, so Andy had to punch his nightstick into the kid's throat. Tonight, Andy was pleased to see him lined up nicely against the back like everyone else.

He made an about-face and scanned the cells on the left side, noting each last name with a slight bob of his head as he passed. But Cell Twenty-six was silent.

Andy stopped and turned around, ready with his nightstick. He didn't know who this kid was, maybe Jones or Jackson—just another black kid—but whoever he was, if he didn't shape up, he was sure as shit gonna come to know Andy real well.

He took in the whole of the cell in an instant. A thin green mattress lay on a thick cinder slab. A brown blanket was rumpled but flat near the steel toilet and bolted stool—nothing else.

Cell Twenty-six was empty.

Fat drops of sweat sprang up on Andy's brow. He smeared them up into his buzzed hair. *Remain calm. Show no emotion.*

He kept walking. Cell twenty-seven called out roll and twenty-eight, too, after a moment's hesitation. Under normal circumstances, Andy would have barked at him, but his mind was racing. All other inmates were accounted for, none doubled up.

He had a missing kid.

At the door once more, he turned around and took a breath to steady himself. "Where is twenty-six?" he asked.

No answer.

"The first person to tell me where twenty-six is might have a shot at getting out of their cell in the next forty-eight hours. The rest of you get weekend lockdown."

No answer.

Andy squeezed the rubber grip on his nightstick until his knuckles went white. He turned, slapped his key card on the reader to unlock the door, then pushed it open and walked out into the night air. His sweat froze to his brow, but he hardly felt it.

The inmates were already jawing behind the closed door. He flexed his fingers and pulled his comm from his belt. "This is Bagshot. We got a problem. South side, Pod A, Cell Twenty-six is empty."

The line was silent. A twinge shook Andy's gut as he waited. He couldn't quite remember the protocol for when an inmate missed bed count. It was in a book somewhere in his locker, gathering dust. He was supposed to be handing off a full pod to the morning shift in a little over an hour. He was supposed to go home and start his weekend off with a long and happy night of drinking malt liquor and diddling himself to his favorite cam girls.

So much for "supposed to."

His comm crackled. "Say again, Bagshot?" Ken Abernethy's tone was icy.

"I think I got a kid missing bed count here in Pod A, boss."

"You *think?*"

"Cell Twenty-six."

The shuffling of papers sounded over the comm, with a few taps on a computer. "That's Jarvis Brown."

Brown, Andy thought offhand. *I wasn't even close.*

"You better be damn sure, Bagshot," Abernethy said. "Because I got my finger on the button here. I press this button, and the valley lights up like a Christmas tree. We'll be neck deep in Baltimore Police."

Andy could hear the boys whispering frantically inside. They sounded scared. Nobody was calling for Jarvis Brown to get his ass in his bed or to knock it off.

Andy had worked for eight years to cultivate the fear in inmates' eyes when he so much as touched his baton. If a boy under his watch didn't make bed check, he wasn't pranking around. He was gone.

"I wish I had better news, boss."

"Hold up, Warden," someone else chimed in—Jack Mitchell, by the sound of it. He would be making the same rounds on the north side right then. "Can I get a description on Brown?"

Andy held his breath. That was an odd request and maybe a blessed stroke of luck. Visions of malt liquor and cam girls crept back into the periphery of his brain.

Abernethy tapped on his computer. "Jarvis Brown. Black male. Six foot one. One hundred and eighty pounds at intake. Raised scarring on the right shoulder. Unidentifiable tattoo on the left."

"Yeah, this is him," Mitchell said. "He's here in Pod D."

Andy let out a breath and pumped a fist in the air. He still might catch shit for this, but at least it wasn't light-up-the-valley shit. Why this dumbass Brown would run from Pod A to Pod D was beyond Andy. No kid in their right mind wanted to be anywhere near D. Then again, most of these kids were even dumber than they looked.

Mitchell chimed in again. "I knew this wasn't Cunningham. He's too fat."

Andy froze with his fist in the air.

"Say again, Mitchell?" Abernethy said.

"Well, we got Jarvis Brown here. He's all doped up in Cunningham's cell. I'd probably have passed him right by if the kid hadn't just fallen out of bed."

Andy closed his eyes. Everything about what Mitchell just said was wrong.

"And where the hell is Charlie Cunningham?" asked Abernethy.

"Don't know, Warden. But I know he ain't here."

Andy didn't even jump when the emergency lights kicked on all down the line, turning night at Ditchfield into day. The sirens overhead worked themselves into a blare as all Andy's weekend plans turned tail and ran.

CHAPTER TWO

SIX YEARS EARLIER

Gordon Pope sat on the edge of his bed and stared at an envelope in his hands. The letter was from Baltimore Urology Associates and was addressed To Be Opened Only by Dr. Gordon Pope. He thumbed the red lettering underneath the address window that read Test Results Inside.

Gordon had been waiting for that letter for a week. Every day, he'd scampered down to the letterbox the moment he heard the mailman, in order to catch it before Karen had the chance to come across it, but now that it was in his hands, he couldn't bring himself to open it.

"What are you *doing* up there?" Karen called from downstairs. "We're going to be late. You know Waterstones doesn't hold reservations."

Gordon snapped back to reality and cleared his throat. "I'm coming, I'm coming," he called back.

He put the letter in his nightstand drawer and stood then wiped his hands on his slacks as if washing them clean of the entire ordeal. He would open it the next day, maybe. Birthdays were bad times to look at medical results, fortieth birthdays in particular. He felt fragile enough already, confronted baldly with the fact that half his life was behind him. *If I'm lucky*, he thought grimly. He smoothed his sparse hair, tucking his tufts behind his ears. *Speaking of "baldly."* The first present he seemed to be opening at the end of his fourth decade was a healthy dose of male-pattern baldness. *Happy birthday to me!*

Karen was already at the door, settling an elegant camel-hair overcoat around her shoulders. She pulled her newly blond hair from inside the collar and checked her reflection in the window. "I don't know why your mother insists upon going to this place all the time," she said. "They haven't changed the menu in ten years."

"I like Waterstones," Gordon said. "It was my idea. And it's my birthday."

"I mean, I get it. The Cobb salad is good," she went on, uninterrupted. "It's been the same Cobb salad for a decade. Your shoes are mismatched."

Gordon squinted at his shoes. "You sure?"

"Yes, darling. That one's black. That one's dark brown."

"Huh," Gordon said. "I think you're right." He turned and took the stairs up again, two at a time.

"I swear, Gordon. What would you do without me? Our reservation is in five minutes. We're going to be late."

"They'll hold it for Mom," Gordon called back, scuffing off the black shoe and dragging on the correct brown one with his foot. He paused by the bed again and glanced at the nightstand.

"Sometimes I wonder what's going on in that head of yours," Karen called from below.

If only you knew.

DEBORAH POPE WAS SEATED in the back of Waterstones, by the window, with a clear view of the Patapsco River feeding Baltimore's inner harbor. It was a prime table. Gordon expected nothing less for a woman who ate there weekly, at least.

"My son!" she said, standing as Gordon and Karen approached.

"You don't look a day over forty." She hugged him fiercely around the waist.

Gordon wasn't a tall man, but Deborah was an even smaller woman. She'd settled naturally into her seventies and never looked back after the death of her husband, a man she described as so self-absorbed that she had no choice but to become a successful couples' therapist just to stay sane living with him.

She turned to Karen and smiled primly. "Karen," she said, with a good deal more reserve.

"Hello, Deborah," Karen replied.

The two women gave each other a delicate embrace.

Karen eyed the half-drunk martini in front of Deborah. "Sorry we kept you. I hope you weren't waiting too long."

"Oh, barely five minutes. The martini was ready for me when I sat down," Deborah said. "They know me here. There's this wonderful waiter, fairly new."

As if on cue, a young Latino with slicked-back black hair appeared and settled another chilled martini glass in front of Deborah, substituting old for new with a touch of flair. Deborah smiled and clapped, her silver bracelets tinkling softly. Karen rolled her eyes.

"Young man, what is your name?" Deborah asked.

"Caesar, ma'am," he said, standing tall, hands behind his back.

"I like you, Caesar. We're celebrating my son's fortieth birthday tonight. Let's start with champagne."

Caesar bowed slightly and backed away. An awkward silence followed, in which Karen arranged her coat carefully behind herself and Gordon stared into the polished cherrywood of the table, thoughts of the envelope lingering in his head. Deborah finished off her martini and reapplied her lipstick. Moments later, three glasses and a chilled bottle were produced.

"This ought to liven things up," Deborah said as Caesar poured.

Gordon was momentarily lost in the whirling tornado of bubbles rapidly chilling his champagne glass.

"Just a little for me," Karen said, and Caesar obliged.

"I'll take the rest of hers," Deborah said, smiling.

"I'm off alcohol at the moment. Caffeine too. And dairy. I've heard it helps with..." Karen rolled her hand as if she didn't want to speak the word.

"Fertility," Gordon said. He grasped his glass and held it aloft. "Karen is doing everything she can."

"I've no doubt," Deborah replied, keeping her eyes on Gordon. "I hope you two aren't beating yourself up too much about all of this."

Gordon took a long sip of ice-cold champagne. By "you two," his mother clearly meant *"you, Gordon."* Karen approached all problems clinically. She never beat herself up about anything. Gordon was the self-loather. Karen lived her life knowing a solution would eventually present itself if she methodically and efficiently narrowed down variables.

He wondered if she knew that one of those variables was Gordon himself.

Before he knew it, he'd taken down the whole glass of champagne. He coughed as the bubbles tickled his nose.

"Gordon, I haven't even proposed a toast yet," Deborah said.

"That's all right," Gordon said. "We'll have another chance." Gordon looked around until he caught Caesar's eye. "Hello, Caesar. I'll take a scotch on the rocks, please. Heavy on the scotch. Thanks."

Both women looked squarely at him. "Oh please, Mother. That was your second martini, and you know it."

"Tough day at work?" Deborah asked.

"Gordon's just feeling fragile at forty. This happens to him on birthdays," Karen said. "As a matter of fact, it was a great day at work. The APF likes the work we did with the Hazel School last summer. They're pushing it for a Rosenblatt Foundation grant."

"*Your* work with the Hazel School. *You* developed the plan to care for the deaf kids," Gordon said.

"Not true. You helped," Karen said, although even she seemed to hear how lame that sounded.

Gordon had "helped" if you called sitting with troubled deaf kids while they angrily signed the answers to a series of questions about their daily routines helping.

"Anyway, it's fifty thousand a year for four years," Karen added offhand, although Gordon knew she was particularly proud of the grant size.

"That's your grant, Karen. You were brilliant in that study." Gordon reached for her hand under the table and gave it a squeeze, to which she responded faintly in kind.

Deborah cleared her throat. "Sounds to me like it could be a wonderful opportunity for Jefferson and Pope, LP."

Caesar came around with the scotch, and Gordon almost picked it right from his hands.

"And you, Gordon? How is work going for you?" asked Deborah. Gordon's mother was very good at redirecting conversations back to focus on her son even if he didn't want the spotlight.

"Well, it's no government grant or anything, but last week, I submitted an appeal on behalf of a kid I worked with briefly when Karen and I did that consulting gig for the Baltimore City Public School System. It's a..." He rolled his hand, not sure he wanted to say the word. "It's a pro bono thing."

"Gordon likes to do the work that takes the most time and makes the least amount of money for the practice," Karen said.

Gordon was pretty sure she meant that as a joke, but she was never very good at jokes.

"I remember that consulting gig," Deborah said. "As if any two psychiatrists on the planet could straighten out the Baltimore public schools."

"Yeah, well, our patient zero in the study was a kid named Charlie Cunningham. I spent a fair amount of time with him before the city cut funding. Very troubled kid—tough upbringing, but bright."

"Textbook antisocial personality disorder," Karen chimed in drolly, ticking symptoms off as she spoke. "Multiple violent run-ins at school and at home. Callous and hostile in general. Almost no empathy."

Gordon swallowed a hefty swig of scotch. "Yes, well, I respectfully disagree. Those markers are extremely difficult to diagnose in a twelve-year-old. I think it's more like standard anger issues, maybe intermittent explosive disorder. I sat with this kid for hours, trying to document the structure of the school day, when he felt like he was spiraling, what his triggers were. He's no sociopath."

Karen pursed her lips. "I wanted to believe you. I almost did. Then Charlie put a pencil into a classmate's eye," she said. "Didn't break a sweat. He partially blinded the kid at lunch and walked away. Cops found him spattered in blood, flipping through magazines in the library. Textbook sociopath."

"He still doesn't belong in Ditchfield," Gordon said, setting his tumbler down with a smack.

Nearby tables perked up and looked over as their pocket of the restaurant grew suddenly quiet.

Gordon looked at the shining red wooden table again. "No child belongs in Ditchfield," he finished quietly. "He got the sentence yesterday. He ships up at the end of the week. So I petitioned the city, crafted a plan of care. I'll take him as a full-time patient if they'll let me."

As Karen shook her head softly, Deborah nodded. "A little life from my son," she said quietly, a hint of pride in the small smile on her lips. "That said, try not to get us kicked out of here. This is one of very few half-decent martinis in Baltimore."

"Long shot," Karen said. "Especially once the courts have ruled."

"I'll take it anyway," Gordon said.

He thought that might have been a great time for Karen to reach out and pat his knee... maybe give his hand a little squeeze under the table. Instead, the three of them sipped in silence until, mercifully, the Cobb salads arrived.

. . .

GORDON FOUND he had to sit on the bed to get his shoes off later that evening. He was a good deal more buzzed than he'd planned, even for a birthday dinner. In fact, he'd been drinking a little bit more than usual across the board recently—nothing irresponsible, just a little bit of a heavier hand during cocktail hour. That was hardly a red flag. Maybe it was a bit of a yellow one, though.

That said, he still wasn't buzzed enough to open the envelope in his nightstand drawer, especially not with Karen just in the bathroom, getting ready for bed.

Instead, Gordon perfunctorily checked his phone before plugging it in for the night. He'd missed a call, one of those generic numbers that was either a spam call or a government office. They'd left a message.

"Dr. Pope, this is Jackie with the Juvenile Board of Appeals..."

Gordon listened to the message, and when it was done, he simply closed his eyes. Not only had the board denied Gordon's appeal, Jackie felt Gordon should know that another incident had occurred.

Charlie Cunningham had broken parole and stolen a car. Then he'd run that car through the wall of a church in east Baltimore during a funeral. Three people were taken to the hospital.

Not only was Charlie Cunningham going to Ditchfield, he was now going to Ditchfield's Pod D under full psychiatric protocols.

In the bathroom, Karen was humming "Happy Birthday" while she washed her face. Gordon took off his clothes and flopped back on the bed then stared at the ceiling fan, slowly rotating above. When Karen came in, he pretended to be asleep.

CHAPTER THREE

PRESENT DAY

Detective Dana Frisco parked her minivan in one of two visitor's spots outside Ditchfield's main manor house. The sun was still hours from rising. The walls of the valley loomed pitch black all around her, but Ditchfield itself was blazing with light, like an angry bare bulb hanging in a cold basement.

She took in the sight of the central manor house in much the same way she took in the old climbing wall at the police academy in Dundalk back in the day, before endurance training and years of dealing with chauvinist cops and petty police politics had turned her from petite to powerfully jaded.

All right, you cruel hunk of rock. Let's get this shit over with and never see each other again, shall we?

The first time she came to Ditchfield, she'd been a regular rank-and-file officer following up on an assignment, volunteering for work nobody else wanted in the hopes of getting her name on the map. Now she was a sergeant, directing the assignments. And that wasn't because she'd taken on more work or volunteered for the tough cases back in the day. She'd found out the world wasn't that simple—the

Baltimore city cops that took on shit work only found themselves rewarded with more until they were buried by it.

The reason she'd made sergeant was that she surrounded herself with people who cared about her and gave her the leverage she needed to keep clawing forward. One of them was Gordon Pope. The other was Detective Marty Cicero, who was sitting in his souped-up Dodge Charger just to her right.

He looked over and gave her a two-fingered salute as he stepped out of his car. "Morning, Sarge!"

"I keep telling you not to call me that," Dana said. "You're the only detective in my unit."

"You got the chevrons?" Marty asked, referring to the three little wonky strips of fabric that designated her current rank.

"They're somewhere in my closet."

"You still got 'em though," Marty said, pointing at her. "And you got the pay bump?"

Dana snorted. "If you could call it that. You're the one who should be wearing the chevrons, Marty."

"Nah," Marty said, waving her off. "I keep tellin' you they took care of me fine. Plus, I'm not a chevron guy."

The case that got both of them commended had also nearly killed Dana. She couldn't run quickly enough from an explosion that put her in a coma for three days. Marty's commendation came because he ran *into* a fire to save Gordon and two others, including a twelve-year-old girl. Marty's writeup cited his "heroic decision to place himself in mortal danger in the hopes of saving others," but Dana knew that the real "heroic decision" Marty made that night was to set aside his dislike of Gordon Pope and save him anyway. Marty didn't like Gordon and never would, for one simple reason: Marty loved Dana. And Dana loved Gordon.

Dana also knew Warren Duke had offered Marty a promotion before he offered Dana a promotion despite the fact that Dana was the veteran. And she knew Marty had declined because it would have meant moving him into another department... away from Dana.

Duke reluctantly gave it to Dana because Gordon Pope had leverage over him. If it was up to Duke, Dana would be pushing papers in some forgotten office and Gordon Pope would be in jail, but the firebug case had involved Duke personally, in ways he wanted to keep quiet, so for once, Duke didn't get what he wanted.

Instead, Duke made her a sergeant over the Child Protective Investigations Unit, a unit of one. That had been a nice little back-handed compliment.

Marty affixed his badge and chain between his sizeable pecs and unzipped his leather jacket. His gun peeked out from its shoulder holster. As far as Dana could tell, the worst part of the whole fire-rescue business for Marty was that the second-degree burns he'd suffered on his hands and arms had kept him out of the gym that first month afterward. He'd made up for it since. Both Dana and Marty were plainclothes officers now. They could wear what they wanted, which in Marty's case was mostly dark jeans and expensive T-shirts that looked about ready to blow off him.

"My first Ditchfield run," Marty said. "Looks about how I pictured it. Is it haunted? Sure as shit looks haunted."

Dana clipped her badge to one hip and her gun to the other. "Haunted? Doubt it. Everybody gets out of here the second they can. Even the ghosts."

EVERYTHING ABOUT DITCHFIELD WAS DAMP—THE air, the ground, the bricks of the walls. The windows looked old and ill fitted. The wet-earth smell of the night had leaked into the hallways of the main manor. Dana and Marty followed a spooked-looking receptionist to the office of the warden, escorted them in, and closed the door behind them.

Ken Abernethy was bent over a drafting table, looking at an over-head topo map of the valley through a brass magnifying glass on a stand. He wore a matching two-piece tracksuit that looked cleaned and pressed, and he held a walkie-talkie in both hands. He reminded

Dana of a gym teacher, the kind that kept even the rowdiest kids in line: clean shaven, gray hair neatly parted, fit but aging.

"BPD?" he asked, looking up as they walked in. "Hate to bother you folks, but we had to call. Protocol's protocol. Take a seat."

"I think we'd like to get right to the boy's cell," Dana said. "Set up a perimeter. We can talk on the way."

"Suit yourself," Abernethy said. "But the young man is long gone."

"You sure about that? This ain't exactly an easy place to get in and out of," Marty said.

"It is if you steal a truck," Abernethy replied. "One of my officers just noticed it missing. Matter of fact, I'd say Cunningham's got a decent shot at being in Baltimore proper by now if that's where he's going. You two could have saved yourself the drive." His tone was even and calm and had a touch of Southern gentility, but his eyes were bright and calculating.

"Your problems don't just disappear with the kid," Dana said. "That's not how this works. You'll probably get a full review from the state. Which, quite frankly, is long overdue."

Abernethy nodded and looked down apologetically, but in the aw-shucks way that meant he wasn't, in fact, worried about any type of retribution. Old white men in places of power often had that look when they messed up. They weren't so different from some of the foolhardy young criminals she came across. Both types thought they were invincible.

"What's the description on the truck?" Marty asked coldly. "I'll call it in."

"It's the groundskeeper truck. An F-150 that's probably twenty years old. Silver with a lot of rust on it." He picked up a scrap of paper on the drafting table and handed it to Marty. "Here's the plates."

"We'd still like to see the cell," Dana said.

"Of course, of course," Abernethy said. "This way."

Dana followed the warden down the hallways of the main house, with Marty close behind, speaking quickly to the city dispatch. The swollen wood of the old main stair creaked and popped under their feet. Outside, the night was still. Mist hung heavy in the air, barely moving in the bright emergency lights. A pair of flashlights swept slowly across the road in the distance, but otherwise, the three of them were all that moved.

They approached a squat brick building with a single metal door front and center. The words Pod C were stenciled above the door in black lettering. Dana thought they might go inside, but Abernethy instead took them around and along a thin concrete walkway that spanned the length of the bunker, about half a football field.

"Don't want to rile up the youths if we don't have to," he said.

Dana looked up at the small slits for windows, evenly spaced above their heads as they walked by. She tried to picture a boy or a girl looking out and almost convinced herself that she saw dark shapes moving inside, watching them.

"Don't worry, Officer... Frisco, was it? The windows are too high for them to see you."

"It's Sergeant Frisco," Dana said.

Abernethy nodded sagely.

"And I'm not worried. Does every cell have a window?"

"No," he replied. "Here we are."

The three of them rounded the corner to the back side of another brick bunker. It had the same flat brick face, the same type of metal door. The black lettering above read Pod D.

Abernethy stepped up and removed a sizeable keychain from his pocket. He plucked up a key card and pressed it against the reader, which showed a red light then a green light. Dana flinched as a lock within the door snapped back like a whip crack. Abernethy pulled open the door and revealed what at first glance looked like a darkened dentist's office. Thin, sharp medical instruments glinted in the light that crept past them. A freestanding chair, inclined slightly, sat in the dead center of the room.

"This is our treatment facility. The cells are just beyond that door," Abernethy said, stepping up and in. His fingers lightly touched the headrest of the chair as he passed. Dana followed, noting the four-point restraints bolted to the chair's arm and leg rests. A machine that looked a bit like a wine fridge whirred softly in the corner. Plastic bottles and metal clamps glowed underneath a magenta light within. Row upon row of cabinets lined the wall to her right, each with a strip of tape scribbled with a name. She scanned them until she found "C. Cunningham."

Marty stepped in last. He'd finished calling in the truck, and the hand holding his cell dropped slowly to his side as he took in the room, muttering under his breath.

"Treatment facility?" Dana asked.

"Yes. Pod D houses criminal youths with severe mental disorders. They often require assistance with their medical regimens."

Marty walked over to a closet-sized door beside the cabinets and looked inside the darkened inset window.

"That's our padded room," Abernethy said evenly, "a place where the youths can fight through episodes without hurting themselves."

Marty muttered under his breath again. "Stop saying *youths*," he said aloud.

"What would you have me call them, Detective?"

"I dunno. Kids? Boys and girls? Little shits? Anything else."

"I run a facility for troubled youths. There are no boys or girls here. They forfeited their childhoods when they made the decisions that led them to my front door," Abernethy said, with a flat finality.

Dana thought of Chloe, almost nine. The Cunningham boy had been shipped here at twelve. That any twelve-year-old could forfeit their childhood based on a single mistake, no matter how bad, made her stomach turn.

Abernethy reached the second door, leading into the bunker. "We also consider them patients, in the case of Pod D," he added.

He pressed his keycard to the reader, and the lock snapped back. The door opened with the scraping sound of a rough broom.

The smell hit Dana first—soiled sheets and greasy hair, not over-powering but ingrained, a bit like opening an old, empty gym bag. She was surprised at the level of light, given the hour. It was more than she'd be able to get to sleep with. And the fixtures all buzzed.

Abernethy led Dana and Marty down the hall. The center aisle was little more than two shoulder widths. The straight shot led to another closed door at the far end, where a big security guard was standing at uncomfortable attention.

They passed cell after cell, each with a single occupant dressed in a single-piece gown, thin and papery. The kids were all behind thick, clear plexiglass. Each was on a bed—a small slab of concrete that most of them hung over at the arms or legs. Their toilets looked more like freestanding bowls than seats. They had no other furniture or adornment of any kind, aside from a series of small steel hoops embedded in the concrete high up on the walls.

Few of the kids moved. One rocked quietly on his side on his concrete bed, arms clasped around his knees. Two were restrained in their beds at the wrists and ankles. Not one of them took any notice of their passing.

Dana was struck by how young they looked.

"How long have those two been in four-point restraints?" Dana asked, her voice a low growl.

"Inmate Fourteen bit a medical assistant today during meds. When patients bite, we restrain them to deliver their doses and keep them restrained until they are copacetic," Abernethy said.

"He looks pretty damn copacetic to me," Marty replied.

"You'd be surprised. The other, Inmate Twelve, is chronically bulimic. It's all we can do to keep him from jamming his hands down his throat. Here we are. Cell Seventeen. Charlie Cunningham." Abernethy ushered them inside with a sweep of one hand.

Dana took a small flashlight from her jacket pocket and clicked it on. "Has this cell been disturbed by anybody?"

"Possibly by the youth they found here, Jarvis Brown. He was supposed to be in Pod A."

Both police paused in their inspection and turned to Abernethy.

"Wait a minute. You found *another kid* in here?" Marty asked.

Abernethy took a deep breath. "We did," he said, disappointment heavy in his voice. "And for more on that, I'll direct you to Andy Bagshot here." Abernethy gestured toward the security guard Dana had seen upon entering. "He'll be more than happy to answer your questions. Won't you, Andy?"

Andy Bagshot stepped forward slightly and nodded. His drawn face and narrowed eyes looked anything but happy.

"If you'll excuse me, I have a good deal of paperwork to attend to," Abernethy said, withdrawing. "Take good care of them, Andy."

"We'll have additional questions for you, Warden," Dana called out, low, after him.

"I'm sure you will," Abernethy said without looking back.

They watched him go until, a few moments later, Marty said, "What a prick, right?"

Dana nodded slowly.

"You can tell him I said that too," Marty said, turning to Bagshot. "Now, mind tellin' us how some other kid ended up in Charlie Cunningham's cell?"

Bagshot was big, taller than Marty—not nearly as cut, but with enough meat on him to make up for it. For a moment, the guard just stared at the detective long enough for Dana to know she didn't like Andy Bagshot at all.

Dana was about to speak up when Andy answered. "Not sure. But the boy we found in here, Jarvis Brown, was pretty messed up."

The way Bagshot said *boy* actually made her prefer the way Abernethy had said *youths*.

"Messed up like injured?" she asked.

"No, he looked drugged. Barely responsive," Bagshot said, only eventually turning to look at her. "Had to shuttle him to Johns Hopkins Hospital. Didn't want him dying on us."

"Did your medical people drug Brown?" Dana asked.

"The same people give the same meds to the same kids every day. They'd notice Brown ain't Cunningham."

Bagshot tongued a bulge in his lower lip and swallowed what Dana assumed was a hefty glob of tobacco juice. She didn't bother to hide her disgust as she turned back to the cell.

"So who did, then?" she asked.

"Ain't that why you're here?" Bagshot asked.

Marty stepped toward him, but Dana laid a hand softly on his back, and he paused. The two men stared at each other in silence.

"Let's check the cell," she said softly.

Marty shook his head at Bagshot but eventually took out his own flashlight and clicked it on, turning away. Dana followed him into the cell. Together, they ran their lights over every inch of concrete, starting in opposite corners.

"Were you on duty when Charlie escaped?" Dana asked.

"I was, but not here," Andy said, adding noticeable derision to the word *here*. "I was doing bed check in Pod A."

"That where Jarvis Brown's cell is?" Dana asked.

"Yes, it is," Andy said after a moment.

"Thought so," Dana said.

"What's that supposed to mean?" Andy asked, peering down at her as she scanned the crevices in the concrete where the slab of bed met the floor.

"You're acting like a man who just got busted down by his superior and needs to take it out on someone else. I had a feeling you screwed up somewhere tonight."

"Listen to me, you—"

"You better think real hard about the next words that come out of your mouth, Officer Bagshot," Dana said, using the hard, sharp tone that always got through to the drunks and addicts back when she booked them by the dozens. She shined her flashlight right in his face. "Or Marty here will arrest you for obstruction of justice, and I don't think I need to tell you they don't take too kindly to prison guards in the holding cells in the city."

"Cameras in there are really shitty too," Marty added, smiling wanly. "And the cops on watch are pretty hard of hearing."

Andy grimaced and clenched his teeth, working his jaw as though the words were hard to swallow, but he was quiet. Dana turned back around and looked at Charlie's bed. She pulled a black rubber glove from her back pocket and popped it on one hand then picked up the thin blanket from where it lay crumpled on the floor. She held it out in front of her, pinched between two fingers, and gave it one good shake. A fine dusting of white powder puffed in and out of the cone of her flashlight. She glanced at Marty, who popped one eyebrow.

"Did Charlie and Jarvis Brown ever interact?" Dana asked.

"No," Andy said flatly. "Pod D is kept separate from all the other kids."

"Could have been anything. Something small, even, like passing by each other for meals," Dana said as she carefully set the blanket down again.

Andy shook his head then appeared to think as his head stilled. "Could be maybe they get close enough to interact when we clear the rec yard for the Pod D boys. Those that can take the rec hour, anyway. One group shuffles out, and the next shuffles in."

"Close enough to touch?"

"Maybe."

Dana focused her light on the bed and found the pillow lumpy and stained. She tried to picture a boy sleeping there, imagining how he might lie after being fed a bucketful of pills or shot up with whatever psychoactive treatment they gave these poor souls. If she was stuck in this place, she would face the wall, curled up in the corner.

She took a closer look at where Charlie's bed slab met the wall. The concrete was whitewashed and pocked. She knelt on the bed and got within a few inches, scanning the wall with her light. The white coating of paint was streaked here and there with stains— blood, maybe, or bloody snot. But the whitewash reflected back for the most part, except in one area near the head of the slab. There, the paint seemed missing in a rough circle about the size of a quarter. The surface looked more like unfinished drywall.

Using one gloved finger, Dana scraped at the spot. A flake of white fell away. She dug some more, and a little chip of white fell out.

"What the hell is that?" Marty asked.

"Not sure," Dana said, but she had an idea.

Dana dug out the entire depression. "Looks like maybe an eye bolt was attached here once. Bad patch job left a little indentation in the wall." She picked up the little chunks of white and put them in an evidence bag she pulled from her jacket.

"You know what kind of meds Charlie was on?" Dana asked, turning to Bagshot.

He eyed the evidence bag warily. "No idea. But probably some pretty heavy stuff. All these Pod D boys are."

She turned around and gave the rest of the cell a sweep, but she'd seen what she came for. Nothing else was there but bare walls and cold concrete.

"We're good here for now," she said. "Just one more thing, and we leave you alone. His effects."

"His what?"

"His personal effects. Whatever he had on him at intake. We're gonna need to see those."

"That was five years ago," Andy said.

"We're gonna need to see them," Dana said again.

"Fine," Andy said. "If it means I'm done standing here, I'll get you whatever you want, *Sergeant*," he said acidly.

Andy brought them to the secretary up front and left them there without another word. Marty watched him go and shook his head.

"Man, they got a special class of people working up here," he said before turning back to find the secretary looking right at him. "No offense, ma'am," he added.

The assistant, a slightly haggard woman with a lot of hairspray in her bob, wore a name tag reading Jolene. She shrugged. "None taken. I'd say, on the whole, you're right. Andy Bagshot might be the most special of all."

"How's that?" Dana asked.

"He has a reputation for being a bit rough with the kids," Jolene said. "And a bit of an asshole to the staff too," she added dryly. "Now what can I get you, hon?"

"We'd like to take a look at the intake paperwork and effects for an inmate named Charlie Cunningham."

Jolene tapped on an old yellowed keyboard attached to a boxy computer that whirred loudly. "Cunningham... let's see. Here he is. One of our long-term kids." She wrote down a number on a pad and tore off the sheet. "Be right back."

Marty leaned on the counter with one elbow, pulled a packet of almonds from his jacket, and ripped the plastic with his teeth. He popped a few in his mouth and chewed thoughtfully. "You're right," he said.

"Thank you. About what?" Dana asked.

"This place is a nightmare."

"You've seen a fourth of it. Probably the worst fourth, though."

"What do you think is in the bag?" Marty asked, gesturing at where she'd stowed the Ziploc and glove.

"Well, we've got one kid, Jarvis Brown, who was doped up to near unconscious. We've got another kid, Charlie, who was probably getting a lot of drugs to dope him up, only I don't think he was taking them."

"You think those are crushed-up pills?"

"Maybe. I used to give Chloe a multivitamin every night before she brushed her teeth, one of those chewy things I thought she liked. I was cleaning her room out a few months ago and moved her bed frame. Fifty multivitamins fell out."

Marty snuffed with laughter. "Little pack rat," he said, smiling.

Marty and Chloe got along effortlessly. Gordon was catching up quickly, but Chloe still considered Marty her best friend, and he had a soft spot for her in return. He'd even started to teach her a few self-defense moves recently. The past four nights in a row, Dana had come downstairs to find her daughter dressed in a pink tracksuit, trying to practice an arm bar on her grandmother.

Jolene returned with a gallon Ziploc bag inside a banker's box. "Here you go. This is what he had on him. When you're done, just leave it there. I'll file it away."

The phone rang, and she looked at it warily. "We're starting to get some calls. Press sniffing around. Not sure how they figure these things out, but they do. If you'll excuse me."

Dana unzipped the bag and emptied it onto the countertop. Charlie hadn't had much on him when he was brought in, although not many thirteen-year-olds did. A keychain had a ticket-sized photograph inside a scuffed plastic covering: a picture of a skinny young black boy trying hard not to smile down at an equally skinny girl, who beamed out at the camera from behind the crook of his arm. They looked like siblings—similar flat noses and big, almond-shaped eyes, although his were slightly more sunken than hers. He also had a chunk missing from his right ear.

"Twins?" asked Marty.

"Looks like it."

The wallet looked like a hand-me-down, with thin and frayed leather and bits of plastic poking through at the edges. In it was another photograph of the girl, school-picture style. She was smirking, dressed in a frilly but worn green dress. On the reverse was written, "Tasha Cunningham—8th Grade."

Dana found a food stamp card where a driver's license might be, but the wallet was otherwise empty. She frowned. Could that really be all the boy had to his name? She checked the itemized list.

Three items were missing, listed as "business cards."

1. Business card for "Reverend Josiah Hill—Elder and Senior Pastor. New Hope Community Church."

"That's the place he ran the stolen Buick through," Marty said. "Maybe he picked up a business card along the way?"

Dana looked at him sidelong for a moment then turned back to the list.

2. Business card for "Brighton and Associates. Thomas Brighton, Esq. —Founding Partner."

Dana knew Thomas Brighton from her days doing grunt work processing cases at the Baltimore City Circuit Courthouse. He was the guy sliding from courtroom to courtroom on tasseled loafers, defending anybody whose check didn't bounce. He was a bit of a weasel but not a bad lawyer, all said and done. He'd fight like a dog if he thought that might get his name in the papers, like he did for Ethan Barrett in the sleepwalker case. She also had to credit Brighton for introducing her to Gordon. They'd first met because Gordon used to moonlight as an expert witness for Brighton in order to fund a borderline drinking problem. That wasn't exactly a storybook start to a relationship, but it seemed to be working so far.

3. Business card for "Jefferson and Pope, LP—Karen Jefferson, MD | Gordon Pope, MD"

Dana momentarily forgot how to breathe. Marty sucked in through his teeth. She held the itemized list up to the light as if it might somehow change. She flipped it over and back again, hoping she'd misread, but no.

"Excuse me," Dana said, gathering Jolene's attention by degrees. "Where are these business cards? They're listed on the intake sheet."

Jolene looked nonplussed. "They let the kids keep pictures and cards sometimes. They put 'em up in their cells."

If that was the case, Charlie had these cards, and he'd taken them when he ran.

That meant her boyfriend's old business card was somehow one of the very few personal possessions of a dangerous young escapee from the psychiatric ward of Maryland's most notorious juvenile detention center—along with the business card of a church the kid had attacked with a two-ton automobile and that of a shady lawyer.

"What do you make of that?" Marty asked quietly.

"I think we need to find Charlie Cunningham," Dana replied, her voice shaky, "and we need to find him quick."

CHAPTER FOUR

Gordon Pope was lying on his stomach in Dana Frisco's basement, his left cheek smushed against the carpet. His right arm was pinned like a chicken's wing behind his back. If it were pressed any farther, he would be scratching his shoulder blade in a way that might compromise healthy rotator cuff functionality down the line.

Chloe Frisco leaned over his head, her long black hair spilling onto the floor. "Do you see how I can just sort of freeze you like that? Just by pushing up a bit more? Can you feel that pinch?"

Gordon winced. "Sure can," he said, trying not to squirm. "I do definitely feel that pinch. That's for sure."

"Marty taught me that," she said proudly.

"How nice of Marty." *Next, he'll have her at the shooting range. Maybe teach her to field strip a nine millimeter.*

Maria, Dana's mother, poked her head around the corner, "Chloe, sweetheart, take it easy on Dr. Pope. That shoulder is forty-five years old. Besides, he came here to talk to you."

Maria smiled down at Gordon. She'd warmed up to him considerably over the past half year. When he first started coming around,

Maria had made herself extremely conspicuous when it came to him and Dana. She seemed to find any excuse to walk through whatever room they were in, sometimes between the two of them. Gordon remembered one time, early on, when Maria squeezed herself between Dana and him on the couch while they watched a movie. She would take Chloe under her wing as soon as Gordon set foot in the door, as if he was just generally contagious.

When Gordon didn't go away, Maria settled into a state of begrudging respect, as if he was a stray dog that wouldn't leave the porch. When Gordon sat watch over Dana in the hospital during her coma, things started changing, but what really won Maria over was when Chloe decided she wanted Gordon around. Chloe had the full-to-the-brim heart of an eight-year-old girl but the observant eyes of an old soul. She was the cornerstone of the family. What she said was law—in matters of the heart, at least.

That was why Gordon was there that day, letting her practice Marty's self-defense tips on him.

"Sorry, Gord," she said, letting up. "I didn't know your shoulder was so old."

Gordon sat up and rubbed some feeling back into his arm. "Well, it's not *that* old. I mean, it's not even seven years old in dog years. Younger than you. It's the knee that's pretty much shot."

Chloe laughed. She'd been fascinated by the concept of dog years recently. Someone at school had told her that most dogs don't live past ten. Beets, their Boston terrier, was eight. She'd been distraught, afraid to let the dog out of her sight lest he poof up to doggie heaven at the drop of a hat. Beets wasn't thrilled with the new helicopter-parenting arrangement.

Finally, Gordon had been the one that talked her off the ledge by explaining the concentrated nature of dog years. That was her first real conversation about death—not an easy topic, but one he'd tackled many times before with kids her age. His approach was to gently remind her that every minute we had here was special precisely because it didn't last forever, and he also emphasized that everyone around her wasn't going anywhere, least of all Beets, who had the constitution and general demeanor of a fire hydrant. It was a good talk.

Still, it was no arm-bar lesson.

Of course, being face-to-face with her, he was having stage fright for some reason. His two-and-a-half decades of experience with kids seemed to have gone right out the window.

"Um. Yeah. So," he began. "I was hoping I could sit and talk with you for a second. About me and your mom."

"Okaaay," Chloe replied warily.

"No, nothing bad. Nothing like that. We're fine. Totally. I just..." He paused, considering his words, then cleared his throat. "May I have a glass of water, Maria?"

Under normal circumstances, Maria would most likely have pointed out the tap. But Gordon had recently had a version of this conversation with her that went mercifully well, and she seemed inclined to help. The glass appeared in his hand, and he drank half of it in one go.

"You're being weird," Chloe said.

"I'm aware of that. Sorry. I'm just nervous. And when I get nervous, I sort of lose my filter, so here we go." Gordon rubbed a dry contact and set his water on the table. "You know I love your mom, right?"

"Yeah," Chloe said.

"Well, over this past year, I've also come to love you too. I hope you don't think that's weird," Gordon said.

Chloe thought for a minute. "No, I don't think that's weird," she said.

"I know how important you are to your mom. And also to me. And I wouldn't want it any other way. So I wanted to ask you something first, before I ask your mom—"

"Are you gonna ask her to marry you?" Chloe asked, and the tiny note of hope in her voice was like a balm to Gordon's racing heart.

He laughed with relief. "If you think it's a good idea, yeah, I was going to ask your mom to marry me. But first I wanted to ask you. You'll always be her number one, but if it's okay, I'd like to be number two."

"Three," said Maria, peering around the corner, wiping tears from her eyes. "You're her three. I'm her two."

Gordon took a patient breath. "I'll take three. I'll take anything as long as I'm in the count with your mom."

Chloe looked at him. He waited, thinking about reaching for the rest of that water, but before he could grab it, Chloe jumped into his arms instead.

"Can you get married tomorrow?" she asked. "Wait, that's too soon. Maybe next week?"

Gordon laughed again, sagging a bit as the force of her hug squeezed out a bit of the anxiety over this pre-proposal.

"Well, it's not quite that easy," he said. "I actually have to ask her first."

"Oh, she'll say yes." Chloe waved him off. "I wonder if mom wants a dress," she said, lost in thought. "I wonder if she'll get a pink one. I'll draw what it should look like." She scampered toward her art station.

Upstairs, the garage door rumbled as it opened. All three of them froze.

"She's home!" Chloe said. "Are you gonna ask her?"

Gordon's stomach flipped again at the thought, but he nodded. "I don't do well with things hanging over my head. So I prepped up a bit of brunch and brought it over."

Maria poked her head out again, her brow furrowed. "You cooked?"

"It's good, I promise," Gordon said, hands up. "Blueberry pancakes from scratch. The only thing I can do, but I do it pretty well. Not like the pork-chop fiasco."

Maria had sole dominion over the kitchen in the household and disliked anyone mucking about in the little slice of linoleum between the stove, sink, and refrigerator. She pondered the idea for a moment before allowing it with a nod.

"Anyway, I was thinking we could all sit down and eat brunch together, have a few mimosas—not you, Chloe, of course, but me—and then when I have the courage, I'd get down on one knee, and you all could be there as backup."

Chloe snorted with laughter. "Backup?"

"Yeah, in case she says no. Maybe you could talk to her. Say you're on board. Sort of like a peer review."

"You've got the ring? Can I see? Can I see?" Chloe asked.

Gordon reached into his breast pocket and pulled out a little velvet box. He found himself smiling, almost giddy. Chloe's enthusiasm was catching. For the first time since he hatched this plan, it was starting to seem real. Even after Maria had nodded soberly and kissed him on the cheeks in blessing, it hadn't seemed real. But with Chloe looking at the center stone his mother had practically thrown at him the moment he'd broached the subject of a ring for Dana, Gordon started to allow that he might actually have a wife again... and one that loved him for who he was.

Dana called from upstairs, "Gordon? Are you here?"

Gordon took the ring box back and tucked it into his breast pocket. "I'll go up and get started. You two come up whenever. Just act natural."

Maria gave a single, solid nod. Chloe bobbed up and down on the balls of her feet.

Gordon nearly ran into Dana on his way up as she was on her way down.

"Oh, thank God," she said. "You're here." She looked disheveled, a few strands of dark hair having escaped her ponytail and gotten plastered to her damp brow. Her eyes were saddled with dark-purple bags. She grabbed Gordon by the shoulders and looked at him like he might disappear on her. Then she looked beyond him and saw Chloe. "But also, you can't be here."

"What? Dana, are you all right?"

"Not really. I've been up for a while. We'll talk about it on your way out."

"Way out? But I was going to make us a nice brunch, my special pancakes. I even brought fresh fruit—"

"That's great," she said. "Perfect. We can take it on the go. I feel like I haven't eaten in forever." She was already up the stairs and opening the refrigerator.

"Can you just slow down for a second here?" Gordon asked.

Dana stopped at the sink and took a deep breath while Chloe peeked around the corner from the basement stairs. "Yeah, sorry. I've had, like, five cups of coffee. I got called in to work at two in the morning. Been at work since 2:00 a.m."

"At the station?"

She shook her head, opened Gordon's Tupperware container of fresh blueberries, and popped one in her mouth. "Out on a call. At Ditchfield. These are delicious."

"You went to *Ditchfield*? At two in the morning?" Gordon asked.

"Yeah. Not by choice. You know how I feel about that place," Dana said then shivered. The cold light of the window picked up the gooseflesh on her slender neck, haloed in wisps of black hair.

"Dare I ask why?" asked Gordon.

Dana looked down at Chloe by his side and seemed to settle herself for the first time. She sagged back against the sink a bit, as if exhaustion had finally caught up to her and jumped into her arms like a fat cat, like it or not.

"Hi, sweetheart," Dana said, sounding tired but much more herself. "How are things?"

Chloe answered her mother much the way she'd answered Gordon earlier: "Okaaay."

"I'm just gonna walk Gord out," Dana said.

"But he was gonna cook pancakes," Chloe said, looking desperately at Gordon to intervene. "And mimosas!"

Dana looked askance at Gordon. "You were?"

Gordon looked back and forth between Dana and Chloe, trying

to square the excitement he'd felt limping up the stairs with the confusion hitting him there at the top. "Chloe, let me talk to your mom outside for a sec. We'll straighten all this out."

Chloe looked like she'd been given a birthday present only to have it swiped from her hands again. She flopped her arms to her sides. "Fine," she said. "But just talk. Nothing *else*. Okay?"

"What's that supposed to mean?" Dana asked.

But Gordon was already ushering her out of the kitchen, an arm around her waist, before Chloe could slip up and his whole plan landed butter-side down.

Gordon navigated the thin confines of Dana's cluttered garage, gingerly sidestepping lawn toys and a pile of snow tires. His knee was better, so he could walk short distances without thinking about it, which was a whole lot more than his physical therapist had told him to expect during the early days of Gordon's recovery. Still, he was one bad tumble away from starting all over again. He still had nightmares of the hellacious exercises that man had put him through.

"How about we start with telling me why you're kicking me out of your house?" Gordon asked once free of the clutter and on the driveway.

"I'm sorry. I didn't want to worry Chloe," Dana began.

"Well what about worrying *me*?" Gordon asked.

"Ditchfield had an escape last night," Dana said, pulling her coat around herself against the pervasive cold. Her breath puffed white, carried away by the light wind. "A boy from Pod D," she added.

Gordon blinked, shaking his head lightly. He wasn't sure what he'd expected her to say, but it wasn't that. *"Let's take a vacation,"* maybe. Or *"Chloe arm-barred another kid at school."* Even *"I'm not sure this is working out between us"* fell higher on his list than a Ditchfield escape from Pod D.

Gordon's mind raced. He'd known a fair number of kids in the Ditchfield system back in the day, but not many of them would still be there. Except...

But that's not possible, not after all these years.

"His name is Charlie Cunningham," Dana said, plucking the name right from the forefront of Gordon's mind.

Eventually, Gordon was able to form and float one word between them: "How?"

"Not completely sure," Dana replied. "Although I have a working theory. Marty and I are going to pay a few visits and try to flesh it out. But that's not why I need you to stay away."

Gordon wasn't fully listening. In his mind, he was walking the cold, shadowed halls of Ditchfield, pacing back and forth on the concrete between the manor house and the bunkers, waiting for the go-ahead to perform a wellness check on one of the handful of patients he'd treated that ended up there. He did so of his own voli-tion—no prompting or state requirements. He did it because he hated Ditchfield. Every patient he'd lost to that institution was a personal failure for him. While he paced those cold walkways, he always wondered what they were cleaning up, what they might have been hiding before allowing him in.

The kids never talked much, not even the ones who were talk-ative before. And he noticed things: little nicks that shouldn't be there, hints of bruises peeking out from collars and sleeves, slight limps, winces when they sat.

Charlie Cunningham was the last of his patients to get sent to Ditchfield. Gordon had only checked on him once. Then came the divorce and his life falling down around him. He gave up child psychiatry for five years. Gave up on himself. Gave up on his practice.

Maybe he'd given up on Charlie Cunningham too.

"Gordon, did you hear me? He had your business card on him when he came in," Dana said. "And he took it when he ran."

Gordon looked up at her as if lost. After another moment, he registered her words. "That would make sense," he said softly. "I worked with him for a while. Even wrote an appeal to keep him out of that godforsaken place, but it never got to a judge before..."

"Before he tried to massacre a church congregation with a car?" Dana said.

Gordon remembered that phone call on the night of his fortieth birthday. He still couldn't quite believe it even though the cops had had Charlie dead to rights. He fessed up to everything and didn't even try to flee the scene.

Gordon had seen a lot of sides of Charlie Cunningham. He could be contemplative, angry, silent, even charming, sometimes all four in one sitting. But he'd never seen the side that might commit mass murder. Then he ran a car into a church and put three people in the hospital. As far as Gordon could remember, all had recovered. *Was he seeking to kill everyone?* The courts evidently thought so. Gordon had his doubts, but that hardly mattered.

"Yeah," Gordon said. "Before that."

Dana put a hand on his shoulder, pulling his attention back. Her face showed her exhaustion, but beyond that, deeper, her eyes looked worried.

"He had five things in his wallet: a picture of his sister, a food stamp card, and three business cards. And one of those business cards was for the church he hit. The last was for Thomas Brighton. I've already given his office a heads-up."

Gordon nodded, understanding what she was getting at. "You think maybe he was on some sort of revenge mission before he got locked up and now he's out again and set to pick up where he left off."

"I think that's a real possibility," Dana said. "One we need to prepare for."

"I get that. I sure as hell don't want to put your family in danger, so I think it's a good idea to take precautions. But from another angle, if you didn't know the kid's history, that wallet looks like it has the contact info for his church—which he relied on to help care for his sister—plus the numbers for his psychiatrist and his lawyer. The car wreck notwithstanding, I don't see anything super strange about that."

"Yeah, well, the car wreck is withstanding. Very withstanding."

"I'll stay away until we find him," Gordon said.

"*We?* No, no. Marty and I will find Charlie Cunningham. You will do no such thing. You'll attend to your patients and live your life with both eyes wide open."

"I know Charlie better than you do," Gordon said, shifting on his feet and easing his knee into motion with a slight wince. "I can help you."

Dana crossed her arms. Gordon knew she was too good of a cop to say no. But he also knew she didn't like it.

"You promise me you'll be careful? Watch your back and not go anywhere stupid or do anything stupid?"

Gordon nodded. That was fair. He would be the first to admit that his habit of waltzing into crime scenes like he owned the place had gotten both of them in a lot of trouble in the past—Marty too.

Dana sighed heavily. "Then I could use any info you have about Charlie's relationship with his sister, Tasha. She's his only living relative as far as we can tell."

"Tasha. He mentioned her. I think they were close. Maybe he broke out to see her? I'll check my files, see what I have," Gordon said.

A car peeled off somewhere in the distance. Dana turned her head quickly at the squealing of the tires and the revving engine even as it faded away.

"Dana, I'm not worth breaking out of Ditchfield for," said Gordon. "There's something bigger going on here."

"You're worth a lot more than you think," said Dana. "To me. To Chloe."

Gordon looked beyond Dana to where Chloe was pressed up against the glass bay window of the living room, her little nose smushed, her breath fogging the cold glass.

"Sorry about the brunch," Dana said, following his gaze. "What was the occasion?"

Gordon caught Chloe's eye and gave a tiny shake of his head. He mouthed *later*. Chloe backed off the glass, slumping a little. It broke his heart and cheered him at the same time, how invested she already was.

"It's nothing. It can wait," Gordon said.

Gordon carefully wedged himself into his beat-up old coupe, positioning his bum leg like an awkward lamp he had to cart around. Chloe gave him a sad little wave. Dana bent down and kissed him goodbye, a little harder than usual. As she walked away, she turned back twice to see him again as he warmed up the engine.

Even if Charlie Cunningham wasn't the mass killer everyone assumed he was, he was still a very troubled young man, loose somewhere in Baltimore, with some sort of agenda. Nobody escaped from Ditchfield just to grab a quick bite and catch a matinee.

Gordon tapped lightly at the ring box in his breast pocket. He could wait.

But something in the air told him he shouldn't wait too long.

CHAPTER FIVE

SIX YEARS AGO

Gordon paced on the cold concrete between the Ditchfield manor house and the north property that housed Pods C and D. The winter-damp brick of the bunkhouse steamed in the weak afternoon sunlight. He checked his watch. In another few hours, the sun would cut behind the canyon, and the brick would freeze all over again. The guards had kept him waiting for going on fifteen minutes. They didn't need fifteen minutes to move a kid from his cell to the visitation room. That took five minutes, maybe ten. Fifteen minutes meant they were stalling.

The door finally opened, and a burly security guard with a buzz cut and a fat baby face stepped out. He looked Gordon up and down, one hand on the butt of his baton. His name tag read Bagshot.

"All right, Dr. Pope," he said, after a few moments.

"About time," said Gordon. "Were you giving him a makeover?"

"Unannounced visitors often have to wait," Bagshot said dryly. "Routine is very important in Pod D."

Gordon stepped up and squeezed past the man, trying his best not to touch him. The visitation room was on the near side of the bunkhouse, shared by Pods C and D. The warden and his band of merry men didn't want civilians seeing that hellacious exam room on the far side, with the restraining chair and the cabinets of sharp steel things. Gordon had only seen it through a window, and that was enough.

Charlie Cunningham was seated like a poseable doll on the opposite side of a thick slab of two-way plexiglass. His back was ramrod straight, his hands shoulder width apart and lying flat on the stubby counter in front of him. The sight of him stilled Gordon in his tracks.

Charlie had been in Ditchfield for only a little over a month by then, but he'd already lost all semblance of childhood. He'd always been a tall kid, but before, he'd been softer, rounder of cheek, his hair in the early stages of what would surely be an impressive afro. All that was gone. His face was longer now, sallower. His head was shaved. He looked like he'd lost about ten pounds from all the places on the body that make a person look full and healthy.

Worst of all, the intelligent glint in his eye was gone, scorched out, no doubt, by whatever drug regimen they had him on.

Gordon sat down slowly. The last time he'd seen Charlie, they joked about him growing out his hair. He'd laughed genuinely when Gordon asked him for advice on how to grow an afro of his own. That was a week before he blinded a kid with a pencil and went from having a few school suspensions on his record to having a jail term at Ditchfield.

A week after the pencil incident, Charlie got into a Buick and drove that jail term from "one year on good behavior" to "no chance of parole," and the powers that be at Ditchfield moved him from a cell in Pod C to a four-point-restraint fishbowl in Pod D.

"Hi, Charlie," Gordon said, speaking through a circular grate about the size of a shower drain. "How are you?"

Charlie stared right through him. Gordon decided to take a mental step back.

"Do you remember me?" Gordon asked.

Gordon watched him carefully. Dilated pupils. Delayed motor response. Eventually, Charlie looked slightly down to find Gordon, but his eyes seemed to have trouble focusing. His irises moved like a spastic camera aperture. He was trying to see clearly but couldn't quite get there.

"I remember you," Charlie said slowly, but he sounded like he didn't care.

Gordon ticked off medications in his head. By then, they could feasibly have built up a crushing base of heavy benzos that would explain the general apathy. He was clearly on some sort of fast-acting sedative as well, probably intravenous. Maybe that's what they'd been doing for those fifteen minutes.

"Pope," Charlie said after another long moment. His mouth began forming a slow smile then gave up, as if he'd forgotten a joke halfway through.

"That's right. Gordon Pope. I'm here to check on you. See if you're being treated fairly."

That was a joke in and of itself. He obviously was not. But Bagshot was standing just behind Gordon, who didn't want to make any more trouble for the kid than he already had. Gordon wished he could see Charlie's inner arms—they were likely all tracked up—but he was wearing a loose-fitting pair of orange scrubs that looked twisted and haphazardly arranged on him, as if thrown on in a hurry. A dark-purple bruise leaked from the left side of his collar, above where the collarbone jutted abnormally.

"What the hell happened to his neck?" Gordon asked, turning to Bagshot.

Bagshot, still looking forward, only shrugged. "I'm not the kid's mom," he said.

"You're going to need to step out," Gordon said. "This falls under physician-patient privilege. It's against the law for you to be here."

In truth, he wasn't sure if medical confidentiality applied to the situation, considering Charlie had already been convicted, but Gordon tried to speak forcefully enough that Bagshot wouldn't question him. The guy gave Gordon the creeps.

Bagshot narrowed his eyes, probably weighing if he cared enough to argue. He looked at Charlie even longer, as if trying to make some sort of silent point. Eventually, he caught the boy's eye, and only after Charlie looked down, defeated, did Bagshot nod.

"Fine. But the clock is ticking. You got five minutes." He turned around and left through the heavy metal door, which wheezed shut behind him, locking with a loud click.

As soon as Bagshot was gone, Gordon leaned in toward the grate. "Charlie, what are they giving you? What kind of medicine? Do you know?"

Charlie's eyes were still on the door. He shook his head a bit as if to clear it then found Gordon. "I dunno. They give me a little cup of different stuff. It's all white. They stand there until they see me swallow and I open my mouth and say, 'Aah.'"

"What about intravenous? Shots. Do they give you shots?"

"They did in the beginning, in the chair. But I stopped talking so much, and they stopped pricking me."

Gordon's mind was all over the place. He had so much he wanted to ask Charlie and so little time, both on the visitor's clock and with Charlie's fading awareness.

"Do they hit you here?"

"Yeah," Charlie said flatly, and his eyes flashed with a bit of that old light. "But that ain't new. Everybody hits everybody everywhere. Here, they make it a lot harder to hit back is all."

"What about that guy?" Gordon asked, nodding back toward the closed door. "Does he hit you?"

"Yeah. Bad. But you snitch on him, he'll make it worse for me," said Charlie. He showed no anger in his voice, only stating flat facts like an accountant.

Charlie seemed more alive. Gordon wondered if the boy had been faking his stupor before and, if so, how. Not for the first time, his wife's words crept back in: *textbook sociopath.*

But Gordon was still skeptical, mostly because that was an easy diagnosis—too easy.

"Why did you run a car through that church?" Gordon asked.

He realized that wasn't the smoothest segue, but they had no time to beat around the bush. He wasn't looking for a criminal motive, really. That ship had sailed. Gordon was concerned with what was going on inside Charlie's head.

But Charlie's eyes glassed over again. An act? He'd seemed all there moments before.

"Charlie. I know you can hear me. You're not a killer. I need to know what you were thinking. Maybe I can help you."

Charlie looked at the door then at the ceiling where a camera perched in the corner like a red-eyed bat. He looked carefully at the grate between them, as if scanning for a microphone. "Nobody died?" he asked carefully.

"A few people had some long hospital stays, but nobody died. How does that make you feel?"

His face was a blank slate. Unblinking.

"Charlie, my wife says you're a sociopath. Help me prove her wrong."

"Tasha," Charlie said, barely above a whisper. His eyes briefly flicked up at the camera again then down. "Find Tasha."

"Your sister?"

He settled back into a dull gaze, as if he'd been wound up, performed his motions, and returned to an inert state.

"You still with me, Charlie?" Gordon asked, tapping on the glass.

The lock on the front door snapped back, and the door opened. Andy Bagshot clomped one boot inside and held it.

"Time's up, doc," Bagshot said. "Out."

Gordon stood, bent low, and tried to look into Charlie's eyes once more, but he'd shut down.

GORDON DROVE the twenty miles back to Baltimore with only the low whine of his old coupe's engine and the wind whipping past the wobbly side-view mirrors to accompany his thoughts. He thought about Ditchfield, about the menace of a place where every threat seemed just out of sight, like a mote in the eye flitting away as soon as one tries to focus on it.

"Nobody died?"

If Gordon had to pin an emotion to those words, which was hard to do given how flat Charlie was, he'd say the kid was disappointed.

Gordon thought about Tasha. He knew Charlie had a sister, a twin. He'd spoken of her before. Once, she came to get him from one of their sessions after school. She was a tall, quiet girl, pretty but deflated, eyes on the floor. She carried herself hunched forward, while Charlie walked with his shoulders pulled back. At first blush, Charlie didn't appear to care much about her or even really acknowledge her.

Then some kid "said something about Tasha"—according to the police report, at least—and Charlie nearly gouged his eye out with the fine point of a mechanical pencil.

Gordon made a mental note to hit the boxes—to check all the recorded sessions, anything he'd written—for any mention of Tasha Cunningham. Obviously, he would search Charlie's sessions, but sessions from the other kids in the study might also prove useful. Maybe something more was going on.

Gordon had plans all itemized and laid out in his head—where to look in the filing cabinets and even a few spare notepads he'd tossed into his everything drawer.

He parked the coupe in the driveway of his home, wincing at the rattle the engine made when it shut off. He would have to get that checked sooner rather than later.

He hung his keys on the hook inside the front door and decided against taking his coat off just yet. The air was freezing outside, and the coupe's heater was a C+ at best.

"Karen?" he called.

No answer.

Her new Benz was in the driveway, though, so she was there somewhere, probably reading in the study. But first things first: he needed a drink. He headed straight to the bar and plucked up a tumbler. *The good stuff tonight. Macallan 15 oughta do the trick.* He poured a generous three fingers and rolled the amber around. He took down one finger in a single sip and felt Ditchfield melt away a bit.

He turned around and found Karen seated with a drink of her own. A glass of wine, almost gone, sat on the table next to a nearly empty bottle. She was holding an open envelope in one hand and a folded slip of paper in the other. Her eyes were a spent color of red.

As soon as Gordon saw the envelope, he closed his eyes briefly then looked away, not unlike the way Charlie had shut down at the end of their visit. His tumbler hung from limp fingertips, waist high.

Karen's lips trembled. "When were you going to tell me about this?" she asked hoarsely.

Gordon tried to put some purpose back into his body by standing up, at least. He grasped his drink like it was a drink once more and not a tissue.

"When I got the courage to open it up," he said after a moment.

"It's been sitting in your drawer for over a week," Karen said.

Gordon decided right then wasn't a great time to ask *how* she'd come across the envelope. Perhaps he deserved to be found out this way. Part of him wondered if he would ever have opened that envelope on his own. Maybe he would've just let it sit there in the back with the phone cords and ancient, unused condoms that they'd never needed to begin with. He knew what the results would say. He didn't need to see them. Opening that envelope only meant he had to act on them.

"Do you know what it says?" Karen asked.

Gordon took a sip.

"It says you're sterile, Gordon. Sperm count is too low to register."

Gordon managed a nod then took another sip.

"How long have you known this?" Karen asked, looking at him like a stranger.

"I've never known. That's why I got the test. But I've had a hunch for a while."

"You care about that Cunningham kid but not this?" Karen flopped the test results onto the table then picked up the rest of her wine and slugged it in one go. "I've been getting cupped, down there. Did you know that? Acupuncture, too, all over, twice a week. Not drinking what I want, not eating what I want. I'm juggling doses of clomiphene and metformin. I've been jamming a steroid pill up my vagina for months. And the problem was never me. The problem has always been you."

"It's not really a *problem*," Gordon said, loosened by the scotch. "It's more the way I am."

"I think I'm understanding that now." Karen pushed her wine glass away and stood.

The glass lolled around on the fine edge of its base until it tipped. Nothing spectacular—just a slow fall until it toppled onto the wood, the delicate bulb shattering.

Gordon moved to his wife, put his scotch down, and started gathering the broken wine glass carefully until she leaned into his arm and started sobbing. Gordon set the broken glass aside on the table and settled himself carefully beside Karen, and she leaned further into his arms. Her hair smelled sharp and clean.

"It's all I ever wanted," she said. "A baby."

"It's not all you ever wanted," Gordon said, steely eyed now, aware of this space in time—of living a watershed moment as it unfolded around him. Perhaps visiting Charlie had prepared him, somehow, to meet this crossroads. "But it's what you want now, as bad as you've ever wanted anything. And I get that."

As she sobbed quietly in the crook of his shoulder, he eyed his scotch, sensing that he had a lot of it in his future... and maybe not much else. He felt his wife firmly in his arms yet slipping away from him at the same time.

"I'll clean this up," he said. "You go lie down."

She pushed up and off him blindly, her lips leaving a red stain on his white shirt. She left the kitchen without another word.

Gordon wasn't sure how long he stayed in the kitchen. Eventually, the Macallan 15 sat empty next to him on the table, and he still hadn't looked at the results. Nor did he think anymore of Ditchfield or Charlie or Tasha. He thought of when he first met Karen. They were undergraduates together at Hopkins, pre-med. Her hair was light brown then but bright with summer sun. He remembered she wore a little butterfly clip that pinned it back at her ear and caught the harsh lights of the lecture hall, flashing every time she bent over her notepad that first week in Psych 101. It caught Gordon's eye one day, and he'd never looked back.

That flash had led him here, to this table in this time. *How strange*, he thought, *what a flash of light could do. How much can change in a single moment.*

When he went upstairs, he held on to the handrail. He wobbled on the edge of the bed and took off his shoes and his clothes as quietly as he could. He knew he'd had too much scotch to be quiet getting into bed, but when his head finally hit the pillow, Karen still didn't move.

She was pretending to sleep. Gordon knew that move well.

CHAPTER SIX

PRESENT DAY

Dana found Marty sitting on a concrete bench outside the entrance to the Children's Center of Johns Hopkins Hospital, eating almonds. *The more some things change, the more they stay the same.* She said a quick prayer of thanks for her staid and steady partner, who always seemed to get there just a few minutes ahead of her. *Or maybe it's just his road-eating car.*

Marty flicked a salute at her, badge glinting on his chest. He wore the same black leather jacket with a different T-shirt—this one was black with a V-neck that stopped just short of nightclub attire—as tight as ever. He fell in place beside her as they walked inside.

The Children's Center at Hopkins was bright and airy, with wide open spaces where kids could run and play while their parents waited nervously. Floor-to-ceiling windows looked out upon a peaceful center courtyard. Dana passed a big piece of functional art, a type of loop-the-loop where a few kids jumped and played. That exam chair at Ditchfield seemed a world away.

"The jewelry's new," Dana said, nodding at a flash of gold peeking out from Marty's cuff.

He looked down at his wrist and started to put his hand in his pocket before stopping himself. "Yeah, just a little bracelet thing. Thought I'd wear it."

"Let me see it," Dana said.

Marty seemed to think twice before popping his wrist out. The bracelet was fine chain link, maybe a quarter inch wide. That type of thing would have looked ridiculous on anybody else.

"I used to wear a chain, remember, but then I started wearing my badge around my neck, and it was too much. She got me this so I could keep a little flash, you know?"

"She?"

Marty cleared his throat. "Yeah, you know, the girl I'm seeing. I thought I told you."

Dana just stared him down—no easy feat when she had to look up. "You told me no such thing, and you know it." Then she smiled, unable to help it. "You're dating someone?"

"Yeah. You could say that."

When they reached the front desk, Dana held up a finger at him. "We will continue this. I have questions."

"It's no big deal."

But both of them knew it was a big deal. Dana thought it was a huge deal. Although she tried not to show it, the fact that Marty had feelings for her that she just couldn't return had kept a sort of distance between them, which she hated. She did love Marty, but not the way he wanted, and she was terrified of showing him the former in case he mistook it for the latter. It had constantly fueled an awkward undercurrent between them. If he really was moving on, or at least trying to, Dana counted that as some of the best news she'd heard in months.

The woman at the front desk looked quizzically between them because Dana's finger was still aloft. But Dana wasn't about to let Marty change the subject.

"Can I help you?" asked the front desk attendant.

Dana let her finger linger in the air.

"Okay," Marty said, exasperated. "Later."

Dana turned to the woman and flashed her badge. "Sergeant Dana Frisco, here to see Jarvis Brown. This is my partner, Detective Marty Cicero."

The attendant looked briefly at their brass and typed something. The printer behind her whirred to life and rattled off some paperwork and two wristbands.

"Sign, please," she said. "Jarvis Brown is on our secure wing. Floor seven. Elevators to your left."

In the elevator, Marty was the first to speak, probably fending off any more questions about this new lady. "So, what's our angle here?"

"According to the ER doc that transferred him, he just slept off enough lorazepam to bring down a horse. They almost intubated him at one point."

"And you think he got it from Charlie?" Marty asked.

"Maybe. The lab got back quick with detail on the white powder. It's a pharmacological cocktail, but mostly fast-acting benzos. So yeah. Same stuff. But we're not playing bad cop here, not accusing him of anything. We want him to open up."

A security guard for the hospital stood outside Jarvis's room. He scanned their wristbands and checked their badges before moving aside without a word.

Jarvis Brown was lying on top of his covers, watching cartoons on TV and eating a cup of pudding like he'd never been fed in his life. Four more empty pudding cups sat on a half table extending over his bed. He turned to look at them when they walked in, but his spoon never stopped moving.

"Hi, Jarvis. I'm Dana. This is Marty. We're Baltimore Police. How are you feeling?"

He looked back and forth between them, blinking. Either he still had a fair amount of the drugs in his system or he just wasn't all that bright. Dana recalled the picture of Charlie Cunningham and his sister in the keychain. The resemblance wasn't dead-on, but it was strong—similar big, almond eyes and high brow. He had the height too. The boys could feasibly pass for one another.

"Jarvis?" Dana asked again.

"That depends," he said, his voice rolling with a drawl. "You takin' me back?"

"No," Dana said. "Only the docs can do that."

"Then I'm doing incredible," Jarvis said, spooning another glob of chocolate pudding into his mouth.

Marty pulled up a chair and sat down while Dana gave a white-board on the wall a once-over. Under the heading Medications, the board had a few scripts Dana didn't recognize, for the purpose of Reversal Agent. Time stamps showed the nurses had checked on him several times already that morning—for pudding requests, by the looks of it.

"Let's talk about how you ended up in Charlie's cell the other night," said Dana.

"Man, I already told everyone. I don't remember shit," he said. "I ate lunch like every other day, and at rec, I didn't feel so good. I sat down for a bit, and next thing I know, I woke up here."

He spoke with authority, even looking Dana in the face, but he didn't look her right in the eye. The anger he put behind his words was trying to cover a lie.

Marty leaned forward, elbows resting on his knees. "You ain't super eager to get back to Ditchfield, are you, Jarvis?"

Jarvis looked warily at Marty. "Man, what do you think?"

"You talk with us, maybe we can see about getting you transferred somewhere," Dana said.

Jarvis turned back to the cartoons, scraping the bottom of his pudding cup, but Dana could tell he was considering it.

"As a matter of fact, one of the reasons you're still here is because we told the warden we needed to speak with you," Dana said. "Maybe we tell him we need another day, say you're still too out of it to answer."

"How many pudding cups you think you could eat in a day?" Marty asked.

Jarvis looked thoughtfully at his pudding cup.

"And these doctors and nurses, they gotta be nicer than what's his face…" Marty snapped his finger to remember. "Bagshot."

Jarvis visibly tensed at the name. The little balsa-wood strip of a spoon trembled for just a moment in his fingers. Marty and Dana shared a glance.

"Andy Bagshot was on patrol that night. He messed up bad. Maybe we can get him removed from his position," Marty said carefully. "You're going back to Ditchfield either way, sooner or later. If you can help us, your time there might be a lot easier."

"What do you want?" Jarvis asked, but his tone was softer.

Dana knew they were in. "Tell us how you ended up in Charlie's cell."

Jarvis put his pudding down with the rest of the empty cups and picked at the thin hospital blanket bunched around his legs. "I told you the truth. I got no idea. I just walked where Charlie told me to walk. That's all. It's hazy."

"You talked to Charlie? How?"

"Before they clear the rec yard, they line the next pod up on the other side of the fence for a while. Ain't no problem to talk. Even fist-bump if you want."

"If you can fist-bump, you can pass something through too," Dana said.

Jarvis looked back up at the TV, but he seemed not to see it. "The Pod D kids that come to rec don't talk much, but Charlie was different. He whispered at me whenever I passed by, like he was working a corner."

"He was dealing in Ditchfield?"

Jarvis shrugged. "He never seemed to call out to anyone else. Just me."

"Because he was targeting you," Dana said. "And it worked."

Jarvis scratched at his neck. "I got sent up to Ditchfield 'cause I worked a few corners of my own pretty hard in West Baltimore. Sometimes I liked to sample. I thought I'd maybe get clean inside, but then someone starts whispering at you, know what I'm sayin'?"

"What did Charlie say he had?" Dana asked.

"Pills. Painkillers. And he'd just hang his hand through the fence. I ignored him for weeks, but then I looked at Bagshot wrong, and he popped me with his stick, and it hurt like a bitch. So the next time I heard Charlie whispering, I took him up on it."

Dana could picture it—one group of kids milling about the exercise yard while the quiet and broken boys of Pod D waited their turn on the other side of the fence, airing out, nobody looking their way. None of those kids could do much more than shuffle about, anyway. But one of them, Charlie, had been squirreling away his tranqs in the broken concrete of his cell wall. He wasn't nearly as quiet or as broken as he looked.

"I asked him what he wanted. He said first hit's free, but I had to take it at a special time. That's how the pills worked. If I didn't, he'd cut me off."

"And you believed him?" Marty asked.

Jarvis nodded. He pulled down the neck of his hospital gown to reveal a mottled patch of black spreading out like an oil slick from a lumpy break in the bone, just recently scabbed over. Marty sucked through his teeth as he looked at it then away. Dana moved in closer, and as she did, she forced herself to contain the cold fury beginning to flicker inside of her. That cold fury came to life anytime she saw a kid taken advantage of, no matter if they lived in a mansion or the projects or a prison.

"Yeah, I believed him. It took everything I had not to sniff it all up right there in the yard, but I didn't want to be cut off. So I waited until the next day, before lunch, like he said."

"And rec is an hour after lunch?" Dana asked.

Jarvis nodded.

Dana counted back the time. The tranqs would be fully on board by then. Charlie knew what he was doing.

"I was feelin' real faded already by the time I went out with the rest of the pod to the yard. It got hazy—that's all I remember."

In Dana's mind, she saw Charlie lined up with Pod D on the

other side of the fence, ready to get his hour in the yard. He scans the yard and finds Jarvis Brown sitting nearby or maybe leaning hard against the fence. As soon as the shift changes, Charlie moves. Swapping places with the boy wouldn't be that hard. All he had to do was shuffle off with the Pod A kids and leave Jarvis sitting nearly comatose in his place behind the fence. Guys like Andy Bagshot, who couldn't even keep the kids' names straight, probably wouldn't notice until it was too late.

"He gave you sedatives, not painkillers. Tranquilizers," Dana said.

"Yeah, I figured that out pretty quick when I woke up here," Jarvis said. "Don't even remember being in Charlie's cell or Pod D. None of it."

"Has Charlie reached out to you?" Marty asked.

Jarvis shook his head and winced a little, favoring his neck. "Like I said, I didn't know the kid in the first place. But even if he did give me stepped-on trash or whatever, at least he got me out of Ditchfield for a day. Worth it."

Dana stood back, signaling to Marty that they were done. She'd gotten what she wanted. Jarvis was already reaching for the call button as they left. That pudding wasn't going to eat itself.

"Hey, wait. You really think you can get Bagshot fired?"

"Maybe. You willing to testify about that collarbone?" Dana asked.

Jarvis looked down at the bedspread again.

"Thought not. But I'll see what I can do," Dana said. And she meant it.

OUTSIDE THE ROOM, Dana started to give her rundown to Marty but stopped when she noticed the guard had changed. Instead of the bored hospital security, a city policeman was standing at attention. He wasn't just any city cop, either, but Tommy Packman, the cop Marty had popped in the jaw a long time before, back when Dana was trying to get Ethan Barrett out of a run-down theater. Marty had laid Packman out after he grabbed her. He'd apologized later, saying he was only doing what Lieutenant Duke ordered.

That lieutenant was now a lieutenant colonel and officially the chief of the Detectives Division. Tommy Packman was one of his chosen ones—an absolute bootlicker and a terrible cop, totally in Duke's pocket. Also, he was apparently guarding the room of Jarvis Brown.

"Morning, Sergeant," Packman said evenly. "Marty," he added after a moment.

"What the hell are you doing here?" Marty asked flat out.

He'd never bought Packman's "apology" either. Others deferred to Packman because of his standing with Duke, but Marty was never one to play politics. That was one of the things Dana liked most about him.

"The chief wanted me to keep a special eye on the kid," Packman said and sniffed.

But Dana knew he would be reporting everybody that visited and probably what they said too. She had no idea how long he'd been there, but the door wasn't thick, especially for a weasel like Packman, who wasn't above pasting his ear to the wood to listen.

"We want to make sure the young man gets back where he came from as soon as possible," Packman added, which came out with the quality of a Duke soundbite, probably word for word.

"Come on, Marty," Dana said, pulling her partner away before he said something stupid that would immediately get back to Duke.

He came reluctantly. On their walk out, Dana spoke with a white coat about maybe letting Jarvis recover for another night. She said she might have more questions for him.

"More questions?" Marty asked when they were in the elevator.

"I lied. I kind of feel bad for the kid. Told him I'd try to buy him another day."

"If Duke wants him back at Ditchfield, he's going back sooner rather than later."

"It's why Duke gives a shit at all that bothers me," Dana said.

Marty pulled out his almonds again and ate them one at a time, lost in thought. "He wouldn't be able to help us find Charlie anyway," Marty said. "He was just a tool. A stooge."

The two of them walked back out into the parking lot, zipping up their jackets. The winter cold seemed to totally ignore the high-noon sun.

"I wasn't holding out much hope of a lead on where Charlie is, in the first place," said Dana. "But Jarvis helped paint a picture. Charlie is very bright. He manipulated everyone and slipped away. He planned this escape for weeks. Maybe months."

"You think this kid is really dangerous?" Marty asked.

Dana sighed. "He's out for a reason. I don't think it's just to go on a crime spree. But there are a lot of different types of dangerous, and he's definitely one of them."

Dana's mind kept returning to that keychain. She wished she'd taken a picture of it. Somehow, she felt that was a better representation of the real Charlie Cunningham than the photo stills and recent mugshots on file with the city. She was less and less concerned with the *how* of Charlie's escape. She wanted the *why*. And the longer she thought about that keychain, the more convinced she was that the *why* had something to do with Tasha Cunningham.

CHAPTER SEVEN

SIX YEARS AGO

The office of Brighton and Associates was located on Bail Bond Row, a short and gaudy city block just south of the Baltimore City Circuit Courthouse. A strip of old-style Baltimore row homes had been repainted in every color of the rainbow and renovated into the offices of bondsmen, lenders, pawn brokers, and various catch-all attorneys—sometimes all four under one roof.

Brighton had opted for a Gilded-Age look. Gordon thought the gold lettering on the sign out front was a nice touch, but the dual-lion setup on the outdoor stairway was a bit much—the same with the hanging chandelier on the porch and the faded golden shutters. Around the city circuit, Brighton had a reputation as a bit of a fop and occasional hustler, but even his colleagues had to admit he was at least a halfway decent attorney. He also didn't discriminate in his clientele, which was why Gordon had decided to reach out to him.

Gordon banged twice with the oversized brass knocker on the front door and stepped back from under the chandelier, waiting. The door comm clicked on.

"Can I help you, hon?"

"Yeah, I'm Gordon Pope, here to see Thomas Brighton. I have an appointment."

During a pause on the line, Gordon could hear the woman chewing gum and flipping through something.

"Here ya are," she said. "He put you down as Gordon Plop. I swear. Come on in."

Buzz, click. The snap of the lock instantly brought Gordon's mind back to Ditchfield. He opened the door and stepped inside.

The interior of the office was narrow and smelled like dusty wood. All around him remained the faded evidence of the home long gone. The receptionist sat behind a desk that took up most of what had likely been the old dining room. She was a young woman, buxom, with a low-cut dress and platinum-blond hair pulled up in a curated mess on the top of her head. She was in the process of spitting her gum out.

"Take a seat, hon. He'll be out in a second. Can I get you a water?"

"No, thank you." Gordon sat in a faded red wingback.

Behind her, a pair of frosted-glass sliding doors led into the back of the house. A figure was walking back and forth inside, loudly wrapping up a phone conversation with, "Thanks, buddy. I owe you one."

Moments later, Thomas Brighton slid apart his office doors with gusto and stepped through into the waiting room. He was shorter than Gordon expected, wider, too, or perhaps that was just the effect of the double-breasted pinstripe suit. He found Gordon and smiled. His face was tan, his dark hair slicked back into a little duck tail.

"Thomas, this is Gordon *Pope,*" the secretary said. "Your eleven o'clock."

Brighton clapped once loudly then pulled Gordon to standing, shaking his hand at the same time. "Gordon *Pope!* Of course. Here I was thinking, *Dr. Plop? That's an unfortunate name.* Come on in. I'm yours for the next—" he popped a gold wristwatch from under his cuff and glanced at it "—twelve minutes."

He ushered Gordon into his office and walked around to the other side of a large desk of worn mahogany. He sat grandly in a large executive chair of slightly cracked leather and steepled his fingers at his lips, waiting.

Gordon took a seat in the companion of the faded wingback out front and tried to shrug off the exhaustion that had been creeping into his day-to-day ever since Karen confronted him about the letter. Karen had suggested they undergo what she called a "period of processing" during which they simply mulled the information over.

They were going on two weeks without really having discussed it. However, Karen had withdrawn in a million small ways—going to bed without him, working away at the office on the weekends, making long calls to her family in California behind closed doors—that told Gordon a lot without her having to say anything. Feeling a sense of unraveling, he knew his window to act on Charlie's behalf was closing, like a child doing chalk art with black storm clouds on the horizon.

"I want to shut down Ditchfield," Gordon said, point blank.

Brighton's laughter dissolved when Gordon didn't join in but only leaned forward and stared at Brighton more intently.

"Wait, you're serious?" Brighton asked.

Gordon nodded. "I hear you're looking for splashy cases. That you're not afraid of a challenge."

"A *challenge*? Running a five-K is a challenge, Dr. Pope. Learning origami is a challenge. Going after Ditchfield is career suicide."

"The evidence is right in front of you. All you've got to do is go see it. Gross negligence at best, straight-up abuse in many cases. I've seen it time and time again," Gordon said. "And it's not going to stop. It's like they don't care who sees."

"I know," Brighton replied.

Gordon looked blankly at him.

"I've only been in this line of law for a few years, but I've already seen what Ditchfield does to kids. You're right. It's like they don't care who sees. Now, why do you think that might be?" Brighton asked.

Gordon supposed he did know. Perhaps the reason he'd been afraid to go right at the beast was because he'd known all along.

"Because it's connected," Gordon said.

Brighton nodded slowly. "Did you know that Ditchfield is a nonprofit?" he asked cheerily. "It's classified as a charity. Funded by a whole mess of special interests. You oughta take a look at their 501c3 filing sometime."

"It doesn't get much splashier than that," Gordon said, grasping at straws. "I could help you. I'm the psychiatrist of record for some kids up there. I can get evidence."

"We would lose," Brighton said, point blank. "Definitely the case. Maybe a lot more."

Gordon sat back in the dusty wingback, rested his head, and closed his eyes.

"You've still got eight minutes," Brighton said. "You can sleep if you want. Wouldn't blame you. You look a little run down. Nothing personal."

Gordon felt trapped between a rock and a hard place. Ditchfield was quite literally a monolithic brick wall that refused to be moved. And on his other side was Karen. He'd never be able to give her a child, at least not the way she wanted. His wife was another immoveable stone. And there he was, trying to wring blood from both like a fool.

"Say," Brighton chimed in, "you ever do expert testimony? I've been looking for someone to moonlight. I'd prep you for the stand. And pay you, of course."

Gordon opened his eyes, stared at the ceiling a moment more, then heaved himself upright. "Thanks for your time. But I'm not that desperate."

. . .

AT HOME, Gordon placed his key on the hook and tossed Brighton's card in the trash. He took off his coat and turned to the bar, only to find Karen already there. In her hands was a dusty bottle of Bordeaux that Gordon recognized at once. It was a rare vintage his mother had given them on their wedding day to drink on their fifth anniversary. Karen cradled it in front of her in two hands, not unlike a swaddled child.

"I keep waiting for my mind to settle," she said, talking to him while looking down at the wine. "For everything to click back in place so I can be fine with not having the child you and I would have had. But it's not clicking."

"You know there are other options," Gordon said carefully, as if talking her off a ledge. But he knew she'd already jumped. "We can adopt. We could look for a sperm donor together. Start researching IVF."

"I don't want someone else's child, not even if it was half mine. Does that make me a bad person?"

"A little," Gordon said before he could stop himself. Gordon was only recently admitting to himself that he'd never be a father any other way.

"I've studied children all my adult life alongside you. I wanted to have a child that was ours. To watch them grow and explore and all the while wonder whether they got more of your heart or more of my head. We would debate it over wine whenever they did something wonderful or stupid."

Gordon didn't know whether to be flattered or offended. *Heart versus head?* He was coming to realize just how good Karen was at disparaging him with a kiss. "Heart isn't all genetics, you know," he said. "Neither is brains."

If Karen heard him, she gave no indication. "I'm going to stay with my parents in California for a few weeks," she said. "My flight leaves in the morning. But before I go, I thought maybe we could share a bottle of wine together."

Gordon's voice caught in his throat. He felt a slow weight pulling him down and reached out to the kitchen island—one finger to steady himself. He thought of the stretch of time in the months after they were newly married, when a new and fresh wind blew at the sails of their relationship. They would work in their shared office, he at his desk and she at hers, while soft classical music played just under the sound of the last rains of fall hitting the skylight above, sometimes sipping a glass from a bottle of red that would glow in the light of the Tiffany lamp between them.

They didn't even need to speak then to communicate. Now, nothing Gordon could say seemed to get through to her. Or, worse, it did get through to her, but she didn't care.

"Yeah, honey," Gordon said, defeated, and he failed to keep his voice from breaking. "Let's have a glass of wine."

So Karen went to the glassware cabinet and pulled out two big tulip-bulb wine glasses and looked at them through the light, wiping away a few stray hard-water stains as Gordon got the corkscrew. The Bordeaux opened with a soft pop, the sound of a peck on the cheek.

They drank the bottle of wine and talked about the past. With each sip, the room took on more of a sepia feel, as if the living colors were slowly draining from the story they shared—the day they graduated as newly minted Hopkins psychiatrists and kissed under the statue of the Christus Consolator in the rotunda of the hospital's old great dome; when Gordon plucked up the guts to ask if they might go into business together—as husband and wife; the room with the skylight, where he proposed.

That night, they made love for the first time in months, holding each other as tightly as Gordon could remember in all their years together. Very early the next morning, Karen woke him with a soft peck on the cheek and said goodbye. Gordon started to get out of bed, but she put a finger on his chest and held him in place.

"Just let me go. The cab is already here," she said.

"Call me when you get there," he said, wanting to say so much more but not finding the words.

Karen took a small roller suitcase and left their bedroom. He heard the luggage skate along the wood then out the front door, which closed behind her with a whisper. Gordon heard the cab pull away and felt the sudden and crushing silence of the bedroom.

He flopped back down and stared wide-eyed at the ceiling like a man who'd just been robbed. He could hear his blood whistling in his ears and thought distantly that he might be having a panic attack. Karen had said a few weeks, but he knew he would be naïve to think she really meant that. He stood up and wandered through their condo, moving from room to room, picking things up and putting them down again in a daze while the coffee brewed.

Half of his brain insisted Karen would be back in three weeks. The other half was in triage mode, working to keep him alive. The triage half wondered about immediate things: how he would work without her, if he even could afford to. His patient pool was deep but not wide. She brought in all the money. In a fit of inspiration, he went to the trash can and pulled out Brighton's card. He dusted it off and stuck it on the refrigerator. His *"not that desperate"* seemed fool-hardy. Everyone was one step from desperation.

A flash of light caught his eye. Karen's wedding ring, on the table, reflected the first rays of sun peeking through the glass doors of their balcony. Gordon was mesmerized. He stood that way for a long time, thinking how strange it was that life could change so completely in the span of a single flash of light.

CHAPTER EIGHT

PRESENT DAY

The address of record for Tasha Cunningham was a housing project in east Baltimore called Lexington Heights. Marty said he'd been out there a few times on wellness checks. Dana couldn't recall visiting before at all. Lexington Heights was the type of place that the Baltimore City Police left alone, one of the many projects where crime had dug in so deep that cops only heaped more trouble on themselves by doing more digging. It was similar to an old box of clothes that had become home to a nest of rats. One didn't dig in. One closed it up and walked away.

The deep cold had apparently cleared out most of the activity in the center yard, surrounded on three sides by brutalist towers that reached five stories high and housed more than five hundred people. Three young men sat smoking on a ratty couch in the center of the dirt, their feet up on rusted school chairs. They spotted Dana and Marty as soon as they turned the corner. One of them hastily put his cigarette out, turned around, and whistled once sharply through his fingers. His whistle was echoed again from a corridor between towers, then again out of a window somewhere a few stories up. Soon, whistles were echoing throughout the towers, then just as abruptly, they stopped.

"Subtle," Marty said as they walked past the pair, smoking again with their boots still up. "Real subtle. No need to get up on account of us, gentlemen. We ain't here for you anyway."

The smokers said nothing, watching them with blank expressions.

Dana could feel the weight of their eyes on her back as they made their way to the south tower. She could feel people staring from all over and had to make an effort to keep her pace steady and her hand away from her gun hip. People who lived in the projects were usually smart enough not to mess with the cops unless the cops messed with them. Usually.

Marty easily pushed open the door to the south tower. Whatever locks these entryways once had were long gone. Dana could see her breath in the hallway despite the hissing rattle of an old steam heater. Dirty cardboard and stacks of phone books gathered dust against the yellowing walls. One of the phone-booth-sized elevators was taped off. Marty pressed the call button for the other, but nothing happened.

"Stairs?" Marty asked.

"Probably smart," said Dana.

The stairwell was erratically lit, and the concrete flooring was stained by foot traffic and what looked like grease from leaking trash bags. The exit to the fourth floor had no lock either. The hallway was deserted, but Dana heard life teeming all around them, behind closed doors. Children yelling, babies crying. The shuddering of pipes. The steady murmur of humanity just out of reach.

They walked the threadbare carpet of the hallway until they found the apartment number on file. Dana knocked three times. The murmuring stopped in the bubble around them. Down the hall, a young girl peeked out from a doorway but shot back inside again as soon as Marty glanced her way.

Dana took another deep breath and knocked three more times.

Just when she was about to pull out her phone to double check with dispatch, she heard a chain clasp slide into place then the bolt lock flip back. The door opened six inches, and a woman with the telltale pitted face of an addict peered out. Her hair was pulled back by a faded red kerchief. She might have been anywhere from twenty to forty years old.

"Tasha Cunningham?" Dana asked although she doubted it.

The woman looked them up and down. She didn't look like an active user. The scabs and scars on her face had faded to a soft purple in most places.

"Nobody by that name here," she said.

"I'm Dana. This is Marty. We're—"

"Cops. I know."

"We're looking for Tasha. She hasn't done anything wrong. We just want to make sure she's safe and ask her a few questions," said Dana.

"Safe, huh?" she said.

"Nobody's in trouble," Dana said.

The woman eyed Marty distastefully, but thankfully, he seemed to know when to take the back seat. He affected a blank face and said nothing. She found Dana again and snuffed a short breath out of her nose.

"Tasha hasn't lived here in years," she said. "She left not long after her brother got sent up. Going on five years now."

"Do you know where she lives now?" Dana asked.

"I wouldn't tell you if I did. But I don't, so all's the same."

Dana crossed her arms then thought better of it, wanting to seem as open and approachable as possible. "SNAP program still lists this as Tasha's primary residence," Dana said, keeping her voice calm.

The woman said nothing but narrowed her eyes.

"Have you been getting her mail? Maybe collecting her benefits?" Dana asked evenly.

As the woman moved to close the door, Dana interjected, "I'm not gonna report you. Looks like maybe the extra help is doing you good. But if you could point us in the direction of Tasha Cunningham, we'd appreciate it."

The woman paused and looked down at the floor as if ashamed. When she looked up again, her eyes were perhaps a shade softer. "I was homeless. She told me I could. Told me she was going to New Hope and they was gonna take care of her. That's all I know."

"Thank you," Dana said, but the woman was already closing the door.

Dana turned to Marty, and together, the two of them simply stood in the damp cold of the hallway and listened to the sound of hundreds of people barely getting by. Dana tried to picture Charlie living there with Tasha. Their father had never been in the picture, according to the police report, but for a time, their mother lived with them. She would have opened the door just like that. However, the scars and scabs on her face would have been fresh right up to the day she died, about three months after Charlie arrived at Ditchfield. Then the two kids were adrift.

"You think he's in there?" Marty asked.

Dana had initially wondered the same thing. They would need a warrant to enter without probable cause, though. And Dana didn't think they had it. She didn't think they needed to get inside, either. That place was in the dark and distant past for both Charlie and Tasha.

"No," she said. "But I think we need to pay New Hope a visit."

NEW HOPE COMMUNITY CHURCH, a simple and classic chapel with a bright white spire that shot into the sky, was a four-minute drive from Lexington Heights. The cross atop stood like a beacon amid the Bermuda Triangle of three of Baltimore's poorest and most dangerous neighborhoods. The sign outside was freshly painted. No graffiti marred the pristine walls of the church house. Nobody was working the corners anywhere nearby. Even the sidewalks seemed less cracked.

Dana and Marty pulled up to find another police car already there. Marty pulled in front and parked while Dana pulled in behind. The cruiser was one of the new supercharged Fords, which usually fell to cops in Duke's retinue. Sure enough, Victor Garcia was sitting in the driver's seat. Garcia and Packman were partners, but Garcia was the smarter of the two. He was less of a bully but more of a weasel.

He looked up from his dash array as they approached. If he was surprised to see them, he didn't show it. Eventually, he rolled down the window. "Can I help you?"

"You working my case now?" Dana asked.

"You want to sit in a church parking lot all day, be my guest," he said.

"Did Duke put you on this?"

Garcia paused for a moment to choose his words. "The chief thought it might be a good idea to post a watch. In case."

Dana was unnerved that Duke seemed to be one step ahead—and keeping her in the dark about it. She seriously doubted he was using manpower to help her. Duke had never helped her in his life. His world was one of swapped favors and land grabs. Every decision he made had an underbelly.

"You see anything?" Marty asked.

"Nope," Garcia said, popping the word with his lips.

"Your rotation is patrol. Duke should have you and Packman following up on the truck," Marty said.

Dana knew he liked Garcia even less than Packman.

"Oh yeah? You speaking for the chief now?"

"Take it easy, Vic," Dana said, rolling her eyes. "We're all on the same team here, right? So, no sign of the truck?"

Garcia gave a sleazy half smile.

"What is it, Vic?" Marty asked, both hands on the open window as he leaned down.

Garcia's face fell, and he leaned away before stopping himself.

Dana smiled. Apparently, Garcia also still remembered the way Marty had connected with Packman.

"We got a hit on the truck early morning. Security camera picked it up, abandoned at a long-term parking lot outside of the airport. No sign of the kid."

Dana couldn't believe it. The airport was the last place she expected Charlie to go.

"Did he try to get on a plane?"

Garcia shook his head. "Never went into the airport. We think he took another car. The security system at the lot shows the car count off. But it's a shitty system, so they don't know which one yet."

"And when were you gonna tell us about this?" Dana asked.

Garcia pouted his lips. "Chief wanted it kept under wraps until we know more about the new car."

"From his own detectives?" Marty emphasized. "Why would he do that?"

"Hell if I know," Garcia said. "Why don't you go ask him yourself?" He nodded in the direction of the church. "He's right inside."

Dana was caught flat-footed as Garcia's lip curled into that aggravating half smile again. He knew Dana didn't want to see Duke. Their relationship worked best when neither was near the other.

Warren Duke had been an oppressive hand on her shoulder for her entire career, but for her first four years on the force, he didn't even know her name. Dana knew he never consciously held her down, but his apathy proved just as effective. The cops in his circle kept moving up, while she stayed in the same place.

Then she started making waves with Gordon. Her cases got press coverage. Duke started paying attention, which only made things worse for Dana. Duke knew he would never get her in his pocket, and he needed his people in his pocket.

For a time, Gordon seemed to have Duke checkmated because Gordon knew a secret. Duke's family was messy. His sister was severely schizophrenic, his niece similarly disturbed. Gordon knew that kind of thing ran in the family.

Everyone knew Duke had his eye on being chief of police. Rumor had it that he was readying for a mayoral bid soon. That kind of position went to people who had others in their pockets—and no whispers of mental illness whirling about their heads.

Dana looked directly at Garcia. "You should have led with that. I wouldn't have had to talk to you," she said, throwing his curveball right back at him. She turned to Marty. "Let's pay the chief a visit, shall we?"

"If you say so," Marty said warily.

As they turned away, Garcia reached for his phone. Maybe they'd called his bluff. Maybe he was texting Duke right then. Duke hated surprises, always wanting the upper hand. Gordon had taken that from him, and for a time, he'd gone quiet.

But recently, Dana had been wondering if her ace in the hole, Duke's family secret, was all that much of an advantage when, in order to play it, she had to sit at the poker table with a psychotic.

"You're not really gonna ask Duke if he's sandbagging us, are you?" Marty asked, his voice low, as they approached the chapel entrance.

"Not in so many words, no," Dana said. "But he's been content to leave us more or less alone for almost half a year. Now we're running into his people left and right."

"Could be a coincidence," Marty said.

The front door was at street level but behind a thick concrete island where a row of young trees grew, their branches winter bare. That was perhaps a new addition, built after Charlie plowed a car through the front doors, to keep anything like that from happening again.

"No such thing as coincidences," Dana replied as she pushed open one of the heavy wooden doors.

The cold light of winter seemed to stop at the front doors of the chapel. Inside under soft lighting, wooden pews the color of dark honey sat empty but expectant, facing an altar that had the look of a ghost-lit stage. The cross behind the altar was tinged in red by light filtering through a stained-glass window high above, which depicted Jesus frocked in red with arms outstretched, ministering upon a small hill. The silence was soft and heavy.

A voice from one side, stern and loud, made Dana jump and Marty spin: "Can we help you?"

Two young men were seated in metal chairs against the wall aside the entrance. Dana and Marty had walked right past them. They stood slowly, and although Dana couldn't see any weapons on them, they had the confidence of men with firepower, as though they were perhaps better suited for the hard corners of the Bermuda Triangle a few blocks over. They were dressed in heavy coats, dark jeans, and stomping boots. They wore skull caps of thick black wool. One had an eye patch.

"We're looking for..." Dana paused.

They were looking for a few people at this point. *Who first? Tasha Cunningham? Charlie?*

"They're likely here with the chief," someone replied confidently from down the aisle, near the altar. A man walked their way with the slow confidence of someone who owned the place. He was broad, but his silhouette tapered, not unlike a coffin. "You'll have to forgive the extra security, but given our history with Charlie Cunningham, we can't be too careful."

He came to rest in front of them. He wore a fitted three-piece suit of dark wool as comfortably as Warden Abernethy had worn his track suit. His black skin was freckled at the eyes, his hair closely cropped and flecked a disarming gray. He held a fedora by the brim in one hand, and an overcoat hung over the opposite arm. He took one look at their badges and nodded to himself before shifting his fedora to his left hand and offering a handshake. "I'm Josiah Hill, senior pastor at New Hope. Warren and I were just finishing up. It's never a good day when your job suddenly becomes police business, but I'm not sorry for the extra eyes on our humble home here."

Dana considered rolling with it, playing like she was supposed to have been here all along, but a second shadow emerged from the door beside the altar, a tall man in a dark sports coat, with a golden ring on his pinkie that flashed in the low light. Warren Duke paused in the act of buttoning his jacket as soon as he saw them. The whites of his eyes narrowed, and his unnaturally tanned face darkened further.

Warren Duke quietly walked down the aisle as Dana shook Hill's hand. He stopped just behind the reverend and said nothing but simply watched and listened, head barely moving, like a rattlesnake emerging from its den.

Dana took a straightforward approach. "We're actually following up on a lead. Trying to get a location on Tasha Cunningham."

The reverend's face flashed with momentary uncertainty as he turned toward Duke, apparently waiting for some sort of confirmation.

Duke shook his head. "They aren't here with me, Reverend," he said, his voice even. "I told you that you should have a lock on that door."

Josiah looked at Duke a moment longer, during which Dana badly wished his back wasn't turned to them, so that she could see what passed between them. When he turned around again, his face was composed once more. "Who am I to lock the house of God?" he said by way of answer then waited in comfortable silence, as if expecting Dana's validation.

Dana felt strangely compelled to give it, finding herself nodding, even.

"These fellas look like a pretty good lock to me," Marty said, still eyeing the two men, who stared back unflinchingly.

Josiah looked upon them with pride and rotated his fedora slowly in his hands. "Brother Alonzo and Brother Dameon are here because of Tasha," he said. "You said you were following up on a lead, Officer..."

"Frisco. Sergeant Dana Frisco," she said, although without her usual vigor.

"Sergeant Frisco," he replied, nodding as if he'd known her for years. "I'll do you one better. Tasha Cunningham is here. We've offered her a home in the church house ever since Charlie was arrested."

Duke put his hands on his hips and looked up at the rafters, his lips a thin line.

"Wait, she's here?" Marty asked, pointing at the ground. "Now?"

"Yes," Josiah said.

"Can we talk to her?"

"No," said Duke. "She's fully aware of the situation with her brother. She hasn't been in contact with Charlie and has nothing more to say on the matter. We've questioned her thoroughly."

"That might have been nice for me to know, Chief," said Dana, "seeing as this falls under my jurisdiction."

"I tell you what falls under your jurisdiction, Sergeant," he said, his voice suffused with simmering anger. He stepped close enough that Dana could smell the sharp punch of his cologne like expensive leather. He ticked off on his fingers. "You missed the truck. You missed the car swap at the airport. You're just *now* following up with Tasha? To the extent we know anything, it is because of *my* people."

Josiah held out his hat as if gently wiping the air between Dana and Duke clear. "Now, Warren. This isn't the place. I'm sure Sergeant Frisco is only trying to help."

For the first time since she could remember, Warren Duke did as he was told. He backed away, although the sound of him breathing through his nose seemed to echo off the altar.

"Warren is correct, though," Josiah said. "Tasha has always been... fragile. She doesn't know where Charlie is. She's scared. We just want to keep her safe."

"Safe from whom?" asked Dana.

"From Charlie, of course," Josiah said, looking down briefly, as if in suffering solidarity. "Tasha wanted out, all those years ago. Out of the hell that her brother was just getting into. Charlie didn't like that. She came to New Hope for help. Charlie didn't like that either. I'm sure you know what happened next."

"You got a new concrete planter," Marty said.

Josiah chuckled. "Yes, we got a new concrete planter. And a new bay window. Whole new entryway, matter of fact."

The reverend ushered them toward the door with the brim of his hat. "Why don't you walk out with us," he said.

And before Dana knew it, they were doing just that. She was walking out alongside Marty, following Josiah, with Duke just about pressing them from behind.

Josiah gestured at the dilapidation and grit painting the city blocks in the near distance. "If you have the misfortune to fall on hard times in this place, it's almost impossible to get your head above water again. Especially if you're a woman." He shrugged on his camel-hair overcoat and donned his hat, in no particular hurry, as if confident the world around him would wait. "Now you see, the young men, they end up in jail or dead. But the suffering of young women is prolonged. Lifelong. We try to help if we can."

He stopped them at the sidewalk and turned to face Dana fully. "We'll take good care of her. Don't worry. But the sooner you can get Charlie Cunningham somewhere he isn't a danger to himself and others, the better. Nice meeting you, Sergeant. You too, Detective. Wish it was under other circumstances."

With that, Josiah walked away, toward an old black town car parked on the sidewalk with REVRND on the vanity plate. Dana knew they'd been redirected, ushered out, and essentially told never to return, but Josiah had a way of doing it that made her feel as though she'd accomplished something and was leaving of her own accord. She'd been snake-charmed.

Duke, on the other hand, didn't give a shit about charming her or anyone else that got in his way. He came up beside her and stared her down out of the corner of his eye. "Josiah is a polite man. A man of God. I am not. I'll tell you this. You fucked up three times now, and I have it documented. When this is all over, your file will finally be big enough that no wrongful termination lawsuit in the world will hold up. And then I'll have you out on your ass."

He lingered.

"Or?" Dana asked.

Men like Warren Duke always had an *or*.

"Or you just let my people take over wherever Josiah Hill is concerned, while you go back to the midlevel bullshit you're best at," Duke said. "And maybe you keep your job."

Warren Duke walked away, toward where Garcia was waiting. He paused by Marty and sized him up. "You backed the wrong horse, Detective."

"We're a team, right, Chief? One big, happy family," Marty said, not quite squaring him up but facing him fully.

Duke snuffed once like a bull then walked to Garcia's cop car and got inside. Neither man looked their way as they passed by.

Dana and Marty found themselves alone together on the sidewalk outside New Hope. A siren wailed somewhere in the distance. The throaty sound of cars revving through a part of town where nobody wanted to stop carried clearly through the cold air.

"That went about as well as I thought it would," Marty said.

"I'm not done with this," Dana said.

"I know."

"What's her name?"

"Who?"

"Your girlfriend."

Marty scratched at the five o'clock shadow already darkening his jaw. "Brooke."

"Brooke. Nice name," she said.

"She's a nice girl," he replied, and his genuine smile warmed her, a sip of hot coffee on a cold day—especially after New Hope. No matter how "open" New Hope claimed to be, she'd found no warmth there at all.

"I'd like to meet her sometime," Dana said.

"If things keep going strong, hopefully, you will," said Marty.

They crossed the street and parted ways to their cars. Dana wanted to do some thinking. Marty said he probably had enough time to do a full cycle at his home gym before Brooke came over for dinner.

They were going on the paleo diet together. He said he'd hit a limit with his BMI and read somewhere that paleo might help him break through. Dana told him to have fun with that.

On her drive home, Dana thought about Marty and Brooke—who, in Dana's mind, was beautiful and probably a yoga instructor or personal trainer, maybe both—dancing around Marty's tiny kitchen, cooking plants and nuts and seeds, which made her smile. She kept her mind there in that place because she didn't want to think about Gordon not being at her home when she got there, maybe not being there for a little while. She tried not to think about how he'd wanted to do a little cooking of his own for her, a wonderfully odd thing for him to propose, and she had ushered him out.

She'd done so to keep Chloe and Maria safe, but still... it felt wrong.

Most of all, she didn't want to think about how Warren Duke was right. She'd missed the truck and missed the car swap, and she was slow on the Tasha lead, so slow that Victor Garcia had gotten there first. She was better than that. Or she used to be, anyway, before a sliver of shrapnel had slipped past her skull and put her in a coma.

Whispers of doubt crept closer, moving in like a cat when her head was turned. Whispers told her that piece of shrapnel had severed something integral inside, something that made her the good cop she used to be, the cop that had rescued that little girl from the dumpster and later carried her, battered but alive, from the old theater. Whatever it was that used to give her that quick jump off the line seemed to have deserted her.

She feared she was going dull at precisely the time she needed to be razor sharp.

So Dana turned up the classic-rock station in the minivan and pictured Marty dancing in his kitchen with a girl he liked. Eventually, she was smiling again. She could still keep that fear—all too familiar now—at bay a little while longer. But she knew she couldn't shut it away forever.

CHAPTER NINE

According to Andy Bagshot, Maranatha High School wasn't very different from Ditchfield. Both were big brick institutions. Both held bunches of kids in little rooms and made them do stuff they didn't want to do. As a matter of fact, regarding looks, Ditchfield beat Maranatha High hands down. Ditchfield manor was a historic place. Maranatha was just big and squat and dirty, like an old airplane hangar.

Both places had another thing in common as well: They both employed Andy Bagshot. And for much the same job, keeping the boys—and girls—in line.

Andy picked up a shift a week at Maranatha on his day off for a little more drinking money. He'd been throwing a bit too much cash at the cam girls recently. Not that it hadn't paid off—after dropping two hundred on his favorite, he'd gotten her cell number. That was step one on the way to buying a night with the saucy little whore.

He knew her rates, though. If he wanted to do what he really wanted to do with the dirty bitch, he would need more cash.

His usual heavy hand didn't go over well at Maranatha. He'd nearly lost the gig when he slammed a kid against a locker for being out unattended and mouthing off when Andy asked to see a hall pass. He pressed the little shit up against the cold metal and held him there by the throat until some simpering teacher had threatened to call the police. Andy liked to hold kids up against things, by the throat. At Ditchfield, he liked to press with his baton. Often, he had to tuck a chub up under the band of his pants afterward.

Andy had a thing for throats in general—especially on his cam girls. Cam girl plus baton plus some throat and some pressing action? That was prime spank material. And expensive.

But they'd never fired him from Maranatha for choking that kid, with a chub in his pants. That was good, especially since Abernethy had put him on temp leave for blowing it on night watch with that shit stain, Charlie Cunningham.

No matter. They wouldn't fire him from Ditchfield either. They would dicker and wring their hands and whatnot, but he'd be fine. Nobody fired Andy, for one simple reason. At all those places—institutions that have to deal with creatures that will steamroll the public if they are allowed to—the top brass want someone willing to press on throats.

Never mind that the principal at Maranatha said he was a "visual presence only." Never mind that he was told to keep his hands in his pockets and baton on his belt. The people who ran these places often said these things, but they didn't mean it. Not really.

Still, with all the drama at Ditchfield, he needed this gig.

And even if he had to keep his hands to himself, it wasn't all bad. He was paid twenty bucks an hour to basically stand by the front door and try not to get caught staring at asses. *They certainly didn't make 'em like that back in my day*, he thought, watching a particularly perky gaggle of girls walk past and inside. As far as he could remember, all the girls at his high school had been fat. And even the fat ones wouldn't put out until he'd gotten them too drunk to see.

One of the little sluts turned and caught him looking. Her head zipped right back around, but Andy swore she gave her ass a little extra bounce.

Not bad at all.

The third time a certain car rolled by, Andy took notice. Part of his gig was rounding up the truants that screwed off in the surrounding neighborhoods and nearby park. The truant kids pulled this little trick where they walked in and through the metal detectors then right out of the gym entrance out back, where they'd parked their beaters—junk SUVs and rusted-out sedans they drove around until they could find a place out of the way to smoke weed.

Andy recognized most of the cars those kids drove. He knew the usual culprits. But he didn't recognize the one he'd seen roll by three times already, a boring white sedan that looked too clean to belong to any high school kid. He stepped out from under the eaves and followed it as it made its third pass, tracking the same square route, down the street out front, stopping briefly at the stop sign leading into the parking lot, then rolling around the corner and down Clifton Avenue, where it turned right.

Andy couldn't get a good look inside the car. He saw only an outline of the driver: thin, bald or shaved head, and tallish, judging by how close his head was to the roof as he looked out at the schoolyard.

He was looking right at Andy.

The guy's head scanned forward until it found him, and it stayed on him as the sedan made its slow way past the stop sign and around the corner.

Andy had the distinct impression that whoever was driving that car only stopped looking at him when he had to physically turn around in the driver's seat—basically at Clifton, where he turned right.

That meant he'd be coming around again.

Andy flicked his baton from his belt and walked slowly across the front entrance to where the parking lot started. He knew he was supposed to be hands off, but he didn't take too kindly to being mean mugged by some pussy hiding inside his car. All those kids were the same—hard-asses until they got punched in the face. He decided to walk out to the parking lot and wait for the kid to pass again, to let him know who was boss or, at the very least, to get a good look at him for later.

Andy's breath puffed and hung in the still, damp air, disturbed only by the lazy spin of his baton.

The car made almost no sound as it rolled around the bend into sight again, nothing like the rattles and chugs most of these kids' cars made. It looked like a rental—no plates, even. Maybe it was Andy's lucky day and the kid was driving a stolen car and he could finally put his baton back to use. He'd been itching twice as bad since Abernethy told him he had to cool it. Funny how that worked.

The car rolled to a slow stop at the stop sign. Andy stepped down into the parking lot and flipped off the driver. He was only mildly surprised when the car made a languid right-hand turn at the four way to move into the lot itself.

Andy smiled. So it was some truant kid after all. And he wasn't even putting up a fight. He squinted to try to see through the windshield, but the glare through the clouds above reflected right at the spot over the driver's face. Andy motioned with a single finger to tell the kid *get the hell over here if you know what's good for you.*

The car crept toward him as if the driver was just letting the automatic transmission do the work for him. Andy bade him come, peering as the clouds ran over the windshield, his finger hooking the boy forward until a break in the sky above finally gave Andy a decent look at the driver.

A boy, like he'd thought. Black kid. Thin and gaunt. Nothing special, save for a weird ear.

Even then, Andy didn't put two and two together. As soon as he clocked out at Ditchfield the day Charlie went missing and the cops were out of his face and the physical evidence of the kid running away wasn't immediately in front of him, Andy had set the entire ordeal out of his mind. He did know Charlie was out there somewhere, doing whatever it was degenerate kids like him did, but when Andy wasn't on the clock, Charlie wasn't his problem.

Twenty feet from where Andy stood, the car lurched forward,

and in the two seconds it took the engine to rev to a roar, Andy remembered about Charlie Cunningham.

Andy folded over the hood like he'd been hooked at the belt and yanked on a line. His boots caught under the grill while his arms splayed over it. Charlie stared down at him like he was nothing more than a scrap of paper he was determined to blow off the car.

Andy recognized that look. He'd seen it a few times while looking in the mirror before paying another hundred for the cam whore. Charlie had made up his mind and turned off whatever part of his brain might see Andy as a person.

Still, Andy didn't think he was going to die, not even when Charlie barreled the car up and over the sidewalk and shattered both of Andy's ankles in the process. He was Andy Bagshot, after all. He was on the thumping side of the baton.

The roar of the engine was so loud, and Andy's face so close to it —mere inches of metal away—that he didn't even hear the earth-shaking cacophony as Charlie plowed the sedan through the double glass doors of Maranatha High School. His senses were thrown into such terrified confusion that he felt the forearm-sized shard of plate-glass window spearing his liver as nothing more than a needle of pressure—then his spinal cord was severed as he was slammed into a metal support beam, and he felt nothing at all below the neck.

Andy had the consciousness of a floating head for a few fleeting seconds, just long enough to see Charlie Cunningham looking down upon him before flipping up a hoodie and disappearing.

All Andy could do was blink. So he blinked as fast as he could... then slower... and slower until his eyelids stuck open and his eyes let go of their focus forever.

DANA WAS PEDALING the squeaky spin bike in her basement—trying to keep up with Marty in the workout department when she could— when she got the call. Dispatch described a potential attack at

Maranatha High School. All available officers were requested. The suspect had slammed a car into the front entrance and was currently still at large. One casualty was confirmed—a security officer named Andy Bagshot.

She was out the door, sweat still dripping down her face, before the bike had even cooled down.

When she arrived on scene, Maranatha High was still in chaos. Dispatch said half of the students had fled to an abandoned parking lot across Clifton Street, while the other half was apparently still inside, barricaded behind classroom doors. They were awaiting an all clear from the Baltimore Police.

Three squad cars were there, junior officers from the northern district patrol division. They were trying to enter the building and fielding panicked questions from the staff in the parking lot at the same time, and they didn't look particularly happy about either job. She beat Marty to the scene, but he was on his way. That's what he got for living in his hip neighborhood across the city instead of in cookie-cutter suburbia up north like her.

Dana's hair was bunched up atop her head in a sweaty mess, and she wore a still-damp workout shirt from some police benefit years before over baggy sweatpants, and the cops looked blankly at her. When she showed her shield and rank, they visibly sagged, as if thrilled to have someone more senior to make the decisions.

She pulled her gun from her holster and left the rest of her rig in her car. "I'm going in," Dana said. "Who's coming with me?"

A pair of the patrolmen pulled away from the crowd and briefed her as they approached the wreckage.

"We were first on scene. After the initial attack, nothing. No shots fired," said one cop.

"Any sign of the suspect?" she asked.

"Car's empty. That's as far as we got."

"All right, keep your weapons out but down," Dana said. "I don't think this is an active-shooter situation, and we don't want to turn it into one."

The patrolmen looked at one another as they walked toward the school, confused. One seemed about to press for further details, but then all three came upon Andy Bagshot's shoes at the lip of the sidewalk, and whatever questions anyone had went out the window.

They followed the thickening trail of blood.

The car door was open, the airbag deployed. Dana could see no blood inside the cabin. Charlie had likely prepared for the impact, but an airbag to the face hurt, no matter what. He would be smarting from the collision as well, but nothing like what had happened to Andy Bagshot.

Andy looked like he was in the middle of a particularly difficult wall-sit exercise, stuck between a metal column and the hood of the car. His head was back, mouth open, eyes looking blankly at the winter sun overhead. His hands were flat on the hood, as if he'd given it a big hug. From the waist up, he looked almost normal.

The space underneath the car looked like a red Pollock painting. Blood dripped in some spots and streamed in others. Andy's legs were splayed awkwardly, bent at unnatural angles. The skin of his exposed abdomen looked like a paper bag full of smashed strawberries.

A shoeprint marred the crisp edge of one spreading dollop of dark blood on the concrete near Andy's hip, a waffle tread, half in and half out. Dana pictured Charlie standing over his handiwork there, perhaps making sure the light fled from Andy's eyes, hoping that a bit of the pain the man had caused him might flee along with it. She wondered if he felt better after all this... or if he felt nothing at all.

More bloody shoeprints led toward the school.

"C'mon," Dana said. "Inside. Stay alert."

Glass glittered like sand thrown across the floor of the entryway. Dana stepped over the twisted metal of the doorframe ripped from the walls. The doors to the rooms immediately inside were locked and dark, but she sensed panicked bodies behind them. The hallways were permeated by the sounds of muffled crying and urgent whispering. She had a quick flashback to the hallway in the Lexington Heights projects.

"Baltimore Police!" she yelled then listened carefully.

Sometimes, the first callout flushed the birds from hiding—not this time. The frightened whispers redoubled.

"Stay where you are," Dana announced. "We will escort you out room by room once we're sure you aren't in any danger."

The bloody footprints ended at the far end of the front hall, where they blended into the everyday scuffs and smudges of a well-tracked floor. Dana walked over to the last remnants of the waffle print and pushed open a nearby door. She edged her way inside what turned out to be the gymnasium and looked carefully around the room before entering. No students were there. All of them had apparently fled out the open back doors.

Dana crossed the squeaky-clean basketball court, eyes down, scanning for anything. She saw a small smear, a bit redder than the other scuffs. Her pulse quickened as her gut told her Charlie had gone that way. She ran across to the open double doors at the far side, and there she stopped, her spirits instantly drained by the sight of hundreds of kids in the parking lot directly across the street.

She forced herself to slow, scanning the crowd for anything abnormal as she approached the tense crowd, but the whole scene was abnormal. She looked for a tall, thin black kid—maybe in a hoodie or a beanie cap to disguise himself a bit—but she found fifty kids that matched that description nearly enough in one glance.

She slipped her gun into the baggy pocket of her sweatpants and pushed through the crowd, trying to get a good look at as many faces as she could. She scanned for anyone that was limping or wincing or standing aside, alone.

"Charlie!" she yelled, but her voice joined the panic of all the others, blending right in.

And that's what Charlie had somehow managed—again. He'd blended his way right out of Ditchfield, and now he'd blended his way right out of a murder scene.

She should have known better. Charlie was a chameleon. He disrupted a scene then slipped right into the chaos with the practiced ease of a child who had lived within chaos his entire life. The Dana of six months before would have had the patrolmen follow up inside the school while she came right here, right off the bat. The old Dana might have had Charlie Cunningham in cuffs already.

Cars streamed in and out of the main lot and the side lot. Charlie was likely in one of them already, a flathead screwdriver jammed into the key block or spliced wires dangling from the console. Maybe he'd found one with a spare key up in the tire well. Maybe he'd scouted it hours before, to secure a getaway. She should have instituted a cordon around the entire school first thing.

She was disappointed in herself. She'd been sloppy. Sloppy and slow.

Camera footage would be more useful to her than scanning random faces. She wanted to see the school and the parking lot from the moment of the attack on and also earlier in the day. Charlie was likely in a new car, and she needed to know the make and model before Duke blamed her for letting him get away and used it as an excuse to get her fired. He was closing his fingers more tightly around this case, while Dana felt she was losing her grip.

She was right about one thing: Charlie was a killer. Gordon's theory that he was simply a misguided kid with anger issues was shattered, along with the entryway of Maranatha High School and Andy Bagshot's spinal column. That didn't make her feel any better. Charlie would be considered armed and dangerous. Duke would likely brief his officers on the use of lethal force. He'd signed his death warrant the second he killed Bagshot.

More than anything, she wished she could talk to the kid and understand what he was thinking. Maybe all he'd ever wanted was a chance to kill Bagshot. Maybe he'd taken one too many hits from the asshole and decided to forfeit his own life to wipe the man from the planet. Given the life Charlie'd had, she wouldn't exactly blame him.

Or maybe this was part of something bigger.

Maybe the time had come to let Duke have the case, to move back under the safety of her little rock with Chloe and Maria. She could hit up Gordon for that home-made breakfast and let Packman or Garcia or any other Duke bootlicker take care of Charlie.

If she did, she wondered when she would forget the little keychain with Tasha and Charlie, smiling, together, holding each other before Baltimore ripped them apart.

Probably not for a very long time.

Marty's midnight black Charger roared into the parking lot. He hopped out and went immediately to work. People seemed to defer to him without even meaning to. That was the kind of cop she used to be. He didn't bat an eye at the hysterical crowds and didn't seem fazed by the car wreck. Before long, he was crouched by Andy's body, doing good cop work.

From where Dana stood, the car wreck looked surreal, like a jagged rip in the fabric of the reality of the school, a run in the stitching of things. Marty was a solid waypoint, something she could focus on and still feel sane.

She gave one last look around the crowd in the adjacent lot, not even really sure what she was looking for, but feeling as though she had to do something. Nobody seemed to be paying her any attention whatsoever. Her gut told her Charlie was gone.

She walked back toward the main lot, stopping at Clifton to make doubly sure the street was clear. She doubted she'd ever look at an oncoming car the same way again. What an absurd idea a car was, really—a thousand-pound metal box you could rev up to killing speed by pressing down six inches on a pedal.

Cars were weapons, all of them. Weapons were everywhere, and all of them in the hands of anybody over the age of sixteen with half a brain. It struck Dana that driving cars was one of the things everyone took for granted, part of the social contract of the working world, but that wasn't the type of thinking that was good to dwell upon. Otherwise, you'd see how crazy it was, blindly trusting complete strangers to stay in their lanes when one swerve this way or that could mean the end of everything.

Marty was directing an evidence shield to be placed around the car and body. Two officers were pulling a screen tight, creating an open-faced box around where Andy lay, still bleeding. *Smart*, Dana thought. *I should have done that. No need to expose these kids to any more trauma than they've already experienced.*

Marty stepped away and walked toward her as soon as he saw her, removing a pair of latex gloves. "I got the students and staff pairing up with their cars if they have them. I bet we find one missing," he said. "And I requested all security-cam footage for the day, yesterday too. We'll find him."

"He took off inside, but I think he just passed right through the gym and out back again in the aftermath," said Dana. "I lost him. Never really had him in the first place."

Marty tilted his head to get a better look at her, and she met his eyes only with effort.

"You all right?" he asked.

"I'm all upside down about this whole thing," Dana said. "I want Charlie in custody, but not for this," Dana said, gesturing at the screen. "I'm not even sure I'm mad he did it," she added, lowering her voice.

"I get it," Marty said. "I'm having a hard time blaming him too. Bagshot was a special kind of shithead."

"Maybe I'm wrong about the whole thing," she said. "Maybe he only wanted to kill Bagshot after all."

Marty cleared his throat, looked around, and nodded Dana over to one side, by his gleaming car. She followed wordlessly.

When they were out of earshot, he spoke. "About that. I found something on Bagshot. Something I decided not to log as evidence. Yet."

He reached into his jacket and pulled out a plastic baggie. Inside was a business card. He handed it to Dana. One corner looked like it had been dipped in red, but the rest was crisp and clean and looked brand new.

Reverend Josiah Hill – Elder and Senior Pastor
New Hope Community Church

On the reverse of the business card was the number one, hand drawn in pen and circled.

"This was tucked between the buttons of his shirt. Andy didn't put it there."

It was a message from Charlie, then, perhaps meant for the Baltimore Police or whoever else followed up on Bagshot's death.

"The start of something," Dana said, thinking aloud.

"Maybe. I can't help but think 'strike one,' like we're not getting something. And another fastball is about to come down the pipe," Marty said, looking back at the screen.

Rapid-fire camera flashes illuminated the outlines of the CSI squad within.

Point taken, Charlie, Dana thought. New Hope was at the center of this. That much was clear. Dana had felt as much since that unsettling run-in with the reverend and Duke the day before. Something was off about that place. *But if Charlie knew something they didn't know, why not tell the cops?* Hell, he could pick up the phone and get Dana on the line any time he wanted.

But he hadn't. Instead, he'd left a calling card at a murder scene. At great cost to himself.

For Dana, the first step toward figuring out what Charlie had to say about New Hope was understanding why he couldn't say it. And she needed to figure it out soon. If Charlie did have a list and if that list was somehow related to the cards in his possession when he was shipped to Ditchfield, the next person he targeted through his windshield could be Gordon.

CHAPTER TEN

When Dana told Gordon that Charlie Cunningham was most likely a killer after all, he did not take the news well. Gordon hadn't thought Charlie was capable of murder, maintaining that Charlie's assault with the car at New Hope was a cry for help. And he was dead wrong.

As soon as Dana finished detailing how Charlie had run Bagshot down at Maranatha High School, Gordon went over to his scotch cabinet and poured a finger of one of the crappy blends he had at the back—he thought he wouldn't deserve a single malt for a long time—and downed it in one go. He paced for a time, wondering where he'd gone wrong. One thing Gordon did know: Charlie had gotten to this point in large part because Gordon had failed him.

Then he found himself back at the liquor cabinet, with another finger of cheap scotch, which he downed in another go.

Things devolved from there until he ended up in his converted broom closet, surrounded by patient files from that public-school study—both Charlie's and others—burying himself in his past to try to find some blueprint to navigate his present. The files were remarkably thin. Soon enough, an empty bottle of scotch was sitting on the floor, with two pieces of his World's Best Doc novelty pencil beside it. He'd cracked it in half after his second drink.

Ethan Barret had given him that pencil after he helped spare the kid from Ditchfield. *Funny how quickly our wins are forgotten in the face of our losses,* Gordon thought drunkenly.

Time had gotten away from him. He'd missed two appointments with his regular, everyday clients. They didn't kill people with cars and actually helped pay his bills, but what had started with rehashing Charlie's case turned into falling down the rabbit hole of the last year of his marriage, and he didn't feel like seeing anyone just then.

The responsible half of his brain was psychoanalyzing the drunk and anxious side, which was likely in the middle of a minor break-down. He had the odd sensation of sitting in his chair and scribbling notes about himself.

Hmm, yes. The scotch. That's always step one, isn't it?

You're thinking of your ex again, aren't you? You're fully capable of handling this yourself, but maybe you'll give Karen a call to talk this all out anyway? Step two.

You're a good psychiatrist, and you know it, but you snapped that pencil in half because you'd prefer to wallow, and now you smell like a dirty distillery. Attractive. And you know Dana loves you, but now you're wondering what the hell she sees in you anyway, aren't you? That's step three. And we've arrived at our final stop of the evening: Full-blown Self-loathing. Congratulations, Gordon. Punch your ticket on the way out.

Knowing the clinical roots of his own anxiety didn't make pulling himself out of a spiral any easier. Ten years at Hopkins then another ten of talking kids off ledges only made his insights into his own neurosis crystal clear—high def.

So he sat in his boxer shorts on a document box with his laptop hot on his pasty thighs until the words of Thomas Brighton from five years before danced to the forefront of his muddled head: *Did you know that Ditchfield is a nonprofit? You oughta look at their public filings sometime.*

The thing about falling down rabbit holes was that at the bottom of them, one often found more rabbit holes.

He started with Ditchfield's 501c3 filing. The mission statement front and center for the entity legally named the Ditchfield Juvenile Rehabilitation Center made Gordon laugh out loud: Empowering Youth to Live Productive and Law-Abiding Lives.

The financials were sobering. Ditchfield had received eight million dollars in donations in the last fiscal year. Brighton wasn't kidding when he said the place was connected.

New donor-disclosure laws allowed many nonprofits to redact donor specifics—Ditchfield included—but Gordon was a pro at navigating old city databases, and he managed to find some older 990 filings that had been spared redaction.

The documents weren't fully digitized, so the online search function didn't work, but Gordon scrolled through page after page anyway. He almost missed what he was looking for because his hangover was well and truly set in, and his eyeballs felt like they were scraping against his eyelids. He left his closet to go the bathroom and get some water, and when he came back, the answer was right there on his screen: a list of donor organizations to the Ditchfield Juvenile Rehabilitation Center circa 1991. First and foremost was an organization called the New Hope Foundation.

He slapped the screen with his thumb and held up his arms to signal a touchdown. New Hope Community Church—New Hope Foundation. The two had to be connected.

He checked his watch—barely three in the morning. *Plenty of time.* Gordon switched tracks and started digging into New Hope.

The going was much easier, almost too easy. Their most recent org filings spelled everything out clearly. New Hope Community Church was just one part of a much larger organization that included four community centers across Baltimore, as well as a small media company.

Also, Reverend Josiah Hill was more than just the senior pastor of New Hope Community Church. He was listed as CEO emeritus and the current chairman of the board of directors for the foundation.

Gordon felt as though he'd stumbled upon some dark secret—a twisted collusion that somehow validated his belief that Ditchfield was a blight, fed by some thread of poison that had its roots deep in the city... but of course, that was because he knew the truth about Ditchfield.

To anybody else, this paperwork would look like nothing more than a wealthy private foundation supporting an institution that rehabilitated juvenile offenders—responsibly and ethically. The mission statement of New Hope Foundation was suitably vague: Uplifting the Underserved of the City of Baltimore. Ostensibly, that aligned with Ditchfield's.

A simple search showed Josiah Hill front and center in the press, as well. A native Baltimorean—what locals called a "Bawlmer"—he'd been born and raised in the Monument Street area east of Johns Hopkins Hospital, which was gritty and had been even grittier in the late seventies. Hill had worked as a community organizer, canvassing for some of the successful local politicians at the time before putting himself through divinity school on a scholarship.

He had an inspiring story, on the surface, at least. He came back to help clean up the neighborhood where he'd cut his teeth organizing. He lobbied for his people and pulled together enough money to buy property. He'd basically been offered the third congressional district in 1992—running against a banged-up incumbent—but he declined. The *Baltimore Sun* article quoted him as saying he "wanted to focus on grass-roots work with New Hope."

Gordon flipped through article after article.

"Rev. Josiah Hill Receives Honorary Doctorate from Hopkins School of Public Health"

"Hill Spearheads Record Grant for Baltimore Performing Arts
Complex"

"Rev. Josiah Hill Breaks Ground on New Community Center"

"Office of Mayor Receives Crucial Hill Endorsement"

The pictures always showed a well-dressed man of presence, aging handsomely throughout the years, usually complete with a fedora. The camera's flash caught moments of deference to the man. People seemed to look up to him naturally. He was a man who didn't want to be the king but who seemed perfectly happy to name the king.

And he certainly seemed to know what his community needed, from his centers to the church to Ditchfield itself. All to serve—all of it tied up with a neat little bow.

Except for Charlie Cunningham.

Gordon set the laptop down. It was nuclear-level hot on his thighs, and the fan was whining like a dentist's drill. He thought about another glass of scotch, but respectable scotch-drinking time was far in the past, and he didn't want to arm his future self with that shame bullet. *Coffee instead.*

Gordon stood too quickly and felt light-headed. He steadied himself on the wall and closed his eyes while the stars subsided. He wondered when he'd last had a glass of water and decided to get one... with the coffee, of course. When he felt like he could stand again, he opened his eyes and found himself looking at a dusty box labeled Tapes. That was odd because Gordon had stopped taping sessions years before, after concluding it negatively affected patients to know they were being recorded.

The connection had to slog through a thin layer of scotch, but it came, and all the more powerfully.

One stipulation of the consulting project with the Baltimore Public School system was that the sessions be recorded. The school board requested it so that they could audit if they wanted, and it was also a way to limit liability. Gordon was given a little microrecorder and about a hundred cassette tapes. Somewhere in all the paperwork, he'd checked a box asking for them back after a period of time.

He'd forgotten all about them, unsure when they were mailed back, even. He must have been in the depths of the divorce. A lot from that five-year time period before Dana was spotty. That wasn't just because of the booze, either. His mind had been trying to save him from himself by blacking out the details.

Gordon popped the box open and looked inside to find row upon row of tapes, stacked in alphabetical order—last name, first initial. They were dated too. He clasped his hands in thanks. *Credit where credit's due. Shout-out to Karen for being anal retentive.* The handwriting was all hers.

He flipped through the tapes with a rapid *clickety-clack* like a toy train running loops on a track. He stopped when he came to Cunningham, C. and pulled out all of them, five full tapes. Those he took from the dusty half-light of his broom closet into the pitch black of his office proper. He almost tripped over a Chinese takeout box on the way to his desk and had to clear the desktop of clean clothes he'd thrown there instead of folded.

Dana asks you to stay clear and you go into full-on bachelor devolution after barely four days, he thought. *Get it together, Gordon.*

There, in the back of the top drawer, sat his old tape recorder.

He spent the next fifteen minutes looking everywhere for eight AA batteries before finally stealing them from the remotes and all the clocks in the loft. Then he went back into the kitchen, set the recorder down in a sliver of moonlight by his pour-over coffee setup, and pressed Play.

"Hi, Charlie. My name is Gordon. Thanks for talking with me today."

A snort of laughter. The creak of an old school chair.

"I didn't have much of a choice, man. But okay. Sure."

The sound of their voices shot Gordon into the past. His was painful to listen to, weirdly reedy. Charlie's was so boyish that he couldn't believe it came from the same kid who would slam a car into a church mere months later and then, years after, run a man down in cold blood.

"Do you know why you're here?" Gordon asked.

"You talkin' to the bad eggs," Charlie replied, and Gordon could almost hear the air quotes. *"Look, man, I was just checkin' handles. If someone leaves a car door open overnight in Baltimore, they oughta get robbed on principle."*

"I'm not here because of that," Gordon said. *"Well, I mean, I am, in a sense. But not the way you think."*

Gordon shook his head as he poured coffee beans into the grinder. He sounded half as confident as the fourteen-year-old boy.

"We're just trying to figure out if there's a way that BPS can help you and other kids like you that seem to have a lot of run-ins with the cops. That's all."

Gordon paused the tape and turned on his bean grinder, packed with nineteen grams of single-origin coffee beans from some shady spot on a hill in Guatemala that he wished he was sleeping on right then. As the burr smashed the beans to pieces, he thought about the interview. More was coming back to him. For a while, Charlie had deflected. Gordon was fairly sure Charlie was simply happy to have something to do. Bright children were like that.

Gordon fast-forwarded the tape. He would give the whole thing a listen later, but right then he was just trying to jog memories loose, to get a sense for the time and place. Quite frankly, he wasn't sober enough for a thoughtful listen. He stopped the tape randomly—a satisfying *thunk*—then set about filling up his electric gooseneck kettle, programming it to heat to 197 degrees. The temp readout glowed red in the dark of his makeshift kitchen, slowly climbing. While it heated, he pressed Play.

"—suspended a few times for fighting. Quick and brutal stuff. Then you get picked up for the door-check thing," Gordon was saying. *"Were you trying to steal a car?"*

"You think I'm gonna cop to an attempted felony on tape?"

"This is covered under patient client privilege. Nothing you say to me can ever be used against you."

That single laugh again. Then quiet. *"Yeah fuckin' right. That shit don't exist for people like me."*

The electric kettle clicked off at 197, just before boiling. Gordon flattened a Hario filter in his V60 ceramic and set it atop a tempered-glass carafe. Then he wet the filter to wash it of its paper taste.

"All right then, how about this? What's running through your head when you do this stuff?" Gordon asked.

"Nothing."

"Nothing? Nothing at all?"

Gordon tapped the ground beans gently into an even layer on the damp filter. The reasons Karen might jump to sociopathy weren't hard to see. But she'd only listened to the tapes. She hadn't been in the room. Gordon clearly remembered a pause, a moment before Charlie said "nothing" that told Gordon it wasn't nothing.

As Gordon recalled, Charlie dodged a bunch of questions then just got up and left not long after. He popped the tape and flipped it over. While fast-forwarding for a bit, he wet the grounds then let them sit. Steam wafted lazily in the filtered moonbeams passing through the skylight.

He pressed Play and started a slow pour from the kettle, keeping the hot water just above the grounds. Pour, stop. Pour, stop.

"—don't you worry 'bout me, man. I ain't the one you need to worry about. I make my own help." Charlie was midconversation.

"Who should I worry about then?" Gordon asked.

"The people you don't see. The people that don't got the strength to help themselves," Charlie answered.

Silence. Then Gordon was tapping faintly on a pad of paper. The sound mixed almost seamlessly with the slow drip of the coffee into the carafe. Gordon was on autopilot in both cases, thoughts surfacing, memories rising.

"You went to the hospital last month. Ended up on the wrong end of a fistfight with a kid named Alonzo Cook," Gordon said.

Silence from Charlie. Then he said, *"Can't win 'em all."*

"School report said you were silent on why it happened. But others there said it started on account of some words Alonzo said." The fluttering of Gordon flipping papers.

"They all start because of words," Charlie replied, flippant.

"About Tasha," said Gordon.

Gordon froze, the pour-over half done. The softly rising steam was the only movement in the kitchen. Charlie was remaining silent, but Gordon remembered that moment in all its clarity. He'd expected the boy to dodge the question with more flippancy, to keep messing with the peeling paint on the desk, but instead he stilled and looked directly at Gordon, right into his eyes. Unblinking, he just stared like that until Gordon was forced to speak to kill the odd silence.

"Is your sister one of the people I should be worrying about? Who can't help themselves?"

More silence—longer that time.

"No." Charlie said eventually. His voice was cold, flat. *"She got me, don't she?"*

At the time, Gordon thought the boy was angry with Tasha, too, just like he was angry at everything. Karen maintained he wasn't angry at anything and that was the whole problem. He felt nothing.

Again, Gordon saw how she might have gotten that, listening to this without the perspective Gordon had. Those last words Charlie had offered him, sitting across the plexiglass at the Ditchfield visitor's room, rang in his head. He'd spoken them as if under duress, like a POW interviewed on camera in a hostile land: *find Tasha.*

He wasn't angry with Tasha at all. He was terrified for her.

Gordon looked down at the coffee as if surprised to find it there. He started his slow pour again, cursing softly. He'd exposed the grind too long, and it would be slightly bitter. But slightly bitter pour-over was still better than nothing at four in the morning when one needed to think. He was looking for that perfect balance of being loose enough to make the mental jumps he needed and focused enough to stay on target.

Charlie excused himself. *"I got no more time for this today. When are you done with your little experiment, anyway?"*

"Another two weeks, then we'll wrap up. Hopefully have enough to get funding for some more counselors in here," said Gordon, undaunted.

Charlie laughed again, that single soft note, a laugh that said another couple of counselors wasn't gonna cut it. At the time, Gordon had written it off as teenage attitude and a healthy dose of reality. The school had a single overworked counselor who also doubled as a case worker, and one man could never attend to the needs of all those kids.

Now, Gordon had a different read. Charlie was angry with a system he knew could do nothing for him, because he had a big problem, one that threatened his sister.

Gordon sipped his coffee as quickly as he could without scalding his lips. He needed more information. His mind was tapping its wristwatch, saying they didn't have much time left. But so was his tired body, saying no amount of caffeine was going to save him from four heavy-handed pours of scotch on no sleep.

Gordon spent the next hour skipping through the tape, but all he got was that Charlie became increasingly distant as their sessions rolled on. By the end, he'd said very little. In their last session together, Gordon had asked Charlie if he was grateful for anything, a question spurred by Karen, who still classified the boy as a sociopath. At the time, Gordon had been doing research into the science of gratitude.

"Anything at all?" Gordon asked. *"Even if it's just one thing."*

The thinking was that a grateful kid couldn't be a sociopath, by definition. In fact, gratitude therapy was being tested as a method for rewiring the dormant areas in the amygdala of actual sociopaths.

He never got an answer, just that single-note laugh.

The question struck Gordon as particularly naïve now. Mere

weeks after the end of the recording, Charlie Cunningham would be taken from the wreckage of the entryway of New Hope Community Church to a holding cell at the city jail, then straight to Ditchfield's Pod D.

Suddenly, nothing was standing between Charlie's big problem and Charlie's twin sister anymore.

CHAPTER ELEVEN

Gordon awoke to knocking at the front door of his office. He'd fallen asleep on his couch, holding limply onto his coffee cup, and when he startled awake, the dregs spilled on his crotch. He stood, and his phone fell from his lap directly onto the corner of the coffee table with a solid smack that made him wince.

The knocking continued.

"Hold on!" he yelled. "Just a minute!"

His contacts felt dry and tacky. He rubbed at his eyes and checked his phone. He saw he'd missed five calls from Dana and one from Karen. It was also two in the afternoon. He'd been dead to the world all day. Dana would be understandably pissed. The call from his ex-wife, though—that gave him pause.

"Gordon! Are you in there?" Dana was at the door.

"Coming!" he replied.

He threw on a robe and hastily tied it while making his way downstairs. He smoothed the frazzled remnants of his hair and opened the door. She was standing with her hands on her hips, staring at him as if dumbfounded by his general being.

"Why don't you *ever* answer your phone?" she asked.

"I was up late, going through Charlie's files," Gordon said. "And drinking a fair bit of scotch," he added guiltily.

Dana rushed in and slammed him into a hug. "Thank God you're safe. I thought you were dead. I mean, not really, but a little bit."

Gordon patted her on the back and took in the glorious smell of her clean hair. "A little bit dead?" he asked.

Dana pulled away, held him at arm's length, and tried not to crack a smile. She scanned him up and down once more, stopping at his crotch.

"That's coffee," said Gordon. "I promise."

Dana nodded and pushed inside, already on to the next. "This Cunningham case is messing with my head. Marty looked at the tapes and figured out that Charlie boosted a white SUV from the Maranatha lot. I kept picturing you half underneath every white SUV on the road, pasted to the hood like one of those Halloween decorations where the witch is wrapped around a tree."

Gordon followed her in, thinking he probably should've opened a window. "Sorry about the mess."

Dana went to the couch, tested the cushion, found it wet with coffee, then pushed over a pizza box and sat on the other side. She sank to the couch, huffing out and leaning her neck back, arms flopped and palms up. "I've seen worse. You should see what Chloe can get up to in three days. I'm just glad you're alive. That's my bar these days. Marty and I have been trying to piece together all these threads while crisscrossing the eastern district. Duke has every able-bodied cop on the lookout for this car."

"He's not gonna find it," Gordon said. "Charlie's too smart for that."

"I know," she said. "Marty found him on tape, casing the parking lot two hours before he hit Bagshot, checking handles, prepping his getaway. He has no intention of getting caught this time around."

"He has a bigger plan," added Gordon.

"Yeah, knocking off everybody he thinks is responsible for making him miserable at Ditchfield, which likely includes you. Then what?

Disappearing with his sister, maybe?" She closed her eyes and rubbed at her temples.

"Hard to say." Gordon moved over to the sink and poured a glass of water. He took a big sip to wash down the fuzz of the morning.

"That's the story Duke is pushing, anyway. He had a press conference about the wreck this morning. Charlie is a 'dangerous criminal' who is 'out for revenge' and will be met with 'lethal force,'" Dana said, using air quotes.

Gordon took another drink. "Pretty cut and dry. Nothing more to see here. That's a Warren Duke special. Maybe that's why I don't like it," he said. *All wrapped up in a nice little bow.*

Dana held up a plastic sandwich baggie with what looked like a bloody business card inside. "I told you about the card from New Hope, but I didn't tell you that there's a number on the back. One. As in 'one of many.' And one of them could be you."

Gordon took another sip. He understood her point. He'd essentially given up on Charlie when he gave up on everything else after Karen left him. He didn't mean to abandon him, but that's what ended up happening. He wouldn't blame Charlie for holding a grudge against him. And since Charlie was now a killer, by all rights, Gordon should be looking over his shoulder.

But he still had time, a small window of time, to maybe make things right. And that was overpowering his fear.

"I need to see Tasha Cunningham," he said.

"Marty and I tried. She's under lock and key at New Hope Community Church," Dana said.

"No, like *see her*. I need to see her with my own eyes."

"I told you we tried."

"You're a sergeant in the Baltimore Police Department, and Marty is Detective Beefcake. What do you mean *tried?* What happened?"

Dana looked squarely at him. "You know that's not how it works, Gordon."

Gordon held out a placating hand. He'd overstepped. "I know. I'm sorry."

"And you should give Marty more credit," Dana said. "He's a good guy. And a great cop. He saved your life."

"I'm sorry," Gordon said, absently rubbing at his scarred knee. "I know he is. That was harsh. But I'm feeling a little harsh. This shouldn't be this hard. We're missing something."

"What *happened* was Warren Duke. And Reverend Josiah Hill," Dana said, standing.

Gordon stood straight, his water forgotten. "They were together?"

"Yeah. Duke was his usual asshole self, but this Hill guy... he's a real piece of work. Had us out the door and basically apologizing for disturbing him before we really knew what hit us. He's that kind of man," Dana said, disappointment in her voice. Gordon knew she'd had her fair share of manipulation at the hands of powerful men and didn't much care for it.

Something was wiggling in the back of Gordon's mind, a sticky piece of memory from the night before. He drummed his fingers on the counter.

"The guy's some sort of powerful community figure," Dana said. "Makes sense that Duke would want him on his side if he really is planning a run for mayor. God help us," she added, crossing herself.

Gordon moved past the couch and back upstairs. He needed his laptop.

"Duke," he said. "I saw Duke somewhere. Not Warren, though."

He popped open the computer and plugged it in. It was mercifully cool after having worked overtime on his lap. His tabs were still open. He clicked through them and landed on the Articles of Incorporation for the New Hope Foundation. He scrolled wildly, the pages flitting by, trying to remember where he'd seen what he half remembered. That had been solidly into the fourth glass of scotch.

He slowed, blurring his vision a bit. He remembered big blocks of text, just like... *there*. He stopped on the Members of the Board.

Rev. Josiah Hill was there, up top. But below him, Gordon found what he'd caught: Archibald J. Duke, member of the board of directors.

"What's Duke's dad's name?" Gordon called downstairs.

"His dad? I don't know. Probably some east-coast blue-blood thing like Higgledy-Piggledy the Third."

"He's the guy with the big-time shipping business out on the docks, remember?"

After a moment, Dana replied, "Archie, maybe? That sounds right."

Another puzzle piece clicked into place in Gordon's mind. The picture was still blurry, but the edges were coming together. He had the borders.

Gordon walked back to the stairs and paused, forcing himself to take them slowly. His knee was already aching, and the day was way too early for that. He'd done himself no favors using it as a computer stand all night.

"He's on the board for the New Hope Foundation. Archibald J. Duke. They're all connected," Gordon said.

Rather than firing her up, that seemed to weigh Dana down. She deflated another inch into the couch. "Of course they are," she said. "They're all connected. It's been that way forever, and it's never going to change."

Gordon limped over behind her and put a hand on her shoulder. He thought about the ring still in the breast pocket of his old tweed blazer, hung on the rack upstairs. He'd patted the pocket every time he passed, as if it might somehow jump out and hit the road if he wasn't careful.

"You okay, Dana?" he asked.

"Not really," she said honestly. "Ever since the coma, I feel like I've been playing catch-up."

Gordon limped around to face her and eased himself into his chair. He said nothing, only listened.

"I'm not sure I can do this anymore," Dana said. "I've mostly slowed Marty down for this whole investigation. I think that explosion took something from me."

"It likely did," Gordon said simply, and before the hurt in Dana's eyes manifested into something too real, he added, "But not the way you think." He tapped his Frankenstein knee. "In medicine, this is what they call a *good* recovery. I can get around just fine, but you and I know I'm not going to be jogging to catch the train anytime soon. You had what they call a *full* recovery. It's possible that there might be some very mild cognitive dissonance every now and then, headaches and the like, but I saw the brain scans, and I took them to some of my colleagues, and every one told me the same story. Fully recovered."

Dana crossed herself again then dropped her hands to her lap. But she still seemed defeated. Gordon sought her eyes and found them.

"What I'm saying is the physical damage we've taken isn't gonna be what stops us. I've got a working knee. You've got a working brain. They'll do the job just fine if we let them. But the psychological damage is a different animal."

Dana's eyes glistened. Gordon knew how hard she had to be outside the walls they shared. He knew the toll that took on her. He wanted nothing more than to give her a space to be herself when she needed it.

"Life isn't often explosions and house fires," Gordon said. "Mostly, we fight little battles. Every day. Without even knowing we're fighting them. The world likes to chip away at your confidence whenever it can, like a horsefly looking for a place to take a bite. I let the world take big bites out of me for a long time until I was convinced I was a fraud, a nobody standing in the place of a licensed child psychiatrist. It's a real thing. Called imposter syndrome. You can look it up if you want."

"Are you gonna charge me for this?" Dana asked, but a hint of a smile flashed in her eyes.

Gordon kept going. "Then I met you, and we saved a little boy named Ethan Barret, and I thought to myself, 'That's weird. You're supposed to be a hack. But hacks don't help kids, so something must be up,' and I realized that there's no difference between the people who succeed and the people who fail. Not fundamentally. I've been both. It's not about who is *best* for the job, it's about who *does* the job."

Dana looked at him as if trying to see what kept him ticking. He didn't know how to tell her that he was running mostly on fear—fear that he'd sit down and find himself unable to get up again; fear that the man he'd been a year before—the man drowning—was just a few steps behind, ready to jump in and take his place again.

She looked over at his desk, where he kept the framed issue of his published work on sleepwalking, his first accepted article in a major journal. Beside it was one picture of his mother and one of him and Dana, both taken at Waterstones. Gordon thought he looked a bit pallid in both, but he smiled nonetheless every time he looked at them.

"Where's your World's Best Doc pencil?" she asked.

"Oh. I snapped it about two drinks in, last night."

"Why?"

"Because I'm not the world's best doc, obviously. Although I'm working on it."

Dana laughed. "You know that's not how those novelty things work."

"It is for me," said Gordon.

"That's why I love you," she said.

Gordon just took that in for a moment.

"I need to see Tasha Cunningham," he said again.

"Then let's go see Tasha Cunningham," replied Dana. "But first, can you make me one of your fancy coffees?"

"On it."

He started measuring out the beans—nineteen grams for an eight-ounce pour. No more. No less.

~

WHEN DANA PARKED her minivan just off the street of the eerily quiet New Hope block of the eastern district, it was already dark. Marty's Black Dodge Charger was already there, quiet, like a pocket of darker black, waiting to pounce.

"Marty's here?" Gordon asked.

"Of course Marty's here. He's my partner. He's gonna be almost everywhere I am for what is hopefully a very long and fruitful career in law enforcement," Dana said, her tone letting Gordon know quite clearly they didn't have time to press bullshit that didn't matter.

Gordon nodded.

Marty stepped from his car when they emerged. Gordon noted he was sporting his regular look, dark on dark on dark. He had to admit the leather jacket did look good on the guy. It made Gordon rethink his own slightly stained ski jacket, still sporting a lift ticket from a fairly crap day of skiing out in Claysburg, years back.

As he gave Gordon a once-over, Marty looked like he wanted to make a quip of some sort but held his tongue. "Hey, doc," was all he said, his voice low.

Gordon nodded at him, slightly ashamed. Of the two of them, Marty was clearly coming across as the adult, and Dana looked like she knew it.

Marty turned to her. "I'm assuming the warrant for this is in the mail?" he asked cynically.

"Don't need a warrant," Dana said. "According to the good reverend, the house of God is always open, is it not?" Dana spread her arms in mock benevolence.

Marty put his hands on his hips and looked back at Gordon. "This sounds like your idea."

Gordon was about to defend himself, but Dana spoke first.

"My idea too," she said, sliding her firearm into its holster at her side. "And your idea, Marty. You showed up tonight for a reason."

Dana pulled her coat over her gun, and the three of them took in

New Hope Community Church, sitting like a silent white monolith in the dead of night. Despite the soft lighting inside, something about the building, about the whole block, made Gordon's eye want to just pass it by. Someone could easily pass the whole block by. All around them, the eastern district teemed—even in the darkness, the expectant, fraught hush of a living, breathing community was still there. But on this particular block, Gordon felt like he was looking at a set piece.

Marty seemed to sense the unnatural quiet as well—he unzipped his jacket a bit and tapped the slight bulge of his shoulder holster as if to reassure himself. "Well, if we're going, let's go."

They walked across the street and around a concrete island with evenly spaced, bare trees that creaked softly in the barely there breeze of the night. Gordon tried to picture Charlie smashing the front door to pieces, looking for evidence of when a car hung half in and half out of this place, but everything had been patched, all of it carefully and cleanly redone.

At the door, they paused. Dana and Marty seemed reluctant, either professionally or personally, and Gordon understood both. He also understood the need for action.

"I'll do it," he said, gently pushing at the doors. They swung open easily, spilling weak light onto the sidewalk. Marty sidestepped him and entered first, his right hand resting lightly on the teeth of his zipper, inches from the gun inside. Dana held Gordon back with a gentle but firm grip on his shoulder.

After a moment, Marty relaxed, but he still scanned the room with a wary eye.

"Looking for someone?" Gordon asked low.

"Two guys were at the door last time. They didn't exactly strike me as the church-going type, if you know what I mean," Marty said. "But I don't see 'em." He didn't exactly seem relieved about it.

Marty walked in, and Gordon followed. Dana brought up the rear, closing the door behind them with a soft click that felt strangely final somehow. Yet in front of him was a chapel that looked like nothing more than a peaceful and open place of worship. Neat rows of pews sat there, each with a soft accent light at the aisle. A centerpiece of stained glass cast a faint red glow on the cross and altar below. To either side were alcoves where rows of votive candles were lit, their singular flames swaying slowly.

Nothing else moved. Still, Gordon felt an ominous undercurrent to the silence that tugged slightly at him, like the surf sliding back from shore.

"Kind of bizarre, all this just wide open in an area of town where if it ain't bolted down, it gets boosted," Marty whispered.

"Maybe the junkies know better than to mess with this place," Dana replied.

"And where is everybody?" Marty asked.

That, to Gordon, was perhaps the more pressing question. From everything Gordon knew about Reverend Josiah Hill, he was constantly surrounded by the community. His other community centers were always busy, day and night.

"Maybe they know to stay away too," Gordon said. "Right now, at least."

"This way." Dana led them down the left aisle, between the pews, down to where she'd seen Hill and Duke emerge at the side of the altar. She pointed at a small wooden door adorned with an upraised crucifix that read Staff Only.

Marty stepped up and tried the handle. It didn't give. He jiggled it again then leaned on the door. "Guess not every door in God's house is open," he said.

"Want me to kick it down?" asked Gordon. "I mean, I've never done that before. But I don't want to get either of you in trouble."

"Kick it down?" Marty replied. "Gord, your leg would blow up."

"Well, maybe I could kind of shoulder into it or something," Gordon said. "That might not cause permanent damage."

"Shh," said Dana. "Someone's coming."

Gordon froze. He heard it, too, footsteps somewhere behind the door and getting louder. He and Marty stepped back.

Gordon stared dumbly at the door until Dana pulled him quickly aside, and the two of them pressed flush against the right side of the altar. Marty withdrew further to the left, blending into the shadows gathered beyond the reach of the votive candles.

They waited.

A young hard-looking black man emerged, ducking through the door and into the sanctuary. He wore dark jeans and a dark oversized jacket that swished in the silence. He was followed by a second man in an all-black sweat suit with a flat-brimmed Ravens baseball cap and a black eyepatch over his right eye.

"Van's about packed. I'll call the reverend and get going to the barn," said the first. "You watch the door while I'm gone."

The first kept walking up the aisle, but the one with the patch paused as if he forgot something then turned around and opened the door again with a key. He reached inside and around and pulled out a dull black nine millimeter.

Gordon squeezed Dana's hand, and she squeezed back. He looked over at Marty across the room. He knew Marty saw it too. Their options were running out. With every step these men took, another path out of this place disappeared. Dana shook her head furiously at Marty as if she could read his mind, but Marty stepped forward anyway.

"Good to see you fellas again. Dameon and Alonzo, right? I was hoping you might help me out," he said, his tone friendly, his hands out and palms up.

Alonzo brought the gun up and fired twice. The sound punched Gordon's ears, obliterating the silence of the church. The fire of the muzzle painted itself on the inside of Gordon's eyelids, and when he opened them again, Marty was down.

"Shit," said Alonzo, looking down the muzzle of the gun as if surprised to find it there.

"Drop the weapon!" Dana shouted, stepping out and in front of Gordon, leading with her handgun.

Alonzo turned to Dameon, already halfway down the aisle. "Go!" he shouted.

Dameon ran, and Alonzo took that moment to spin around and aim again. Gordon saw the dark metal of the barrel twirl around as if in slow motion. In the reddish light, it cast a shadow that looked a bit like an accusing finger.

Dana fired twice. Alonzo's nine millimeter loosed one more round, as if in animalistic response, but the bullet went high. Alonzo dropped into a moaning heap on the ground, and the gun clattered down afterward. Dameon was already out the front door. Gordon saw him hook left before passing out of view, running full tilt.

Dana ran up to Alonzo, still leading with her gun. He was clutching his right shoulder and seemed to be having trouble breathing, but he was very much aware. Dana kicked the gun away and pushed him down with a hand planted firmly on the other side of his chest.

He moaned again. "You know what..." He took another breath. "You fuckin' done?"

Gordon ran past both of them to where Marty was pushing himself back against the nearest pew. He was hitching for breath that didn't seem to come, pawing wildly at his chest.

"Marty, please," he said although he didn't know where to go from there.

Marty's jacket was in tatters, still half zipped. Blood was running from tiny black specks above the V-cut of his T-shirt, and when Gordon unzipped his jacket, he fully expected to find a ruin of ground meat.

Instead he found a vest of body armor.

Gordon dropped to his other knee and almost collapsed on the man. "Oh, thank God."

Marty grabbed Gordon's arm with one hand, and with the other, he popped the vest open at the buckle underneath his shoulder holster. It came free, and he took in a huge breath.

"The key," Marty said, squeezing Gordon's arm hard. He pointed at the little door.

Gordon looked at the handle of the little door, where the key still dangled, then back at Alonzo. Dana snapped up to them.

"Marty?" she asked, her voice brimming with tremulous hope. "Marty, are you—"

"Go!" Marty said.

Gordon pushed himself up like an old dog and limped over to Dana. He looked down at Alonzo, who was clenching his jaw against the pain—and likely against a string of words he would've liked to fire at all of them. But he'd been trained well, it seemed. Silence was golden.

"He had a vest on," Gordon said, and as he spoke, he still couldn't believe it himself. Somewhere out there in the floating cosmos was a timeline where Marty Cicero got blown to pieces in a church in east Baltimore, and it had almost been their timeline. But it wasn't. And it wasn't their timeline because Marty was a hell of a lot smarter than Gordon had ever given him credit for.

Gordon squeezed Dana's arm. "I'm going in," he said. He hoped his eyes conveyed everything else. He hoped they even conveyed all he wanted to say about the ring tucked safely away in his jacket pocket back at his flat, stupidly unused. But he doubted she saw anything more than the man she'd always seen.

He hoped that was enough.

"Be careful," she said. "I love you."

Gordon turned around without another word, clicked the key into place, and opened the door with his shoulder. He stepped in and left the acrid gun smoke behind, but the ringing in his ears followed him as he made his way down a narrow, dimly lit hall. He heard frantic movement ahead. Heavy things were dropping, and what sounded like a table's worth of metal gear was being shoveled somewhere.

Gordon picked up the pace to what he might call a fast lurch. A door sat open ahead, heavy and steel. Dameon was flitting in and out of view within, shoving things into a bent cardboard box filled to the brim with papers and computer parts. He knew he was in no shape to confront a young man, terrified and possibly armed. If he tried to analyze him with impromptu therapy, he'd get beaten senseless at best. But maybe he could bluff his way through.

"Police!" he shouted. "Get on the ground! Face down, hands on your head!"

That sounded about right. It checked out with the few times he'd seen Dana in action and the hundreds of cop shows he'd watched.

Dameon froze, and Gordon pressed against the far wall, hoping he'd think a burly city cop was barreling down on him and not a forty-six-year-old psychiatrist with a bad knee. Apparently, Dameon didn't care to see either. He grabbed the box and bolted out the back door without so much as one backward glance.

A crunching sound was followed by the slamming of doors. Gordon followed as quickly as he could, navigating a harshly lit office in disarray. When he pushed open the steel double doors after Dameon, the man was already peeling away in an unmarked white van. Tires screeched as he took a corner hard. Gordon waved his way through a cloud of exhaust, limping down the alleyway after the car without really knowing why. Then he remembered the steel doors and reversed course, sticking a leg out just before they closed. He hissed in pain as his shin became a doorstop, but the way back remained open.

Gordon heard sirens in the distance as he pulled open the doors and went inside again.

The office looked like it had been hit by a tornado. It seemed to be a stripped computer lab, with dangling cables and hastily unplugged wires. Dead monitors spread out evenly along a series of desks that faced a blank brick wall. The only other door was white-washed nearly the same color as the brick. Gordon might have missed it if the lock hadn't caught his eye—a big, industrial-grade thing with a throw bolt the size of a ruler. Gordon slid it aside and pulled the door open.

He was met again by the sounds of the night and a small enclosed patio that extended out from the secret doorway. At the far end was a small window leading into what looked like a budget apartment. He pushed through the bones of an overgrown bush and crossed the small, open courtyard as quickly as he could to reach the front door. He tried the handle, fully expecting it be locked, but it was open—his first welcome surprise of the night.

He hesitated even as the door swung easily inward. He caught it and pulled it back then knocked. "Hello? Anyone there? I come in peace."

Silence. Darkness.

He pushed open the door and found a dorm-like living quarters that had the empty echo of fresh abandonment. A common space attached to four rooms, all doors open. A few papers lay on the floor, with some cables and wires strewn about. A heap of what looked like baby monitors was piled in the corner.

Gordon's gut told him Tasha had lived here. Maybe others had lived there too. But they were gone. Gordon popped his head into the nearest bedroom. The walls were dark red, with no windows. Most of the space was taken up by a sagging twin bed, stripped down to a yellowed mattress. More baby monitors sat on the floor. The smell of old sweat mixed with dust raised the small hairs on his neck. The entire area had an air of oppressive sadness, not unlike Pod D at Ditchfield. The longer he looked, the more it glommed on to him. He felt a powerful urge to run.

The sirens were very close, and one wound down, clipped. He heard car doors opening and slamming shut.

Nothing was there any longer but the ghosts. Gordon turned back, crossed the courtyard, and entered the office once more. He saw the computer lab for what it was now: a surveillance station. They'd recorded things there, things those monitors showed.

He eased himself down onto his knees and looked flatly across the floor. Dameon had been hurried. The place probably wasn't as stripped as they wanted it to be. Papers were strewn across the floor.

Maybe Gordon could still salvage this operation and glean some tidbit of info that might help Tasha and Charlie.

He flipped a piece of paper near to hand, a grainy print of a photograph. When he saw the picture on it, his resolve redoubled. He picked the rest of the papers up, all of them, not even looking, only gathering. He jammed papers into his pants pockets, scrunching and folding. Underneath a small pile of receipts in a corner, he found a thumb drive. He pocketed the drive and the receipts, thanked God for small miracles, then left the way he'd come.

Gordon was halfway down the narrow hallway when he heard someone approaching from the chapel side. A series of scenarios flashed through his mind of what might happen if he was found there, and none of them were good.

He about-faced again. A wonky soft-shoe trot took him quickly to the double doors through which Dameon had fled. He pushed them open just as he heard the inner door slam shut. He flipped around outside the doors and closed them as quietly as he could, then he pressed himself up against the frigid bricks of the outer wall of the church.

Gordon took three deep breaths and wiped the sweat from his brow. The freezing night air turned him from hot to cold in an instant. He stepped softly down the alleyway and turned the corner just as he heard the double doors open. He wanted badly to look and see who emerged, but he would've been spotted in an instant. So Gordon kept walking.

He hooked a left then another left then one more until he was nearing the front of the church again. At no point did anything he pass give any indication that a horror-show dorm and an oddly quaint courtyard lay somewhere within. Nobody passing by would ever know, which was exactly how Josiah Hill had likely designed it.

Not for one second did Gordon think the good reverend wasn't completely aware of everything that happened under his roof. Or on his block. Or in his city.

From a shadowed vantage point just around the corner, Gordon watched the scene unfold.

Four police cars and one ambulance were outside. Marty Cicero was being wheeled out on a stretcher, but the head was elevated, and he was sitting up, talking to the medics. Dana came after, followed closely by Warren Duke.

She held up a hand in stoic farewell to Marty. He gave her a thumbs up and pushed it farther out as if to impress it upon her, then the rear doors of the ambulance closed after him.

Dana turned around and faced Duke. He was a good foot taller than she was, and he used all of it to tower over her. Gordon couldn't hear what he said—he knew Duke preferred the low growl—but he got the gist when Duke held out his hand and Dana unclipped her gun and handed it over. She followed it with her badge.

Through it all, she stood with her shoulders back and her head held high, unflinching, even after Duke turned away and stalked off. Gordon had never been prouder of her than at that moment. He had half a mind to run up and propose to her right there, ring or no ring.

The other half of him, the one not soaked in fading adrenaline, told him right then probably wasn't the best time.

He texted Dana: *Around the corner. Meet at car?*

Her phone lit up with the text, and she exhaled into the night. Some of the tension left her shoulders. He realized that, up until that moment, she'd thought he was still trapped somewhere inside that madhouse of a church. *I really do need to get better at the phone-communication thing.*

Gordon waited until the cold from the brick started to seep through his jacket, then he set off toward Dana's minivan, keeping out of the pools of white light thrown by the streetlights. When he got there, Dana was already inside, looking blankly out the window. When he tapped the glass, she started then quickly reached over and lifted the wonky lock on the passenger-side door.

He sat down and put his hands in front of the heating vents. His nose was running. Dana looked at him expectantly, grabbing one of his hands in both of hers. She seemed to be processing, looking for words while her brain raced back and forth over the events of the past half hour. Gordon had no doubt she was in shock.

"Okay," he said. "I'd say that went pretty well."

Dana snorted once then started laughing. Soon, she was crying with laughter. At least, Gordon hoped that's what was happening. She was still holding his hand in a way that suggested a fair number of other tears were in there as well.

"Pretty well?" Dana asked when she was composed enough. "My partner got shot in the chest. Twice."

"Yes, that did happen, but—"

"I'm on unpaid leave. No badge. No gun. That's the first step toward removal for dereliction of duty," said Dana.

"I saw that. And I'm not saying there weren't some hiccups—"

"And for what?" Dana continued, undeterred, her head in her hands.

"For this," Gordon said, taking the picture he'd found and floating it down to rest on the center of the steering wheel.

Dana lifted her head and looked at the print. Then she looked harder, picked it up, and turned it sideways.

"This looks like a glamour shot gone wrong. Is it Tasha?"

"No, I don't think it is," Gordon said.

He'd been looking at it in the cold light of the night while he waited for a clear exit. The woman in the picture was made up heavily—big eyelashes and lips painted as red as apples. Her cheeks sparkled with a blush that was many shades lighter than her skin. But Gordon had seen the pictures Dana had of Tasha—up until almost a year ago—and that was a different woman.

In silence, Dana looked at the picture for such a long time that the weak light of her cell phone clicked off three times, and she clicked it back on again each time.

"I saw cameras," Gordon said after a minute. "And beds."

"How many beds?" Dana's eyes were getting that sheen that

came over her when she saw things that struck her deeply—grave things that affected children.

"Four," Gordon said quietly. "They were... bad. The place smelled like fear."

Dana whispered a prayer in Spanish that Gordon couldn't make sense of, but he felt it was a prayer of lament, one that spanned dialects and languages. Her voice was hoarse and broke at the end. She had probably known since the beginning somehow that Tasha Cunningham was being taken advantage of. She was a lost woman with only one place to turn, and that place had been New Hope.

The tears she cried then—quietly into her hands then into Gordon's shoulder as they sat side by side on the darkest block of their city—were entirely tears of sorrow.

CHAPTER TWELVE

SIX YEARS AGO

Four of the lightbulbs in Thomas Brighton's outdoor chandelier were burned out. Gordon counted them while he waited for Brighton's secretary to answer the door. The chandelier was up high too. He doubted the bulbs would get changed any time soon. He couldn't imagine Brighton in his shiny oxfords and his double-breasted suit fifteen feet up on a ladder. Nor could he imagine the buxom secretary up there in her red heels.

"I don't see a Pope," she replied through the speaker.

"Try Plop," Gordon said, rolling his eyes.

"Oh! Here you are!" she said, buzzing the lock. "Come right up."

The lock snapped back, and Gordon stepped inside. The entryway had been spruced up with a gilded mirror and a vase of fake flowers since his last visit. A small space heater rotated in one corner and smelled faintly of burning plastic.

As he approached, Brighton's receptionist looked up from a gossip rag and smiled around her gum. Her hair looked freshly blasted, so blond it was almost white. "Water?" she asked. "We got some bubbly water too," she added proudly.

"No, thanks," Gordon said, taking a seat in the same chair as before.

He put his head in his hands before realizing that might make him look as strung out as he felt. For the first three weeks Karen was gone, he'd held out half a hope that the phone would ring and she'd say she'd changed her mind. For two weeks after that, he just hoped the phone would ring at all. Then, the previous week, the phone did ring, and it was Karen, and she asked him how he was holding up.

He said not great.

She spoke of the difficulty of processing trauma while within it. She told him to give himself time. Then she said, in a very clinical tone, that she was beginning divorce proceedings.

Gordon said he wasn't surprised. Even though he was. The unraveling of his married life over the past month and a half still occasionally hit him with the jump scare of a jack-in-the-box.

Brighton slid open the doors with as much flair as ever, although his smile seemed a tad forced. "Dr. Pope! Thought I might be hearing from you again. Come on in."

Gordon moved from chair to chair, resituating himself in one of Brighton's faded wingbacks with a bit of a grunt. Brighton's receptionist picked up her reading again as Brighton closed the doors behind them.

"I'll save us both some time here," Brighton said, walking back to his cracked-leather desk chair. "No, I haven't looked further into criminal negligence at Ditchfield, and no, I don't plan on it."

Ditchfield. He'd gone almost a month without thinking about Ditchfield. That might have been the only silver lining in this whole mess. But that meant Charlie Cunningham was well and truly institutionalized. His support systems were almost completely broken down.

A flash of anger surprised Gordon, bubbling up from somewhere within, tapping emotions he thought had gone cold over the past few weeks.

"You know where I got your card, Thomas?" he asked. "Where I first found it?"

"Courthouse?" Brighton replied, looking idly out the window, his tone humoring. "Maybe the Fells Point bars? Some strip club on The Block? I drop cards like candy everywhere trouble finds people."

"Ditchfield," Gordon replied.

Brighton came around again and met Gordon's eyes then looked away. "That must have been a long time ago. I don't go up there anymore," he said with none of his usual swagger.

"You did though, once. There's a whole stack of them on the intake desk. A few here and there in the administration building too."

Brighton cleared his throat. "Early on, I was trying to build my client list," he said. "That's all it was, drumming up business."

"Were you working for Abernethy?" Gordon asked softly, genuinely curious. The anger was already dying down again, and with it went all his drive to care.

"All I did was follow up on a few tips for potential representation. Kids that were already on the fast track, understand? I just... I basically filed the paperwork. That's all," Brighton said, his eyes darting around the room, looking at everything but Gordon.

Brighton was just short of pleading, but Gordon didn't know what for—a crack in the slick-lawyer persona. Maybe if he pressed, he'd open that crack a bit wider and peel off some of the patina, to see more of the man underneath.

But pressing took energy. And while he was surprised that Brighton was being as genuine as he'd ever known the man to be, what didn't surprise him was that Ditchfield's reach extended to an attorney that walked a blurry line on Bail Bond Row. If anything, it gave him more reason to shelve Ditchfield.

Brighton seemed to take Gordon's silence for further probing.

"Did you look at the filings? Do you see what I mean when I say *connected*?" Brighton asked, his voice a harsh whisper.

Gordon hadn't dug into the Ditchfield filings. He'd planned on it, but then he got punched in the heart. He was too busy trying to bail out the capsizing boat that was his own life.

"Last time, you mentioned an expert-witness gig. I need some extra cash," Gordon said. "I'm having some marital troubles," he added lamely.

Brighton seemed confused by the sudden turn of topic. Then, relieved, he laughed and steepled his fingers again. The polished veneer returned.

"That's why you came?" he asked. "To ask for a job?"

"Just a gig every now and then, if you have it," Gordon said, and it was his turn to avert his eyes from the conversation.

"Marital troubles? You need a lawyer? Not my specialty, but I know a guy—"

"No," Gordon said. The word came out like a sigh.

Brighton leaned forward on his elbows. "No offense, Doc, but you have the look of a guy that's gonna get run over in a divorce."

"I don't want to fight for anything," Gordon said, rubbing at his temples. "The clients are all basically hers anyway."

"That's exactly what I mean," said Brighton.

"Look, do you need an expert witness or not?" Gordon asked.

Brighton held up his hands. "Yeah, yeah. Sure." He dug around in his desk, opening and closing drawers until he found a little black address book. "Fill out your info here: full name, email, occupation, credentials, and all that."

Gordon stood and took the notebook and flipped quickly to an empty page in the back, half afraid of what he might find within if he looked too closely. He figured any little black book Brighton owned was best held like a hot potato.

When he handed the book back, Brighton looped it closed with a tether and tucked it away. "I'll send over court documentation when we need you," he said.

On his way out, Brighton's secretary waved cheerily at him, and he made a nearly herculean effort to muster a smile so that he didn't look so pathetic. Nobody wanted to put an Eeyore on the stand, no matter how expert his testimony might be.

Walking back to his car, Gordon thought vaguely about all the things he needed money for. The flat he and Karen shared... that would have to go. He couldn't pay the mortgage solo. He might have been able to keep up the rent on the office if he cheated on code and figured out how to live there too. He'd slept on the couch plenty of times before, and it had a small washroom and shower. That was doable.

He could keep up appearances if he put himself out there more, establishing himself as a solo act. But he'd been a part of Jefferson and Pope for so long that he wasn't sure he could do it alone. Karen was the funding part of their duo, while he was the client part. He would need a lot of clients—new clients.

And he didn't care enough anymore.

He was drowning in apathy. He would say he was a textbook case for moderate-to-severe depression, the hallmark of which was complete lack of feeling, were it not for one thing: he felt very strongly that he never wanted to treat kids again.

He knew his sterility wasn't his fault. He knew that Karen was, in all likelihood, the bad actor here. None of that mattered to Gordon.

The most terrifying outcome of the entire mess wasn't that it had ended in divorce. The relational implosion of Jefferson and Pope had taken away something even more special.

Whenever he thought of kids, he now thought of personal failure.

And he didn't see how anyone, anywhere, could ever make it right again.

Gordon walked along the cold concrete sidewalk, past winter-stripped trees and the rattling bones of bushes, caught trash twitching within as the wind picked up off the bay.

And scotch, he thought. He cared about scotch too. Strongly.

He thumbed the edge of Brighton's card in his pocket as he wrapped his coat more tightly around himself. He hoped the little snake had some work for him soon. Gordon's liquor cabinet was looking rather pathetic.

CHAPTER THIRTEEN

PRESENT DAY

Thomas Brighton settled down for lunch in his office and sipped on a glass of iced vodka. He was feeling fairly pleased with himself. He'd just snagged a big client in a carbon monoxide poisoning case with a long tail—the woman's son had gone hypoxic after a furnace in their apartment leaked in the middle of the night a little over a year before, and he was having mental issues. The kicker was that the detectors had no batteries. They had proof too.

Best of all, it was a civil case—people vs. money, not people vs. people. The criminal stuff was weighing on him of late. The last time he felt really accomplished in the criminal-defense arena had been with Ethan Barret, almost a year before. And that had been a bright spot. Brighton had no problem taking cases where the innocence of his client was suspect—everyone deserved a fair trial, after all—but recently, he'd been feeling strange. This Charlie Cunningham stuff, along with Ditchfield, all brought back memories that made him feel... not guilty, of course, never *guilty*. But not *great*.

That day, though, he felt pretty good. He felt pretty good because of the civil case he'd bagged, and he felt pretty good because he'd been able to decline the offer of representing a juvenile criminal case that didn't sit right with him. Also, he was halfway done with a glass of vodka and had a famous crab-cake sandwich from Darrow's Barrel in front of him, ready to chow.

He topped off his vodka, turned to his crab cake, and just as he was about to take his first bite, the front door buzzed.

Annoying. Probably a package, though. Brighton purposely kept his lunch hour free every day. He fought for it. Meeting-creep was real even though he was essentially a one-man show, no offense to Natasha.

He tried not to listen in as he ate—he often tried to will his office to be bigger than it was—but he couldn't help it.

Natasha was being her usual semi-helpful self. "Who?" she asked. "I don't see any reverend on the schedule today."

Brighton stopped chewing.

He didn't quite catch the reply, but he recognized the deep voice. His first bite of crab cake felt like it dropped another six inches into his gut.

"Mr. Brighton is at lunch right now. And like I said, he's booked all day." One bright-red heel was bobbing up and down with increasing vigor past the glass doors. "Next time, I suggest you call ahead first—"

For a span of moments, Brighton wondered what would happen if he just sat there behind the glass in his little office with its big desk. He could let Natasha turn away his troubles at the door while he spun his old leather chair toward the window and ate his lunch.

Likely, he'd get another visit, a little less friendly than the first, perhaps. Some things—and some people—just wouldn't be put off. Some handshakes stain. Some choices that seem small at the time can reverberate. One might think the noise had quieted, but in reality, the echo was just bouncing off the rocks on its way back.

He pressed the button on his intercom, cutting off Natasha. "This is Thomas Brighton," he said. "With whom am I speaking?"

"Hello, Thomas," came the reply, like an old friend. "It's Josiah."

Brighton closed his eyes for a moment. When he opened them again, Natasha was turned toward him, arms out in question.

He waved her off. "Hello, Reverend. What a nice surprise," he said, trying desperately to sound like he meant it. "Come on up."

He pressed the lock's button and buzzed up Reverend Josiah Hill. After looking longingly at his crab-cake sandwich and gingerly rolling it up in its paper wrapping, he set it aside. He finished his vodka in a shot and slid the glass next to the wrapped sandwich, then he stood and straightened his suit.

Brighton opened the double sliding doors reservedly. Hill emerged from the hallway, along with another young man, an acolyte or a bodyguard. Both were dressed in dark suits, and Hill had his wool fedora in hand.

"Sorry to bother you at lunch, Thomas. Unforgivable, I know. I'll be quick."

He nodded to the young man, who took a seat in the waiting room and rested his hands on his knees. Somehow, Brighton found himself following Hill into his own office. As he closed the doors, he caught a glimpse of Natasha watching the big young man, wide-eyed.

Hill took a seat, crossed his legs, and set his fedora neatly over his knee. He waited until Brighton rounded the desk and settled himself before speaking.

"How have you been? It's been a little while," Hill said kindly.

"Good, good," Brighton answered. "I've been exploring the civil side of law recently..." Brighton said then trailed off. He wondered if his professional pivot might have had something to do with the reverend's little visit.

"I saw that." Hill looked around the office. "New ventures, new clients, I'm excited for you," he said, although he didn't sound particularly excited. "This place hasn't changed a bit."

"New chair," Brighton said. "Fixed the chandelier too. The wiring was shot for about a year. Turns out Baltimore winters aren't good for outdoor chandeliers. Summers neither. But the rest of the place... I like it the way it is."

Hill laughed, low and slow.

"Always thought that chandelier was tacky," Hill said. "Tried to get the previous tenant to take it with them when I bought the place. They politely declined."

Brighton's uneasy laughter drifted off to a heavy silence. Hill just watched him with a look as though he was about to break out into a smile even when he wasn't.

"This place has treated you pretty well, hasn't it?" Hill asked. "You've made a bit of a name for yourself. Got a decent reputation."

"You gave me a place to call my own," Brighton said. "I've tried to pay back that first year's rent several times—" he began, fidgeting with the vodka glass.

"I don't want your money, Thomas," Hill said, and that smile went across his face, sad and slow.

Brighton nodded. Hill had no shortage of money. What he needed was more lawyers in his pocket—specifically, Brighton and Associates.

Brighton wet his lips. He felt he should say something, apologize for something. But he didn't know what.

"There was a young man caught selling stolen phones. Bit of a rap sheet. I believe you were supposed to represent him?" Hill asked, furrowing his brow as if he didn't know exactly which young man and exactly which case were in question.

It was the one Brighton had just declined to take up, the one he was celebrating passing on with the glass of vodka and crab-cake sandwich, now lukewarm and congealing in its wrapping paper to his left.

"I was offered a fairly big civil opportunity—"

"The young man was supposed to go to Ditchfield, Thomas, and you were supposed to see to it that he did," Hill said, as if reminding Brighton of something very obvious, like where he'd parked.

Brighton began to sweat under his collar as he saw flashbacks from years before of the boys he'd sent there, almost all of whom probably deserved it. At least, he'd told himself that over the years, especially at three in the morning, when he often woke up and had trouble finding sleep again for reasons that eluded him at the time but were becoming clearer by the second.

"I was under the impression that Ditchfield is a little... precarious at the moment?" Brighton said. He meant it as a statement, but it came out as a question.

"Ditchfield's never been better," Hill said easily. "In fact, we're investing heavily in it as we speak." He shifted his position, recrossing his legs and settling his fedora. "Old knees," he said offhand.

"Charlie Cunningham's been found?" Brighton asked.

For the first time since he'd arrived, a slight shadow of a cloud passed over Hill's face. But it was quick. "I'll take care of Charlie," Hill said. "You just concern yourself with the criminal trial I handed you. Fair? Otherwise, there are a few people on the Maryland Bar Association that owe me a few favors."

Brighton took his meaning clearly but tried not to let his creeping fear show.

"Why do you care that the kid who stole the phones ends up in Ditchfield?" Brighton asked before he lost all courage. *That kid and all the others over the years*, he wanted to add, but he faltered, suddenly aware of a headache creeping forward from the back of his skull.

Hill looked directly at Brighton. "Do you really want to know?"

Brighton looked down at his old desk, with its cracked leather writing table and its seamed wood, lacquered again and again over the years.

"Because I'll tell you if you really want to know," Hill added, and he seemed genuine. Then again, Hill always seemed genuine.

A lot of words ran through Brighton's head. Chief among them was the phrase *plausible deniability*.

"No," he said quietly. "I suppose I don't."

Hill smiled and eased himself to standing. "Smart man," he said. "That's why I like you, Thomas. I look forward to seeing our new young ward at Ditchfield soon. I do apologize about butting in during lunch."

"Not a problem," Brighton said, dazed.

"I'll be in touch," Hill said over his shoulder, helping himself through the doors and walking out in step with the young man he'd set as watch outside.

In short order, both were gone and the office was quiet, as if they'd never been.

But Brighton's lunch was cold. And he felt he'd just agreed to dive deeper into a deal he'd been trying to side-step out of for the past five years. Somewhere, he'd made a wrong turn. He'd been bewitched again.

He needed to think.

He pressed his comm. "Natasha, please clear my schedule for today," he said.

"But—"

"I'll make it up to them. Whoever they are," Brighton said forcefully. "Please," he added, calming himself. *No need to bring Natasha down too.*

"Fine," she replied flippantly.

Brighton topped off his vodka and spun his chair toward the window and sat for a long time.

AT FIVE ON THE DOT, Brighton saw Natasha's blurry visage through the clouded glass as she stood, smoothed her skirt, and set her hair. She picked up her purse and called, "I'm leaving!" unnecessarily loudly.

"About time," he replied, their standard friendly parting.

Brighton's words were a bit slurred. A fair amount of the vodka was gone from the bottle, but he was no closer to figuring a way out of Hill's pocket, not without ending up disbarred. He wasn't sure how Hill could do that, but he knew he could. Hell, Hill could probably get him disbarred for the work he'd done for Hill. He had no doubt the man could incriminate him while staying above the fray. Above the fray was Hill's specialty.

Natasha's heels clicked evenly on the creaky wood as she left. The glow of her phone was visible through the glass. She was totally checked out. *Must be nice to set aside your work like that. Be on when you have to be then forget all about it.* Sometimes, Brighton thought he should have just gone to work at a bookstore. He liked reading. That was the only reason he got through law school passably. If he was at a bookstore, he'd just clock in, talk about books, sell a few here and there, and clock out.

The problem was that selling books didn't buy suits. Books didn't buy watches or sedans. Books didn't buy fine vodka or nice dinners out or an office of one's own.

Right then, though, Brighton would have swapped all the nice things, including the suit right off his back, to be out of this mess with Hill. Whatever Hill did with these kids, whatever he needed them for, it felt bad. And if it felt bad on the surface, it was likely evil at the core. That's how those things worked.

He heard Natasha coming back down the creaky hallway. *Probably forgot her keys*, he thought. Or her jacket. Or her head. She was a good woman but totally scatterbrained, and in hindsight he likely should have called a few more references, but she had managed to keep the place from burning down for years, and that was enough for Brighton.

She was walking heavy, though... and slow.

"Natasha?" Brighton asked. "Everything okay?"

Thomas Brighton did not scare easily. He was street savvy enough to avoid most trouble and had the legal chops to save himself from pretty much anything else. Even Josiah Hill didn't make him *scared*. Hill brought on a sense of existential dread, perhaps, that was vague and ephemeral and all-consuming, but he wasn't a scary man. That's precisely why he was so dangerous.

But when Brighton called out for Natasha and was met by

nothing but the creaky sound of heavy footsteps on old wood, he became very afraid.

He kept a gun in the office. Bail Bond Row wasn't in the greatest area of town, and the people that frequented the establishments there weren't often of the highest caliber. He'd shoved the weapon somewhere in his locked desk drawer four years before and promptly forgotten about it until right then. He had a mild distaste for guns. They didn't go well with double-breasted suits. But he dug furiously in the top drawer of his desk for the key to the bottom drawer.

A man stepped into Brighton's waiting room. And even though his view through the clouded glass of his sliding doors obscured any defining features—pretty much all he could see was that the man was skinny and black—Brighton had no doubt at all about who'd come in.

Charlie Cunningham was paying him a visit.

Busy day, Brighton thought darkly, fumbling with the stupidly small key to his bottom drawer. *Lot of drop-ins.*

Charlie opened the sliding glass doors slowly, one in each hand, almost theatrically slow, in a way that struck Brighton as a macabre reversal of what he'd been doing to clients for years.

Brighton paused, key in lock. He couldn't help it. He had to get a good look at the kid giving the city such fits.

Brighton knew he'd represented Charlie poorly. But he was ashamed to find he didn't recall him, not specifically—no details that he could place and think, *Aha! That's him!* What he saw was a rangy young man with a ragged left ear and a singular, driven look in his eye. Brighton was old hat at picking out emotions through eyes. He saw furious anger inside Charlie, barely kept in check by a deadly purpose.

While Brighton was frozen, Charlie kept moving, constantly, fluidly. By the time Brighton's hand was in the drawer, grasping for the gun, Charlie had come around the desk. Without a second's pause, Charlie lifted a boot that looked two sizes too big for him and planted it right in Brighton's chest like he was trying to kick open a door.

All the air left Brighton in a huff, and he collapsed forward, still seated. His chair hit the window behind him hard, and his head popped backward, bouncing against the puffy leather. The glass window cracked with the sound of a stick snapping.

Brighton tried to speak. His words were his best weapon, but the air was maddeningly slow in coming. By the time he got half a breath, Charlie Cunningham had reached in and pulled out the handgun—a snub-nosed .32 revolver—and turned to face Brighton. He looked carefully down at him and idly picked up a mechanical pencil off Brighton's desk with his free hand.

Charlie looked very much like a man caught between two paths: a gun or a pencil.

In the eternity it felt to get air back into his lungs, Brighton had chosen his words carefully.

"I'm sorry," he said.

Charlie brushed off the apology with a faint twitch of his upper lip. "You knew?" he asked. His voice was curiously childlike. Not high, but not yet shed of the reedy timbre of youth. The contrast between his appearance and his voice was disorienting.

"Sort of," Brighton admitted, defeated. "I knew Hill needed to keep the inmate count up. He had specific targets. Kids he wanted."

Charlie's eyes narrowed, but the emotion was still there. Brighton felt that if they went blank, if Charlie stepped away and let whatever else was inside take over, he'd be dead.

"I didn't want to know why. So I didn't ask. But I knew enough. Knew it was wrong."

Charlie advanced slowly. The gun wasn't pointing at Brighton yet, but it wasn't pointing at the ground anymore either. As Brighton watched it rise slowly, his vision grew blurry. He found himself crying—a stranger sensation than getting kicked in the chest. Brighton couldn't remember the last time he'd cried for any reason. And he found he wasn't even crying for himself, not totally. He was crying for all those kids he'd sent to that godforsaken prison.

"Did they abuse you?" he asked, barely getting the words out.

That seemed to give Charlie pause, and his eyes narrowed. "This ain't about me," he said. "But you knew that, right? I saw Hill come in here. Saw that pig come back out, lookin' pleased with his shit."

"Not about you?" Brighton asked, confused. "Then it's about all of you. All those kids I helped send up there. Hill got me by the balls early, and he kept squeezing, but that's no excuse. I got no excuses left."

Charlie's eyes flashed, his brain almost humming audibly. "Man, fuck them other boys," he said. "This ain't about them neither."

Charlie stepped forward, and Brighton instinctively pushed backward. The window creaked ominously. Brighton got the sudden impression that he was being tested somehow. And his life depended on if he passed or not.

"Who is it about, then?" Brighton asked.

"Tasha." Charlie's eyes bored into Brighton. "It's about Tasha. And how Hill's gonna pay."

Brighton's mind raced. He checked the name against everything he had, inside and out. Gut reactions, old cases, new cases, bad cases, good cases—nothing.

"Who the hell is Tasha?" Brighton asked desperately. He didn't want to die because of somebody he'd never known.

"Where is she?" Charlie snapped. He raised the gun until it was pointed squarely at Brighton's chest, an angle that seemed past the point of any return.

"I have no idea who you're talking about, Charlie," Brighton said, his voice jittery. His words were deserting him, fleeing his head and abandoning ship. Obviously, he'd failed whatever test Charlie was giving. He had an acrid taste on his tongue like licking a battery and somehow knew he was tasting his own fear, so acute that it was a real thing in his mouth.

Brighton's day in court had come, and Charlie Cunningham had found him guilty. But the worst part—the part Brighton knew he'd take to the grave and be forced to dwell upon forever—was that he probably deserved what was coming to him.

CHAPTER FOURTEEN

Dana felt strangely exposed without her badge and gun. She kept tapping her hip out of habit as she sat in an uncomfortable plastic chair against one taupe wall of Marty's room in the bustling Hopkins ER.

The weightlessness of the empty spot on her hip where her gun should have been unsettled her. It was a microcosm of the general free-falling sensation that had taken over her entire life, as though she'd reached what she thought was the bottom of the stairs only to find one more surprise step.

"What are you gonna do?" Marty asked, sitting up without the need for the hospital bed at his back.

The Kevlar had absorbed both slugs, barely. The blasts, clustered top left, would have blown right through his heart. Instead, he had a monster bruise on his chest and a cracked sternum, along with a lot of shirtless recovery time that Dana knew he would secretly enjoy—the shirtless part, anyway.

"You just got shot, and you're asking me what I'm gonna do?" she replied, smiling wearily.

"I only got shot. You're getting axed," Marty said, wincing a little as the nurse rewrapped his trunk of a chest.

"We got a comedian over here," Dana said.

"Sorry," he added. "Bad joke."

Dana waved it off with a fleeting smile.

She'd been placed on leave before but never suspended without pay, never told to hand in her hardware. Next came a token internal review, likely headed up by Duke, then she'd be fired. Firing a cop was hard in Baltimore, but Duke had basically done it. He'd been gunning for Dana since the day he realized she wanted to succeed in his department despite him, and she was about to be out of the way.

She could fight the suspension. They hadn't trespassed at New Hope Community Church. There was no illegal entry of any sort. They'd been fired upon first, and Dana only returned fire when she thought she was in mortal danger. Theoretically, she had a case, but if she wanted to stand in front of Internal Affairs and look Duke in the eye and tell him she still deserved to be a sergeant in the Baltimore City Police—if she really wanted to pick that fight—she needed to believe it herself first, one hundred percent.

She wasn't even at ninety percent. She was hovering somewhere near fifty and losing more faith in herself every day the Charlie Cunningham case went on.

Duke would chew her up and spit her out.

"Duke'll probably come for me too," Marty said, testing out some deep breaths and gritting his teeth a bit. "I didn't discharge my weapon, so it's less of a whole thing, but it's only a matter of time. Hill will make sure of that."

"Maybe," Dana said. "Or maybe this is a good time to..."

Marty looked carefully up at her. "Good time to what?"

"Move on?" Dana offered tentatively.

Marty started to say something then stopped himself, calmed his demeanor, and turned to thank the nurse, who said she'd notify the doctor for discharge papers. When the door closed behind her and the two of them were alone, he turned back to Dana, who was patiently waiting. She wasn't sure what she expected. Yes or no, either answer would chip at her heart.

On the surface, Marty had everything Duke liked in a cop. He had a healthy respect for authority and process. He was also, crucially, not a woman. He would do better without her. In fact, the only thing Duke likely held against Marty was his steadfast loyalty to his uppity partner who kept breaking rules.

Dana was about to say so when Marty interrupted her.

"You don't get to tell me to move on," he said with forced calm. "The first time, with you and me and you and Gordon... I got that one eventually. It's been hard, but I'm doing it. And it's working, I think. But this, about how I get to be a cop, this is different."

She found herself stammering, at a loss for words. "I was just thinking that—you know—you've been doing so well. Personally, professionally. We sort of switched. You're the grown-up now, Marty. We're on different trajectories. I thought maybe you ought to cut me loose. Chuck the dead weight."

"You're not dead weight," he said, exasperated.

"You know what I mean," Dana said. "I asked the impossible of you with me and Gordon. To show up and do your job with me *and* to let me go? And you did it. And you're better for it. Maybe it's a sign."

"A sign?" he asked. "I don't do signs. I do cop stuff." He tapped his chest and winced again but gamely recovered. "So do you. And what *I* need is to be able to have you in my life in a way that we can both live with."

He got up slowly and went to the coat rack, where his badge hung on its chain next to his tattered Kevlar vest and his destroyed leather jacket. He shook his head sadly at the jacket but patted the vest like a good old dog and flicked his badge affectionately.

He paused and moved back to the vest. He stared at it so long that Dana started to take a second look. The impact zone was clearly delineated, the protective layers of Kevlar warped and crumpled. She knew he'd specifically left instructions that it be kept close to hand because he needed to log it as evidence. But the sliced-up top quadrant was new.

He turned to Dana. "Did you take the chest camera out?"

Dana shook her head. A look passed between them that said everything without saying anything at all. Hill had gotten to it somehow, likely through one of Duke's lackeys while he was in surgery.

Marty took another pained breath and shook his head, exasperated. "These assholes are good. Thorough. But we're better. So long as we keep working together."

His continued friendship and dogged loyalty warmed her heart, but she felt he wasn't facing the facts. Charlie had been two steps ahead of her since the beginning. She'd risked the lives of the two most important men in her life in a barely legal raid for a bunch of papers that Gordon was still sifting through and that could realistically be of little evidential support. And to top it all off, she'd gotten her partner shot.

A sane cop would run screaming for the hills. But Marty was stubborn and loyal to a fault. And somehow, he still thought she could do her job.

"What about *suspended* don't you understand, Marty?"

"If we can crack this case, who knows what might change," Marty said, keeping his voice low and glancing at the door.

Dana took his meaning. Hill was a sterling monument in this city, but they both knew that if you tipped him over, a lot of squirming bugs would be exposed underneath. Ditchfield was one of them. The Duke name was another. All of them were tied together.

"What can I do?" Dana asked helplessly.

Marty tapped his shield again. "You'll figure it out. I'm going to go do cop stuff like file the incident and ballistics reports as best I can and try to avoid getting fired. But first, I'm gonna try to explain all this to Brooke."

Dana got up to go. She didn't want to intrude anywhere Brooke might take offense. Marty seemed to understand.

On her way out, he called after her softly. "Dana, this is a heavy piece of metal," he said, holding up his shield. "But it's still just a piece of metal. It doesn't make you a cop. That comes from somewhere else. Somewhere deeper."

Outside the room, a young woman was nervously pacing by the intake desk. Brooke was as pretty as she'd imagined but more genuinely so. She was obviously giving them time, and Dana felt an overwhelming sense of gratitude to the woman. She walked right up to Brooke and hugged her by way of introduction, knowing no other way to thank her. She was a little surprised to find that Brooke returned the hug completely.

"Will you watch out for him?" Brooke asked.

"He's the one that watches out for me these days," Dana said.

"He's a softie, you know. He needs watching too," Brooke said.

"I got his back," Dana said. She didn't feel like she did, but she knew that was the right answer, the one Brooke wanted to hear, anyway. "We'll all get a glass of wine one day, once all this dies down. I promise."

Dana concentrated on putting one foot in front of the other as she walked out of the ER. She felt aimless and tired, as if she'd been the one admitted. She needed to eat some real food and to hug her daughter. She needed the substance of her life around her.

She needed Gordon. Maybe he'd found something in the meager haul he'd scooped from the back rooms of New Hope.

She picked her phone from her purse and froze. He'd flipped the script on her: she'd missed five calls from him.

CHAPTER FIFTEEN

Gordon called Dana the first time once he'd spread out everything he'd stolen from New Hope on the floor of his loft. Each document lay side by side between his big chair and the little therapy chair he kept for the kids.

Only two pictures were among the documents, but they were more than enough to cement his suspicions. The second one was very similar to the first he'd shown Dana in the car: a young black girl—maybe fifteen, probably younger—heavily made up. She sat awkwardly on a small bed in a bikini that was far too big for her. She had an expression like she'd been asked to look sexy and was trying her best but wasn't quite old enough to know how.

Gordon had to take a break then. He called Dana and tried to swallow his low-level nausea. When she didn't answer, he got a drink. That helped a little.

The rest of the documents proved less immediately abhorrent. Spreadsheets had lines of numbers in one column and dollar figures in another. Other spreadsheets used abbreviations Gordon couldn't make heads or tails of, each associated with more dollar figures. Receipts for random, everyday things like paper towels and Clorox were there, along with other receipts for stranger things Gordon had never heard of—things like video borescopes, FLIR cameras, and T30 servers, all paid in cash.

He tried to open the thumb drive on his computer, but it was encrypted. He hesitated to guess at passwords too long for fear that some self-defense mechanism would rewrite the drive after too many failed attempts. He went back to the paper trail.

Gordon called Dana two more times when he recognized that some of the numbers on the spreadsheets were repeated. He saw the vague outline of a pattern weaving through the documents on his floor, but no matter how many times he shuffled them around, he couldn't quite grasp it. Dana had cop-fu. She was better at evidence, not to mention paperwork.

He realized he'd unconsciously set the pictures of the girls aside. He found them physically hard to look at. He almost went to get another drink, but he stopped himself when he realized the only reason he wanted to drink was to try to blunt the fact that the girls looking up at him from those photographs were very likely being sexually abused. Maybe right now. Another scotch might help him to avoid that, to hold more tightly to a false thread of thinking that, while these pictures were certainly in poor taste, maybe they weren't blatantly sexualized. Maybe this was all one big mistake.

He put the bottle back. This wasn't one big mistake. This was a horrendous reality. He dialed Dana again—still no answer.

He picked up his keys. He didn't need a scotch right now. What he needed was a lawyer.

GORDON POCKETED his phone and rubbed at his eyes. Five calls, three texts, and no answer from Dana. *She's right*, he thought. *It really is incredibly annoying.*

He knew she was with Marty, and Marty basically got a free pass for a good long while on account of having been shot in the chest with a nine millimeter, but still, *answer the phone!* His stolen evidence was sitting in a banker's box to his right, on the passenger's seat of his rattling coupe. He was sitting at a red light at the intersection of Madison and Broadway, willing his heater to hold up.

The last time Gordon had gone down this road with Brighton, the man had basically escorted him out of his office. But this wasn't just about Ditchfield anymore. This was about New Hope and about Hill. Even Thomas Brighton had to take a side on this one. Nobody could just wash their hands of the matter once they dug into that box.

Finding parking was difficult even in the early evening. Bail Bond Row was a twenty-four-hour operation, with people coming and going regardless of working hours. Gordon knew Brighton often stayed late—he'd hit the man up for work several times in the evening, back in the dark days, and once for an advance, which Brighton had laughingly denied. Gordon hoped to catch him in that sweet spot after all his appointments but before he packed up to go home.

By the time he approached the offices of Brighton and Associates, the time was almost six. At least one light was still on in the back, which was a good sign. Gordon walked up the creaking outdoor staircase and stood underneath the chandelier. He had his hand on the buzzer and was about to press when something crunched underneath his shoe, a large splinter of painted wood. He looked up at the chandelier, thinking maybe the dodgy thing was finally pulling away from its old wooden moorings, but it looked as stalwart and out-of-place as ever.

When he dropped his gaze again, he noticed the door had been forced.

Gordon took this in abstractly. The break-in was clean. Something had snapped the bolt side clean off. The front door, like the rest of the place, was old wood. It probably hadn't even protested much.

He pressed the comm. "Hello?"

Nothing.

He pressed the comm several more times but got nothing in return. The buzzer didn't even seem to be working. The doorknob didn't turn, but the door pushed open easily. Gordon let it swing inward until it bumped on the backstop.

"Thomas? Natasha?" he called.

Silence from within.

Just a break in, Gordon thought. *They're long gone home.* But his ears were ringing, faintly, in a way that told him the blood was racing through his body.

Just a break in, he repeated because if this was only a smash-and-grab for whatever fancy baubles Brighton kept in his office, that meant Dana was still wrong about Charlie Cunningham's "list." It meant Karen was still wrong all those years before when she said Charlie was a sociopath, pure and simple, and would never be understood.

With each step down the dusty wooden hallway, he felt less and less sure of himself. Nothing was disturbed in the outer room, where Natasha sat. Her desk was tidied up, pencils and pens all in a row, a rainbow of highlighters ready for another day.

Then he turned toward Brighton's office, dreading what he might find. The sliding glass doors were open. The desk lamp was on. The intercom was smashed, the cords cut. Drops of what looked like spilled ink flecked Brighton's old wooden desk, but Gordon knew they weren't ink.

Brighton's chair was turned around, facing the big window at the back of his office. A nasty crack split the pane from corner to corner, feathering out around an impact point in the center.

Gordon licked his lips. "Thomas?" he ventured.

No answer. Gordon really, really didn't want to turn that chair around.

He could smell the blood in the room and something else, too, a strange whiff of ozone, like burning plastic, that some ingrained, ancient response locked deep within his brain told him was the lingering smell of fear. Strong, animal fear.

The ringing in his ears was a high keen as he grasped the old leather and spun it his way.

Nobody.

"Just a break in," he said aloud to himself. *Except for a decent spattering of blood.*

Gordon allowed himself a few deep breaths. The ringing had receded, and in its place, a sound like running water was coming from somewhere in the back of the house. He turned around to follow it and found himself face-to-face with the bloody ghost of Thomas Brighton.

"What's this now?" asked Brighton, wild-eyed.

Gordon yelped like a rat had run across his shoes. He dropped the box, spilling papers all over the worn wooden flooring. He scrambled to gather them then felt the best thing to do was deal with this fresh hell first by putting Brighton's desk between himself and the apparition.

"Gordon?" asked Brighton in a very alive tone. "What are you doing here?"

"I thought you were dead!" Gordon said. "You're not dead, right?" he added. He felt far too fragile in general to deal with ghosts at the moment—real or imagined.

"Not yet," Brighton said, "although it was a damn close thing." He was pressing a wad of paper towels to the right side of his face, and it was sopping wet and running with red. His pristine white cuffs were pink. "I thought he was gonna kill me. But all he did was slice me up with a pencil then bash my head with my own revolver. My lucky day."

Brighton took the wet red mess away from the right side of his face to reveal a jagged rift in the skin of his face, starting just below his right temple and ending about halfway down his chin. It looked black in the low light but wept blood evenly and consistently.

Gordon took an involuntary step back, cringing. *That's gonna leave a mark.*

"Who?" Gordon asked.

"Who do you think?" Brighton asked, applying pressure once more.

"Charlie was here?" Gordon asked, looking around as if he might jump out from behind the wingback chairs at any moment.

"Yes, he was here," Brighton said.

"What did he want?" asked Gordon. "What did he say?"

"He asked me if I knew. I said yes. But I think what he knows and what I know are two different types of knowing." Brighton flipped his compress and steadied himself against the doorframe.

Gordon's mind raced over and around Brighton's words. *But first things first.* "Maybe you should see a doctor, Thomas. That's a bad gash."

Thomas shook his head, the whites of his eyes visible all around. "I'm not going anywhere. I deserved this—deserved worse, to be honest. You can patch me up. Come on, I got a first-aid kit back here somewhere. Natasha made me buy it, God bless her."

Brighton turned on his heels and walked back around the corner toward the rear of the office. Gordon stood blinking for a minute before he realized half the papers were still scattered across the room. He hurried to gather them all back into the box.

"Come on, Pope! I'm bleeding here!" Brighton called.

"I'm not that kind of doctor!" Gordon replied, following with the box in hand. He turned a second corner and came upon a little half bathroom that looked like a small animal had been sacrificed and swung around by the tail.

"Good Lord," Gordon said, stepping back out again.

"Here." Brighton shoved a small red plastic suitcase into his arms and turned back toward the sink. He tossed the old soaked wad into an overflowing trash can and wet a new, partially bloody wad.

Gordon set his box down and reluctantly popped open the first-aid kit. "What do you mean *knew*? What do you know, Thomas?"

Brighton looked at Gordon in the mirror then turned off the faucet and braced himself against the lip of the sink with his free hand. He looked down, watching the slow and steady drip of his blood as it spattered against the white porcelain.

Gordon waited. If Brighton was in deep in all this, too, Gordon didn't know what he was going to do—certainly not help the man stop bleeding.

"In the early days, when I had no money, no clients, nothing, I made a handshake deal with Josiah Hill."

Gordon closed his eyes.

"I made sure certain kids went to Ditchfield, kids he tapped. In exchange, he got me under this roof."

Gordon waited for more. Brighton shook his head, watching the blood fall. He looked genuinely disgusted with himself. That was a new look for Brighton.

"That's it?" Gordon asked after a moment.

"Isn't that enough?" Brighton replied. "Some of these kids... they maybe didn't deserve Ditchfield."

"Nobody deserves Ditchfield," Gordon said, "but that's beside the point. Is that all Hill asked you to do? All he asked you to cover up?"

"Yeah, why? Is there more?"

Gordon blew out an enormous breath, feeling that he could finally breathe for the first time since having seen that splintered door outside.

"Yeah. There's more," Gordon said.

Brighton dabbed at his face, looking about as lost as Gordon had ever seen him.

"Do I want to know what it is?" Brighton asked.

Gordon said nothing. This was a decision Brighton would have to make for himself.

Brighton looked down at the banker's box pressed up against the wall then back up at Gordon. He nodded. "Patch me up first, as best you can."

"I'm not that kind of doctor," Gordon said again.

"You'll do better than a hack lawyer," Brighton said, and he tilted his weeping cheek toward Gordon. "Blast it with rubbing alcohol first. I want to feel the burn."

. . .

Brighton sat in his big leather chair, holding his head in his hands, Pope's papers spaced evenly across the dark wooden desk in front of him. An hour before, he'd thought he was going to die in that chair. But as the full weight of what he was seeing in front of him pressed upon his heart, he wondered if perhaps he should have.

Gordon sat in a wingback across from him and downed two ibuprofen with a slug from one of Brighton's water bottles.

"Just so we're clear," Gordon asked, "what do you see here? I've been up for a while, and I've had a lot of coffee and a little scotch, and I want to be sure I'm not crazy."

Brighton looked at him. Gordon had patched him together with five Steri-Strips like little railroad ties spaced evenly down the right side of his face, but it was starting to feel really swollen. He wondered if it was medically possible for a cheek to burst. "You said you saw the rooms? And camera equipment?"

Gordon nodded, grimacing slightly, as if those memories were going to stick with him for a very long time.

"These receipts, they're for hidden cameras and private encrypted servers," Brighton said.

"They managed to take off with all that stuff by the time I got back there," Gordon said.

"He was whoring these girls out from inside a *church*?" Brighton asked.

Gordon set his head back on the chair, apparently vindicated. Brighton knew what he was seeing. He also knew what he wasn't seeing, which was enough to convict Hill of something that would put him away for life.

"At least online," Gordon said. "Maybe in real life too."

"My God," Brighton muttered, trailing off. He picked up the photograph of the particularly young-looking girl in the bikini and tossed it down with disgust. "What is she, thirteen, maybe?" he asked.

"It's a lot to take," Gordon said.

"It's a goddamn horror show," Brighton said, looking up at

Gordon. "You gotta believe me when I say I had no idea about this mess," he said.

"I do," Gordon said. "Evidently, so does Charlie. That's why you're alive right now."

Brighton stood and looked over the desk, hands on his hips. "But it's still just pictures and numbers. There's nothing linking them. I'm sure that whole place has had a bleach bath by now and looks nothing like what you saw. This won't hold up in court, certainly not against New Hope."

Gordon held out the thumb drive. "There's this too. But it's encrypted. I can't get in."

Brighton quickly walked around the desk, his shoes tapping lightly on the hardwood. He plucked it from Gordon's fingers and turned it around in the light from his Tiffany lamp. "It's a USB drive," Brighton said, smiling.

"I thought maybe you knew somebody who could hack it," Gordon said.

"Of course I do," Brighton said. "Me."

Gordon looked skeptical. Brighton knew he must be a sight: a middle-aged fop with limp hair plugs and a puffy face, soaking wet and slowly bleeding. But he didn't care anymore. Somehow, when Charlie had spared him, he'd dug out a hole in Brighton's heart where a bunch of junk had been. Then Gordon had come by and ripped it wider but also planted a seed of something like hope.

Maybe he could redeem himself somehow in all this mess.

"You don't work for years on Bail Bond Row without picking up a few tricks when it comes to accessing evidence," Brighton said, rummaging around the bottom drawer of his desk. He paused when he saw the empty place where his revolver had been. Charlie had it currently. *Problematic*, Brighton thought. *But one thing at a time.*

He found what he was looking for, a small electronic box with a USB port and a digital display. He held it up and attempted a smile before gingerly patting at his wound to make sure nothing had popped.

He flipped open his laptop and logged in, then he plugged the box into one of the ports on its side. The box blinked on. After a moment, the digital panel said Ready in retro red lettering.

"It's called a USB sniffer," Brighton said, taking the thumb drive and inserting it into the port on the opposite end of the box. "I bought it off a shady software developer a few years back. He was getting sued for intellectual property infringement and needed some cash."

With the drive inserted, the box whirred softly. The panel showed a rotating stylus. "I don't claim to know how it works. Something about listening in on the conversation between the drive and the computer, a security flaw on almost all USBs, where the password gets passed right along with the request. I don't really care."

The sniffer beeped once, and a string of characters appeared on the panel, nothing recognizable at all. They could have guessed for years and never hit it.

Brighton smiled. "It worked," he said. He ripped a sticky note from a pad on the desk and wrote down the password then popped the sniffer out and plugged the USB directly into the laptop.

By that time, Gordon had come around behind the chair and was holding onto the leather for dear life. Brighton shared his trepidation. He entered the password at the prompt and was brought to a file explorer screen with just two folders. One was named Contact and the other Sample.

Brighton swallowed a sickly-sweet wave of nausea. He looked over his shoulder at Gordon, who nodded grimly. He clicked on Contact. Within was a spreadsheet that, at first glance, looked very similar to the paper copies he had on his desk.

The disappointment was clear in Gordon's voice. "More numbers," he said.

Brighton scanned the document quickly: two columns and forty-five rows. The first column contained combinations of two letters and two numbers. The numbers were sequential, while the letters seemed random: AC01, RY02, LB03...

The second column was names: first name, last initial. A quick scan showed all of them to be male.

"Client list?" Gordon asked, squinting.

"Maybe. Looks like it."

Brighton hovered over the second folder, the one labeled Samples. He kept having to swallow acid indigestion down. He double-clicked before he lost all nerve.

Inside the folder were four video files, each labeled in the same style, two letters and two numbers. Gordon was breathing with forced calm behind him. Brighton clicked on one labeled BY39.

The video opened on a view of a room with bare white walls and a maroon bed. A young girl was adjusting the camera. Her smooth black skin was smeared with gold rouge at the cheekbones. Her lips were a candy-apple red.

"Her pupils are dilated," Gordon said evenly, clinically.

The girl sat back down on the bed. She wore black underpants and a lacy black bra with one strap falling off at the shoulder.

The purring voice of a man came from off-screen. "Hi, Brianna. How are you feeling?"

The girl didn't respond, only stared at the screen for a time.

"She's in shock," Gordon said, pain noticeable in his voice. "And likely drugged."

"I'm fine," said Brianna, slowly and slightly slurred.

"I want you to do some things for me. Okay, Brianna?" asked the man.

Brighton tried to place the voice but couldn't. It sounded like it was coming from elsewhere, outside the room, over a speaker.

After another long pause, the girl nodded.

"I want you to take your clothes off, okay?" the man said.

Gordon let go of the chair and turned away toward the window, breathing heavily. "Shut it off," he said.

Brighton was only too happy to oblige. He'd seen many things in his years in criminal defense, many bad things. At first, he'd insisted nothing could get to him, but then, gradually, as he started to shake hands with people like Josiah Hill, he wondered if perhaps each terrible thing he'd seen had taken a piece from him after all, without him noticing. He was happy to feel disgust welling up within himself. Disgust was a defense mechanism, after all. Maybe he wasn't completely lost.

He closed the video, feeling strongly that if he watched the whole thing right then, with everything and everyone still up in the air, he would lose a piece of his soul through his eyes.

He flipped back to the spreadsheet and found the entry for BY39, the same label as the video file. The date next to the initials was from the first week of January.

"I think it's safe to say the letter-number combos are designations for the girls," Gordon said. He seemed to have recovered and was back over Brighton's shoulder. "The names have to be a customer list."

"First name, last initial for the men," Brighton said, shaking his head. "Not much to go on." Although a few of the names struck Brighton as vaguely familiar for some reason.

"Wait a second," Gordon said, stepping around. "Go back up. To the top."

Brighton flicked the track pad back to the top of the spreadsheet.

"There," Gordon said, pointing.

Beneath the gnawed tip of his fingernail was a name: Charlie C. The corresponding code was TC09.

"Charlie Cunningham?" Brighton asked.

"Maybe," Gordon said. "And TC for Tasha? It fits."

Brighton highlighted the row, and when he did, a date appeared next to each name in the formula bar. Charlie C.'s was 02-24-15.

"That ring a bell to you?" Brighton asked.

Gordon scratched at the scruff on his chin. "That would have been around the time he ran the car into New Hope, I guess. But the day itself, I have no idea. I wasn't in a great place then."

Brighton highlighted the cells and scrolled down, exposing all the dates behind the names, then he leaned back and crossed his damp sleeves over his chest, taking everything in.

"Some of these are in the future," Brighton said. "Look, that's in four days."

Brighton was struck again by a sense of familiarity, but this time because of the dates. He knew that date, the one from the future. He clicked out of the cell and brought back the name on top: Jamal M.

The two came together with a nearly audible click in Brighton's mind, and with that click came a new wave of terrible understanding —and more questions.

"Jamal Martin is the defendant I declined to represent in a criminal case set for four days from now," Brighton said wearily. His face throbbed fiercely in time with his racing heart. "Josiah Hill visited me this morning and told me that declining wasn't an option."

"Wait, Hill was here?" Gordon asked.

Brighton felt a stray rivulet of blood coming from the bottom of the gash. He dabbed at it with his cuff. *Shirt's ruined anyway*, he thought. "I hadn't heard from him in years. I thought I was rid of him, but I should have known. Hill wanted to bring back the old business. Said he was *expanding*."

"Did Charlie see him?" Gordon asked.

Brighton nodded. "He said he followed him. I think he might have killed him if he knew where Tasha was. But that's the missing piece for him."

Brighton closed out of the hacked drive and opened up the BCDC Court Records database, wanting to double-check Jamal's court date. Sure enough, the date on the court record matched the date on the decrypted spreadsheet.

Brighton's shattered resolve was piecing back together, shard by shard. If it had been a mirror, it would be reflecting a very different man than the one who'd walked into the office that morning.

Just to make sure, Brighton looked back at the latest date in Charlie Cunningham's court records. The final hearing that sent the boy to Ditchfield was held on February 24, 2015, another date match.

"These are court dates," Brighton said. "They're the day these boys got shipped to Ditchfield."

"And also the day that Tasha Cunningham was left alone," Gordon said, moving back over to the desk, to the pictures. "The day New Hope could close in on her and all the other girls like her."

Brighton spun back around to Gordon. "You think they're related. The girls and the Ditchfield boys."

"Most likely. Dependent on each other, at least," Gordon said, picking up the picture again.

Brighton was struck by the depth of the pain on Gordon's face. The good doctor looked like he wanted to reach through the grainy ink and pull the girl out of that room himself.

Until that night, he'd always thought of Gordon as a desperate sort of person, a man barely treading water in the world around him and, regarding the expert-witness stuff, a man he could use to further his own agenda. For the first time, Brighton considered that maybe the reason Dr. Gordon Pope always seemed barely above water was because he was the type of man that kept throwing himself back into the deep end every time he managed to climb out.

"I think the boy and the girl are a package," Gordon said. "Hill gets one then gets the other."

Brighton flipped back to the court appointment of Jamal Martin, set for four days hence—the first half of Hill's next twisted package deal... if his pet lawyer followed instructions.

But Thomas Brighton wasn't feeling much like following instructions at the moment. He knew what he had to do, and he knew what it would cost him.

"I'll stand up to him in court," Brighton said. "I'll go after him."

Brighton was surprised—and relieved—to find that the good doctor did not look shocked. Perhaps Gordon saw something inside him that was still worth redeeming. He was a shrink, after all. He probably had more than an inkling of what was going on in Brighton's head.

"But none of it sticks unless we have a girl on the stand, testifying," Brighton said. He knew which girl too.

Gordon looked down at the photo again. "That's a hell of an ask," he said. "Even if we somehow find Tasha, she may be too damaged to testify."

"Without her, we've got a bunch of disgusting movies, creepy pictures, and old receipts," Brighton said. "Even child-porn charges won't stick if there's nothing tying the computers specifically to Hill, and the computers are gone. Right now, it's your testimony about what you found while borderline trespassing on private property."

Gordon inhaled then exhaled. Brighton knew he understood what would stick on Hill and what wouldn't. Brighton also felt that charges of possessing child pornography was too lenient by far, and Gordon would surely agree.

"So we're back to where we started," Gordon said. "Chasing Tasha Cunningham."

"Except now I got a gash down my face," Brighton added.

"And Dana is about to get fired," Gordon said, raising a finger.

That was news to Brighton. He knew Dana Frisco tangentially, mostly through bumping into her in the courthouse. But he'd always thought she was good people.

"And Marty Cicero got shot," Gordon said, ticking the two off on his fingers. "He'll be fine, just bruised up," Gordon added after seeing the look on Brighton's face.

"Who shot Cicero?" Brighton asked.

"One of Hill's men," Gordon said offhand. "A man named Alonzo." He was looking at his phone, distracted. "Dana had the *audacity* to fire back," he added, heavy on the sarcasm.

Brighton had a flicker of an idea. "Did she kill him?" he asked.

Gordon shook his head. "He's at Hopkins."

The flicker caught. "He knows where she is."

Gordon furrowed his brow. "Maybe. But he's almost certainly

under Duke's watch. And I doubt he'd talk to me, not after all that mess. Not with Hill on his side."

Brighton checked his watch, already moving. He counted back the time since the shooting at New Hope. Depending on how bad the wound was, the surgery could take four, maybe five hours. Then another hour in step-down recovery.

Maybe nobody had seen the guy yet.

"He's not gonna talk to you," Brighton said, taking off his suit coat and rolling up his bloody sleeves to pass for clean. "He's gonna talk to his lawyer, the one with years of experience shoveling Hill's shit for him, the dutiful lapdog."

Brighton shrugged on his camel-hair overcoat, picked up his leather suitcase, and spun back toward Gordon with a flourish. "He'll talk to Thomas Brighton, Esquire, of Brighton and Associates."

CHAPTER SIXTEEN

Gordon Pope looked at Thomas Brighton across his desk as if seeing an entirely new man. Getting his face misaligned had realigned something else inside him, something Gordon sensed had been slowly breaking of its own accord, incrementally weighing him down for some time. Five years before, the guy wouldn't advance Gordon twenty bucks to get a sandwich and a few beers. Now he was talking about walking into the lion's den on behalf of Charlie and Tasha Cunningham, two people that, as far as Gordon was aware, stood to gain him nothing, financially or otherwise. They could, in fact, spell the end of Brighton's career.

"Isn't impersonating an attorney illegal?" Gordon asked finally.

"Well it's not exactly what I'd call *best practice*. But I'm not looking for admissible testimony from the guy. I want a location. That's all. Hopefully, you and your cop buddies can do the rest. It's our best shot."

Brighton was right. Not only was it their best shot, it was likely their only shot. Tasha and the other girls held in those horrendous rooms were the key to bringing down Hill's castle.

"I gotta go. Time's ticking." Brighton looked around at his disaster of an office as if seeing it for the first time. "Yikes. Uh, how about you get all of this together and lock up on your way out? I'll be in touch."

Gordon blinked. "Lock up? The door's busted."

"You'll figure it out!" he called over his shoulder, already down the hall. "You're a doctor!"

The front door creaked halfway shut, and Gordon found himself alone in the offices of Brighton & Associates. Everything had happened in such a whirlwind that the sudden silence was heavy. The roughed-up office, the creaky old repurposed house, the smell of wet blood mixed with old plumbing—all of it brought home what he had to do.

He set about gathering the evidence as quickly as he could while he listened to his messages. Two were waiting for him, which he hoped were from Dana.

"Gordon, it's Karen..."

Gordon froze, phone pressed between his ear and shoulder, his hands full of papers. He had completely forgotten he'd missed a call from his ex-wife sometime during his drunken record diving in the broom closet.

"Listen, I know it's short notice, but I'm coming out to Baltimore tomorrow to speak at a Hopkins APA dinner, and I wasn't even going to tell you, but then I thought how childish that was, so I thought we might meet up for dinner at Waterstones. My accountant's been on me for years to finalize the split of the business, so I thought maybe we could kill two birds with one stone. Catch up over a Cobb salad and get some paperwork signed. Anyway, call me."

Gordon dropped everything in his hands and grabbed the phone. He looked at the time stamp just to be sure. Karen had called at 8:15 p.m. the night before. That meant she was in town already, and for some reason, the thought of Karen coming at this time, with all these knives still being juggled, made him deeply uncomfortable.

Then he saw a business card.

He'd missed it before because it was on the far corner of the desk, where the comm system used to sit, before Charlie destroyed it.

Gordon had seen the card a hundred times over the years, at the courthouse, around Baltimore, and of course, up at Ditchfield... where he'd seen it first.

Brighton and Associates
Thomas Brighton, Esq.—Founding Partner
Mental Health Attorney | Psychiatric Defense Specialist
Illuminate. Enlighten. Brighton & Associates.

Nothing unusual about the man's business card being on the desk in his place of business, Gordon thought. Yet something about that card struck him as different. For one, it was older, frayed. The font looked outdated, the design different from the stack Brighton kept neatly situated in a crystal cardholder on the opposite side of the desk.

Gordon recognized it as an older model, one might say, the kind still kept out at Ditchfield, the place that time forgot. It was from an era when Thomas Brighton was a different kind of lawyer.

Gordon realized he was shaking slightly as he picked it up. He flipped it over, already dreading what he knew he'd see there.

The number two was circled in pen, hand drawn, like the crooked bullseye of a target.

Dana's words echoed in his head, underneath the slow and steady return of the ringing: *He has a list. And like it or not, you're on it.*

He recalled her imploring face on that cold morning that felt like a million years ago, when she said she had to keep Chloe safe by keeping him away. He remembered the strange weight of the engagement ring in his breast pocket and the question unasked.

That was not Thomas Brighton's business card. It was Charlie Cunningham's business card, or rather, it was a calling card of unfinished business.

Dana had said three cards were in Charlie's possession when he took off. The first was for New Hope, which he'd left on Andy Bagshot's ruined corpse. The second was for Brighton and

Associates, which he'd just left on the blood-spattered desk of Thomas Brighton.

The third was the business card for Jefferson and Pope.

His phone buzzed and startled him nearly to jumping. He snatched it up. A reminder was indicating a second voice mail, also from Karen Jefferson.

The ringing in his ears picked up a notch. He had a feeling of impending collision, like he was parked on the tracks at a crossing, stuck between the closed crossbars, with trains careering toward him from both directions.

He listened to the voice mail.

"Gordon, it's Karen again. You're still terrible with the phone. Good to see some things never change. Anyway, I'm at the office. I let myself in with my key. I'm going to wait here for a bit, grab a few things I'd always been meaning to pick up. If I still can't get hold of you in half an hour or so, I'll just leave the papers. Call me."

He looked at the time stamp. She'd called him a mere ten minutes before, when he and Brighton had been knee-deep in all the darkness from Ditchfield.

Gordon had an awful feeling, distinct and clear, more a premonition than anything, that Karen Jefferson was about to meet Charlie Cunningham.

He threw everything back into the box as quickly as he could and tried to recall whether Charlie would have any cause to remember Karen specifically. He had a vague memory of mentioning her in a session or two, and not favorably. Something like:

"My wife deals better with red tape than she does with patients."

That wasn't bad, not damning. But then, like dominos, one memory felled another. He'd dropped little seeds in their weekly meetings about how he and Karen had totally different views about how to help the boy. And then, at Ditchfield, the first time he'd seen him:

"Charlie, my wife says you're a sociopath. Help me prove her wrong."

Gordon felt sick to his stomach. He yanked the USB drive from Brighton's computer then turned toward the door and was reminded that it was nonfunctioning. He cursed and looked around for some way to lock up.

He dropped the box, grabbed a wingback chair, and dragged it to the creaky hall. It was a tight fit. *Good.*

Gordon got behind the wingback and pushed it down the hall. The wing tips scraped along the paint, leaving dark little trails of crushed red felt. At the door, he tipped the chair back and jammed it under the knob.

He trotted back down the hall as fast as his knee would allow, picked the box up on his way, and headed toward the back. He passed the bloody bathroom, where the sink was still dripping. He left out the back door, stopping only to make sure it latched behind him before quick-limping down the outer stairs on the way to his car.

CHAPTER SEVENTEEN

The drive from Brighton's office on Bail Bond Row to Gordon's loft in Mount Vernon was normally fifteen or so minutes, but he was hoping to make it in ten. Gordon dialed Karen as he sat, sick to his stomach at a red light on East Biddle. The phone rang and rang and rang. The light turned green, and he almost pitched the cell against the passenger door. Karen always answered her phone. Even during the divorce when he was drunk and pitiful, she answered. It's what she did.

Gordon dialed Dana again. She picked up on the first try. *Small miracles*, Gordon thought. Then he was immediately confronted with how to frame the fact that his ex-wife might be in serious danger on account of him.

"Dana, I think you're right," Gordon said, speaking quickly.

"Gordon, thank God," said Dana. "I miss five calls from anyone, I assume the world is ending."

Gordon got caught first in line at another red light. He inched forward by degrees.

"The world's always ending," he said. "It's all about how we live in it."

He looked both ways then gunned it, with a small prayer that Dana was the only cop he'd end up speaking to on his drive.

"Charlie broke into Brighton's place. Slashed him up. He's alive. Doing better, actually, than I think he's been in a long time," Gordon said as he took a hard right and gunned the coupe up to a rattling sixty miles an hour on Hartford.

"What? Gordon, slow down, what are you talking about?"

"The business cards. Charlie left one of Brighton's behind. It had the number two written on it."

Silence from Dana.

"You there?" Gordon asked.

"Yeah, I'm here," said Dana.

"You were the one that said it. He had three cards on him. He's dropped two of them. That leaves one."

"Where are you?" Dana asked.

Gordon's mind was racing. "He was listing. Ordering. Planning his approach. I dismissed it initially because I had an idea of who this kid was, but I think I'm wrong. I think we're all wrong."

"Are you in the car?" Dana asked. "Focus, Gordon."

"Yes, I'm on my way to the office. And get this: Karen is there," Gordon said, holding his outspread fingers to the windshield as if he wanted to squeeze his frustration out of the orange clouds in the evening sky.

More silence from Dana. Gordon could picture her leaning back on the counter, one hand holding the phone to her ear, the other stroking an eyebrow as she thought. That was a tic of hers.

"You want me to call this in?" Dana asked. "Marty is out on recovery, but there's a handful of other good apples on the force still—"

"With the rap sheet Charlie's got? They'll kill him. You know it, and I know it," said Gordon. "I need you."

"Gord, I'm not technically police right now," she said, her voice wavering.

"Bullshit. You're every bit the cop you always were and more," said Gordon, leaning into a hard right that made his tires squeal softly.

He got a long honk from someone and didn't care.

"I don't even have a gun," Dana said.

"Good," Gordon said.

More silence. Gordon pictured her nervously fussing with her eyebrows. "Dana, please."

"My whole fear with this business card theory was that you would be placed in danger. I wanted you to stay *away* from all this," Dana said, helplessly.

"You know I can't do that. Especially not if Karen is walking into some kind of trouble she knows nothing about."

"Okay," Dana said. "Okay." She sounded as if she had to rev herself up, give herself an internal pep talk that she wasn't quite buying. But she was coming.

"I'm five minutes out," he said.

"I'll be there in fifteen," she replied. "I'd say be careful, but I'm not totally sure you know what that means."

As Gordon was trying to think of a witty reply, she hung up.

FOR A FEW FLEETING moments on the awkward run from his car to his loft, Gordon thought perhaps he was overreacting. Nothing he'd thought about the case, neither the criminal case nor the psychiatric case, had turned out even remotely the way he'd predicted. Maybe his instincts here were wrong as well.

Then he saw neat slivers of his doorjamb sprinkled across the entryway. *Of course,* he thought grimly. *The one thing I get right.*

The door opened easily. More shards of wood lay on the floor inside. A stab of fear mixed with sickly sweet nostalgia at seeing Karen's bag and coat in the foyer, just like they always used to be, way back when, before everything.

His place was still a mess and smelled vaguely of old Chinese food. He couldn't see anyone right away, but he felt them. The darkness inside was expectant.

"Hello?" Gordon ventured.

He flicked on the lights and heard a shuffling from around a corner, as well as heavy, panicked breathing.

"Charlie?" he asked. "It's just me, Gordon. I'm coming in alone."

A man cleared his throat somewhere inside, a soft sound that was still somehow a violation. Gordon worked to unclench his teeth. If he hoped to get out of this encounter alive, he would need to be at the top of his game, to find that space where he could glide, effortlessly working in both his own mind and that of his patient.

Then he turned the corner and saw Karen bound to his desk chair with an ethernet cable, a strip of duct tape slapped over her face, her eyes wide beyond the whites and into the reds at the far edges. He took a step toward her, and as if on cue, Charlie stepped out from behind the stairway and pointed a gun at him.

All his training fled him in an instant.

He didn't know what he was expecting Charlie to look like, but it wasn't that: a skinny pole of a young man in a baggy black hoodie and a loose pair of jeans that fit like he'd stolen them off the line in a hurry. His hair was bushy and unkempt, his cheeks hollow, and even his ragged ear looked different, more lived in, like the old war wound of a street cat. He held the gun awkwardly, at a bit of a lean, like he could barely support its weight.

Only his eyes were the same, piercing and steady, simmering just before a boil.

"Charlie, what did they do to you?" Gordon asked, his voice barely above a whisper.

"You know what they did," Charlie said, eyeing Gordon up and down as if squaring away the sight of him with whatever memory he had. "What they still doin'."

"Trying to crush you," Gordon said.

The words simply came out, but they rang true. From day one, everybody wanted to squeeze the life out of that kid—his parents, who never gave him a shot; the teachers who couldn't deal with him; the court system rigged against him; Ditchfield, quite literally. The city itself was set against him from the very beginning because he lived in the projects, hustling to survive with the added weight of responsibility for Tasha.

Everything and everyone seemed designed to hold him down... everyone but Gordon. Somehow, Gordon had to make him see that.

Charlie pulled a business card from his baggy front pocket and held it up. Gordon could see the even black lettering of Jefferson and Pope LP on one side. He flipped it to reveal the number three in a scrawled circle.

"Last stop," he said, and he flicked it at Karen, who let out a muffled whimper.

"You don't have to hurt her. You don't have to hurt anyone, but especially not her. She isn't even supposed to be here," said Gordon, willing himself not to sound as desperate as he felt.

"Two questions," Charlie said, all business. "First, did you know?"

"No!" Gordon exclaimed. "I mean, I knew Ditchfield was horrendous, but I had no idea Josiah Hill was involved in any of it. Especially not when it came to those girls."

"Two. Did you find Tasha like I told you the last time I saw you, through the glass?" Charlie asked.

"No," Gordon said again, but without strength. "I should have. But my life sort of fell apart, and..."

"And you gave up, same as the lawyer," Charlie said. "Let me get sent up to that hellhole and then went back to your lives." He shook the gun at Gordon and spoke through gritted teeth. "You gave me no choice! This is what I gotta do to get through to you!"

"You're not a killer, Charlie," Gordon said.

"I sure as shit killed Andy Bagshot," Charlie said. He looked like he was trying for a merciless smile, but it came across as a grimace of pain.

"This is different, and you know it," Gordon said. "Andy was torturing you. Karen and I were just bad psychiatrists."

Charlie's eyes seemed to go unfocused, which Gordon thought was a bad sign. "You don't know the half of it," Charlie said.

"Then tell me," said Gordon.

Charlie came back a bit, finding the room again. "Dirty Andy's been fuckin' with me for years, sayin' he buys black girls on camera. Talkin' 'bout how he's gonna step up his game, maybe buy one in real life. Maybe somebody I knew. Then he showed me a picture on his phone, right before they came in with the needles. I recognized Tasha."

Gordon could picture it: Andy pulling out a greasy cell phone as Charlie lay strapped to that dentist's chair from hell and flipping through his filthy pictures, just like the ones Gordon had in the box. A brother would recognize his twin sister no matter what she'd been turned into. He wondered if Charlie screamed at him, straining against the four-point restraints to get to him as long as he could. Or maybe the fast-acting benzodiazepine had paralyzed him already.

"I put most of it together after I popped that bitch Alonzo's eye for saying he'd already taken her down. After he got out of the hospital, he tried to swagger back. Got a message through to me about raping her at New Hope like it was a walk in the fuckin' park. Like they let it happen."

"That's why you stole the car. Why you ran it into the church," said Gordon. He remembered seeing Alonzo, eyepatch and all, the night Marty was shot. He was the man that got away. Gordon understood finally. Charlie wasn't going on some sort of spree. He was looking for help.

Charlie's gun trembled slightly, and he looked like he wanted badly to squeeze the trigger. "New Hope was supposed to help her," he said, his voice cracking slightly. "Instead, they let Andy and Alonzo and whoever else use her like a rag. Then Brighton was supposed to help me. But he got bought off. Then you two were supposed to help me, but you gave up, and *this one* never thought I could be helped to begin with!" He stepped forward and pushed the stubby barrel of the revolver against the back of Karen's skull so hard that he bowed her head until her chin touched her chest.

"Charlie, I only see this going one of two ways. Either we help you tell your story, or you pull that trigger and Josiah Hill and Alonzo and half the Baltimore Police who are out there right now, trying to paint you as nothing more than a sociopathic killer, win."

Karen looked up at him, and he truly met her eyes for the first time, her focus wholly on him.

"Sometimes Karen is thoughtless. She has a thousand-foot view in a world that requires seeing eye to eye. But she's not the one that failed you. She never promised to help you in the first place. I did. And that is something I'll live with for the rest of my life."

As he spoke, all the conversations he'd had with the boy came back in one fire hose blast, snippets of conversations layered over one another in one big synaptic firing squad of memories. One, in particular, struck him.

"I asked you one time if you were grateful for anything," Gordon said calmly, evenly, with the kind of clarity that can only come when someone quite literally has a gun to their head.

Charlie's eyes glanced up and away, but the mania he'd been showing receded a bit. He was recalling the conversation.

"That was a dumb question to ask. Lazy too. I was trying to build a plan of care around making you reassess your past, thinking maybe you'd overlooked something wonderful, some beautiful memory you could hold on to. But your past was brutal. Sometimes, no amount of reframing can fix a shattered picture. Sometimes, you've just got to start painting again. I should have worked with you to paint something new. So how about we start right now? Give me a chance to find Tasha. If I can't..." Gordon didn't want to say it, but some contracts needed to be signed in blood. "You can take what you feel you're owed from me."

Karen's cries were muted, but her tears were real as Charlie pulled the gun back from her head and pointed it squarely at Gordon once more.

"You know where she is?" Charlie asked, his voice deadly calm.

Gordon thought it a particularly ridiculous bit of irony that his entire life was now in the hands of Thomas Brighton, probably just then waltzing into the secured ward of JH Emergency in his fancy leather shoes with a freshly jagged smile. But that was the hand he was dealt.

"I think we may have a lead," Gordon allowed.

Charlie looked carefully at him then back down at Karen. He put the gun inside the baggy double-sleeved pocket of the hoodie. The snub nose was still there, but the immediacy of death seemed a mile away.

"You got one night to prove it," Charlie said. "And you and I do it together. Let's go."

Gordon cleared his throat. "Well, I'm not one hundred percent sure where to go just yet," he began, stammering a bit. "I was hoping we could just take a seat here. Maybe get a cold glass of water? Think through our options?"

"We're going now," said Charlie. "We take your car."

"My car? It's a piece of junk. Really. Our chances of getting killed go up substantially as soon as we sit down in that thing."

The revolver pressed through the fabric of his sweater like a pointing finger. Dana was about five minutes away. Gordon wondered how he might stall. *Offer the guy a cup of coffee?* That would take a good five minutes to make, easy.

"How about if—"

"Go," Charlie said.

Gordon took one last look at Karen. Her eyes pleaded with him, trying to convey something he couldn't quite grasp: anger, fear, but also gratitude. From kissing under the Christus, to being in and out of a divorce, all the way to getting bound and gagged. What a ridiculous ride.

"All right," Gordon said, clapping his hands together lightly. "You say go, we'll go."

When Gordon pulled the keys back out of the front-door lock where he'd left them, he thought about that flash of light he'd seen on the coffee table all those years before. The roll of duct tape was sitting where she'd left the ring.

Charlie followed him out and closed the door softly behind them. On the walk to his car, Charlie kept the distance between them to within a step.

CHAPTER EIGHTEEN

Thomas Brighton was a man who lived by a handful of tenets. One of those tenets was "Never forget a favor." Another was "Get the shit you dread done first." A third: "Drink twenty ounces of water for every ounce of vodka."

But by far, his most sacred tenet was "Fake it till you make it."

That sacred tenet was what allowed him to walk, briefcase in hand, right up to the security desk at the Emergency Department of Johns Hopkins Hospital, looking like he was born to be there. He pulled out one of his cards, flashed it to the officer behind the desk and said he was there to see his client.

The officer eyed the card perfunctorily, barely even looking up from her computer. "Who is your client?" she asked.

"Alonzo Cook," Brighton said, as if it was obvious.

Of course, it wasn't. Up until about ten minutes before, he hadn't even had the man's full name.

He'd called Natasha on his drive over and begged her to tap one of his contacts at the records department inside BPD. He needed a full name. At first, she demurred, saying she was on a date, but he must have sounded a special kind of desperate because she eventually agreed. It was a crap date anyway, she'd said.

So Brighton flexed one of his tenets and called in a favor. In fact, Marty Cicero had just filed the ballistics report for a recent shooting at New Hope Community Church. Two were wounded. One was Cicero himself, and the other was a man by the name of Alonzo Cook.

A quick cross-reference with the county courthouse told Brighton that Alonzo Cook had quite a rap sheet—right up until he didn't. He'd been arrested five times in his teens, everything from drunk and disorderly to assault. He'd entered a probationary program at seventeen as part of a plea bargain to stay out of Ditchfield, a reform program run by the venerable New Hope Foundation. He'd been squeaky clean ever since, at least on paper.

Brighton knew better.

"Alonzo Cook is in step-down under guard," said the officer, looking up for the first time. Her eyes widened slightly at the jagged new addition to his visage.

Still, he never let his smile waver. "That's exactly why I'm here," he said. "He's expecting me."

But of course, he wasn't.

The officer eyed him a moment more then pulled out an electric-orange sticker badge marked Visitor. She wrote the room number in the top right: 102.

Brighton pulled the sticker off its backing and pressed it above his gold chrysanthemum lapel pin. He tapped it a few times for good measure then thanked the officer and walked inside.

No matter how orderly an emergency department was—and the ED at Hopkins was among the best—Brighton still cringed inwardly every time he walked inside. He'd been in and out of hospitals all his career—on behalf of others, for the most part—but it never got easier. He could sense a consistent undercurrent of panic, along with the sounds of pain, both heard and unheard, because even the guys that suffered in silence seemed to emit a kind of dog-whistle keen just too high to hear. All of it made Brighton slightly nauseous.

The important thing was that Brighton cringed *inwardly*. His exterior was as stalwart as ever as he pressed the button to unlock the heavy double doors that would take him to the step-down rooms, where patients fresh out of surgery awaited transfer to the recovery floor.

Brighton saw a police officer right away, a beefy fellow in full uniform, standing beside the door and unabashedly gawking at the asses of the nurses as they came and went. Brighton pulled his shoulders back to present as confident a front as possible. He slowed his stride until he was walking the hospital hallway as assuredly as he would his own living room. A glance at the officer's badge gave him the man's name before the cop even realized Brighton was approaching him.

"Officer Packman, right?" Brighton said, nodding as if in answer to his own question. "The chief told me you'd be here."

Who "the chief" was, Brighton couldn't be sure. But that hardly mattered. He knew that type of cop. The dolt would be flattered that "the chief" was thinking about him and probably a little amazed that Brighton knew his name, despite it being stitched right there on his shirt.

"Duke sent you?" he asked.

That was the guy, Warren Duke. Brighton knew of him—total asshole, the kind of guy that the Thomas Brighton of a few days ago might have admired a little.

"He did." Brighton nodded sagely and pulled a card effortlessly from the breast pocket of his eight-hundred-dollar camel-hair overcoat. "Thomas Brighton of Brighton and Associates LLP. I'm Mr. Alonzo Cook's defense attorney. Warren sent me himself with instructions to speak with him and only him as soon as he wakes up."

He hoped the first-name familiarity would also cement his persona, and evidently, it was doing the trick. Packman was nodding slowly while he looked at the card, eager to have been in on the decision the entire time, eager to make it look like he knew what was going on.

Brighton decided to take a gamble. "Feel free to call it in if you want," he said offhand, as if such a thing was an absolute waste of Packman's time.

The gamble paid off. "No, that's all right. Go on in. He's been out of surgery for a few hours now."

Brighton nodded thanks and stepped past Packman, who was already uninterested in everything but the nurses' asses once more. He flicked down the handle of the door and walked inside.

Alonzo Cook was attached to all sorts of machines. IV lines trailed from both inner wrists, leading to what looked like a coatrack sporting bags of liquids. A tube was running out from under the covers at his side, draining thin red liquid into an evil-looking hazmat box on the floor. Brighton counted three monitors, each displaying a different set of numbers.

Alonzo was also wide awake, tapping a fingertip clipped tight with a heart-rate monitor slowly on the top of the covers, and staring straight at Brighton with one good eye.

"Who are you?" he muttered. His voice wasn't strong, but it was crystal clear, not the voice Brighton would associate with a man fresh out of surgery that had a bullet removed from his chest.

The other blockers on this mission—front desk security, the officer on duty—those were nothing compared to what he'd have to pull off next. Alonzo was Brighton's true test.

He felt oddly elated. "I'm Thomas Brighton, your attorney."

"I don't know nothing about any attorney," Alonzo said slowly, pausing every few words but never taking his eyes off Brighton.

"Hill sent me," Brighton said, returning gaze for gaze.

Alonzo didn't bite. "This is the first I heard."

Brighton looked around, found a rolling stool, and pulled up a seat. He situated his empty briefcase carefully at his side and looked squarely at Alonzo. "That's because you were in surgery, Mr. Cook. Because you got shot. By a cop. For shooting another cop."

Alonzo leaned back on his elevated bed and took in Brighton through hooded eyes.

"Hence, your need for an attorney," Brighton said, holding out his arms in a mock welcome.

"I didn't shoot nobody," Alonzo said.

"Good," replied Brighton. "That's good. That's exactly what you're gonna say in court. And with any luck, that will be the end of it."

The tapping stopped. He'd gotten Alonzo's attention. *Time to set the bait.*

Brighton leaned in and lowered his voice. "What you certainly will not be saying is anything remotely related to the New Hope Foundation, especially New Hope Community Church and what you may or may not have been doing there on the night in question. Nor will you mention the Reverend Josiah Hill's name anywhere whatsoever. In fact, once I leave this room, you will remain silent."

"Where you goin'?" he asked, wary but less confident.

"I have to clean up my second mess of the evening, concerning a certain acquaintance of yours on the night in question, caught running a red light in an unmarked van at midnight, who subsequently mouthed off to the officer and ended up in holding."

Alonzo's eyes went wide at that. Brighton had struck a nerve.

"They caught Dameon?" he asked.

"Yes, they did," Brighton said, affecting a tried-and-true note of disgust as he stood, which had proven particularly effective in court. It wasn't hard. He picked up his briefcase and made a show of getting ready to leave but slow played it a bit by checking his phone. He'd set the bait—time to wait for the bite.

"What about the van?" Alonzo asked quietly, in confidence.

"Thankfully, the reverend has friends in the department. We were able to swap the driver, but it was tricky," Brighton said, leaving the statement open to interpretation.

"But it made it to Ditchfield?"

Bingo.

"Yes, Mr. Cook. It made it to Ditchfield. If it hadn't, we'd be having a very different conversation right now," Brighton said.

Brighton had it. All the cameras, all the computers, all the recording equipment was now up at Ditchfield. That made sense. A big place like that, a lot of refurbished old buildings, some left derelict over the years—anything could be hidden up there, even a bunch of terrified young girls.

Brighton paused at the door and looked back at the man who had almost killed Marty Cicero, a cop that Brighton knew only tangentially but who nonetheless felt like a guy that played on his team. "Remember what I said, Mr. Cook. Speak to nobody. And for God's sake, try not to shoot any more cops. It really taxes the reverend's legal team."

He let those words hang in the air as he pushed open the door and left Alonzo's darkened recovery room for the antiseptic white of the hall. Saying nothing to Packman as he passed, he only walked away, already dialing Gordon Pope.

CHAPTER NINETEEN

The slow rattle coming from somewhere under the hood of Gordon's coupe sounded like a lazy castanet as he sat in the darkness with a white-knuckle grip on his steering wheel. From their vantage, the sharp steeple of New Hope Community Church shot high into the sky, but the rest of the place was obstructed by a shuttered auto-parts store and a ratty off-brand gas station.

"I'm telling you, Hill's not there. Nobody is there," Gordon said. "They cleared everything out."

"Go around the block again," Charlie said. Brighton's revolver sat crosswise in his lap, the muzzle pointed right at Gordon's liver.

Gordon eased the coupe out. Traffic was sparse, both foot and automobile. People that weren't working the corners were walking quickly from one to the other, keeping to the shadows. Or they were buying and bolting.

Crime scene tape crisscrossed the big white double doors of New Hope just beyond the concrete island. No light could be seen through the windows, not even weak candlelight. Despite his guarantees otherwise, Hill's house of God appeared to be temporarily closed by the power vested in the Baltimore Police, likely by order of

Warren Duke, specifically, until he could get things under control his way.

When they swung around the back, Charlie gazed intently at the high brick walling off the inner courtyard and that miserable inner sanctum. Gordon felt like he could still smell the place.

"This used to be the only spot Tasha and I could get food, back in the day," Charlie said, his voice distant.

Gordon said nothing.

"I remember Hill handing me a bologna sandwich when I was ten years old. He gave Tasha an extra chocolate milk that first time and every time after." Charlie seemed lost in the memory, as if he was trying to examine it from every angle in his mind. "You think he was whoring little girls out then too?"

For a moment, Gordon didn't realize he'd been asked a question. He was still grappling with the fact that he was being held at gunpoint in his beat-up two-seater by a guy that he'd spent the better part of the entire week and much of the end of his married life trying to connect with.

When Gordon found Charlie looking at him, waiting for his answer, he couldn't do anything but speak the first words that came to mind. "Probably. Men like Josiah Hill don't just wake up one day and decide to prey upon children. His setup might not have been as sophisticated, but he was likely grooming his next victims even then."

"With chocolate milk," Charlie said softly, almost a mumbled whisper. "How the fuck does a grown man..." He trailed off, eyes on the church again. He seemed to have gone down that line of questioning before, probably hundreds of times, knowing he'd find no answers.

"Likely, Hill was sexually abused himself," Gordon said simply. "That's almost always the case with sexual predators. Especially pedophiles."

Charlie sneered. Gordon could tell he didn't like hearing that. Anything that made the monster look like more of a man likely didn't align with Charlie's worldview right then. But to Gordon, that was simply a medical fact.

"It's no excuse," Gordon added. "There is no excuse for what Hill did, what he continues to do. I'm just saying that these cases are vicious cycles. You and Tasha were pulled onto a runaway train that was a long time coming. It probably left the station before you and I were ever born."

Gordon's eyes drifted down to the gun and wondered if they'd reached the part where the runaway train rounded the bend, one side lifted, wheels barely touching the steel, only to find that the track is out ahead.

He felt a vibration in his pocket and reached for it out of instinct then paused as the gun dug into his side.

"My phone is ringing," Gordon said quickly. "It could be the lead I told you about."

Charlie considered it and nodded once. "You say one word about me or where you are, I'm gonna end that call real quick."

Gordon squirmed to get the phone out of his pocket and answered it without even looking at who was calling.

"Hello?"

"I got it out of him, Doc," Brighton said, a bit breathless. He was walking somewhere, the tapping of his shoes audible. "Ditchfield. It's all up at Ditchfield."

Ditchfield. The word settled itself in his stomach like a stone at the bottom of a lake.

"Hello?" Brighton asked, his voice tinny and distant. "Gordon?"

Of course it was all up at Ditchfield. He felt the truth of that as surely as he felt the cold of the night closing in around him. It was as inevitable as the deepening winter. In some ways, perhaps, he'd always known.

All roads eventually lead to Ditchfield.

"You hear me, Pope? I think it's all there. The cameras, the equipment, even the girls."

Gordon's voice came out slightly panicked. "Yeah, I hear you. Makes sense."

"What's the plan? Where are you?" Brighton asked.

Gordon felt the barrel push in slightly, like a probing finger. "Uh, I'm... around."

Brighton paused. "What?"

"Tell Dana," Gordon said suddenly and cringed a bit, half expecting to get shot for it.

But Charlie held his fire. He'd likely heard Brighton too. Maybe his mind was on a crash course with Ditchfield, just like Gordon's.

"You're being weird, Doc. What's going on?" Brighton asked.

"I'm fine. I'll take it from here. You start building a case."

"Okaaay—" Brighton began.

But then Charlie snatched the phone and hung up.

Gordon turned toward him. Charlie had heard, all right. Gordon could see in him a mute fear that filled his hollow eyes and made them look more ancient, as if the word had triggered a primal flight response he was trying to wrestle back into its cage.

Maybe this was where their story ended—in Gordon's beat-up coupe idling on a run-down street outside New Hope. Charlie couldn't possibly have the strength to return willingly to the prison from which he'd fled, to waltz right back in to the scene of what was likely almost ritualistic abuse, day after day, for the most formative years of his life.

Gordon certainly wouldn't blame him if he put an end to it all right there. One way or another.

"We're gonna need gas," Charlie said.

Gordon cocked his head, not quite sure he'd heard correctly. "Excuse me?"

"You're almost empty. It's a long way to Ditchfield," said Charlie.

Just like that, the young man's decision was made. Gordon had no choice but to act it all out with him. He tried to think of where the nearest gas station was. Charlie returned the gun to a cautious rest in his lap, like a cat eyeing Gordon with a one-eyed stare.

∼

As soon as Dana saw the evidence of forced entry at Gordon's front door, she reached for the spot on her hip where her gun should have been, and her fingertips lightly brushed her pocket. She muttered a curse. *Time to improvise.*

She pushed open the door and grabbed the first thing that came to hand: a cheap plastic umbrella from the stand just inside. She flattened against the near wall, using the angles of the entryway to limit her exposure while maximizing her view. Most importantly, she kept moving. The last thing she wanted was to get caught in a standoff with Charlie Cunningham while holding an umbrella. He would close in on her from one end while her own self-doubt closed in from the other, and she would be a sitting duck.

She was about to announce herself as police but thought better of it. First, it wasn't technically true, and second, that might spook Charlie into doing something stupid.

"Anyone here?" she asked instead.

A muffled scream came from somewhere inside. She took the roundabout way, skirting the main room by dashing across the waiting room to the right. She hugged the far wall and peered into the back of the main floor.

A woman she'd never seen before was tied up to a chair, her hands bound behind her, forcing her shoulders square and jutting her chest out. A strip of duct tape was wrapped around her head and covered her mouth. Another, longer strip wrapped her tightly to the back of the chair around her waist.

"Where is he?" Dana asked before realizing the woman couldn't answer. "Nod if he's here."

The woman shook her head furiously. Wisps of perfectly dyed blond hair fell over her face.

"Is anyone else here?" Dana asked, looking up the stairs, back toward where Gordon's cave was.

Another furious shake preceded muffled speaking that Dana

couldn't make sense of. She let the umbrella fall to the ground and moved to the woman. The tape was triple wrapped around her head and arms. She tried to pull it down off her mouth but got nowhere.

"Karen?" Dana asked, more hesitantly than she would've liked. The woman finally nodded.

"Hold up," Dana said and moved quickly to Gordon's desk to rifle through the main drawer until she found a pair of scissors.

She came back and carefully slipped one shear in the gap just behind her jaw and cut the wrapping apart. One quick pull opened up the front and exposed Karen's mouth. She took in a deep, gasping breath.

"Charlie took him," she said raggedly. "Took Gordon at gunpoint. They left in his old coupe."

Dana paused in her unwrapping and plucked out her phone. She hadn't missed any calls. She dialed 911 but held off on pressing Send at the last second. She couldn't be sure who would get the call on the other end. If she gave Duke a description of the car Gordon and Charlie were in, he would do anything to silence the kid. She could imagine Duke calling in some sort of SWAT intervention that treated Gordon as irrelevant collateral damage.

She had to trust that Gordon was handling the situation as best he could and take a second to think.

"Where did they go?" Dana asked, moving down to Karen's bound wrists.

She slit the tape neatly and pulled it off in a single motion to limit the pain. Still, she winced. Since neither of them was in immediate danger, Dana took a second to look at her fully. Karen Jefferson. Right there. In the flesh.

"I don't know. He didn't say," she said, pulling her arms slowly in front of herself and rubbing at the wrists. "Thank you," she added.

She was quite pretty, nicely dressed in a billowy pants suit that looked expensive. The light jacket looked tailored, and a tasteful diamond pendant around the neck had notably been left undisturbed by Charlie. Her diamond studs, too, looked like they cost a small fortune.

"Karen Jefferson," Dana said, as if the name was the punchline of a particularly flat joke.

"Are you a colleague of Gordon's?" she asked.

"I'm his girlfriend," Dana said.

Karen assayed Dana in a new light. "Dana Frisco?"

"You know me?" Dana asked.

"Of course I do. I know *of* you, at least."

Dana stopped cutting. She stepped back and sized her up again. After a moment in which Dana simply held the scissors and looked at the woman who had almost irreversibly cracked the foundation on which Gordon had built his life, she spoke again, mistaking Dana's shock for confusion.

"Yes, well, in addition to being Gordon's ex-wife, my name is one half of that shingle out front. Which is actually the whole reason I came here. I was waiting for him to return so I could discuss full divestiture, but I got Charlie instead."

"I know all about you," Dana said flatly.

Karen looked about to speak, but then she paused. A clinical look came over her, which Dana recognized as the same that struck Gordon when he went into doctor mode. "Am I not what you expected?" Karen asked evenly.

In the old pictures Dana had seen, Karen was always a somber figure, pretty but conservative. She'd expected a severe woman, a shrew, a type-A monster. This woman was striking and colorful and surprisingly calm, even for having been taped to a chair.

"You destroyed him, you know," Dana said.

Karen eyed the scissors briefly then settled her gaze back upon Dana. "Evidently not. Gordon turned the tables here. He talked Charlie out of killing me. He certainly didn't seem destroyed to me."

So he'd bargained for her life with his own. *You loveable fool,* she thought. Then again, frantic self-sacrifice always was one of Gordon's strong points.

Dana's heart panged. She missed him terribly, and not just because he had thrown himself into immediate danger... again. She'd actually missed him from the moment she told him to stay away for the safety of her family.

What an idiot she'd been. Gordon *was* her family. She never should have pushed him away, never mind that he went willingly, that he probably thought that was a smart idea. She should have pulled him in tighter with Chloe and Maria in their happy little home at the first sign of danger to any of them. Because that's what family should do. Family drew in. Family did not push away.

Karen was feeling around the tape stuck firmly to her fresh haircut. She pulled a bit and winced then took a deep breath and held the tape at the base before yanking the first wrapping off. Chunks of blond came with it, and Karen hissed in pain.

"You're a police officer, right?" Karen asked after gathering her composure. "Can't you get people out there on the streets to find him?"

"It's complicated," Dana said. "Not something you can just drop in on and get up to speed."

Karen looked at Dana sidelong while grasping at the second wrapping. "That's fair," she said.

Dana knew she had to decide right then and there whether or not to hate the woman. She had a right to hate her. She knew how toxic Karen was to Gordon, the man she loved more than anything else in her life save, perhaps, her own daughter. And she wasn't toxic in a clean and simple way where the wound could just be cauterized. She was insidiously toxic, having struck at Gordon where he was most vulnerable, by turning his love for children into a personal failing he was just managing to overcome.

Yes, she could hate Karen Jefferson quite easily. But she wouldn't... for one reason: Gordon didn't hate Karen. He knew her better than anyone, and he didn't hate her.

She snipped the shears once in the air. "I can help you get it off. Might have to cut a little bit."

Karen looked carefully at Dana then nodded. "Thank you," she said again. "Cut whatever you need. I was planning on going short anyway."

For the next minute, the only sound was the snip of shears. Dana worked quickly and surely and only had to snip off real length in a few areas. Soon, Karen was free. She stood and looked back at the chair as if offended by it. When Dana's phone rang, both women started.

Dana didn't recognize the number, but she scrambled to answer anyway. "Hello?"

"Is this Dana Frisco?" came the reply, a voice she recognized but couldn't place.

"Who is this?" Dana asked.

"Thomas Brighton. You may remember me as the asshole lawyer that paid Gordon Pope by the hour as an expert witness. Paid pretty poorly, actually."

"Yeah, I know you," Dana said, failing to keep disappointment from her voice.

"Anyway, long story short, I'm pretty sure Tasha Cunningham and all the rest of this mess is up in Ditchfield right now," Brighton said, as if it were the perfectly ordinary progression of things.

Dana didn't trust that she'd heard him correctly. "How do you know—"

"Gordon and I had one hell of a late-night working session," Brighton said. "This was the last piece of our puzzle. I called him and told him, but he just told me to tell you for some reason. I think something's up. He was being weird on the phone. Even for him."

"Charlie's got him," Dana said. "They went for a drive."

Brighton was silent on the other end of the line for a moment before coming back with surprising calm. "I figured something like that," he said. "The kid doesn't quit. But I don't think he wants to hurt Gordon. Not if he can get around it."

"Oh? And you know this how?" Dana asked, fully recognizing that she was getting defensive.

Somehow, she was the last to know about everything recently, the last to get hit by whatever bolt out of the blue seemed to smack everyone else regarding Charlie and Ditchfield and everything. She was tired and scared for Gordon and under no illusions that things were going to end well, no matter what come-to-Jesus moment Brighton had gone through.

"Charlie and I had a nice little chat last night," Brighton said. "I think we're all straight on who the bad guys are. Plus, now you know where he's going with your boyfriend."

The full weight of his words hit Dana, and she had to lean against Gordon's ring-stained coffee bar for a moment to process. His sprawling coffee setup rattled in warning.

"You think they're going to Ditchfield? Now?" Dana asked.

"From what I've seen, Charlie's not exactly the hurry-up-and-wait type," Brighton replied.

Dana's mind felt like it was buckling. *A kamikaze run at Ditchfield in the dead of night?* She tried to think of the myriad ways that might end. None of them were good.

"I got some work to do on my end. I'm gonna leave the cop stuff to you. Listen, though, we got a hell of a case brewing. It'd be nice if Gordon lived to see it through."

Dana muttered thanks and hung up. She found Karen looking at her, waiting. She realized that the woman was expecting her to move immediately—she knew Gordon was expecting her to take charge right then too. He'd told Brighton to call her, after all. Right then was the time to do what she supposedly did best. Whether or not she thought she could do it anymore no longer mattered.

For so long, Dana had maintained that all she ever wanted was to rise up in the Baltimore Police, to lead. But the longer she lived around Gordon Pope, the more things changed. Recent promotions, future accolades, more money, more chevrons—they were all false gods.

Gordon mattered. Righting wrongs mattered. She might never be a sergeant in the Baltimore Police again, might never be a cop again at all, but she could be the kind of person that Gordon was proud to stand beside.

She zipped up her coat and checked her pocket for her keys.

"I'll clean up here," Karen said. "I was never very good in these types of situations. The trench work was always Gordon's specialty."

"I know," said Dana.

"Please keep him alive," Karen said with every ounce of pretense dropped.

All Dana could do was nod.

Her hurried walk to the minivan was surreal. She felt as if everything was converging. It only made sense that things would come to a head at Ditchfield. The place had mocked her for years from its ancient nook, embedded like a tick in the foothills. Dared her to return.

And so she would return. But she wasn't going all by herself—not anymore, not if she could help it.

MARTY CICERO COULDN'T SLEEP. After gingerly rolling from side to side for the fourth time that night, he knew he was keeping Brooke awake, so he got up. At first, he thought he might just pee and get a glass of water, but after he peed he thought, *Why the hell not pad around a bit downstairs?* Maybe Brooke could get some sleep if he wasn't fussing around. She certainly needed it. He'd told her right off the bat that being a cop's girlfriend wasn't easy, but he'd never thought she would be picking him up from the hospital that early in their relationship.

He stood for a while in the darkened kitchen, surrounded by the lingering smells of the meal she'd cooked him: organic chicken breast, grilled, on a bed of spaghetti-squash noodles. It was delicious, and he didn't have the heart to tell her that swallowing hurt, so he ate it all and gutted the pain. His discomfort didn't matter, not when the rest of his life felt so good. Even his kitchen felt good, lived in. No longer was it some distant part of the house, used only for blending single-portion protein shakes and microwaving lean single-serving meals.

He took a few more ginger sips of water and wandered to the garage, where he'd set up a small gym next to his Charger. It was nothing special, just a small weight rack, bar and bench, and some handholds bolted into the wall, enough to do whatever cycles he needed. He looked wistfully at the bench press—his favorite lift. He was well aware of his meathead tendencies, but even he wasn't going to power through lifting seventy-five on either side with a cracked sternum. Not for a while, at least.

Bye-bye, sweet gains.

Funny thing, though. A year before, he would've been devastated. Now, he was happy to be alive. *Turns out getting clocked broadside with two slugs from a nine has a way of reordering a guy's priorities.*

Brooke was the one who'd made him promise to start wearing the Kevlar vest when he went out. She was the one who held it out to him before he left the house and watched as he buckled it on. Without her, he would've been a dead man, a pretty corpse lying in a casket and not seeming quite right in the middle because there was chicken wire in spots where his chest should be.

He sat down on the bench and watched the moonlight cut a white knife across the liquid black of his car. He wondered what a more practical car might look like in this garage, something with some room for more than Brooke and her purse. *Would a minivan like Dana's fit in here?*

His heart started beating a little too quickly. "Don't worry, baby," he whispered to the Charger. "You know I'd never do you like that."

But still... that girl had him thinking thoughts—that girl and the two slugs. Another couple of inches north, and one of them would have slipped through his trachea and out his spinal column. No ambulance would have been fast enough then.

He thought he would've been angrier at being shot in the line of duty, like he'd want revenge. But then it had happened, and he was so happy to be alive afterward that all he could think about was preventing the people he loved from ever feeling that kind of fear—the kind after the slug hit but before he got a chance to check if the vest held up, and he didn't know if what he was feeling was pain from his chest getting a good thump or pain from his insides being scrambled.

Revenge didn't matter. If what Dana had told him was true, whatever was happening at New Hope was about a lot more than a crooked pastor and a few bad cops. It was a deep evil, the kind that didn't care if a few of its branches were snipped here and there. It had lived too long and dug too deep.

He wondered what it would've been like if the tables had been turned, if the great dice roll in the sky had sent Dana's wonderful daughter, Chloe, to grow up in the projects in East Baltimore—spitting distance from the darkness at the core of New Hope—and put Tasha and Charlie in Dana's comfy little house up north in suburbia, each with a room of their own. And the twins got home cooked meals every night instead of stringing out a food stamp card as long as they could.

What if Chloe was the one Hill forced to perform on camera, all painted over and drugged up?

Marty found himself balling his fists and clenching his teeth until his jaw trembled and the tightness in his chest fired a warning shot of pain across the bow.

The house whispered movement upstairs. Brooke was padding around in their bedroom on tiny feet. She hardly made any noise, moving with a dancer's grace. When she first told him she was a professional dancer, he'd thought she meant stripper, which was all the same to him. In fact, she'd meant the Baltimore Ballet. She laughed every time she remembered that conversation.

He felt bad for waking her. He'd spent enough late nights to know that once someone got out of bed, they were pretty much giving in to the insomnia. But truth be told, he wanted to be with her, wanted to sit with her and know she was there. By holding her, he could be reassured that he was not, in fact, lying dead on the ground in a false church. Whenever he wasn't with her, he was only ninety percent sure, sometimes less.

He walked back into the kitchen and set down his empty glass and waited for her to find him. She padded around the corner like a little white fox. Even his tight tees swam around her frame.

"You okay?" she asked.

"I am now," Marty said.

"Your phone's been buzzing," she said, seeming reluctant as she handed it over.

He felt some reluctance, too, to look down and see who was trying to get hold of him this soon and this late... and this many times. *Dana.*

She called again, and the phone vibrated in his hand, the screen glowing brightly in the dark kitchen. He picked up.

"What's going on?" he asked.

"Ditchfield," Dana said. "They're all at Ditchfield. Tasha, the other girls, all the gear. Charlie too. He took Gordon. They're on their way in Gord's car."

Ditchfield. The dark heart. Maybe this was their chance to shed some light.

"I wouldn't ask you if I..." Dana said but trailed off.

"I know," Marty replied.

He looked up at Brooke. She knew. She could hear every word Dana said too. And what was more, he'd shared with her just earlier that night that he was worried about Dana. She hadn't been herself lately.

He wasn't worried that Dana was physically incapable or somehow mentally damaged or anything like that—she was just too much in her own head. She needed him to help nudge her straight again.

He looked questioningly at Brooke. If she shook her head, pulled him closer, and whispered that they should just return to bed, he would probably do it. He could call in the few good cops he had left on his side and bring them up to speed as best he could. Maybe by the time they formed a bigger plan and got more people involved, the girls would still be there.

Or maybe not.

And then he would try to sleep in his own bed, in the peace and quiet of his little duplex, with Brooke's warm body beside him. But the whole time, he knew he would be thinking of what his night of peace cost those girls that night... and every night thereafter.

Instead, Brooke nodded. But when she did, she dropped her head a bit, and her eyes were swimming in tears. Marty knew she would nod, knew she would never keep him from finishing this one way or another.

"I'll come pick you up," Marty told Dana. "Just hold on."

Dana thanked him in a half-choked voice, then she hung up. He pulled Brooke gently against himself. She was small and soft and warm, like a kitten against his chest. She was crying, little quiet tremors that shook her even though she hardly made a sound.

"Wear a vest," she whispered.

"I will," he promised. And he meant it. He had a spare in his trunk, right next to the one Alonzo had destroyed. This whole affair had a charged air. Things were primed to blow. If lightning struck twice, he wanted all the protection he could get.

He had a lot more to live for.

CHAPTER TWENTY

Gordon had been to Ditchfield eleven times over the course of his career. He remembered each visit and each patient clearly and wore each of them on his heart like a notch carved in the crumbling concrete of a cell wall.

The first time he rounded the soft bend on I-70—the one just after the Patapsco River crossing—he'd been in his twenties. A short-coat doc fresh out of school, finishing up a clinical rotation with the prison system, he'd been shadowing a psychiatrist who had to sign off on a transfer and was reluctant to do so. Watching her dicker over the paperwork, he wondered why. When he caught his first glimpse of Ditchfield in the distance and his heart sank without warning, he understood why she'd balked.

The place just had a bad air about it.

Rounding that soft bend never got easier over the years. In fact, the more he went out to Ditchfield, the more he felt like the Patapsco River marked some sort of barrier. It was an invisible toll booth beyond which hope started to bleed from the body, slowly but surely, the same way a car sips gas. He was reminded of the old wives' tale about running water keeping vampires out. But at Ditchfield, the vampires were already inside.

When Gordon and Charlie crossed the Patapsco late that night, the water below the bridge was ink black. The crescent moon above looked like a shard of ice, and the shadows of the forest pressed down all around them. Charlie sat silently with his gun still trained on Gordon. He'd been diligent about it the entire trip, diligent enough that every time Gordon's crappy suspension hit a broken section of Maryland's crappy roads, Gordon held his breath.

"There it is," Gordon said grimly.

Charlie didn't respond. Gordon glanced over and found the kid staring numbly at the compound. The main manor was lit like a gothic mansion, windows for eyes, the big double door a toothy mouth. The pods were arrayed to the right and left like little Monopoly houses, hemmed in by chain-link fencing topped with razor wire. The entire length of the property was lit up at intervals by banks of spotlights.

"How the hell did you get out of there, anyway?" Gordon asked. Strangely, that question had never occurred to him. At the time, it wasn't important. Now, though, it could be very useful to know.

"Swapped places with Jarvis," Charlie said.

"No, I mean physically. How did you get through the fence?"

"Hop's truck. He's the groundskeeper. I'd been watching him for a while from the yard. Knew where he parked it. Knew when. Knew he had all sorts of shit in the back, too, including clippers—the big two-handed kind. And I figured I could hotwire it. Turned out I didn't even have to. The ol' man kept the keys above the visor," Charlie shook his head, but he smirked, almost smiling.

"You clipped the fence?" Gordon asked, impressed.

Charlie nodded slowly, still watching Ditchfield as it grew in their view. "Clipped a big door, left one side whole. Took all of five minutes. Scraped the shit out of the truck, but I got it through. Then I shut the door again."

Gordon cleared his throat and wiped his sweaty hands on his

slacks for what felt like the hundredth time. "I take it we aren't going to just waltz up to the front gate, then?"

Charlie shook his head. Gordon had figured as much. He'd had a nagging premonition ever since Charlie had made him fill his gas tank to the very top, back in Baltimore. Gordon never filled his gas tank to the top. Ditchfield was far, but it wasn't that far.

"You can't possibly think the break in the fence is still there," Gordon said, feeling clammy all over.

"You better hope so," Charlie said. "The front door'll be a whole lot messier."

They were almost at the turnoff. Up ahead, just visible in the weak lights of the coupe, a sign read State Prison Next Exit in reflective white on official turf green. Below that, it said Do Not Pick Up Hitchhikers.

Charlie sniffed at the sign as they turned off. Gordon had been carefully watching him for any signs of erratic behavior, something that might tip him off that he needed to take drastic measures like crashing the car in order not to get shot. But Charlie was vacillating between youthful bravado and an almost robotic calm. He guessed Charlie was running through scenarios in his head, psyching himself up to do something terrible, perhaps, then running through a sort of advanced postmortem of his actions.

When Gordon took the exit to Ditchfield, the clock on the dash turned to midnight.

"It's my birthday," Charlie said, as if in passing, like he was pointing out a particularly interesting rock.

"Are you serious?" Gordon asked.

Charlie nodded minutely. "Eighteen today. An adult in the eyes of the law. Likely, they'd be prepping to ship me to North Branch or some other max lockup," he said. "If I hadn't busted out, I'd just be leaving Tasha to the wolves when they transferred me."

"You know, if they catch you—I should say *when they catch you,* you'll be tried as an adult too," Gordon said. "You'll likely end up at North Branch anyway if you go through with this."

"I'm not going anywhere. This is my last stop," Charlie said.

"What does that mean?" Gordon asked, and a bit of the emotion he'd been trying to tamp down during the whole car ride bled through in his voice. "What's your endgame here?"

"I'm gonna take as many of the fuckers with me as I can," Charlie said, and his voice cracked involuntarily, breaking Gordon's heart a little.

"That's not going to save Tasha," Gordon said.

"You still don't get it, man," Charlie said, turning toward him. "Ain't nothing can save Tasha. Nothing can save me neither. Not against this place. But maybe I can see her one more time, show that I didn't abandon her. That I ain't forgot." Then Charlie recognized some turnoff. "Hold up."

Gordon's brakes squeaked as the coupe skidded to a stop. For a split second, Gordon thought maybe he'd changed the boy's mind, and strangely, he felt a pang of disappointment.

I'm going to need to unpack all this in therapy when all is said and done. Maybe have a chat with Mom about it, he thought. Then he reminded himself that when all was said and done, he'd likely be leaving Ditchfield in cuffs. Or in a body bag.

But he'd thought about it, thought and thought. And unless he was willing to risk those girls' lives, they had to strike against Ditchfield right then, however they could. Gordon was far more aligned with Charlie than Charlie was likely aware—not about killing anyone, of course, but about making a big bang, maybe the kind of big bang that got attention and lifted up this poisonous old rock to expose the wriggling filth underneath.

"You gotta cut left," Charlie said. "There's an access road that runs 'round the back side, where D is."

Gordon cranked his window down and peered out into the night. The land was dark, a no-man's zone before the floodlights where everything looked like prickly shades of black. His headlights seemed to die about fifteen feet out, but he was pretty sure he saw an overgrown two-stripe dirt road in the near distance.

"You know, if my car falls apart out there, this is going to be pretty awkward for both of us," said Gordon.

Charlie allowed a quick snort that might have been laughter under different circumstances. "Too late now. Just drive."

Gordon eased his way forward, picking a route that avoided the biggest rocks. Then he heard something in the distance. At first, he thought trucks might be downshifting on the highway, but the throaty roar seemed to be coming their way, increasing in volume, and what was more, he recognized the sound of that engine.

Only one car was that overpowered, that obnoxiously loud at full throttle.

Charlie was listening, too, his head cocked to the side, out the window.

"What is that sound?" Charlie asked, wary.

"I think that's a Dodge Charger, Hellcat edition," Gordon said, a bit embarrassed that he remembered the whole title.

"Your people?" Charlie asked, and he pointed the gun at Gordon with real intention again. "Kill the headlights. Out of the car. Now."

Gordon did as he asked, put the coupe in park, and fumbled with his seatbelt. He stepped out and held his hands up. Charlie kept the gun trained on him until they were both standing in the ratty grass just off the main road.

"Likely it's Marty Cicero, the cop that Alonzo shot. If we're lucky, he's with Dana Frisco."

"Who's she?"

"She's my girlfriend," Gordon said. "And she was a cop, a very good one. Until another one of Hill's men, a gangster disguised as a high-ranking official named Warren Duke, took it all from her."

Charlie was thinking again. Gordon pressed.

"Neither of these people is any friend of Hill. As a matter of fact, they have their own reasons why they might want to sort some things out tonight. Most important of all, they know your story."

Charlie looked back, behind himself, where a pair of xenon headlights rimmed with orange appeared in the distance like the bloodshot eyes of a rabid robot. At the rate the car was approaching, they'd drive right past them.

"And they believe you," Gordon added. "They're not here to arrest you. They're part of the child-protection unit. They want this finished as bad as anyone. Except maybe you."

Gordon could tell Charlie wasn't convinced. This would change his suicidal plan. He was recalibrating.

"They'll tell your story," Gordon said desperately. "If you blow yourself up tonight, trying to take this goddamn place down, they'll tell everyone why."

Gordon thought he might be getting through to the kid. *The man, now*, he thought, belatedly.

"Please, Charlie," Gordon asked, blatantly begging now.

"Turn on the headlights," Charlie said.

Gordon scrambled to reach in the window and flicked on the coupe's weak headlights again. The Charger's engine slowed abruptly. They'd seen him.

Charlie lowered the gun. He kept his eyes on the approaching car until the headlights illuminated him from the boots up. By the time Gordon had to shade his eyes, Charlie had the gun back in his front pouch, but he was still holding it.

The Charger growled low as Marty shifted it into park, then both doors opened. Gordon was afraid Marty was going to come out shooting, but instead he held his hands out first then followed with his body. Dana did the same until both partners stood in the harsh backlight as if they were the ones being held up.

"Charlie?" Dana asked, hesitant. "We just want to help."

Charlie looked between them then at Gordon. The young man needed to decide his way forward. Gordon had done all he could.

After a moment more, Charlie said, "Then shut those high beams off."

Marty dipped back in and, with a flick, plunged them all into a purply darkness. Nobody moved while their eyes adjusted to the night again.

"Gordon? Are you okay?" Dana asked.

"Yeah, I'm fine," Gordon replied. "I think we're all on the same page here."

"Yeah?" asked Marty, a slab of shadow like an obsidian rock face in the darkness. "And what page is that?"

"We're going in," Gordon said before Charlie could snap off something provocative.

"Well, looks like you got lost, then," Marty said. "Road is thataway."

"If we go in the front door, it's not going to end well," Gordon said. "For any of us."

"So where are we going, exactly?" Dana asked. She was finally resolving in Gordon's eyes and lowering her hands slowly until she had them at her sides. She looked slumped and unsure.

"There might be a break in the fence this way. It's how Charlie got out," Gordon said.

"I can speak for myself," he said. "I'm gonna blow a hole in Pod D. Then when everybody is scrambling, I'm going to find Tasha. If I die in there, I want her to know I did it fighting for her. That I didn't abandon her."

In the dark, without the gun visible, he sounded heartbreakingly young again.

"And ain't nothing any of you can do to stop me," Charlie added when none of them responded. "Not least 'cause I think Hill wants all you dead only a little less than me."

"He ain't wrong," Marty said. "Came damn close with me already. I think they'd like to finish the job."

"So that's it, then?" Dana asked. "That's your big plan? Same as the old plan? Smash shit up and pray?"

"My plan is to find Tasha, to die by her side if that's what it takes. She's all I got left. That's always been the plan," Charlie said.

"No, it wasn't," Dana continued, stepping forward. Charlie pulled the gun from his pocket again but kept it pointed at the ground.

"Dana—" Gordon began, trying to calm the situation with his hands.

Dana ignored him. "You didn't alert the world to all this by killing Bagshot so you could *die by her side*. You didn't slash Brighton's face to *die by her side*." Her voice was strengthening as she grew a little more confident with each step.

"You didn't strap Karen Jefferson to a chair and carjack Gordon because you wanted to die. You did it to get all of us here. And here we are. So give us better than *die by her side*," she said.

Charlie backed up in the face of her approach. "Maybe so," Charlie said. "Maybe I thought you could help. But that was before I knew where she was. Breaking into New Hope is one thing. This is *Ditchfield*. You know once we go in, there ain't no coming back from this. Especially for me."

Dana exhaled hugely, her breath puffed out into a blue cloud lit by the moon.

"Great. So instead of crashing and burning separately, we get the pleasure of crashing and burning together. Unless we do something about it," said Dana.

"And fast," Marty said, tugging at his vest uncomfortably. "We're sitting ducks out here if anyone cares to look."

Charlie turned toward Gordon. "We're going to the fence. Now." He turned back to Dana and Marty. "You can follow if you want. Whatever."

"Follow?" Marty said, incredulous. "Absolutely not."

"Fine," Charlie snapped.

"No, it's not like that. I'll scratch the shit out of my car," Marty said.

In the silence that followed, everyone looked at Marty.

"I've got ground effects on that baby. It's five inches from the pavement. Plus, I just shined it up."

"Are you serious?" Gordon asked.

"Dead serious," Marty said. "We're squeezing in your Pinto or whatever the hell it is."

"I don't even know what to say to you right now," Dana said, but with a smile in her voice.

"How about 'Get in the Pinto, Marty'?" he replied, already moving toward the car. He tugged down at his vest again and winced.

Dana wrapped her arms around her chest and looked out at the stadium lights of the prison. She seemed like she was trying to capture a thought that was as elusive as the cold mists around her.

"Pop the seats forward. I can jam in the back. If it means saving my car," Marty said.

Charlie said nothing, but he did pop his seat forward and watch as Dana climbed in and squeezed herself into the dinner-plate-sized space next to Marty.

Gordon eased his way in last. His seat wouldn't even lock. He was literally resting on Marty's knees. He closed his door gingerly, like the whole coupe might explode.

"Off we go," he said. He threw the car into drive and started praying to whoever was listening to give them enough horsepower to get where they were going.

CHAPTER TWENTY-ONE

Gordon killed the coupe's headlights a few hundred feet back from where the forest broke. The last incline was proving to be too much for the car. Twice already, the wheels had spun out. Gordon eased the pedal again, and they moved minutely, then the wheels lost traction again, kicking pebbles that clacked loudly against the undercarriage.

"You want me to get out and push?" Marty asked.

Gordon couldn't tell if he was being sarcastic or not, over the raking sound. He threw the car into park and pulled up the emergency brake.

"How about just get out?" Gordon asked. "We've got to be getting close anyway."

"Fine by me," Marty said. "Haven't been able to feel my legs for ten minutes."

Dana nodded but was quiet, watching Charlie carefully. While Gordon had nursed his car's four-cylinder engine and bald tires through the wilderness, she'd laid out the plan.

They'd revised once and had to stop the coupe to go back for supplies in Marty's car. All the while, Charlie remained aloof, nodding along, but faintly. Gordon knew her plan was extremely risky for all of them, but none more so than Charlie. If the chips didn't fall the way Dana thought they would, their lives were likely forfeit. But for everything to work, they absolutely had to keep Charlie alive.

The problem was, Gordon knew Charlie had come to Ditchfield expecting to die, maybe even hoping for it. Dying for his sister was easy, though. Living beyond Ditchfield would require a different kind of sacrifice from him, one he was having to wrap his head around.

Gordon turned the car off and got out. Marty squeezed his way free from behind. Charlie and Dana did the same until all of them were standing around the car in the dead of night. The wind was flat. Exhaust from the coupe floated lazily up and over them, hazing the moon. The engine ticked as it cooled.

Gordon waved the smoke away, coughing. "Look, before we get ahead of ourselves, let's at least see what we've got working against us up there."

Gordon also wanted to give Charlie time to think, to weigh the options and tally up the balance book in his mind the way he seemed to whenever he made a decision.

As the four of them walked toward the clearing ahead, the fence came into view: a long, straight line that boxed off the western edge of the property and ran away into the distance for at least a few football fields. It looked about twelve feet high and was topped with shimmering loops of razor wire. Charlie had chosen the spot well. It was halfway between the corners on the west side, where the reach of the spotlights was weakest. It was also probably an eighth of a mile away from anything. The closest building was Pod D, and it looked small in the distance. They would be crossing a lot of land exposed, but that wasn't Gordon's immediate concern.

The fence was mended. Gordon couldn't see a break anywhere.

"Shit," Dana said. "There goes everything."

"Maybe we can ram it," Gordon said lowly.

Marty turned to him. "Your car would have trouble knocking over a trash can, much less reinforced chain-link fencing."

"Well, we have to get through somehow," Gordon whispered furiously. "This gets a lot harder without the car. Impossible, even."

"Let me think for a minute," Dana whispered, rubbing her temples.

All the while, Charlie was walking toward the fence. He assayed the distance to the corners along the right and left, counting off ticks in measured time with a pointing finger.

"There," he said, walking quickly to an area of the fence that looked slightly wavy. The other three went quiet as Charlie found where he'd clipped through, shook it a few times, hard, then fingered the edges of the break. He turned around again.

"Zip ties," he whispered.

"That's it?" Marty asked. He fished in one of the tactical pockets of his Kevlar vest and pulled out a small box cutter. "That's no problem at all."

"Ol' Hop always struck me as the lazy type," Charlie said. "Get the quick fix and worry about it later."

As Marty moved toward the fence, snipping out the razor, Gordon said, "Wait."

Marty paused until Charlie had joined them again back in the shadows of the trees.

"So does this mean you're in?" Gordon asked Charlie. "To do it Dana's way?"

Charlie stood still, his breath clouding his hoodie. He nodded. "You all would really do that shit for me?"

"It's the only way," Dana said.

"Unfortunately, I agree," Gordon said. "Unless we make a clean sweep tonight, even if we get out of here, they'll never let us live. Not for long. Not with what we know."

Charlie looked specifically at Marty. "You too?"

Marty's answer was longer coming, but eventually he nodded too. "It's the only way."

"Remember, Charlie. Whatever you do, don't shoot. If you shoot, it's all over."

They'd debated getting rid of the gun entirely, but Charlie had simply shaken his head in silence. His trust went only so far. Ultimately, the final test of whether Charlie was on board or not would be if he kept the gun under wraps.

"All right," Dana said. "Then let's get to it. We got a few things to do and about five minutes to do them."

Marty tugged at his vest again, stretching his neck as if he had a terrible itch somewhere in there. Gordon had never cracked his sternum, but he bet when it wasn't hurting like hell it was itching like hell. Marty never complained. He flicked open the box cutter and got to work. Each zip tie popped like the slow tick of a metronome, counting down.

CHAPTER TWENTY-TWO

The office of the warden had been occupied at Ditchfield for eighty-two years running. Ken Abernethy had been sitting in that hallowed chair for almost twelve of those eighty-two years, longer than any of his predecessors. From fence to fence, Ditchfield was his home. The second someone turned off I-70 at the sign, they entered his dominion.

Over the years, Abernethy had assured many a donor, board member, frightened parent, and furious child that his primary concern was rehabilitation. *Empowering Youth to Live Productive and Law-Abiding Lives.* That was the Ditchfield mission, and by then, he was very good at messaging. Abernethy had an easy Southern bearing that won over Marylanders despite themselves. His confident gentility lulled people. He could spin up a speech so stirring, so impactful, that it might bring his audience to tears. Sometimes, he even came close to convincing himself that it was true.

But in reality, as far as Ken Abernethy was concerned, he had one aim in life, and that was to hold tightly to his dominion.

He'd had his fair share of trouble over the twelve years he'd sat in the warden's seat. Josiah Hill wasn't the first major donor he'd had to appease to keep the taps flowing. Positioning Ditchfield for a piece of the state-penitentiary pie as a psychiatric hospital was most notable among them. A lot of people had to be greased—and quieted—to get Ditchfield that dual government designation. He'd done worse over the years than turn his back to let Hill move his operation into the northern border property.

He was quite sure that whatever Hill was doing out there was illegal and immoral. He'd seen tarted-up girls ushered quickly and quietly into the old barn at the base of the mountain. He had an idea of what might be going on. Nothing happened in his dominion without his at least being aware of it. He just didn't care. He had bigger problems, namely, keeping the financial support Josiah Hill had earmarked for him. That support would allow him to secure a second one-hundred-year lease on the one-thousand-acre property upon which his throne sat.

Abernethy was in his office, surveying his maps underneath his antique brass magnifying glass and thinking about how Charlie Cunningham was placing all of it in jeopardy. *A boy.* That one boy had been a nonentity in Abernethy's life until recently—safely *stuck and stowed*, as they said.

Until he wasn't anymore.

When Abernethy heard Cunningham had run down Bagshot in cold blood, that was the first blip of good news he'd had all week. After the way that fat-body loser had botched his watch rotation, Abernethy had been afraid if Bagshot showed up at his penitentiary again, he might kill the moron himself.

Even Duke, for all his steely-eyed fury, hadn't been able to corral the boy. And he had half the Baltimore Police in his pocket. He was just another bureaucrat, unable to do what needed to be done. Abernethy would remember that fact when the time came to vote on the mayoral ticket, on which the trust-fund baby was all but guaranteed top billing.

Abernethy stood straight again, arched backward, and rubbed at his aching back. He shut off the desk light and plunged his office into darkness. Usually, when he couldn't sleep, surveying the building plots and plans for Ditchfield's expansion to the north served to calm him—not that night.

Abernethy could've used a bit of good news, but he firmly believed that while good news rained off and on, bad news poured. Thus, he wasn't at all surprised when the comm to his right, quiet all night save for the all-clear calls after the bed checks, suddenly chirped to life. It was Jack Mitchell, who had graciously stepped up to fill in on night watch for the week after Bagshot got waxed.

"Looks like activity along the west fence. Midway in," Mitchell said.

Abernethy snatched up the comm. "Is it Hop?" he asked, knowing full well it wouldn't be Hop, not at one in the morning.

The old groundskeeper had probably been asleep in his little A-frame at the south end of the property for at least five hours by then.

"No, not Hop. A little junker car I don't recognize," said Mitchell. "We doin' repair work on that break tonight, boss?"

"No," Abernethy said.

Outside of himself, Hop, and the ten men in his employ, only one other person knew about that break. Cunningham was back. Maybe it was Stockholm syndrome or some sort of obsessive vendetta on Ditchfield. Either way, Abernethy felt a break in the clouds that had been gathering over his head. The fool boy was serving himself up on a platter.

"Mitchell, you engage with extreme caution, you understand me? Take Horowitz with you. He's closest. But do it now. Report when you have visual," Abernethy said.

"Roger that, boss. Who you think it is?" asked Mitchell.

"I think our flown pigeon has come back to roost," Abernethy said, smiling.

∼

DANA AND GORDON held tightly to the handles fixed above the windows—the oh-shit handles—aptly named for that night as Gordon drove his coupe at a bone-rattling twenty-five miles per hour over the lumpy, uneven earth of Ditchfield's inner grounds. She watched him warily. She'd thought this part of the plan was solid until she saw how much he was jiggling all over the place. When her teeth weren't clacking together, she managed to get out a full sentence.

"There's no way you're rolling out of this car," Dana said.

"What?" he asked. The thumping and rattling was too loud.

"You've got a bum knee, and you're on the far side of forty!" she said more loudly. "There's no way you're rolling out of a moving car!"

Gordon glanced at her, but then the coupe hit a particularly nasty sounding rock, and both looked forward again. *That definitely punctured something*, Dana thought, but that didn't matter. All this bucket of bolts had to do was get them about another hundred yards, hang on while they made some adjustments, then...

Straight on till morning, she thought grimly.

Instead of responding, Gordon nodded hard, in a way that said *We've already discussed this. It's happening.*

Something caught her eye behind Gordon, through the driver's side window. Flashlights were bobbing in the distance. Gordon saw them too. They shared a look that said everything without speech. *No backing out. See it through.*

Dana was surprised they'd gotten that far without being noticed. *Pretty shoddy security for a prison.* Then again, Ditchfield was way more than a prison. For years, they'd done whatever they wanted and never had cause to fret about a damn thing. They'd gotten lazy.

Gordon pressed the gas. Dana winced as the coupe rattled at a higher pitch, but perhaps sensing her swan song had arrived, the old car pressed on. The flashlights receded in the distance. The guards giving chase were on foot. That was good. That would buy them a little time.

"There," Dana said, pointing.

Ahead, the blacktop of the main road stretched out in the

distance, illuminated at intervals by the cold blue light of overhead halogen lamps. They'd come around the long way, but they'd bypassed the front gate and guard station.

Once they passed Pod C on their left, the main manor came into view. Only a few lights were on, lending it a jack-o-lantern glow. The intake room looked empty. The whole manor looked empty, which was a good sign.

Gordon hit the sidewall of the road and bounced both of them an inch into the air where they sat. He swung the car hard left and gunned it down the straightaway. Both looked back over their shoulders—no flashlights yet. Then Dana saw a second pair coming from the other side of the property. She lost them behind Pod B as the car picked up speed, but they would be back soon.

After another hundred feet, Gordon screeched the car to a halt, midway between overhead lights, where the road was darker. The main manor was less than a hundred yards away, yet it looked much farther. Dana didn't think Gordon's hunk of a car could stay on target for that long. When they'd planned this all out, hastily, in the freezing dark of the forest, still safe behind the fence, she'd asked Gordon when he'd last gotten his steering aligned. He'd said sometime in the nineties.

Too late now. See it through.

Gordon threw the car into park, and they both jumped out. Dana picked up the old rag they'd dug from the depths of the trunk earlier. It still reeked of siphoned gasoline. She raced around the back end while Gordon worked furiously at the base of the driver's seat. They worked in silence, a two-person pit crew in the dead of night.

She popped the gas tank open and jammed one end of the rag as far down the hole as she could while leaving a bit exposed.

"Ready," she whispered.

Gordon grunted, lifting something heavy into place. The rock they'd hauled in from the Maryland wilderness beyond the fence was perhaps a tad overkill, but better safe than sorry. He got back in the car and lined up the steering wheel straight.

He took a deep breath. Then he popped the cigarette lighter out and handed it to her. Before she could think, she pressed it against the rag, which started to smolder.

"C'mon, c'mon," she whispered, pressing more tightly.

She thought she heard yelling in the distance. They were running out of time.

"Twenty-five feet," Dana whispered to Gordon. "That's it. Then you roll."

The acceleration on the coupe wasn't good, so she hoped it wouldn't be going faster than twenty miles an hour at that point.

The rag smoked. She turned to Gordon to remind him to guard his head, to tuck and roll. But suddenly the rag burst into flames.

"Go!" she whispered harshly, stepping back.

With the driver's side door still open, Gordon lifted the rock off the floorboard and dropped it onto the gas pedal. He was jolted backward in the driver's seat as the coupe took off down the straightaway.

INSIDE THE CAR, Gordon gritted his teeth and counted down from twenty. He figured that was the easiest way to count out distance, the way least prone to panic blindness. That was a good thing because he was fully panicking, no way around it.

Once the steering wheel was as straight as it was going to get, he snapped his old Club antitheft bar fully across, locking it in place. Ditchfield manor was rapidly approaching. He found himself grinning grimly. *Knock, knock, assholes.*

One last time, he slapped the dash of the coupe he'd driven for twenty-two years. "Bye-bye, ol' gal. Do us proud."

He looked down at the blacktop whizzing by, feet from his shoes.

When his mental countdown hit three, he gave himself a little push and rolled out into the empty air to the left of his moving car.

He remembered to cover his head, and he remembered to tuck and roll, but when he hit the road, it still felt like a baseball bat to the side, then a second baseball bat to his elbows, and so on and so on, a mob-style pummeling all over his body. But not his head, and not his knee, which was why, when he finally came to rest in the dead grass off the side of the road, he was still conscious.

Dana was there in an instant. He found her eyes and tried to speak, but his wind had left him. He nodded instead. He wasn't dead. Of that much he was sure.

"Anything broken?" she asked.

He eased out his arms and legs. They felt a little numb, but nothing like the deadness punctuated by shooting pain that he'd felt when he broke his leg before. He shook his head and pushed himself up to sitting.

He followed the car as it careened toward the manor. The flaming rag looked like a little streamer in the dark. Dana started to speak, but just then the two flashlights appeared again, rounding the nearest pod. Dana dropped beside him and pushed him back down flat.

Dana whispered something about not moving. Gordon could only watch, mesmerized, as he witnessed the last flight of his coupe. He'd locked the steering as true as he could, but the car was definitely veering right. *She always veered right*, Gordon thought, his cheek pressed on the cold ground, watching through strands of scraggly winter grass.

For a few terrible seconds, he thought they'd done all that only to watch their ratty little rocket miss the entire manor house or maybe run weakly into the hedgerows to either side. As if echoing his fears, the little red streamer seemed to sputter out in the distance.

Gordon turned to look for the two officers they'd seen coming closer on their other side. He expected to get called out at any time and told to stand with their hands up. They were inconspicuous, but they weren't exactly hidden. Then his car blew to pieces.

Luckily, his startled yell was covered up by the echoing clap of his coupe turning into a fireball, like the final thump of thunder that comes after a warning crackle of lightning. He turned back in time to see what was likely the undercarriage sailing through the air at about ten feet.

She would have missed the manor house, Gordon thought in wonder. But the explosion set her right. When the gas tank blew, it cracked the whole car in half. The front end clobbered the front of the manor, just to the right of the old double doors, shattering the old brick and caving in the ancient stone until it lodged like a bizarro impressionist piece of art, smoking and burning four feet up.

When he squinted, Gordon could still see through the back half and out the shattered windshield.

The guards screamed, and all their attention turned toward the main house. They cut quickly to the paved road and took off running toward the wreckage. Dana kept a hand pressed on Gordon until they were well out of range. Gordon tried to speak again, but she pressed a finger firmly to his lips.

The first two guards to give them chase broke from the pods directly behind them. If they'd stood, they probably would have run right into them. Instead, the guards paid them no mind, running at full tilt after the others, boots smacking the blacktop loudly, all their equipment clinking and jostling.

The lead man was screaming into his comm, "All watch to the main house! There's been an explosion!"

They clanked away. Dana pressed on Gordon for another minute, then she stood. She held out a hand, and Gordon carefully rose alongside her, completing a litany of physical health checks as he did so. *Legs bear weight? Check. No nausea or vomiting? Check. No double vision? Check.*

He was scraped up but not bleeding profusely. All in all, he'd come out of that a lot better than he'd thought he would. He was fully expecting Ken Abernethy would be scraping him off the pavement in the morning.

"Ready to move?" Dana asked.

Gordon felt a bit like he was playing on house money. Or perhaps that was just the adrenaline talking. Either way, he had to take advantage of it.

"Let's go," he said.

The two of them stood and looked toward the north, where he hoped the second half of the plan was already in motion. Gordon had taken two steps when he heard a yell from behind.

"Hands in the air! Don't move. I see you move, I kill you."

Gordon put his hands in the air and looked at Dana and found her doing the same, her eyes already seeking his. *I love you*, he mouthed.

I loved you first, she mouthed back.

Gordon and Dana turned around to find a guard shining a high beam directly at them, perched above the barrel of a gun. The guard's aim shifted twitchily back and forth between them.

"We don't want any trouble," Dana said.

"Well you fuckin' got it, sweetheart," said the guard. He switched his comm on quickly then got back to standing them up with the gun and light. "Boss, it's Mitchell. I got two trespassers here. I saw them roll out of the goddamn car that just smashed into the main house."

There was a crackly pause on the radio as all three waited. White smoke wafted through the space between them. Then the comm chirped.

"Bring them to me," said Ken Abernethy, not sounding happy about it.

Marty watched the old coupe take off through the field toward its rendezvous with the main manor and said a little prayer to the big guy upstairs. *Don't let it blow up with them inside it. It can crap out on the grass or blow an axle somewhere between here and there if it means they won't die, but just don't let it blow up with them in it.*

"It'll make it," Charlie said. "The old cars got the most fight."

They stood side by side just inside the fence. They'd helped push the coupe up the hill then given her one final push to get her up to speed and through the fence, and just like that, phase one of the plan was underway.

"All right, we're up," Marty said. "You sure you want to do this? Breaking and entering goes on your permanent record, you know."

Charlie turned to him. "Is that supposed to be some sort of joke?"

"Yep," Marty said, adjusting his vest again and unzipping his backup leather jacket, which Dana had been surprised to see he owned. Marty was surprised she was surprised. If you had a leather jacket, you had a leather backup. That's how it worked. "Just trying to lighten shit up a bit. C'mon, try to keep up."

Marty didn't bother crouching or concealing himself. They were all going to be found sooner or later. The key was what they did in the meantime. So he ran, taking off straight through the inner grounds, heading due north at the spot where Gordon and Dana had peeled off toward the main manor. Charlie had to hold his loose jeans up with one hand, but he seemed like an old pro at it, and he settled in solidly behind Marty soon enough, keeping to his line and matching him stride for stride.

Before Gordon went careening off in his little car, he'd told Marty he was "fairly sure" an abandoned barn marked the north edge of the property. He'd seen a large structure surrounded by several smaller structures in the original plat that had been attached to the 501c3 filing. Gordon also admitted he was "kind of drunk at the time" and "in a bit of a mania."

So that wasn't perfect intel, but it was as good as they were gonna get. Hill's man had mentioned the barn back at New Hope too. Marty was confident that if they could find it, they'd find the girls. And barns, being barns, were usually pretty big—not something one missed if one got near enough.

They passed Pod C in a blur. Marty wasn't sure how long they'd been running, but his lungs were burning. His chest itched like a whole nest of ants were using it as an elevator. He badly wanted to rip the vest off and scratch like a dog.

"Hey," Charlie said, breathless. "Company up ahead. Right."

A flash of light peeked out from around the back side of Pod D. Marty slowed and dropped low, and Charlie followed. A guard came around the far side, flashlight panning the windows high above him. They were still out of earshot, but if the guard looked their way, he would likely spot two lumps that shouldn't have been there. Pod D was the last structure before the north side, the only thing standing between them and the barn somewhere beyond. But if they moved any closer, they'd be spotted instantly.

"Do we take him out?" Charlie whispered.

"No, we don't *take him out*," Marty whispered, still breathing hard. "Jesus, kid. I'm tryin' to like you, but you gotta meet me halfway."

"So we wait?" Charlie asked, sounding unhappy about it.

Marty wasn't pleased either. Every second they wasted would make succeeding harder. The guy might linger and possibly have a smoke. Maybe his job was to watch Pod D all night long. If that was the case, Dana and Gordon would be in a cell of their own before he and Charlie could even find the damn barn.

Charlie crouched like a runner on a starting line, looking like he was about to bolt for it and see if he could make it past. But the angles, the visibility... Marty knew about these things, and it wasn't gonna work.

Then something exploded.

A single pulse of the hungry orange color unique to fire warmed the black sky in a spot just above the buildings to their right. The sound followed half a heartbeat later—a cracking boom that bounced around the box canyon until it escaped into the night, lessening by degrees.

Marty and Charlie looked at each other. *Please don't let them have been in the car,* Marty thought again.

The guard swung his light east toward the source of the sound. He pressed his comm and frantically repeated something a few times that Marty couldn't catch in the reverberations.

"Get out of here," Marty whispered, mentally urging the man onward. "Go check it out."

The guard shook his head and gave the door one last sweep with his light before he took off at an ugly gallop toward the main house. Once he disappeared behind the far side of the pod, Marty nodded at Charlie, and the two of them resumed their pace, racing past the form and function of Ditchfield until they crossed beyond the spotlight banks keeping the darkness of the north side at bay.

The light bled from the landscape as they pressed farther north until they both had to slow to avoid turning an ankle or tripping over the brush.

Charlie stopped Marty again, with a light touch to the shoulder. "You see that?" he asked, pointing ahead and to the right.

Marty squinted. Sure enough, the more he focused on the darkness, the more there seemed to be a strange glow in the distance.

"That's it," Charlie said. "It's gotta be it."

They increased their pace, focusing as hard as they could on the ground while still picking a line through the trees. The forest was weak there, but that almost made it worse. Twice, Marty slammed his hip against little runt trees, and Charlie tumbled once over a knotty patch of bushes that Marty only narrowly avoided himself. Charlie landed hard on his shoulder but rolled out of it, pressing on without a word.

A fence appeared out of nowhere. Marty almost ran full sail into it but stopped himself by sliding, thankful it wasn't electrified. Nor was it as high as the fencing on the front of the property.

Still, it had razor wire that caught the moon like shards of glass, daring them to climb. Marty looked left and right down the fence line, which had to have a break somewhere, an entrance gate for construction, but he couldn't see one, and they were running out of time. They were close enough to see well-defined lighting in the distance—a single spot that cast an eerie redness. The sound of a generator hummed faintly.

Charlie didn't wait for Marty's say. He gripped the fence and started climbing.

Marty grabbed his hoodie at the back. "You'll slash yourself to pieces."

"I don't care," Charlie hissed.

"Razor cuts don't heal, kid. They bleed and bleed. That's the point."

Charlie ignored him and tried to climb again.

"Goddammit, Charlie, wait!" Marty said. He looked around as if seeking a witness for the sacrifice he was about to make. Of course, he found none, only backcountry Maryland hell.

He shrugged out of his backup leather jacket and handed it up to the kid.

"Climb up *carefully* and lay this across. Make a gap. I'll follow."

Charlie looked down at him inscrutably then grabbed the jacket, turned, and climbed. At the top, he picked his spot. He scraped lightly against one big looping set of razors, rattling the whole line softly like a can full of rice. He cussed.

"Told you," Marty whispered.

Charlie ignored him, rebalanced himself at the top, and pressed the jacket until it caught the razor wire. He pushed one sleeve through a loop in the chain link and hastily tied it with the other sleeve on the other side to hold the razor wire at bay. It wasn't much, but it was a gap. Then he flipped over and scrabbled down.

"Good luck, big man," he said from the other side. He sucked at a cut on the back of one hand.

The last time Marty had scaled a chain-link fence was three months into the job, when he was still working the East Baltimore project beat and had to get into a chop-shop impound lot. The last time he'd scaled a fence with razor wire on top was never. But he wasn't about to let Charlie know that. He visualized the gym in his garage, where he'd put a few rock-climbing grips because he wanted to work his way up to three fingered pull-ups, then he started climbing.

His chest hurt abominably every time he reached up for the next link, but he kept reaching and kept the pain off his face, and eventually, he was up top. He threaded through the narrow gap in the razor wire as best he could, but he knew he was too broad to come out unscathed. Instead, he just decided where he'd take the hits: the vest kept his chest and back clean, but his arms and shoulders were fair game.

He pushed through the bright flares of pain and managed to flip around with minimal agony. His sternum grinded once, and he was forced to grip the top crossbar for a few seconds while the spots in his eyes faded, but soon enough, he was on the other side.

He looked at his backup jacket mournfully. By the time he worked it free, it was slashed cleanly apart at the pockets and sleeve, like some wily pickpocket had assaulted it. But he wasn't about to leave it perched like a huge dodo bird atop the fence. He didn't have a backup backup.

By the time Marty hit the ground, Charlie was already running again. Marty hurried to keep up.

They found the barn. It was a weather-worn Quaker structure that seemed to want to fade away into the side of the mountain. Under different circumstances, it might have been hard to spot. As it was, it was hard to miss. The explosion behind them had set off a beehive of activity inside.

Marty pulled back on Charlie while they were still far enough away. Charlie stopped reluctantly.

"What?" he asked, exasperated. "Tasha's in there," he added, desperately.

"Let's just take a minute," Marty whispered harshly. "We don't know what we're running into."

One man was outside, watching the glow to the south. He was talking on a comm, his voice coming to them in unintelligible snippets, but he sounded frantic. Marty looked backward for the first time and saw why. They couldn't see the main manor from where they were, but the sky was reddening in the area over where he knew it stood. The campfire smell of wood smoke was tingeing the air.

"I think Gordon's car put on one hell of a final show," Marty said. *Please let them have gotten away. Please don't let that wood-smoke smell also be little bits of them.*

The barn doors swung open, pushed from inside by two men. Marty saw movement within. Shadowy figures scrambled about in that unsettling red light, some of them cowering, their shadows thrown large against the walls.

"That fire can probably be seen from I-70," Marty said. "This place is about to get a lot of visitors."

A van rumbled their way along the fence, bouncing violently along a barely there path. It cut hard toward the barn well before it reached them then swung a tangent toward the open barn doors before backing up, beeping the whole way. Soon, its rear doors were bathed in the red light as well. Another man jumped down from the driver's side and moved quickly around to open it up.

Two of the four men standing outside, including the one yelling into the comm, took off into the night, tracing back the way the van had come. At the same time, a line of crouching young women was ushered out of the barn toward the van.

"They're trying to move them again," Charlie said. "Now or never."

Marty doubted he could stop the kid if he tried, but as things stood, he agreed with him. He laid a hand on Charlie's shoulder one last time. "None of this works if you fire that gun you got in your front pocket. Remember that. You kill anyone, it's over for all of us. Tasha too."

Charlie looked like he understood, all right—understood that he was about to meet the architects of his misery. But at that point, Marty had to let go.

"I'll be right beside you," Marty said.

Charlie stood up, adjusted his hoodie, and pulled down on the neckline. Marty straightened his shield and laid it flat on the outside of his vest. He adjusted his jury-rigged camera setup as best he could.

Charlie started walking toward the van, his arms in the front pocket of the hoodie. Marty walked beside him, step for step.

When they were still about a hundred feet away, Marty called out, "Ahoy, there!" while holding up his badge to the smoky moonlight. "I'm with Warren Duke!" Riffing then, he added, "We got a fire at the main house that's getting out of hand."

The two remaining men swung flashlights into blinding focus, right in their eyes.

"Don't move!" one yelled.

Marty recognized the voice. It was the other man from the church, the one Hill had called Brother Dameon. He'd taken off after Alonzo blasted Marty in the chest.

Marty stopped. No shots were fired this time. That was something, at least.

"I have something for you," Marty said. "Some*one*, actually. You've been looking all over for him."

Charlie kept walking forward. He had to get close, had to see the girls. Marty's job was to get him there.

"I said don't move!" said Dameon.

But Charlie kept walking.

"Don't you recognize him?" Marty called. "Charlie Cunningham? The whole city's had an APB out for him for most of the week." Marty tried to shade his eyes, but the glare was too intense.

Charlie was walking in totally blind, but they were past the point of no return. All Marty could do was keep talking. "No? Look, can I talk to your manager or something, then?"

He was answered by the two-click snap of a cocking handgun. He couldn't tell if it was pointed at him or at Charlie. He certainly *felt* like it was pointed at him. He'd always wondered what he'd think of in this circumstance. At New Hope, the trigger was pulled before he had any time to take stock.

What came to mind was a single image, frozen in time: Brooke, pulled into his embrace, her heartbeat like a fluttering butterfly against his raw chest, her tears wet on his neck.

"Wear the vest."

He wondered if she would be disappointed in him.

Then another man spoke. "Now, just hold on there, fella."

Marty recognized that voice, too, from his first visit to this hell-hole what felt like a century ago: Ken Abernethy, the sweet-talking warden.

"Take the damn lights out of their eyes, son. You're gonna blind them," Abernethy told Dameon. As Marty blinked to clear the glare, Abernethy added, "Well, how about that? Charlie Cunningham in the flesh."

Abernethy plucked the gun from Dameon's hands and held it loosely, like a marksman waiting for his shooting target to slide fully out on the line. Marty had a bad feeling about the way Abernethy was holding that gun. He was way too comfortable with it.

"Charlie," Marty said, "hold up a sec."

"No, by all means, Charlie, come on in. Who you lookin' for, boy?" Abernethy asked. "One of Hill's whores?"

Charlie seemed to neither hear nor care—not about the men, not about the gun, not about the fire or the barn. He cared only about the girls huddled back against the barn door, shuddering and cringing but weirdly silent, as if their whimpers and screams were on some other bandwidth, too high to hear.

One, in particular, drew Charlie in. She was tall and thin, like him. Swimming in loose and faded sweatpants and a sweatshirt stretched out at the neck, she crouched against the rough wood of the door and seemed folded over, as if trying to hold herself together and hide her height at the same time.

"Tasha?" he ventured. All bravado, even the false kind, was swept clean from his voice. This was a brother asking for his sister.

Tasha Cunningham looked up at the sound, but Marty could see she wasn't all there. She quested for Charlie's voice like a woman swimming in the depths of a bad dream. Dameon stepped toward him, but Abernethy held him off with an unsettling why-the-hell-not gesture that Marty read as the same type of allowance he might give to a man asking for a smoke on his way to the electric chair.

"Charlie, come on back," Marty said, trying to keep his voice level. "I got it all on camera." He tapped his vest. "Let's just back away."

Tasha caught on to the name and seemed to focus for a span of moments, but no relief showed on her face, only shame. As Charlie reached out, she pushed away and tried to hide.

"Don't look at me," she whispered weakly.

"There, see?" Abernethy said, "You got what you wanted. Was it worth it?"

Charlie reached toward his sister again but checked himself. Stunned, he backed away until Marty was able to pull him gently back out of the red light from the barn and into the glowing night. In the distance, sirens wailed.

"We got a shitstorm on our hands, boys. I don't want to have to explain anything, and I'm damn sure the reverend doesn't want to explain anything, so get gone, and get gone now."

Charlie pulled away from Marty and walked like a shell-shocked soldier to the van. He pulled out his gun, and before any of them could react, Charlie pointed it at Abernethy.

"Charlie, no!" Marty yelled.

The revolver lingered on the warden, but only for a moment. Then Charlie turned to the van. He fired once into the front left tire then once into the front right tire. He unloaded another shot into the engine block before the handgun Abernethy held came alive, and the warden shot Charlie full on in the chest three times.

Charlie left his feet, danced for a moment an inch in the air, then swung around and planted face-first on the ground, unmoving. The girls screamed as one. Tasha's voice cracked highest above the others.

"Goddammit!" Abernethy yelled, turning his gun on Marty. "No cop of Duke's gonna let that boy anywhere near a gun."

Marty barely heard the warden. He ran to Charlie but was cut down at the knees by Dameon, a low body tackle he never saw coming.

"I know this cop," Dameon yelled, leaning hard into Marty's side, pressing him to the ground. "He ain't got nothing to do with Duke. Alonzo shot him at New Hope."

Marty registered all this only peripherally. He was looking for any sign of life from Charlie, even with his own face pressed into the dirt and pine needles poking into his cheek. But he saw nothing.

Dameon said, "I think Alonzo got him right *here*," and he slammed an elbow into Marty's sternum.

His entire chest felt like it caught fire, like his skin was being raked by claws from within. He bellowed in rage. His pain gave him strength, and he jerked out from directly underneath Dameon and into a bit of leverage. He lifted hard at the knees until both men were standing, Dameon with his arms halfway around Marty's chest and throat from behind.

Marty drove himself backward with his heels. Dameon was big, but Marty was more powerful. When he felt the man lose his footing, he threw himself backward with total abandon. Both of them fell back, Dameon under Marty.

Marty loosened his bull neck and made sure that when Dameon hit the ground, he snapped the broad back of his skull right into the man's face. The squelchy pop of Dameon's shattering nose brought a grim grin to Marty's face. He barely felt the pain as the man's front teeth caved in on his skull.

Dameon was unmoving underneath him. Marty scrambled toward Charlie again and almost ran right into another bullet that blew a clod of dirt into his eyes. Abernethy had sighted Marty again. Marty froze, blinking, guarding his head and waiting for the punch that would end him.

"A dead escapee is one thing," the warden said. "A dead cop is another. So we gonna do this a bit differently."

The sirens were loud by then. The glowing sky pulsed faintly red and blue. Marty heard Dameon groan and shuffle into a sitting position. If Abernethy had any sympathy for the wounded goon, he didn't show it.

"Leave the boy. I'll clean him up later. We bring the cop with us."

Marty was staring numbly at Charlie's broken body when Abernethy whip-cracked him neatly at the temple with the butt of the nine millimeter, and he lost consciousness.

CHAPTER TWENTY-THREE

The fire that started when Gordon's car exploded spread quickly up the face of the main manor house. By the time Ken Abernethy was able to deal with the Charlie Cunningham situation on the north side and get back to the main property, three fire trucks had arrived, along with three police cars.

Catastrophic destruction aside, Ken Abernethy thought the sight of the grand old house burning was spectacular, like something out of another era. The flames were so bright and so high that they seemed to suck the light away from everything else until Abernethy felt displaced, as if he was watching an ancient temple in a lost city burn in an unknown time.

A firefighter hailed him, pulling him back to this place and time. He walked over, full gear rattling, and confirmed what anybody within a mile of this place could plainly see.

"It's a total loss, Warden. We're setting up a defensive line to make sure it doesn't spread to the housing units."

Abernethy nodded grimly. The flames were consuming the structure from front to back with the relentless surety of a mass of lava. The car itself, or what was left of it, was pinned like exposed rebar to the glowing stone. The warden's office, seat of his dominion, was a firestorm with a single smoking window for an eye. When the car exploded out front, it had jostled everything in the office. His mirror and art, his coat stand and computer. When the front half slammed into the house, the place fairly shook. Tokens of gratitude, awards and accolades, all of them were jarred off his desk. His magnifying glass had tipped off the map and clattered to the floor.

Abernethy had just enough time to look out that window and down at the burning wreckage before the fire alarms went off and the overhead sprinkler system activated—poorly, it would seem.

After he evacuated, he figured it best to deal with the whole mess up north and shut off the lights before the cavalry came to town. And boy, had they ever.

"Think you can keep it contained? I've got guests in those pods," Abernethy said. "They're the most important thing."

The firefighter squared his oxygen tank and reset his mask. "You got lucky cause there's no wind and it's muggy as shit. Ayup, I think we'll keep it to the one structure. Still, I agree that evacuating the prisoners is the right thing to do."

Abernethy realized the firefighter mistook his words for fatherly concern. He nodded sagely anyway. Abernethy was able to stare clear-eyed into the destruction of the manor house because it wasn't really the heart of Ditchfield. He could rebuild the house and might even be able to spin some charitable campaign out of it. He'd officed in that house, but the true seat of his dominion was on the shoulders of the boys in the four pods arrayed around it.

They were the most important thing because they were the actual monetary value of Ditchfield. Prisoners. And the unrealized future value of Ditchfield was the space for more prisoners—that and the moonlighting Josiah Hill had to do up north. Palms needed greasing, after all, especially if those palms held sway over a thousand-acre lease at the foot of a national forest.

Looking at the hungry way the fire consumed the ancient wood of the manor house, Abernethy already knew it would eat itself there.

The pods would be safe. The three trucks showered the house from above with a triple punch of high-powered water. He could feel it briefly cool his face in between bouts of wafting heat. Still, he would prep to evacuate to the safety zones even though that would be a colossal pain in the ass. He would do it because when the press arrived, it would look bad if a hundred kids were a solid stone's throw away from a five-alarm fire and nobody had given an evacuation order. Thankfully, Duke had sent six city police who were in his pocket. Abernethy would need them to assist his guard unit in keeping the pods in line.

Abernethy called Mitchell over and pulled him close, even though nobody could hear a thing they said even at an arm's length away, given the roar and hiss of the fire surging and being beaten back.

"You take care of the two insurgents that burned down my manor house?" he asked.

Mitchell cleared his throat and covered his comm. "They're put away."

"Good," Abernethy said. At first, he'd thought he would have to spare the detective. He was active duty and distinguished. The woman was a sergeant. She was on the dishonorable discharge track, but still... a sergeant was a sergeant.

Duke had told him otherwise, saying that even if all three went missing, he would find a way to shuffle it off, especially the doctor and the woman.

So at some point in the very near future, Ken Abernethy was going to have to figure out how to bury one current cop, one former cop, one psychiatrist, and four underaged hookers.

The day was shaping up to be perhaps the strangest in his tenure, which was saying an awful lot.

But first, he needed to make sure of one thing.

He pulled Mitchell close again. "You take point. When the press shows up, you keep them focused on that manor house burning to the ground. Nobody looks north, you understand me?"

He pushed Mitchell out but still held him at the shoulders, boring right into his eyes. Mitchell nodded gravely.

"Good," Abernethy said.

Then he turned without another word and went back to his truck, where one of Hill's strongmen sat complacently, watching the raging inferno like it was about as interesting as the daily weather readout. Blood was streaming down his face from a buckled front tooth, but he didn't seem to mind.

As soon as Abernethy was strapped in, Dameon pulled the warden's truck around in a slow circle, and the two of them headed back north.

One of Abernethy's most prized possessions—currently burning in the manor house he stoically watched in the side-view mirror—was a surveyor's packet for Howard County, dated June of 1863. The packet referred specifically to his thousand acres as the "leveled acreage," at that point owned by a wealthy farmer named Thomas Beck, a pro-slavery spitfire who took up cause with the Confederacy at an advanced age and never came back from the war. His derelict sons eventually sold the land to Richard Ditchfield to cover gambling debts. Such was the inglorious birth of Abernethy's dominion, ever striving for better and ever succeeding... allowing for a few bumps along the way, of course. The surveyor's packet was notable to Abernethy for many reasons, not least because it outlined the true legal dimensions of the plot, but also because it documented a cave at the far north of the property.

At the time, Baltimore was a smuggler's cove. Abernethy would argue very little had changed in the ensuing century and a half— mostly just the nature of the contraband. Back then, the rum runners and gun jockeys needed a place to store their goods away from the eye of the port authority. Ditchfield was private and was the perfect distance from Baltimore to avoid eyes and make a lot of pirates a lot of money.

Again, Abernethy had to allow that not much had changed.

Dameon killed the headlights of the truck a quarter mile out and drove the rest of the way to the cave by moonlight. They'd blacked out the barn too. Hill's operation would have to be put on hiatus for a while, until things died down again.

But they would die down eventually. They always did.

Still, Abernethy wondered how he could quietly be rid of seven human beings. Part of him wished they'd just shot the whole lot the second the fire broke out. Nobody had been around for miles. But now, the Howard County Fire Department would be putting out embers all night. In short order, four pods of boys would be spaced in shivering rows in the yard, under the careful watch of ten guards and six cops. That was a lot of ears.

Dameon slowed the truck until he rolled to a stop at the base of a pocked formation of basement rock. The fist-sized indentations up top got wider and wider as they went down until one could walk right inside at the base—or get thrown inside, as the case may be. Some old bootlegger had fashioned a steel-plate covering God-knew-how-long ago, but it still sealed the front of the cave well enough. Abernethy could hear weeping within.

"I think we've got to smoke 'em," Abernethy said. "No way around it."

"Say what?" Dameon asked, his words lisping through his battered maw.

"Can't shoot 'em. Too much noise. Plus, it's two against seven, and two are cops. So here's what we do: let's take the gas tanks on the truck, dose some logs, light them, and chuck 'em in. The smoke will take care of them eventually. Plus, we can say the cops and the doctor succumbed at the manor fire." The more Abernethy thought the plan through, the better it sounded. He had nothing against any of his new prisoners—nothing personal—but they had to go. He was simply protecting his domain.

"They'll put it out. They got clothes on. They'll take 'em off. Smother it with their bodies if they got to," Dameon said.

"Then we'll put more logs in," Abernethy said.

"What about the body cam?" Dameon asked.

"Body cam?"

"On the big cop. The one Alonzo shot. He wears vests. They got cameras."

"Christ almighty," Abernethy said.

The big man had mentioned something about a vest cam. Abernethy had let it flit from his mind on account of his entire livelihood burning down around him.

"Some of them hook up to the internet now," Dameon persisted. "Maybe it's got a suicide switch or something. He saw everything. He was right there."

Ken Abernethy muttered and cursed. He kicked out at the dead grass at his feet. It was a five-percent chance, maybe. But a five-percent chance sealed up in a cave was still a five-percent chance. A body cam's battery could take a long time to die and maybe or maybe not send one last gasp to some police server somewhere that would ruin his life. And Reverend Hill certainly didn't like loose ends.

"Goddammit," he hissed. "Fine. Open up the hatch. And get your gun up."

Dameon thunked the lock open—it sounded like some Civil War–era version of the power locks they used on the pods—and swung the hatch open. The smell of wet dirt and body odor seeped out on the wave of the desperate cries of the girls.

"Anybody comes at us, they die," Dameon said with the flat and even tone of a man who means it.

Expecting a bum rush, Abernethy instead heard scrabbling away and then silence and counted that as another small victory on a day full of defeats.

"Detective?" Abernethy asked, peering into the full darkness of the cave. Beyond the moonlit perimeter, he couldn't see a damn thing. "You still alive in there, or you been concussed out of the game?"

Just when he thought he might actually have to go into the damn place, Marty Cicero responded. "I'm here."

"Step forward, please," Abernethy said.

Silence. Stillness. Inaction when Abernethy knew well they couldn't afford it.

"Do it now, or my associate here fires one shot randomly into the dark. Maybe it hits you. Maybe it hits one or two of these girls," Abernethy said.

That got the bleeding-heart bastard moving. He could hear the shuffle.

Marty Cicero appeared, oozing blood from the forehead, his face a smoke-dusted, mud-smeared mess. He had his hands up, which was good. He also had the vest on.

"Take off the Kevlar," Dameon said. "Easy. Then head back in. Nothing funny."

Marty never even looked at Dameon despite the fact that he was the man holding the gun. His eyes shot death at Abernethy, though, which made him want to wrap this up even more quickly.

Marty took his vest off and handed it to Dameon on a single outstretched finger.

Dameon snatched it, backed away, and threw it to Abernethy, keeping his gun trained on the big cop.

The second Abernethy took hold of it, he knew something was wrong. It was lumpy, fractured, mutilated. He felt around to confirm.

"Did you shoot that fella outside of the barn?" he asked Dameon.

Dameon gave him a brief, confused glance.

"I thought not. This vest is worthless. It's been blasted and looks like the camera was stripped already," Abernethy said. So much for that. Case closed.

The detective backed away, fading into the darkness of the cave again. But he had a look on his face that Abernethy didn't like.

While Dameon rolled the steel plate back in place, Abernethy held the vest limply in one hand and thought of loose ends.

Something wasn't right. And over the past week, whenever things had taken another turn for the worse, his thoughts came back to Charlie Cunningham.

"Give me the keys," Abernethy said.

"What? I thought we were gonna—

"You stay here and make sure things stay in line. I'll be right back."

Dameon tossed Abernethy the keys. "I'd just as soon get this done if we're gonna do it," Dameon said.

"Five minutes," Abernethy said, helping himself into the old truck.

Dameon muttered something Abernethy didn't hear as he fired the engine and flicked on the low beams. He drove south.

The barn came into view as a hulking mass of angular lines. It was cold and dark once more, the way it had been since being abandoned in the early nineteen hundreds when the estate moved south. Abernethy wasn't there for the barn, though.

He swung the truck around out front, looking for where he'd shot Cunningham. He thought he found the place but realized he was too far out. He was amazed at how disoriented a man could get in the pure blackness of the place. He thought it strange that he couldn't immediately see the body. He would be the first to admit he was getting old, but he could count on two hands the number of men he'd killed. He knew he was in the right place.

Creeping fears of loose ends had made their way from his gut all the way up his back by then.

Abernethy thought about flicking the high beams on, but at least twenty nonaffiliates were now down at the southern end, and he couldn't risk one of them looking his way and spying a glow, not with what was in that cave.

Abernethy killed the engine and took a small Maglite from the glove compartment, along with the standard Ditchfield service-issue .357. His boots kicked up dust as he stomped down out of the vehicle. He focused the business ends of both tools on the ground and started sweeping.

Three times Abernethy repositioned himself, triangulating his location with the barn doors, the shot-up van, and the trees. He reenacted the entire encounter, top to bottom, from the moment the detective had walked Cunningham onto the scene to the moment he'd killed the boy with three shots to the chest.

He stood over the packed patch of dead land where he was ninety-nine percent sure the boy had died. But the boy wasn't there. His flashlight glinted off flat metal instead of a body. He eased himself to one knee and picked his ill-gotten prize off the ground. The warped-pancake shape gave it away. It was a slug stopped by a Kevlar vest.

He looked briefly for the other two but found no trace and no blood, either. If they'd hit home, blood would've been everywhere.

Dameon had said the vests had body cams, said the detective had seen everything. Well, Cunningham was even closer. Cunningham had run up to his sister among the gaggle of other terrified whores, for Chrissakes. *Talk about seeing everything.*

The other two slugs were likely still embedded in the vest he'd worn, along for the ride to wherever he was going with the footage that would spell the end of Ditchfield.

He always thought if things were crumbling down around him, he would have some grand gesture to make, some final rage into the dying of the light.

Instead, he had the .357 loose in his hand and the glowing embers of his domain laid out before him.

He leaned against the driver's side door, his arm draped across the crook of the mirror. Scenarios spidered out of his brain. If Cunningham made it out with that cam footage, things weren't going to get better for Ditchfield.

If Cunningham had limped, slowly dying, into the dark winter brush, they would find his body somewhere and the cam footage with it. Maybe if Abernethy had a full shift of guards and some peace and quiet instead of half a shift and a five-alarm fire, he could go after the boy. But that wasn't happening.

In the best-case scenario, the boy limped off to die, and nobody ever found him. But if Charlie had come into Ditchfield wearing the vest, that meant he probably had a plan to get out. From what Abernethy had seen, the boy wasn't a quitter.

And an investigation into the fire was sure to follow, along with the rehousing of a hundred boys, many of whom were, to be blunt, not well treated. Things would come to light.

To say nothing of the cave. It was up north a ways, but to think it would never be found was folly. If he had time and help, he could probably gas all of them and carry them down to the fire like they'd been there all along, but time was running out. With Charlie on the lam, Hill's men would stay away. Dameon had probably already bolted. That young man was born and bred on the bad blocks of Baltimore's east side. He'd done time for a botched robbery before Hill "reformed" him. He could read a room.

Abernethy saw no scenario in which he ever sat on his throne again.

The .357 twitched in his hand.

CHAPTER TWENTY-FOUR

T homas Brighton was gliding. He didn't know what time it was and was only vaguely aware of the day. He'd been working nonstop to help the boy who'd slashed his face open from the moment he'd done so.

Piles of paperwork surrounded Brighton's desk. He held one highlighter in his hand and another in his teeth. Every now and then, he would get to studying one of the photocopied receipts or printed photographs or detailed spreadsheets too long, and a drop of blood would dribble off his chin and splatter on the paper, snapping him briefly back to the present.

Whenever the blood spattered, he knew he had to change his dressing. He was no doctor, but sopping dressings on his face struck him as reckless. He liked the scar, but he didn't want to lose half his face to gangrene for it, so he blasted it with rubbing alcohol and slathered it with Neosporin every few hours, and he barely felt the pain. He was too eager to get back to the case.

Brighton built legal cases—the ones he cared about, anyway—from the ground up. He used a pillared system. One big truth, the point he was trying to prove, was up top: the New Hope Foundation aided and abetted the sexual trafficking of underaged girls.

That was a big truth. Very big. It was so big, in fact, that it needed several legs to stand on. So Brighton built those legs.

One leg was that Ditchfield was an accessory to said trafficking.

Another was that Warren Duke and select members of the Baltimore City Police Department were complicit in said trafficking

A third was that Thomas Brighton of Brighton and Associates was an unknowing accessory to said trafficking.

Brighton had pictured several scenarios in which his career ended, but he could honestly say that building a case that indicted himself was not one of them. But facts were facts. He was a knowing accessory to legal malpractice—legal abuse, in fact. He was a corrupt attorney.

He'd written it all out on his legal pad before he knew what he was really confessing to, but when it was there in plain black ink on yellow paper, he knew it was the right thing to do.

His case needed legs to stand on. Duke was as slippery as an eel and far more connected, and that leg of the case would likely crumble. The one in which he damned himself would have to bear the weight.

After he'd pieced together his own paper trail such that he was confident it would hold up in court even if Hill threw a curveball at his own confession, Brighton took a break and poured himself an ounce of ice-cold vodka. He sat back in his chair and stared at the whirlwind of self-incriminating paperwork surrounding him. It was strong but not strong enough. If he walked into a courtroom right then, he would certainly succeed in putting himself behind bars. *Josiah Hill? Not so much.*

He needed evidence pinning the girls to New Hope, and he didn't have it.

Brighton was so lost in thought that, at first, he barely registered the throaty rumble of an approaching car engine. Kids dragged up and down the streets outside Bail Bond Row all the time, but even they usually dispersed a little after one. Not at four in the morning. *How did it get to be four in the morning?* Brighton got up to change his dressing again.

When the guttural growl crept right up to his front door, he took notice, especially when headlights illuminated his foyer.

The engine shut off.

Brighton was done with surprise visitors. He dropped the pen and paper from his hands and spat the highlighter from his mouth. Gordon had wedged one of his thrift-store wingbacks against the front door, which seemed to have done the trick so far. Brighton had come in the back way. He hoped the wingback would hold.

Heavy clomping sounded up the old wooden stairs. Brighton peeked around the corner leading to the hall, but the lights washed everything in a disorienting black-and-white relief.

During a pause, a shadow hovered by the door, lit weakly by the chandelier overhead. Brighton reached over to his desk lamp and switched it off. He couldn't afford any more scars.

The person tried the door, pushing it open as far as they could, which was about three inches until the overstuffed chair clogged up the works. *Good thinking, Doc.*

Whoever it was leaned in hard, too, even slamming against it once. All they succeeded in doing was ripping up the felt on the chair. It was jammed in tighter than an otter's pocket.

During another pause, Brighton thought of his gun, how it might be nice to have right then. Then again, maybe not. The only thing that gun ever did was sit in a drawer until it got stolen right out from under him. Even if he had it, he'd probably end up shooting himself in the ass somehow.

Then he heard something. Either he was hallucinating, or someone was politely knocking on the front door.

Brighton peeked out again. He still couldn't see anything but a shadow, but he was fairly sure the knocker and the would-be break-ing-and-entering suspect were one and the same. *Baltimore. Where wonders never cease.*

"Hey," came a harsh whisper. "Brighton, it's Charlie. You let me in now, or you got a lot more blood on your hands."

That got Thomas Brighton up really quickly. First and foremost, he needed to shut off the outdoor lighting that was shedding a halo on the most wanted man in the city as he stood like a Jehovah's Witness on his front porch.

After flicking the switch that dropped them all under a curtain of darkness, Brighton leaned awkwardly over his fat chair. "Are you alone?"

"Yes. Let me in."

"I can't move the chair. Come around back."

"Are you serious?" Charlie whispered.

"Yeah, I'm serious. Am I supposed to leave my office open to the whole inner city? You were the one that crowbarred the lock, remember? Not my fault. Now, come around back, and I'll let you in."

Charlie faded back, and Brighton scrambled through the office to kill the back lights and meet him at the rear door. He heard Charlie trip once and curse, but the kid kept coming.

Brighton opened the door and ushered him in. Then he locked it in two places. The first thing he noticed, upon turning around, was that Charlie seemed to have trouble taking a deep breath.

"What the hell happened?" Brighton asked, still whispering.

Charlie spoke at a normal volume. "I got shot. Three times. Then I had to drive for a little under an hour, feeling like I was gonna choke and puke at the same time. That's what happened."

Brighton looked for the blood. He'd been no stranger to blood recently, and he figured he'd see a lot of it on Charlie, even if the shots grazed him. But no blood was visible. For the first time, he noticed Charlie was carrying something that looked like a ratty harness.

"How are you standing?" Brighton asked. He guided Charlie into his office and flicked on his fake Tiffany lamp to get a better look.

In the boy's hand was a bulletproof vest, well used.

Brighton thumbed at an embedded slug then looked back up at

Charlie, who seemed to unconsciously rub at a tender spot on the left side of his ribcage.

"You should see a doctor," said Brighton.

"So should you," Charlie replied, drawing a line down his cheek to mimic the rift in Brighton's face.

Brighton tongued the weak back side of his newly forming scar through the inside of his cheek.

"That's fair," Brighton said. "Sometimes, you've gotta gut it out."

"The vest ain't important no more," Charlie said. "It's the camera that matters. Can you get that footage out?"

Brighton flipped the vest around and found the camera rig. The memory card was a standard flash drive. He wouldn't even need a sniffer. He pushed a little slit on the camera's side, and the chip popped right out. Brighton held it up to Charlie.

"Play it," Charlie said.

"Do I want to see this?"

"You're gonna see this," Charlie said, with the same razor edge to his voice that he'd had when he picked up the pencil last time around. "And then you're gonna go to Ditchfield and find everyone."

"Find everyone?"

"By the time I could get up, they'd moved the girls. And Marty. But they can't have gone far. No idea about the other lady cop or Pope."

Brighton opened his drawer and dug around until he found a flash reader. He plucked it out and plugged it into his laptop. The chip slid in with a simple click.

Brighton downloaded the contents of the folder to his computer then to his external drive, just in case. Then he opened it up.

It had one file, a video twenty-eight minutes long. Brighton clicked Play.

He saw muddy footage of what looked like a football field at night, viewed from the cheap seats. Somebody whose voice he vaguely recognized said, "All right, we're up. You sure you want to do this? Breaking and entering goes on your permanent record, you know."

"Fast forward," Charlie said.

Brighton clicked and dragged right. Suddenly, they were outside a ratty old barn. A single spotlight lit the immediate surroundings and threw everything else into harsh relief. Brighton glanced at Charlie but found the boy's gaze impenetrable.

The same voice again: "Charlie, hold up a sec." But the camera moved forward. Brighton peered into the screen, moving his face up close. That was Ken Abernethy in the lights, holding a gun.

"No, by all means, Charlie, come on in. Who you lookin' for, boy?" Abernethy asked. "One of Hill's whores?"

Brighton's jaw dropped. That certainly helped their cause. One leg of the case just got a steel-beam reinforcement.

Charlie's camera thumped forward, jostling slightly left and right as he walked. Brighton found himself donning his legal armor, analyzing the footage for how it would hold up in court and also removing himself by a degree to make the whole unearthly scene easier to process.

The way the girls appeared reminded him sickeningly of a time last fall when animal control scoped his attic for a bat's nest. They just appeared, huddled against a barn door, drenched in low red light, screeching softly. The camera footage turned their eyes to black pits. He heard Charlie call for his sister and saw the heartbreaking way she pushed him away in shame.

Got 'em, Brighton thought grimly. *Checkmate on Ditchfield. Now, to save Charlie.*

No matter how noble Charlie's cause was, he was a convicted criminal, and he'd murdered Bagshot in cold blood. He would never walk, but Brighton had a best-case scenario of twenty-five years less time served if all the cards fell their way.

He took time-stamped notes of who appeared when and what identifying words they used. He noted the vaguely menacing way

Abernethy held his weapon and also noted when Charlie seemed to slip away from reality and point a gun at the warden—Brighton's gun.

I knew nothing good was ever gonna come from that revolver, he thought again as he winced and waited for Charlie to kill Ken Abernethy. The court wouldn't like that. *Sure-fire life sentence right there.*

But at the last moment, Charlie relented and unloaded three shots into the van before Abernethy unloaded on him.

In Brighton's mind, the court swung back in Charlie's favor.

After Charlie had been shot, the rest of the footage was dark.

"Ditchfield is done for," Brighton said, looking over his notes. "Ken Abernethy is too. Hill is always a wild card, but if we can get one of the girls on the stand, he'll go down too. As for you..."

When Brighton looked up, he was alone.

CHAPTER TWENTY-FIVE

G ordon's thoughts wandered toward despair in the pitch black of the cave.

Once Gordon had determined none of them were in immediate mortal danger, they talked through their options. They were limited, to say the least.

It had to be a cave, Gordon thought. *Of all the places in all the world to get forgotten and shrivel up and die, it had to be a cave.*

The four girls, Tasha included, took their confinement in silent misery. Gordon knew they'd been conditioned to be resigned, and they likely still had some sedatives or opiates in their systems, but their quiet defeat still crushed him.

Only the feeling of Dana's shoulder pressed up against his kept him from devolving into a gibbering ball of panic. He didn't even know what the time was. He guessed they'd been in the cave for four or five hours. They'd tried cell phones for a while, but none of them had any shot at service, and the roam and flashlight features were draining battery life.

They didn't know how long they would be in there, so they agreed to turn them off in case they needed the light down the road.

What went unspoken was the fact that they would likely die of thirst before they drained the rationed battery juice of three cell phones. But they all knew it.

Marty shuffled where he sat with his back up against the rough rock on the other side of Dana.

"Hey," Dana said to him, "stay awake. No sleeping on a concussion."

"I'm just drained is all," Marty said, his deep voice echoing.

"Then let's talk. What are you thinking about?"

Marty sighed in the darkness. "How I should have bum-rushed Dameon."

"He'd have killed you," Dana said. "He had every advantage, and you had none. So set that out of your mind. What else are you thinking about?"

In a strange twist of fate, Dana seemed to be the only one *actually* keeping it together. She'd rallied them to try to speak with the girls even though they didn't make much progress. She'd explored the cave as far back as she could, but it wasn't deep. Then she'd suggested they all shut off their phones until they really needed the light.

She'd kept them talking when the spaces between words grew too long, and she'd reached out and held Gordon's hand in the dark as if she could somehow sense the revving of his panic. Gordon knew she was holding Marty's hand, too, a human link that kept them both from spinning out.

"Come on," she urged Marty again. "What else?"

"Brooke," Marty said after a moment.

"Good. That's good. Keep thinking about Brooke because that's what's gonna get you through this. Chloe is out there somewhere too. And when we get out of this place, I want Chloe to meet Brooke. I think she'd like her. What about you, Gord, what are you thinking of?"

Gordon was thinking about a lot of things: whether Charlie was alive; how reckless and low-percentage the plan was to begin with; how much his butt hurt sitting on the cold rock; whether anyone could ever get those girls talking again; the steps he would take to try to unpack their pain and anguish; how much air was in the cave.

"To be honest, I didn't think we'd make it this far," Gordon said. *If you can even call this* making it *at all.*

"Neither did I," Dana said, a hint of bewilderment in her voice. "But we did. And we're together. And for the first time in a while, I don't have to share your attention with anyone or anything else. So, whatcha thinking?"

"I'm thinking how I should have asked you to marry me that day I brought pancakes, like I was planning to," Gordon said.

The cave was silent then and so dark that Gordon could halfway convince himself he was alone. Then Dana laid her head against his shoulder.

She said nothing, just listened. Gordon knew that trick, but he still took the bait and kept talking.

"It would have been better than here. Chloe was at the window, you know," Gordon said, and he didn't know when he'd started crying, but he was doing it. Maybe a part of him had started crying the second he and Charlie crossed the Patapsco in his coupe.

"She was in the window. She was so disappointed when I didn't pull the trigger. I can remember her face. I had the ring in my pocket and everything."

"You asked Chloe if you could marry me?"

"Of course," Gordon said. "After I asked your mother, that is. I know how mothers are."

Dana buried her face in his shoulder and let out a few deep sobs. Then she stopped. When she picked her head back up, she wasn't crying, but she was holding his hand more tightly than ever.

"You listen to me, Gordon. We are getting out of this cave, and then you are going to propose to me, and then I'm going to say yes. Do you understand me?"

Gordon tried to find where her eyes would be, were the dark not so saturating.

"I understand," he said.

"Did you just get shot down?" Marty asked.

Gordon heard Dana give him a friendly thwap on the arm.

"Technically, I think I did," Gordon said.

"He did not get shot down. He got postponed," Dana said.

"That's good," Marty said with a tired chuckle. "Because believe it or not, I think you two might actually be good together."

GORDON HAD SLEPT. He knew he'd slept only because he awoke from a dream in which he was buried, and when the darkness behind his eyes and the darkness in front of his eyes were identical, the panic deepened. He jerked to sitting and was trying to stand, but Dana grabbed his shoulder firmly and sat him down again.

"You'll wake the girls," she whispered.

He took deep breaths to gather himself and felt his face to make sure it was there. His hands came away grimy with sweat. He was powerfully thirsty.

"How long was I out?" he asked.

"Not long, maybe thirty minutes."

Those thirty minutes felt like a lifetime and like nothing at all. He was in purgatory, floating and sensory deprived... or rather, deprived of all the good senses. All he felt was grime and dampness. All he heard were wheezing breaths. His nose seemed blasted of everything but the rank, coppery smell of fear sweat. When he stared at one patch of black long enough, his eyes played tricks on him, exploding in muted reds and yellows. Phosphenes, those were called, his own brain trying to make sense of the pure black by putting on a light show to stay sane.

"I'm turning on a phone," he said. He expected resistance from Dana but didn't get any, which struck him as a bad sign.

The phone powering up was so bright that it felt like it physically burrowed into his brain. Even closing his eyes didn't shut out the screen completely. He waited for a span of minutes before looking around the cave. The girls were huddled over one another like puppies, sharing the warmth of Gordon's coat and Marty's shredded leather jacket. They weren't much but had helped ease their tension enough to let them sleep.

Even unconscious, they shied away from the light. Before Gordon turned the phone away, he saw Tasha at the center of the group. The girls had known she was the most damaged. Even if Tasha herself had yet to fully process having seen her brother shot in front of her, the others knew. They kept her at the core like a queen bee. She was deeply asleep.

He shined the light toward the front hatch, which was enough to peripherally light Dana, who looked at him through baggy slits of eyes. Marty had his head back and eyes closed.

"Marty?" Gordon asked.

"What," he replied flatly.

"Just checking."

Red was smeared all over his upper lip, but a little bead of black still seeped from his right nostril. On the one hand, that could have been a nosebleed—on the other, a hemorrhage.

"So how long have we been here?" Dana asked.

"Let's make it a game. Closest guess wins," Gordon said.

"I like Chutes and Ladders more," Marty said.

"Oh, I'm sorry. Do you have something else to do, Marty?" Gordon asked lightly.

Marty rewarded him with a slight smile. "Ten hours."

"I'll go ten hours and one minute," said Dana.

"That's bullshit," said Marty. "You can't *Price Is Right* me."

"And the lady wins it," Gordon said, "with a time-in-cave of twelve hours and nineteen minutes! Which showcase would you like to choose, Dana?"

Dana was smiling. "You've lost your mind."

"One hundred percent," Gordon agreed. "Now, which showcase would you like to choose?"

Dana looked mournfully at the cold, sweating circle of steel plating that covered the entrance. She pointed at it like the Grim Reaper.

"I'll take what's behind door number one," she said.

"Wouldn't we all," Gordon said.

Then the steel plate shook with the reverberation of three hammer blows.

Everyone jumped. The girls started screaming. The entire cave erupted in a deafening cacophony.

Marty turned to Dana in semiconscious wonder. "What did you do?" he asked.

Gordon didn't wait to hear her answer. He ran toward the steel plate, intending to stop and knock back, but he'd forgotten that he'd passed out sitting on a rock floor for thirty minutes, and instead he tipped forward on pins-and-needles legs and slammed shoulder-first into the steel. His yelp of pain was drowned out by the reverberating boom.

Muffled sounds came from outside. He could hear them as clearly as the ear picks up a siren in the dead of night. He started slamming his fist again and screaming as if the entire cave wasn't full up with cries already.

Rusted metal creaked and groaned. Muffled speaking became audible. Gordon pressed his ear to the steel but couldn't catch anything. He went back to pounding with his fist. Something outside went *pop*, like when Marty had snipped the zip ties, but heavier.

Someone yanked from the outside, and the plate groaned again until a sliver of blood-red sunlight slipped through, hurting his eyes. The chorus of cries behind him turned from painful to grateful. Marty was up and at Gordon's side, along with Dana. Together, they all pushed until all three of them emerged into the misty gloaming of a winter sunset in Ditchfield, blinking like newborn animals, a full spin of the clock after they'd been shut in. Two Baltimore City cops had snapped the U-lock. They stared at each other, wide-eyed.

A man slowly emerged from the twilight, and Gordon's eyes adjusted enough to see. The man wore a camel-hair overcoat over a double-breasted suit, held a briefcase in hand, and had what looked like shopping bags over his shoes.

"Hiya, Doc," Thomas Brighton said, pure relief on his face. Then he turned to Dana and Marty in turn. "Are the girls okay?"

"You found us" was all Gordon could say.

Brighton held up a copy of the surveyor's assessment Gordon recognized from his own boxes of paperwork. "Funny thing. Long time ago, Josiah Hill made me hammer out the property line with the county. I remember this cave. If I recall correctly, I said it could be a liability to him." He stood watching Gordon until Brighton cracked a smile. "Get it? Liability? Come on, I planned that line out like an hour ago on the drive up—"

He might have said more, but Gordon enveloped the man in a fierce and tribal bear hug and drowned out the words.

"Watch the face," Brighton managed, but he did pat Gordon lamely on the back.

The girls came out last, holding each other. For a span of moments, they simply stood in the fading light, looking lost and frightened, as if waiting for the next fresh hell to arrive.

"Officers, your jackets, please," said Gordon.

The two patrolmen looked at each other only briefly before they removed their heavy canvas coats and handed them to Gordon. He carefully approached the two girls without coats and handed them over. Tasha was still wearing Marty's shredded leather coat.

"Does she want my overcoat?" Brighton asked. "It'll be a little long, but I don't care."

Gordon looked at Tasha to see if she understood and saw that she did. Her eyes were clearer. Still, she shook her head and gripped the coat proudly, looking at Marty with pained gratitude. Perhaps she hadn't been as far gone as they had supposed when she saw what he did for Charlie.

He exchanged a glance with the big detective, who only shrugged. Marty was in a thin T-shirt himself, steaming in the still night. His body was likely running hot, still trying to fight off infection from the trauma to his chest, as well as the gun butt to the head. He flashed down a short list of the toughest people he'd ever met in his life—most of them were children—but he had to put Marty Cicero right at the top.

Brighton spoke to the girls. "I know you've been through the unimaginable. But do you think you can walk with us for a bit? Until we can get you somewhere safe?"

The four of them looked at each other—conferring without ever talking, which struck Gordon as a very sensible mode of communication for four young women imprisoned in a place where someone was always listening.

Tasha said the first words Gordon had heard her speak: "We'll walk with you."

Brighton motioned Gordon, Dana, and Marty over as they headed down the slow, rolling slope leading from the north side back to the heart of Ditchfield.

"A few things," he said. "One. We've got a great shot at shutting this place down forever."

Gordon's heart quickened as Brighton looked meaningfully at him, and Gordon recalled when a certain green psychiatrist had walked into the office of a certain crooked lawyer and said, *"I want to take down Ditchfield."*

"Two," Brighton continued, stepping carefully down a small embankment in his grocery-bag shoes and slipping a bit before recovering. "Ken Abernethy is dead. Shot himself sometime in the night by the fence. Which means he can't testify, which means it'll be harder to get Hill."

Gordon hung his head. Marty cursed under his breath.

"I said *harder*, not impossible. Especially if we can get one of the girls to take the stand. So buck up. Three..." Brighton paused, pressing back on Gordon with the flat end of his arm like a mother might a child who isn't buckled in at a hard stop. "We don't have a case against Duke and won't be pursuing one."

"What?" Dana hissed. "Are you serious? After all he's done? His father is on the fucking board of this unholy organization."

"I know. I know," said Brighton. "But we gotta pick our battles. Especially you, Dana. Because it's time to get ready for the Duke show. He's down at the scene of the fire."

"He's here?" Marty asked. "Now?"

"You better believe it," said Brighton. "Duke knew he was cornered, so he flipped the script. Went full surprise and delight. He would have come to the goddamn cave himself, but he got caught up in a mess of press that just happened to show up because I just happened to tip them off."

Gordon looked down the property and could just make out flashes through the trees. The cameras were probably focused on Duke talking his way into another promotion.

"Pick your battles," Brighton repeated, looking specifically at Gordon.

Dana seethed. He could hear the air pumping in and out of her nostrils. He didn't know what to say to her, what comfort he could give her, but thankfully, Marty stepped up. He threw an arm around her like they were about to take a team photo at the sandlot.

"Think about it this way, Sarge. We got a rap sheet a mile long on the chief. And he knows it. Maybe once we win this case, we take that sheet to his desk and ask for your badge and gun back. Or else."

Dana's anger didn't quite melt away, but it did thaw. She looked at Marty as if half amazed still to see him standing, much less offering comfort.

"Brighton," she said. "Let's spare the girls as much of this shit-show as possible."

"One step ahead of you," Brighton said.

And he was. As they broke through the brush line and into the lights of the press—just as the cameras started to target the girls—a chardonnay-colored minivan pulled onto the grass between the Duke press conference and where they stood. The door slid open automatically. Natasha was behind the wheel.

"C'mon in, ladies," she said between smacks of gum. "I got donuts and hot tea and cold fancy water and everythin'."

The girls didn't move, although Tasha almost smiled, probably at the severity of Natasha's platinum-bleached updo.

"Look," Natasha said, "it's a lot warmer in here, and you won't get creeps taking your picture."

That got them moving.

One by one, they filed into the minivan, then the door closed, and they were behind enough tinted glass to stymie the flashes of what Gordon judged was probably fifteen photographers—way more than the local press and way more than the state, even.

Good.

He turned toward the ad hoc press conference Warren Duke was holding. The smell of burning wood was campfire strong, and intermittent waves of wet heat shifted on the breeze across the collapsed wreckage of the main building. One fire truck was still dousing the place, aiming to stamp out glowing embers.

"Shall we?" said Brighton. "Smiles, now. Duke isn't our enemy. Not today."

Gordon walked forward as if in a dream. He shielded his eyes against the camera flashes and made sure to keep his eye on the tall man in the navy sports coat and jeans. He was even sporting a ball cap that was no doubt meant to look tactical.

And Warren Duke kept his eyes on Gordon.

"We couldn't be prouder of these three," he heard Duke say. "They are the personification of Baltimore, honest, loyal, and determined. I may be the one standing here today, talking about winning this battle in the war on sex trafficking, but it's only because of Detective Marty Cicero"—a brief pause—"Sergeant Dana Frisco, and—"

That was his longest pause, almost as if his years of finishing school had failed him and he simply couldn't say the words. But then he recovered.

"And Dr. Gordon Pope." He added, "Please, no questions at this time for these three. They've gone through a terrible ordeal them-selves, and I'd ask you to respect that."

Warren Duke shook their hands, each in turn. Gordon was last.

He wasn't sure what Marty or Dana had said, if anything. But when he got in close enough to smell the chief's expensive cologne, he leaned in toward his ear. "Tell your sugar daddy we'll see him in court," he whispered.

He didn't wait to see Duke's reaction because he didn't really care. Instead, he walked back toward the minivan, along with Dana and Marty. He wouldn't get any sort of last laugh that day. Nothing about Ditchfield was a laughing matter.

But if Gordon put in the work and the cards fell the right way, he might just get the last word in court.

CHAPTER TWENTY-SIX

Waterstones restaurant continued. Gordon wasn't quite sure why it shouldn't, but he found himself strangely surprised to see the place running like a Swiss watch, the same as always—as if perhaps it might be slightly reeling just like he still was, even two weeks out of the cave. But no, Waterstones was a rock in the river. Its charm came from the fact that it was unchanging in the face of a constantly changing world.

His mother was similarly unchanging. Deborah Pope was seated at her table, wearing a light-gray dress and a faded denim jacket that somehow looked both thrifty and outrageously expensive. She was taking up too much of her favorite waiter's time, as usual, but Caesar was only too happy to catch up with his favorite customer. He was the one that first noticed Gordon's party, which was a good deal larger than their usual standing reservation.

Deborah stood, surprised but looking thrilled nonetheless. Caesar picked up her martini and shifted it to a larger table to their right and started resetting.

"My son! And with an entourage? What a wonderful surprise."

Marty Cicero looked back and forth between Gordon and

Deborah with a half-suppressed smile on his lips. "Entourage? No, ma'am. Your son showed up in my life one day, and he ain't left since. All due respect."

Deborah moved to the big detective and patted his forearm. "He tends to do that, dear. You must be Detective Cicero. I've heard all about you. You are twice as handsome and half as beefy as Gordon said. It's wonderful to meet you."

Even though she was less than half his weight, she pulled Marty into a hug he couldn't help but return. Gordon saw it all happening and was powerless to intervene. They were on his mother's stage, now.

"Mrs. Dr. Pope, this is Brooke, my girlfriend," said Marty.

Brooke stepped up with her hands clasped demurely in front of herself. She looked at ease in Waterstones, or at the very least like nothing could faze her. And Gordon couldn't blame her. After having nearly lost Marty twice, she'd been through quite a trial by fire.

"Thanks for having us," she said.

"My, you're gorgeous," said Deborah. "I'd say I used to look like you when I was in my thirties, but I'd be lying. Come sit. Come sit."

"Hi, Deborah—" Dana began until Deborah cut her off with a pre-emptive hug that lasted a long time.

"You saved my son," she said. When Dana started to protest, his mother simply shook her head. "He told me the whole plan was your idea. And also how you kept everyone sane in the cave."

"I was just doing what I could," said Dana.

"That's what they all say," said Deborah. "Now, I know there's someone else here, but she's hiding behind her mom for some reason and not saying hello to me."

Chloe stepped out boldly from behind her mother and stood with her hands in the pockets of her pink jumpsuit. Still, she looked slightly bewildered by the scene until Deborah somehow bent down to her level, all eighty-two years of her.

"How've you been, Chloe?" she asked. "Tell me honestly. Your mom, Gord, Marty, everyone has been running all around Maryland doing all sorts of scary stuff, and I want to know how you feel about it. One word."

She answered, "Sucks."

Deborah nodded with an instant approval that had eluded Gordon himself most of his childhood. "I bet you were scared. I was too. Scared to death. But that's over now. Let's get you a drink."

Deborah stood and found her waiter. "Caesar, would you bring a Shirley Temple for the young lady? That is your drink, right, sweetheart?"

Chloe nodded somberly, and Gordon found he had to hide a smile, especially when Chloe pushed herself up and into the seat right next to his mother.

"As a matter of fact, Caesar, it looks like I finally have an excuse to order a bottle of champagne." She looked around the table, now seated. "Five glasses?" she asked in a way that brooked no argument.

Caesar nodded and departed.

Marty and Chloe seemed to have settled in well enough. Gordon always worried about such things, the mixing of worlds personal and professional, especially given the history. But, as usual, he found his overthinking was far worse than the reality. Everyone looked happy.

That was good. That was step one.

Step two was proposing to Dana.

Chloe hadn't stopped staring at him since she'd sat down. When Caesar brought her the Shirley Temple, she sipped it with one unblinking eye upon him, like some old-time tough in a Western saloon.

She was the only one he'd told about what was happening that night, and she looked like she'd been ready for it to happen for a whole month. Gordon knew the feeling. In fact, if he didn't do the deed immediately, he would never be able to stomach the champagne, much less the Cobb salad. All of it would sit right at tonsil level until he took care of business.

It had to be now. But she was talking, apparently in a genuine conversation with Brooke. Marty looked at him skeptically. He knew something was up too. He glanced at his mother, who was also staring at him with a strange intent. He knew at once that she also knew. *Am I that obvious?*

Gordon cleared his throat. Dana didn't notice. Chloe rolled her eyes. Caesar came over with the chilled bottle of champagne and started working the cork, but Deborah stilled him with a soft touch.

"Dana," Gordon said, which slowed her conversation. "Dana," he interjected again, grasping for her hand and holding on for dear life.

The conversation slowed, and Dana looked at him as if he might be ill. "Gordon, is everything okay?"

He hobbled out of his seat and somehow managed to crank down onto his one good knee. By then, his surroundings had narrowed to a binocular view in which he only saw her.

He had a speech. He'd written it out then turned the highlights into bullet points to try to remember—something about when he first saw her in the courthouse and then progressing through their first date in the sleep lab and so on. All of it fled him. In its place, he pictured a flash of light: Karen's ring on the side table.

How devastating that had been at the time, and how little it hurt him now. That was all because of her. She was stronger than everything the world had thrown at him, and she made him strong too. He wanted to make her understand all that.

"Dana, until I met you, I was convinced that this world never gives you anything you want until the moment you no longer need it. But the longer I live next to you, the more I realize there is nothing in this world I need more, and nothing that I want more, than you."

He grasped her trembling hands in his, barely registering her swimming eyes.

"Will you marry me?"

Silence. Shock, maybe, although she certainly knew it was coming. He wondered if he'd stuttered. She was wiping at her eyes. He heard Chloe clear her throat heavily. He looked over at her, along with Dana.

Chloe tapped her chest just below the shoulder, as if trying to signal in secret.

The ring!

Gordon let go of Dana's hands and fumbled around in his breast pocket. He couldn't believe he hadn't brought it out first thing. That was supposed to be the order: take a knee, pull out the ring, ask the question.

Smiling, Chloe nodded encouragement. He managed to pull the ring out from where it had been marinating for weeks. He held it out to Dana like some sort of peasant offering wheat for taxes.

"Gordon," Dana said, her eyes looking at the ring and past the ring at the same time. Her voice instantly calmed him. "Do you remember Erica Denbrook?"

Of course he did. She was the young girl that sleepwalked herself right into a construction dumpster. Dana had risked her life climbing a trellis, only to dive down a trash chute in the hopes of finding her.

She took his hands and held them surely between hers. "My heart was yours the minute I saw how far you'd go to save a child you'd never even met. And what's funny is that back then, I thought it was a one-time thing for you. But you sacrifice yourself for these kids every day. How wonderfully wrong I was."

"Is that a yes?" Gordon stammered.

"Yes, Gord. It's a yes."

He held on to her as she helped him shakily to his feet and didn't stop until Caesar popped the champagne. Chloe was clapping like a maniac.

A COBB SALAD and two scotches later, Gordon was feeling as fine as he ever had in his entire life. Outside, Baltimore was dark and cold, and the Ditchfield trial was set for ten the following morning, but in Waterstones, at that moment, the pressing darkness was kept at bay. Dana's ring caught the low light easily, in single flashes, each of which was a marvel to Gordon. She wore it like a natural.

Deborah made many toasts. She said that she'd known all along, of course, that his son was going to marry Dana, that she knew the day he'd first mentioned her name. She even pointed out the seat where it had happened.

Marty tried toasting twice. Each time, he was overcome with emotion that only doubled when Brooke came to his aid and rubbed his broad back. His snappy Baltimore accent devolved into a sort of husky bark, but Gordon understood.

Chloe stepped in when Marty had to gather himself. She was eloquent as ever, and at least four Shirley Temples deep.

As for Gordon, he found himself at peace, saying very little after having said so much, content to observe and take in. That was why he saw Josiah Hill stand from his place at the long mahogany bar.

He turned and looked directly at Gordon—no nod, no acknowledgement, no dapper aw-shucks charm—only a dead, flat stare before donning his wool fedora and walking to the doors and outside.

Nobody else at his table saw, which Gordon thought was a good thing. Still, the darkness of the Baltimore night felt closer than ever... until another well-dressed man stood up from the bar.

Brighton turned toward them and gave a single wave, hoisting the remains of his martini glass high in salute. He was wearing his very best, a soft gray suit—double breasted, of course—with forest-green pinstripes. A camel-hair scarf was draped lazily around his shoulders. Anyone that glanced his way could easily think he owned the place until they saw the scar. Then they might start to wonder.

He gathered his things and was making his way to the door when Gordon called to him and waved him over.

He came reluctantly. And when he arrived at the table, he nodded at each of them in turn, as if he'd known them all for years. To Deborah, he said, "You must be Gordon's mother."

His mom cut right to it. "Thomas Brighton. For a long time, I thought you were nothing but an ambulance-chasing fraud. When I heard my son was taking your money, I told him to wash his hands."

"Probably smart," Brighton said, distractedly. He was watching the door as if Hill might spring back in at any moment. "Gordon," he said, as if in a daze, "I don't suppose you've heard anything good from Brookhaven, have you?"

Gordon had not. He'd called the chief attending at Brookhaven Clinic—a workhorse of a psychiatrist he'd leaned on before, named James Cohn—multiple times a day for two straight weeks. According to Cohn's report, they ate and drank in survival mode, huddled close, and said nothing. They'd been weaned of the opiates in their systems through a step-down regimen of methadone and naloxone that he said was a fairly brutal experience, but they'd gotten through it with round-the-clock care.

It was the anti-Ditchfield, in other words. But none of that seemed to matter. The girls still weren't talking.

Cohn kept them together in a calm, minimal-stimulus room with one of three primary care providers on constant rotation. Gordon himself had been there five times. He'd tried everything he knew to get them to open up: group therapy, individual sessions, speaking, silence. Nothing worked. They couldn't seem to find the words.

Gordon felt strongly that Tasha Cunningham could break the cycle of silence. The others seemed to look to her. If she decided to stand up, they might too. But according to Cohn, Tasha had so far done nothing but stare out the window and sleep.

He had an idea who she might be looking for.

Brighton pulled his cuffs straight under his overcoat. "This is probably my last night out for a while. I wanted a martini in a place about as far as possible from Ditchfield," he said. "I should have figured Hill would show up and find a way to ruin it."

"Did he threaten you?" Dana asked.

"Of course," Brighton said easily. "He reminded me what jail is like. As if I don't know. Said he had people inside. Blah blah blah. I don't want to talk about Josiah Hill. I want to say congratulations, Dana, and you too, Doc. That's what I came over here for. I saw Gord drop to one knee. I think the whole restaurant figured he was either having a heart attack or proposing."

Dana stood and grasped Brighton's limp hands. "Thank you, Thomas. God only knows where we'd be right now without you—"

"In a cave," Chloe interjected.

"Thank you, honey," Dana said in stride. "But, Thomas, listen to me. If you think we're gonna get blown out of the water tomorrow in court, maybe we file for a postponement? Maybe we need more time."

Brighton shook his head. "We've sprung the trap. He knows he's caught, but he's probing the walls. It's now or never."

"What happens if we win?" Gordon asked. "To you, I mean."

Brighton buttoned his overcoat and fluffed his hair. "Well, best-case scenario, Ditchfield gets shut down. Hill gets a life sentence under Title Eighteen for child trafficking." He cleared his throat again. "And I'll probably serve five for legal malpractice. Maybe less. But I'll certainly go bankrupt."

The table was silent.

"Now, now, please, hold yourselves together. There's a child here," Brighton said.

"Thomas—" Gordon began.

Brighton shook his head and staunched Gordon's words. "This is my decision. And it's one I want to make."

Dana cleared her throat. "Have you heard from him? Since?"

Brighton buttoned his overcoat. "No. And I suspect I'll never hear from him again. In my mind, he's boosted a '57 Chevy and is taking Route 66 out west. Far away from here."

That was a nice thought. Gordon could picture Charlie with the top down, one arm out, surfing the wind blowing by.

But that wasn't reality. The Charlie he knew would never leave the job unfinished. He wouldn't rest until he knew Tasha was somewhere out of the clutches of the shadow land into which she'd fallen. And judging by the way Marty was hiding behind his beer, he wasn't the only one who felt that way.

"Anyway, congrats on the upcoming wedding, Doc. You clearly outkicked your coverage," Brighton said, nodding at him and then turning to Dana. "Sergeant. Watch out for him. He tends to stumble into messes. Yours truly included."

He spun on the heel of his leather shoe and walked away. Gordon thought about calling after him, but by the time he could think of what to say, Brighton was out the door.

CHAPTER TWENTY-SEVEN

At nine in the morning and not a moment later, Gordon Pope walked through the doors of the Baltimore City Circuit Courthouse and slowly shuffled through security.

He nodded at Harold, the security guard, who looked exactly the same as he had the day Gordon first set foot in the building all those years before. Either the man didn't age, or he'd been born old. Gordon would've put his money on the latter.

Gordon beeped as he walked through the metal detector. He always had. The wand beeped at his belt, a few notches wider than in the early days. *That'll happen when you're happy*, Gordon thought in a flash.

And he was. The realization struck him like a bolt out of the blue.

He didn't know what was going to happen in the courtroom that day, whether Josiah Hill would sweet-talk his way out or say nothing at all and just cash in on favors—or maybe the long arm of the law would extend all the way out to Ditchfield.

Either way, Gordon was happier walking through BCC security than he'd ever been. Maybe that came with knowing he'd literally burned the house down at Ditchfield, knowing that if Hill somehow walked now, Gordon would dedicate his whole life to waiting until the man slipped up again. And there he'd be, along with his friends.

Or maybe it had to do with Dana.

Probably, it was because of Dana and the ring she was wearing on her finger.

Harold pointed at the pass-through basin. Gordon slid in his ID. Harold looked at it blandly.

"I look a little constipated because I had to sneeze," Gordon said.

Harold raised an eyebrow.

"At the DMV. I had to sneeze. They made me take the picture anyway. They aren't patient people."

Harold huffed like a walrus and handed the license back. Gordon was walking away when he paused and backtracked.

"Did I just make you laugh, Harold?"

Harold looked up at him blankly.

"I'll take it," said Gordon, and he moved along.

He sat down at his old spot, by the vending machine, and eyed the moon pies, as always. He thought about getting one but decided against it. God knew how long they'd been sitting there. One of them had a bit of yellowing on the package.

Brighton was not late that time. He walked right up and sat next to him, eyeing the moon pies himself.

"I don't suppose you have any last-minute good news about how the girls have become a font of information, do you?" Brighton asked.

"I do not," Gordon said. "They're all silent. But Tasha wanted to come here today. Dana is going to sit in the stands with her. The only reason I can think is because she's trying to piece together the reality from the nightmares. Maybe she needs to convince herself that Josiah Hill is a real person. It's healthy, believe it or not."

Brighton leaned all the way back on the bench until the back of his head rested upon the hard wood.

"But it doesn't help the case," Gordon added.

Brighton stood and assayed the halls of the Baltimore City Circuit Courthouse as if seeing them anew. "You know, they're building a new dedicated juvenile justice center down the street," he said. "I think things might get better for these kids. Not any time soon. But maybe someday."

Gordon pushed to his feet and eased out his knee. "Lay out the case. Hill will be right there, probably with his stupid hat and a mess of lawyers, but they still have to give you your turn. So tell him. Tell everyone."

Thomas Brighton took a deep breath and let it out very slowly. He gingerly patted at the scar that raked his cheek.

"Does it hurt still?" Gordon asked. "Your face?"

"Not anymore," Brighton said. "It's just that sometimes I'm afraid it'll disappear. Is that weird?"

Gordon came up alongside him as the two of them walked to their courtroom.

"Not at all," Gordon said. "But you earned that one. The ones you earn never go away."

Marty's head was itching. Just when the bruising in his chest calmed down, the split at the side of his dome woke up. *Been a bit of a rough week,* he thought as he waited outside the courthouse, eating almonds slowly because each crunch sent a little flick of pain to his temples. But Marty always got hungry when he got nervous.

The air was freezing even at ten in the morning. No amount of weak winter sun could chase away the bone-deep chill of a cold snap in Baltimore. The trial was underway presently. They liked to keep things timely. The judge probably had a full docket. Marty thought it was crazy that the fate of all they'd worked for was just another line item for somebody else.

Ah well. That was the system they had.

Truthfully, Marty was happy to be outside. He didn't have much faith in the court system and didn't want to be around when Josiah

Hill walked, not least because he wasn't sure he'd be able to restrain himself if the man passed by his bench in the cheap seats.

And while Marty had taken a late liking to Charlie Cunningham, the cop in him thought he was probably dead. One could place only so much on a kid, especially one as banged up as Charlie was. That any of them were alive and in the sun at all was a testament to the kid's tenacity. He'd done plenty... and not nearly enough.

Ah well. Such is life.

Yet Marty waited... long past when the almonds were gone. He watched every car and looked at every face that walked up and past, and the more time went by, the more he slumped. He felt strange, like he might cry again. He'd gone twenty years without crying, but there he was with a hat trick. The first time was when he'd seen the kid gunned down outside the barn. The second, when Gordon proposed to Dana. And then this.

He missed the kid, the reckless, murdering juvenile delinquent. It made no sense, but there it was. Marty missed him.

At quarter to eleven, Marty walked back inside. He had no plan to go into that courtroom. He just wanted to sit down where it wasn't so cold.

At the door, he felt a tug on his shoulder. When he turned around, Charlie Cunningham was there. He was wearing a clean pair of jeans and a puffy jacket, both of which had a just-stolen look about them. They stared at each other for several moments, but Marty couldn't hide the relief on his face.

"I knew you'd come," Marty said.

"Yeah? Is that why you were walking away?" Charlie asked, a hint of a smile on his lips.

"I'm freezing my ass off. I've been eyeballing every car for almost an hour."

"You think I'm gonna drive a stolen car onto the lot of the city courthouse?" Charlie asked.

The kid had a point.

"I didn't hear that," Marty said. Then he paused. "I gotta cuff you," he said.

"I know," Charlie said, and he turned around, placing his wrists together behind his back.

Marty found himself in tears for the fourth time. "I wish I... that it didn't have to be..."

"It is what it is. We can still win," Charlie said, looking over his shoulder.

Marty cleared his throat and clicked the cuffs into place. "All right," he said. "Let's go."

BRIGHTON HAD GIVEN it his all. The defense came at him exactly as he expected, claiming total innocence when it came to the sex-trafficking charges. They outlined the many organizations in which Hill was involved, charitable and business entities alike—forty-eight, to be exact. He had a passing knowledge of Ditchfield and supported it only because he thought they were a great reform institution for wayward boys. Not all investments hit.

The evidence that they said Brighton "claimed to have found" at the site of New Hope was nothing but a bunch of nonsense spreadsheets and, yes, a few very unfortunate photographs and videos, likely placed there by one of the churchgoers. Hundreds of people came and went in that building every week.

After all, "The house of God is always open," they said. "Reverend Hill seeks to shepherd his flock, but he is not legally responsible for them," they said.

Through it all, Josiah Hill sat complacently, as if waiting at a bus stop, happy to engage in conversation if you sat down next to him but just as happy to sit quietly. And he did have his stupid hat. It sat on the table, right next to his gloves and the meticulously prepared defense of three attorneys whom Brighton knew personally as very capable and a little desperate—in other words, a perfect fit for Hill's pocket.

Hill never even glanced at Tasha Cunningham, who sat in the far back, a small, thin creature who clung to Dana but never looked away from the proceedings. Brighton lost his train of thought several times during the prosecution when his glance happened to fall upon her, staring back at him.

Every time he faltered, Gordon urged him on with a sure nod, but Brighton knew. He knew before he'd set foot in that courtroom. He'd known when he was sipping his martini. He was buying time—that was all—because he was going to lose.

Then the door of the courtroom swung open, and Charlie Cunningham walked in with his hands cuffed behind his back—followed at a fair distance by his escorting detective, Marty Cicero—and everything changed.

Charlie looked around as if he owned the place, as if nothing could hurt him. That, Brighton supposed, was the rare positive you were awarded when you hit rock bottom.

He found Tasha well before Tasha found him. Brighton kept talking, not even knowing what he was saying, only knowing that the tables had turned and he had to see the reversal through. The rest of the courtroom seemed to follow his eyes, though, Gordon especially, who was closer to the front and the first to stand.

Soon, everyone was looking at Charlie.

Brighton watched as Charlie knelt down, his hands behind his back, and placed his head on his sister's shoulder. She flinched terribly, but Charlie kept his light touch until she turned, and in an instant, she knew him. She encircled him around the shoulders and leaned against him to stand, and Brighton finally saw the twin in them as they leaned on each other in an embrace. For a moment, there was no Charlie and no Tasha. There was a family.

Brighton couldn't hear what Charlie said to her when he was close to her ear in that embrace. He doubted anyone in the courtroom could, although he was fairly sure the word *never* was in there somewhere.

"I never abandoned you."

Or maybe *"I'll never leave you again."*

Or maybe Brighton's favorite: *"Take the stand, and you'll never see Hill again."*

Whatever it was, it worked. Brother and sister looked at Brighton. She was ready.

"Your honor," Brighton said, clearing his throat. "The prosecution would like to call Tasha Cunningham to the stand."

Hill's team went mad. They objected on every ground imaginable, but Brighton knew no self-respecting judge who wished to maintain their seat in this city would keep a victim like Tasha Cunningham from the stand if she was willing to take it. He'd banked on that, and he was right.

So then Hill's team went after Charlie, objecting on legal procedure, claiming their client felt unsafe. Brighton pointed out that Charlie Cunningham was in cuffs, escorted by a city policeman—a detective, in fact. And no law prevented suspects—or convicts, for that matter—from attending an open trial when in custody.

Eventually, the judge overruled them all and offered up the stand. Tasha seemed reluctant to leave her brother's side, but he urged her forward then sat in her place next to Dana when she moved to the aisle.

Tasha took the walk.

Brighton thought she might look away as she passed Hill, but instead, she peered at him sideways as if trying to see and understand who this quiet animal was, stretched languorously in the depths of the cage.

She sat on the dais, behind the bench, a little lower than the judge, who watched her curiously.

Brighton came up to the stand and rested there easily. He saw her look at his scar and smiled. "Tasha, a lot of people did a lot of very brave things to get us here, to this moment. But I want to tell you, no matter what happens, that what you just did was the bravest of all."

She nodded weakly. Brighton pulled himself together by the lapels of his suit. Standing tall, he turned to address the court.

"Your honor, I've laid out in painstaking detail the evil Josiah Hill presided over at New Hope, and the evil he was building in Ditchfield. You've seen the ledgers, the codes, the photographs, and the videos. But pictures and words are one thing. People are another."

He turned to Tasha, feeling his sad smile tug unevenly at his cheek. "Would you please state your name for the court?"

Tasha looked back at Charlie, who nodded encouragement at her.

"Tasha Cunningham," she said.

"And Tasha, is that your brother there?"

"Yes," Tasha said, and the love in her voice was palpable.

"Your honor, meet Charlie Cunningham. He is a wanted man, with good reason. But the crimes he committed should be viewed through the lens of the trap that Josiah Hill set for him years before he ever stole his first car. A trap I sprang myself."

Brighton looked at Hill's table. The man himself met his gaze unflinchingly, but Brighton got the sense that it was in defiant pride despite the iceberg that had just smashed into his ship.

"Josiah Hill has a lot of lawyers. Until very recently, I would have been at that table myself, furiously taking notes, thinking of any way to get my client out of the mess he made for himself, because I was on the take. In exchange for money, I tipped the scales of justice the way Hill wanted: toward Ditchfield. But only for certain young men. Men who were the only support system for vulnerable young women. Men like Charlie Cunningham."

The judge leaned forward, arms flat across the bench. She looked down at him over her glasses. "Mr. Brighton, are you incriminating yourself?"

"I am. Although I submit to the court that I thought I was helping to pad the books of a prison. It's no excuse, but I want it on the record that I had no idea of the depths of this man's true plans."

Having said that, Brighton turned back to Tasha, feeling lighter than he had in years.

"Tasha, do you remember how you met Josiah Hill?"

Tasha looked at Hill in a series of fleeting glances as she spoke, as if she couldn't quite stand to place her eyes fully upon him. "He gave me a sandwich and chocolate milk when Charlie and I were hungry."

"And how old were you at the time?"

"Ten."

"A simple sandwich. A kid's carton of chocolate milk. That's how it started. And maybe that's how it would have stayed if Charlie didn't get sent to Ditchfield."

One of Hill's attorneys objected. "This is hardly relevant to the case," he said, but the objection had no vigor behind it.

"Overruled," the judge said simply. "Although since the young lady took the stand, I'd like to keep this to ask and answer, Mr. Brighton."

Brighton bowed in acknowledgement. "Tasha, when did you move into New Hope Community Church?"

"Not long after Charlie went to jail," she said. "I had no money for the apartment. I was running out of food. Reverend Hill offered to take me in."

"And how long until he asked for payment?" Brighton asked.

"He never asked for money," Tasha said. "But one day, he asked if I could take some pictures for him. He introduced me to Alonzo."

Brighton turned to the judge. "Alonzo Cook, your honor. Currently recovering from a gunshot wound sustained after firing upon detective Marty Cicero inside the walls of New Hope."

Hill's lawyers objected again. "Your honor, the shooting at New Hope is not relevant to this case. There is not one shred of evidence supporting Ms. Cunningham's claims."

"Overruled," the judge said.

Brighton jumped right back in. "Pictures like this?" he asked, holding up one of the two Gordon had found in his slapdash raid. Tasha looked at it out of the corner of her eye then looked away.

"That's not me. That's Brianna. But yeah."

"And after pictures weren't enough for payment, what then?" Brighton asked carefully.

"Movies." Tasha's eyes glistened.

"And after movies weren't enough?"

"Men," she said. "They brought in men and asked me to massage them. And... and have sex with them."

"Who did?" Brighton asked.

"Alonzo and Dameon."

Josiah Hill sat back in his chair and repositioned his fedora on the table. He crossed his arms.

"But when I said no, they took me to Reverend Hill."

"And what did Josiah Hill say?" Brighton asked.

"He told me I had nowhere else to go. Said if I wanted to stay warm that winter, I had to do what Alonzo and Dameon asked. And he gave me pills. Said they'd help with the pain."

Brighton let that settle. Not even Hill's lawyers seemed able to surmount the weight of Tasha's words.

"Thank you, Tasha," Brighton said. "You've been very brave."

"Brianna said she'd come to the courthouse too and testify if nothing bad happened to me," Tasha said. "The other girls too."

Brighton drummed his fingers on the wood of the bench. "Let's hope it doesn't come to that. Thank you again, Tasha. No further questions, Your Honor."

Hill's team looked blindsided. When the judge looked at them for cross-examination, they seemed caught unawares. One stood, shuffling papers, looking at the materials in front of him and coming up short. "Your Honor, given this new testimony, we'd like to request a brief recess to confer with our client."

"I think that sounds like a good idea," the judge said in a tone that didn't bode well for Hill or his team.

As Hill's party gathered their things, Josiah Hill approached Brighton.

"You think I'm a pervert," Hill said lowly. "I'm not. But you would not believe how many powerful men are. No matter what happens, you've turned many dangerous eyes your way."

"I don't think you're a pervert," said Brighton. "I think you're a monster. And the best way to deal with monsters is one at a time."

Hill watched him coldly for a moment longer before donning his hat and following his legal team down the aisle. He walked like a weight was slowly settling upon him. For a split second, Brighton had a vision in which Charlie Cunningham threw himself at the man as he passed, never mind that Charlie was cuffed. He pictured Charlie tackling him, somehow, and bashing his head into the man's face until both of them were brainless.

And maybe, in another life, Charlie would have done just that. But in this one, Charlie stood tall, squared to face Hill, and said, "Goodbye, Reverend," in a tone so quiet and final that it gave Brighton goose bumps.

CHAPTER TWENTY-EIGHT

TWO MONTHS LATER

The dining room table in Dana's kitchen was covered in little pink scraps of paper from Chloe's arts-and-crafts closet. Each scrap had a name scribbled on it, and each was arranged around a series of overturned teacups meant to represent tables at the wedding venue.

Dana and Chloe had rearranged the seating three times already as they weighed the pros and cons of putting certain members of the extended family together. After a healthy back-and-forth about separating a pair of cousins and some surprisingly mature observations from Chloe about how they might want to split up a table she felt was "too fun" so that "other tables could be more fun," they decided to rearrange again.

Gordon had politely excused himself after their first rearrangement and set about making his famous blueberry pancakes, the reason being that Dana was already up to a hundred guests at the wedding—with more RSVPs coming in daily—while Gordon's list maxed out at twenty. And even twenty wasn't a true reflection. Half of those were his mother's friends.

"Where should we put Karen?" Dana asked.

"Not by my mother," Gordon said from the kitchen. "Anywhere but by my mother."

He heard Chloe muttering something about how Karen was lucky to get an invite at all, which drew a knowing look from Dana.

"Hey, I did almost get her killed," Gordon said. "Inviting her to an open bar is the least I can do."

"Fine," Chloe said, plunking her name along with *Chaaad*, her husband and plus-one, at a table designated by a cracked coffee cup in the far corner of their little layout.

"So we got Gordon and myself at the head table, of course—"

"And me," said Chloe. "Of course."

"Of course," Dana echoed. "Plus Marty and Brooke. Who else?"

"Brighton and Natasha," Gordon said. "You know he earned it."

"Fine, fine," Dana said. "If he can make it, he has a spot."

Gordon whisked vigorously. "Oh, he'll make it. He might have to walk right from prison to the venue the day he gets out, but he'll be there."

Thomas Brighton had to serve one full year then four more on probation. Gordon had seen him three times already in visitation. At first, he was concerned how an attorney might be treated in jail, even at a minimum-security place like Brockbridge, down south. As it turned out, instead of being known as the man who'd sent kids to Ditchfield, like he'd feared, he was known as the man who'd helped burn Ditchfield to the ground. He said he'd been mostly left alone.

"The scar helps," he'd added.

That reminded Gordon. "Make sure we get good vodka on the spirits list," he said. "Brighton's gonna need it."

In addition to jail time, Thomas Brighton had been disbarred. Brighton & Associates was no more. He could apply for reinstatement to the Maryland State Bar Association after his full sentence was complete. Gordon had thought that would destroy the man, but again, Brighton surprised him.

"I'm thinking about trying something else," he'd said.

What that was, Gordon couldn't fathom. But he knew it would

be successful. As for Natasha, she'd gone on to a secretarial position at another attorney a few houses down on Bail Bond Row, but she said she was ready to jump when Brighton was.

"And Mimi, too, at the head table," Chloe said, putting Maria's name next to hers. "And Deb," she added, moving Deborah's marker to the other side of hers.

"Honey, we can't have everyone at the head," Dana said, which led to another back-and-forth and the reshuffling of tabs all over again.

"The batter has to rest for a few minutes. I'm going out to get the mail," Gordon said.

The girls didn't acknowledge him. They were deep in the new redesign.

Spring had finally managed to hang on in Baltimore. The sun felt like more than a set piece, and the lawns and flower gardens seemed past the delicate green phase, ready to grow in earnest. A month back, Gordon had had his mail forwarded to Dana's house and was in the process of turning his loft back into the office it was originally meant to be.

This was his home, and he couldn't have been happier about it.

In the distance, an engine roared, and Gordon followed the sound on instinct. He remembered when Dana had been spooked by a similar sound a lifetime before, when Gordon still had her ring in his pocket and Chloe was hanging her head in the window.

Dana had been right to worry... and wrong. Charlie wasn't the enemy, but he was the fuse. In the end, he'd gotten twenty-five years less time served at Ditchfield. So twenty to go.

"There's always a chance at parole," Brighton had said when the sentence came down. "It's better than we could have hoped for."

Still, it stung, especially considering that Josiah Hill got the same sentence, although with no chance of parole, and given Hill's age, it was effectively a life sentence. The weird equivalency bothered Gordon. He wanted a grand gesture for Hill, like life plus a hundred.

"It gets the job done," Brighton had said.

That was true. Sometimes grand gestures were hard to come by in Baltimore. The longer Gordon lived there, the more he realized it was a city where the small things got the job done. The things nobody else wanted to do.

Gordon had gone to see Charlie as soon as he was able. He was serving his time at Jessup, a federal penitentiary that was well regarded, as far as those things go. It was not the supermax Charlie had feared, and it certainly was nothing like Ditchfield, still in the depths of a federal audit that, according to the word on the street, was never going to climb out of.

On Gordon's first visit, Charlie came out dressed in an orange jumpsuit, clear-eyed and unmarked and also a fair bit thicker. He nodded to Gordon like an old friend before he picked up the pass-through phone.

During their chat, Gordon had told Charlie about Hill's sentence but was surprised to find he already knew. Word traveled fast in lockup. Charlie also said that he doubted the good reverend would have the luxury of dying of old age wherever he ended up.

"He committed two sins," Charlie said. "Bad ones. One, he hurt kids. Two, he hurt kids on his block. There's a lot of people don't take kindly to that shit in here. Or out there. Just ask Dameon."

Gordon couldn't ask Dameon, of course. Nobody could. After he'd disappeared from Ditchfield, he was at large for a week before showing up dead in an impound lot on the east side of the city, not far from the Lexington Heights projects, a bullet blown clean through the back of his head. Alonzo probably would've been dead, too, if he hadn't gone straight from Hopkins to solitary confinement at the Chesapeake supermax.

So debts had been paid, in a manner of speaking. But none of it really felt like justice to Gordon, not when it got stacked against all those lost children. *How much is a childhood worth?* he wondered. *One where you're kept and cared for. Told you matter. Told you're loved.*

He was bringing himself down. *Enough of that.* He walked back toward the warmth of the house, back toward the world where plans were unfolding and futures were being written.

On the way back, he pulled the mail from the box and sifted through each piece. Three more little envelopes were there— incoming RSVPs that would no doubt throw Chloe into a fit of giggles and wreck their most recent seating plan.

One of them gave him pause. It looked like it had been inspected and carefully taped up again, and the return address was Jessup Correctional Institution.

Could it be? On a lark, Gordon had mailed Charlie a wedding invitation. He'd been thinking about the kid, as he often did, and was in the depths of the invitation grind. He'd doubted Charlie would ever see it but thought it was worth a shot.

He popped open the return envelope and pulled out their standard response card. The name field read, "From: Mr. Charlie Cunningham."

And in the response section, he'd ticked Regretfully Declines, to which he'd appended "On account of prison."

In the comment section, he'd written:

I'll make it up to you when I get out.
Thank you.
—C

ABOUT THE AUTHOR

B. B. Griffith writes best-selling fantasy and thriller books. He lives in Denver, CO, where he is often seen sitting on his porch staring off into the distance or wandering to and from local watering holes with his family.

See more at his digital HQ: https://bbgriffith.com

If you like his books, you can sign up for his mailing list here: http://eepurl.com/SObZj. It is an entirely spam-free experience.

ALSO BY B. B. GRIFFITH

Gordon Pope Thrillers

The Sleepwalkers (Gordon Pope, #1)

Mind Games (Gordon Pope, #2)

Shadow Land (Gordon Pope, #3)

The Vanished Series

Follow the Crow (Vanished, #1)

Beyond the Veil (Vanished, #2)

The Coyote Way (Vanished, #3)

The Tournament Series

Blue Fall (The Tournament, #1)

Grey Winter (The Tournament, #2)

Black Spring (The Tournament, #3)

Summer Crush (The Tournament, #4)

Luck Magic Series

Las Vegas Luck Magic (Luck Magic, #1)

Standalone

Witch of the Water: A Novella

Made in United States
North Haven, CT
15 November 2021